THE LT. KATE GAZZARA
SERIES BOOKS 7-9

BLAIR HOWARD

CASSIDY

A LT. KATE GAZZARA NOVEL BOOK 7

CASSIDY

A Lt. Kate Gazzara Novel Book 7
By
Blair Howard

DEDICATION

For Jo
As Always

CASSIDY
PROLOGUE

Hank Reese had no idea what was waiting for him just a couple of miles down the road. If he had, he would probably have turned around and taken the longer Frog Lane route home that evening. Evening? Well, it was almost six-thirty so, yes, early evening.

It was already dark; he'd had a couple of beers... Okay, so he'd had four, but being the drinker he was, they'd had no effect on his ability to keep the little machine he was driving on the straight and narrow... the road, that is.

He'd spent most of the afternoon with his buddy Joe, lazing around, watching TV, and just generally hanging out and shooting the shit. They were both in their twenties, no girlfriends—ha, with his schedule how would that even be possible? Now he was on his way home to bed.

His family owned a small dairy farm, and he had to be up at four-thirty in the morning with the cows, literally. They had to be milked and, though he would never admit it to anyone, especially Joe, milking time was his favorite part of the day. It was quiet, the cows were always happy to see him, and dang if they weren't easy to talk to. Not like talking to a girl. Somehow, he always managed to say the wrong thing no matter how hard he tried. *Now cows... Well, they understand, don't they? And they never talk back.*

He made the left turn off Calumet onto Route 18 and cranked up the gas, pushing the little machine to a hair-raising forty-two miles an hour, which would have been exhilarating in daylight. In the dark, however, on the narrow rural road, it was pretty damn dangerous. Dangerous or not, his bed was calling and there was little traffic so on he went, the wind in his face, a knight riding into battle... *Shit!*

He hit the brake, braced himself, closed his eyes, and waited for the impact. It never came. He opened his eyes to find himself on the wrong side of the road, almost nose to nose with a car. The dark vehicle he'd almost smashed into was parked half on and half off the side of the road. *Stupid son of a... What the hell?*

He backed up a little, climbed off the machine, set it on its stand, pulled a flashlight out of the toolbox, took a step forward, and stopped. He took a deep breath then shone the flashlight on the car.

The passenger side of the car's windshield was shattered...

He stepped to the driver's side door and peeked in, the small beam from his flashlight illuminating the inside. The driver's seat was empty, but the passenger side... He gasped. There was a man with a gaping hole where his nose should have been. The dash, console, and window were awash in blood and... "Holy shit!" he whispered, as he staggered two steps backward, fumbling in his pants pocket for his phone. He dragged it out and punched in 911: nothing. He looked at the screen... *Shit, no service!*

He ran to his bike, hopped on, turned around and drove back the way he'd come, holding his phone in front of his face, waiting for service. Two miles on he was able to make the call and was told by the dispatcher to return to the scene and wait for assistance, and under no circumstances was he to touch anything.

Ten minutes later, and stone-cold sober, he was sitting in the darkness on the shoulder some twenty yards from the car, his elbows on his knees, his head in his hands, wondering what the hell he'd gotten himself into, wishing to hell that instead of being nosey he'd just driven right on by. But deep down he knew that would have been the wrong thing to do. *Unneighborly even.*

He lifted his head quickly; something rustled in the cornfield behind him. With his heart pounding, he sprang to his feet and headed to his bike to retrieve the flashlight.

And then Hank heard the distant wail of approaching sirens.

1

I knew my workday was going to be rough when I woke to find the sun had already set—yes, I was on the night shift—and I'd just showered and was drying my hair when I noticed several gray hairs just above my left temple. *Holy cow... really?*

For a minute I just stood there and stared at them. There are some women I know who would freak out at such a devastating discovery, don a baseball cap, dash to the nearest drug store and grab a box full of chemicals. And I have to tell you that, for a moment I was tempted to do just that, but I didn't. For one thing, I knew no one would notice since I'm a blonde... well, a dark blonde, and second, I was working nights, and only the freaks come out at night, right?

I'd been working the late shift—seven to seven—for the past several months. It came with my promotion to Captain.

Captain Catherine Gazzara. You have to admit, it does have a nice ring to it; the pay's not bad either. But with the promotion came new responsibilities, so it really was no surprise to see those gray hairs. I guess the surprise was that there weren't more of them.

I was, after all, forty-two years old. Do I sound like I was obsessing? Maybe I was, but not for long; I had a job to get to.

So, I shrugged, accepted the inevitable, finished my morning routine, drank a cup of lukewarm black coffee, and then dressed in jeans, a white top, and a black leather biker jacket that had set me back a week's pay. I tied my hair back in a ponytail, drank another cup of coffee, and headed out into the burgeoning night.

It was almost seven when I arrived at the police department that Tuesday evening in December, to find my partner, Sergeant Janet Toliver, nervously awaiting me, which was not a good thing and I felt my skin begin to prickle.

"Good evening, Captain," Janet said, unusually formal and looking even more like a teenager than she normally did. Her looks, though, were deceiving. She was a bubbly little thing, only twenty-five years old with red hair, green eyes, an upturned nose, freckles and, well, you get the idea. As I said, looks can be deceiving. The girl was more than capable of handling herself on the job, on the street, and in a scrap. She'd been with me almost two years and had had my back more times than I cared to admit.

"What's up, Janet?" I asked.

"Chief Johnston's waiting for you, in your office." She looked over her shoulder then back at me. "He's been in there for about fifteen minutes. He looks like he's loaded for bear."

"He always looks like that," I said with more confidence than I felt. "What's he doing?"

"Just sitting there with his eyes closed, waiting for you. Was I supposed to ask him what he wanted?"

"No," I replied, pursing my lips.

The Chief waiting in your office can never be a good thing.

I tried to think back on all the cases I'd worked over the last few months and who I might have upset during the course thereof. A cop's life isn't easy these days—not that it ever was. Thirty-eight officers killed nationwide in the line of duty already that year; thank God it was almost over. And God only knew how many false accusations had been leveled at hard-working officers. There was always a perp claiming a cop had roughed them up or someone had forgotten to read them their rights. It had happened to me more than once. But try as I might, I couldn't think of anything I'd done that could have gotten me into trouble, but that didn't mean there wasn't something, something I'd overlooked that had caused a major-league logjam for someone. In this case, the Chief of Police, Wesley Johnston.

And suddenly I felt like I was back in high school, called to the principal's office. Hell, I knew I wasn't the best student in class, so what I could have done wrong was anyone's guess.

"Okay," I said. "I'll go see what he wants. I'll give you a call when we're done."

I adjusted my purse over my shoulder, checked my Glock and badge on my waist, made sure my top was tucked properly into my jeans, and headed to my office. My new office. Another perk of my promotion. I had tons more shelf space, my desk was bigger, there was a round table for meetings with a half-dozen straight-backed chairs, a coffee table and... Lordy, Lordy, a small but comfy couch; I even had a small, personal coffee maker, but that was between me and nobody else.

"Hey, DG. The Captain is waiting in your office," Lennie Miller shouted from his cubicle as I crossed the situation room. Lennie is a junior detective and something of a computer wiz, another perk of my promotion. I nodded and hurried before he could yell something else.

Chief Johnston was seated on my couch. His long legs stretched out in front and crossed at the ankles, his arms folded across his chest. Had I not known better, I might have thought he was taking a nap.

"Evening, Chief," I said, brightly, closing the door behind me and dumping my bag on my desk. "What's the haps?"

"Catherine. I need to talk to you."

Catherine? He was the only one that ever called me that, and then only when I was in trouble or he wanted to make a serious point. I figured I was in trouble.

"Look," I said, "I can vouch for my team. Whatever the accusations are they are false. Internal Affairs can come talk to me." I blurted the words out before I even realized I was speaking.

"Relax, Kate. You're becoming paranoid. No one has made any accusations..." He paused, like he'd had a sudden thought. "At least that I know of. But the fact that you're so willing to talk to Internal Affairs makes me very nervous."

He wasn't smiling, just stared up at me as if he was waiting for a confession.

"Oh," I said, offhandedly, "you know the old saying: hope for the best but expect the worst." I smiled and slipped behind my desk, shoved the small stack of files aside, folded my hands, and leaned forward.

Even seated as he was, Chief Wesley Johnston cut an imposing figure. He was, as always, impeccably dressed, his uniform pressed to perfection, which was probably why he was stretched out the way he was.

"Kate, fifteen minutes ago a call came in, a report of a robbery-homicide on Rural Route 18 just before it intersects with Pellmont Road. The car's registered to a Jack Logan, an accountant. I want you and your team to handle it."

He unfolded his arms, sat up straight, rubbed his shiny bald head, and looked at me across the desk, obviously waiting for me to speak.

"Sure, Chief, but... isn't that area kind of iffy for jurisdiction? I'm not going to run into an angry Sheriff White, am I?"

"It's within the city limits, but not by much... maybe ten or twenty yards. You shouldn't have any problems. I'll talk to Whitey. But, Kate, I need for you to be extra careful with this one." The Chief swallowed hard, as if he had a sore throat.

"Of course. Can I ask why?"

"I knew the man. Well, I did, but not as well as my neighbor did."

He cleared his throat and continued, "My neighbor, Jimmy, and I became friends the day he and his wife and kids moved in about twelve years ago. Our kids played together. Our wives went shopping together. Holidays and birthdays, we always spent at least some time together."

Chief Johnston had a smile on his face, something I rarely saw. Then the smile disappeared and he said, "That's how I became acquainted with the victim, through Jimmy Boyd. Jack Logan was Jimmy's sister's ex-husband. Logan's ex-wife's name is Cynthia, by the way."

"I see," I said.

"According to Jimmy, they preferred Jack's company to Cynthia's, even though she was Jimmy's own sister. I met Jack and Cynthia on more than one occasion at Jimmy's house, and quite frankly, I could see why. Cynthia was a... Well, never mind."

The Chief cleared his throat again. "Jack was just a nice guy. A good conversationalist, knowledgeable, knew a little something about everything, but he wasn't a know-it-all. He was a good guy. You felt comfortable around him. It's a real shame."

"And what about Cynthia, the victim's ex-wife? You were about to say something and then stopped... So what's she like?" I asked.

"She's a trip..." The Chief shook his head. "Has a foul mouth. Laughs at her own jokes though they were never that funny. I think she's in denial about her age, wants to be twenty-one again but that ship sailed about twenty years ago."

"Is she a suspect?" I asked.

He thought for a minute, then said, "She could be. According to Jimmy, Cynthia wasn't happy that Jack remarried. Be careful when you talk to her, Kate. She's an alligator looking for someone to eat. Don't let it be you."

He shook his head, ran a hand over its shiny surface, did that slicky thing men do with their mustaches, then stood and smoothed the front of his pants.

"Oh, and Catherine, if there *is* anything Internal Affairs might be wanting to talk to me about, I want to know about it. I don't want to be blindsided, so tell me... Now!"

"There's nothing, Chief. Not a thing!"

He nodded, turned and walked out of the room, closing the door behind him.

I let out a long sigh of relief, looked at the stack of files on my desk and sighed again. I'm no desk jockey; never will be. It was something I'd made clear when Chief Johnston offered me my promotion to captain. I'm a detective, not an administrator. Paperwork gives me gray hairs, literally, as I'd found out just that morning.

So I slid the stack of files back to the center of my desk, patted the one on top gently and smiled to myself, feeling proud that if nothing else I had at least touched them. Then I grabbed my purse, called Janet and, like Captain Jack Sparrow, headed out to the edge of my world, the Chattanooga city limits and the end of my jurisdiction, stopping only to fill my thirty-two-ounce flask at the incident room urn. Yuk!

2

Driving along Pellmont Road, even in daylight, was like heading off into a David Lynch movie. At night, it was a dark, lonely narrow two-lane at the northwest city limit dotted here and there by glowing porch lights set back off the road like unblinking eyes. Occasionally, we'd see the gleaming green and gold eyes of a raccoon or possum caught in the headlights, sometimes in the middle of the road, sometimes in the tall grass on the roadside.

Finally, in the distance, we saw the cluster of red and blue flashing lights of the police vehicles and the red and white lights of an ambulance and, every few seconds a bright flash of white light. Mike Willis' CSI team had positioned three portable high-intensity lights and were already working the scene and taking pictures.

"If they're taking pictures, that means Doc is already here," I said.

Doctor Richard Sheddon, Hamilton County's Chief Medical Examiner, was one of the few people I could rely on to keep me sane in a world where death is the norm rather than the exception. He was, still is, my friend, a rock to lean on when things get tough.

He's not a big man... well, not tall anyway. He's around five-eight, in his late fifties, overweight, almost totally bald, with a round face that usually sports half-glasses and a jovial expression. He treats unnatural death as if it's nothing more than part of the natural order of things, which I suppose it is.

"He makes me nervous," Janet said.

"Doc? Why?" I asked, glancing sideways at her.

"I don't know," she said, keeping her eyes on the road as she negotiated a sharp bend. "He doesn't really talk, does he? He barks. And whenever I have to meet him at the Forensic Center, he offers me coffee cake with raspberries or cherries or something that resembles something he's just removed from a body." Janet pulled her lips down at the corners. "He's weird."

I smiled. "Yeah, I suppose he is, a little. That's why I like him."

"I'm not talking bad about him, DG. I like him well enough but... well, he makes me nervous. Sorry. I'm just saying."

"No need to be sorry. I understand what you're saying. He's been talking to the dead for more than twenty-five years. So yes, he's different. Don't tell me that wouldn't make you a little weird, too."

She nodded, then shrugged as she pulled up and parked behind one of the cruisers.

"I guess you've got a point," she said, as she snapped on a pair of latex gloves while I grabbed my coffee from the cup holder, and we exited the car.

"Wait," I said, putting a hand on her arm.

"Why? What's wrong?"

"Nothing. I just want to look for a minute."

Mike Willis's crime scene unit was parked almost in the ditch some twenty yards or so back from a metallic silver sedan that appeared to have run off the road almost into the cornfield, and it would have, had its passenger side front wheel not dropped into a shallow ditch.

I stood for a moment, staring at the sedan, then looked back down the road; beyond the dome of light put out by Mike's lights it was dark, really dark.

"Come on," I said as I walked toward the car. There were no skid marks that I could see, so it didn't look like the driver had lost control of the vehicle and swerved off the road. None of the tires were flat. I wondered if the airbags hadn't gone off. It looked more like it had been deliberately parked, that the driver had intentionally parked out in the middle of nowhere.

"Hey, Kate," Doc said from somewhere behind me. "You brought coffee and something to eat, I hope. Hey, Janet. Nice night for it, right?"

"I think there may be a Twinkie from 1998 in my glove box. You can have it if you want," I said, handing him my coffee without looking up as I studied the outside of the car.

I took a pair of latex gloves from my pocket and put them on, then took a step forward... A head bobbed up above the car's roof on the far side of the vehicle, the passenger side.

"Hold on, Kate. Give me a second. I'm not quite done here yet."

It was Mike Willis, standing at the edge of the ditch, taking pictures. I nodded.

He disappeared again and a couple of seconds later reappeared.

"Okay," he said. "I'm done. We haven't opened the doors or moved anything... yet. The flatbed truck should be here soon, but take your time."

The car was a Chrysler Sebring and, thanks to the Chief, I already knew that it was registered to a Jack L. Logan. I took another step forward and shined my flashlight in the driver's side window. Logan, what was left of him, was in the passenger seat, slumped against the door, his head lolled to the right resting against the door frame. There was what looked like a bullet wound to his left temple, and his left eye and most of his nose were missing. There was a hole in the windshield surrounded by blood spatter and a large smear of thick, viscous blood on the dash...

Geez, he must have been shot in the back of the head, thrown forward and then... And then what? The killer pulled him upright, positioned him? Why is he in the passenger seat? What the hell? How the hell? Why?

I heard a car door open nearby and then a moment later slam shut again, then the rustle of plastic wrap. I stood, turned, and stepped aside so that Janet could take a look.

"I had to run out of my house," Doc said as he stuffed the wrapper in his pocket with one hand and took a bite of the Twinkie in the other. "No time to eat anything. Umm, I haven't had one of these in a coon's age." He smacked his lips.

"Where's my coffee, Doc?"

"Oh... yes, sorry." He returned to my car, retrieved the cup from the hood.

"Here you go," he said, after taking a huge gulp and then handing it to me.

I hefted the cup; it felt like it was almost empty. I cut him a dirty look. He grinned back at me unperturbed.

"What do you think, Doc?" I asked.

"Pretty damn good for 1998..." he mumbled, his mouth full. "Oh, you mean... Well, probably a nine-millimeter weapon, judging by the exit wound. Anything larger would have removed most of his face, not to mention the windshield. He was also shot in the left temple. There's another exit wound at the right side of his head."

He finished the Twinkie, licked his fingers, dried them on his pants, snapped on a pair of purple latex gloves, then held out his hand for my coffee. I handed it to him and he closed his eyes and took a huge gulp.

"Oh my," I said sarcastically. "Would you like some coffee?" I looked from him to the cup and back again.

"Took you long enough to ask," he grumbled, then took another sip and handed it back to me... empty. *Damn it, Doc!*

I hefted the cup, sighed resignedly, handed it off to Janet, opened the driver's side door, leaned inside for a closer look at the body, and said, "So, time of death?" The inside of the car had that coppery smell about it. *Geez, I hate the smell of blood.*

"You know better than to ask that question when we have yet to extract the body from the vehicle... Judging from how much the blood has coagulated... not long, two hours, three at the most. Once we get him out of there, I'll check the liver temperature... My question is, though: what the hell is he doing in the passenger seat?"

It was a question I was asking myself, so I didn't bother to answer.

"So," I said, checking my watch—it was just after eight, "it was called in at six-thirty-one, so that narrows it down to... sometime between five and six-thirty... Hey, there's something under the seat." I reached beneath the seat and felt a soft, thick object. It was a wallet. I opened it.

"Jack L. Logan," I muttered. "I knew that."

There was a wedding picture of him and his wife, several credit cards in designated slots, but no cash. *Robbery, then? Petty cash? Not something to kill for, but I've seen people shot dead for the price of a burger, so...* I let the thought go, extricated myself from the car, and stood back, the wallet still in my hands. I wouldn't know if anything was missing until I spoke with his wife... *his current wife.*

"Janet?" I called.

"Yeah, DG," she replied. She was standing on the road with Mike Willis.

"Any word on the tow truck?" I asked.

"On their way," Willis replied. "They called and said they're about five minutes out."

I nodded, stared at the wallet, then at the interior of the car, and shook my head. *I just don't get it... If he was jacked... surely the jacker would have been in the passenger seat. And where the hell did he go? At five-thirty it would have been getting dark. It's more than three miles back to civilization. Did someone pick him up? Did anyone see him? I kinda doubt it. Why here?*

This was not a strategic execution. This was a murder either for the joy of killing or for the money. I was leaning toward the second option. Jack Logan was in the wrong place at the wrong time. A carjacking that escalated. Maybe. Maybe he picked up a hitchhiker.

No good deed goes unpunished... but again, why was he in the passenger seat?

I snapped a couple photos of the body with my iPhone: a close-up of the head and the wound to the temple. Then I went around to the passenger side of the car, opened the rear door and snapped a couple of pics of the wound to the back of his head. *How the hell did the killer do that... and why? Two... of them?*

"Where's the person who phoned this in?" I asked Doc, closing the car door.

Doc shrugged; he was focused on the paramedics who were beginning to extricate the body.

I looked around. There was a weird glow over the scene from the LED lights: shadows, flickering shadows as the techs went about their tasks. Darker shadows beyond the reach of the lights. Beyond that, nothing but blackness.

I saw three uniformed officers standing together beside one of the cruisers. There was a man with them. He was talking to one of the officers. *That's him,* I thought, *has to be.*

He was wearing jeans, a flannel shirt and a heavy jacket, shifting from one foot to the other, back and forth. I walked over and joined the group.

"Detective Gazzara, this is Hank Reese," the uniformed officer said. "He called it in."

"Thank you, Officer," I said.

The officer nodded, stepped backward and away to join the other three who were now helping Doc and Janet with the body.

"Hello, Mr. Reese," I said. "Thank you for staying. I really appreciate it. What can you tell me? Oh, just give me a minute, please. I'll be right back."

Out of the corner of my eye, I'd spotted the flatbed arriving. I stepped over to the truck where Mike Willis was talking to the driver.

"Mike. Don't let them take it away until I've had a word. I'm talking to that guy over there. I should be finished with him shortly, okay?"

"You got it, Captain," Willis replied.

I went back to my car and retrieved my iPad.

Hank Reese was a thin guy with a long neck in his late twenties. He had that farmer's build: wiry but muscular from bailing hay or whatever it is those people do all day.

"Now, Mr. Reese," I said, turning on the recording app. "I'm going to record our conversation, please tell me that you consent."

He did. I asked him to provide his name, address and phone number for the record. I added the time and place, and then said, "Talk to me, Mr. Reese."

"Well, see, it was like this. I was coming home from my buddy Joe's house... that's down along Calumet off 18, you know, where the Gas City is on the corner."

I nodded as he pointed off into the distance. Then I looked around for the beat-up truck I imagined he likely drove, but I didn't see one.

"So you were walking, then?"

He looked at me like I was crazy.

"What? Walking? Course not. I was ridin' that." He turned and pointed to a spot between two cruisers.

I looked at it, then at him, then at it again, and then I couldn't help but smile. It was a bright blue, Alibaba electric motorcycle.

"That's yours?" I asked, smiling.

"Yeah, so?"

I just shook my head, then said, "Go on, Mr. Reese."

"Well. As I said, I was comin' back from Joe's. We'd just been hanging out, had a few beers, watched a couple movies, just shootin' the shit. Oh, pardon me, ma'am." Reese paused, looked embarrassed.

I said nothing.

"So I was heading back. See, I gotta be at the milkin' shed by four-thirty each morning. They get ornery if I'm late... the cows, you know?" I nodded and he continued, "Anyway, I didn't see it, see. An' I almost run into it. The car, right there; it was just parked... At first, I thought maybe the dude had been drinking and drove into the ditch. But then when I got closer, I could see he hadn't... drove into the ditch, at least I didn't think so. It looked like he'd tried to park but drove a little too far off the pavement." He paused again, his mind obviously somewhere else.

"See, I lost my father last year. He'd gone to start one of our tractors and had a heart attack right there in the seat."

"I'm sorry," I said, wondering where the hell he was going with it.

"Thank you," he said. "But I thought maybe, that is, maybe this man had the same thing happen to him, a heart attack, like. I got a flashlight in the toolbox." He nodded toward the bike. "You never know when it's going to run out of juice... So I shined it in the car. But when I got close to it, I saw all the blood." He shook his head and ran his hand through his hair again. "I just about lost my lunch... know what I mean?"

I nodded, then said, "Did you touch anything, Mr. Reese?"

"No, ma'am. I freaked out. I went back to my bike and called y'all. Part of me wanted to ride away and get home, but I figured that wouldn't look all that good. Besides, I wouldn't want to be just left out here if it was me. Even if I was dead. I'd hope someone would wait around to make sure I got found."

I gathered a few more details from him and informed him that I'd be checking his alibi.

"Of course, Detective. I'm telling the truth. No doubt about that," he stuttered.

"Mr. Reese, did you notice anything unusual when you pulled up, or while you were waiting? Another set of taillights? Did anyone pass you going in the opposite direction? Did you hear anything strange when you stopped? Did you smell anything unusual?"

"I held my breath when I saw that body in there." He looked at the ground and I could tell he was giving it his best shot to remember everything. "I'm sorry. There wasn't anything."

"Thank you, Mr. Reese," I said. "I'll need a formal statement from you. You can do it here, or at the department later tonight; your choice."

He nodded. "I need to get to work. Can we do it later, say after three this afternoon?"

I told him he could, gave him my business card, and told him someone would be expecting him. He looked at it and then at me. "I never met a female detective before." He looked at me and grinned.

"All the ones you met were men, huh?" I said as I started to walk away.

"Oh, no. I never... I mean... I never met even one detective before."

He was trying to clarify even though I knew what he meant. I just liked to put people on the spot. It was my job and hard to stop when I found it so much fun.

I watched him climb onto the incongruously tiny electric bike and ride wobbly away, then I walked to where Jack Logan's car was being winched up onto the back of the flatbed.

Doc Sheddon was at the back of the ambulance with his patient, Jack Logan. The body was in a bag ready for transportation to Doc's little shop of horrors.

3

"Okay. Guess what happened while you were interviewing the witness?" Janet said as we drove back toward the city. She waited two seconds and then said, "I'll tell you because you'll never guess. We were loading the victim onto the gurney, and his cell phone fell out of his pocket."

"That's a plus," I said. "Anything interesting on it?"

"Dunno. It's got a passcode, so I'll get Miller on it as soon as we get back to the office. The uniforms are going to inform the victim's wife, but we need to talk to her, too, so I thought I'd take Ann with me... You'll be going to Doc's place, right?"

I nodded.

"You know," she said, "two women: his wife and his ex-wife... maybe he was having an affair? If there were any domestic issues... well, you never know, do you? We could have it wrapped up by morning."

"That's what you think, is it, that he was having an affair?" I asked.

"I don't know what to think," she replied. "He seems like a good guy to me, based on what the Chief told you, but... Look, I ran his record before we left the PD. He has no priors. Not so much as a traffic ticket. You said there was no cash in his wallet, but his credit cards were all still there. Maybe someone was trying to make it look like a robbery."

"We don't know that all of his cards were there," I said. "Not yet, anyway. Yes, take Ann and go talk to the wife. See what you can find out."

Detective Ann Robar was a transfer from another department. I'd known her a long time. At forty-four, she was a couple of years older than me and had more than twenty years as a cop, fifteen of them as a detective. Although Janet's perkiness got on her nerves sometimes, Ann had been showing rookie Janet the ropes. Which I appreciated.

"I want Hawk to stick with Mike Willis," I said. "I want that car processed ASAP."

"I'll call him," Janet said.

I t was almost ten o'clock when we arrived back at the PD that evening. The weather was good, though cold, and I began to wish I'd brought a heavier coat.

Janet dropped off Logan's phone with Miller, then she and Ann left to go talk to Sheila Logan while I went to my office with a stop along the way, in the incident room for a refill of my coffee mug. I could have made my own, but I just couldn't be bothered.

I checked my messages—fortunately there were none—and then spent the next hour going through the recording of the Hank Reese interview, making notes, and listing questions that still needed to be answered. I had it at the back of my mind that I was dealing with something more than a carjacking gone wrong. Those two head wounds bothered me.

I took out my phone, pulled up the images I'd shot inside Logan's car, and sent them to my printer. Then I taped them up on the whiteboard and, with a black marker, drew a large question mark alongside the photos of the head wounds.

I started the list of questions:

1. Why shoot him twice?
2. Why was Logan in the passenger seat?
3. Why take the cash but leave the wallet and the credit cards behind?
4. One perp or two?

I had no answers, nor would I until I'd talked to Doc and Mike Willis.

I leaned back in my chair, put my hands behind my head, and closed my eyes, trying to imagine how it could have happened. I couldn't. All I could see were two dark, unidentifiable images of someone in the driver's seat and someone in the back seat.

Two people? Hitchhikers? I doubt it. No one in their right mind would risk picking up two strangers, not these days. Friends, then? Possibly. Shit! Who the hell knows?

I let myself fall forward onto my feet, grabbed my coffee and, with a final look at the images on the board, I left and headed over to the medical examiner's office.

4

When I pulled into the parking lot out front of Doc Sheddon's Forensic Center, it was empty, no vehicles; it was, after all, almost midnight so I had to assume that the front door was locked. That being so, I drove around back. The parking lot there was also empty, except for Doc's car. I parked next to it and sat for a moment, as I always did before entering what I liked to think of as the dead zone, gathering myself for the ordeal that was to come.

The Forensic Center—I often wondered why they called it that, because the only forensics that went on inside were medical examinations; Mike Willis ran CSI from a suite of offices and a lab inside the PD. Anyway, the Forensic Center was a small, unremarkable building located on Amnicola just three blocks from the police department—The Police Services Center. Try saying that three times quickly when you've had a couple of glasses of red.

Doc's place was, and still is, comprised of a suite of three offices, two examination rooms, several labs and a nasty little section—I don't know what else to call it—where Carol Oats, the resident forensic anthropologist, stripped unidentified, unclaimed bodies down to their bare bones, literally. I hate the Forensic Center.

I hit the buzzer at the outer door and Doc's tinny voice asked, "That you, Kate?"

I confirmed that it was indeed me, the lock clicked, and I pushed the door open and stepped inside.

I made my way along the corridor to the first of the two autopsy rooms and found Doc inside bending over a naked body on one of the three stainless steel autopsy tables.

He, Doc, was dressed from head to toe in green scrubs, a face shield, and a vast rubber apron already liberally smeared with blood. He'd already made the "Y" incision and peeled back the flesh revealing the ribcage still in situ; he looked like frickin' Frankenstein.

"Better cover up," he called as I stood in the doorway. "And hurry up, you're letting all the cold air out."

I took a deep breath, sighed, turned, and did as he asked. I joined him a couple of minutes later dressed in a pale blue Tyvek coverall, safety glasses, and a breathing mask.

The naked body on the table was, of course, that of Jack Logan. His clothes had been bagged and tagged and set aside ready for transportation to Mike Willis' department for processing.

"Don't tell me you dragged Carol in at this time of night," I said, eyeing the evidence bags.

"I did. You just missed her."

I approached the table and stood opposite him, Logan's body between us.

"So, Doc," I said resignedly. "Tell me what we've got."

"White male, one hundred-ninety-three pounds, five feet ten and one-half inches tall, dead as the proverbial dodo bird. Cause of death... one of two gunshot wounds to the head. It's impossible to tell which shot killed him, because it's impossible to determine which was fired first. Either one would have killed him, instantly. My considered opinion is that... he was shot first from the driver's seat, in the left temple, then in the back of the head, probably by someone sitting in the back seat, though why... Well, one can only speculate; it was certainly overkill."

"So," I said, "it could have been a carjacking?"

"It could indeed, which would account for him being in the passenger seat. But carjackers usually want only the car, don't they? They usually toss the driver... So why would they take the vehicle and its owner, and add kidnapping and, in this case, murder to their crime? No, I'm not sold on carjacking."

"What about an old-fashioned robbery?" I asked.

"Nope. You see, he was shot in the side of the head, but that might have been an accident. Whoever was driving was probably pointing the gun at him, may not have had any intention of actually killing him. But say as they are driving, the car hits a pothole or the shoulder, and the gun goes off... but that still doesn't explain the bullet to the back of the head."

"Execution style, you think?" It made sense, but then again, it didn't.

"Your guess is as good as mine," Doc said with a shrug.

"Anything else?" I asked, somewhat dejected.

"I'll be able to tell you what he ate for dinner in an hour or so. Might be helpful for tracking his movements." Doc handed the file to me to look over. "The weapons were both probably nine-millimeter. Both bullets exited so I won't find them, maybe a fragment or two, but that's all."

"That narrows it down to just three-fourths of a haystack to find that needle," I replied. "Time of death?"

He shrugged. "It was nine-oh-four when I checked the liver temp. It was ninety-five point two. Normal body temperature is ninety-eight point six. The body normally cools at a rate of one point five degrees per hour, so between five-thirty and six-thirty, give or take a few minutes either way."

I looked at the diagram that showed where the bullets entered and exited the victim's head. "All right, Doc. I'll let you finish up here. Call me if you find anything new. When can I have the report?" I handed the slim file back to him.

"When it's done, Kate, when it's done. Now, if you're going... well, you know the way out," Doc said as he grabbed a set of bone shears and positioned himself over Jack Logan's torso. He was about to remove the ribcage, and I wasn't about to hang around to watch. I hated that part; the crunch and crack of bones. I had to get out of there.

"Thanks, Doc. Not going to wish me 'good luck'? No 'let's be careful out there'? Nothing?"

"Don't forget to lock the door when you leave," Doc said without looking up. "And let's be careful out there."

I smiled, did as I was told, left through the rear door, and walked to my car, my mind already churning with possibilities. As I punched the starter button and drove slowly back to the depart-ment—it took all of two minutes—I began to think again about the location of the two entry wounds and how the body was positioned in the passenger seat.

Logan had been shot in the left temple. The impact of the bullet would have shoved his body to the right. Then, he was shot in the back of the head at point-blank range. The stippling of gunshot residue around the entry was plain to see. The impact from that wound should have thrown his body forward, but he was sitting upright in the passenger seat.

I sat for a moment in the parking lot at the rear of the PD and pulled up the images I'd taken with my iPhone: *seat belt's not fastened... hmm.*

It wasn't much, but I felt like it was at least a little grease to get the gears moving. I couldn't even say why. So much of police work is guesswork based on a hunch, and I'll even go so far as to say divine intervention. I think maybe it's God's way of helping people like me stay sane when we have to face so much insanity every day. If He didn't drop a clue directly in our laps every now and then... well; my own opinion, of course. Anyway, something about those tiny images triggered a memory and I had to check it out.

So, instead of checking in with my team, I snuck into the elevator and went down to the basement—to the morgue, this one being where the cold case files are stored, not dead bodies.

The morgue is a sad place that few of us visit more than the obligatory once a year—to update the files we've never solved but put to rest, nonetheless. Somehow, though, I always felt comfortable down there among the lost. Not because I was particularly proud that I'd been able to shift a few of them to the closed list, but because I knew I'd made a difference, and would continue to do so. But that was not why I was there that day. As I said, my cell phone images had triggered a memory and... a name.

Some twenty minutes later I found what I was looking for.

"Ah-ha!" I said, breaking the stillness in the room. "There you are, Mr. Cappy T. Mallard."

Who wouldn't remember a name like that? More to the point, who would name their child Cappy? It must have been hell for the kid, having to go through middle and high school with a name like that.

I heaved the cardboard banker's box down from the shelf, carried it to a nearby table, and lifted the lid. The murder book was at the top of the pile of paperwork: reports, interviews, etc., etc. I picked it up, opened it, and flipped quickly through the pages to the photographs, and there he was. It was as if I'd taken the photos myself. Cappy was in the passenger seat of his car. The positioning was almost identical to that of Jack Logan, as was the cause of death: one shot to the temple and one to the back of the head. Cappy's car had been discovered in an industrial park about a mile away from Rural Road 18.

I closed the murder book, put it back in the box, put the lid back on, and then hauled it over to the elevator.

I dumped the box on my desk and returned to the incident room.

Lennie Miller was seated at his desk between two stacks of files, one on either side of his desktop. A third, sloppy but smaller stack of papers was in his inbox; his outbox contained only a couple of single sheets of paper. His laptop was closed and there was an empty coffee cup in front of him.

Lennie was the fourth member of my team. Younger looking than his twenty-eight years and wearing a dark blue, two-piece suit with a white T-shirt. He was tall, maybe five-eleven, with the soft almost pudgy build of a guy into all things techie, but a happy kind of individual with one of those "unshaved look" beards that made him look both scruffy and handsome at the same time. Me? It did nothing for me. He was a good guy, though, and still lived at home to help out his widowed mom.

"What do you have for me, Lennie?" I asked, startling him.

"Oh, hi, DG. I didn't see you come in." He coughed, as he usually did before he started to explain what he was doing. "This was pretty simple." He held up Logan's Samsung phone.

I could see he was about to dive right into a long-winded explanation, so I put my hand up to stop him. I had little interest in what he did to make things work, or his expertise at hacking, computers, phones, codes, GPS, or the Dark Web. My only interest was in the results of what he did.

"I know you're good at what you do, Lennie. Just tell me," I said. "Were you able to unlock it?"

"No problem, DG. He used his wife's birthday for his passcode. You'd be surprised at how many people do that. I wouldn't recommend it. It's too easy to figure out. Plus, anyone can get access to all your basic personal info, you know, the stuff people say isn't important like birthdays and anniversaries and the kind of cars you've owned. It's really rather spooky how much you can get from—"

Geez, he's Tim Clarke made over. Are they all like that, I wonder?

"Spare me the lecture on internet fraud, Lennie," I said impatiently. "Just tell me what you found?" I gave him a quick smile. He was a chatty Cathy. But he was amazing when it came to the gadgets... Not as good as Tim, but better than I probably deserved.

"It looks like the last person he spoke to was his wife, Sherri, at five-oh-eight," Miller said. "The call originated from somewhere in this area here."

He opened his laptop and turned it to face me. I knew what I was looking at. It was a map of Chattanooga pinpointing all the cell phone towers and where our victim's phone had pinged. There were three towers within the radius we were looking at where Jack had called his wife. I looked at my watch and hoped Janet and Ann would be back soon.

This was good information, which of course prompted more questions. "He must have just gotten off work,

I said. "What businesses are there in and around that area that are open at five o'clock in the afternoon?" I mused.

"Good question. I'll take a look," Miller offered.

"Thanks. And I'll want a full background on him too. I'll be in my office. Let me know what you find out."

5

It was more than two hours later when I finally heard back from Doc Sheddon.

"Our friend had a burger and a couple of beers just before his demise," Doc said without saying hello. "Onion rings, too. I don't think he was watching his weight."

"Wow. That helps a lot, Doc," I said, sarcastically, and suddenly realizing how hungry I was.

"He had no tattoos, no distinguishing marks. A couple of moles he should have had checked out, but it's too late for that now, of course. He was a plain Jane if ever there was one," Doc said sadly.

"How about trace? Anything?"

"On the body? Nothing I wouldn't expect to find. No foreign hairs, particles... Both bullets exited, as one might expect from a close-quarter wound. No fragments. The shot to the left temple was fired from about twenty-six inches. The one to the back of the head was a contact wound. Other than that, the state of the corpse was quite unremarkable."

"Okay, Doc. Thanks. I'll share it with the team," I said, my mind already starting to piece together some possible directions we could take.

"Yeah, well, don't say I never gave you anything," he grumbled.

"You know I'd never do that, Doc. You're one of my favorite people. And I've only got two."

"There are *two* people who'll tolerate you? Just remember I'm paid to. Who's the other, I wonder?" The smirk in his voice was evident.

"I could tell you but... well, you know how the saying goes," I said. "Would you mind emailing the photos to me, please?"

He said he would and I hung up, just as there was a knock on my door.

"Come in," I called.

"DG, do you have time for us?" Ann Robar said as she stuck her head inside.

"Sure," I said and set my cold case file aside and picked up what was left of my now cold cup of coffee. "Come on in; sit down; talk to me. What did you learn from Mrs. Logan?"

Ann sat on the couch. Janet took one of the chairs from the table, turned it around to face the middle of the room, and sat down.

Ann Robar was a striking woman, not quite a beauty but... well, striking. Her closely cropped hair, prematurely graying, framed an oval face. Her hazel eyes were clear and intense, though the crow's feet indicated that the woman had spent far too long in the sun without protection, and now her skin was suffering for it. At five-ten, she was almost two inches shorter than me, but she carried herself well... almost arrogantly. She was short on patience and didn't take crap from anyone. She was also married with two teenage boys, both of them still in high school. She was a senior detective and a good one. Could have been a higher rank, but family was her priority, and I admired her dedication to them. She was dressed, as she almost always was, in a white T-shirt and jeans.

I don't think I ever saw her wear slacks or a blouse, certainly never in a skirt.

"She already knew her husband was dead," Ann said. "The uniforms had informed her. She seemed genuinely distraught."

She opened her iPad, flipped through several screens, then said, "Mrs. Sherri Logan, age forty-two, was his second wife. They married in 2005, so they were married for almost fourteen years. They had no children. She said that they had their problems, like all couples do, but the good times outweighed the bad. I saw nothing in her behavior that indicated she might have had anything to do with his death." She looked at Janet.

Janet nodded and said, "She said he called her after work and told her he was going to have a beer, something to eat, and maybe watch something on ESPN, and he'd be home by ten. She also said she had a headache and went to bed early, around nine. The next she knew was when the uniforms were knocking on her door."

"We asked her if he stayed out often," Ann said, "and if he was in the habit of coming home late. She said usually only if the Packers or the Braves were playing, but sometimes, whenever he'd had a rough day, he'd stop off somewhere and watch whatever's on, just to relax.

"She also claimed that she isn't into sports and doesn't like to drink, so in deference to her he usually watched the games at a sports bar. He was never out later than eleven and gave her no reason to worry about him, where he was or what he was doing. He treated her well, so she saw nothing wrong with him blowing off a little steam on his own, enjoying what he liked, baseball and football."

"What about enemies?" I asked.

"Sherri couldn't think of anyone who would want to hurt her husband," Janet said. "Apparently, he must have been quite saintly, an all-around good guy. She handled the money. They had a healthy bank account and were saving for a trip to Australia. She said that Jack wanted to go to the place furthest from where they lived but still speak English."

"Nobody's that good," I said. "I've asked Miller to run backgrounds on Logan, his wife, and his ex-wife, so we'll soon know." I paused, then said, "So do we know where he was, which bar?" I asked.

"No," Janet said, "Sherri mentioned several favorites, most of them on his way home from the office, but he'd been at a meeting with a client yesterday on the other side of town. So where he might have stopped off on the way home, she just didn't know."

"Did you get a list?" I asked.

"Yes, of course," Ann said. "D'you want a copy?"

"Not right now, but we need to check them all, no matter where he was last night. We need to find out who his friends were." I stood, went to the board, and with a marker added the words "Bars?" and "Friends?" to the list.

"Well," I said, sitting down again and leaning back in my chair. "Miller's checking the businesses in the area. Until he brings me a list, we wait. In the meantime..." I checked my watch. It was almost four in the morning. "We can't do anything now, not until morning, which it already is..." *Damn, we can't work like this. We need to be working days.*

Thankfully, I had the authority to change our schedule. A handy perk that came with my new rank.

"Go home, both of you. We're switching to the day shift. Tell Lennie to go home too. Get some sleep, a couple of hours anyway, and then go check Logan's place of work. Talk to his co-workers. We'll meet back here at ten o'clock. By then we should know something, okay?"

"Thank God we're back on days," Ann said. "What about Hawk?"

"He's with Mike Willis processing Logan's car," I said. "They should be done in time for breakfast."

They should have been, but they weren't. Anyway, Janet and Ann left my office, leaving me with my thoughts, and I had plenty.

Did Jack Logan have an encounter with a lady of questionable reputation and take her out to Rural Route 18, where things got out of hand? It happens, as I well knew, and with a guy whose entire existence seemed to be as vanilla as his was, I couldn't help but think the worst. It was always the quiet ones that had the dirtiest secrets.

"But Doc would have found proof of that, right?" I muttered to myself.

Wait until Hawk gets back. See if they found any DNA. Stop jumping the gun. Assume nothing.

I grabbed my cold case file and flipped it open, then closed it again. *I can't do this now. I need to get some rest too. It's going to be a long day.*

I set the Mallard file aside, looked up at my almost empty whiteboard, shook my head, and went home.

6

I t was just after five in the morning when I fell fully clothed on top of my bed. I think I must have been asleep even before my head hit the pillow. I woke four hours later at nine o'clock, feeling like death warmed over. I stripped off my clothes, staggered to the bathroom, turned on the shower, stepped into the cold water and almost died from the shock of it. I counted slowly to ten then turned up the heat, reveling in the warm blanket of water.

I shampooed my hair and then stepped out into the cold air of the bathroom, and I shivered, caught sight of myself in the mirror and wondered who the hell was the witch glaring back at me. *You're the one who wanted to switch to days*, I reminded myself.

I dried off, wrapped myself in a towel and went to the kitchen. Two minutes later I was seated, still wrapped in my towel, at the breakfast bar, sipping on a cup of steaming black coffee. *Thank you, Mr. Keurig, if that's what your name is.*

And suddenly I felt better... no, I felt great. I would have loved to have gone for a short run, but time was passing and I had a job to do. And I was hungry. I dressed quickly, gathered my bits and pieces together, and headed out into the wintery sunshine; it was nine-forty-five.

I stopped only to get coffee and an egg and sausage sandwich at the Bagel Shop and was in my office at the crack of ten o'clock. Janet was already there waiting for me. *Why am I not surprised?*

"Good morning, Janet," I said. "Where is everybody?"

"Ann and Lennie are getting coffee. They should be here soon."

"What about Hawk?"

"He didn't get to go home. He's still with Mike Willis processing Logan's car."

"Damn, I was hoping they'd be done. Oh never mind. Maybe they found something... or not," I said, gloomily. "Look, I have a couple of things I need to do... and I really don't want to get started on this thing until I know what, if anything, Forensics found in the car. So, why don't you and Ann run on over and talk to Logan's co-workers and see if they can add anything—friends with issues, enemies, affairs. You know the drill. I don't have to tell you how to do your jobs. Be back here by noon and we'll take it from there, okay?"

"What about Lennie?" Janet asked.

"Don't worry about him. I have a job for him to do while we're waiting for Hawk."

And she left, not looking too happy, but she left.

Me? I grabbed the cold case file, didn't I?

Poor Cappy T. Mallard. I looked first at the photos. Like Logan, he'd been found in his car. And, also like Logan, his body was in the passenger seat, but it was folded over on itself and slumped over the center console onto the driver's seat. He, too, had been shot in the left temple. And, according to the medical examiner's report, he'd also been shot in the back of the head. Mallard's blood-alcohol level was 0.19, more than twice the legal limit.

So... I thought. *He was legally drunk, unfit to drive. If someone was driving him home...*

I scanned quickly through the remaining pages of the report, looking for more similarities and differences in the two cases. A nine-millimeter handgun was the probable murder weapon in both cases. The time of death was much later for Cappy, but that was about it.

Then my heart jumped at something curious when I saw the signature. It wasn't Doc's. The name on the report was that of a Doctor Terrance Boddinger, ME.

I grabbed my phone and called Doc's office.

"Medical examiner," Doc answered.

"Hey, Doc. It's me, Kate."

"No, absolutely not. I will not leave my wife for you no matter how much you beg," he said loudly.

I grinned. Same old same old.

"Tell Sophie I say hello and that she should quit bringing your lunch this early; it's not yet ten-thirty."

Every time I called when Doc's wife was around, that was how he answered the phone. I'd love to have Chief Johnston call from my phone and see what his reaction would be.

"It's not lunch," he said. "It's breakfast. I have not yet been home since you darkened my lab at midnight. Now, what d'you want? My sausage, bacon, and egg biscuit is getting cold."

"I want to know why you didn't do the autopsy on a Cappy T. Mallard on September 3, 2013?"

"Are you serious? That's more than four years ago. I can't remember that far back... September 3, 2013, you say? Hold on, Sophie's saying something... Apparently, I was on vacation. Sophie and I took a cruise around Sicily. We were gone for twelve days. I remember now. I came home with Montezuma's revenge, and I had jet lag for a month."

"Montezuma's revenge? What the hell is that?"

"An upset stomach would be the polite way to describe it."

"Oh, I see," I said, and I did, and I decided to pursue the subject no further. "Doc, are you sure, about the date? You don't need to check your calendar to make sure?" I asked.

"*Excuse me?*" he said.

Whoops, wrong question, but...

"Come on, Doc," I said soothingly, "you know I have to ask."

He sighed. "We were on a boat," he said with an edge to his voice. "I can send you Sophie's scrapbook, if you like. It has a dozen pictures of me in a swimsuit."

I shuddered at the thought of Doc in a swimsuit.

"Okay, I believe Sophie. So, do you have Doctor Boddinger's contact information? What d'you know about him, by the way? What's he like?"

"Kate, I am eating my breakfast, but since you obviously want me to starve, and because you always want your information *immediately*, and even though the law entitles me to eat now and then—"

"You can text it to me, Doc," I replied hopefully, interrupting him.

"Of course I can. Well, Sophie can... Sophie, will you send this information to Kate from your phone? Just the address and phone number... Dear, you know I hate texting. It always comes out wrong. You're the only one who can do it right. No, not because my fingers are too fat... Kate, are you still there?"

"Yes, Doc," I whispered, shaking my head.

"Sophie is sending it to you right now."

Doc's wife took care of him and kept him in line at the same time. I couldn't help but chuckle as I thanked Doc for his help and cooperation. He grunted something unintelligible and hung up on me without saying good-bye. I wasn't a bit put out. He did it all the time.

Sophie's text came through a few seconds later, word perfect; again, I had to smile. *What the hell would he do without her, I wonder?*

"So," I muttered, "Doctor Boddinger. I'm going to need to talk to you, but not right now." I made a note of his phone number and address and set it aside.

I knew that if Doc had worked on Cappy Mallard, he would

have remembered it and made at least a comment about the similarities of the two cases during his examination of Jack Logan. I wondered if Boddinger would remember the case.

I stared at the Mallard murder book, flipped through the pages, looking at them, but not seeing them, lost in thought; what if... *No, surely not!*

And then, on a whim, or maybe it was that divine guidance coaxing me along again, I put out a request to my brothers-in-blue across the tri-state area. I sent my request to all jurisdictions as far as and including Nashville, Knoxville, the Tri-Cities, Huntsville, Alabama, and finally to Atlanta. Several hundred departments in all, and then I wondered if I hadn't over-reached. But no, if any of them had open cases that fit my MO, I would hear about it. A forlorn hope? Yes, but in my game, hope is often all you have. Whatever, I figured it was worth a try.

After all, a man gets shot and left in his car on a deserted road; that was hardly a distinctive calling card, right? It happens all the time, right? *No, not as often as you might think...What the hell am I doing opening up this can of worms?*

Was I having second thoughts? You bet, but I'd learned a long time ago, from a man I still liked to call my friend, to go with my gut. Yes, it was a hunch. The chances of this Cappy T. Mallard case sticking in the back of my head for all these years only to resurface today was a mystery all its own. The urge to tie the two cases together was something I couldn't explain. I just had to go with it.

So, I fetched myself a second cup of coffee and settled down to wait. And, wouldn't you know it? I didn't have to wait long.

7

I spent the next hour working through Cappy's case file. The lead detective, a Sergeant Paul Hicks, a guy I knew quite well, which is probably why I remembered the case... Anyway, he'd chalked it up to the work of some drifter, maybe a drunken argument gone wrong. It was his last case before retirement, so it probably didn't get the attention that it deserved.

Cappy had no family. He was, so the report said, just a guy who was in the wrong place at the wrong time and met up with the wrong guy, or guys.

Yeah, right! I thought. *Time to call the good doctor, I think.*

I dialed the number Doc had given me and waited for Boddinger to answer, and I waited, and I was just about to give up when there was a click and a stern voice said, "Who is this?"

"I'm a police officer. Is this Doctor Terrence Boddinger?"

"It is. Please properly identify yourself."

Sheesh, really?

So I identified myself and then said, "Doctor, I'm investigating a homicide that took place here in Chattanooga last night. There are similarities between my victim and the death of a Mr. Cappy T.

Mallard some five years ago, and I think the two cases might be connected. I see from the autopsy report that you did the post. Do you think we could meet to discuss it?"

"I doubt that very much, Detective." He sounded annoyed. "I have a full schedule all the way through until Christmas."

"You do understand that I'm conducting a homicide investigation, perhaps more than one?" I said. "You were the pathologist filling in for our regular medical examiner, Doctor Richard Sheddon. I really would appreciate your help, sir."

"Oh, I see. You think I, as an outsider, forgot to cross a "T" or dot an "I" and you feel a need to question my work? I can assure you, Detective, that my skills meet, if not exceed, those of your... regular ME."

What the hell is this guy talking about?

"Doctor Boddinger, no one is questioning your findings, just the opposite, in fact. As far as I can tell, everything is in order. I was hoping to discuss the case with you on a hunch that the two cases might be connected. You *do* understand two men are dead, and that Mallard's killer is still out there somewhere?"

"Detective, I understand your position, but you need to understand mine... Yes, I did the autopsy. It was, as I recall, an unremarkable case. I'm sure if there was anything unusual, I would have mentioned it in my report."

"Doctor Boddinger, I understand when you say that you're extremely busy, and I also understand that you might not be able to remember everything about an autopsy you did five years ago." I felt my chest tightening as I choked back the urge to start shouting. I was tired and aggravated by the man's attitude. "That's why I'd like to go over the file with you and have you look—"

"I remember it perfectly," he snapped, interrupting me. "Cappy T. Mallard was a transient, a visitor, passing through, from somewhere in Ohio, as I remember. He was a loner and more than likely fell in with the wrong person who robbed him and then killed him. It happens all the time. I'm sure I don't have to tell you that, Detective."

"Doctor Boddinger, you do know that if you don't comply with my request, I can have you picked up and brought in for questioning?"

"I don't like your tone, Detective. You can be sure I'll talk to your captain when I file a formal complaint. I've more things to worry about than the death of a bum more than four years ago. Now, if you don't mind, I have a speaking engagement before the Chattanooga Society of Physicians. I am also a close friend of the current Mayor."

"First of all, Doctor, I *am* Captain. Second, when you file your complaint, you'll want to talk to Chief Johnston," I said calmly. "Third, I don't give a damn who you know or where you have a speaking engagement. I'll have a unit waiting to pick you up when you return. Fourth, I'm sure the press will be interested to know that you're refusing to cooperate in a murder investigation, but hey, any publicity is good publicity, right?"

He clicked his tongue and muttered something. This was the kind of guy who would call the police because a lunatic broke into his house, then sue the department after they saved his life because they damaged a vase in the process.

He was quiet for a moment then said, curtly, "One moment, please."

I heard him walking through his house, then I heard a door shut, and then a file cabinet open and slam shut. He must have put the phone down on his desk because I heard pages being flipped. There was an interruption when someone came to his door. It was a female voice asking a question I didn't quite catch.

"I'm on the phone!" he snapped, and I heard no more of the female voice.

"Are you there, Detective?"

"Yes, I'm still here."

"Mallard, Cappy T. He was forty-eight years old. Died of two gunshot wounds to the head. One entry point at the left temple. This I believed to be the first of the two wounds. The other at the base of the skull. There was also a bruise to his right thigh I never established had anything to do with his death. He had a blood-alcohol level of zero-point one-nine, more than twice the legal limit. You see? It was as I clearly stated. It's my considered opinion that this was nothing more than a robbery gone bad."

"Yes, I know, Doctor. All of that's in the file. But didn't you think it odd that after the assailant shot Mallard in the temple, someone in the back seat shot him again in the back of the head?"

"Detective, every case of murder is odd," he said, sounding bored.

It had become obvious that I wasn't going to have a worthwhile discussion about the oddities of Cappy T. Mallard's murder with Doctor Boddinger.

"You don't remember anything else? Nothing outstanding?" I asked without much hope in my voice.

"No," Boddinger said. "Detective... you and I both know that sometimes people get killed because they make stupid decisions. Mallard was one of those people. He had too much to drink and thought he could trust the person he allowed to drive him... to wherever it was he was staying."

So, you think he let someone drive him home too? That's interesting.

"That's what you think?" I asked.

"I do. He was legally drunk and likely chatting with someone at the bar. People who drink too much often make bad choices; you know that, Detective. It's the scenario that makes the most sense. Someone sees he's intoxicated, starts a conversation with him, and offers to drive him home with the intention of robbing him. The next thing you know, the man sobers up at the last minute and by then it's too late. The viper has already slithered up your pant leg, so to speak."

He's right, of course, I thought. *But still... Maybe they didn't intend to kill him, but simply intended to rob him and take his car; they sure as hell weren't going to walk back to town... And now there were two murders, at least. Could it be that there are two predators targeting the local bars? Geez, if the press gets hold of it they'll have a field day.*

"Detective? Detective Gazzara, are you still on the line?" he snapped.

"Yes, uh... yes. Sorry, Doctor."

"Look, if you really insist on carrying on with this conversation, I must ask that we continue at another time. If not, I'll be late to my speaking engagement."

"No. I think I have enough, for now anyway. You've been very helpful; thank you... I would remind you, however, that the investigation is ongoing, and I may have to contact you again."

He didn't answer.

"I appreciate your assistance, Doctor."

He hung up without saying goodbye. *Hmm, are all doctors like that, I wonder?*

I sighed, stared at the iPhone screen, shook my head, dropped the phone onto my desktop, then leaned back in my chair, linked my fingers together at the back of my head, closed my eyes, and thought back over my conversation with the good doctor. Unfortunately, that didn't get me anywhere new, except more irritated at the doctor's arrogance.

I let my chair fall forward, set my elbows on my desktop, my hands over my ears, and I stared up at the whiteboard and my half-dozen cell phone photos of Jack Logan's body.

"You're jumping the gun, Kate," I mumbled. "Two murders do not a serial killer make. Three are required before we can call it that. Follow the trail and see where it leads."

I sat up straight, opened my laptop, and began to read through my emails...

8

It was the last email in my inbox, the one that set my world on fire. Even before I opened it, my instincts told me life was about to get harder. Why else would I be receiving an email from Sheriff Lyndon Cane in Dalton, Georgia?

The subject line read: *Regarding your cold case request.*

In a nutshell, Sheriff Cane was more than happy to share the details of a cold case that had stumped him for more than four years.

I sighed and wrote down his contact information, intending to call him as soon as I could get my act together. Even so, I couldn't help but wonder if I now had a third victim. I hoped not... but deep down, somewhere in the depths of my soul, I also hoped that it was. Then again, I wondered if maybe I was seeing ghosts and specters where there were none, where there was nothing but shadows? I needed to bring in my team; get some input, second opinions.

I shook off the feeling of impending doom and began to make a list of what needed to be done.

First, I had to track down Jack Logan's ex-wife. If she had anything to do with his death, I could put my case to bed and forget

Cappy and Sheriff Cane. It would also put to rest the tiny voice inside my head that kept telling me, *Kate, you've got a pattern killer here. Hunting season on middle-aged men is open.*

Second, I needed to get a hold of Hawk. He was working with Mike Willis's forensics team; they were still processing Logan's car.

I reached for my desk phone to call him, but before my fingers hit the handset, all hell broke loose.

There was a beep and my message light started blinking. I picked up and tapped in my code. An electronic, female voice informed me that I had five messages. That wasn't unusual, and neither were the first two messages: they were run-of-the-mill demands for overdue paperwork. The third message, however, was a punch in the gut. Sheriff Pete McGraw from Huntsville, Alabama, informed me, in a voice that sounded like gravel, that he had a cold case that matched my description.

I swallowed hard. I needed more coffee in the worst way. Even the crap in the situation room would help. I grabbed my to-go mug from the credenza and headed out, returning a few minutes later. I hadn't been seated more than a minute when there was a knock on the door and Janet, Ann, and Lennie stepped inside.

"We have news for you, Cap," Ann said.

"Sit down, all of you, round the table. We need to talk. Has anyone heard from Hawk? Any news on the car?"

"I called him last night, but it went to voicemail," Ann said as she sat down. "He texted me back that he'd be in today, but he didn't say when."

"Damn," I muttered. "Fine. So what's the news?"

"We, the three of us, have been doing research and interviews. A few months ago, Logan's current wife took out a restraining order on the ex-wife. It's good for a year," Ann said. "And someone called Lester Harris also took one out on the ex-wife six months ago; it's still good, too."

"Really, that's interesting, but just hold that thought for a minute. I have some bad news."

I stood, grabbed my coffee, stepped around my desk, and took a seat at the table between Ann and Miller.

"On a hunch I did a little digging," I said. And then I explained finding the Cappy Mallard cold case, sending out the email for a tri-state search, and the responses I'd received so far.

"So... that's four then," Miller said hesitantly. "You're thinking that we have a serial killer?"

Miller was one of those happy individuals who always seemed to be smiling, but having said the dreaded words, he looked as if he'd just seen a ghost.

"It's too soon to say," I replied. "Right now we have two victims; both died in a similar manner. We have two more possibles, but until I've talked to the two sheriffs, we can't assume anything. Yes, I have a hunch, but that's all it is. Right now, other than the similarities of these first two cases, we've nothing to go on."

It was true, but deep down, I was convinced. A hunch? I'd rather call it intuition: I had a feeling that we were going to be in for a long haul, that nothing was going to come easy. And after everything was said and done, I was almost certain we were looking for a predator, maybe two.

"Do you still want us to interview the ex-wife?" Janet asked.

"Yes. We need to eliminate her... or not," I said. "Not would be good. If she killed her ex-husband or paid someone to kill him, it would be over and done with; we could put it to bed. You and I, Janet, will go pay her a visit later. Miller, how about the bars and restaurants in the area around the three towers, what did you find?"

"Unfortunately, there are plenty of options. There's a string of eleven bars—some of them just holes-in-the-wall—several restaurants, mostly small BBQ joints and the like, and there's an Applebee's. There's also a handful of carry-outs."

"Okay, you and Ann start canvasing the area. Start with those that have security cameras. Take Jack Logan's photo with you. See if anyone remembers seeing him."

There was a tap on the door. It opened and Hawk entered.

"Hawk," I said with mock surprise. "How nice of you to join us. How was your vacation?" I said, waving him to a seat at the table.

Sergeant Arthur "Hawk" Hawkins, the third member of my small team—there were five of us, including me—was sixty-four years old. He'd been a detective for twenty-nine years and had less than a year left to go before retirement. I used to think he'd been transferred to me so that he could work out the rest of his term in relative peace, but on reflection, I think the Chief was making sure I had what I needed to get the job done. Hawk was not a huge team player, but a real asset nonetheless.

He was a handsome man, five-ten, a little overweight at two hundred ten pounds, clean-shaven, with white hair, piercing blue eyes, a sharp nose, sunburned face. I'd known him a long time, too. He came across as a tough old man, but his heart was big and soft.

He nodded, sat down, looked stone-faced at everyone, then said, "You know what I've been doing. I've spent the last eighteen hours with Willis and his team processing our victim's freakin' car."

"And?" I said.

He reached into his inside pocket and pulled out a worn notebook, flipped through the pages, and cleared his throat.

Janet looked at me and I knew what she was thinking. *How come he gets to use a paper notebook?* A couple years ago when she'd started as my partner, I made her give up her paper notebooks for an iPad.

"It's not a frickin' novel, Hawk. Just spill it," Ann said.

"Just cool your jets, Robar," he said, staring at his notes. "Okay, we did recover a bullet fragment on the dash. Willis thinks it was from the shot through the base of the skull that shattered the windshield. He's not sure, but he thinks it's a frangible."

Hawk looked at Janet, and said, "For those of you that might not know, frangible bullets are designed to break apart, to fragment on impact. That, however, doesn't always happen. The earliest versions can still go clean through a person, and even a wall, because the bullet will not always break apart and release its energy inside its intended target."

Janet's fair skin was flushed, but she listened and gave Hawk a single nod when he finished.

He flipped another page, then continued, "There were several medium-length blond hairs on the driver's headrest, obviously out of a bottle—according to Willis—and obviously not the victim's. We found plenty more, most of which probably belonged to the victim, Logan. We may get some DNA from those. And there were some brunette hairs that probably belonged to the wife. Mike's running them through the system as we speak. We also found a Band-Aid, a small one, on the floor in the back, but under the passenger seat. He's working that too, but it will take a while; always does."

"Do we know what color the ex-wife's hair is?" I asked. They all shook their heads.

"Well, Janet," I said, "you and I will soon find out. If she's a bottle blond, she goes to the head of the suspect list. Since Sherri Logan has taken out a restraining order against her, seems the ex-wife might have a temper... What else, Hawk?"

He stared at his notes.

"Fingerprints?" Janet asked.

"Oh yeah, plenty. They are being processed, but I'm afraid, they're just those of the victim and, we assume his wife... We're assuming that because there are a lot of them, all over the car. We'll need prints from her and the ex for comparison."

I nodded. "We'll get the ex's this afternoon. Ann, you and Lennie go get them from..." I glanced up at the board, "from Sherri Logan. Get a swab from her too, turn them in to Willis, then start making the rounds of the bars. What are your plans for the rest of the day, Hawk? You probably should go home and get some rest."

He shook his head. "Nah, it's too early for me. Look, Willis hasn't yet been able to properly process the scene; it was too dark last night, and he's heading that way in..." he checked his watch.

"Well, as we speak. I thought I'd go with him, snoop around a little, if that's okay with you, Cap."

"Good idea. They had to have left the scene somehow, probably on foot... unless there was a third person with them." I shuddered at the thought. "So yes, go ahead."

And before I could say another word, he was on his feet and heading toward the door.

I looked at the rest of my team and said, "Let's go to it," and they too upped and left the room, all except Janet, who remained seated, searching through her own notes on her iPad.

"Something on your mind?" I asked.

"This one is a real mystery. I hate to use the term. But I'm coming up with nothing. No ideas. No guesses. Nothing. It's like someone just leaned into Jack Logan's car, shot him in the head, and took his money."

"No," I shook my head. "There's more to it than that. They didn't lean into his car. He was in the passenger seat, which means someone else was driving. Go grab Hawk and bring him back. I need to ask him a question."

Janet returned with Hawk a few minutes later.

"You summoned?" he said.

"Hey," I said. "The driver's seat, how was it positioned? Had it been moved during the crime, d'you think?"

He shrugged. "Hard to tell. Mike Willis removed it. You'll have to ask him."

I nodded, disappointed. "Okay. Check-in with me when you get back."

"You got it, Cap."

He left and I said to Janet, "I need to talk to Mike, then we'll go talk to the ex-wife. It should be fun. I hear she's a real sweetheart."

9

Mike Willis confirmed that both seats were not in an unusual position. In fact, had he not been found in the passenger seat, Jack Logan might well have been driving.

I listened to what he had to say, asked a few questions, made an appointment to visit with him later the following morning, then we headed out to beard the lioness in her den.

It was just after three o'clock that Wednesday afternoon when we arrived at Cynthia Logan's home. I hadn't called ahead, wanting to retain an element of surprise. It's a tool that almost always works in our favor.

I already knew that the house was a rental, set in a quiet, middle-class neighborhood; what I didn't expect was the size of the home, and the sparkling new Ford truck parked in the driveway.

I had a job, no kids, and could comfortably afford a one-bedroom apartment and a used Toyota, so I figured it was a pretty nice set-up for a woman who, according to court divorce records, was singing the blues about her finances.

As we approached the front door, we could hear music playing inside, the kind of music you hear at carnivals on rides called The Barn Burner or The Cyclone. It wasn't loud enough to disturb the neighbors, but it was loud enough to be heard as we stepped up the porch steps. I knocked on the door hard enough for it to be heard over the music. A few seconds later, the door opened and Cynthia Logan took one look at us, then shook her head and laughed out loud.

"Sooner than I thought," she said. "I knew it was only a matter of time before you showed up on my doorstep. My but you're quick."

Hmm, the lady has blond hair. Just the right length, too.

"Quick?" I asked. "You're Jack Logan's ex-wife. He's dead. His current wife has a restraining order against you. So quick? Yes. What else would you expect, Ms. Logan?"

I introduced Janet and myself, flashing my badge and identification. I had a certain feeling this woman knew just enough about the rules of the game and that if I didn't follow them to the letter I would indeed be facing an Internal Affairs investigation.

"May we come in, Ms. Logan?"

"So you're here to talk to me about that idiot I married. Well, I didn't kill him." She made no effort to let us in. Instead, she folded her arms across her chest defiantly and shifted from her right foot to her left.

"We didn't say you did, Miss Logan," Janet said with a smile.

"Call me Cynthia." Her snarky tone made it clear she wasn't happy we were there.

I thought for a minute that she was going to make us conduct the interview on the front step, if at all, but then she relented, her voice softened as she said, "Yes, fine, come on in."

We followed her into the living room. The music was coming from a small, somewhat aged boombox with a CD player. It was set next to a large flat-screen television. An open laptop on the table was showing one of those social media sites where people post every move of every day, make connections, hookups, and argue about politics.

Me? I have a love/hate relationship with social media. On the one hand, I hate it because of the phoniness of it all, the lies, the subterfuge, the photos people post of themselves. But I love it when the geniuses on the other side of the law post their wrongdoings with live footage of their crimes. Dumb? Yes, I know, but it happens more often than you think. It's law enforcement's secret weapon, and it isn't even a secret.

Janet was ahead of me and I knew she'd also spotted the open laptop; so did Cynthia, because she quickly slammed it shut. I smiled, because there was nothing she could do about the joint smoldering in an ashtray next to it.

"It's for medicinal purposes," she said as she pinched it out and moved the ashtray to the mantlepiece. "I have a license."

"I don't care what you're smoking, Ms. Logan. I'm here to talk to you about your ex-husband."

She shook her head, smirked and said, "You know, that asshole died owing me more than fifty thousand dollars."

She waited for a response but got none.

"That was the least of what I gave him over the course of our marriage," she continued. "Then he ditches me and marries that whore, Sherri, and leaves me holding the bag."

"Holding the bag for what?" I asked.

"All of my medical expenses, of course." She clicked her tongue and slowly eased herself down into a leather recliner.

"Sit down," she said, "wherever you like."

Janet and I sat down together on a couch that must have set her back a couple of grand. I opened my purse and took out a small digital recorder and turned it on.

"I'm going to record our conversation, Ms. Logan. Do I have your permission?"

She looked at the recorder as if it were a cobra readying itself to strike. I thought for a minute that she was going to refuse, but she didn't; she nodded, reluctantly.

"Out loud, for the record, please, Ms. Logan."

"Yes, okay, fine."

"So, you mentioned medical expenses," I said, setting the tiny machine down in front of her on the coffee table.

"Yes, I suffer from depression and have back problems."

"Do you work?" I asked, already knowing the answer.

"Not anymore. I can't. Some days I just can't bear to get out of bed. I can't hold a regular job so money is tight. I'm on disability. I barely get by, but d'you think that son-of-a-bitch would help me out? Nope. Not one red cent."

She ran her hand through her hair. She didn't look at all depressed. She looked pissed off. Her eyes were blue and almost completely concealed when she smirked, which seemed to be just about all the time. Her face was heavily wrinkled, leathery from years of overexposure to the sun. Her hair was blond, not quite shoulder length, and the roots were showing. She was wearing jeans and a tight T-shirt that made it painfully obvious that she had implants that had increased her breast size by at least two cups. She was also wearing three thin gold bracelets around each of her wrists and another around her left ankle.

"So, Ms. Logan," I said, "you and Jack divorced in 2003; fifteen years ago. That's a long time... How did you meet him, by the way?"

She ran her hand through her hair again and let her hand slap on her thigh. "We met at a bar. If you can believe that."

I certainly could, but I didn't say anything.

"He always loved sports," she said thoughtfully. "You know, baseball, football, basketball. I wasn't interested... in sports, but he seemed nice, and he bought me drinks, so I started seeing him. We'd usually meet at a sports bar and go on from there. He was lonely, and kinda sad-looking. I sort of felt like... sorry for him, you know? He was a Cubs fan; the Braves, too."

She smirked. "But he was actually a lot of fun. Not a party

animal, but he'd walk me to my car after the game was over, and sometimes he'd bring me a little present like this." She picked out one of the delicate little bracelets around her wrist with her pink manicured nails.

"How long did you date before you got married?" I asked.

"Three months," she snapped, looking at me as if daring me to say something snarky.

I obliged.

"A whirlwind romance, then?"

"That's right. We went to the Grand Canyon for our honeymoon and spent a few days in Vegas. I remember I won four-hundred-and-eighteen dollars." She lifted her chin as if we'd all be impressed. "Jack didn't win anything. He didn't even bet. Then, once we were married, he changed, and it was like pulling teeth trying to get a dime out of him."

"How long did you stay married?" I asked.

"Four years."

"Jack wasn't your first husband, was he?" I asked.

"I was married before, yes." She rolled her eyes. "The first time when I was eighteen... Sam was twenty. That lasted almost four years. Then again when I was twenty-nine, to Ray Watson. That lasted until..."

"That lasted until you met Jack," I said.

All the while I was talking to her, Janet was doing what she did best. She was slowly, carefully taking in the scenery and putting together a profile in her head as she listened to us talk.

"Yes, two years, give or take. I left Ray to be with Jack. But Jack didn't know that, of course." She shifted in her seat. "My marriage to Ray was over. He cheated on me with someone I knew. At least I had the decency to find a stranger."

I couldn't help but note that she was actually proud that her cheating standards were a fraction of an inch higher than those of her second husband.

"So, you were what, thirty-three when you married Jack in 1999?"

"Yes, that's right."

"And Jack would have been... thirty-four?"

She nodded.

"And you expected life with Jack to be different?" I asked.

"Yeah, of course I did. He had more money, a steady job: he was an accountant, you know. I was supposed to be taken care of. That was what he was always saying. That he was going to take care of me. But I still had to keep working. I still had to do everything around the house. It wasn't fair."

Her eyes widened as she looked for a nod or smirk of approval from me. She got neither.

"If anyone should have been asking for a divorce, it should have been me. I had more reasons than that son-of-a-bitch. And then he goes and marries that whore. She's driving around in a Cadillac, you know. A freaking Cadillac for God's sake!"

"Is that your truck out there?" I jerked my thumb toward the window. "I wouldn't say that was a beater."

She blushed, probably for the first time in a long time. "That's not mine. I'm just borrowing it from a friend. I had some errands to run."

"Ms. Logan, we know that Sherri Logan took out a restraining—"

She cut me off quickly. "Yeah, a restraining order. I know. She didn't want me contacting him when I needed help." She raised her right eyebrow, and said, "He wouldn't answer his phone, damn it. I had no choice but to show up at their house."

"Why would you do that?" Janet asked. "He filed for the divorce. Not you. Why would you want to stay in contact? You have no children, not even a pet to share."

"Look, I know our marriage wasn't perfect, but he led me to believe... swore to me that we were going to be together until death do us part." She pointed at Janet. "He made it so I came to rely on certain things, and then he took it all away. He *owed* me."

"What about Lester Harris, what does he owe you?" I asked. "He has a restraining order out on you, too. What's that all about?"

"Lester Harris..." she stuttered. "That was... is... Look, I threatened to take out a restraining order on him, so he beat me to it; he took one out on me first... to make me look bad. He's been stalking me, you know. We went out on a couple of dates and now he thinks he owns me. I think he could be dangerous. In fact, I wouldn't be surprised if he did something to Jack just to get at me. He's that kind of crazy."

"If he's that dangerous, why didn't you get a restraining order immediately?" I asked. I have to admit I was enjoying watching her back herself into a corner.

"I had hopes for Lester, at first, but... well, I was wrong. I thought if I just showed him some kindness, he'd leave me alone." She sniffled. Was she really trying to cry in front of us? "No good deed goes unpunished, right?" she said.

"Where were you between the hours of five and six o'clock on the evening Jack was killed?" I asked.

"Oh hey. Here it comes," she said. Her sniffles quickly disappeared and her tone turned angry. There was no doubt that she believed that she was a victim, the victim of a cruel and vindictive ex-husband. *And there's your motive.*

"Where were you, Ms. Logan?" I asked again.

"You know, you people have a lot of nerve coming after me," she snarled. "There are rapists and murderers out there and—"

"And one of them got your ex-husband," Janet snapped. "Now tell us where you were."

"I don't remember," Cynthia said, biting her lip.

"What do you mean you don't remember?" I said, rolling my eyes.

"I was here till... Oh, I don't know... maybe eight o'clock. No, there was no one here with me. Then I went out to a bar. I met a guy. He bought me a drink... and that's the last I remember until I woke up in my car... in a damn ditch. You can check. My car's at the collision center on Rossville Boulevard. The damn front end is shoved in. Luckily, I have insurance, but my shoes were gone, so was my cash. The bastard must have drugged me." She jerked her chin toward the front window. "That's why I have the truck. I borrowed it from the woman who does my nails."

"We're in the wrong business, DG," Janet said, looking up at me, wiggling her fingers, and then rising to her feet.

I stared at the woman, not knowing what to make of her so-called alibi that wasn't an alibi at all. She was at home, so she said, when her ex-husband was killed, but was she? Was all that stuff about her being drugged just so much BS? Oh, there was no doubt we'd find her car was indeed involved in a wreck when she said it was, but drugged? Maybe, maybe not.

"This man you met," I said, "can you describe him? What was his name?"

"He said his name was Will something. He was kinda small, maybe five-nine, nicely dressed, good-looking... That's all I remember. I was only with him for about thirty minutes."

"What about the bar?" Janet asked.

"Roper's Sports Bar on Battlefield Parkway. Look, I know what you're thinking, but you're wrong. I didn't kill Jack. If I was gonna kill anyone... and I wasn't, it would have been that stupid little woman he married, not him."

"Can you think of anyone who might have wanted to hurt Jack?" Janet asked. "Did he have any enemies?"

"No, not that I know of. Well, um, like I said, Lester Harris, maybe. He's obsessed with me. Maybe he thought Jack and I were getting back together or something, and—"

"Where would he have gotten an idea like that?" I asked. I was beginning to understand this bitter, self-victimized woman. I'd seen it before, more often than I cared to admit. She loved attention, was addicted to it. And I knew exactly what was coming next.

"I don't know," she snapped, pulling her shoulders up to her ears. "Maybe I said something. I might have told him that Jack still loved me," she said, her eyes lowered.

Yes, of course you did.

"Did you still love Jack?" I asked.

"I loved his money." She tried to smile cutely, then giggled, like a flirting teenager. More play-acting, but it didn't work. It was pathetic, and I didn't like Cynthia Logan, not one bit. I decided to change tactics.

"Have you ever been to Huntsville, Alabama? Or Dalton, Georgia?" I asked, looking down at my notes.

"Dalton, of course I have, many times. I've been all over," she bragged.

"You've been to both cities? When?" I asked.

"Dalton? Dozens of times, mostly to the outlet mall. The last time... I don't know. A couple of months ago, maybe? Huntsville? Oh, it has to have been a couple of years ago. Just a short getaway, in the spring as I recall, May, I think it was. A change of scenery. They say that's as good as a rest, don't they?" She nodded. "I've also been to Colorado, Wyoming, California, Wisconsin, New York, Washington, and... lots of places."

I made a note of everything she said, but I knew I didn't dare reach out to those states at this early stage in the investigation. What I did know was that things weren't looking good for Cynthia Logan. The fact that she'd visited Dalton was inconsequential; I'd visited Dalton many times myself, and for the same reasons she had. That she'd also visited Huntsville, well, that was something, but coincidental and circumstantial, and I wouldn't know better until I'd spoken to Sheriff McGraw.

I had nothing solid, and I felt like I was trying to put a set of cuffs around the steam coming out of a kettle.

"Miss Logan," Janet said, conversationally. "Lester Harris said you showed up at his house and threw rocks through three of his windows, and that you also threatened to kill his dog and then him.

Was that before or after you told him you were going to file a restraining order against him?"

"Look, that was a mistake. I had had one too many drinks. I'll admit that. I'm not perfect. Who hasn't let the alcohol do the talking for them at one time or another?"

She was right, but most people don't resort to throwing rocks and making threats.

"You didn't just talk, Cynthia. You threw rocks and threatened him and his dog," Janet continued. "It seems to me that you have a bit of a temper?"

"Well, I've been through a lot. It's only natural," she said matter-of-factly as if we were supposed to smack our foreheads with our palms, nod our heads and say 'oh, well, that explains it then.'

"Does that mean yes, you have a temper?" Janet was like a dog with a bone.

"Oh, come on, nobody likes to be jerked around, do they? Or maybe you do. You look like one of those stupid young girls that believe in happily-ever-after," she said, staring at Janet.

"That's enough, Ms. Logan," I said. "I think we've taken up enough of your time." I stood and reached into my pocket for a business card. "If you can think of anything else that might help us, please give me a call."

She didn't make any effort to get up from her seat. I set the card down on the table and picked up my recorder, but I didn't turn it off.

"I didn't kill Jack, you know," she said, the smirk back on her face.

"You've made the point several times," I said.

"Do you mind if I use your bathroom?" Janet asked.

Cynthia rolled her eyes and let out a sigh and said, "If you must. It's down that hall on your left." She pointed. "I'll ask that you respect my privacy. I didn't see a search warrant with those badges."

"Of course. Thank you," Janet said and disappeared down the hall.

"I get the feeling you don't believe me," she said. "I know you've probably spoken to Jack's wife already, and I can just imagine what she had to say about me. She has a vivid imagination, so don't let that innocent act of hers fool you."

"What I believe isn't the issue here, Ms. Logan. I go where the evidence leads me. As they say on television, 'just the facts ma'am.'"

"So what did happen to Jack?" she asked. "Do you know if he had life insurance? I'm sure you do. You people have to look into that kind of thing, don't you? I'm sure Sherri had a hefty policy on him. She'll be laughing all the way to the bank; just you mark my words. A fricking Cadillac. Would you believe it?" She clicked her tongue, scowled, and shook her head, almost violently.

"I wouldn't know about any of that," I said.

The look on her face was pure evil. Was I looking at a killer? I didn't know, but one thing I was sure of was that her moral compass sure as hell wasn't pointing north.

Janet returned, adjusting her badge on her belt. Cynthia looked her up and down as if she suspected that she'd stolen a roll of toilet paper.

I stood up and said, "We'll be in touch, Ms. Logan. Thank you again for your time."

"I was thinking, Miss Logan," Janet said as we approached the front door. "Do you own a gun?"

"According to the Second Amendment, I am allowed to own as many as I want. But no. I used to have one. I don't know what happened to it. It got lost sometime after Jack and I got married." She stared at Janet. "But I think I should probably consider getting another one, don't you? Who knows, the person who killed Jack might come after me next."

"Boy, it must be tough having the whole world against you," Janet said sarcastically.

I'm going to have to talk to her, I thought. *She's going to get herself into trouble.*

"You're a real smart ass, aren't you?" Cynthia snapped back.

Janet chuckled, then stared at her and said, "Don't leave town, Miss Logan."

Oh... my God, I thought. *Really?*

I opened the front door and we stepped out onto the porch. The door slammed shut behind us. I turned off my recorder and said, "What the hell were you trying to do in there?"

"She's hiding something. I know she is. I was just trying to prod her a little, hoping she'd lose her temper; we know she's got one, right? D'you think she's really suffering from depression, or a back injury? I sure don't. And I'm certain she doesn't have a prescription for medical marijuana either. Oh yeah, she's bad, and... well, I guess we'll find out sooner or later."

"You're probably right," I said, "but you need to be careful who you're poking. You haven't had a brush with Internal Affairs yet, but what you did in there... well, she knows I was recording the interview, and if she makes an official complaint, you could be in for a wild ride. Tone it down a little, okay?"

"You think?"

"I do."

She nodded, but she didn't say she would. Instead, she said, "Oh, and did you notice her blond hair?" She pulled the car door closed.

"Yes, so?"

"Well, here you go," she said as she pulled a small plastic baggie from her pocket, grinning. "There was a hairbrush in her bathroom. I couldn't help myself. Maybe Mike Willis can find us a match."

10

Miller and Ann had still not returned when we arrived back at the PD. Janet went to find Hawk, and I went to get coffee. It was some ten minutes after I returned to my desk when Hawk came into my office.

"Hey, you," I said. "Did you talk to Janet?"

"Yeah. She gave me this." He waved the small baggie with a sample of Cynthia Logan's hair in it. "She asked me to give it to Mike for analysis. I'll do it on my way out. You got a minute, Cap?"

"Sure. What's up?"

He took up his usual spot on the corner of my desk. The knees of his pants were dirty like he'd been crawling around on the ground.

I raised my eyebrows and said, "You were going to the scene with Mike Willis. So, what have you got for me?"

"Mike got sidetracked. I went out there by myself," he said, smiling like I've never seen him smile before.

"Well, are you going to tell me, or do I have to rip out your fingernails?"

"A bullet..."

"No shit," I said excitedly. "Where? How?"

"Don't get too excited. It's, well it's a partial, kinda flat, but I reckon there's enough to work with. It's a nine, looks like a range round, FMJ. Pretty common around here."

FMJ is the acronym for full metal jacket.

"So Doc was wrong when he said the killer was using frangible rounds?" I said. "That's another piece of luck. How the hell did you find it?"

"Yeah, the harder I work, the luckier I get. It's always there... somewhere. The perp always leaves something at the scene, or takes something away, or both. You just have to buckle down and look for it."

"Yes, I know; that's Forensics 101. So come on, Hawk, give."

"So I told you I was going out to the scene to snoop around. Thankfully, that road isn't traveled much," he said as he pulled a folded piece of paper from his pocket and handed it to me. It was a simple sketch of the scene.

"I'd spent hours with Willis processing the car and all we could come up with was a couple of hairs." He scratched at the stubble across his chin. "I knew I was missing something. I was literally banging my head against the hood of the car, trying to figure out what it was. Then it hit me like a ton of bricks. The window was rolled up."

"What do you mean?" I asked.

"It was one of those blatantly obvious clues that can get missed because we're so focused on looking for the small stuff." He shrugged, then continued, "See, Logan was shot in the side of the head first—"

"We don't know that," I said, interrupting him, "not for sure."

"Yeah, we do," he insisted. "It's the only thing that makes sense, especially when you know what I found. We saw an exit wound for both bullets. The second shot to the back of the head went out through the windshield and is lost forever, but the first shot..." He paused for dramatic effect. "It went out through the *open* passenger side window. Our perp rolled it up *after* shooting him."

"How d'you know that?" I asked.

"Because if the window had been closed, not only would there be blood and tissue all over it, the bullet would probably have shattered it. But see, there was none of that. The window was spotless except for along the very top where Logan's blood sprayed."

I stared at him. He grinned back at me. It made sense.

"So that's why you wanted to go to the scene?" I asked.

"Yeah, I had no hopes of finding the slug, but hey, stranger things, right? And this time, as you say, I got lucky. It wasn't easy. It's open country out there. The crime scene tapes are still there, and the tire marks, so I knew the exact position of the vehicle. Here, gimme that," he said, reaching for his map.

"See this?" He pointed to a small square to the east of the car. "It's an old barn. It's about... oh, maybe a hundred yards from the road. You wouldn't see it at night, not in the dark. Here..." He took his phone from his pocket. "I took photos. I found the bullet here, right at the northwest edge of the building; two more inches to the left and it would've been gone forever. Fortunately, that old barnwood is as hard as iron. This is where I found it in relationship to the car." He pointed to his drawing and the dotted line that connected the car to the barn.

Hawk had an eye for details, and that's what made him a good detective. There was no disputing what he'd found, and he'd backed it up with the drawing and photos.

"I think maybe Logan tried to exit the vehicle while it was still moving, and that's what got him shot," Hawk said. "I'm not sure that spot was supposed to be his dumping ground, so I'm not going to speculate about that. So, Cap, what d'you think?"

"I think you did great," I said, shaking my head at my own understatement.

And I knew what he was getting at about where the car and body ended up. If Logan was being taken to another location, the perpetrator might have a place where he likes to dump the bodies. The thought of there being more bodies out there somewhere made my stomach flip.

Hawk continued, talking more than he had in months, "Here's the thing though. When I left here this morning, I wasn't really going looking for a bullet. I mean, what were the chances? No, what I was going after was footprints... See I figured there was only one way the perp, or perps, could have left the scene, and that was on foot. And that meant there was a possibility I might find prints, and I did. I found one about twenty yards south of where the car was discovered, right on the soft shoulder."

He paused and grinned at me, then continued, "I'm a size eleven. This one, a right foot, looks to be a nine, maybe nine and a half. I made a cast. Mike has it. See?" He showed me a photo of the cast on his iPhone; it had a yellow and black measure next to it. It looked to be about eleven inches long.

"That's kind of small, don't you think? Are you sure it's not the photographer's or one the techs?" I asked.

"Yeah. I already checked with forensics. None of them have this make of shoe or fit the size. It looks like it was made by a boot of some sort, by a small guy."

"So what do you have planned next?" I asked. "Janet is confirming the ex-wife's alibi." I gave Hawk the gory details of our visit with the lovely Cynthia Logan. "If her hairs match those you found at the scene, we at least know she was in his car."

"What about his wife?" Hawk asked. "Do we know the color of her hair?"

"I don't, but I'm sure Janet does. I'll check."

"I bet she's a brunette. We found plenty of those, and his. How long has Logan owned the car? If he had it before the divorce, his ex-wife's hair inside it means nothing."

"True, but—"

"And what if they don't match?" Hawk asked.

"Back to the drawing board. Come on, Hawk. You know the drill," I said and took a sip of my now cold coffee.

"Does she own a gun?" he asked.

"Said she lost it a while back," I replied.

"Of course she did. I'm not saying the woman did it, but she sounds just like every other bitter ex-wife. Hates the guy but not enough to kill him herself. So she pays some poor dope to do it," Hawk said as he slid off my desk.

"Is that what you think happened?" I asked.

"Yep."

"Simple as that?" I shook my head.

"Simple as that. I mean no disrespect, Cap, but women can be just as cruel and heartless as any man, even more so. Evil doesn't favor one sex over the other."

"You've got that right," I said, but my mind was on other things.

I checked my watch. It was almost three o'clock. "What are your plans now, Hawk?"

"I'm gonna take these to Mike." He held up the baggie with the hairs. "And then I'm going home. I've been on my feet for two days straight. I need some sleep."

"That you do. Okay, so, do me a favor on your way out. Tell Janet what your thoughts are about an accomplice, and then tell her to talk to this guy Lester Harris. He took out a restraining order on Cynthia Logan. That could all be smoke and mirrors. Then again, he might be able to tell us more about Cynthia."

Hawk nodded and headed out the door.

Me? I had some phone calls to make. The first of which was with Sheriff Lyndon Cane in Dalton. I tapped in his number and my call was answered by his secretary. I explained who I was and that Cane was expecting the call, and she put me through.

"Captain Gazzara," he said when he came on the line. "I've heard a lot about you. I wish we were talking under different circumstances."

"Yes, sir, me too," I said. "Thank you for your time. I have to tell you, though, that I wish this conversation wasn't happening at all. To be honest, when I sent out my request, I was hoping I wouldn't hear back from anyone. But here we are, and again, thank you for getting back to me. So, please tell me what you've got."

He was silent for a moment and I heard papers rustling, then he said, "Okay, Captain, the victim's name is Lawrence Berryman. Age forty-eight. Caucasian. Average height of five feet ten and one-half inches. He was a plumber. Married. Clean record. No priors. Cause of death, either one of two gunshot wounds to the head. One to the left temple, the other the base of the skull.

"He was found in his car at seven minutes after eight—that's the time the call came in—on Wednesday, November twenty-fifth, 2015, just outside the city limits on Cleveland Highway. He was in the passenger seat. Both bullets exited the head. The one to the back of the head exited the car through the windshield. The one to the left side of the head impacted the passenger side door frame. There was no way to tell which shot came first, but we assumed it was the one to the temple. It was fired from a distance of about eighteen inches, the one to the back of the head from less than two inches."

Sheriff Cane sighed and then said, "How does that compare to your victim?"

As I listened to him relate the details, with every word he spoke, my heart sank a little lower.

"I hate to say it," I said, "but it sounds identical. Would you mind FedExing a copy of the file to me, please?"

"Of course. I'll have Lily do it just as soon as we finish."

I nodded, even though I knew he couldn't see me, then said, "Anything else I should know, Sheriff? You said something about the time the call came in. I'm assuming there was a delay between the time the body was found and the finder calling it in, right?"

"Yes, that's right. The car might have remained undiscovered longer but for a guy by the name of Michael Hartwell. Apparently, he was heading home after an office Thanksgiving party in Cleveland, Tennessee. I think he may have had a little too much to drink, though he wasn't charged. Be that as it may, he had to pull over to take a leak..."

The Sheriff cleared his throat. "Er, sorry, Captain. Anyway, he pulled over and stepped just far enough off the road into the woods to have a little privacy when he saw the rear end of the car. He approached the vehicle, saw the shattered windshield and the blood, then the body, and he panicked... at least that's what he said, and there was no reason to disbelieve him. He went back to his car and tried to call it in, but there was no cell reception, so he left the scene and drove until he could make the call. That's why there was a delay of, well, probably just a few minutes."

"You don't think he had anything to do with it?" I already knew the answer, but I had to ask.

"No. He was cleared almost immediately. He was an accountant. We checked his alibi. It was solid. He left work at seven-forty-five. It's no more than a thirty-minute drive from Cleveland to the crime scene, so the timeline fits."

"Any idea how long the body had been there?" I asked.

"The ME put the time of death between six and eight o'clock, so no more than a couple of hours. God only knows how long he would have been there if Hartwell hadn't decided to... relieve himself."

"How about forensics? Anything helpful?"

"They recovered a nine-millimeter bullet from the doorframe, pretty much deformed, not much use, but you never know. The autopsy showed he had some alcohol in his system, just enough to be legally drunk."

"That's it then?" I asked. "No hairs, fibers, fingerprints?"

"Nope... well, plenty of prints, and hairs, but they were all accounted for. Other than that, nothing."

"Sheriff, did you have any thoughts as to what might have happened to Mr. Berryman?"

"Yeah. I think he had a few drinks, met up with the wrong

guy... maybe for sex, or maybe he was giving the guy a ride home, and something went wrong. A robbery that went sideways. Simple as that. All of his cash was gone, but we found his wallet outside the car. His credit cards, ID, and photos were all still present. We figured someone wanted to make a quick score, and Berryman didn't want to part with his cash. He paid with his life. Pitiful."

I thanked Sheriff Cane for his help and disconnected the call, then sat back in my chair to think.

So now I had three murders. That meant I did indeed have a serial killer on my hands. I sighed. I felt like crap. I was bone-tired, my shoulders ached, my neck was stiff, and I wanted to go home and drown myself in red wine, but I didn't. I forced myself to call Sheriff Pete McGraw of Huntsville, Alabama.

He was a man of few words, but we talked for maybe ten minutes. He gave me the facts and, in just those few minutes, I learned that William Leeds died in May 2017 as a result of two gunshot wounds to the head, left temple and blah, blah, blah. This time, however, there was a witness who saw Leeds leave a bar with a man smaller and thinner than him with short blond hair.

Yes, I now had victim number four, and by the time I got off the phone, I also had a splitting headache.

It was just after eight o'clock that evening when Ann and Miller came into my office. They both looked like they'd been ridden hard and put away wet. Janet had arrived a few minutes earlier just as perky as ever. *Oh, to be that young and energetic,* I thought, sighing to myself.

I wanted to hear what they all had to say, and I wanted to tell them what we were dealing with, but my heart wasn't in it. I was tired and wanted to get out of there. I needed a long hot bath and a bottle of red... and a pizza.

"What the hell happened to you two?" Janet asked, looking at Ann and Miller. "You look like I felt after last year's Christmas party."

"I only wish we had that much fun," Miller said.

I don't think I ever saw him drink anything harder than a Coke, but that didn't change the fact they both looked exhausted. Miller had dark circles under his eyes, and Ann's eye shadow was smudged from rubbing her eyes. It was a look that, as crazy as this might sound, made her look... sultry.

"We covered almost every bar and hole-in-the-wall in the northeast quarter," Ann said. "There are about five left on our list that we didn't get to."

"Can it wait until tomorrow?" I asked hopefully. "I don't know about you, but my body clock's all out of whack. I need to get back on track, and I'm sure you do too."

"Sure," Ann said, sounding more than a little grateful. "It can wait."

"Okay. Go on home, all of you. Get some rest. We'll get to it tomorrow morning."

11

It was eight-thirty when I arrived home that night. The first thing I did was wrench open the refrigerator door and grab the last of the summer wine, a third of a bottle of Cabernet. I poured the lot into a half-pint glass, flopped down on the couch, cradled the glass in both hands, closed my eyes and sipped, and sipped and sipped until the damn glass was empty. Then I got up, opened a new bottle, poured another half glass, and headed to the bedroom. There I stripped completely, went into the bathroom and took a long hot shower, glass in hand, ducking my head in and out of the water every now and then for a sip.

I toweled myself off, washed the glass in the bathroom sink, returned it to the kitchen, and grabbed the last two slices of a two-day-old pizza from the refrigerator and ate it in... I dunno, three, maybe four bites. Nah, it was more like six, but it was cold, and it was good, and it filled the gap. I looked next at the wine bottle, was tempted, but told myself no, and went to the bedroom where I crawled under the covers, naked as a jaybird. I stretched out between the cold sheets, luxuriating in the feeling of total relaxation. I closed my eyes, a contented smile on my lips, but sleep didn't come easily.

When it did finally come, after what seemed like hours of tossing and turning, it wasn't the deep sleep I craved, but more a sort of balance between sleep and wakefulness.

I was thinking quick, disjointed thoughts that jumped from one victim to the next, leading me around and around until I felt dizzy and nauseous. Cynthia Logan was still a suspect in her husband's death, but her involvement in the other cases was melting away. Actually, it was melting away in Logan's case, too, but I felt I had to hold on to the idea that at least in this case, my case in Chattanooga, she might be the perp. If she did it, or paid someone else to do it, I could close the case and consign the file to the warehouse where it belonged, and Cappy T. Mallard could go back to the morgue.

No, that really wasn't an option. I was already in too deep. And so, eventually, I drifted off into a troubled sleep to dream dreams of shadowy figures in bars and the backs of cars, until finally I woke at six-thirty to the strains of "Don't Worry Be Happy" blasting out from the iPhone at my bedside.

Damn it, I really must change that alarm ringtone.

My head was aching slightly, but it was nothing a couple cups of coffee and two aspirin couldn't cure.

I lay on my back for a few more minutes, breathing deeply, trying to gather my wits. Then I gave up and headed to the kitchen, and then the bathroom, and then stood under a hot shower while my coffee brewed in the kitchen.

I rinsed the shampoo out of my hair, took a deep breath, and turned the water to cold. It hit my body like a bolt of lightning, took my breath away, made my eyes bug. *Now* I was awake.

I dried off, got dressed—jeans and a pale blue blouse—tied my hair up in a ponytail, filled my to-go mug with hot coffee, and sat down at my computer and took a few minutes to answer some of my work emails. At seven-thirty I refilled my to-go mug and left for work, wondering what the day might have in store for me, and knowing that I had to bring the Chief into the loop and tell him that there was a serial killer on the loose somewhere in the city.

12

"Is the Chief in yet?" I asked the duty sergeant as I walked in through the rear entrance to the department. It was just after eight o'clock and raining outside like it was the end of days.

"Isn't he always?" the man said with a curt nod.

I made my way along the hall to the Chief's suite of offices, stood for a moment at the outer door, took a deep breath, knocked, and then entered the outer office where Cathy, his PA, was already at her desk.

"Captain Gazzara," she said with a smile. "You're early. He only arrived a few minutes ago. You know how he is. Could you come back in say... an hour? Give him a chance to compose himself?"

That was a laugh. I'd never known the Chief when he was anything but composed.

"That's not an option, I'm afraid, Cathy. He won't want to be kept waiting for what I have to tell him. D'you mind?"

She tilted her head, frowned slightly, but picked up the phone.

"Captain Gazzara is here. She says it's important."

I heard him growl something. She looked up at me, raised her eyebrows, then said, "Yes, sir," and hung up.

"Take a seat, Captain. He'll be with you shortly."

Shortly was exactly fifteen minutes, and by the time Cathy's phone buzzed and she picked up, I was a nervous wreck.

"You can go in now, Captain." And I did.

Chief Wesley Johnston was seated behind his desk, reading what appeared to be a report, and he was indeed composed: he had a scowl on his face that made him look even more like Hulk Hogan than Hogan did. My heart sank. I'd been hoping he was in a good mood; he wasn't.

"Sit down, Catherine," he said, without looking up.

I sat on a hard seat in front of his desk.

"Chief—" I began, but he held up his hand, his eyes still not rising from the report. He continued to read for several more seconds, seconds during which I grew more and more agitated. Then finally:

"So," he said, looking up and placing the report carefully and deliberately to one side. "What is so important that it can't wait for a more civilized time of the morning?"

I took a deep breath and dived right in. For almost fifteen minutes he listened to me, without saying a word, as I took him through the events of the past three days until finally, I ran out of breath and things to say, so I shut up and waited for him to speak.

He'd been leaning forward as he listened to my diatribe, his elbows on his desktop, eyes narrowed, concentrating. The man never took notes. I figured he must have some sort of eidetic memory.

When I finished speaking, he leaned back in his chair and stared at me.

"How many people know about all this?" he asked quietly.

"About Logan? Just my team. About the victim Mallard, just me. About Berryman and Leeds... me and the two Sheriffs. That's it, so far. I'll bring my team up to speed when I go to my office."

He thought for a moment, then shook his head slightly and said, "What leads do you have, Kate?"

I looked down at my knees, then back up at him and said, "None... Well, I was thinking the ex-wife, but I'm beginning to think that's one hell of a stretch. I'll follow it up of course, but... Other than that, none."

"You have to keep this under wraps, Kate. No, I'm not suggesting a cover-up, but we have to keep it out of the hands of the press until... We can't have this go public, not yet. When we do it, we do it together. In the meantime, keep the circle as small as possible: just your team and Mike Willis, and tell them to be extra careful in their inquiries. They are not to mention the word 'serial' ever, understood?"

I nodded, and I did understand. Ours is a small city, and the idea that there was a psycho killer at large, well, it was disconcerting, to say the least.

"I trust you, Catherine, but I want you to keep me informed every step of the way."

I nodded.

He said, "Go do your thing, Captain."

I stood, opened my mouth to speak, thought better of it, nodded, and left him to his thoughts; my own were spinning almost out of control.

13

From the Chief's office I went straight to the incident room. My intent was to gather my troops and spend the next hour planning strategy, but as I exited the elevator, I heard someone shouting.

"You don't know what you're talking about!"

Then I heard Ann's voice. "Mr. Brown, you need to calm down!"

Ann was sitting at her desk, talking to a small man who looked to be about thirty years old. It was him who was doing the shouting, at her. He was wearing one of those camouflage hats with the panels that hang down the back like he might suddenly be transported to the desert and need his neck protected from the sun, a red and black flannel shirt over a T-shirt and baggy jeans, with a heavy camouflage jacket on top of that. The laces of his boots were untied and, as he talked, he slipped his left foot in and out of its shoe. A nervous tick of sorts?

"I am calm! This is calm! Believe me! You'd be sorry if I wasn't calm!"

What the hell?

"Sir, if you don't calm down," Ann said quietly, as Janet and Miller, both at their desks, looked on smiling, "I'll have you tossed in the tank until you do. Now, take it easy and tell me what happened slowly, so we can get you the help you need." Ann pinched her lips together and waited for him to speak.

I went to Miller's desk and stood by, watching.

"I told you. All right?" he said, somewhat mollified. "I was assaulted."

"From the beginning, please?" Ann didn't look up from her notes.

"I was on my way home last night, from Mickey's tavern. There was a girl I used to know. She was waiting for me in the alley by my apartment. She and her sister came out of nowhere." He looked around. By then everyone in the room was watching and listening. "I know what you're all thinking, but I was raised that you don't hit a girl."

Janet shrugged.

Miller nodded in agreement. "That's how I was raised too," he concurred and was gifted with an enthusiastic nod from the man.

"Yeah, well, she jumped out of the alley and slapped me," he said, then waited for the collective gasp he thought he deserved but didn't get. "And two weeks ago she vandalized my car."

"Did you file a police report?" Ann asked.

"No. But I know she did it. She knows my car. She told me she'd get me back. It's a red Bronco."

"Everyone knows my car, too, Mr. Brown, a red Monte Carlo," Ann said sarcastically. "Sometimes it gets dinged, scratched, dented, a tire goes flat. It happens. Okay, okay, I hear you," she said as he opened his mouth to protest. "How long have you been with this... girl?"

"We've been on-again, off-again for about six months," he said with a shrug.

"Had you been drinking?" Ann asked.

"I had two beers," he replied.

I smiled. They all only have two beers, don't they? The guy arrested for plowing into a car full of nuns only had two beers. The woman who drove her car onto a railroad track also had only two beers. The guy that drove through the drug store window only had two beers.

"What about your girlfriend? Had she—"

"Ex! My ex-girlfriend!" He sat back on the steel chair and spread his legs wide, slouching, his hands in his jacket pockets.

"Had she been drinking?" Ann asked loudly.

"Probably," he snapped.

"But you don't know for sure," Ann replied.

"No, I don't know. I wasn't with her, was I?"

"What's her name?" Ann asked, then said, "Look, Mr. Brown, are you sure you want to do this? Do you really want your ex-girl-friend hauled in here in handcuffs and processed?"

Brown chewed his thumbnail, thinking, then said, "Can I think for a minute?"

"Take all the time you need, Mr. Brown. Do you mind if I talk with my captain while you're thinking?" Ann said, pointing to me.

He turned in his seat to look at me. He was wearing glasses, big glasses that gave him an owl-like look. His face was thin and pale. He turned back to Ann and shrugged. She stood and joined me at Miller's desk.

"You need to get rid of him ASAP," I said. "We have real work to do. Where the hell did he come from?"

"He walked in through the front door about thirty minutes ago," she said. "He said he wanted to file an assault complaint. I happened to catch it, sorry."

I shook my head. It happened more often than you'd think.

"What's the plan, DG?" Janet asked.

"I need everyone in my office. Where's Hawk? Anybody know?"

"He went to get coffee," Janet said.

"Okay," I said, "Ann wrap that thing up and let's get to it. My office in fifteen minutes, everyone."

"You got it, Cap," Ann said, turning to go back to her desk. "Hey, where'd he go?" The man was nowhere to be seen.

"Obviously had a change of heart," I said, and I left them to it.

Ten minutes later they all trooped into my office and took seats around the table, Miller to my left, Janet to my right, Robar and Hawk opposite.

Miller opened his laptop, connected it to a small projector, and before I could stop him began tapping away on the keys.

"Hold on, Lennie," I said and looked at them each in turn. "There have been some developments... a lot of developments. It appears that we're dealing with a serial killer."

I swear, you could have cut the silence with a knife.

14

"**Y**ou gotta be shittin' me," Hawk growled. "How the hell did you come up with that idea?"

"We now have a total of four victims, that I know of," I said, standing and stepping over to the board.

"Jack Logan," I said. "Cappy T. Mallard." I wrote the name at the top of the board, added the date, 2013, and taped up the five photographs from the murder book.

"Lawrence Berryman, Dalton, Georgia, 2015," I said, adding his name and the date of his demise to the board. "And William Leeds, Huntsville, Alabama, 2017." I added his details to the board and then sat down again. "And there may be more, many more."

I looked at the board, then at my team.

"All four were killed over a period of five years and found in exactly the same way, our friend Logan being the latest, with Cappy Miller, the first, that I know of. Comments?"

And they came in a deluge. It took more than an hour for me to relate my findings. Through it all, Hawk sat stoically across the table from me and said barely a word. The result, in the end, was a confounded silence all round with everyone staring up at the board, still horribly bare.

Finally, Hawk said, "Okay, I believe you. There are too many coincidences for it not to be true, but we need more information. When are we getting the goods on Berryman and Leeds?"

Talk about coincidence; just as he said it there was a knock at my door. I called for the knocker to come in, and a uniformed officer stepped inside.

"From Sheriff Cane," he said, dumping a sealed banker's box on my desk. "One of his deputies just dropped it off, said it was urgent. He's waiting downstairs, needs a signature." He handed me a form. I scanned through the list of the box's contents, and signed the form, tore off my copy, and handed it back: the chain of evidence was complete. No, I didn't check the contents of the box; that would've taken too long. I took the list at face value and signed: not the best practice, but you have to exercise a little trust now and again, and this was one of those times.

I thanked the uniform and he nodded and left, closing the door behind him.

"Looks like we already have Berryman," I said, opening the envelope taped to the top of the box and reading aloud the note inside. "I thought I'd send it on, rather than have you wait for FedEx. Let me know if you need help. Best, and good luck. Cane." *Nice of him to rush it. Not solving this one must have bothered him.*

"How's that for service?" I said, unsealing the box and opening it.

Together, we searched through Berryman's files, reports, trace evidence, and found little more than we already had. There were, though, several sealed evidence bags inside the box. One contained Berryman's wallet, another several strands of blond hair, and another contained a badly damaged, full metal jacket nine-millimeter bullet. Cane had been right when he said there wasn't much evidence, but as he also said, you never know what might help.

I set all of the evidence bags aside for transfer to Mike Willis, and together the five of us concentrated on the reports and photographs.

By the time we'd finished, it was almost noon, and the big board was beginning to look like we had the germ of a plan; funny how looks can be so deceiving.

It was at that point that I noticed Miller was growing more agitated almost by the minute.

"Hey, what's wrong with you?" I asked.

"I... I've been running security footage, where there was any, and I found something, I think."

"Why the hell didn't you say something earlier, Lennie?" I asked. "Damn, we need direction and if you found something... Okay, come on, spill it."

"If you'll just give me a minute... while I..." He tapped on the keys of the laptop, the projector lit up, and, "Here we go," he said. "This is footage from one of the bars Ann and I visited."

I watched as the wall behind Hawk and Ann lit up with moving images as Miller pulled up the grainy black and white video.

"Geez," Janet griped. "Is that the best we can do? We can put a man on the moon but we can't get half-way decent footage on our security cameras. Look at that. It's crap!"

Miller, feeling the need to defend modern technology, tried to explain why the footage from such places was almost always poor.

"Do you have any idea the damage that cigarette smoke does to the camera lenses, or any other kind of electrical devices?" he asked. "The only time fresh air gets into a bar is when the doors are open, which is only when someone goes in or out; the rest of the time the air is like pudding. There's moisture, dust, dirt, grime, *smoke*, and grease if there's a kitchen, and yes, most of them do provide food in one form or another. The lens ends up with a thick film of grease on it, thus the deterioration of the image. It's not like the pristine conditions we have in our homes where—"

"Miller, have you ever kissed a girl?" Janet teased.

"Does family count?" he replied innocently, making me choke back a chuckle. Ann was not so discreet and laughed loudly.

"All right," I said, "that's enough. Just tell us what we're looking at, Lennie."

"This is from the bar Second Base," Miller said. "You remember it, right, Ann? That place where—"

"Yeah, I remember," Ann said, interrupting his flow.

"Cute name," Janet replied.

"Yes, well, Mr. Logan will show up in a minute. It's just a small sports bar. There's nothing fancy about it. Nothing special about the crowd. But look, here we go," he said as Ann went to stand behind him, her arms folded.

I watched intently and, after a minute or so I saw a man enter and take a seat at the bar.

"That's him," Miller said. "See, look at the photos. It's him, Jack Logan." And it was.

Logan had sat down. Then he looked along the bar to his left and saw something that seemed to upset him, because he stood up again, turned away, and walked quickly out of the bar. Lennie stopped the projector. The final image of Logan walking to the door still on the screen. It was time-stamped four-oh-nine, roughly an hour before the opening of the ninety-minute window during which he died.

"Well, that's weird," I said. "Did you interview the bartender?"

"Yeah," Miller replied. "I went down there this morning. He was cleaning up. He remembered Logan coming in and then leaving right away when he saw a woman at the far end of the bar. She's a regular, and she'd had an altercation with Logan several weeks earlier. He said her name was Cynthia. He didn't know her last name."

My eyebrows shot up, my mouth hung open, and I was sure my heart stopped for a brief second.

"Shit! Seriously? Is she on the video? When did she leave? Did she go after him?"

I prayed for Miller to tell me yes, but he just shook his head and said, "The bartender said she didn't leave until after last call; that was at one o'clock in the morning."

"Did she make any calls?" I asked. "Did anyone follow him out?"

"No, she didn't, and she was just about legless when she left. I can run the footage, but there's nothing more to see. No one left the bar until almost forty minutes after Logan did."

"Looks like Cynthia Logan has an alibi," Ann said.

"Unless she paid someone to do it for her," Janet said.

"So what's the next step, DG?" Ann asked as she walked back around the table and sat down.

I thought for a minute, then said, "Ann, you and Miller go check out the remaining bars on your list. He went somewhere after he left Second Base. We need to find out where.

"Janet, I need you to take those evidence bags down to Mike Willis. And see if he has any news about those hairs, and if he was able to match the bullet Hawk found. Also, Miller, before you and Ann head out, I need Cynthia Logan's phone records. Jack Logan's too... Good work, Lennie."

He grinned, nodded, and said, "Thanks, Cap. Check your printer. I sent both sets of records to you before we started our meeting. I thought you'd probably need them so—"

"Well done, Lennie. I appreciate it. Now, both of you get out of here. Go find out where Logan ate his last meal. It has to be somewhere close to Second Base."

And they left.

I spent the next fifteen minutes or so talking to Hawk about the Cappy Mallard case, my idea being that he could begin following up with the witnesses, especially the lead detective, a Sergeant Paul Hicks, now retired.

I was about to send him on his way when I heard footsteps in the hall outside my office. A few seconds later, my door burst open and Ann Robar charged in, followed by Miller.

"You're not going to believe this," she snarled. "Some son of a bitch has slashed my freakin' tires!"

15

We pulled the security footage from the cameras in front of the building, and none of us were surprised to see the enigmatic Mr. Brown—Ann had somehow neglected to get his first name—walk calmly around Ann's car and slash all four tires. *Boy, she must have really pissed him off,* I thought. *How did he know it was her car?*

Ann called for a wrecker to come get her car, and then the motor pool for an unmarked cruiser. She put out a BOLO for Brown, and the two of them left again to go finish their canvassing.

~

By the time I was done that day, it was already dark outside and I was starving. We'd missed lunch, and I hadn't eaten a thing other than the sausage and egg sandwich earlier that morning.

I stopped off at Publix on the way home and bought a whole rotisserie chicken and two bottles of a halfway decent Cabernet, and by decent, I mean they had corks instead of screw caps.

It was almost seven o'clock when I parked my car in my spot outside my apartment. I was beat, so I just sat there for a minute with my eyes closed, thankful that the long day was over.

Finally, I took a deep breath, shoved open the car door, grabbed my groceries, and headed to the front door, wondering how many other folks were about to settle down for the night with a whole chicken and two bottles of wine.

For a minute, and only for a minute, I felt guilty. My body was going to suffer for what I was about to do, but I didn't care. All I wanted to do was eat and sleep... and drink a little.

As I approached the steps to my apartment, I was greeted by a neighbor and his dog. He was talking to a woman I didn't know but assumed must be another of my neighbors from the adjoining block. I'd chatted with the guy a couple of times before about the weather and work and such. He was in construction if I remembered right. He was just a nice guy who liked to watch sports and drink a few beers.

The woman was petite. Her hair short and blond and she was wearing jeans and a short black leather jacket over what looked like a tank top.

"How are they treating you down at the station, Detective?" he asked.

"Can't complain. And if I did, no one would listen," I said, smiling as I walked past them and on up the steps.

"She's a detective, can you believe that?" my neighbor said to his friend.

"She's pretty," I heard the woman say.

For a moment, I felt a little better about myself. I guess after a day like I'd just endured, a little normalcy put things back into perspective.

I tended to forget that sometimes, no matter what crap I have to deal with on a daily basis, the rest of the world keeps right on turning. *Don't it just, though?*

I closed the door to my apartment, and on the rest of the frickin' world, dumped my chicken on the kitchen counter, opened one of the bottles, poured myself a half a glass, and said, "Alexa, play some mariachi music."

Yeah, that's what I said, mariachi. I don't know why. Maybe it's the cheerfulness of it, but mariachi always does it for me.

I added some ice to my glass of Cabernet, tore a leg off the chicken, and all but fell into my recliner and then tried to let go. It wasn't easy, but I forced myself to listen to the trumpets and not to think about work.

As I sat there, glass in hand, my eyes closed, listening to the music of Mexico, I suddenly realized I hadn't had any time off in almost two years. I needed a vacation. I had time coming to me. Maybe I'd go someplace cold. Colorado maybe. I'd never been skiing. Maybe I'd meet someone to snuggle under a blanket with and sip hot cider, with a little rum in it, of course.

Nah, I need hot sunshine, a bikini, turquoise waters, and calypso music. I wonder if Harry could put in a word for me at Calypso Key... Shit! Where the hell did that come from?

Calypso Key was where Harry married Amanda. That was the last place I needed to go. *Ah, forget it. Who needs a vacation anyway?*

Finally, as my eyelids grew heavy, I struggled out of the recliner, pulled the curtains closed, stashed the rest of the chicken in the fridge, poured myself another half glass of wine, and went to bed.

In the darkness, I turned off my phone—something I rarely ever did—stripped off my clothes, climbed into bed naked, took a last sip of wine, lay back on the pillows, closed my eyes and was soon lost among the white-topped mountains, log cabins, snowflakes and hot chocolate. And, for the first time in weeks, I slept well. I didn't wake until the alarm went off at six-thirty the following morning.

16

The next morning was Friday the thirteenth. Now, I'm not usually superstitious about such things, but that one started with a bang, literally. And from that point on, events began to move very quickly and all downhill.

It was just after eight-thirty when I walked into the incident room that morning to find most of my team already there, primed and ready to go. I'd stopped along the way to get my usual breakfast sandwich and a fill-up of my metal coffee tumbler. After the best night's sleep in many a long day, I was feeling pretty chipper.

"Hey guys," I said brightly. "How y'all is this rainy Friday morning?"

I was answered by a chorus of good mornings and smart remarks, and I smiled and thought that life was good, probably better than I deserved.

"My car should be ready later this morning," Ann said, her voice was cheery or at least as cheery as Detective Ann Robar ever got.

"How about I run you over to get it?" Miller said, suggestively, giving her a playful nudge.

She smiled, shook her head, and said, "Not today, sonny." And Miller looked suitably chastened.

"I... I didn't mean—"

"I know you didn't, sweetie," Ann said. "Of course you can take me."

"Where's Janet?" Hawk asked. "It's not like her to be late."

I looked around at her cubicle. Her computer wasn't on. Her notebooks hadn't been disturbed, and her chair was still tucked neatly beneath her desk. I took out my phone and called her. She didn't answer.

"She probably stopped somewhere to get coffee," I said. "Give her a few more minutes; she'll be here."

I stood there talking to them about the case for several more minutes, ending with a repetition of my warning that Chief Johnston wanted everything kept under wraps for as long as possible. Then I turned to go into my office, and my phone buzzed in my jacket pocket. I barely heard it, and I certainly didn't feel it. *Damn, I forgot to turn the ringer back on... Un-for-frickin' believable.*

"Gazzara," I answered, and then my world turned upside down; Friday the thirteenth had begun in earnest.

"Captain," the receptionist said. "I'm sorry to call you on your cell, but you're not in your office. I have a Doctor Joon Napai on the phone. She insists on talking to you; says it's an emergency."

"Put her through, please."

"Captain Gazzara?"

"Yes, doctor. What can I do for you?"

"I tried calling you last night, Captain, and again this morning. I even left messages. Your Sergeant Janet Toliver was brought into the hospital last night—"

"What?" I asked, stunned, interrupting her. My mouth had gone completely dry.

"She's conscious, and talking, and she insisted I call you to let you know. I'll go now—"

"Wait, what happened to her? How is she?"

"According to her boyfriend—he's here with her—she was assaulted and beaten. She received a very nasty crack on the back of the head, and she has a hairline fracture of the skull that should heal quite quickly. She also has some superficial facial trauma that will also heal nicely. Her two broken ribs, though; they will take a while to heal. Now, I have to go. She's in room 2007. Please feel free to visit." And with that, she hung up, leaving me standing there in a stupor. I just couldn't believe it. Janet wasn't a careless person, nor was she easily fooled.

What the hell could have happened?

"Cap? Is everything all right?" Hawk asked.

I know I told them what had happened and I remember the looks of shock and worry on their faces, but for the life of me, I can't recall exactly what I said.

"I'll go with you to the hospital," Ann said.

"No. I want you and Miller to finish canvassing the bars. Go shake some trees and see what falls. Somebody somewhere must have seen something.

"Hawk, I need your help. I need you to study the files and put together a map. I've been looking at it by myself way too long, and I'm going cross-eyed. I need a fresh pair of eyes on it, yours. By the time I get back, I want something we can work with and a full breakdown of all four cases, including Huntsville and Dalton. FedEx should deliver Huntsville before ten, any minute in fact. Go to it, people."

Without another word, I walked out of the building and drove to the Erlanger Hospital Emergency room. I barely remember the ride over there. My mind was in a whirl. I parked in the lot opposite the emergency room, half-ran inside, flashed my badge and asked where I'd find room 2007.

A kind-faced, elderly gentleman sporting a volunteer's badge that proclaimed his name was Bill led me through a set of double doors, down a long corridor until:

"Here you go, Detective," Bill said. "Let us know if you need anything." He smiled and his brown eyes twinkled. As much as I didn't feel like it, I couldn't help but smile back.

"Anybody home?" I asked quietly as I pulled the curtain aside and stuck my head through.

Janet was in the bed, with her boyfriend sitting next to her, holding her hand. She looked... awful. Her left eye was swollen shut and her top lip, puffy and purple, looked... well, she had a fat lip, and that described it perfectly. Her chest was heavily bandaged, and she looked like hell.

"It's part of the job, right Detective?" The boyfriend smiled sadly as he rose to his feet. "At least, that's what she tells me." He looked fondly down at her, then back at me, offered me his hand and said, "I'm Adam. You're Detective Gazzara, right?"

He was a big bull of a guy, did something in construction, as I recalled.

"You can call me—" I began.

But before I could complete the thought, Janet opened her eyes and interrupted me, "Hey, Kate," she muttered and tried to smile, but all she managed was to wince with pain.

"What the hell, Toliver?" I said, patting Adam's arm and stepping to her side. "Look, if you wanted time off, all you had to do was ask, okay? Can you talk? Can you tell me what happened?"

She nodded slightly, winced, then said, "Yeah, but I don't know what happened. Adam and me, we'd arranged to meet outside that bar, you know, Second Base where Logan was last seen. I arrived first, but instead of waiting for him, I decided to go take a quick look. I parked curbside and was just getting out of my car when there's this tremendous blow to the back of my head and... and then I'm on the ground. My head's spinning, I can't see anything, and then I get kicked in the face. Next thing, someone is kicking the crap out of me, see?" She tried to look down at her bandaged ribs, but couldn't. "And that's all I know," she said.

I turned to her boyfriend and said, "Did you see what happened, Adam?"

"Like she said, we were supposed to meet outside the bar. When I got there, I see her car but she's not in it, not so far as I could see. So I step up and look inside... nothing. Then I hear a moan, like, so I go around the car and I find her lying on her back, on the ground, in the street next to the car, bleeding from her face."

"Did you get a look at the guy who did this to you, Janet?" I asked.

"No. I went down like a sack of potatoes. But I think I got a glimpse of his girlfriend. I saw a tattoo on the back of her hand when the bitch reached for my purse. But my head was spinning, and everything was wavy and out of focus." She looked at Adam, who was, I could tell, holding back tears.

"I'll be right back," he said and slipped quietly out of the room. And that seemed like a good time for me to go talk to the doctor.

Doctor Joon Napai was just a little thing, no taller than Janet. She had smooth skin, and I figured she must be somewhere in her forties, but gray strands were already present among her jet-black hair. Her job in the Emergency Room probably took its toll on her, like mine was doing to me. She informed me that she would be keeping Janet in the hospital, probably for several days—standard procedure for anyone with a serious head injury—to make sure she didn't have a concussion and to make sure she'd give herself the time needed for her ribs to mend. For that I was grateful, because knowing Janet as I did, she'd be back at work as soon as she could stand up.

I returned to Janet's room and had a few words with Adam, who assured me he intended to stay with her. For that I was also thankful. I asked him to give me a few minutes alone with her, and he nodded and said he'd go get a bite to eat.

"You still feel like talking?" I asked.

"Absolutely," she said, wincing.

I shook my head, then said, "Will he be okay, Adam?" I asked.

"Yeah, he'll get over it," she said. "This is the first time I've gotten hurt... I tell you what, Kate. These are some fiiiine pain-killers."

"I'll bet they are." I smiled.

"So, you think there were two of them, then?"

"I guess."

"You said the woman reached for your purse?"

"Yes, she took my cash, all of it. I had almost three hundred in my wallet. Damn it."

"That's all they took, just your cash?"

"Yes, just the cash."

"Not your credit cards?"

"Nope."

"Tell me about the tattoo."

"It was kinda blue... and swirly..." She shook her head, then said, "I'm sorry. That's all I can remember."

"Interesting," I muttered, more to myself than to Janet.

17

"Hey Cap, I need to show you something," Hawk said when I walked into the situation room. "How's Janet, by the way?"

That's Hawk for you. He knew she was alive, so that was good enough; she'd get over it.

"She's banged up quite a bit," I said. "But she's doing okay. I'll fill you in later. What d'you have for me?"

I was happy for the distraction, but more than a little bothered by the odds that two people, two police officers, both members of my team, Ann and Janet, had been targeted within forty-eight hours. It was too much of a coincidence.

"Sheriff Cane's people in Dalton recovered a badly damaged bullet from the victim's car door frame," he said. "And, as you know, I recovered another from the barn on Route 18..." He paused, stared at me, a sloppy grin on his face.

"So?" I said impatiently.

"Mike Willis made the match," he said triumphantly. "They were both fired from the same gun."

Try as I might, I couldn't feel as excited about it as he obviously was. So they matched? So what? I'd already figured they would. Big deal. It didn't help the investigation. In fact, it complicated it—confirmed that we did indeed have a predator on our hands.

"That's good, right?" he said. "But there's more. McGraw's ME took one out of Leeds' head. It also matches."

And there it was, confirmation. We were now officially dealing with a serial killer. Whoop-de-doo.

"Come on, Kate," he said. "This is big."

"Okay, Hawk. I agree. It's good to know. Now, all we have to do is find the gun and we have our killer. Any ideas how we might do that?" I didn't mean to be so bitchy to him, but I was frustrated and upset about what had happened to Janet, and even more upset that I was now dealing with something that could quickly get out of hand. Oh yes, I was worried the press might get hold of it.

I put my hands on my hips and waited, not really expecting him to give me an answer, but of course he did.

"Well, according to what we know, the perp has been using the same weapon for more than five years," Hawk said. "I doubt he's going to toss it in the river and go find a new one now. These people are creatures of habit. They also believe they're invincible."

"Did you see anything in the case files that could give us a lead on where they might strike next?" I asked. "Our victims are all over-weight, middle-aged men. Some are single. Some are married."

"There isn't a sexual component involved," Hawk replied. "As far as I can tell, it's all about the money."

"That's bizarre," I said. "We've got a maniac prowling the bars and killing for a few dollars. None of them had more than two or three hundred bucks on them, right? Sure, people have died for less, but I get the feeling there's more to our subject's motivation—"

"Kate." I heard my name and whirled around to see Chief Johnston approaching. I'd been hoping I'd be able to skate through the day without having to talk to him.

"Hey, Chief. I was just going to call you," I said, lying through my teeth. "We're making progress, not much, but some. Willis has been able to establish that the bullet Hawkins recovered from the Logan scene matches three other cold cases—"

"That's all very interesting," he said, "but that's not what I want to talk to you about. Your office, Captain, I think. Now!"

What the hell? I wondered.

We sat down together at the table. He put his elbows on the tabletop, clasped his hands together in front of him, stared at me over them, and began, "You remember when I asked you if you had anything you wanted to tell me, so I wouldn't be surprised if I heard from Internal Affairs?" His eyes bore into me.

"Yes, I remember. So?"

My heart skipped a beat as I waited for him to explain.

"Captain Volker called me about an hour ago."

Volker ran the IA department. My heart skipped another beat.

"A Mr. Alvin Brown called him and said that he came in yesterday morning to file a complaint against his girlfriend, and during his interview, you made an inappropriate suggestion to him. What the hell did you say to him, Kate?"

I couldn't help but grin. In fact, I almost laughed out loud.

"What's so funny, Captain?"

"That man's a nut case," I said. "First, it was Ann Robar that conducted that interview, not me. I just happened to stop by while he was yelling at her. Second, she asked him to think about if he wanted to go through with what he was doing while she talked to me for a minute and, while we talked, the idiot disappeared. Third, he went straight out of the building and slashed all four of Ann's tires; we have him on surveillance footage doing it. I made an inappropriate suggestion? Seriously? Ann's about to have him arrested, if she can find him. Maybe she'll get lucky, now that we know his full name." I stopped talking. I could see by his face I'd said enough.

"I thought it sounded a little off-the-wall, Kate," Johnston said. "If he'd claimed you'd slapped him, I might have tended to believe him, but sexual harassment? No. Forget it. I'll handle Volker. So, now that we have that out of the way, what's the situation with the Logan case?"

"There's something going on, Chief, something I can't quite get a handle on. This guy slashed Ann's tires. The same guy files a complaint against me, and Janet got beaten half to death outside the bar where our victim Logan was last seen. It's all a little coincidental, don't you think?"

I folded my hands and leaned forward. "I have a bad feeling about Brown. We need to find him, and quickly. I'd hate for something to happen to Miller or Hawk or both before we can grab him, if it is him."

"I agree," he said. "How's Toliver doing? She'll recover fully, I presume?" The corner of his left eye began to twitch; something I'd never seen before.

"She's at Erlanger," I replied. "She has two broken ribs and a fractured skull. It's not quite as bad as it sounds. It's just a hairline fracture, but still, they're keeping her for a few more days, worried about a possible concussion. She should be able to go home next week, if all goes well. Her boyfriend, Adam, is staying with her."

"There's no security footage of the attack, I assume?" he asked.

"Unfortunately, no."

"So, we don't know if it was Brown... Better get a uniform over there, just in case. I'll go see her this afternoon. She is allowed visitors, correct?"

I nodded, thinking about what he'd just said. *Could it possibly be Brown we're looking for?*

"And you," Johnston said. "Do I need to assign a uniform to follow you around, too?"

"Are you serious, Chief?" It was a stupid question, because I could see from the look on his face that he was.

"No, Chief," I said. "You don't need to worry about me. I'll be doing things by the book. I promise." I don't know why I said I promise. I knew damn well it was a promise I couldn't keep, and that he didn't believe me.

"Chief, have you ever known a case like this?" I asked.

He slowly shook his head and said, "What do you think, Kate? Of course not, but then, I was never a detective." He stood, looked down at me, and said, "That'll be all for now, Kate. Get back to work. Catch this guy before he kills again."

I nodded, and he left my office. I picked up my desk phone and called Hawk. Miller and Ann had returned. I asked him to join me and bring them with him.

"Everything okay, DG?" Ann asked.

"Oh yeah," I lied. "What have you got for me?"

"Yes, I can see that," Ann said sarcastically. "Well, I think I have something that'll make you feel better. We found the place where Logan ate his last meal, a bar and grill called The Sovereign. It's a half-assed sort of establishment: just a long bar, a couple of tables, two big flat-screen TVs, a griddle, and a couple of deep fat fryers. The place is... let's just say, I think a call to the restaurant inspector might be in order."

"And we've got video," Miller said, slipping a thumb drive into his laptop. His fingers flew over the keyboard, and instantly, we were watching video footage from inside the bar.

"You can see our victim clearly," Ann said, pointing at the screen. "This is him sitting at the bar, alone, drinking a beer and eating a burger. He doesn't look intoxicated to me."

I said nothing. I just watched as the scene played out. There were some dozen people in the bar, none of them doing anything out of the ordinary. Most of them were staring up at one or the other of the two TVs on the wall behind the bar. Some patrons were talking to each other, but not a lot; no sound, unfortunately. The footage was time-stamped four-twenty-eight, just nineteen minutes after he'd left Second Base. *He must have driven straight over there,* I thought.

"It looks depressing," I said. "Is this all there is?"

"No, wait, there's more," Ann said. "Here we go: enter our suspect. That's him, there."

A small man walked into the bar and sat down next to Logan. We couldn't see his face; he seemed to be consciously avoiding the camera. He had blond hair, that was obviously in need of a trim, and was wearing a heavy camouflage jacket over what might have been a white T-shirt and jeans. He said something to Logan, then looked at the bartender, then again at Logan, all the time keeping his head down. Logan gestured to the bartender and two beers were placed in front of them.

"Looks like they're getting along fine," I said. "I wish to hell I could see his face. Is that him, Ann? Is it Brown?"

She slowly shook her head, then said, "I dunno. Could be, but this guy isn't wearing glasses. Brown was... And he was wearing that hunter's cap, so I never did see his hair. It's hard to tell, DG... Might be."

We continued to watch as Logan bought the man another drink, stood, slapped him on the shoulder, and moved to leave. The man in the camo jacket turned, stared after him, said something, and Logan returned and stood beside him, and the two became engaged in an animated conversation.

"I think Logan's new friend wants him to stick around," Miller said.

Hawk leaned closer to get a better look at the man then pointed to the screen.

"Look at his hair. It's about the right length and color. We may have a match. What d'you think?"

"Hey, don't touch the screen," Miller said, slapping the back of his hand. "You'll mess it up."

"Yeah, okay, nerd," Hawk said.

"Hey, I'm just saying," Miller snapped back.

"Would you two knuckleheads quiet down," Ann replied. "Leave his shit alone, Hawk. You know how sensitive he is."

"Oh hell, Robar," he said, without looking up from the screen. "I didn't even look in your direction, so as I see it, you don't need to be interjecting yourself into the conversation."

"One of these days, Hawk," Ann said, "someone's going to teach you a lesson," and she bumped him with her hip as she scooted past him.

"Yeah, yeah, so you say," Hawk said, still not looking up. "Cap, I think Logan is wanting to leave, but the little guy is trying to get him to stay. Then look, see? It's the little guy who leaves first, not Logan, he didn't finish his beer and he looks pissed."

"He waited for him, outside," I muttered thoughtfully. "The little bastard ambushed him. You think it could be Brown, Ann?" I asked again.

"I don't know. It could be... If we could just get a look at his face."

"Did you talk to the bartender?"

"We talked to a bartender, but he wasn't on duty that night. He didn't know anything," Ann said. "But the bar owner who provided us with the footage said that the bartender that did work that night was off until this afternoon; his name is Mickey, by the way, the bartender, that is, not the owner."

I looked at my watch. It was almost two-thirty.

"What time do they open?" I asked.

"They're open already, since eleven," Miller said.

"Come on, Ann," I said. "Let's go talk to Mickey. The rest of you stay on it. Keep digging. Lennie, see what you can find out about an Alvin Brown. And I need a screenshot of those two. Can you send it to my printer?" He nodded, and I continued, "Hawk, you check in with Willis. See if he's come up with anything new. We'll be back, okay?"

I grabbed the image from my printer, then my jacket, and we left.

18

The Sovereign was just as nasty in real life as it was on the video footage. We walked through the front door into a dingy, half-lit world where the air was awash with the smell of stale beer and cigarette smoke. It wasn't quite as bad as the smell of my grandmother's basement after it flooded in 1996, but it was damn close, and I wondered about the people who habitually congregated in such places. Surely there was something better.

The barstools, those that weren't occupied, were old and made of wood with short, stubby backs. The walls were papered with promotional beer posters featuring sports heroes from a bygone era: the Atlanta Braves, the Falcons, and for some reason, some featured players in Green Bay Packer uniforms. There was even one poster featuring the great Spanish bullfighter, El Cordobés, a tribute to the bar's Hispanic clientele, I presumed. There was also a dartboard and a long row of small, framed photographs of people I could only assume were regular customers.

Ann and I took seats at the bar, trying to ignore the attention we—two seemingly single women—had attracted from the moment we walked in, and we waited for the bartender to see us. He was at the far end of the bar, talking to a young woman while washing glasses at the same time.

He was a pleasant-looking guy, despite the burgeoning beer belly. His heavily muscled arms bore an assortment of tattoos, including an American flag crossed with the red flag of the Marines. The words Semper Fi were tattooed in big letters over the flags, and God Bless America beneath.

The bottles on the shelves behind him were nothing special either: cheap bourbon, off-brand scotch, gin I'd never even heard of. It was a place where Absolut was the most expensive vodka and Budweiser came in a can.

He glanced at me, jerked his chin up, and held up a finger, signaling he'd be right with me. I discretely opened my jacket and displayed my badge. He grinned, nodded, and came right over, still wiping out a glass. I showed him my ID.

"D'you mind?" he asked, taking it from me. He held it up to a light over the shelves, nodded, and handed it back to me.

"Was that just to impress me, or was it routine?" I asked.

"Can't be too careful, can we, Captain?" This guy was either a stickler for the rules or he was full of shit; I figured it was probably the latter.

"You Mickey?" I asked.

"Mickey O'Donnell, at your service. What can I do for you two lovely ladies?"

"Cut the crap, Mickey. You were working on Tuesday, so I'm told. Is that right?"

"Yes, ma'am," he said, smiling, obviously unperturbed by my tone.

"Do you remember seeing this man come in here?" I handed him a copy of a photograph of Logan, one his wife had provided.

"Yes. Sure. He came in to watch the ballgame."

"Had you ever seen him in here before?" I asked.

"Once in a while, not often. Loves his football. I felt kinda bad for him though."

"Why is that?" Ann asked.

He shrugged and said, "The guy came in to watch the game, right? But he got himself tangled up with one of my regulars. He made the mistake of buying the guy a beer. After that, the guy just wouldn't leave him alone."

"Do you have a name?" I asked.

"Nate. He goes by Nate."

"Is this him?" I showed Mickey the screenshot taken from The Sovereign's surveillance footage. Mickey nodded and handed the photo back to me.

"Yeah, that's him."

"And you say he's a regular here?" I asked as the front door opened behind me. I turned and looked, hoping I was about to get lucky and Nate would walk right on in. But no such luck. The guy who did walk in was at least six feet tall with a heavily weathered face and Dumbo ears. He sat down at the far corner of the bar, next to the woman the bartender had so recently been talking to, waved at Mickey, and yelled in a high-pitched voice for a Bud.

"Go ahead," I said. "I'm in no hurry."

I looked around, checking out the clientele, and I noticed a woman staring at me. She was by herself, an older lady who looked as worn out as the posters on the walls. She had a cigarette between her fingers and kept flicking it nervously. I had a feeling, from the way she kept looking at me, then down at the cigarette, then back at me again, that she wanted to talk to me.

"Hold the fort for a minute," I said to Ann, then I got up from my stool, walked over to the woman and sat down next to her.

"You're a cop?" she asked. Her voice was scratchy, raspy; she was obviously a heavy smoker.

"Detective Gazzara, Chattanooga PD." I showed her my ID.

She glanced quickly at it, nodded, then said, "You're looking for Nate, aren't you?"

I felt my heart rate multiply, almost like I was going into AFib, not that I'd ever had that experience, but you know what I mean, right?

"Why would you say that?" I asked. "Who are you?"

"My name is Bobbie Lynn Wilkesen," she said, extending her hand. I wasn't sure which reached me first, the alcohol on her breath, smoke from her cigarette, or her hand. It was a safe assumption that Bobbie Lynn Wilkesen had been drinking for a while.

I shook her hand politely. She didn't really grip my hand, just my fingers in a very feminine way. Her nails were acrylic and her hands were very soft, yet the signs of age were creeping into them. Her knuckles were deeply wrinkled and there were dark spots on the backs of her hands and wrists.

"I read in the papers about that man who died," she said quietly, taking a huge drag on the cigarette, then tapped it over the ashtray with her forefinger, sending a shower of sparks into the overflowing pile of butts. "He was in here you know. Tuesday afternoon. I saw him. He was talking with Nate. Nate isn't a nice person."

"Really?" I said. Then I showed Bobbie Lynn the two photos of both men and asked her to confirm that we were talking about the same people.

"Oh, yeah, that's him, and that's Nate. I know who he is, and I know who he will be, too." She stubbed out her cigarette and took a new one from a silver beaded cigarette case full of those long, thin cigarettes. They're usually packaged in pastel-colored boxes with the slogan, "You've come a long way, baby."

I frowned. "What can you tell me?"

"Nate has issues," Bobbie Lynn said as she lit the cigarette and took a long, deep drag. Then she turned her head and blew a stream of smoke away from me.

"Issues? What do you mean, issues? And how d'you know about them?" I asked.

"Let's just say I knew him before he changed. It was the Army that did it to him, the Marines," she said and gestured to Mickey.

He nodded, made her a drink of some dark liquor and a mixer, added a cherry, and brought it to her.

"Nate was in the Army?" I asked, as Mickey set the drink down on the table in front of her.

"No," Mickey said. "He's a Marine."

"This guy was in the Marines?" I held up the picture from the surveillance footage. "He's too small."

Every Marine I've ever known was huge and had an even bigger ego. I'd heard recruitment was down but come on, really?

"He's five-eight and tough as shit," Mickey said. "Yeah. He was in the Marines. And then he was out of the Marines. Except, they're never out of the Marines, are they? Once a Marine, always a Marine." He rolled his eyes. "The guy is full of shit. He got kicked out when they found out what he was there for."

What the hell are they talking about?

I looked at Mickey and then to Bobbie Lynn.

"You have no compassion, Mickey," Bobbie Lynn said.

"Compassion isn't what Nate needs. He... What the hell am I saying... SHE! She needs a swift kick where the sun don't shine!" Mickey smirked down at me.

Me? I felt like an anvil had just fallen on my head.

"What?" was all I could utter.

"Yeah. That's right," Mickey said, so obviously enjoying himself. "He's a she, a woman, a girl, a female. And when she comes in here, most of my customers get antsy because she gives off a bad vibe. Not only that, but she doesn't have two nickels to rub together, and she's always on the hunt for new faces to buy her a round."

"This is a woman?" I held up the picture again. "You're sure?"

"He's going to be mad as hell when he hears you're still talking about him that way," Bobbie Lynn said to Mickey.

"Why do you keep saying he?" I asked, bewildered.

"What's he going to do about it? I'm not going to lie to the police. He's a she who wants to be a man... Look," Mickey said, looking down at me, "I don't care what people do, how they do it, or what frickin' gender they are or want to be. I'm just a bartender. But when someone starts hassling the customers or making people feel uneasy, then that interrupts business. And when that happens, I have to say something."

"You said Nate had issues," I said to Bobbie Lynn. "Is what Mickey said true? That at birth he was a... female?"

"I'm just saying he's got issues. He has a temper, and he has a chip on his shoulder," she replied, picking her teeth nervously with her manicured nails. "I think he wants so badly to be something he isn't that he overcompensates, and because of all that, he starts trouble with people."

"You didn't answer the question," Ann, who'd now joined me at the table, said. "Is he a woman?"

She looked away, obviously not wanting to answer.

"Yes he is, she is... Damn, you've got me going now," Mickey answered for her. "She's still a woman, yes!"

"When was the last time you saw him, her?" I looked at Mickey and then at Bobbie Lynn.

"The night that guy was killed," Mickey said.

Bobbie Lynn nodded.

"Did he... she say anything out of the ordinary?" I asked.

"Are you kidding?" Mickey said. "She says the same horseshit every time she comes in. She's making progress with her hormones. Her doctors have never seen anyone respond so well to treatment. Bullshit! She looks the same today as she did a year ago. Frankly, I don't think she's seeing any doctors. I think she's just playing dress-up."

I couldn't believe what I was hearing. I'd spent the last several days looking for a needle in a haystack, and the first solid identification I get comes from two people telling me I've been wrong all along? That my man is a woman? Hell, I needed a drink and I was about to ask Mickey for one when the door opened.

Mickey and Bobbie Lynn both looked around and then they froze.

"Son of a bitch," Mickey said. "Speak of the devil."

I turned, so did Ann. Nate had just waltzed in wearing the same camouflage jacket and baggy jeans he'd been wearing in my photo and was jauntily heading for the bar, his shoulders swaying from side to side.

"Shit!" Ann said. "That's him. That's Brown."

What happened next took no more than a couple of seconds.

I jumped to my feet, headed in the same direction, and said, "Excuse me. Can I talk to you for a minute?"

"Who, me?" Nate said, nervously, and began inching back and toward the door.

"Yes, just a quick word." I smiled... well, I thought I did, but I think it may have been more grimace than smile. I held up my ID and said, "I'm Detective Gazzara, Chattanooga Police."

"Oh, yeah. Cool. Uhm, yeah, okay. Just give me a sec while I go tell my ride that I'll be a few minutes," and she bolted toward the door. Yeah, it took less than ten seconds and he, she, whatever, was gone.

I ran after her, out through the front door. I stopped outside, listening. I heard the sound of feet running fast to my right. I ran after her, my weapon in hand, my heart pounding as the adrenaline surged through my body. She turned right into an alley. I was less than twenty yards behind her, the sweat already beading on my face.

And then I made a rookie mistake, and the next ten seconds almost cost me my life.

As I ran after her, I was trying to process what the hell and who the hell I was chasing. So instead of slowing down and taking precautions, I continued running headlong around the corner and into an empty alley, or so it seemed. And then it hit me, literally. Something slammed into the back of my head. I went down and my forehead hit the ground, hard.

I felt hands on me. I tried to roll over, my gun still in my hand. Something slammed into my ribs, and then a boot crashed down onto my wrist. The Glock flew out of my hand. The weight of the boot on my wrist increased. I tried to roll. I couldn't.

"Keep still, damn it," she snarled. "Don't frickin' move. I don't want to hurt you, but I will," she said.

Then the weight lifted off my wrist and she got in one last kick to my gut. It knocked the wind completely out of me. I lay there gasping for breath. Then I heard footsteps, running, and I was afraid she was coming back. With a supreme effort, a grunt, and a couple painful gasps, I reached out, grabbed the Glock, rolled up onto one knee, my weapon in one hand, the other cradling my ribs. I could still breathe. *Maybe I don't have any broken ribs,* I thought.

"Whoa, don't shoot. It's me!" Ann yelled as she ran toward me with Mickey close behind her.

Ann ran on past me, weapon in hand. Then, realizing Nate was gone, she stopped and bent, her hands on her knees, breathing hard. "Damn," I heard her say to herself, "I need some frickin' exercise. This is ridiculous." Then she turned and came back.

"You okay, Kate?" she asked, as Mickey took one of my arms and helped me up.

"No," I said. "I got stomped on and hit in the head. I hurt all over."

"You need to sit for a minute," Mickey said. "C'mon, I'll give you a hand." And he did, he took my arm and we returned to The Sovereign.

The place had emptied, all but for the crinkled old guy with the Dumbo ears. He was still working on his drink.

"Geez, where'd everybody go?" I asked, wincing.

"You sort of scared them off," Mickey said, grinning. "The people we get in here like to stay out of sight, if you get my meaning."

"That I do," I replied. "That I do."

"You look like you need a drink, Detective, both of you." He looked at Ann. She shook her head. "Detective?" he asked. "I won't tell if you don't, and I know old Ralph won't, right, Ralph?"

The crinkled old guy grinned hugely and shook his head.

"Thanks, but no thanks," I said. "But I will take a glass of water."

"Coming right up." Mickey turned away, grabbed a large tumbler, and went down the bar to fill it with ice.

"Her name is Nate Cassidy," the crinkled man called Ralph said.

"What's that?" I said softly.

"Nate Cassidy. Her real name is Natalie. I heard her talking once when she didn't think anyone was paying any attention," Ralph said, taking a sip of his drink. He winked at me and then went back to his brooding.

"Thanks, Ralph," I replied quietly.

Mickey returned and handed me my water. I drank about half of it down then asked for the lady's room.

"I'll be just a minute," I told Ann.

She nodded, then said, "Take it easy, okay? You want me to come with you?"

I shook my head and left her sitting at the bar. I could feel the goose egg already beginning to grow on my forehead. *Shit!* I thought as I made my way to the restroom. *This is all I need.*

And the lady's room at The Sovereign did nothing to boost a girl's mood. The mirror over the sinks and the florescent light above the three stalls and the green paint on the walls made my skin look beyond sickly. *Geez, I look like a freaking zombie.*

The greenish tinge to my skin contrasted with the cut and trickle of blood at my hairline. My shirt, the thighs and backside of my pants, my palms, and my right cheek all had some kind of unnamable grime on them. God only knew how many patrons from The Sovereign had vomited in that alley or used it as a bathroom. My stomach flipped at the thought.

I brushed the crap off my clothes as best I could, washed my face, scrubbed my hands, dried off, and stared again into the mirror. My face, now devoid of makeup, looked back at me, and I shuddered. I sure as hell didn't want to be seen out in public looking like I did. I wanted to get out of there, in a hurry, go home, take a long hot shower, but I had little choice. I needed to find out who and what the hell this woman was.

19

I had Ann take me back to the PD, and I went to the locker room where I showered and cleaned myself up as best I could. There was little I could do about my clothes, but I always keep a couple of pairs of jeans and tops in my locker so I changed, threw the dirties on the locker floor and slammed the door shut on them. Some lipstick, a little foundation, and a touch of blush worked wonders on my face, or so I thought.

By the time I was done prissing and primping, it was after five. I wanted to go home, but I didn't. I needed to talk to Janet. One, I wanted to make sure she was okay. Two, I wanted to compare notes. Following the dynamic shift in the focus of the case, I wanted to see if I could jog her memory, so I again headed to the hospital.

I didn't go through the emergency room entrance. Instead I parked in the multi-story lot and went straight to her room on the second floor.

"Knock-knock," I said as I entered.

"Oh wow, Kate," she said. "What happened to you?" *So much for the makeup!*

"Not much. How're you feeling?"

"Better. I can't wait to get out of here... You look like you were hit by a truck. So what happened?"

"Geez, Janet. Thank you for the kind words."

"Oh, oh no. I didn't mean... I'm sorry, I just—"

"I know," I said. "I was kidding, okay? You're right about the truck, though, well, sort of. It's been quite a day. Where's Adam, by the way?"

"Doctor Joon sent him home. So tell me. What happened?"

"We found the guy who did this to you, is what happened. Well, we think it was him, but as yet there's no proof of anything. I'm hoping you can help."

"Oh, Lord. You arrested him, right? He's in custody?"

"No! He got away. I was chasing him down... Hey, it's good to see that you're feeling better."

"I am. In fact I'd like to get out of here, but they want to keep me for at least another day... Kate, did you really think it was necessary to put a uniform outside my door?"

"That was the Chief's idea," I said as I made myself comfortable on the edge of her bed and took out my mini recorder. "So, Sergeant Toliver," I said, smiling at her, "you know the routine. Start at the beginning. Tell me what happened."

"I've already told you most of it," she said. "Adam and I were supposed to meet at that bar, Second Base, where Logan had been spotted. I hadn't planned anything. We were just going to have a beer and get the lay of the land, maybe ask a question or two, show Logan's photo around. I knew Ann and Miller had already covered the place, but it was a date and something to do. I'd just gotten out of the car when bam, and that's about all I know."

"Did you get a look at him? Did you see anything at all?"

"Aha! Yeah, it came to me earlier today. I was trying to remember what happened and I... well, you remember I told you his partner had a tattoo on the back of her hand? It was one of those blue things, a jailhouse tat. It was a Marine badge. You know, the anchor and globe thing... Look, the guy who jumped me only got the upper hand because I didn't see him coming. If I had, things would have been different. He'd be in my place right now, and a lot worse off than me, I can tell you that." Janet shook her head.

"You didn't get a look at his face?"

"No."

"How big was he?"

"Hm, not hugely big, in good shape... I guess."

"What about his hair?"

She shook her head. "No. I didn't see it... Kate, what is it? You look like you know more than you're saying."

Before I could answer and tell Janet the full story, Doctor Napai entered the room.

"Visitors at this hour?" she said and clicked her tongue disapprovingly. "She needs to rest... What happened to you?"

She took a penlight from her coat breast pocket, put her hand on my head, and pulled it toward her.

"I'm okay, Doctor," I said. "It's just part of the job."

"No," she said, sternly. "It's not okay. This is a nasty bump. And..." She rubbed the back of my head, making me pull back and wince. "You also have another bump here."

She let go of my head, took a step back, folded her arms, and glared up at me. If I hadn't been in the state I was, I would have found it funny. She was about the size of a thirteen-year-old girl—I towered over her. But there I was, standing in front of her, feeling like an idiot.

"Captain," she said, "you need to have your head properly examined."

"I've been told that on more than one occasion," I joked nervously. "I'm okay, doc, really I am. I promise. How about I come back when I get done... with my work. I mean, I have to go back to the police department, and well, there's paperwork I have to finish, so it might take me a while, I mean..." I could see she wasn't buying it. "I will. I'll come and let you take a look, doctor. I promise."

She snorted, fussed around Janet for a minute, checked her chart, gifted me with a look that would have frozen a waterfall, then left, shaking her finger at me.

"Wow! She scares the hell out of me," I said when she'd gone.

"That's only because you know she's right," Janet replied.

I rubbed the back of my head as if to say *See, no big deal,* but I wasn't fooling anyone; it hurt like hell, but I ignored Janet's look of concern and continued.

"So, back to our perp," I said, and then I relayed to her all that had happened over the past few hours, the short version, of course, and then I dropped the bomb. "Brown is not Brown. She's Natalie Cassidy."

Janet looked stunned. "What? Are you telling me it was a woman who did this to me?"

"I can't say for sure, but it sure looks like it," I said.

"Are you... You're not sure? Wow!" she stuttered.

"Not yet," I said, "but we're working on it. As far as we can tell, she's the last person to see Jack Logan alive. She was seen talking to him, and we have it on video, not more than thirty minutes before he died. According to the bartender and the Wilkesen woman, this Cassidy person is taking some kind of hormones and seeing a doctor for a gender swap."

"I want to help," she said, obviously excited. "I need to get out of here."

"No you don't," I said. "You need to take it easy and get well. We have her name. Miller will track her down, get her background and an address, and we need to find that doctor. Sheesh, how many shrinks can there be who handle this gender transformation thing?"

By the time I got out of the hospital, the pain at the back of my eyes was killing me. I blamed it on the bright lights, but I knew what was really happening: a migraine. Every once in a while, usually in stressful situations, I'd get a real humdinger and they all started the same way, at the back of my eyes.

The idea of quitting for the day was sounding better and better;

it was, after all, almost six-thirty. But I had to stop off at the PD and talk to my people. What I didn't know at the time was that Doctor Joon was right, and I was in trouble. As I was driving back to Amnicola, I missed several turns and had to back-track. I'd driven that route, back and forth, a thousand times, but now... Well, I just couldn't stay focused. Finally, though, I pulled into the parking lot at the front of the PD, shut off the engine, let out a deep breath, and laid my head back against the headrest: not a good idea. Pain speared through my head like a red-hot knife.

I sat for a minute, my eyes closed, waiting for the pain to subside. Then I stepped out of the car, made it into the building, took the elevator to the second floor, and from there to the incident room where I found Miller still at his desk. I'd forgotten what my face looked like until I saw the expression on his face.

"Hey DG," he said. "Ann said you'd gotten into a kafuffle, but she wouldn't elaborate. What the hell happened to you?"

"That's what she told you, huh?" I said, unaware I was rubbing the back of my head. "You should see the other guy."

"Did you make a bust?" Miller asked, not catching my joke.

"No. I'm the one who got busted... upside the back of my head." Involuntarily, I rubbed it and winced.

"Your eyes are all... You're not well, Cap. I'll call the Chief," he said and turned and reached for his desk phone.

"Whoa! Stop! Do *not* call the Chief. That's an order. If he finds out he'll take me off the case, and I can't have that, not when we're about to crack it wide open." I closed my eyes, breathed deeply, pinching the bridge of my nose.

"Well, okay, but—"

"No buts," I said. "We keep it to ourselves, okay?"

"Okay, but you went to see Janet at the hospital. Did they check you out while you were there?"

"Oh come on, Miller, you're not my moth-er. Oh shit. I'm sorry. Yeah, Janet's doctor checked me out." It wasn't a total lie, but a little voice at the back of my head was telling me that I was doing the wrong thing. As usual, I ignored it.

"Look," I said, "I just wanted to bring you and Hawk up to speed, let you know what Ann and I found out. Specifically, that the guy we're looking for is a woman."

"No way! DG, I think you must have hit your head harder than you think."

"Nope," I said. "I'm serious. Look, I need everything you can find on a Natalie Cassidy. She's ex-military, so there should be a record. She certainly has a history of psychological problems. I also want to know who she works for, where she lives, and who she lives with. Your priority, though, is to find me the address. I have to take this monster off the streets."

"You got it, DG. But first, I'm going to take you home. It's past quitting time, and you need to rest up." And before I could refuse, he was on his feet, keys in hand.

Any other day, I would have made a fuss and told him to get off my back, but I didn't. I knew he was right. I let him drive me home. He got me there in no time and parked his car at the door.

"I'll walk you to the door," he said.

"We're not on a date, Miller. I can get into my apartment," I grumbled.

"Okay, but I'll wait here until you get inside."

"Fine. Thanks," I muttered ungratefully as I opened the car door and stepped out into the darkness and the rain.

I pulled my collar up around my neck and hurried up the steps and heard him say through his open window, "You're welcome, DG."

I waved my hand dismissively, unlocked my front door, stepped inside, and closed the door.

Later, I'd be sorry that I'd been such an ass.

20

I was never so happy to get behind closed doors in my life. I didn't even turn on the lights in my apartment. I stood for a minute, leaning back against the front door, and allowed my eyes to adjust to the darkness. Then I turned and slipped the dead-bolt into place. The green numbers of my iWatch read seven-oh-two.

I went to my bedroom, peeled off my clothes, slipped into bed and within minutes was sound asleep, but it wasn't even twenty minutes later when my phone rang. I thought my world had exploded, and even though the room was totally dark, I had to squint my eyes as I picked up the phone.

"Gazzara," I muttered.

"What the hell, Catherine? I just heard that you have a head injury and that you haven't seen a doctor," the male voice shouted, making my head ring.

"Mom, is that you?" I said, knowing it was Chief Johnston, but I just couldn't help myself.

"Don't be smart with me, Gazzara!"

"All right, Chief," I said, now fully awake. "I'm sorry. Look, I did see a doctor. I just didn't... I promised I'd see her again later. I'm fine. I just got a little banged up, is all. I'm okay, really I am." I pushed myself up onto one elbow.

"Bull. Miller will pick you up. He said you'd be pissed at him for letting me know you got jumped," the Chief barked at me. "I told him not as pissed as I am that you didn't get yourself checked out!"

"Chief, I've got some news you need to hear about the Logan case—"

"I don't want to hear a damn thing about it until you've been cleared by a doctor," he growled, interrupting me.

"Ok. I'll go with Miller and get myself checked out." I sighed.

"And don't even think of setting foot in this department without a doctor's note. I mean it, Kate. Don't screw with me." I could see in my mind the Chief's teeth clenched and his left eye twitching.

"Yes, sir." But there was a click as he hung up. He didn't say good-bye. *Damn! I should have seen this coming. What was I thinking?*

I took a deep breath and carefully crawled out of bed, trying not to move my head too much. My headache was almost gone, but I figured there was no point in pushing my luck: I still had a tiny spear sticking into the back of my right eyeball.

I took a quick shower, dressed in my sweats, grabbed my purse, badge and Glock, and headed to the front door. I figured that Miller should already be pulling up outside. I couldn't wait to hear his excuse, and apology, for ratting on me and then insisting he did it for my own good. I knew it was, and that his intentions were good, but I still felt like I didn't need a damn babysitter. And then I began to wonder if maybe I'd forgotten what it felt like to have someone who actually gave a shit about me.

I grimaced, knowing that if it was true, it was because I chose it that way. The life I lived wasn't conducive to close friendships, close relationships. Let's face it; there's nothing more dangerous than a policewoman with a weapon on her hip and a broken heart beneath her badge.

I knew Miller was just looking out for me. Janet would have done the same.

I opened the front door. *Where the hell is he?*

It was raining outside and bone-chilling cold. I closed the door and waited, watching the parking lot through the window at the top of the door, and I waited.

Ten minutes later Miller still hadn't arrived, and I was getting seriously pissed. I took out my phone and called him. His phone rang four times then went to voicemail.

"What are you thinking, Kate?" I muttered to myself. *It's a horrible night, and he's driving, so he's not going to pick up the phone and risk an accident. Not Lennie Miller.*

So I hung around the front door, checking the parking lot every couple of seconds through the window, but time continued to tick by and there was still no Miller. I was beginning to panic, thinking he must have had an accident or something. I called him again; still no answer, so I called the Chief.

"What now, Catherine?"

"He hasn't shown up," I said. "You did tell him to come here, right? Could he have misunderstood and gone... Hell, I don't know; he's not answering his phone, Chief."

"No. He offered to pick you up at your place," Johnston said in a low voice.

"Maybe he's had an accident," I said.

"I doubt it. It's been almost an hour. We would have heard something from the emergency services."

"Right... that's right," I said, thinking. "Okay, I guess I'll drive myself to the hospital. It's not a big deal—"

"You'll stay right where you are. I'll send a unit. In the meantime, keep trying to raise Miller on his phone. I'll try his apartment." The line went dead.

I called Miller again, still no answer. I was beginning to have a really bad feeling that something had happened to him.

Finally, I saw a blue and white cruiser turning in through the gates and I stepped outside. It had stopped raining, so I paused on the top step and hit redial. I put the phone to my ear and heard his phone begin to ring... and then I heard his ring tone. *What the hell?*

I hit the red stop button and then the redial again. Sure enough, somewhere close by I could hear Miller's phone ringing; it was faint, but that's what it was, I was sure of it, the theme from Star Wars, what else?

"What the hell?" I muttered out loud as the uniformed officer got out of the car.

"Good evening, Detective. Chief sent me to—"

"Yeah, I know, to take me to the hospital. Stand still for just a second and listen." I hit the redial again. "Do you hear a cell phone ringing?"

"Yes, ma'am." He looked to the left of the lot, then pointed and said, "That way."

My apartment is an end unit. The parking lot circles the block. My front door faces north, my living room window faces east. Miller's car was parked under my window on the east side of the building. Its driver's side window open and I could see he was asleep at the wheel.

"Miller!" I shouted. "What the hell? The Chief is going to skin us both alive! How could you fall—"

"Oh shit," the officer said from the driver's side of Miller's car. And he grabbed his radio. "Officer down, officer down!"

I ran around the car, stopped, both hands to my mouth, staring in through the open window, the bile boiling up into my mouth. I was sure I was about to throw up.

Miller had been shot in the left temple, through the open driver's side window. His jacket was open and his wallet was on the ground beside the car. My mind went blank. I could see nothing but the wound at the side of his head. It seemed to grow bigger and bigger as I stared at it. I tried to go to him, but the officer grabbed me and held me back.

"Hold on, Detective," he said as I struggled to break loose. "There's nothing you can do for him."

"*I need to help him,*" I screamed. "*Where the hell are the paramedics?*"

They arrived a few minutes later, lights flashing, siren blaring, along with several police cruisers.

I watched as an ambulance careened into the complex, screeched to a stop, and three paramedics jumped out and ran to the car.

With deadpan expressions on their faces, they went quickly to work only to stop again almost immediately and turn away; there was nothing they could do for him. And I knew then that there was no hope of resuscitating Miller. And then the tears came. I tried to hold them back, but I couldn't. It's not good for a woman police officer to be seen crying in public. It looks weak, especially when there are male officers around, but I couldn't help it. I just stood there, my right elbow supported by my left hand, my right fist in my mouth, the tears rolling down my cheeks.

Miller was dead, no doubt about it, and I knew it was my fault. If I had done the right thing and had myself properly checked out, he would have been back at the office doing his thing on his computer instead of sitting in his car outside my apartment with his brains blown out.

What the hell was wrong with me? When was I ever going to learn? My eyes stung and my headache was back.

I stood there, watching as more and more officers arrived, everyone around me moving, at least to me, as if in slow motion. None of it was registering. How could a member of my team be dead? *My* team.

"Kate?" I heard a quiet voice behind me say.

I turned. It was Doc Sheddon.

"It's my fault, Doc."

"No. It isn't. It's the fault of the person who pulled the trigger," Doc said, but I was having none of it.

"How am I going to tell his mom?" I asked, more for something to say than for an answer. "He was everything to her. How am I going to face her and tell her it was my fault? I don't think I can do it."

"Yes, you can," he replied. "You'll do it the way you do everything else, Kate. Now, I suggest you get out of here and let us do our jobs."

That's what I should have done, but I didn't.

Out of the corner of my eye, I saw a red Monte Carlo drive through the gate. It parked beyond the tapes and Ann jumped out and ran to us, ducking under the tapes. I quickly turned away so she couldn't see my tears. I wiped my eyes; not that it could have done much good, they must have been as red as... Well, you get the idea.

"DG? Is it true?" she shouted, as she stopped short, a good two car lengths away from where we were standing. It was like she didn't want to get any nearer to the crime scene for fear that might make it all the more real. That maybe, if she stood far enough away, Miller would somehow be all right. I knew exactly how she felt, but all I could do was nod my head.

"I heard it over the radio," she said. "I can't believe it." She began to pace back and forth, constantly wiping her eyes as she watched the paramedics slowly packing up their gear.

Doc squeezed my shoulder as he left me and went to Miller. I followed him, wanting to get another look at the friend who'd driven me home just a short while ago, this time as a professional. It wasn't easy. I had to block out the personal stuff and see it for what it was, a crime scene and a victim. It wasn't quite the same as Logan or any of the three other cases. Lennie had been shot only once, but in the left temple. It looked similar to me.

I stood back, away from the car, looked around at my apartment building. It was like I was seeing it for the first time. Lennie's car was right under my window. Why hadn't I heard the shot? Why had no one heard the shot? There were people gathering now beyond the tapes, staring... at me. Most of them were my neighbors and knew what I did for a living. I hated to think what might have been going through their heads that night. Nothing good, of that I was certain.

I turned and looked at the building opposite mine. It was just across the street, maybe thirty yards away. All of the widows had drapes; all the drapes were closed. Nobody could have seen anything unless they were peeping, and why would they be? All I needed was one person, just one person... and then I spotted it: a blue light next to the front door of a ground floor apartment, not quite opposite mine, but two doors up on the other side of the street, about forty yards away.

That's a frickin' doorbell camera. Nah, I couldn't get that lucky, could I?

"Ann, I think that's a doorbell camera over there," I said, pointing. "I know the owner."

"Let's go," she said without looking at Miller's car.

Together, we hurried across the street and... it was, it was a doorbell cam. *Yes!*

I rang the bell and we waited.

21

It took Mr. Himel, my neighbor across the road, about ten minutes to contact his security company and download the footage to his laptop.

"Detective, I am so sorry for your loss," he said as we waited for the huge file to download, more than three hours of it, all the way back to ten minutes before Miller dropped me off at just before seven o'clock that evening. Finally, it was done. With a couple taps on the keyboard and a few clicks of his mouse, he cued up the small window of time when I knew for a fact that Miller was still alive.

I had to choke down my feelings as I watched the video. Ann, I think, was also having trouble, but I didn't look at her to find out.

The quality of the image wasn't bad, but it wasn't great either, and we were dealing with a distance of more than forty yards, but it was enough, just.

We watched as I got out of Miller's car and went to my front door. Sure enough, like a good Boy Scout, he waited until I was in the building before pulling away... except that he didn't pull away. Instead, he backed out of the parking space and pulled around to the east side of the building, then stopped in a parking spot under my window.

"That must have been when he called the Chief," I muttered.

"Can I ask what you guys were doing?" Ann asked.

As we watched, I gave her the short version of what had happened when I arrived back at the PD. How Miller had insisted on taking me home. Again feelings of guilt almost overwhelmed me.

"Wait until I get my hands on the freakin' bitch," Ann whispered as the footage continued to roll.

As I watched, I continually checked the time stamp at the bottom of the screen. At seven-oh-eight, I leaned closer to the computer screen and squinted. A minute later, at seven-oh-nine a shadow, someone running, slipped around the back of the car to the driver's side door. For a moment we saw nothing. It was her, though; there was just enough light from the window next to mine for me to tell. She was leaning forward, bent low. I figured she must have been talking to him. And then there was a tiny flash of bright light.

Shit! That's a muzzle flash, but she's using a suppressor. No wonder no one heard the shot.

And then nothing, at least for a moment, and then the shadow was off and running, fast. It hopped over the fence and ran across the empty scrub between the complex and the mini-mall on Brainerd Road.

"Freakin' hell." Ann slapped the table. "Are you freakin' serious?"

"It was her, Ann," I said quietly. "Nate, Natalie Cassidy didn't figure on us catching her on a doorbell cam." I felt the bile rise again in the back of my throat; this time I was in trouble.

As calmly as possible, I asked Himel if I could use his bathroom. As soon as I closed and locked the door, I turned on the faucet, lifted the toilet lid, dropped to my knees and heaved. There was nothing much in my stomach but my body still insisted on trying to expel my guts. After what seemed like an hour, but was probably less than a couple of minutes, and with my stomach in a knot, I was finally able to stand upright again.

I washed my hands and face and tried to pull myself together, but the problem was that no matter how hard I tried, I couldn't get past the idea that what had happened to Miller was my fault. If only... yeah, well, you know what they say about if only, right?

There was a knock on the door.

"Hey, DG? You all right in there?" Ann asked.

"Yeah," I lied. "I'll be right out."

22

It was midnight before Ann left on that terrible evening of Friday the 13th. Doc was long gone and he'd taken poor Lennie with him—that was one autopsy I would not be attending. The crime scene unit was still there when I went to bed after Ann left, and they were still there the following morning.

I didn't get much sleep that night, what was left of it. I tossed and turned, watched the clock, then sometime around two o'clock I fell into a sort of half-life: half asleep and half awake. And I dreamed, oh how I dreamed. I must have watched, close-up, a dozen times as the woman shot Lennie in the head.

I woke early the next morning just before six-thirty... Hah, I never was really asleep. I called and scheduled an Uber for seven forty-five. Then I showered, dressed, drank four cups of coffee in the space of less than an hour, and then, trying to push aside the headache that lay waiting in the dark backroads of my brain, I gathered up my gear and went outside to wait for the Uber. I arrived at the police department a few minutes before eight o'clock.

The mood in the situation room was somber... No, it was downright dismal. The place was packed with uniforms and detectives.

Word had spread throughout the department about the demise of Detective Lennie Miller. Conversations were being conducted in hushed voices. Heads were held a little lower over the desks. Phone calls were being answered a little slower. And I was conscious of the sidelong glances I was getting from just about every officer present. It was a nightmarish situation, and I'd never experienced anything like it before. Sure, officers had died in the line of duty before, but somehow this one was different; Lennie had a lot of friends.

The only people who didn't feel the melancholy were the criminals who were being brought in. They got yelled at just a little louder than usual, treated a little rougher by officers who already had short tempers, and there wasn't a damn thing that anyone could do about it. It was a bad day; one of the worst I'd ever experienced, and it wasn't about to improve.

So, when I walked into the situation room that morning, all eyes were upon me; not a good feeling, and I wondered what everyone was thinking. Was I being blamed for Lennie's death? It wouldn't have surprised me. But then came the outpouring of sympathy and good wishes, for which I was grateful, but didn't make me feel any better.

Lennie's desk had already been cleaned off. His laptop was gone, his chair was pushed tidily under his desk, and I... felt like shit. Hawk and Ann had not yet arrived, and Janet was still in the hospital. For several moments I stood there alone, then I pulled Lennie's chair out from under his desk and sat down on it, stretched out my legs, laid a hand on the desktop, closed my eyes, and drummed slowly on it with the tips of my fingers. I remember nothing of the next ten minutes or so.

And it must have been at least ten minutes later when I felt a presence behind me. I turned my head and looked up. I didn't need to. I knew who it was, and I also knew I wasn't even supposed to be there. I should have been either in bed or at the hospital getting my head examined. Doctor Joon had never uttered truer words.

"My office, now," Chief Johnston said.

I rose to my feet. Ann, who had just arrived, grabbed me and hugged me, and then whispered in my ear that it would be okay and gently patted me on the back, and walked on over to her desk.

I heard Hawk speaking to someone too. Who it was or what they were talking about, I don't remember, but I do remember that I didn't care.

"Chief," I said as I followed him into his office. "I know I'm not supposed to be here, but I—"

"Shut up and sit down, Kate," he said and walked slowly around behind his desk and sat down.

I did as I was told. I said not a word—nor did he—as I watched him open the bottom desk drawer, reach inside, and take out a bottle of Jack Daniels and two double shot glasses. He unscrewed the cap, poured one and placed it at the edge of his desk in front of me, then poured the other and set the bottle down.

"To Lennie," he said and raised his shot glass.

"To Lenn..." My voice trailed off. I grabbed the glass and tossed the double measure back in one hit. I almost choked as the fiery liquid burned its way down the back of my throat. I closed my eyes and waited, and slowly my head began to clear.

"Kate," Johnston said, replacing the bottle in the drawer, "this is the kind of situation where nothing I can say, or anyone else can say, will bring you any comfort. But the one thing you have to know and understand is—and I'll never stop telling each and every one of you—this is not your fault."

I felt the tears begin to well up, and I bit the inside of my mouth, trying to fight them off. Somehow I managed it, but I knew that he knew.

"It's the bad guy's fault," he continued. "This sack of excrement is who's to blame for what he did to Lennie. And we'll find him, Kate," he hissed. "You'll find him."

"Her," I said quietly.

"What?"

"It's not a male. It's a woman. We have her on surveillance footage from a doorbell camera. It's not really clear enough to recognize her, but I know it's her. It was the same woman who put me down yesterday, too. And she's our serial killer. She's transgender. Goes by the name Nate Cassidy. Her real name's Natalie. That's what I wanted to tell you last night before you sent me home."

"You're sure about all this?" the Chief asked.

"Yea," I said, staring down into the now empty glass. "I'm sure. I talked to some of her... acquaintances; I don't think she has any friends. None that I know of, anyway." I was waffling, trying to put my thoughts in order, but I couldn't. I figured it must have been the Jack Daniels.

"Anyway," I continued, "that's what came up. I don't have all the details yet, but I'll get it done. You can count on that. Her friends claimed that she was seeing a doctor for her *reassignment* procedure." I spat the word out like I'd spat out the bile at the Himel residence the previous night. *Freakin' bitch. I'll reassign you, to the freakin' grave.*

"Kate," Johnston said. "I know this is not going to go down well, but I need you to take a step back."

"What? Why? Oh no. Not now. Not after Lennie... You can't do this to me."

"I can, and I must, and especially now after what happened to Detective Miller. You can either do as I ask, or I'll suspend you. Either way, you'll leave your badge and gun here with me."

"Oh come on, Chief. Please don't do this... You can't do this to me. Every one of my team is suffering. We have to catch this monster. We have to find her, and fast. She's dangerous. If she was at my apartment building, she must have been looking for... me."

I knew I'd been babbling, but that thought struck me dumb. I stared at the Chief then grabbed my glass and said, "I need another."

He obliged. I tossed it back like it was nothing and yes, I know, it wasn't even nine o'clock yet.

"That's it, isn't it?" I asked. "She was waiting for me. She didn't expect Miller to give me a ride home and wait while I went inside. And she killed him, Chief. She knew I was onto her, and she decided to stop me." I wasn't sure if it was the Jack Daniels or the weight of the situation, but I was suddenly overwhelmed by a serious case of the jitters.

"All of that makes sense," he said. "But how? How did she know you were all working the Logan case? It can't be just dumb luck."

"From the incident at The Sovereign, probably. I questioned several people there. She's a regular, right? Other than that... I don't know, Chief. I can't think of anything else."

"Kate, you're babbling; you're not thinking clearly, and that's because of the crack on the head." He paused, stared at me.

I knew what was coming and shook my head so violently it hurt.

"I'm sending you to the doctor," he said, "and then you're going home to rest. That's it. No arguments."

"Chief, please."

"I said no arguments, and I'm sending the rest of your team home as well. Working in the state you all are in now is... well, it isn't going to change a thing. But a good night's rest and some food in your stomach will help. We now know who she is, so don't worry. There's nothing more you or your team can do. I'll have them put out an APB on this Nate... Natalie Cassidy person. We'll get him... her."

He leaned forward, folded his hands in front of him, and said, "You need help, and your team needs rest."

He picked up his desk phone, punched a button, and said, "Cathy, come in here please, and bring your notebook."

She came in almost immediately, notebook in hand.

Johnston looked at me and said, "I want the name of that neuro-surgeon you talked to yesterday."

I sighed and told him.

"Cathy. Call the doctor. Use my name. I want her to see Captain Gazzara this morning, as soon as possible. Let me know."

Cathy nodded and left.

He punched in another number. "Charles, have a car brought round to the front, and then come and get Gazzara and take her to the hospital, and stay with her until she's seen the doctor. Don't let her out of your sight until the doctor's finished her examination, and then take her home. Make sure she gets safely inside, okay?"

He listened to whatever Charles replied, nodded, and hung up.

"Okay," I said, resigned to my fate. "You win."

He pointed to his desktop, and said, "Gun, badge."

Reluctantly, I handed them over.

"Now, get the hell out of here and don't come back without a release from the doctor."

I shook my head at him, rose to my feet, staggered a little, then turned and left his office, and boy was I ever pissed.

I did manage to pull myself together for my interview with Dr. Napai. I insisted I was fine, lied through my teeth in answer to her questions, complained that the Chief was just being an ass, and tried to get her to declare me fit for work. It was one of the best acts I'd ever put on, and she fell for it, sort of. She didn't do as I asked, though. Instead, she went along with the Chief's request and told me to go home and rest and made an appointment to see me again the following Friday. But said nothing about me going back to work.

In hindsight, it was in fact one of my worst acts of rebellion. Had I done as I was told; had I let her examine me properly, the course of events over the next several days might well have taken a different direction.

23

The next time we were gathered together in my office, two days later, after two days rest I neither wanted or needed, or so I thought, the whiteboard was no longer white. We had the photos of the other three suspected victims up there along with their autopsy photos, and those of Jack Logan. Unfortunately, they also included Miller's photos, and those of his killer. And she, Cassidy, was still at large. The Chief's APB hadn't produced a single sighting.

Me? I was relatively clear-headed and headache free, though I still wasn't over Miller's death, nor would I ever be. I just had to make sure I stayed out of the Chief's way. I didn't dare go ask for the return of my gun and badge for fear he'd send me home again.

It was Ann who had taken over from Miller, and she collated and printed out the information on our subject and then handed it out.

"Natalie Cassidy, or Nate Cassidy, as he likes to be called, is who we are looking for," Ann said. "She's twenty-nine years old, brunette turned blond, five-seven, size nine shoes, or boots. She has no criminal record, but she was briefly in the Marine Corps, one of the few women fit and strong enough to make it through the selection process. She served about fourteen weeks before she received an ELS—Entry Level Separation."

"So, she's a Marine," I said. "Was a Marine, though I'm told there's no such thing. Ooh frickin' rah."

"ELS?" Hawk asked. "Do we know what happened?"

"If you can read through all the military jargon," Ann replied, "Natalie Cassidy, as she was when she enlisted, intended to use the military to get her... gender reassignment surgery, and it probably would have worked for her had she played by the rules. The problem was, it was all she was focused on. She couldn't, or wouldn't, keep up with the Marine Corps basic training. Oh she had what it takes physically, but not mentally. She didn't have the fortitude to carry it through. Her Sergeant's report indicates that they tried to help her, but her attitude made it impossible for her to continue. Let's face it, for a woman, joining the military is hard enough; joining the Corps is—"

"Ooh-rah," Hawk muttered, interrupting her.

"Even harder," Ann continued, glaring at him. "So, since she didn't get into any real trouble, and was just more of a thorn in their side, they gave her an out."

"Does she have any family?" I asked, thinking there might be somewhere she would run to if she found herself backed into a corner.

"She does, though her mother died when she was a teenager back in oh-four. Her father is still alive and living in Norton, Texas, and has been for the past four years. According to military records and a psych evaluation, they didn't get along. But no report of abuse of any kind."

"Has anybody talked to him?" I asked.

"Yes, I did," Hawk said. "He claims he hasn't spoken to his daughter in more than two years." He shrugged. "But who knows? He sounded like a dumbass. We should probably follow up."

I nodded. It was something to think about.

"Anything else?" I asked.

"Oh, I haven't even gotten started," Ann said. "Janet's been making calls from home."

Geez, why am I not surprised?

"She called me. Apparently, Natalie's been seeing a specialist and a shrink. She's still trying to make the transition from female to male. Janet talked to her shrink, a Dr. Reginald Morgan—apparently, he's British—but he wouldn't discuss Cassidy; claimed doctor-patient confidentiality. The specialist, though, a Dr. Audrey Harmon, admitted that she'd met with Cassidy on three occasions and agreed to be interviewed. I made an appointment to see her at two this afternoon. You want to come with me?"

"Excellent, but d'you think you can handle it by yourself? Janet won't be back for at least a couple more days and—"

"You think?" Janet said as she barged into the office. "Count me in."

"Wow. Doctor Joon released you early?" I said.

"Yeah," she said, avoiding my eyes. "I told her what had happened and that I needed to get back to work. She wasn't happy about it, but she released me... Okay, she did release me, really, but for light duties only. That's not going to cut it, DG. I need to be in on this. I need to..." She paused, her lower lip trembled, than she sat down, opened her iPad and mumbled, "I need to work. Don't try to stop me."

"Welcome back, Janet," Hawk said. "Robar is just getting started."

"Ann has an appointment with Doctor Harmon this afternoon," I said to Janet. "You can go with her."

Ann folded her arms across her chest and rocked back and forth on her heels. "We also have a place of employment and an apartment," she continued. "I had officers check out both places, but she hasn't been seen at either one in more than a week."

"Why am I not surprised?" I said. "Where does she live and where does she work? Who's her boss?"

"She lives in an apartment off 23rd. She works at Happy Henry's Family Fun Center," Ann said, shaking her head. "Her boss is Happy Henry Pierce."

"Now why didn't we think to look there first?" Hawk said and slapped his thigh.

"Hawk, you can go interview Pierce, now," I said. "We can't go slow on this. We have to find her—before she kills again."

Hawk nodded, stood up, and adjusted his badge and gun.

"Any news on the DNA found in the car?" I asked.

"No. They're still working on it," he said, shaking his head.

"Okay," I said to him, "call me when you're done with Happy Henry. We'll need a warrant to search the apartment... Oh shit. That means I have to talk to the Chief. Never mind, I'll just have to bluff my way through it. I need to get my weapon and badge from him anyway." I took a deep breath, then continued, "Remember, emotions are high, and so they should be, but we can't afford to screw up. We have to do it by the book."

I paused, looked at Hawk, then at Janet, then at Ann, and continued, "I don't care what kind of issues this person has, she has to go down. We need a solid case so we can lock her up for good. But here's the thing..." I hesitated for a moment, because I knew what I was about to say, if it was leaked to the press, could cause problems; Internal Affairs would be all over it.

"This is a high-profile case. We have a serial killer, a woman with this special 'condition,'" I said, making air quotes with my fingers. "You can assume that she will land herself a lawyer who's looking to make a reputation. There will be no hole too tight, black, or dirty that he won't crawl through to say that we violated her rights. So we do it right, by the book, okay? Let's deliver Christmas to the Chief early this year."

They all nodded, collected their things and went to work. Cathy wasn't in her office, so I knocked on Chief Johnston's door and waited.

"Come in."

"Hey, Chief," I said. "It's me."

"Yes," he replied without looking up from the paperwork he was reading. "I heard you were back. I've been expecting you. How are you feeling?"

"I'm good." I swallowed noisily and continued, "I need a search warrant, Chief. Robar found a residence for Natalie Cassidy." I put the paperwork on his desk and stood back.

He looked up at me and said, "Kate, did you see the doctor as I asked?"

"I did. She checked me out and I went home and went to bed, just as you ordered. Now I'm fine, well-rested and back at it. Now—"

"The doctor's release please, Catherine," he said, holding out his hand.

"I... don't have it with me."

"Go get it."

"Chief, I need that warrant."

"I'll get you your warrant when you get me your doctor's release. Either that or I'll take you off this case until you do. Take your pick."

There were a million things I wanted to say. This was practically blackmail. I was being strong-armed by my own chief to do something that I didn't think needed to be done. I was furious, but I had to choke it down.

All I could say was, "Yes, sir." And I stood and walked out of the room. I was tempted to slam the door, but I didn't.

My car had been left at the station when the uniformed officer drove me home. So when I climbed in, windows rolled up, I screamed. I banged the steering wheel. I swore like only a trucker knows how. And then I called Dr. Joon.

Of course, I didn't get her. I got her nurse practitioner.

"I need to see her, now," I said belligerently: big mistake. "I'm a police officer. I need a release to go back to work."

"Your follow-up appointment's not until Friday," she said, even more belligerently than me.

"I know that," I snarled, "but I'm conducting a murder investigation. I need to go back to work, now!"

"I'm sorry, Captain. Doctor Napai has a full schedule. You'll have to wait for your appointment."

"Oh, come on... special circumstances, please... Can't you give me a release?"

"I'm sorry. I can't. And, as I said, the doctor has a full schedule. You'll have to wait until she sees you on Friday."

And she hung up, and I lost it. I banged my hands on the steering wheel and I screamed, and I screamed, and then I gave up and leaned back against the headrest and closed my eyes. I thought about what the hell I could possibly do to get myself out of the mess I'd gotten myself into. And then I did what anyone in my position would do. I called the one person who I knew could help.

"Doc, I need a favor."

Doc Sheddon and I have always had a special relationship—no, nothing like that. We were just... He was more than just the medical examiner who I worked with regularly; he was my friend. And at times like this... Well, I hate to say it, but he was also my accomplice.

"A doctor's note? Are you kidding? I can't do that. And, you are missing the crucial element that would allow me to see you professionally. You're still alive. Come on, Kate, you know I can't give you one. Johnston would take one look at it and toss it in the trash, and you along with it, and then he'd come after me."

"I know, but I'm desperate and... Don't you know someone, a doctor, who owes you a favor, and might be willing to bend the rules a little?"

"That won't work either," he said. "No one can release you, but your own doctor."

"Please, Doc. Do something. I'm begging you."

There was a moment of silence, then he said, "Where are you?"

"I'm in my damn car at the police department."

"Wait there while I make a call. Give me five minutes."

I smiled and nodded—stupid, right?—and he hung up without saying good-bye, as usual. But, true to his word, less than five minutes later he called back.

"Get yourself over to Erlanger. Doctor Napai will see you."

"Oh God! Thank you. You're a dream boat. I owe you one."

"Take it easy. Don't speed." That was all he said before hanging up.

Me? I said a quick prayer to St. Christopher, the patron saint of travelers, that if he could, would he please give me as many green lights as possible. He must have felt bad for me because I don't think I hit a single red light or even a yellow the whole way to the hospital. I made it in less than ten minutes.

Dr. Napai wasn't in the best of moods, in fact she wasn't happy at all.

"I take it you have a special friend," she said as she came into the examination room and sat down in front of me.

"You mean Doctor Sheddon? Yes, he's my friend."

"You understand that I am making an exception for you, yes?"

"I do and thank you so much. I really need to get back to work, Doctor. I'm conducting a murder investigation."

"Yes, I know. Doctor Sheddon explained the situation. I'm going against my better judgment here, Detective. But under the circumstances..." she said, slowly shining her flashlight into my eyes, one at a time. "Hmm! Hmm!" She paused again, stood back and glared at me.

"I will allow you to return to work, but I must insist that you keep your Friday appointment."

"Yes, Doctor," I replied, feeling like a naughty child.

I left the hospital with my note in my pocket and when I got to my car, I called Chief Johnston. Somehow, though, I didn't feel like I'd accomplished a whole lot. I had the uneasy feeling that I was balancing on the edge of a cliff and that at any minute someone would step up and push me over the edge.

I was starting to get another headache. Then I realized I hadn't had but one cup of coffee. That's it, I thought. Coffee. I need a booster.

"I've got your judge," Johnston said when he finally answered. "Meet me out front of the Federal Courthouse, and you'd better have a doctor's note."

It took me a little longer to get to the courthouse, and when I arrived, I couldn't find a spot and ended up parking in Harry Starke's secure lot. I didn't have time to ask permission, but I figured that after our long history together, he wouldn't mind. From there I walked the two blocks to the courthouse where the Chief was waiting for me.

The first thing he did was stick out his hand for the note. I gave it to him. He glanced at it and handed it back to me along with my gun and badge.

"Have you read it?" he asked.

"N-o... Should I have?"

"Light duties."

"Light duties?" I asked, completely confused. "What the hell does that mean?"

He smiled, something he rarely ever did, and said, "In your case, I shouldn't wonder, not a damn thing."

24

J udge Amiel Seagal was almost a midget, or should I say a little person, or just plain old short. Yeah, I know; none of them are politically correct, but what the hell, I never was that anyway. However you might describe it, though, regardless of his stature, he had a tough reputation and was a stickler for doing what's right.

I hate lawyers. They are a distraction and a disruption for just about everything I have to do, and it pains me. The only thing worse than lawyers are politicians. What was it Shakespeare said? First, kill all the lawyers, or something like that? Maybe he did, maybe he didn't. Whatever; I certainly understood the sentiment.

"Hello, my friend," Judge Seagal said to Johnston. "Take a seat, if you would." Then to me he said, "Captain. I hate that we should have to meet under such sad circumstances. My condolences to you and your team. Let me see the warrant, Wesley." He held out his hand.

"Thank you, Judge," the Chief said and handed it to him.

Seagal briefly scanned it, nodded, then signed it and handed it back. Johnston handed it on to me.

"Detective Gazzara, where'd you get that lump on your head?" the Judge asked.

Instinctively, I raised my hand to touch my head, but quickly stopped and said, "From the person named on this warrant."

He nodded, sympathetically, and said, "It's a sad truth that sometimes the bad guys win, Detective. We've all seen it. Me more than most, I think. Make sure you lock it down tight."

"Yes, sir, and thank you."

"Good luck to you, Captain."

"You can leave now, Captain," Johnston said. "I need to talk to the judge."

Oh, those heavenly words. I was so pleased that I didn't have to ride the elevator down to the lobby in close proximity to one of the most intimidating men I'd ever known. I'm talking about the Chief, of course.

I hurried out of the courthouse, down the steps, turned right and then almost ran back to my car at Harry's offices on Georgia. I didn't go inside, though I dearly would have liked to have said hello to Jacque and the guys and, yes, even Harry, but I really wasn't in the mood.

And then that decision suddenly was taken out of my hands. No sooner had my backside hit the driver's seat than Hawk called.

"I'm at Happy Henry's. Can you meet me?" he asked.

I had the engine running and my foot on the gas before I even got the words "give me ten minutes" out of my mouth.

Happy Henry's is a legend in the Tri-State area... well, in its day it was. It's called a family fun center, but I think it would be better described as a "have to see it to believe it" kind of place. I'll admit, I've been there only once in the last five years, and it was exactly the same then as it had been the first time I went with my mother when I was ten years old.

The trippy '60s-style decor could have used a coat of paint, the three mini-golf courses were in serious need of renovation, and even on a captive course such as these, you could expect to lose at least three balls per game. As for the go-carts, you can get into a worse accident colliding with someone walking than driving one of them at top speed. And the baseball batting cages... the ball machines were a relic from the past, from the Jimmy Carter era, and even when they worked, all they could produce was a slow, soft pitch.

But that's not all: the place is poorly run. Employee turnover is high. Teenagers work for half a summer before the regular employees creep them out enough for them to leave. Background checks are rarely done. Most of the staff are paid under the table in cash. Poorly maintained as the place is, though, it still manages to turn a small profit. It's one of those places everyone has to experience at least once. And it is also well-known as a spot where people getting out of rehab or jail can get work.

I parked my car and walked to the turnstile where Hawk was waiting for me. Thankfully, the place wasn't too busy.

"What have you got?" I asked.

"I talked to Pierce. He's a clown. He's never heard of Natalie, or Nate, Cassidy. He told me he leaves the everyday running of the park to his manager, a Mary Sanek. She's been here for years. I think she's the only one who has, other than Henry himself.

"I've already spoken to her," he continued, "but I couldn't get her to open up. I have a feeling they have some unsavory characters, maybe even felons or registered sex offenders working around the kids, and I spotted at least a dozen violations of the health and safety codes. I can't believe the place is allowed to stay open.

"Anyway," he continued, "I told her I wasn't interested in any of that. I just wanted some information on someone who once worked, or still works here, but she wouldn't go for it. Maybe you can get through to her. Come on, it's this way."

And Hawk led the way to a trailer-cum-office at the western edge of the park.

"It was when I mentioned Cassidy's name that she clammed up," Hawk said as we walked toward the office. "She wouldn't say another damn word, so I called you. I thought maybe another woman might—"

"Yeah, yeah, I know," I said. "Did you tell her what it was about?" Maybe it was my state of mind, the stress, or the fact that I was still grieving for Miller, I don't know, but I was angry. There's nothing more frustrating than to have someone you think might have some good information shut down and refuse to talk.

"Let's do it," I said as I pulled my hair back from my face and winced as I touched the knot under my hairline.

The trailer was probably the most modern piece of equipment in the entire park. More steel box on wheels than habitat, it was painted a sickening pee-stain yellow color and had an air conditioner sticking out of one of the only two windows on the structure. The original aluminum door had been replaced with a clunky wooden one that was about two inches too short, leaving a significant gap at the bottom. The security was a hasp and padlock. The steps were also made of wood and had seen better days; they creaked under Hawk's weight.

"Did you go inside?" I asked Hawk as he raised his hand to knock.

"No. She wouldn't invite me in. We talked out here. When she decided she didn't want to talk any more, she went inside and slammed the door."

He knocked loudly on the door and waited. He knocked again, and eventually we heard a scratchy voice from inside tell us to come in.

The inside of the trailer was even more depressing than the outside. A permanent haze of cigarette smoke clung to the ceiling, fed by a spiral of smoke that rose slowly upward from a huge ashtray full of half-smoked butts at the center of the steel desk.

Mary Sanek was seated behind the desk. She wore a dirty, crimson sweater, and her brunette hair was cut short but stood out in spikes at odd angles and looked to be in serious need of a shampoo. Her body had that classic pear shape of someone who spent most of her life seated. Her shoulders were narrow, her neck long, and her chin slanted back from her bottom lip to her neck. She reminded me of a Dr. Seuss character.

There were stacks of paper everywhere: on each side of her, piled up on a card table to her left, and on top of a row of filing cabinets to her right. The threadbare carpet, judging by the bits of crap I could see in the pale, green light of a single fluorescent tube over her head, probably hadn't seen a vacuum cleaner in under a decade. The place smelled of mold, wet dog, and stale cigarettes.

"Miss Sanek." I stepped further inside the trailer—much further than I felt comfortable with—and held up my badge. "My name is Captain Gazzara. You already know Sergeant Hawkins, I believe."

"Hello, Detective," she said, sighed, and lit another cigarette. The one she'd just stubbed out still smoldering in the ashtray.

"I'd like to talk to you about Natalie Cassidy," I said. "D'you know where she is?"

"No, I don't. Haven't seen her since Friday. Sit yourselves down," she said, waving at the three steel folding chairs in front of her desk.

I took my recorder from my pocket and asked her permission to record the interview. She rolled her eyes, coughed violently, then spluttered, "Yeah, whatever."

I spoke the usual ritual into the machine for the record, then asked her to confirm that her name was Mary Sanek.

"Oh geez," she said. "Seriously? Yeah, that's me. Look, I told Detective Hawkins here everything I know."

"That's not true," Hawk said. "You said nothing about her."

"There's nothing to tell," she replied.

"Yeah, well, I don't really buy that," I said. "Why don't you start from the beginning. When did Natalie Cassidy start working here? Or was she calling herself Nate?"

She took a long drag off her cigarette and began to speak. Each word was accompanied by a small puff of smoke.

"*Natalie* started working here about five months ago. Well, that was this time. She'd worked here before. Last year, I think. And the year before that, maybe nine months prior." She shrugged, then continued, "We employ a lot of people. They come and go. They stay a few weeks, make a little money, go spend it, then come back again. We're one of the few places in this town that don't judge people. Henry likes to give everybody that needs it a second chance." She squinted at me as she sucked hard on the cigarette.

"What does she do here? What's her job?" I asked.

She shrugged, then said, "She does like all the others. Everybody pitches in where they can. Sometimes she'd collect the tickets in the arcade. Sometimes she'd work the mini-golf, sometimes the pettin' zoo, clean up the shit, and such. It ain't rocket science."

"How does she get along with everyone? Does she have any friends?" Hawk asked.

Mary's facial expression changed from easygoing to wary. She looked to the left, pinched her lips together, and then coughed so hard I thought she'd lose her lungs.

"Look, I don't care what people do in their personal lives—" she began.

"You're not running for office, Ms. Sanek," I said angrily. "This is a murder investigation. Political correctness is not a necessity, so please answer the question."

She glared at me, as if to say *fine, you asked for it.*

"Natalie's... different," she began. "When she first came to work, as Nate Cassidy, everyone thought that she was a dude. She was always in baggy camouflage pants and clunky boots and that hat with the panels down the sides and back. She has a deep voice, and she's strong as a frickin' ox, and she strutted around and joked with the guys about the women they'd see out there in the park. All guys do that sort of thing, don't they?" she asked, looking at Hawk.

"She sure looked and acted like a guy," she continued, "and there didn't seem to be any problems until she made her big announcement, back in 2017, I think it was."

"Which was?" I asked, already suspecting the answer.

"That her name was really Natalie, and that she was a girl, but not for much longer. No one could believe it, at first, then everyone started to say, 'yeah, now that you mention it... I should have noticed this or that,' you know."

She took another drag on her cigarette and stubbed it out.

"And you," I said, "what did you think? Were you surprised?"

"Not really, not once she come out. I was like the others: once I knew... well yeah, it made sense. Her size, for one thing. If she weighs a hundred and twenty pounds soaking wet she weighs an ounce. And she never took her shirt off like the other guys did, or wore T-shirts or those singlet undershirts, not even when it was hot outside. Always a long-sleeved flannel shirt or something similar. Then it was obvious, wasn't it? She didn't want no one to know she was taping down her breasts."

"Was she accepted after she came out?" I asked.

"Yeah, mostly, at first. Most folks around here have baggage of one sort or another. It was sort of like... Okay, so now we know you're really a girl, but that's okay. But then it became a grind, you know?"

I shook my head.

"It got to be too much, like. Everything was about her, getting her surgery and about being a guy. She bragged about the weights she could lift and how the medications her doctor had given her were working and how horny she was. She kept going on and on about how she couldn't wait until stage four or whatever to get her new parts attached."

She took another cigarette from the pack on her desk and continued, "She bragged about her time in the Marines, and that she broke her arm in basic trying to beat some record and got discharged. But I think she was full of it."

"Why do you say that?"

"My second ex-husband was a Marine. He told me if you so much as rolled your eyes at a drill instructor you'd find yourself in a world of shit. But Nate, well she insisted that she yelled at her DI on more than one occasion and had even threatened him too. But that he didn't do anything about it. Jim, my ex, said that was a load of shit; she'd never get away with it. She was constantly trying to prove how tough she was. She claimed it was because of her DI that she broke her arm, that it was his record she was going to break and he made sure she didn't."

She paused, coughed, and licked her lips. I swear her tongue was the color of a corpse. "She's full of shit," she said, shaking her head. "I don't believe a word of it."

"Did any of your employees?" I asked.

"Hell no. It got to the point where some of them would ask her silly shit just to get her talking and see how much crap would come out of her mouth. She drank like a fish. And when she drank, she really changed. Screw the surgery. She was a regular Jekyll and Hyde."

"Did she ever turn violent?" I asked.

"Not that I saw on the premises. But I was told by some of the high school kids who worked over the summer that she tried to pick fights with some of them."

"You've got high school kids working with ex-cons?" Hawk asked.

"Are you kidding?" she asked. "Half the kids who work here have rap sheets some of the ex-cons would be proud of. You should know that detective." She sucked on her cigarette and blew out a cloud of smoke Mount Kīlauea would have been proud of.

The atmosphere inside the trailer was becoming thicker, unbearably so. I figured I was going to have to take a bath in tomato juice to get the smell out of my hair and off my skin.

"What about relationships?" I asked. "Did she have a boyfriend... girlfriend?"

"Nah. Not that I know of. She's a loner," she said. "But she liked to impress the kids. Spent most of her time with them. When they went back to school and she was left with the grown-ups, she took another turn." She tapped the cigarette with her forefinger, letting the ashes fall to the floor.

"What do you mean?" I asked.

"She was always braggin' but when the kids were gone, she started telling stories about how she's hurt some people, that she'd hurt a couple of guys and stole their wallets. She said she went into a bar and put some guy's head through a jukebox and *strolled* out of there. I'll never forget that because she said she was talking with a woman at the bar and that the woman's boyfriend had come in and gotten pissed. So, she took him down and then just *strolled* out of the place. Just *strolled*. That's what she said. No one called the cops. No one tried to stop her. That she was so badass that she could just bust up a place and walk right on out and no one could do anything about it.

"More than one of the guys told her it was all bullshit, because she wouldn't name the bar. That was when she said she killed a guy in Huntsville."

"She said that?" I asked.

"Yeah, but no one believed her. She's crazy, full of shit, a narcissist, and a regular pain in the ass. She doesn't need a dick attached; she already is one. Look, I don't care what you do. Do what you want. Pierce your damn tits, if you want, but don't come around here stirrin' up shit, okay?"

Just then Hawk's cell phone rang. "It's Robar, DG," he said. "She's done with the shrink."

"Tell her to meet us at Cassidy's apartment. Make sure she has the location," I said. I was ready to get out of the smoky hellhole.

Hawk nodded. "I'll be outside," he said and went out of the door, leaving it wide open.

I felt the cold air rush in like an arctic blast. Unfortunately, it did little to alleviate the blanket of smoke.

I stood up, picked up my recorder, and said, "Is there anything more you can tell me that you think might help?" I asked.

"Yeah! I can tell you you're dealing with one messed-up crazy.

She thinks she's a man, for God's sake. The sad thing is, she'd be kind of pretty as a girl. I don't get it."

"Did you ever feel threatened by her?" I asked.

"Nah." She shook her head. "I don't think she has what it takes to take me on. Some of the younger people, maybe, but me? No!"

I thanked her for her time, left a business card, turned off my recorder, and asked her to call me if Cassidy turned up. Then I walked outside and took a deep breath. It was heavenly.

"Glad to be out of there, I bet," Hawk said.

"Yeah," I said feeling my head swim.

"Also, DG, while I was waiting for you, the lab called back about that Band-Aid they found in Logan's car. They've got a profile."

"Great. Now if we could get a match... Maybe we'll find something in her apartment."

25

Natalie Cassidy lived in a large, multi-story apartment complex on the south side of town in an area it was wise to avoid, especially after dark. Hawk and I waited outside on the street until the rest of the team arrived. The team consisted of me, Hawk, Ann Robar, Mike Willis, two techs from forensics, and three uniformed cops.

We gathered at the street door, and I gave everyone a few final instructions, mainly that I was looking for physical evidence that would tie the woman to one or more of the crime scenes. This would include trophies, trace evidence—hair, fiber, fingerprints, blood, and, in particular, a pair of boots that matched the cast Hawk had retrieved from the Logan crime scene. We also needed to gather a DNA sample in order to try for a match with the blood on the Band-Aid. I knew Cassidy was my killer, but knowing's not enough to convict her; I had to prove it.

The lock on the street door—steel, painted olive green—was broken. Hawk turned the latch and we pushed on through into the lobby, an open area maybe twenty feet square with two elevators facing the door and a flight of stairs to the right of the elevators. The north wall was devoted to a bank of mailboxes, seventy-two of them in twelve layers of six; which meant, of course, that the building had twelve floors. Attached to the elevators, one on each door, were signs written in black marker on cardboard, torn from what once might have been an Amazon packing box. They stated that the elevators were "out of order." Wouldn't you know it? Cassidy's apartment was number 1105; it was on the eleventh floor.

"Oh crap," Robar said, eyeing the stairs. "Are you kidding me?"

I was in no mood for hilarity, but I couldn't help but smile at that; I knew exactly how she felt.

"Let's do it," I said, and I headed for the stairs followed by Hawk and then the rest of the team.

I swear it took the best part of ten minutes to mount those eleven flights of stairs—well, that's what it seemed like—and by the time we reached Cassidy's floor, I was all but done for. So was Robar. Hawk? What d'you think? The man is an animal. He wasn't even breathing hard.

We stood outside apartment 1105. I hoped to hell we weren't going to have to break it down; those apartment doors are made of steel for a reason, to keep people out.

No, I was hoping that Natalie was home and that she would cooperate. But that didn't seem likely. If she was willing to kill Miller, she was probably more than willing to kick up a fuss. My one concern was that we knew she was armed...

Don't get me wrong. The idea of thumping the back of her head against the wall was more than a little intoxicating; revenge is sweet, and I needed a little sugar.

So, we stood together at the door to apartment 1105. I had an officer draw his weapon and cover the stairs in case she came upon us unawares. The other two officers stood ready with me, Robar and Hawk.

I drew my Glock, nodded to the others to do the same, then I covered the peephole with my free hand and knocked on the door with the barrel of the gun, and then we waited. No answer.

"I don't think she's home," Robar said.

"I think you're right," I said. "Damn! We're going to have to kick that steel slab in."

"Step aside, Cap. Gimme a little space," Hawk said, taking out his wallet.

I stood back, my gun trained on the door. Hawk extracted a set of picks from his wallet and set to work on the lock. It took him less than thirty seconds to open it.

It was a small studio apartment: a living room, a kitchen, and a bathroom. I switched on the light. Nothing. No electricity. The living room was empty of furniture, just a sleeping bag on the floor and a cooler with a 10-inch, battery-powered TV set on top at the foot of the sleeping bag. In one corner, there was a pile of men's clothing. I poked it gingerly with my foot, half-expecting an exodus of... hell, who knows what? Rats, maybe? I sure as hell hoped not. I hate the little bastards.

And then there were the walls. The one facing the sleeping bag was covered with photographs, all of men. Some of them were obviously models. Some were bodybuilders. Some were sports personalities. Many of them had cutouts of a girl's head taped over the heads of the models or bodybuilders. I assumed it was Natalie's head.

"So, this is what our girl looks like," I said, squinting; I couldn't see too well in the dim light, and I had another headache coming on. *Hey, I think I know that face...* I thought. *Where have I seen her before?* I couldn't remember; I wasn't even sure that I had seen her. *Maybe she just has one of those faces.*

I took several of the photos down and handed them to Hawk. "Go back to the office and have them copied and enlarged," I said, still staring at one of the images of her face. *I do know her... but from where?* "Then get them out to patrol. Maybe someone will spot her, though I have my doubts: she's got to know we're after her by now."

I stared again at the images on the wall. She looked like an older high school senior with a crooked smirk.

"She's over the edge... way over," Robar said, shaking her head, staring at the photographs. "She's fixated, frickin' nuts. She belongs in Moccasin Bend. DG, we have to get this crazy bitch, and fast... But see here, this is the kind of guy she wants to be, right?" she asked, pointing to one of the altered bodybuilder images. "So why would she go after someone like Jack Logan? He didn't look anything like these guys. I doubt he did even when he was younger."

"You understated it when you said she was crazy," I said. "The woman is insane..." I stared at the images. "I don't know what to think," I said as I studied each picture in turn. There were scribbles alongside many of them, unreadable notes with arrows and circles pointing to pecs and thighs and genitals. I shook my head and went into the kitchen.

The kitchen was almost as bare as the living room. It didn't appear that Cassidy was much of a cook. Empty cereal boxes littered the counters. Empty cans that once had contained Beefaroni, Vienna Sausages, and Miller beer were piled high in the overflowing trash can. Milk cartons, fast food containers, and napkins, along with cigarette stubs in makeshift, aluminum foil ashtrays, and a whole collection of other garbage lay scattered around everywhere. It was disgusting.

From the kitchen I went to the bathroom, turned on one of the faucets, and then off again. At least she had water.

"Yikes," Robar said, as she carefully stepped into the tiny bathroom and saw the shattered mirror over the sink. "I guess she didn't like what she saw."

The bathroom was a mess. Aside from the broken mirror glass, there was a stack of mutilated porn magazines. All of the important... maybe I should call them interesting anatomical parts had either been scratched out, scribbled out, or cut out. Bits of paper lay scattered all over the floor in front of and around the commode, along with a utility knife, the blade of which was covered in blood.

"Get forensics in here," I said. "Looks like we have our DNA sample."

"Mike," I said when he entered. "We could get lucky." I pointed to the knife.

He nodded, stepped forward, lifted it carefully, and bagged it.

"And grab her toothbrush, just to be sure," I said, and as I said it, I couldn't help but wonder if maybe Cassidy had used that knife on herself. Had she harmed herself? Did she look at herself in the mirror and not like what she saw, as Ann had suggested?

"Kate? *Kate?*" Ann said, interrupting my thoughts. "Did you hear what I said?"

"I'm sorry. I was just thinking... What did you say?" My head was spinning. I was having trouble concentrating.

Robar pointed to a small leather kit that was on the corner of the toilet tank.

"I asked if you thought that might be her father's shaving kit."

I looked at it, chuckled, and then carefully picked it up. "No. It's not her dad's shaving kit. It's a hormone injection kit, if I'm not mistaken. Forensics can take it, too."

"I think we've seen enough here," I said. "We got most of what we came for. Hawk's gone to get the images copied. Now all we need is a DNA match with the Band-Aid. Maybe we'll get lucky. If so, it would make life a whole lot easier."

"I need to get out of here, DG. I have an appointment with Doctor Harmon at two, remember?"

"Yeah," I said, still thinking, my eyes on one of the photographs. "Don't forget to drop by the department and pick up Janet."

"I hadn't forgotten. What are you going to do now, Cap?"

I looked at my watch and squinted. It was just after one o'clock in the afternoon, and my head was really beginning to bother me. *What the hell's wrong with me?* And then I realized I'd still had only one cup of coffee since I left home that morning, and none since before Happy Henry, or had I? Damned if I could remember. *So no coffee, then?* No wonder I felt like hell; coffee to a cop is like gasoline to a car. I needed a fill-up.

"I'm going to go get something to eat," I replied to Ann, "then back to the office. I'll see you both there when you get done with the doctor. Mike, you'll be a while, right?"

He nodded. I told the uniforms to remain stationed at the door and the stairwell to protect Mike and his team, and I left the building.

26

As I drove back to the office, I stopped by a Five Guys restaurant and grabbed a burger with everything, a sack of French fries, and a quart of black coffee, all to go—yes, I know, the calories, but what the hell. I spend too much time on my feet for them to matter a whole lot. And, with what I was dealing with, I had no doubt my body could handle the extra intake with ease.

And so I drove, and as I drove, I munched and I drank, but most of all I wondered where on God's green earth Natalie-Nate Cassidy could be hiding; she had to be somewhere in the city.

I thought about the cutouts on the apartment wall. It was obvious she had some sort of love-hate relationship with herself, that her dream was to be like the muscular, chiseled men in the images, which is why she'd taped her own head to many of them. But why was she targeting older, harmless guys who didn't look anything like them, or her dream? Was it a power thing? Domination? And did she or did she not have an accomplice? If she did, who the hell was it? If she didn't, what was behind the shots in the back of the head?

Then it dawned on me.

"That's why!" I said to the steering wheel. "These guys, her victims, would never hit a girl; they couldn't or wouldn't fight back. A jock, a bodybuilder on steroids, or even a younger guy could easily backhand her into the middle of next week." *Especially if she was prancing around like a dude with a smart mouth and a chip on his shoulder,* I thought. *Hmm. Jack Logan was the kind of guy who liked his sports and maybe a beer or two, but then he went home to his wife every night, lived a plain and simple life. And he was over-weight and about as fit as a Bundt cake. He wasn't a threat to anyone. Neither was Miller, for Pete's sake.*

The thought made me angry. She didn't know Lennie Miller was just a nice young man with a penchant for all things technical. A guy who thought a gun was too dangerous to touch, let alone carry, even though his job required it. Janet was smaller than her, but not much, so she was an easy target. With Robar, Natalie was smart and didn't confront her directly. So instead, she vandalized her car. But what was it about Miller that made her think he was the easy mark?

And then I realized two things. One: it wasn't my people that were the actual targets. It was me. By attacking them, she was attacking me, the one person who could and would bring her down. Two: I realized where I'd seen her before. She was the woman I'd met talking to my neighbor outside my apartment: the bitch was checking me out.

"I'll kill the frickin' bitch," I snarled to myself as I banged my wrists on the steering wheel. And suddenly I was in big trouble. I was sweaty and cold, and my stomach was flipping. I had to pull over at an auto parts store and before I knew it, I was outside my car at the rear bumper saying goodbye to the burger, fries, and coffee. *Damn it all to hell.*

"Hey, are you okay?"

It was a guy in a red company polo shirt; he obviously worked at the store. And I could see another, inside, watching me through the plate glass window with interest, a snide smirk on his face.

"I'll be fine, but thanks," I said, gulping at the air and spitting the final remnants of a fourteen-dollar meal onto the ground. "I'm sorry about the mess." I held my stomach and my head swam for several seconds before I could focus and stand up straight.

"Don't worry about it," he said. "I'll hose it away. You look like shit. D'you want me to call someone for you?" He looked genuinely worried.

"Geez, thanks for the compliment." I managed a small smile, then said, "No, but thanks. I'll be fine. Again, I'm sorry."

He nodded and went back inside. The guy in the window was still grinning at me. I was tempted to give him the middle finger, but I didn't. Instead, I climbed in back behind the wheel, started the engine, and drove away.

Ten minutes later I pulled into the parking lot at the rear of the police department, fully recovered from my embarrassing encounter at the auto parts store, but still feeling like crap and in need of a shower, which is what I did. I went to the locker room, stripped off my clothes, and washed away my blues: mood, that is, not my uniform. I was wearing plain clothes, remember?

Like the proverbial Boy Scout, I was always prepared, and thus I kept a couple of spare pairs of jeans, several sets of clean underwear, and a couple of clean tops in my locker. That being so, when I emerged from the locker room, I felt like a princess and ready for just about anything. Unfortunately, I still looked like hell.

The feeling of euphoria? It didn't last for more than a few minutes... just until I walked into the situation room and saw Miller's empty desk.

I stood for a second, staring at it, looking at it, but not seeing it, if you know what I mean. And then I realized that it was only a matter of time before someone else would be sitting there, and I felt my eyes begin to water. I turned away. I couldn't let it happen; I could cry, but not in the situation room.

I hurried to my office and closed the door, happy to be able to shut out the rest of the world, at least for a few minutes, but still I choked it back. And then my phone rang.

"Gazzara," I muttered, barely loud enough for me to hear, let alone the caller.

"Good afternoon, Captain. This is Chief Gunnery Sergeant Wilcox Dorman of the United States Marine Corps over here in Columbus, Georgia. I hope I'm not disturbing you."

Who? What? I don't know any...

"Good afternoon, Gunnery Sergeant. This is a surprise. What can I do for you?"

"Well, I think it's more what I can do for you. I understand that you've had the unfortunate luck of meeting Miss Natalie Cassidy."

He had a nice voice and spoke as if he was giving orders. I liked the sound of him.

"Not yet, not to speak to I haven't, but I'm working on it and hope to meet her *very* soon. And you know this... how?"

"Let's just say a little bird told me. The truth is that with an Entry Level Separation like hers, we try to keep an eye on them, at least for a while, to make sure they get properly acclimated to civilian life again... or, as in this particular case, not."

"Yes, not, and that's putting it mildly, Gunny. So, what is it you can do for me? Would it be breaking the rules if you told me the reason for her separation?"

"It would, but in this case, I'll tell you. Miss Cassidy had it in her pretty little head that joining the Marine Corps would be the perfect way to get the government to pay for her gender reassignment surgery. When she found out that it wasn't going to be quite that easy, and that she would be required to complete the six-year active status commitment she signed up for... well, it was a dealbreaker for her. In a nutshell, she went nuts. Hers was a psychological separation."

I sat there for a moment, unsure of what to say next. Fortunately, I didn't have to.

"Miss Cassidy had no intention of serving out her term," he continued. "She was convinced that Uncle Sam would pay for her change of gender, and then she'd be on her merry way to go bone Miss Teen USA. Pardon my language."

"No apology necessary, Gunny. I've said far worse myself over these past couple of weeks... Look, I shouldn't be talking to you about it over the phone. In fact, I'm under strict orders from my chief of police to keep what I know under wraps until I can make an arrest, but I will tell you this: she's responsible for the death of a member of my team."

I don't know why I spilled my guts like that to him. Maybe it was the sound of his voice. Maybe I felt that somehow I could trust him, or maybe it was just because at that moment I needed to talk to someone who understood how I was feeling. Whatever! The words just spilled out, and suddenly I felt like someone had sucked the poison from my wound.

"I am sorry, Detective. May I offer you my condolences?" So he did understand. "So, she's not in custody?"

"Unfortunately, no. But we're closing in," I lied. I didn't want to sound completely incompetent.

"Well, I am glad to hear that, but the reason for my call was because I thought you might like to know that when Cassidy was with us, she corresponded often with a friend by the name of Tilly Montgomery. She was listed as Cassidy's emergency contact, the only one, in fact. Montgomery lives in Chattanooga."

Oh... m'God! Are you serious? Oh Lordy, I think I'm in love.

"Gunny, if you ever find yourself in the Chattanooga area, I'd like to buy you a drink. Now, if you wouldn't mind, please give me that address."

27

It didn't take me long to grab Robar and for her to drive me to
Tilly Montgomery's home. *Light duties, my ass.*

Her house on the north side of the river looked like it
hadn't seen an update since its construction in the early sixties. It
was tiny, situated on a tired, worn-out street and looked like it had
barely enough room for one person to live there, let alone a couple.
But that wasn't the worst part; there were cats, hundreds of 'em—
okay, so there were eight—lying and roaming around the front
porch, and that made me afraid of what we might encounter on the
inside. I am *not* a cat person.

"A crazy cat lady?" Robar asked and, evidently, from her tone,
she wasn't a cat person either.

"Looks that way," I said as I knocked on the front door. "You
want to go check round back?"

She nodded and left.

"Who ith it? Who'th out there?" the voice lisped.

"Someone doesn't have her dentures in yet," I muttered.

"Miss Tilly Montgomery?" I asked and then identified myself.
"I'd like to talk to—"

"Who did you thay you are?"

"My name is Detective Gazzara," I repeated. "I'm here to talk to you about Natalie Cassidy."

One of the dirty lace curtains that hung across the window in the front door moved to one side, and the woman peeked through at me. She wasn't as old as I'd expected from the sound of her voice. She was maybe in her late fifties; her weather-worn skin made her look older.

"Nate isn't here," Tilly Montgomery said through the closed door, frowning.

"I didn't ask if she was," I said firmly. "I said I want to talk to you. Please open the door."

The curtain dropped back into place. I listened and watched. I could see the woman through the curtain. She seemed to be talking to herself, mumbling. I couldn't make out what she was saying or who she was talking to, but after what I'd just been through, I was taking no more chances. I drew my weapon and held it down by my thigh, ready.

Finally, after a couple clicks and the swipe of a security chain, the door opened and... "Oh geez," I muttered as the wave of ammonia from an overabundance of cat litter wafted through the opening, almost overwhelming me.

Mary Sanek's trailer was a palace compared to this place. I took a step back and took a deep breath.

"Nate isn't here," she said. "I haven't seen him in months. You'd better come on in then." And she shuffled backward, pulling the door open to make room for me to step inside.

It was dark inside, gloomy, and the woman was obviously a hoarder. It was like something out of an old movie. I was unnerved, but not by the atmosphere; by more than twenty pairs of golden eyes that stared at me, unblinking. *Holy cow!*

"Mrs. Montgomery—"

"Call me Tilly," she said as she waved for me to follow her into the kitchen. I heard a knock at the back door and saw Robar's silhouette through the door window.

I looked around. It appeared that Montgomery lived alone in the small house... with her cats.

I holstered my weapon. She didn't seem to notice. The back door was secured by two large bolts, a chain, and a lock. Ann knocked again.

"Who's that out back?" Montgomery asked, making sure I was between her and the door.

"It's just my partner, Detective Robar. Is it all right if I let her in?"

She nodded and I drew back the bolts, undid the chain, turned the key in the lock, and opened the door for Ann to step inside.

"This is Detective Robar," I said as Ann flashed her ID. "I'm sorry to bother you, Ms. Montgomery—"

"I told you to call me Tilly," she said, interrupting me.

"Tilly, yes. As I was saying, Tilly, we're worried about Natalie. She's in a lot of trouble. D'you have any idea where she might be?"

"No. I told you. I haven't seen her in... three months, it must be."

"What is your relationship to Natalie?"

"It's not Natalie. It's Nate now, ain't it?" she asked, plonking herself down at the kitchen table.

Ann sat down across from her. I remained standing. I had no idea what might be on those seats... I don't like cats.

"Didn't he get all his stuff done like he said?" Tilly asked.

She was looking at me as if I might be the bearer of the big news she'd been waiting for.

"What stuff are you talking about?" Ann asked.

"His surgery, of course. The last time I talked to him, he said he almost had enough money to get his new bits attached, you know." She wrinkled her face and pointed down at her crotch.

I actually shuddered.

"No. She hasn't had the surgery yet," I replied. "How well do you know her?" I asked, finding the whole situation weird.

"I've known *him* since *he* was a kid. I'd say that I met him when he was about thirteen years old. Maybe fourteen. I'm the one who helped him, you know," Tilly said as she looked me squarely in the face. She was wearing a housecoat with sweatpants underneath and a thin necklace made of seed beads around her neck. Her hair was a patchwork of gray and mousy brown cut into a bob style.

I looked around the room. The sink was filled with dishes, the counter cluttered with coupons and junk mail flyers and cans of pork and beans, corn, carrots, Dinty Moore stew and half a loaf of bread.

"What did you help him with?" I asked, taking out my recorder and turning it on.

She looked at the little machine as I set it down in front of her.

"It's just so I don't forget what we talk about," I said. "D'you mind?"

She glared at it, then at me, then at Ann, then at the recorder again. Finally, she shrugged and nodded.

"I suppose it will be okay," she said, still staring at the machine. "Nate was wrong from the get-go. He was born in the wrong body; he wasn't meant to be in that body at all. He was a strong young man inside a weak body, he was. I could see it all along. I just knew it. I told him so."

My heart began to race.

"Are you trying to tell me that you convinced a young girl that she was really a boy?"

"I didn't have to convince him. He knew it, just like I did. I just offered him my support. I didn't judge him. Like I can tell you're doing right now." She raised her chin and looked defiantly down her nose at me.

"You've got to forgive me, Tilly. It isn't every day I hear someone claim responsibility for persuading someone to reject their gender. Why would you do that?" I looked down at Robar. She looked as bumfuzzled as I was.

"He wasn't happy, you see. He wanted to be a boy, a man. Strong. He hated wearing dresses and heels and bras and panties and all. When I let him wear my late husband's shirts and pants, he was a different person, happy, like. You know, you could just see how much better he felt. Even after all these years, I can still see it as clear as day. He looked so much like my Albert." She smirked up at me.

And there it was. I'm no shrink, but I knew instantly what had happened. This stupid woman had tried to replace her dead husband with a vulnerable young girl and had turned her into a serial killer. The old bitch was as responsible for those deaths as was Natalie.

I stood for a moment trying to figure out what to say next, then Ann stepped in.

"When Nate came back to see you, did he say anything about where he'd been or what he had been doing?" she asked.

"The last time I spoke to him, he left rather quickly."

"Why is that?" Ann asked.

"I don't know... You know how men are. They're always nice to you when they want something, but when you want something in return... well, they are not so nice then, are they? They're not giving creatures, not like my pussy cats," she said, a tight smile on her lips.

I say smile, but it was more half sneer and half smirk, as if she'd at last noticed the smell in her own house. Her lips pinched into a pout, and she wrinkled her nose. And then I got it, and I almost puked. I looked at Robar. She'd gotten it too; at least I thought she had. Together we stared at the woman, disbelieving what we were thinking... well, *I* was.

"And what was it you wanted in return from him?" Robar asked, and I could tell she was dreading the answer.

Tilly licked her lips and pinched her eyebrows together. "After all the years I helped him, nurtured him, accepted him. Well, he was coming along nicely, becoming more muscular... you know, and I knew he had feelings for me."

"Were you and Nate in a sexual relationship?" I asked while attempting to stay calm, stoic.

"Oh no. We never had sex," Tilly said, looking first at me than at Robar. "No, we never had sex."

"Were you intimate in other ways?" Ann asked.

She looked away, avoided the question, and said, "Look, like I said, I haven't seen Nate in nearly three months. I doubt I'll see him any time soon."

"So you *were* intimate with him?" Ann persisted.

"Intimate? What does that mean? I told you already. We didn't have sex."

And then I remembered the words I'd heard so many times over the years on TV. "I... never... had... sex... with that woman."

I shook my head and turned away. I needed a break from the old woman, so I wandered out of the kitchen, into the living room.

"Where's she going?" I heard her say.

"She'll be back. Now please, answer the question," I heard Ann say, then I shut the rest of it out and concentrated on the living room; big mistake.

First, I came under the stare of all those eyes. Second, there was no place to sit that wasn't covered in newspapers or cat hair. The television was on with the volume turned down. Third, the most repulsive thing I think I ever encountered was the huge, pink vibrator on the table next to the recliner. *Oh... m'God! Are you kidding me? That's freakin' disgusting.* I swear, I've seen horses less well-endowed. I backed out of the room, turned, and went back into the kitchen, the image of the giant dildo stamped indelibly on my psyche.

"Did you know," I said, "that you were the only person listed in her military file as her next-of-kin? You must have meant something to her. And if you did, mean something to her, don't you think there's a chance she might come back?"

Tilly's eyes lit up for the first time since we arrived. She reminded me of one of her cats, waiting beside a hole in the baseboard, knowing there was a mouse inside, and that it had to come out sooner or later.

"Him," she said. "You mean him. She's a him."

"Yes, I meant to say him. I'm sorry, Tilly," I lied. "So, if Nate does come back, will you call me? He's in trouble, Tilly. Big trouble. He needs help. And if you try to hide him, spare him from taking responsibility, you could find yourself in trouble too," I said plainly, watching the fire in her eyes fade and finally die.

She looked at me suspiciously.

I continued, "The truth will have to come out, Tilly. All of it. It always does."

I set my card down on the table and picked up my recorder. Tilly looked at the card as if it had legs and might scurry at her any second. She looked up at me, then at Ann, but she said nothing. I turned off the recorder and we left her sitting there, alone with her thoughts... and I shuddered to think what they might have been.

"Oh, my God," Ann said as she opened the driver's side door and got in. "I need to go to the fire department and have 'em put me through the hazmat unit. What the hell *was* that?" she asked, shimmying her shoulders with the willies. "Just when I think I've seen humanity at its lowest, someone manages to shove it down a couple more notches."

"She was... I'm at a loss for words," I said, and I was, truly.

I sat beside Ann for a moment. She pushed the starter button and eased the car away from the curb, made a U-turn, and headed back in the direction of Amnicola Highway.

"Find us a coffee shop," I said. "I need to wash my mouth out."

She pulled into the drive-through at Starbucks at Hamilton Place and ordered two large black coffees. Two minutes later we were back on 153 heading toward the police department.

I decided I didn't want to be the only one that had had fun at Tilly Montgomery's home, so I told Ann about the dildo.

"Holy shit!" she said. "Why did you do that? I didn't need to know that. D'you have any idea what's going on inside my head? It's disgusting. You really do need to wash your mouth out."

And for the first time in days, I was able to sit back and relax, and even smile, just a little. But, at the back of my mind, I couldn't help feeling that Tilly Montgomery was more than partially responsible for the way Natalie Cassidy had turned into a monster.

Ann pulled into the parking lot at the rear of the PD, shut off the engine and said, "It's almost five. If it's okay with you, I think I'm going to call it a day, Kate. That was just too much to handle. Wait until I tell Hawk about it."

"Yes, sure. Go on home to the kids. Relax. We can talk to Hawk in the morning. You and him... you get along well, right? I think he likes you, Ann."

"Ha! Don't even go there, Kate. Hawk and I are just friends. I can talk to him like I can talk to no one else. You name it, he's been there, done that. He understands." She smiled, then continued, "You know how hard it is to find someone to talk to about this stuff. Could you imagine talking to say... oh, I don't know, my husband, about Tilly Montgomery? He'd cringe and tell me for the umpty-eleventh time that I shouldn't be in this line of work, or that there's something radically wrong with me. And Lord knows, he might even be right."

"Yes," I said. "You're right about that." And suddenly, for no reason I could think of, I remembered my conversation with Gunnery Sergeant Wilcox Dorman, and I wondered what it would be like to talk to him about Tilly Montgomery, sans the dildo, of course. I smiled at the thought and made a mental note to call him when the case was over, or not.

What was I even doing thinking about it? One thing I *was* sure of was that I stunk from the cat house... *Yeah*, I thought. *That's what it was, a freakin' cat house.*

My head was aching again. It wasn't bad, but it was there,

lurking under the surface and just didn't seem to want to go away. *Maybe it's because I'm hungry*, I thought, as I sipped my coffee.

I tried to think of something I could eat that might hit the spot, that would stay down, or wouldn't take too long in the oven. *Not a burger, that's for sure, nor a frickin' pizza!* In fact, the idea of eating anything at all made my stomach turn. *Maybe some chicken broth and crackers. That might do the trick.*

"Did you hear what I said, Kate?" Robar said, interrupting my thoughts.

"I'm sorry. What?"

"I said we need to take up a collection for Lennie's family to help pay his funeral costs. We should help his mother do Lennie right."

"Of course. Count me in," I said, climbing out of the car. "I'm going on home. I'll see you tomorrow."

It was a pleasant afternoon. The rain had stopped, finally, and the sky, already dark, was clear. The roads were also clear, which was unusual for a Monday. I was looking forward to a quiet evening, another shower, my sweats, and a good night's sleep. Yeah, that's what I was thinking, and I couldn't have been more wrong.

28

I t was just after five-thirty when I got home that evening. I went straight to the bedroom, slipped out of my clothes and then into the shower. I left the bathroom light off and showered by the soft glow from the lamp on my bedside table. After dumping half a bottle of my lavender shampoo on my head and rubbing myself down from head to toe, I felt that maybe I'd managed to scrub the smell of cat litter from my skin and out of my hair.

I toweled off, wrapped the towel around me, went into the living room, sat down on the couch, and began to think back over the events of the past several days. It was a circus. There were more weird twists and turns than I could count, and I still had no physical evidence that Natalie Cassidy had killed anyone, not even Lennie Miller. I knew it; deep down I knew it, but that wasn't enough.

"Why him?" I whispered. The sound of my own voice set off an alarm in my head and I winced. "How in the world did she know about us? That we were onto her? The only one who hadn't been attacked was Hawk. Why?"

Then I thought of all those pictures in Natalie's apartment, and I knew why. Hawk was more than she could handle.

I went to my bedroom. It was cool and dark, and I was sure that once my body relaxed on the soft mattress, my head cradled on a pillow, I'd soon fall asleep. But I didn't. I was wired. It was as if someone had hooked me up to an IV of liquid caffeine. My eyes popped open; my mind raced from one uncomfortable topic to another: Lennie, Hawk, the gunnery sergeant, the cold cases on my desk, Janet lying in the hospital, the images on Cassidy's wall, the images on the whiteboard in the office, Lennie, that annoying TV blurb for my insurance company I'd heard a million times and kept barging into my thoughts like a child screaming for candy in WalMart, the giant dildo, Ann... Lennie, that damned great dildo... *Geez!* I couldn't focus on anything. I couldn't keep a single real thought in my head for more than a couple seconds. I was experiencing bouts of dizziness, my body ached and wanted to rest, but it was impossible.

I sat up and went to the kitchen and grabbed a new bottle of red wine from the fridge. I uncorked it, grabbed the aspirin bottle, opened it, shook two of the little tablets into my hand, and washed them down with a single huge gulp of wine. *That should do the trick.* I was sure of it.

I sat down on the couch, waited for a minute, then swung my legs up, laid my head back on the armrest and... Thankfully, I dozed off. Unfortunately not for long, not more than thirty minutes, and it wasn't the deep sleep I needed, and I was still aware of where I was and that I couldn't sleep.

Finally, I gave it up. I opened my eyes feeling like I'd just spent five hours in hell, and I suppose, on thinking back, that was precisely where I'd been.

I decided it was time I faced the fact that I wasn't going to get any real sleep that night. I thought about going for a run, but that idea brought on an attack of the jitters. That bitch could be out there somewhere waiting for me.

I thought of reaching out to Janet or Ann but quickly backed away from that idea. I was their Captain. They could come to me, but I couldn't go to either of them. I even thought about calling Harry Starke, but quickly gave up on that idea.

I paced the floor. I tried to watch television. Reading was out of the question, and doing any kind of work that required I stare at a computer screen also didn't appeal to me. I straightened up the kitchen. I put on the radio and listened to some talk show but just got more aggravated. When I looked at the clock, I was shocked to see that it wasn't even ten o'clock yet; I had the whole damn night ahead of me... and I freaked. I was frickin' desperate... and then I had a thought.

With my brain feeling like cotton candy, I went to my bedroom and sorted through my purse and found Dr. Joon Napai's business card. I'd remembered she'd written her personal cell phone number on the back of it, in case of an emergency. Well, this was it; this was an emergency. She answered almost immediately, bless her. Her voice, the Indian accent, was soothing, calming, and I asked her for help.

"If I can," she said. "Please tell me, how have you been feeling?"

"My mind's a mess. I can't sleep. I can't seem to focus on anything. Oh, I'm okay. I'm not in any kind of trouble, or danger, or, whatever but, like I said, I can't sleep... and I'm dog tired. I have to sleep, Doctor. I took some aspirin, but they didn't help."

"Aside from not being able to focus," she said, "have there been any other symptoms that you've noticed that are out of the ordinary?"

"Well... I haven't had much of an appetite. I've been a bit dizzy, at times. The thought of eating makes me feel like I want to vomit."

"Detective, you sound like you are under a lot of stress. "Can you drive? If not, call an Uber and come and see me. I'm at the hospital."

"Oh geez, thank you. I'll be there as soon as I can."

"And breathe, Captain, breathe deeply. It will help."

"That wasn't so hard now, was it, Kate?" I asked myself as I slipped into a clean sweat suit, a navy blue one with a Civil War-era cannon on the front along with the numbers 186 stamped in yellow over the right breast and over the right hip bone. I put my tennis shoes on and tied my hair up in a ponytail. Then I grabbed my purse and headed downstairs, out through the front door and onto the steps where I paused to do some deep breathing, as Dr. Joon had instructed. It was at that moment I was overcome by a terrible feeling of impending doom. I swear I felt the hair on the back of my neck stand up.

"Don't say a word, bitch," a voice to my right said, "or I'll shoot you right where you are."

I turned and looked toward the end of my building and, just a few yards away, almost hidden in the shadows at the corner, I could just make out the shape of a person pointing a gun at me. I couldn't see her face, but I knew instantly who it was.

"Just walk to your car," Cassidy said, gesturing with the pistol. "Don't do anything stupid."

Reluctantly, I did as I was told.

"Stand still. Reach behind you and hand over the keys. Don't look, just keep facing forward. Good, now get into the car... on the driver's side... That's it. Easy now. Slide over into the other seat. Just remember I have my gun on you, and I won't hesitate. I killed your partner right here, and I'm not afraid to kill you, too."

I did exactly as she said. She waited until I was in the passenger seat, then, without taking her eyes off me, carefully, slowly climbed into the driver's seat, keeping the gun trained on me, her hand steady as a rock.

Now I knew how Jack Logan, Cappy Mallard, and the others had gotten into their seats, and I also knew how they must have felt.

Me? I felt strangely calm. I knew I was about to face the final conflict, maybe my own personal end of days. Was I ready for it? No, but I knew deep down that I would rise to the occasion; I always did. She had the advantage, but I was a smartass and knew exactly how to take it away from her... at least I thought I did.

When she got into the car, slammed the door shut and pressed the lock button, I turned sideways in my seat and stared at her. She was wearing the same camouflage pants, the same baggy shirt, the same stupid hat with the flaps. I thought it was stupid that night I first saw her—him—in the incident room, sitting in the seat next to Robar's desk, complaining about his ex-girlfriend assaulting him.

"You really need to change your look," I said, casually. "You're dressed exactly the same as when you came to the PD to piss on your girlfriend."

"Ex-girlfriend, and I like the way I look."

"Brown, you said your name was, as I recall. Good choice, Natalie. You look like shit." The headache was gone. I felt good. I was in my element. I had no fear of this strange little man-woman that was holding me at gunpoint. I doubted very much that she was planning to kill me, but what was she planning?

"I'm not Natalie anymore," she said. Her voice was deep for a female but not overly masculine either. "I haven't been for a long time. My name is Nate. Now, you and I are going for a drive."

And so I sat there, in the passenger seat, a hostage in my own car, and I cursed my stupidity. There was little I could do but sit still and wait for something to break, or not. The only plan I had was to try to piss the woman off to the point where she would lose it and maybe make a mistake. It wasn't much, but it was all I could come up with. One thing I was sure of, though, was that things were coming to a head; it was almost over. No matter that I was a hostage, I had her. She'd either have to kill me or I'd put her away for good.

If she killed me, it would only be a matter of time before Hawk and Ann took her down.

"You know," she said, still driving with one hand, the other holding the gun almost at my head. "I saw you that day, after I'd killed that fat guy, Jack. I was in the field, just a few rows down. You guys," she shook her head. "Pathetic. You didn't even conduct a proper search of the area," she taunted.

I clenched my fists and wondered if I could smack the gun out of her hand. Without turning my head, I glanced sideways. She had her finger on the trigger. *Too risky!*

"I knew who you were, big shot," she rambled on. "You've been in the news a lot lately. So I thought I'd check y'all out. See what you were doing to catch me."

She waited for me to answer. I didn't.

"Cat got your tongue, miss fancy detective?" Natalie chuckled. "I have to admit, I was impressed, but that Detective Robar... The silly bitch actually told me what car she was driving. You know, I hated to slash the tires on that sweet ride, but she gave up the information without even being asked, like she was daring me to do something to it."

"You're delusional, Natalie. That wasn't what she was doing. She was just making conversation. You don't impress me."

"I told you, my name is Nate."

"Sure it is. And believe it or not, I understand how you feel. You were born in the wrong body. You identify as a male. I can buy that. But the killing? What good does that do?" I hissed. "When did ambushing good, decent guys who never hurt anyone... when did that become a guy thing?"

"Are you kidding?" she asked. "It's always been about that. I've always known that I'm really a male. Men are strong. They have muscles. They fight and hunt and kill and screw. That's it. It's the natural order of things, always has been, ever since Abel killed Cain. It's called the survival of the fittest. Guys are born to kill... and that guy at The Sovereign? He was just like all the others: fat, weak, stupid. He wasn't a man."

"It's Cain that killed Abel, dumbass. His name was Jack Logan, by the way," I snapped. "And he was someone's husband."

"Abel Dumbass? Hahaha, that's just too funny... He was a disgusting blob." The laughter turned to a snarl. "One too many chili dogs and supersized Mountain Dews made him soft, slow, and ignorant. You should have seen what he was eating. It was frickin' disgusting," she said, and she actually shuddered.

"He was kind to you," I said. "He didn't come onto you or assault you. You killed him just for the hell of it. You really are certifiable. You're nothing. Just a silly little girl playing dress up and killing for the fun of it. But you're not going to get away with it, Natalie."

"It's Nate! Bitch!" she shouted at me. "And you know nothing about me. Yeah, I'm getting' away with it, and you're in no position to do a damn thing about it."

She was right there. I didn't have the upper hand at all. She held all the cards.

"I killed him because he was a fat slug, the same reason I offed your fat friend with the blond hair."

My stomach tightened; she was talking about Lennie. I didn't answer; I couldn't.

Her eyes constantly darted back and forth as she drove, from the road to me and back again. Never for a second did the gun waver, and never once did she give me an opportunity to make a move. *Geez, I would have thought her arm would have been getting tired by now.*

"I guess the so-called mandatory fitness guidelines for the police department are just a suggestion." She laughed again, giggled. "He looked like he was well on his way to being a fat-ass desk jockey, too fat to chase anyone down on the street. Unless they were carrying a greasy sack of Krystal's or something and he was hungry."

"You piece of shit," I snarled. "You know nothing about him. He was a good man."

"Right. Sure he was."

I watched her knuckles whiten as she squeezed the grip of the gun.

"See," she continued, "there are two kinds of men in this world. There are men who see life as just a day-by-day occurrence. And then there are men like me who grab onto life and make it their own."

I snorted and turned my head to look at her. "That's just frickin' dumb," I said. "Even if it made any sense, it wouldn't matter because you're neither one. You're neither woman nor man. As I said, you're just a silly little girl with delusions of... not grandeur, that's for sure. Look at you, even your coat's too big for you."

"Shut up!" she screamed.

Her voice had taken on a wild edge, and I knew we were getting closer and closer to that point of no return. I also knew that whatever the outcome of the next several minutes, it wasn't going to end well. Natalie Cassidy was a killer, and a cop killer to boot, but she was also transgender. She'd become the media's favorite victim, and my name would be shit. But at that moment, I couldn't worry about that. I had to keep the crazy bitch off balance, if I could; if she was flustered and upset, I figured she'd eventually screw up, and I'd get my chance.

"What? You thought you were something special, right? But now you're just confused," I said, chuckling.

"Me confused?" she said, calmer now. "Not hardly. Tell me something. What did your boss say when he told you I'd filed a complaint against you? I'll bet he was pissed that his superstar had screwed up." She laughed, but not as hard as I did.

"Are you kiddin' me?" I asked, laughing at her. "D'you think for one minute that you fooled anybody? If you did, you're a frickin' idiot, as well as a confused little girl."

"Stop calling me that," she yelled. "I'll shoot you in the head; I swear I will."

"You're not going to shoot me," I said, with a whole lot more confidence than I actually felt. "You don't have the balls to look me in the..." And then I really laughed. "You don't have the balls... Ha ha ha. Oh, that's funny. You really don't have the balls, do you?"

"You freakin' dyke," she howled.

"Not me, Natalie. You're the dy—"

And then she hit me, sideswiped me in the mouth with the barrel of the gun. I swear I felt my teeth move, and the pain... Geez, my entire body froze. I felt the warm blood drip from the side of my lip down my chin and the bitter taste of copper in my mouth.

"My name is Nate, you bitch! And if you don't stop calling me Natalie, I'll kill you right now and dump your body where they'll never find it!" She was becoming hysterical.

"I know what you're trying to do!" she yelled. "You're trying to piss me off, so I'll make a mistake. Well you can forget it. I'm gonna put a bullet through your pathetic little brain. You're gonna make me famous."

"Famous?" I ran my tongue along my teeth. They were all still intact. I put my hand to my mouth. My lip was split, top and bottom, and blood was dripping from my chin. "Why don't you put that thing down and stop the car and step outside? I'll make you famous. I'll beat your silly little girly face to a pulp."

"You don't have what it takes," she muttered, more to herself than to me, and then she continued, muttering, shaking her head, "You have no idea what my end game is. I joined the military. They were supposed to help me get my surgery. But they expected—"

"They expected you to serve out your contract," I said and braced myself for another crack on the head. It didn't come. And then I became aware of where it was we were going. We'd just turned onto Rural Road 18, and I realized I had to do something quick or I was going to end up like Jack Logan.

"They expected me to wait six more years," she mumbled. "How could I serve with my body like this? It was all their fault." And then she began to curse and swear, calling everyone in the

United States Marine Corps, including Gunny Dorman, the vilest names I'd ever heard, and I've heard some.

"If that was all you wanted, why didn't you just save your money and pay for the surgery yourself? Why did you have to kill all those people? It wasn't their fault you're what you are. They didn't do anything to you."

"You'll never understand," she said as she hit the gas and we tore off down RR18 in the direction of Jack Logan's demise. Her face had changed, softened. Her eyes looked blank. She was in another world.

"D'you think this is what I wanted to be? D'you think I chose to be like this? I could have been okay with it, you know? Being a girl. I could have been okay; really I could. But it was all wrong, see? She told me I was all wrong and that only I could fix it," she stuttered.

Had my face not been hurting, I might have almost felt sorry for her. I had a feeling the girl inside was trying to come out. And then I got it. She wasn't a transgender at all; she was suffering from multiple personality disorder. And Nate was the dominant entity, and I knew who was responsible for it: Tilly Freakin' Montgomery.

"Natalie," I said carefully. "I saw Tilly Montgomery today. Did she hurt you?"

"No! She helped me! She's the only one who ever did."

"Your father is still alive, you know," I said. "Why didn't you ever go to him? Why didn't you ask him for help?" I was stalling. There was no telling when she was going to pull over and put me out of my misery.

"I couldn't... He's wonderful... I couldn't let him see what I'd become." Those were probably the first honest words the woman had uttered in a long time.

"Put the gun down, Natalie," I said as she squeezed the steering wheel until the knuckles of her left hand were white. She was beginning to feel the strain in her right arm; her hand was trembling.

Holy crap, I thought. *I hope that thing doesn't have a hair trigger.*

"We can talk it through," I said gently. "We can straighten this mess out, Natalie, if you'll just put the gun down and talk to me for—"

"I warned you not to call me that name," she screamed.

29

The car, speeding now, was almost out of control. She was driving so fast everything was a blur. The moon was a silver disc, the sky a field of stars. It was a beautiful night, but I saw it only in short glimpses as the car careened onward. My mouth was dry, my lips and teeth hurt like hell, and there was nothing going on between my ears. It was as if my brain had quit working. I tried to shake it off but couldn't, and all the while Natalie was muttering to herself as she drove, saying vile and hateful things about women and girls and me... and even Janet.

"You people," she said. "You have your badges and your guns and all sorts of other shit, but you're nothing. You don't know how to use any of it. You're so easily manipulated, clueless, stupid, weak... *women.*" She spit out the last word as if it was something foul, which to her, I suppose it was.

"Tell me," she said. "The cute one; the redhead who looks like a schoolgirl; is she still in the hospital? I felt sorry for her. I really hated to leave her there on the ground, but..." She shrugged. "Silly little bitch. She was just like you. Careless."

And she continued to blather on and on. Most of what she said made no sense. She talked about the cruelty of the doctors she visited, the incompetence of the counselors she'd spoken to, and the co-workers who judged her. It was a never-ending list of people who she thought had done her wrong.

Finally, we were out of the city, and she seemed to relax a little and slow down. I braced myself, looked into the side mirror: nothing, no cars, no lights. The road in front and back was shrouded in darkness. I readied myself. If she slowed down below forty, I planned to throw myself out of the car. I looked out through the side window. Everything was a blur and almost pitch black. And then I lost my nerve. I figured I'd probably break my legs, or worse, my head, and then I'd really be done for.

I had no choice but to wait.

"So," she said. "I bet you're wondering what I did with all the money I took from those guys." She smiled proudly. "All together over the years I've collected almost five thousand dollars."

"Five thousand?" I asked. "How the hell many have you killed?"

"Your cop friend was number eleven. D'you know that tight piece of shit had only fourteen dollars in his wallet? Geez, I heard cops didn't get paid much but fourteen dollars…"

My guts almost turned inside out at her words.

"I'm sure you used it to feed your habit. Steroids, right?"

Her smile faded. "Screw you," she snarled.

"I saw your little kit in your apartment. In the bathroom."

"You were in my home?"

"We sure were… So what's with all those pictures on the walls and in the bathroom? And what about the hormones you bragged you were taking? I didn't find them. How long have you been a junkie, Natalie?" I asked, looking out of the side window, trying to gauge if the car was slowing.

I turned and looked at her. *Is that a tear?*

"You had no right to do that," she whispered. "How would you like having strangers go through *your* things?"

She'd lowered her hand. It was resting on the center console, the gun still pointing at me, her finger still on the trigger.

"You're wrong there. I had every right. I had a search warrant. You've got a lot of baggage going on in there. Come on, Natalie. Give it up. You can't win. I'm a senior police officer. You kidnapped me. They'll be on you like a duck on a June bug."

"They won't find me. I'll just disappear. I almost have enough for the down payment. I'll be a new person, a perfect person. I'll get a job, a good job, a man's job."

"In your dreams," I said. And then I saw lights in the side mirror, a car was approaching from the rear and it was approaching fast.

"I've never killed a woman," she said. "Not ever. I was brought up never to hit or hurt a woman, but I'm looking forward to killing you. I'm gonna shoot you dead, then I'm gonna shoot you in the back of the head..." she tailed off, dreamily. She was losing it.

Then she started to slow the car down. I watched the speedometer, then the headlights behind us, then the gun in her hand.

"It's really fun, you know, to shoot someone in the head. And it's even funner shooting them in the back of the head, from the back seat."

Funner? What the hell kind of word is that? I thought, as I prepared myself to pull the door handle and roll out.

"See, I get to watch when I do it from the back seat. When I'm still steering the car, and I pull the trigger like this," she said as she raised the gun and pointed it again at the side of my head, "I don't get to see what happens... not really."

I squeezed my eyes shut and clenched my teeth. But Natalie just started laughing and lowered the gun again, her wrist on the center consol.

"See, when I sit in the back seat and put the muzzle to the back of the head and pull the trigger... You can actually see the head expand as the gasses fill it, then the slug. You know, you can't hardly hear it. It's like the head is a silencer... weird." She was all dreamy again. It was like she was a completely different person, and I wondered if maybe it was Natalie, not Nate. Then her voice suddenly changed, hardened and she snarled, "I can't freakin' wait to see your tiny brains splattered all over the windshield."

That would be Nate, I thought, my hand now on the door handle. *Come on, bitch. Slow down. Just a little more.*

"You're not going to get away with it, Natalie. Killing one cop has put you on the Chattanooga Most Wanted List. Killing me will make you public enemy number one. You won't even get out of town."

"I am not Natalie!" she screamed. She began beating the steering wheel with her left hand. She spewed out a string of obscenities, naming me, the department, and anyone else she could think of. She'd lost it; she was spluttering. It was almost as if she was speaking in tongues except the words weren't Divinely inspired, but a raging diatribe of filth and hate.

"I'll teach you," she screamed. "You'll learn!"

And she slammed on the brakes. I wasn't prepared for it. I'd chosen not to fasten my seatbelt in the hope I might be able to jump out of the car. My head hit the dashboard. I saw stars. Everything went white. For several seconds I could see nothing. I sat up, blinked, put my hand to my head. Nothing helped. My brain was reeling; it wouldn't function.

"Bitch!" I heard her snarl. "Bitch, bitch, bitch... Frickin'... frickin' bitch. I'll frickin' teach her to screw with me. Nobody frickin' screws with me, not no hoity-toity bitch, that's for frickin' sure."

I heard the driver's side door open. I shook my head, trying desperately to clear it, but before I could, my door was flung open and Natalie had her gun in my face.

"Get out of the car, bitch," she hissed.

I shook my head, raised my hand to push the gun away from my face, then screamed in pain as she brought it down hard across my thumb. I tried to turn my head to look at her, and it was then I knew I was in trouble. I could barely see at all, and what I could see was fuzzy, out of focus, blurred. And I couldn't think, couldn't focus my thoughts, and I was sure there was something wrong with my hearing, too, because when Natalie screamed at me, it sounded like she was inside a giant clamshell.

"I'm going to enjoy this. You just wouldn't learn. You just…"

She grabbed my arm and pulled. I fell sideways out of the car onto the grass shoulder. I struggled to my knees. She kicked me in the ribs.

"I told you, didn't I?" she yelled. "I told you. I said I'd teach you." She laughed, bouncing on her toes like a damned boxer. "Now. Tell me. What's my name?"

"Natalie Cassidy," I replied defiantly and received a kick to my shoulder that spun me over backward; my face slammed into the hard dirt beneath the grass.

"Come on," she said, punching the air with her fist, waving the gun in the other, and dancing on her toes.

"Say it again, bitch. I dare you! You… frickin'," and she screamed more obscenities and stamped on my fingers, and kicked my legs, and then my thighs as I tried to protect my head and ribs.

And then I saw the lights of the car. *Oh, thank God!*

I needed to do something. I couldn't risk her taking off running across the field. And then I saw another kick coming. I grabbed her foot, wrapped my arms around her ankle and tried to pull her down.

"Leggo!" she yelled and punched me in the back of the head.

I balled up and wrapped my body around her leg and held on tight, my eyes clamped shut. She continued to swipe at me with her fist, but her blows were awkward and carried no real weight.

The car lights disappeared.

"Ugh," I grunted, hanging onto her like a boa constrictor. It was all I could do, and I was embarrassed when I thought about it later: big bad old me hanging onto that pathetic little thing, but what the hell was I supposed to do? I couldn't see worth a damn, and I was hurting like I'd been put through a trash compactor.

Where the hell did that car go? I thought desperately. Was there a road back there? Did they see what was happening and turn their heads away and drive on by? I didn't know. I just kept right on hanging onto her leg. I knew she couldn't kick me. If she raised her free foot off the ground, she'd fall over.

I knew I had to do something more, and quick. The only thing that came to mind was something I'd learned at the academy during self-defense training: go for the genitals.

Okay, so Natalie wanted to be a man, she had better get prepared to be treated as such. I turned her loose and with everything I had, steeling my stomach, I brought both fists up between her legs. The double blow landed perfectly, but it didn't faze her one bit: the bitch was wearing some sort of padded cup, to enhance her manly appeal no doubt. She barely felt a thing and, if anything, she became even more enraged. I got to my knees, raised my hands and looked right into the barrel of her Glock 17.

"Goodbye, bitch." She smiled and placed the barrel of the gun against my forehead, her finger already white against the trigger.

30

I don't remember exactly what happened next. From off to the side, out of the corner of my eyes, I caught a glimpse of a shadowy form come flying in from the cornfield. At first, I thought it was a deer, but then it slammed into Natalie, sending her spinning sideways. She somehow managed to twist in the air and land on her back with a thud. She grunted as she hit the hard ground. The gun discharged harmlessly into the air and flew out of her hand to land several yards away in a shallow ditch just beyond the hard shoulder.

Still on my knees, my hands on the ground in front of me, supporting me, my ears ringing from the noise of the shot, I looked to my left and saw the "cute little redhead" Natalie had thought she'd put out of commission straddling the woman, sitting on her belly, pounding the living crap out of her. Janet was not holding back. Her fists were hammering Natalie's face and I could hear her, Janet, sobbing loudly as she gave way to the feelings we all had for the woman who'd killed our friend.

And then another dark figure appeared, gun in hand. The other hand grabbed Janet by the collar of her jacket and hauled her off the now barely conscious Natalie Cassidy.

"Get your hands where I can see 'em, *now!*" Hawk yelled at Natalie. "I said, put your hands up. If you don't get your hands up..."

Janet stepped back and away, shaking her hands from the pain of her busted knuckles. Now I wasn't the only one with a busted lip; Natalie had one too.

Janet spit on the ground next to Natalie and with two long strides she was at my side.

"Don't move, Cap. Help is on the way."

"I'm okay," I said. Ha, no. I tried to say it, but my lips wouldn't move. The words came out as an incoherent mumble even I didn't understand. I ran my tongue over my lips. They felt like a couple of Polish sausages. I touched the bottom lip tenderly with my finger, not the split, and a small speck of blood came away with it. At some point, I must have bitten it. When that had happened I wasn't sure, but as the past several minutes came slowly back into focus, I figured it must have been when my face hit the dashboard.

"Just stay still, Kate," Janet said soothingly. "There's an ambulance on the way."

I looked up at her and couldn't help but think how far she'd come over the past two years, since the first case we'd worked together. She'd almost become the latest victim in a string of murders. She'd just saved my life, and now she was taking charge. She was a rookie no longer.

Hawk holstered his weapon and turned Cassidy over onto her stomach, wrenched her hands behind her back and cuffed her. She struggled like a demented cat, screaming about her rights. Hawk recited them to her, then stepped away, put his hands on his knees and scowled at her.

"If I thought for one minute," he snarled, "that I could get away with it, I'd pound your face into the dirt." Then he stepped forward again and yanked her up onto her feet by her cuffed wrists.

She was a mess, and I had no doubt that there would be an investigation into why she was as bruised about the face as she was. I didn't care. It was what it was; no regrets. It was one of those bridges we'd have to cross when we came to it. Why should I care anyway, about what had happened to her? She was a cold-blooded murderer, of five that I had personal knowledge of, and six more, according to her. I was to have been number twelve. *Lucky me!*

"How did you know where I was, Janet?" I asked as I tried carefully to stretch my lips.

"It was just dumb luck. Hawk and I were on Brainerd Road. He'd just had a phone call from forensics. The DNA from the Band-Aid in Jack Logan's car matched what the Marines had on file for Natalie Cassidy. That puts her in Jack Logan's car. He was excited.

"As I said, we were passing your place and he didn't want to wait until morning to tell you the good news, so we decided to stop by, maybe drink a glass of red to celebrate. We'd just pulled through the gate into your complex when we saw Cassidy walking you toward your car. Hawk wanted to rush her right then, but I knew she had a gun and I was afraid she'd shoot you before we could stop her. So we decided to follow you.

"Even when she pulled over, we weren't sure what to do. So we drove on by. Hawk turned off the lights and pulled over, and I jumped out and ran through the cornf—geez, Kate, that was really scary, in the dark, and all. Anyway, by the time I reached you, you both were out of the car and I could see... Well, that's when I lost it."

"Wow," I mumbled. "Thank God you did. She was just about to pull the trigger."

"They're coming," Janet said. "I can hear the sirens."

I could hear them too.

"There's something else," Janet said.

"Janet, I don't know if I can handle any more. Okay, go on.

What is it?" I rubbed my forehead. My face was swollen. It felt like my skull was trying to push out through my skin.

It was right about then that two ambulances arrived. The paramedics helped me walk to the nearest one, and I sat down on the tailgate to listen to what Janet had to say.

"Tilly Montgomery came in earlier," she said. "She's still there locked up in an interview room. She talked to Ann for almost a half-hour. When they were done, Ann took her to Room B and locked her in and left her there, so she could come and talk to me. Apparently, something had spooked Tilly. She told Ann that she had a prior conviction for lewd behavior toward a minor, a five-year-old boy. She was concerned because she knew what happened to child molesters in jail."

"So what?" I asked. "Why would she go to jail for a prior?"

"Not for the prior," Janet said, shaking her head. "For molesting and aiding and abetting Cassidy."

"What?"

"Yep, apparently she's known for years what Cassidy's been up to. She even feared for her own safety, so she kept it to herself. She said if Cassidy confessed, it would all come out and she'd be screwed, so she wants immunity. In return, she said she'd testify against Natalie. She said Cassidy is responsible for nine murders that she knows of, and there may be more. I guess it's your lucky day, Kate; you get to clear up your cold cases," Janet said. "Maybe you should buy a lottery ticket."

I tried to laugh, but I couldn't; it hurt too much. So I huffed and tried to smile. What the hell I must have looked like, God only knows.

"Oh yeah," I said wryly. "I look like I got lucky, don't I?"

We sat together and watched as they escorted Natalie to the second ambulance. Just as they were about to pass by, however, she made them stop, and she smiled at me.

"You think you've won, don't you?" she said. "Well you haven't.

I'll get my surgery in prison, you know, and I won't have to pay for a thing."

One of the paramedics tried to hustle her on past, but she looked back, and she scowled. "And then, missy, I'll be back to pay you a visit." She made an obscene gesture with her tongue and laughed... No, she cackled, like the damn witch that she was, and the EMTs hauled her away by both arms, and up into the back of the ambulance and slammed the doors.

I wouldn't see her again for almost two weeks. I didn't even get to do the interviews; Janet had that pleasure.

"Okay," one of the other EMTs said to me, "let's get you loaded. Up inside, please, and onto the gurney with you."

"I don't need that," I said.

"Why don't you just relax, Detective? Let us make that call. You've been through a tough time." It wasn't really a question, and they didn't give me a choice. In fact, they paid no attention to my protests at all.

Once they had me loaded, they began to question me. No, I'm not seeing double. You're holding up three fingers. Yes, my lip hurts. Yes, I have a headache. No, I'm not dizzy, well, not much, and on and on it went until finally they shut the doors, turned on the siren and away we went to Erlanger Hospital.

It seems funny now, but I remember the ride out at gunpoint seemed to last for hours, though it couldn't have been much more than twenty minutes or so. The ride back to the hospital seemed to be over almost before it had begun. Before I knew it, I was being unloaded into the emergency room. And then time really did stand still. They were busy that night, really busy, and I guess that since I wasn't bleeding out through my eyeballs, I was the low man on the emergency room totem pole; I didn't see a doctor for almost an hour.

My head still hurt, and that bothered me a lot. I was beginning to think that maybe I did have a concussion after all, but not from what had happened that night. I'd been having problems ever since Natalie had jumped me outside The Sovereign.

And then I got to thinking again. Yep, I know. I'm my own worst enemy when it comes right down to it, and I couldn't help but think how different things would have been if I'd only followed orders, done what I was supposed to and gone to the doctor. If I had, Miller would still have been alive... and maybe, just maybe, this whole nasty business could have been—

"Ah, there you are," a familiar voice said, interrupting my thoughts. I turned my head and saw the smiling face that went with the voice.

"I heard they had brought you in. I was waiting for you, but you didn't turn up. I was wondering what had happened to you. Now I know. How are you feeling, Captain?"

I chuckled as Doctor Joon Napai stepped into my little space.

"I was on my way to see you, Doctor. Honest Abe, I was," I said. "But I got... sidetracked."

"Yes. So I was told," she said, as she took a pen flashlight from her breast pocket and stepped to the side of the bed. "Look up, please. Hmm, now down... and the other... hmm."

"Will I live, Doc?"

"Undoubtedly, Captain. What happened to you? A cage fight perhaps? A bar brawl?" She pointed at my lips with her penlight.

"You should see the other guy," I said and tried to smile.

"Yes, so I heard. Well, you will not be leaving here tonight. I will order an MRI for first thing tomorrow morning."

"Thank you," I said. "I should have told you before. I've been having some real headaches, and dizzy spells. Nothing seemed to help. Sleep, eating or not eating. Aspirin. Wine." I shrugged.

"Well, we shall see," she said. "In the meantime, I suggest you try to get some rest. I'll have the nurse bring you an Ambien." She smiled kindly... and I started to cry.

She sat down beside the bed, picked up my hand and said, "It will be all right you know. You're just having a reaction. There's nothing to worry about."

"I know," I said, "and it's not that I'm worried. It's just..." And then I shut down.

She nodded sympathetically and said, "It is not your fault, any of it, not what happened to your young redheaded partner, Janet, or the officer that was killed in the line of duty."

"Miller? How do you know about that?" I asked.

"Word gets around. Doc Sheddon called me. He was worried about you. He said I should keep an eye on you. He attended to... Miller, you say his name was?" I nodded. "He attended to his remains."

I wiped my eyes, careful not to bump my sore lip. I looked at her. She was so calm, so... together. I wanted to say something, but there was nothing to say. For the first time since the Jack Logan case was handed to me, I was at a loss. It was over, done with, finished. No more insane deadlines, no bodies piling up, no one breathing down my neck, not even the Chief. The case was closed, wrapped up in a nice neat little bow, but you know what? I still felt like crap, and I told her so. All she did was click her tongue and shake her head.

"It's all about the anticlimax, you know, and your sense of loss, of course."

"His funeral is in two days," I said. "I'll never be able to keep it together, Doctor. I'll be a mess."

"And that is okay. You can be a mess. No one will blame you for that, and you will not be the only one."

31

I was released the following afternoon with strict instructions to go home and stay there for the next week; the only exception being that I could attend Miller's funeral.

The MRI had revealed nothing but a slight swelling of the brain and...

"How are you feeling today?" Doctor Napai had asked when she visited me earlier that morning.

"Fine, I think."

"Good. Well, you will be pleased to know that you do not have a concussion. Your head must be hard as a rock."

"I remember my father saying something similar when I was growing up."

She chuckled and said, "I am sure that he did." She stuck her hands in her coat pockets and smiled down at me.

"So what about the headaches?" I asked. "The loss of appetite, the pain at the back of my eyes? What's all that about?"

"Stress, Detective. Nothing more than stress. Something you will have to learn to live with... By the way, when did these symptoms begin? Can you remember?"

I thought about that for a minute, then I realized what she was getting at, and I nodded. They began when Harry Starke left the police department and I had to go it alone, but I didn't tell her that. I felt better just knowing.

"Years ago, when I received my first case as lead detective," I said. "And they've stayed with me over the years, but more so since I received my promotion to Captain..."

She nodded again. "As I thought. New responsibility. Stress. As far as your skull and brain are concerned, there is a little swelling, but that will get better quite quickly. Other than that, your head looks normal."

"So, when can I go home?"

"This afternoon, if you promise to be good. Detective, I am going to prescribe something for you and I want you to take some time off—"

"What for?" I asked, interrupting her. "If I don't have a concussion then—"

"Detective, you may not have a concussion, but you *are* suffering from Post-Traumatic Stress Disorder."

PTSD? I was stunned.

"Now, I know there are many doctors who prescribe drugs to treat the disorder," she continued. "I do not. I'm going to prescribe a very mild sleeping pill, and I am going to recommend that you talk to someone. That is it."

"A shrink? I don't think so. Look, I know what you're thinking. I know I broke down yesterday, but that was just a reaction. You said so yourself. I don't need a shrink. That lunatic who shot Miller, she needs a shrink. I don't need to talk to anyone. Especially not some kid fresh out of college who couldn't even imagine some of the stuff I've seen, let alone what happened to Lennie. No. I won't do it." I stared back at her.

"Oh, I think you will, Captain. I will not allow you to go back to work until you have completed twenty hours of therapy with a psychologist." And she looked at me as if to say *checkmate*.

"Damn it, Doctor... Okay, you win. Now, can I get out of here, please?"

And so that's what happened. She released me, I called for an Uber, and I went home and, for the most part, I did as I'd been told. Sheesh, I had to. I hadn't but stepped into my apartment that afternoon when Chief Johnston called and told me he'd have me shot if I even tried to step foot inside the police department until my seven-day respite was up.

As I expected, Hawk and Robar visited me a couple of times, but as far as work was concerned, they clammed up; I couldn't get a word out of either of them, not gossip, not anything. It was their idea of tough love. But that wasn't the worst of it; even Janet was holding out on me.

"Can't do it," she said when I called in to get the status on a couple of things I'd had on my mind. "It's doctor's orders, DG. You are off for the week. If I break the rules and the Chief finds out, he'll have me back filing reports, and that ain't gonna happen. Be a good captain and do as you're told for once."

"You cheeky little... Just you wait till I—"

"Bye, DG," she said, and hung up, leaving me staring at the blank screen of my iPhone. *Damn it!*

32

I did get to go to Miller's funeral the next day after Doctor
Joon released me. It seemed to me that every off-duty cop in
the Chattanooga tri-state area was also there.

Me? I accompanied his mother, who did more to help me than
any doctor ever could. I held her arm throughout the service, trying
to hold it together for her. But you know, when it was over that
sweet lady took me aside, took both my hands in hers, and said,
"You mustn't do it, you know, blame yourself. He wouldn't want
that." She had tears in her eyes.

"He talked about you... a lot," she continued. "He thought so
much of you." She patted my hand.

I looked down into her soft blue eyes and felt my own eyes
begin to water.

"Lennie wanted to be a policeman all his life, ever since he was
a little boy," she said. "He never wanted to be anything else..."

She paused for a moment, squeezed my hands and continued,
"When he was just a little guy, fourteen or fifteen years old, I
remember asking him, 'But honey, what would I do if you got hurt?'
He said, 'Mama, if I died in my uniform, I'd be happy knowing I'd

helped make the world a better place.' It's the God's honest truth. He did, he said those words to me."

I looked down at her, and I lost it. I burst into tears. I cried and I cried, in front of everyone. I put my arms around her, and we just stood there, holding each other. I tried to tell her how sorry I was, and that I wished I'd done so many things differently. But she would hear none of it.

And so, almost three weeks later, I stood in front of the mirror looking at my reflection, recalling that awful day when we laid Lennie Miller to rest. The display of respect had been amazing. You see it on TV: hundreds of officers, motorcycles, and it's impressive, but to see it in your own hometown, for one of your own, for one of your friends... Almost eleven hundred officers, the mayor, the sheriff, Chief Johnston, Harry and his entire staff including my old friend TJ Bron. It was beautiful, but it was something I never want to go through again.

After the funeral we, that is me, Hawk, Robar and Janet, we went to the Boathouse for lunch, not that I felt like eating... none of us did. I remember it was a cold, clear day with not a cloud in the sky. We sat together inside by one of the windows. The river was quiet that day, a ribbon of dark glass that meandered almost imperceptibly slowly toward the city center. It too seemed to recognize the solemnity of the occasion.

We talked shop for a while, but not about the Cassidy case. When I think about it now, the conversation at the table that day was forced. I think now that each of us would rather have been anywhere else but staring out of the Boathouse window that day. But we were there to pay our respects to Lennie, and that's what we did. We raised our glasses to his memory and in celebration of his short life, drank a couple of beers, and told stories about him through the tears.

Me? No matter what they said, no matter what anyone said, I still couldn't shake the feeling that I was to blame; still can't. Oh, they all tried to console me. It was the nature of the game, they said;

we lay our lives on the line every day, they said; you never know when it's your turn, but we do it anyway... blah, blah, blah. They all meant well, I knew that. They were such a great team. But with Lennie gone, there was a hole in the dynamic.

I remember we tossed back quite a few drinks that day, but they had little to no effect. When we left the Boathouse, we didn't go back to work; we all went home.

Cassidy is still awaiting sentencing. I was right, she did get a hotshot lawyer. Some TV personality type from Atlanta more interested in himself than his client. Sure, he made a big deal of the transgender thing, and the way his client had been treated, even demanded retribution for the beating she'd taken. But it went nowhere. When he saw what she'd done to me, and Hawk had testified that Cassidy had received her bruises while violently resisting arrest, he dropped it. He did manage to cut her a deal, though. The ADA, Larry Spruce, agreed to take the death penalty off the table if, in return, she'd plead guilty. She did. She confessed to a total of eleven murders and revealed where the bodies were hidden.

Me? I completed my twenty hours with the psychologist, a young PhD by the name of Holly Ferris. Did she do me any good? I think so. She must have thought so too, because I was released as fit to return to work yesterday, Friday. My first day back in the office would be on Monday and I was looking forward to it, sort of, but we won't get into that now.

So, there I was, staring at myself in the mirror, early on a Saturday evening, three weeks after Lennie Miller had been laid to rest. I was wearing a black skirt and a white blouse with a light blue blazer. I thought I looked nice, but professional. Not too fancy, but respectful and modest.

When my doorbell rang, I almost jumped out of my skin. I

went to the intercom, pressed the button, and said I'd be right down. I checked myself in the mirror one more time, grabbed my purse and keys and headed downstairs. I was nervous. I'd never done anything like this before, but I was sure that Chief Johnston and Doctor Ferris would approve.

I opened the door and... my heart flipped. He was freakin' gorgeous. The man stood at least six-four. He was wearing a dark blue suit with a stiff, white button-down shirt and red tie.

Oh m'God. Are you serious?

"Sergeant Dorman?" I asked. It was all I could do to get the words out without stuttering.

He nodded. "Detective Gazzara?" It was that same deep soothing voice I'd heard over the phone.

"Yes, but please, call me Kate."

The End

Thank you. I hope you enjoyed reading *Cassidy* Book 7 in the Lt. Kate Gazzara series as much as I did writing it. If you did, and you'd like to read the next book in the series, *Georgina*, just CLICK HERE or simply copy and paste this link. https://readerlinks. com/l/1079919
Again, thank you,
Blair Howard

ACKNOWLEDGMENTS

As always, I owe a great deal of thanks to my editor, Diane, for her insight and expertise. Thank you, Diane.

Thanks also to my beta readers whose last-minute inspection picked up those small but, to the reader, annoying typos. I love you guys. Thank you.

Once again, I have to thank all of my friends in law enforcement for their help and expertise: Ron, Gene, David for firearms, on the range and off. Gene for his expertise in close combat, Laura for CSI, and finally Dr. King, Hamilton County's ex-chief medical examiner, without whom there would be no Doc Sheddon.

To my wife, Jo, who suffers a lonely life while I'm writing these books: thank you for your love and patience.

Finally, a great big thank you goes to my oh so loyal fans. Without you there would be no Kate, no Harry, Tim, Doc... well, you get the idea.

GEORGINA

A LT. KATE GAZZARA NOVEL BOOK 8

GEORGINA

For Jo

A Lt Kate Gazzara Novel Book 8
By
Blair Howard

1

It was September 26th, 2004, a balmy fall day under a turquoise sky broken only by the occasional fluffy white cloud. It was a truly glorious morning, and no one appreciated it more than Mike Phillips as he stood on the perimeter of Swiss Valley Park football field. He gazed around the field, smiling, stuffed his hands into his pants pockets, closed his eyes and breathed deeply of the sweet smells of the unexpected Indian summer morning.

For more than a minute he stood there, savoring the moment, then he opened his eyes, turned and shouted to his son, "Logan! I'll get the tables. You get the coolers and—I'm not going to tell you again—they're heavy, so use the cart!"

They needed two tables, one for each team, and it was Mike's job to make sure they arrived on site and on time, this because he was able to borrow them from his wife's arts and crafts business.

"Friggin' things," he muttered to himself as he dragged them across the grass, the steel frames digging into his fingers.

Mike had been the head coach of the Mavericks, a local peewee football team, for almost five years. He took his responsibilities seriously, hence he'd taken on bringing the damn tables.

It was a special day, a serious game, so Mike had arrived early to get set up. The Mavericks were playing their rivals, the South Side Trojans: last year's division finalists. And all Mike wanted to do was dump the tables and run through the plays he'd drawn up for the kids and figure out how they were going to win with their best runner out with the chicken pox. It never failed that when they were on the cusp of a real victory, whether it be for the Regional or State Championship, Professor Murphy always managed to throw them a curveball that squashed any hope of them winning. But it was a beautiful morning for football, even when he knew his team was sure to lose. He was determined he was going to enjoy it.

His boy, Logan, was at the minivan loading the coolers into a large, red Radio Flyer wagon, along with the footballs and some fluorescent cones Mike used to delineate the warm-up area.

Mike was particularly proud of his team's coolers. He'd purchased them himself and had the Mavericks name painted on them along with the team logo, a silhouette of a wild horse rearing up on its hind legs.

It took only a few minutes to get the tables set up. Plenty of time left to sit quietly and reflect on the coming match before the parents would begin to arrive with their tiny warrior sons and daughters. It was in those moments that Mike liked to enjoy the quiet and get his act together. And why not? The field was freshly mowed. The birds in the forest at the edge of the field were singing and traffic on Dresden Road was almost nonexistent. *What the devil is that boy doing?* he wondered.

"Logan! What's taking you so long?" Mike shouted, then turned to see his son struggling across the grass towing the cart behind him. He chuckled a little, then jogged over to help him.

"Sorry, Dad. This cooler is one heavy son-of-a-bitch," the eight-year-old muttered.

"Language, Logan," his dad said, sternly, but smiling to himself.

"Where did you hear that?"

"You, Dad. You said it the other day when you were pulling the spare tire out of the trunk. Remember?" Logan said, his eyes wide and innocent.

"I did? Okay. But don't tell your mother or she'll wash both our mouths out with soap," Mike said as he grabbed the handle of the cart.

"Deal," Logan said, grinning a crooked, toothy grin.

"Good, now grab a couple of those lawn chairs and put them over there by the tables."

Logan did as he was asked, loaded himself up with two folding chairs, one under each arm, and awkwardly wobbled across the field toward the tables, close to the end zone where Mike's in-laws liked to sit. They always brought an extra cooler, snacks, and drinks and invited just about anyone who attended to join them for chips and a chocolate chip cookie.

The Fagan family, Mike's in-laws, were a pain in the ass, but... well, he put up with them for the sake of his wife and the kids; he loved kids. Unfortunately, the Fagan girl seemed to be allergic to just about everything but the grass on the field and the pigskin. Thus Faye Fagan—his wife's sister—and Ralph insisted that no one *ever* offer their daughter, a lovely eight-year-old young lady by the name of Zoey, anything to eat.

The thought of being around those people gave Mike a headache. Faye insisted her daughter be allowed to play. Mike had agreed. He had no problem with girls, and he really didn't care who played as long as they all played to the best of their ability. But, there was always an issue. From practice days to the snacks, from when phone calls should be made to notify families of schedule changes to who could post pictures of whom on social media. Everything was an issue.

"There's always one," Mike muttered to himself for at least the tenth time that week as he lifted a cooler from the cart and set it on one of the tables. *Where the hell's that boy?*

He was about to go looking for Logan when he spotted him
beyond the end zone on the edge of the trees. He opened his mouth
to shout, but before he could, the boy turned and began to run
toward him.

"Dad!" Logan shouted.

"What?"

"Dad! I think someone's hurt over there!" he shouted as he ran
to his father, pointing back over his shoulder.

"What... where?" Mike squinted as he looked at his son.

The boy looked scared, like Mike had never seen him before.

"In the trees. Over there." He pointed.

"Show me."

Logan took his father's hand and together they walked toward
the trees. They were some twenty yards out when Logan stopped
and said, "There. See?"

He obviously didn't want to go any further. Mike looked
toward the trees in the direction the boy was pointing and saw what
he thought was a small heap of trash and junk just inside the tree
line. That wasn't unusual. "The Woods" was a hot spot for
teenagers. They'd gather there after dusk and make a mess for Mike
and the other parents to clean up.

He told the boy to stay put and went to check it out. He was
still some fifteen feet away when he stopped, stared, and scratched
his head. There was a lot of trash all right, but... *What the hell is
that?* he thought. *It's a practical joke, right? Has to be.* Lying among
the trash was... *What is it, some sort of department store
mannequin?*

But it wasn't, and for a second, Mike's mind refused to accept
what he knew he was seeing. His mouth went dry as he inched
closer. *Oh, my God... No!*

What he was looking at was no department store mannequin. It
was a body, a girl, half-naked, skin the color of week-old oatmeal.
Her clothes were torn, exposing her... and then he saw her eyes.
And he put his hands to his mouth, turned and began to run toward

his son. His first inclination was to grab the boy, run to the car and get the hell out of there, but then he saw several more cars arriving, and he felt his heart go into A-fib.

"No! No, no!" he shouted, waving his arms over his head. "No game today!"

The people in the cars looked at him as if he'd gone crazy. Fortunately, one of them was his good friend, Tony Ricco.

"What's wrong, Mike?" Tony asked, rolling his window down.

"Call the cops, Tony."

"What?" Tony asked, trying at the same time to quiet the four kids in his car.

"Just do it. Call 9 1 1 and tell them to get here quick."

And then he began to run from car to car telling the occupants that the game was canceled. But no one was listening. They piled out of their cars, oblivious to the fact there was a dead girl at the edge of the field.

The situation soon got out of hand. Mike ran to the picnic tables to try to keep people away from what was obviously a crime scene until the police arrived.

Tony had his phone to his ear as he ran across the field, his kids following.

"What the hell are you doing, Mike? Here, they're on; the police." He held the phone out to his friend, who quickly snatched it out of his hand.

"Hello? Hello? Police. Yeah. My name's Mike Philips. I'm at Swiss Valley Park. There is a dead girl here. Yes. Dead! Right. I don't know if she's breathing or not. I didn't get that close; she looks dead to me. Look, you'd better hurry. We had a game today and people are starting to arrive," Mike said, looking at Tony, who clapped his hand over his mouth and quickly gathered his kids to him.

Within minutes they heard the sirens in the distance, but by the time the police arrived, so had both peewee football teams and all the parents. The crime scene was a circus.

2

I woke with a start. It was that day again, September 26th, sixteen years to the day, the very day. The thought punched me in the head like some kind of morbid alarm clock. I didn't think about it yesterday, and I probably wouldn't think about it tomorrow, but today... *Geez, here we go again.*

I lay there in bed, eyes wide open, staring up at the ceiling, fully aware of the horrible realization of what day it was staring me in the face.

I closed my eyes and it all came flooding back. The case was a bad one from the get-go. When I set foot on that football field with Harry Starke all those years ago, we were mad as hell at everyone who was there: at least sixty people, adults and kids. It was a homicide detective's worst nightmare: a half-a-hundred people tramping around the crime scene. That poor girl was being treated like some sort of sideshow, a spectacle.

My name, by the way, is Catherine "Kate" Gazzara. I'm a homicide detective, a captain with the Chattanooga Police Department. At the time, I hadn't been a detective very long, not even a year, and I was partnered with Harry Starke, which was cringeworthy enough all by itself, but just imagine arriving at a murder scene... That was bad enough, but it was the way all those people were behaving that makes me dread thinking about it. Yet, every September 26th, I recall that long-ago morning in vivid detail.

"Georgina Harrison," I muttered out loud and shook my head on the pillow, hoping the images would go away; they didn't. They never do.

Every cop has an unsolved case they can't let go... Actually, if the truth be told, I think every cop has at least a half a dozen cases that stick with them. Georgina Harrison was mine. I can't tell you why... Maybe it was because she was just a teenager, sweet sixteen, that it stuck in my craw. Maybe it was the sight of... you don't want to know. Maybe it was because I was still a rookie when I accompanied Harry to the crime scene that god-awful day. Maybe it was all of those things, but try as I might to move on, I couldn't. And every year on September 26th, the memory of that terrible day came flooding back to haunt me. And every year I opened the case file, flipped through it, and then closed it again. *This time though...*

The following morning, Monday, September 27th, I woke late. I looked at my bedside clock. It was almost seven. And damn, I didn't want to get up. The blankets were warm, the temp outside was in the low forties, as I recall, and it was raining. I thought about calling in sick, something I've never done. The thought lasted but a moment before I pushed it aside. And then I heard the coffeepot coughing and spluttering. It was on a timer—much better than an alarm clock—and within seconds I could smell the coffee so I threw off the covers, sat up, my head swimming, swung my legs off the bed, stood, and staggered out into the kitchen.

Dressed only in a tee and underwear, I sat shivering on a bar stool, cradling my first cup of the day. I sipped, sipped again, closed my eyes and let the bitter nectar go to work on my brain and body.

I finished my coffee and headed to the shower. Minutes later, my skin the color of a lobster, I stepped out a new woman... Well, hardly new. I would be forty-three next month, but you get what I mean, right? Anyway, I dressed in my usual work attire: jeans and a white V-neck sweater over a navy shirt and then made myself a piece of toast. Routine, right? It would have been but for a couple of things: Georgina Harrison and Chief Gunnery Sergeant Wilcox Dorman; more about him later.

~

I finished my coffee, stuffed the last bite of toast into my mouth, went to the bathroom and checked my makeup—I never wear much, just a touch of blush and a little Pink Porcelain lipstick. Then I clipped my weapon and badge onto my belt, slid into a tan leather jacket and headed out the door.

It's about a ten-minute drive from my apartment to the police department on Amnicola Highway. I checked the time—it was just a couple of minutes after seven-thirty. *Yay! Time enough to swing by Starbucks and grab a Venti to go.* And I did.

I walked into the PD at five minutes to eight, went to my office, closed the door, set my coffee on my desk, and sat down. I glanced at the coffee maker on the credenza at the far side of the room, picked up my big black Venti, and smiled to myself. I love my coffee maker, but there's something about a Venti... But I digress.

"September 26th," I muttered, then sipped my coffee and closed my eyes. I took a deep breath, opened them again and looked at my desk phone: the glowing red button told me I had messages. *No, not this morning!* I thought and, rising to my feet, and with my coffee in hand, I left my office and went down to the morgue.

The morgue! An apt name for a dreary basement room that most cops avoid like the plague. Well, not all of us. Some of us, like me, are gluttons for punishment and drawn like flies to a dead body to the place where cold cases go to die. Oh, we all have to go down there once a year to review our cold cases, which usually means a cursory glance through the files, a signature, and we're out of there, back to the real world. There were literally hundreds of them, packed in banker's boxes and stacked on shelves eight feet high. All of them labeled, dated, and with the investigating officer's name appended thereon, but all of them were missing that one important word that would allow them to be laid to rest forever: CLOSED.

And so, that morning, September 27th, 2019, when I entered the morgue, as I strolled slowly between the racks, I glanced at the labels, half-hoping I might spot something else that would distract me from my nemesisicle quest—is that a real word? Well, I didn't, though it might have been a whole lot more fun to solve someone else's cold case.

Oh yeah, I thought about it, but I couldn't shake that guilty feeling... *Yeah, that's what it is, guilt.*

Try as I might, I couldn't shake it. Every year I'd told myself it wasn't my fault, and every year, deep down, I knew we could have done better. I felt like I owed it to the victim to try one more time. And so I was drawn like a magnet to the banker's box, discolored with age, the label with Georgina Harrison's name thereon peeling away at the edges, the corners of the lid broken. There it sat, my own personal Elf on the Shelf, at eye level, exactly where I'd left it a year ago to the day, and I knew it was waiting for me.

3

I pulled the box down from the shelf. It seemed heavier than I remembered. *Yeah, that's because it's loaded up with my guilt of sixteen years' inaction... Well, not this frickin' time. This time I'm going to put you to rest once and for all. Come on, Sweetheart, let's go talk to the Chief.*

And so I hauled the box up to the first floor, entered the Chief's outer office only to find that Linda, his PA, was absent from her desk.

I hesitated, shrugged, dropped the box onto a chair, took a deep breath, and knocked on Chief Wesley Johnston's office door.

"What?" he shouted. And I knew immediately I'd caught him in a bad mood. *Shit! Just my frickin' luck.*

With teeth clenched, I grabbed the door handle, turned it, pushed the door open, stuck my head inside, smiled sweetly, and said, "Hey, Chief, it's me. D'you have a minute?"

"I do. I'm glad you're here. Sit down, Captain."

Oh hell. I'm in trouble again.

Oh yeah, those were never good words to hear from the Chief.

They either meant more work or I was in trouble with Internal Affairs... again.

I rolled my eyes and sat down in front of Chief Johnston's massive oak desk. And as I did so, I sighed, annoyed, a little louder than I'd intended.

He narrowed his eyes and said, "Something wrong, Catherine?"

He used my full name. That was another warning sign that I was in the...

"I don't know, Chief. You tell me. What did I do now?" I asked, resignedly, expecting to hear the worst.

He smiled, and that was even scarier. Two rows of perfect teeth shone below the famous Hulk Hogan mustache. That and his shiny baldness made his head look like a grotesque grinning skull, and then he chuckled. It sounded like water gurgling in the drain at the back of my washer.

"Relax, Kate. I did want to see you, but not because you did anything..." He paused, glared at me across the desk and then continued, "Unless there's something I don't know about. Is there?" he said ominously.

"No, no... NO!" I spluttered. "Of course not. I just wanted to—"

"Good," he said, interrupting me. "We'll get to your wants in a minute. I want to talk to you about Lennie Miller's replacement. He'll be with you in a couple of days. There are... hmm, a few things you should know about him." The Chief cleared his throat. "His name is Jack North. This is his last stop, Kate," he said seriously. "If he doesn't work out with you, he won't work out at all. His IA file is six inches thick and, like you, he doesn't work well with others."

"What are you talking about? I work just fine with others." I tried to sound wounded; it didn't work.

"Oh yeah?" Chief Johnston looked at me like I'd just insulted his wife.

"Well... usually," I said. "Chief, I have a good team now. That makes a big difference. I get along."

"Sure you do. Instead of the complaints coming from other officers, they now come from the civilian population, the media people in particular."

"What you call civilians I call criminals, and as for the media, there's not a cop in the department that has a good word to say about any of them. Do you really think I care if their feelings get hurt? Cut me a break, Chief." *Geez, did I just step over the line... again?*

It was true, though. I'd had a couple of incidents with a couple of my co-workers, and one, in particular, was a superior. But that was all water under the bridge. I'd closed some difficult cases and even a couple that weren't just cold but on ice. I didn't deserve this kind of "talking to." But I also knew better than to keep needling the Chief.

"Like I said," he said wryly. "North will be here in just a couple of days. I want you to welcome him. Lennie's gone and we're all hurting. You maybe most of all, even if you still refuse to show it."

Those words stung like a smack in the mouth, and I had to bite my tongue to make sure my eyes didn't begin to water.

"But, Kate," Johnston continued, "North's going to need help if he's to salvage his career. Consider it extra credit and keep him busy and out of trouble."

There was no arguing about it; it was a done deal as far as the Chief was concerned. So, I inwardly took a deep breath and said, "Yes, sir. I'll look after him."

I looked at my watch, then I looked at the Chief, my eyebrows raised in question. You don't change the subject on the Chief unless he tells you to.

"Was there something else, Catherine?"

"There was, is."

"Let's hear it then."

"Do you remember the Georgina Harrison case?" I asked.

"Of course. How could I forget it?"

"I'd like to take another look at it," I said quickly.

Johnston leaned back in his chair, set his elbows on the armrests, steepled his fingers, set them to his mouth, pursed his lips as if he was kissing his fingertips, and stared across the desk at me.

"You worked that with Sergeant Harry Starke, didn't you?" he said after a long moment. It was a question to which I knew he already knew the answer.

"Yes, sir."

He nodded again.

"And you've already pulled the case file from the morgue?"

"I have."

I could have bleated about how every anniversary of the girl's death, I... but I didn't. Johnston would have taken it as a sign of weakness, which it wasn't.

"That was a bad one, Kate... All right. Give it another shot. But if you find you've hit the same wall you did back in '04... well, no big loss. Just don't get too wrapped up in it. You already have a full caseload." He switched his gaze back to the papers on his desk in front of him.

"Anything else?" he asked without looking up at me.

"No, sir," I said, standing up quickly. I opened my mouth to speak again but changed my mind and turned and headed toward the door.

"Kate, don't forget what I said about North. I'm counting on you."

"I understand," I said and left.

I picked up the box, nodded to Linda, now back behind her desk, and I went to my office just a few doors down the hall from the Chief's. I kind of inherited it when I was promoted to captain and its previous occupant, Assistant Chief Henry Finkle, was transferred.

It was a nice office, probably better than I deserved, and I loved it. It was huge, with an expensive walnut desk, a round walnut conference table, big enough to seat six, and chairs to match, and... the thing I loved most, my own personal coffee maker.

And so, having set my Venti down while I was in the morgue and left it there, I put my box down on the table and set about making myself a fresh cup of Italian roast. You know where I got that from, right? Right, it's Harry Starke's favorite beverage, and I have to smile every time I push the button to set the coffee brewing.

I sat down at my desk to await my brew, and I couldn't help but stare at the weathered banker's box. It held a strange fascination for me, magnetic. I almost gave in to the urge to open it, but I didn't. I had other things to worry about before I could dive into that.

It was my fault that Lennie was dead. Of course, there are a million people, including the police department's resident shrink, who continue to insist that it wasn't my fault, but I know better.

Had Lennie not been forced to babysit me, he'd still be alive today. And now I had his replacement to babysit, and he sounded like a real head-case, too. I still wasn't ready. I wasn't ready to see anyone in Lennie's seat or taking on his job. And that in itself was another problem. Lennie was my computer guy, my own personal geek, and this guy, North, I didn't care how well trained he was, he'd never fill Lennie's shoes. And I knew I wasn't the only one who felt that way; my entire team would too.

"Okay, Kate. Let's get it together," I said to myself. "We have things to do, people to meet, coffee to drink, yay!"

4

And that's what I did. I grabbed the cup from the machine and sat down at the table with the big box in front of me... and I stopped to think. *How the hell am I going to tell my team about Lennie's replacement?*

Lennie's cubicle in the situation room was still just as he left it. It was almost like he hadn't died at all, but had just left the room for a few minutes. Once his replacement took up that space, however... When Detective Jack North dropped his backside onto Lennie's chair, the fact that none of us was ever going to see Lennie again would hit home like a kick in the gut. They had to be warned, but that wasn't something I wanted to handle, but I also knew it was one of those "the sooner, the better" deals.

So, I decided to make myself a second cup and call the guys in, and we'd discuss Detective North and Georgina Harrison's cold case.

I stood, went to my desk, and picked up the phone to make the call, and then I put it down again. There were a million things I needed to address before I talked to everyone. I looked at the clock. It was still only a little after nine. *Plenty of time... Not!*

My desk was a mess, not that that had ever made a difference. I had about two dozen emails to answer that were already a day old... Okay, so what was a few more minutes? *More than I want to waste, is what!*

My muscles tightened. I would have given almost anything to be able to go to the gym and get in a few reps, maybe even a jog around the park.

Of course, I was sure the ladies' bathroom needed cleaning, and the drunk tank, and had someone told me I could get out of telling my team about Jack North if I'd just scrub them down, I would have done it. But there was no such offer on the table and time was running out.

Not only that, but I also had that sinking feeling in my gut that Chief Johnston was keeping an eye on me, ready to pounce if I didn't get it done. So, I shook my head, girded up my loins, grabbed the phone again and made the call.

"Janet, I need everyone in my office, like now. Handle it for me, will you please? Oh, and tell them they'll need to bring coffee; we're in for a long session."

Now, I think, would be a good time to tell you about my team. The word team might be a little ambiguous; there are only three of them... There were four but, well, that's what the meeting was about, that and the Harrison case.

Sergeant Janet Toliver: she's an enigma. A bubbly little thing of twenty-six, she still looks like a schoolgirl, and she never seems to change. Her hair is fiery red, her eyes as green as emeralds, nose upturned, freckles. She comes across more as a cheerleader than a detective, which can be a two-edged sword: at first meeting she gets little respect, but that soon changes when you realize she has a brain like a scalpel and that she can cut you to pieces with her repartee.

When my old partner, Lonnie Guest, retired a couple of years ago—actually he just up and quit—Chief Johnston decided I needed a partner and—would you believe—he assigned his own PA to me. At first, I wasn't happy about it. She was young, and a rookie, and I didn't want to have to fool with the new kid, but I soon found out that she's a natural and proved herself to be one hell of a good detective.

Sergeant Arthur Hawkins is the oldest member of my trio, affectionately called Hawk. He's a good-looking dude, a detective of the old school, a suit and fedora man—though the fedora is long gone—a crusty, stoic old bird that says little but sees everything. He's rapidly approaching retirement, but you know, I've always had the feeling that the man would never accept full-time retirement. He was a handsome guy for someone pushing sixty-four.

Detective Anne Robar, the third member of my team, is a few years older than me. Anne lives in a house full of males: her husband, two teenage sons and two dogs: Fang and Brutus. I'd often heard her say that dealing with Chattanooga's derelicts was not much different from dealing with teenagers, especially the ornery ones who had unengaged parents. While she never could be called a beauty, she is a striking woman: prematurely graying hair cropped very short, a round face, hazel eyes surrounded by crow's feet—the woman had spent far too many hours in the sun without protection and now she was suffering for it. At five-ten, she's not quite as tall as me, but she carries herself with attitude, and she doesn't take any crap from anyone.

Janet arrived first as she almost always did, armed to the teeth with her phone, yellow note pads, digital recorder, iPad, laptop—the works.

"Morning, Captain," she said, dumping her gear on the table. "I need to go back and grab my coffee. Back in a mo!" and she left again without waiting for me to speak.

That young lady is beginning to take me for granted. Hah, I'll soon put a stop to that.

Hawk followed Janet, sans anything, his hands stuffed into his pants pockets, jacket wide open revealing a Glock 17 and his badge. He took a seat at the table as far away from my desk as he could, folded his arms and rocked the chair back onto its hind legs.

Ann walked in carrying her iPad and also took a seat at the table, her back to me, on the opposite side to Hawk. They got along together well, but Hawk always managed to say something that...

"Hey, Janet. Leave the door open, please," I said as she returned.

"Forgotten anything?" I asked her sarcastically, poking fun at her for all the stuff she carries around. She took no notice—she knew me only too well—and sat down smiling sweetly.

"I'm not going to wish y'all good morning," I said, stepping around my desk and taking a seat at the table between Hawk and Ann, "because it isn't. I've just come from an interview with the Chief."

I looked around. All three faces were expressionless. They all knew that an interview with the Chief was never a good thing.

"All right," I said, tapping my fingers on the table. "The first item on the agenda you're not going to like, so I'm just going to get it done with and out of the way. Lennie's replacement, Detective Jack North, will be joining our team in a couple of days, and I want y'all to make him welcome."

They looked at each other then back to me, but no one said a word.

"Now," I continued, "I know it's not going to be easy, but we have to face it: Lennie's not coming back, and we need a computer guy. So, I want everyone to play nice, got it?"

I looked at Robar. I had a feeling the news would hit her the hardest; she and Lennie had had a special back-and-forth relationship that was more like a pesky younger brother and his too-cool big sister. I was right, her eyes began to water, but she said nothing.

"When's the big unveiling?" Hawk asked.

"I didn't get an exact date. No later than Wednesday, I think." I shrugged.

Janet sniffed loudly. She also had tears in her eyes but wiped them quickly away. I took a deep breath.

"Any questions, anyone?" I asked.

"Yeah, I do," Hawk said, his arms still folded, his chair still on its back legs. "I know North. He's a bit of a rebel. Almost got himself fired a couple of times. He's a loose cannon. We're going to have to keep a close eye on him."

That didn't go down well with Ann and Janet. Me? My first instinct was to snap back at Hawk, tell him to give the new guy a break before he made judgments, but I didn't. I figured it was just as well to get North's perceived lack of discipline out in the open. While such shortcomings were almost always detrimental, they could also be an asset, Harry Starke being an extreme example.

"Agreed!" I said dryly, gifting him with a look that should have withered him, but it didn't; he just sat there looking at me with that oh-so-enigmatic expression he does so well.

"Now, let's move on," I said, "unless anyone else has something to say." No one did.

"This," I said as I tapped the banker's box, "is why I went to see the Chief, not knowing that he wanted to see me, but that's beside the point. This was one of my first cases... well, it wasn't mine. It was Harry Starke's. I was his partner back then. Again, that's beside the point. The point is, we never solved it... and it's been bugging the hell out of me ever since. Yesterday was the anniversary of Georgina Harrison's death and we're reopening the investigation, and I want it solved; I want it *closed*..."

I quickly took them through the details of the case then said, "Janet, I want you to make copies of the casefile and pass them around, and then you can make a start on the storyboard." I waved my hand at the big whiteboard on the wall opposite my desk.

"Then I'd like you all to read the casefile and thoroughly familiarize yourselves with it. In the meantime, I'm going to talk to Doc Sheddon. He handled the autopsy. Maybe he'll remember something helpful. We'll meet here again this afternoon at two o'clock, and I'll want input from you, okay?"

They all nodded. I could see that Janet was itching to get her hands on the box.

"One last thing," I said, "and then y'all can get out of here. Ann, when Detective North shows up, I want you to take him in hand, bring him up to speed."

She rolled her eyes but nodded. With that, I sent everyone on their way to get started. Me? I made a quick phone call, then grabbed my purse and my to-go cup of coffee and left to go meet with Doc Sheddon at the Medical Examiner's Office. *Geez, just what I need to clear my head... oh yeah!*

You may think I wasn't looking forward to my foray to Doc's little house of horrors, but you'd be wrong... On that day anyway. If I'd have been attending a postmortem, I certainly wouldn't have been looking forward to it, but I wasn't, and I was, looking forward to it, I mean. If any of that makes sense.

You see, there's something about the smell of strong disinfectant, the squeaky-clean environment, the bright lights and Doc Sheddon's tacit sense of humor that usually made me feel better. He had an unusual way of reminding me that life wasn't all dead teenagers and unpunished bad guys, that there was still order in the chaos if you knew where to look for it. And, if you were lucky, there was a person who never let sudden death get to him. Doc, for me, is that person and the epitome of the gallows humorist. No, he wasn't a morbid man; far from it. It was just his way of dealing with reality, and I liked it... I liked him.

5

When I pulled up at the ME's office, I was surprised to see another car parked beside Doc Sheddon's. *Who does that belong to, I wonder?*

I walked through the front door into the small reception area to be confronted by a face I'd never seen before. It wasn't a surprise. It wasn't uncommon to see a new receptionist at the Medical Examiner's office. Doc was hard on his receptionists; most of them had no idea what they were in for when they applied for the job. He used a temp agency, and they always did their best to warn the applicants that it wasn't a job for the squeamish.

Nor was it a job for anyone who thought they could bring change to the way things were done at the ME's offices, had been done for the past two and a half decades. Moving files or ordering tea instead of coffee or staring at the cadavers was enough for him to request a replacement. That always took time, and so when that happened the inestimable Mrs. Sheddon would fill in which, in my opinion was Doc's plan all along. He wanted his wife to work with him; she, however...

"Hi," I said, pulling aside my jacket to show my badge. "Captain Gazzara to see Doc Sheddon."

"Oh, uh, do you have an appointment? I don't see you on the calendar," the young woman said. She was nervous and skittish as a mouse as she flipped through the pages of her appointment book.

"I do," I replied. "I called him earlier."

"Oh, good, well, just give me a second while I let him know you're here." She picked up the phone, tapped the screen.

"Yes? What is it?" I heard Doc snap.

"I'm... I'm sorry to bother you, Doctor. There's a Captain Gazzara here to see you. Do you want me to bring her back?"

"Bring her back? Of course not. She knows the way. Send her through."

I wanted to smile, but I didn't. The poor girl had a lot to learn, and I wasn't about to make her life any more difficult than it already was.

"You can go on through," she said, sounding a little chastened.

I nodded, started for the hallway, then turned to her and said, "Don't let him get you down. He's a pussy cat, I promise, but you have to stand your ground. He respects that. You'll see."

"Thank you," she said. "I'll try my best."

I nodded and continued along the hallway to find Doc in Examination Room 3; I could see him through the window in the door. I knocked, opened it and stuck my head inside, but before I could speak...

"What are you doing standing out there?" he shouted. "Waiting for a bus? Come on in."

"I wish. One that would take me away to Florida for some sunshine. Do you have any coffee?" I said as I stepped into the room.

As usual, he had a guest stretched out on the table. An older man, in his late fifties, I guessed, and overweight with thinning hair and naked as the day he was born. *Oh dear. I was hoping... Oh, never mind!*

"Over on the counter. But it's cold," he said. "You can warm it up in the microwave or make a new pot; your choice."

I chose cold. I wasn't there to make coffee for him, and cold coffee was better than none.

"You sure do know how to impress a girl," I said as I strolled over and filled a Styrofoam cup with what was left in the pot.

"I do, don't I?" he said seriously. "Come here. Look at this. Fifty-nine years old. Heart attack. Family is squabbling over his finances and one of them insists there was some kind of foul play, which is why he's here." He shook his head. "The poor guy probably died just to get away from them."

"Well, if you wouldn't mind taking a break," I said, "I'd like to take you on a stroll down memory lane. The Georgina Harrison case. I'm sure you remember it, right?"

"Yes, I remember that one." Doc furrowed his brow and closed his eyes. "A real mess, as I recall." He opened his eyes and continued, "Senseless. Absolutely senseless. Such a pretty girl."

"It was, wasn't it?" I said. "So, I'm taking another crack at it." I grabbed a metal stool, set it at the head of the examining table and sat down.

He grinned at me and sat down opposite me on the other side of the table.

"Don't mind Mr. Jenkins, here," he said, tapping the corpse gently on the shoulder. "He won't mind if we speak over him. Yes, I remember it well. It was the one where the crime scene was completely destroyed by the rubberneckers. Unbelievable how people can act." He shook his bald head and looked down his nose at the cadaver.

"Give me a minute, Kate. I'll go find the file. No point asking Mary to do it; she'll be all day."

"The new receptionist?" I asked as he got up and headed for the door. "She seems nice. You need to give her a chance."

But he hurried on out without replying and returned a couple of minutes later with the file.

"I did give her a chance," he said. "I gave her a job, didn't I?"

"That's not what I meant and you know it, you old reprobate. Be nice to her. Let her find her feet. She'll do fine."

"Hurumpf," he growled as he sat down, opened the file and flipped through papers and photographs. Harry always said that Doc reminded him of Bilbo Baggins, but to me he was more the Doc of the Seven Dwarfs. He had white hair at the sides of his head, was bald on top, wearing half-glasses, and his cheeks were fat and rosy. When he smiled his eyes became crescents that glittered in the harsh light of the examination room.

I spoke up while he was looking through the file. "She had dirt and debris under her fingernails," I said. "And of course, apart from the wound to her neck, there were the cuts on her breasts. Other than that, nothing found at the crime scene could be used because of contamination."

"Yes," Doc replied pensively. "Those markings on her breasts were not precise, yet they were indeed deliberate carvings. Hmm... I determined that they were made by a different weapon than the one that was used to slit her throat." He looked up at me and said, "I stand by my initial finding that this was some sort of ritual killing."

I rolled my eyes. "Doc, that whole satanic panic vibe that was popular in the 1980s... It doesn't really translate to the new millennium."

"Are you saying you don't accept my findings?" Doc looked shocked.

Careful now, Kate. Think before you answer that.

"I don't know what to believe," I said. "I didn't then, and I don't now. I'm not sure that almost decapitating the girl and then stabbing her multiple times—how many was it, twenty-three? And cutting her makes for a ritual killing. You of all people know that the world produces evil people with evil needs and desires. We see their handiwork almost every day; that's the worst of being a cop. This was a bad one, Doc, but we can rest assured it won't be the worst thing I see before I retire; neither you nor me." I took a sip of my cold coffee.

"What is your opinion then?" he asked.

I shrugged, and said, "The usual: jealousy, rage, love, hate. One of those. It always is, isn't it?"

"Not always, Kate. You left out money and fun. It couldn't have been about money; she was too young. There are, however, people out there that do this kind of thing just for the fun of it. And I don't see any other reason for what they did to her postmortem; the cuts to her breasts were made after death."

He paused, cleared his throat, and then continued, "Look, Kate, I'm not saying they conjured Satan himself by torturing this poor girl. I'm just saying that if they, *whoever they* are, thought they were doing Satan's work, then it doesn't matter if the vibe is prevalent or not... Richard Ramirez—remember him?—thought he was doing the righteous thing by serving the Prince of Darkness. It still got him locked up in jail until 2013 when he died of lymphoma. Hardly a glamorous exit for Satan's right-hand man."

"But Ramirez was a serial killer, and a rapist," I said. "There have been no other murders to match this one. Not once since this one in 2004. It was a one-off, Doc. Don't you think that if it was a ritual killing, *they* would have done it again?"

It wasn't that I thought Doc was wrong. He could well have hit the nail on the head. But if I had a nickel for every lunatic with blood on his hands that said, "the devil made me do it," I'd be rich.

"I can't say, and neither can you," he replied. "Maybe there have been more that we don't know about. Maybe the perpetrators learned from Georgina and have perfected their craft." Doc shrugged.

"Geez, Doc. Thanks for that. It's bad enough I have to figure out what happened to Georgina, but now you've gotten me thinking I should be peeking under every rock for more victims. That's all I need." I shook my head. "I guess I need to have my new guy do a search, whenever he gets here."

"Oh, I'm sorry if I made more work for you," Doc said, smiling happily.

"Sure, you are," I muttered. "So, you think it was more than one person?"

"I do. There were no injuries to the head, so she wasn't unconscious, poor thing. She must have been held down, hence the debris under her fingernails," he said as he flipped through his notes. "I'll ask you again, did you ever look into these markings? Maybe there's a clue there?"

"Doc, I'm telling you, they're just torture wounds made by some psycho who's managed to blend into society for all these years."

"When she was already dead? Oh, do come on, Kate."

I have to say that I didn't see what Doc was seeing. He was sure the cuts to Georgina's upper chest: on her breasts to be precise, were symbols of some sort. But I wasn't convinced. To me, they looked like someone had taken a blade to her and enjoyed the moment.

"As you wish," Doc said, flipping through several more pages. "We'll agree to disagree until you come to your senses and see that I'm right. We did find marijuana in her system but nothing noteworthy. She'd had sex prior to her death, but there was no tearing or bruising and there was no semen present—her partner used a prophylactic—so I have to believe it was consensual."

"A condom?" I asked, wrinkling my nose. "You think?"

He gave me one of his "are you questioning me" looks and said, "Yes. I found traces of lubricant. That good enough for you?"

"Yes, sir," I said, suitably chastened.

Doc closed the file and laid it down on the table at his side. "I'll take the file home with me and give it another look... Yes, that's what I'll do, and I'll ask Mrs. Sheddon her opinion."

"It's pretty graphic," I said. "Do you really think you should be showing it to her?" I asked, knowing full well that Doc's wife was a steel magnolia if ever there was one.

"It'll give her something to do other than bothering me," he grumbled.

"I don't know why you don't just go ahead and hire her," I said. "She'd make a great receptionist. You do go through them like crap through a goose. At least she'd be reliable."

"Are you insane, Kate? Has the heat in here affected your brain?" he said, rising to his feet.

"You're the boss," I said amiably, also rising. "I take it we're done, right?"

"Right! Now go on, get out of here. If I find anything new, I'll call you," he said, shooing me out of the examination room.

"Please do," I said as I headed back toward the front entrance.

I was saying goodbye to the receptionist when Doc came bustling after me.

"Kate, a minute, if you please. There is something else worth mentioning, I think. Do you, by any chance, remember all the hoopla back in 2004? It was all over the news... about the night sky?"

I stared at him, uncomprehending.

"Of course you don't. You wouldn't, would you? Well, let me tell you then: from September 21st through September 27th there were some weird happenings going on in the night sky. Very interesting, as I remember it. There was one of those meteor showers and there was a blood moon that year too." He smiled triumphantly. "Those are very rare eclipses, but they usually occur in November... I think. Oh well, never mind. There certainly was a full moon the night she was murdered," Doc said, putting his hands on his hips. "And you know all about the full moon, don't you, Kate?"

"You're sure about that?" I asked, and immediately bit my tongue. That's not a question you ask Doc Sheddon. But he didn't seem to notice. He just nodded, absentmindedly.

Now I know exactly what you're thinking. You're thinking we're both full of it, that the effect the full moon has on the crazies is just a myth, an urban legend. Well, I'm here to tell you that it isn't. It is a well-known fact at every police department around the world that during a full moon, the crime rate goes up. You don't believe me? Just ask any cop and he or she will tell you it's true.

If Doc was right, and Georgina's murder took place during a blood moon, or even a full moon, and the crime scene was destroyed by a bunch of crazies, then hell, maybe there was something to his theory.

I stared at him, not knowing what to say.

"Ah-hah!" he said. "Not quite so skeptical now, are you? I remember because there's supposed to be another blood moon quite soon."

I slowly shook my head, not wanting to believe but, though I hated to admit it, it was an interesting factoid, and one worth thinking about... or was it?

"I still think," I said hesitantly. "I think... Hell, I don't know what to think; it's nuts. The Chief will pitch a fit if I lay that one on his desk."

He smiled benignly at me, and once again I was reminded of Doc from the Seven Dwarfs.

I nodded, smiled weakly at the receptionist who was staring at us bug-eyed over our conversation. I wasn't sure what she expected from her new job, but she must have known that many of Doc's patients would be murder victims. Well, if she hadn't before I arrived, she sure as hell did when I left, and I was sure I left the poor girl reevaluating her career choice.

I said goodbye, gave Doc a wry look, to which he gifted me with a wide smile, and I went to my car. I slid in behind the wheel and sat quietly for a few moments, contemplating Doc's theory. I let the engine run to warm up the car. I made notes, I thought about it, made more notes and as I did so, I tried to visualize what might have happened that moonlit night back in 2004 and... I shivered: not from the cold, but from the images my vivid imagination conjured up. And I felt infinitely sorry for the kid and shuddered at the thought of what she must have gone through.

Truth be told, I was feeling pretty shitty myself. All this talk about blood moons and ritual killings and Satanists in Chattanooga. Unbelievable! Yeah, that's what it was, and I didn't believe it. Not really, but then again, Doc's point was well taken. Just because I didn't believe in any of that crap, didn't mean my killer, or killers, didn't. *Oh geez. He will. Johnston will pitch a fit!*

I thought some more, then gave it up as a lost cause. I got hold of myself, jerked the car into drive, and then drove the three blocks back to the department and my office, hoping that my team had come up with something... anything.

6

The short drive from the forensic center to the department seemed to take much longer than its usual couple of minutes. I wondered why. No, not really; I had a lot to think about.

Fortunately, my office is on the ground floor, far away from the hustle and bustle of the situation room on the second floor, so I was able to sneak in unobserved. I closed the door, set the coffee maker to work, and then sat down at the table—Janet had returned the banker's box to its former resting place, *so thoughtful of her*. She'd also made a start on the storyboard.

And so, as I sat at the table waiting for my brew, I stared up at the big board and studied the photographs and the notes Janet had added in her oh-so-precise script. *Geez, how does she do that?* Good question: my own handwriting was abysmal; only I could understand it, and not even me after a couple of weeks.

An 8x10 headshot of Georgina Harrison took the top center spot on the board, and my gaze lingered there for a minute until I heard the coffee maker utter its last strangled gasp. I stood to go get my brew, never once taking my eyes from the haunting photograph of the sixteen-year-old murder victim. *She sure as hell looks different than the girl in the crime scene photos,* I thought as I stirred a little cream into my coffee.

I sighed, returned to my seat, set my cup down, leaned across the table and dragged the box toward me. I opened it, took out the casefile, opened that, flipped through the pages until I found the autopsy report and began to read:

Hamilton County Medical Examiner's Office

Postmortem Examination Of The Body Of

Georgina Harrison

Case Number DS-903-Autopsy

A postmortem examination of the body of a 16-year-old Caucasian female identified as Georgina Harrison is performed at the Hamilton County Medical Examiner's Office. The examination is conducted by Richard Sheddon, MD.

In Attendance:

In the performance of her usual and customary duties, Forensic Anthropologist Carol Oats is present during the autopsy. Also present during the autopsy is Detective Sergeant Harold Starke of the City of Chattanooga Police Department.

. . .

Clothing:

The body is received clad in black shorts, white sweater, white bra, white underwear and white Zebo brand tennis shoes.

Property:
Yellow gold hoop style earrings are present in both earlobes. A yellow gold bracelet is on the left wrist.

Identification:

There is a Hamilton County Medical Examiner's record tag on the right toe.

External Examination:

The body is that of a well-developed, well-nourished adolescent Caucasian female 110 pounds and 68 inches, whose appearance is appropriate for the stated age of 16 years. The body is cold. Rigor mortis is present. Livor mortis is purple, posterior, and blanches with pressure.

The scalp hair is blonde, approximately 10 inches in maximum length. The irides appear hazel with the pupils fixed and dilated. The sclerae and conjunctive are unremarkable, with no evidence of petechial hemorrhages on either. Both upper and lower teeth are natural, and there are no injuries of the tongue, gums, cheeks, or lips. The nose and ears are not unusual. The abdomen is flat. The upper and lower extremities are well developed and symmetrical, without evidence of clubbing or edema.

I dentifying marks:

N one

E vidence of Medical Intervention:

T here is no evidence of medical intervention.

E vidence of Injury:

.   .   .

Sharp Force Injuries of the Neck:

1. Sharp force injury of neck, left side, transecting left and right internal jugular veins. This sharp force injury is complex, and appears to be a combination of a stabbing and cutting wound. It begins on the left side of the neck, at the level of the midlarynx, over the left sternocleidomastoid muscle; it is gaping, measuring 6 inches in length with smooth edges. Dissection discloses that the wound path is through the skin, the subcutaneous tissue, and the sternocleidomastoid muscles with hemorrhage along the wound path and transection of the left and right internal jugular veins, with dark red-purple hemorrhage in the adjacent subcutaneous tissue and fascia. The direction of the pathway is slightly upward from left to right...

And so the damn thing went on, and on, and on, but I'll spare you those mostly technical details, mainly because I spared myself. I'd seen enough.

I stared unseeing at the report for what seemed like an age, my emotions running rampant. Finally, I shook my head and laid it aside, then looked once more at the photograph of the pretty young woman who once was Georgina Harrison. And my blood ran cold when I realized she was staring back at me... or was she? Or was it simply a trick of the light, a photographic anomaly? I didn't know, still don't, but what I do know is that whenever I looked at that photograph from then on, I always had the feeling that she was watching me.

I returned my attention to the casefile. Janet had made copies of the original suspects' photographs and returned the originals to the box. I glanced again at the wall; the five copies were taped to the board in a row just beneath the photo of Georgina, the names appended below each, along with a few cryptic notes.

Also inside the box were several more files and a large plastic evidence bag, sealed with red evidence tape that indicated it hadn't been tampered with since it was sealed in 2004. Inside that bag, I could see several more paper evidence bags; they too were sealed and signed.

I returned the plastic bag to the box unopened—I decided to do that later—and turned my attention again to the file and the five suspects.

1. Shelly Pinkowski-Brenner
2. Regis Taylor
3. Buck Halloway
4. Junior Cole
5. Lillith Morris—Now Lilith Overby

Not unexpectedly, Janet had managed to find them all, and all five of them were considered suspects in 2004. In the eyes of the law, back then, they were children, minors, making it necessary for their parents to be present during interviews. And that was always a trial, for the parents, and for Harry and me. The parents were, understandably, protective of their offspring, confrontational even. And, even today, I can't blame any of them for wanting to answer for their kids. Let's face it, no one wants to think, much less admit, that their child might be a killer. But kids are notorious liars, especially teenagers. I remembered those interviews. At sixteen, they were savvy enough to understand the system, and they, all five of them, worked it to their advantage; They covered for one another, lied for one another, and when lost for words, they shut up.

It was then, as it is now, so important for kids to blend in, to be accepted by their peers, especially when cliques are involved, even when it turns out that blending in might be the last thing they needed to do, given a situation like the one these five found themselves in.

But now we were sixteen long years on. They all were in their early thirties; thus the pool of suspects was older, more mature with families and careers to protect. I figured all I had to do was find the weak link, give it a jerk, and voila, goodnight, goodbye, case closed.

But where to begin? I scanned the five baby faces, looking for inspiration, though deep down I knew exactly where to begin: Shelly Pinkowski-Brenner. After all, she was Georgina Harrison's best friend. If anybody knew what happened that night, she did.

I looked at my watch, it was almost eleven o'clock. *Plenty of time to make a start before we're supposed to meet at two.*

I picked up the phone and called Janet.

7

Shelly Pinkowski-Brenner lived with her husband Thomas Brenner on Duane Road, a quiet street in Hixson. Traffic at that time in the morning was fairly quiet, so it was a few minutes before noon when I turned my unmarked cruiser into the semi-circular drive of a very nice two-story home and parked at the left side of the house.

It was one of those abodes you see on HGTV that boasted a mudroom, bonus room, play area, powder room, and a guest bedroom: because calling it what it really was—a four-bedroom, three-bathroom house—wasn't sexy enough.

"Doing well for themselves by the look of the house," Janet said as we stepped out of the car. "He does something in local government, I think. I didn't know those jobs paid that well."

I smiled at her and shook my head. "Do you never think positively?" I asked.

"Always," she replied brightly, "especially where a suspect is concerned. For instance, I'm positive I'm not going to like Shelly Brenner," she said as I thumbed the bell push and took a step back from the door.

"Oh, and why's that?"

"Didn't you look at her photo? She's a dyed-in-the-wool snob if ever I saw one, and she was a cheerleader. I hated cheerleaders when I was in high school; them and the jocks that fawned all over them. Talk about the high and the mighty... Well, some of them have been known to fall."

"Janet, are you speaking from personal experience?"

She just made a face and said nothing.

The door opened and Shelly Pinkowski, sixteen years on, stepped out wearing a puzzled look and a frown on her heavily made-up face.

"Yes? Can I help you?"

"I hope so, Mrs. Brenner," I said, showing her my ID. "My name is Captain Gazzara, Chattanooga PD—"

"Yes, I remember you," she said, her face hardening as she interrupted me. "You and that Starke man. What do you want?"

Do you now, I thought. *Two can play your game.*

"Yes," I said dryly, putting away my ID. "I remember you too. This is Sergeant Janet Toliver." Janet pushed her jacket aside to reveal her badge and Glock.

"We'd like a few words, if you don't mind, Mrs. Brenner."

"It's Pinkowski-Brenner. You want to talk to me about Georgie, I suppose. I can't believe this is coming up again after all this time."

"I can understand that, Mrs. Brenner," I said, ignoring her implied request for me to use her full hyphenated name.

"But the killer was never found, and there's no statute of limitations for murder. I think Georgina deserves justice, and her family needs closure. Don't you? May we come in, please?"

"Well, if you must," she said, stepping to one side to allow us to enter.

The inside of the house was... overdone, might be the right word to describe it. Built in the 1990s, the house had obviously recently been renovated, expensively. The open plan ground floor and kitchen were something I'm sure Hillary Farr would have been proud to have designed.

"Please, won't you sit down?" she said, indicating the stools at the massive kitchen island. "Can I get you some coffee? Anything at all?"

"No, thank you," I said, giving Janet a hard look—that girl never says no!

"Well then," she said, sitting down on a stool at the end of the island. "What would you like to know?"

I nodded, took my digital recorder from my purse, turned it on and set it down on the marble top in front of her. She visibly leaned away from it.

"If you don't mind," I said, "I'm going to record the interview—"

"Yes, I do mind," she said haughtily, interrupting me. "I don't know if you know who my husband is, Officer Gazzara, but he's the Assistant Public Works Director. I don't think recording a conversation about an incident that took place sixteen years ago would even be necessary," Shelly snapped, looking down her thin, pointy nose at us.

"And that's fine, Mrs. Brenner," Janet said, without a hint of hesitation and, at the same time, sliding off the stool. "Grab your purse. We'll continue this at the police department."

I so wanted to smile—Janet was right; she didn't like her.

You know, it never ceases to amaze me the way some people think the mere mention of a name or position means they don't have to abide by the same rules as everyone else. Me? I don't take that crap anymore; Shelly was going to learn pretty damn quick that she wasn't above the law.

She stared at Janet, then at me and narrowed her eyes to near slits. I thought for a minute that she was going to tell us to go to hell and then call her lawyer, but she didn't; she didn't move on her stool either. Finally, she broke, looked away, shrugged.

"Fine," she snapped. "Have it your way. Go ahead and record."

She leaned against the backrest of her stool, crossed her legs and folded her arms. *I see*, I thought. *Okay then, let the battle begin.*

I turned on the recorder and then asked her permission to record the interview.

"I just said so, didn't I?" she snapped.

"For the record, please, ma'am."

"Yes, all right. You have my permission to record. Is that good enough for you, officer?"

"That would be Captain, if you don't mind, ma'am," I said, sweetly, and smiling to myself.

I looked around, spotted a framed picture on the mantlepiece. It was a photograph of Shelly, her husband and their child.

"How old is your son, Mrs. Brenner?" I asked, looking down at my iPad.

"Justin is eight," she muttered defensively, obviously trying to let me know that she was on to my attempt to butter her up by talking nice about her kid. She was wrong! That wasn't at all my intent.

"I want you to try to imagine that what happened to Georgina that night has happened to Justin, and the police are interviewing one of his friends. Now, what do you say?"

I stared at her, silently. Janet didn't move. The color drained from Shelly's face as she pinched her lips tightly together.

It often helps to paint a picture for an interviewee. Sometimes it doesn't work, but this time it did. She'd been there that night: I knew it and she knew I did. Whether or not she'd had anything to do with Georgina's murder remained to be seen.

It took her a minute to compose herself but, finally, she took a deep breath, looked at me, tilted her head, raised her eyebrows questioningly and said, quietly, "Please, Captain, ask your questions."

I obliged.

"Would you like to tell me what happened that night, Mrs. Brenner?"

She looked away to the left—she was about to lie to me—closed her eyes, thought for a minute, then opened them again and said, "We met in the forest at our usual spot... We called it The Woods. It was, well, just a nice place where we could get together and be ourselves, talk, laugh, make out, you know," Shelly said, looking over her shoulder toward the stairs.

"Are you expecting someone, Mrs. Brenner?" I asked.

"No. I just don't want my son to hear any of this." It was probably the most honest thing she'd said so far.

"We were good kids," she continued pensively, obviously reliving the moment in her mind. "Sure, we stayed out past curfew now and then, and maybe smoked a little pot once in a while. But none of us were bad. Well, except Regis Taylor, that is, and we all know where he is."

I nodded but didn't say anything. I knew to what she was referring.

"Who is *we?*" I asked.

"Myself. Georgie. Regis Taylor. Buck Halloway, Junior Cole, and Lilith Overby. We were always together," Shelly continued. "It was Saturday, late, after midnight. We had permission. It was a special night. We were allowed to stay late to see the meteor shower... Only we didn't. Buck's father had gotten the date wrong. It wasn't due until November." There were tears in her eyes.

"Georgie and Regis were all over each other, as usual," she continued, with some difficulty. "They weren't dating, not officially."

"What were they doing, then?" Janet asked.

"What d'you think they were doing? They were screwing each other. Everybody knew, except her folks, of course." She paused, thinking.

"Georgie's family was," she continued, "quite ordinary, shall we say."

I heard Janet gasp. I knew what she was thinking: *freakin' little snob.* I knew because that was how I felt, and with what Janet had told me at the door about her feelings for cheerleaders, I figured I'd better keep her on a tight leash.

"You see," she continued, "Georgie was very pretty, and they were expecting her to land a well-to-do husband someday and lift them up a notch in society. It wasn't that they were trash. Far from it. But it was obvious from the things Georgie told me that her mother expected her to marry well. Of course, isn't that what every Southern Mama wants for her daughter?" Shelly chuckled.

Janet looked... incensed.

"However, Georgie had a thing for Regis. He was good-looking. No doubt about that. But he was trouble. You could see it in his eyes."

"How about you?" Janet asked sharply. "Did you have feelings for Regis too?"

She blinked, startled by the question, hesitated.

"No. Of course not," she replied, blushing. There it was again, the tell.

"Of course you did," I said, pushing gently. "He's a good-looking guy, right? It would be only natural for you to feel something. It wouldn't be human not to, would it?"

She looked down at the recorder, then up at Janet.

"Well, perhaps I did have a little crush on him; all the girls did. But I knew better than to act on it. First of all, Georgie was my friend. I wouldn't do something like that to her. Not only that, unlike Georgie my family does have status here in town."

Janet almost choked, but she turned it into a cough and Shelly didn't seem to notice.

"It's one thing to show kindness to a boy like Regis and be his friend," she continued. "But it would have been quite another to know him *intimately*. Besides, I was seeing Buck Halloway. We had a lot more in common."

"Buck Halloway came from a better family than Regis?" I asked, at the same time shooting Janet a warning look.

"Oh, it wasn't anything like that. I don't think I'm better than anyone else." She rolled her eyes, coyly.

"Buck and I just knew our places in society. I don't know how long it took you to develop that southern drawl, Detective, but when you've been here long enough, you'll learn that here in Chattanooga, people tend to learn your business pretty damn quick. Knowing too many intimate details about Regis could be very dangerous for someone like me."

Now it was me who was pissed. *Who the hell does this woman think she is?*

"I was born and raised on Missionary Ridge," I said dryly. "But never mind that; you did know him intimately, didn't you? Not sexually, perhaps. I mean, you guys all hung out together in high school. You were the best of friends, so you said." I had my iPad open and was reading from my notes.

Shelly took a deep breath, looked at her manicured nails, adjusted the big diamond ring on her left ring finger, but didn't reply.

"Mrs. Brenner? Isn't that what you said? You were the best of friends?"

She nodded.

"I'll take that nod as a yes," I said for the recorder.

"Your *friend* Regis. He's fallen on hard times, as you know. Have you offered him any help recently? No? I thought not! How about Buck Halloway? He was your sweetheart. Have you two ever gotten together over the years, to reminisce about the good old days, perhaps? And what about the fifth wheel in the group, Junior Cole, when did you last see him?" I asked. Yes, I was aggravated. I was letting the woman get to me, and I knew it.

"I see what's happening here!" she snapped. "It's all becoming very clear." She pursed her lips. "This is because of who my husband is, isn't it? You're looking for a way to embarrass him. And digging up this old case and tying me to Regis Taylor—the person most likely to have killed Georgina—is just the right way to smear us. Isn't that right, Detective?"

"Why you—" Janet began angrily.

"Janet, don't," I said, interrupting her before she could do any damage that would bring about an official complaint. Then I turned again to Shelly Brenner.

"I can assure you, Mrs. Brenner, that's not my intent. I was part of the original investigation in 2004. We failed to find Georgina's killer then, but I intend to set that right and bring him—or her—to justice. I couldn't care less who or what your husband is, unless he can shed some light on my investigation and the happenings the night Georgina was almost decapitated," I snapped.

Again, Shelly's face went pale. She'd obviously forgotten that Georgina's head was almost severed from her body.

I flipped through the screens on my iPad, then handed it to her and said, "Here! Take a look!"

She gazed at it. Her mouth dropped open. Tears ran down her cheeks.

"I... I didn't... know. Oh, my God! I didn't know."

I knew then that I'd probably made a mistake by showing her the photograph, but I didn't care. I had to do something to jerk this silly woman out of her crazy affected world of semi-luxury. And that it did, but it also shut her down.

"I think it's time for you to leave," she said, wiping her eyes with the back of her hand.

I nodded, picked up the recorder and turned it off, then said, "I'm sorry I had to show you that photograph, Mrs. Brenner. I know what a shock it must have been, but none of you could possibly have known what that poor girl went through that night, except her killer of course; now you do."

She sniffed, wiped her eyes again, but didn't look at me, said nothing.

"If you think of anything that might help us, anything you might remember... or have been holding back, please come and see us or give us a call," Janet said, standing and handing her a business card.

Brenner looked at her as if she was some punk kid trying to horn in at the grown-up table. Janet took no notice; she was used to it. But if I had to bet, it would be Janet that Shelly Pinkowski-Brenner would call before she called me, thinking her good cop act was for real. Little did she know that I was the one playing good cop.

We left the Brenner home without much more than we'd gone in with.

"What's your take on Mrs. Pinkowski-Brenner?" I asked Janet as we settled back in our seats in my cruiser.

"She's a first-class freakin' cow, is what I think of her. I told you, didn't I? Frickin' cheerleaders. I hate 'em! And I don't trust women who hyphenate their last names worth a damn either, and I sure as hell don't trust her," she replied flatly.

I had to chuckle. The look on her face was a picture, and well, you would've thought she'd just put her hand into something nasty.

"Is that all?" I asked, smiling.

Janet was quiet for a minute and then looked down at the notes on her yellow pad.

"Did you spot the small altar on the bookshelf in the corner and the trinkets from her high school? You didn't see it, did you?" Janet smirked. "I'm not surprised. It wasn't in the center. It was off to one side, near the window. There was a trophy: one of those things with big gold numbers—2004—and a group photograph that I assume was of the six of them. One was definitely Georgina, and one certainly looked like a younger, thinner Shelly Pinkowski. There was a votive candle on each side, and a couple of other things I didn't recognize."

"I can't believe I missed it." I shook my head.

"I can't believe she didn't say anything about it," Janet said. "You'd have thought she'd have showed us the photo, if nothing else. Maybe she forgot it was there. But there wasn't any dust around it, so the display was kept tidy."

The girl doesn't miss a thing.

"That doesn't mean anything," I said. "The entire house was spotless, but I bet she's not the one who does the dusting. In fact, I'd be willing to bet that she hasn't touched a duster in years. So, she'd probably forgotten about it... Look, she had no idea we were going to pay her a visit. If we come back in a week, though, I wonder if it'll still be there."

"I'll put it on our calendar." Janet smirked as I put the car into drive.

8

W e stopped at Hardee's for a sandwich and arrived back at the police department at one-forty-five to find Hawk and Robar at their cubicles in the situation room. They'd wasted several hours trying to talk to Buck Halloway, and it appeared they'd made no more progress with him than Janet and I had with Shelly Pinkowski.

"According to the notes in the file, Buck Halloway was Shelly's beau," Robar said, sitting on the edge of her desk, scanning her notes. "It was the weirdest thing, wasn't it, Hawk?"

Hawk, seated in Robar's chair rocking back and forth with his arms folded, his jacket off and his shirt sleeves rolled, merely nodded, his eyes half-closed.

"See," Robar continued, "we didn't get to talk to him, just his wife, Lena."

"Yeah, we didn't get but a glimpse of him," Hawk grumbled. "Damn nut case if you ask me. I spotted him when we left. The fool was peeking out of an upstairs window like some ghoul in a horror movie."

"His wife gave us some fairy story about him suffering from

depression," Robar said, swinging her leg, "and that talking to him now about Georgina's murder after all this time would be enough to trigger some kind of episode. But we did manage to squeeze a few details out of her. I don't even think she realized what she was saying.

"Anyway, when I asked her about Buck's past relationship with Shelly Pinkowski, she just shrugged and said, 'it is what it is,' present tense. That made me wonder if they were still an item, so I asked her if Buck was still seeing Shelly. She shrugged again, looked to her left and said no; a clear indication that she was lying."

"Really?" I took a seat at Lennie's empty desk and spun around on the seat so I could look at them.

"Yeah, really," Ann said.

And Robar and Hawk spent the next ten minutes describing their interview with Lena Halloway.

Their house, although it didn't sound as grand as Shelly Brenner's place, was in a nice part of town at the end of a cul-de-sac off Igou Gap Road.

"I rang the doorbell," Hawk said. "Mrs. Halloway answered, but she only opened the door a couple of inches, like she was expectin' us to bust in on her. When we identified ourselves, she stepped out onto the porch."

Hawk went on to describe Lena Halloway as a good-lookin' woman, well-proportioned, with jet black hair—obviously dyed—piled high on her head. "A real southern belle that'd make Scarlett O'Hara pea green with envy, and with an accent to match that sounded as phony as hell."

Robar flashed him a withering look, then said, "And she was definitely acting strange. We flashed our creds and told her we wanted to speak to her husband. She refused to let us in and told us in no uncertain terms that Buck was unable to talk to anyone, about Georgina Harrison's murder or anything else; he wasn't well. Here, listen," she said, tapping her iPhone and then holding it up so we could all listen.

"You thought I didn't know about it?" Lena said. "That I didn't know that Buck was sweet on that Pinkowski woman? Well I did. I know all about it. And someone just called him—I don't know who —and warned him you were coming. He won't be speaking to anyone. He has depression and is indisposed."

"Mrs. Halloway," Hawk said softly but firmly. "You do realize this is a murder investigation? Just because your husband isn't feeling good doesn't mean he can avoid talking to us."

"It's not going to happen. Right now he's in the crawl space, clinically unable to talk to anyone," Lena said.

We all looked at each other. The replay continued.

"In the crawl space?" Hawk asked. He sounded incredulous.

"It's his safe space. Look, I know all about that night. Buck told me. He said that he and his girlfriend, that Shelly Pinkowski, were in the woods at Swiss Valley Park. They were just doing what teenagers did back then. They had words, and he left early. He said he offered to walk Georgina home since they didn't live all that far from one another, but she insisted on staying with the group. That's it. That's the end of it. He left. That should satisfy any of your interest in Buck. Now please leave."

"I'm sorry, but it really doesn't work that way..." Ann tapped her phone and stopped the replay.

"Did you catch it?" Ann asked. "Lena called her 'that Shelly Pinkowski.' I'd say there's some tension between the two women. That might be something that works to our advantage. And it must have been Shelly that called him, right? No one else knew. Anyway, I handed her a card, and she went back inside and closed the door."

"That was when I backed up from the front porch to look up at the windows," Hawk said. "I guess he thought he was safe, peeking through the curtains. If it was him, had to be... didn't it?"

I had to scratch my head because we had left Shelly's house around one o'clock and according to Hawk and Robar, they arrived at the Halloway house at just after one. They'd spent an hour or so studying the file and then headed out. Whoever made that call must have known Buck's number, or even had it on speed-dial. And, since Shelly and he were a "thing" back in the day, it might not be too surprising if they'd stayed in contact.

"I'm going to guess it was Shelly who called him," Janet said.

"Couldn't have been anyone else," I said. "Add it to the calendar for our next visit."

"Halloway's wife is obviously very protective—" Ann said.

"Bossy bitch is what she is," Hawk said, interrupting her.

"Yeah, and that's coming from the guy who likes his women at home in the kitchen chained to the stove," Robar snapped, barely looking over her shoulder at Hawk.

"I never said anything about being chained," he replied, smiling.

"All right, you two," I said. "That's enough. What else happened?"

"Well, it seems that the Buckster has this weird habit of disappearing down into his crawl space whenever he's feeling low," Hawk said. "You heard the woman say that's where he was. I found that hard to believe, so I checked around the house a little. There's a crawl space all right, but it's no basement. I'd say there's barely enough room to stand upright down there."

"But you said you saw him in the window?" I looked at Hawk.

"That's right." Hawk replied.

Now, that's a strange thing to tell the police, I thought as I tried to imagine the boy from the file photos, now a grown man, scurrying down through a hole in the floor to deal with his depression. And I wasn't sure how I felt about it. Part of me wanted to laugh. But then part of me thought that maybe there was something to his behavior that we weren't seeing. I'm no shrink, but the urge to run and hide usually meant the runner had a guilty conscience.

"You didn't call her back when you saw him in the window?" I asked.

"No," Ann said. "We, that is I," she continued, glancing at

Hawk, "figured it would be a waste of time. It wasn't like he'd come down and talk to us, and maybe letting him stew a day or two might make him more willing to talk next time we pay them a visit."

"That's not good, Ann," I said. "You should have called her out; she was obviously lying, and lying to the police—"

"Yeah, that's what I said." This from Hawk.

Ann simply shrugged, unfazed, and said, "I don't think so. I made a decision and I stick by it. I'll get her next time, and him, if I have to drag him feet first out of his hole."

I nodded and said, "See that you do. Hawk, see if you can find out what Buck Halloway does all day besides huddle in his hidey-hole. Ann, I need you to get that phone number. It had to have been Shelly, but we need to know for sure. Janet, you see if you can find out what Shelly was talking about when she referred to Regis Taylor. We should probably talk to him next."

I stood up, looked down at Lennie's desk. It seemed they'd all forgotten that Lennie's replacement would be arriving soon. Now, if only I could forget it myself. I figured I needed a project of my own, and I had a good idea what that might be, so I went to my office and made a call.

9

There was something about walking into Eastwood High School that instantly transported me back to my own high school days in East Ridge. Maybe it was the smell of hand sanitizer and reams of paper, or maybe it was the colorful banners promoting the upcoming homecoming game and dance. The rows of lockers and the maroon and cream checkered floors were identical to at least a hundred other schools across the country. Seeing it all made me thankful those awkward, awful times were long in the distant past. You might think from hearing that, that I didn't enjoy my school days, and you'd be right. I didn't. I knew exactly what Janet was talking about: unless you were one of the in-crowd—which I wasn't—well... you get the idea.

With the threat of unwanted visitors entering schools these days, I had to call ahead and let the Vice Principal, Marty Egan, know I was coming. He, along with the school resource officer, was there to greet me at the doors.

I introduced myself, as did he and the officer, a Johnny Larkin, whom I knew slightly, and we were about to go inside when I happened to adjust my jacket, revealing the Glock 17 on my hip.

He looked hard at it, then at me, and I could tell Egan was considering asking me to leave it outside.

"I have to keep it on," I interrupted his thoughts. "Try and remember I'm one of the good guys. Right, Johnny?"

"She's good, sir," Larkin said.

But Egan still looked uneasy. He was a rather effeminate man with a head that looked too large for his twiggy body, and his long, boney fingers fidgeted with the green and yellow tie he was wearing.

"I'm sorry," he said, rolling his eyes. "I just don't like guns."

"No one does, until they need a cop," I replied. "Look, Mr. Egan, as I told you when we spoke on the phone, all I want to do is take a look at the 2003 and 2004 yearbooks."

"Yes, all right. I had Miss Hennessy in the library pull them for you. Can I ask what it is you're looking for?"

Inwardly I also rolled my eyes. Egan, like so many people who don't like guns, would lick his chops over the gory details of a violent crime, so I obliged him.

"One of your students, a girl, was brutally murdered back in 2004. We've reopened the case and I'm the lead investigator. I assume you weren't here in 2004, is that correct?"

"Right. I assumed the role of vice principal here five years ago. I'm originally from Virginia," he said, smiling a big toothy grin like coming from Virginia was something we Tennesseans saw as a plus.

"Well, bless your heart," I replied with a smile. "We certainly won't hold that against you, will we, Johnny?"

Johnny didn't answer; he knew better than to be dragged into a spat between me and the vice principal. He needn't have bothered. There was no spat. In fact, Egan ignored my remark and continued as if I'd said nothing.

"A murder, you say? How awful. I do think the world we're living in is getting more and more violent every year. Why, just this past spring I had two of my flowerpots broken by vandals. I called the police and made a report, but they never caught the culprits," he rambled as we walked the corridor. "And, would you believe, a lady-friend of mine had a person walk across her yard at six in the morning even though she has clearly placed signs that state: 'stay off the lawn.'"

"What do you teach here, Mr. Egan?" I asked.

"Oh, I teach geometry. I have a master's degree," he replied proudly.

"Congratulations. When did you graduate?"

"In 2006." He continued to smile pleasantly.

"Who are you related to here at the school?" I slipped the question in seamlessly.

"The principal is my cousin," he said sheepishly, looking over his shoulder, suddenly realizing what he'd let slip.

"Well now, you know what they say," I said, trying to hide my attitude but not succeeding, "It's not what you know... right?" It was bitchy of me, I know, but there was something about the man that brought out the worst in me.

Fortunately, the exchange ended at the library doors before he could reply. He held the door open for me.

"Miss Hennessy should be at the desk," he said, following me inside.

"I asked her to pull the books you were looking for," he said. "Just have her call me if you need anything else, and I'll be happy to oblige." And with that, he left me to it.

Several of the students seated at the tables looked up and studied me, whispering among themselves as I approached the desk where a middle-aged woman with a round face and pug nose also looked up at me and smiled.

"You must be Detective Gazzara," she said, in a whisper.

I nodded and whispered, "Yes."

"I thought so," she said conspiratorially. "I'm Mrs. Hennessy, the librarian. Please sit down. Mr. Egan said you wanted to review some of our yearbooks. We keep a copy from every year since 1963 when the school first opened," she continued in a hushed voice, her eyes twinkling. I had the idea that she had a litany of things she wanted to talk about but didn't know where to start.

I stuck out my hand, introduced myself, and sat down opposite her.

"It's nice to meet you, Detective... and you're a captain, my, my. Here are the yearbooks you requested."

She slid two red hardcovered books across the counter to me. They were clearly labeled in gold letters: Class of 2003 and Class of 2004.

"How long have you worked here, Mrs. Hennessy?" I asked as I picked up the Class of 2003.

"Oh, let's see," she whispered. "I came here when my own children started attending high school. That was twenty-four years ago, in 1996." She shrugged and nodded.

"So, you were here in 2004." I set the books back on the desk and leaned forward so I wouldn't have to whisper so loudly. "Do you remember Georgina Harrison?"

Her face drooped, she blinked and nodded, then said, "So that's why you're here. I should have guessed. Yes, I knew her. It was such a shame, what happened to her. She was a nice girl, and I always thought that she had a lot of potential, and would make something of herself, but..." She shook her head and stopped speaking.

"But what?" I asked.

She looked around the room, took a second to give a deadly glare and point her pencil at a table where five kids were giggling among themselves, quickly bringing quiet back to the library.

She took a deep breath, sighed, then said, "I was fond of Georgie, but you know how it is when adolescents form cliques. No matter how hard the administration tries to stop that sort of thing— we don't encourage it here—and try to persuade the children to all be friends together, it rarely works. That old saying: birds of a feather... It's so true."

"I agree," I said, still leaning on the desk.

"Georgie was part of a clique," she continued. "They were a diverse group in that Georgina and Regis Taylor were not born with silver spoons in their mouths like the other kids in their group. That always struck me as very mature. It does say something about them, doesn't it? Maybe some of the adults in the school could learn a lesson from their kids," she mused.

I flipped open 2003 and found the freshman photos of Georgina, Shelly, Lilith, Regis, Buck and Junior. They looked a lot younger than they did in the file photos.

While I looked at the photographs of the six victims: *Yes, that's what they are,* I thought, *all of them. One of them I'm sure is a killer, but the rest of them... How they all must have suffered through the years.*

Somewhere off in the background of my mind, I could hear Mrs. Hennessy droning on about the students, her memories of Georgina's class and how everyone was so disturbed by the news of what happened to her.

And then she said something that jerked me back from the past.

"It's the kind of thing that happens in the big cities, isn't it? Not here. Not in our peaceful Chattanooga." She shook her head. "Had they not made such a big deal about the moon that year, I really believe Georgina would still be here."

"What?" I asked, clearly and loudly. Behind me a group of students shushed me and then giggled among themselves.

"The moon. It was a special moon. They called it a blood moon, but I hate that term. The school was encouraging the students to get out and see it because it only happens every couple of years. I went out to see it myself. I took photos. It was beautiful. So big."

She looked at me, obviously expecting some sort of reaction, so I gifted her with a smile and a nod.

"A lot of the teachers were offering extra credit if the kids wrote about it, took pictures, did research, they really were making a big deal of it."

I flipped through the book and found several color photos of Georgina with the other kids in her group. And, like she did from the photograph in my office, she stared back at me, eyes full of life... And that was when I noticed that she and the rest of the kids in her group had red strings tied around their wrists. I'd read an article somewhere, recently about the significance of these red strings. It signifies some kind of religious belief or membership in some sort of club... Whatever it was, I couldn't readily remember exactly what it was supposed to symbolize. But it was around each of their wrists and none of the other kids in any of the other pictures had them. *Hmm, I need to check that out.*

"Mrs. Hennessy," I said, looking up at her and closing 2003 and laying it down. "Could I trouble you for the yearbooks for 2005 and 2006?"

I don't know why I didn't ask for them to begin with. Georgina's life might have ended in 2004, but the rest of them continued.

"Of course. I'll be right back," she said, standing up and stepping around the desk.

She paused at the unruly table and gave the kids a strict warning that if they didn't behave, they'd be spending Saturday morning with her.

I watched as she continued her trek across the library and smiled when the kids made faces at her back as she walked away. They saw me watching and lowered their eyes, pretending to be studying. I continued to smile: *been there, done that.*

10

I turned again to the yearbooks. Opened 2004, Georgina's sophomore year, and sure enough, Georgina and her friends were still wearing those red threads around their wrists.

The kids looked happy, like they were having fun. One thing I noticed was that Georgina always seemed to be standing close to Regis Taylor. In some instances, he had his arm around her shoulder. In others she was looking up at him.

Even at sixteen they were a serious couple, I thought. *But Shelly Brenner insisted that their relationship was nothing more than a physical attraction. It sure as hell doesn't look like that to me; those two kids were in love... well, she was.*

I opened my iPad and looked at my notes, flipped to those that referenced what Georgina's friends had said back in 2004. None of them said the two of them, Georgina and Regis, were anything more than friends. They couldn't imagine anyone hurting her. They were scared it could have been any one of them.

Mrs. Hennessy returned with the two yearbooks. Again, she glared at the unruly table as she passed by. The students had their heads down and in their books; they didn't make a peep.

"Here they are," she said as she placed them on the desk in front of me.

As I didn't have any more questions for her, at least not then, I asked if there was somewhere I could sit quietly while I studied the books.

She nodded and pointed to a row of seats that lined the back wall.

"We don't allow the children to sit back there during study hall," she said quietly. "None of them know how to behave. You should find it relatively quiet."

It was indeed quiet and before I began my review of the yearbooks, I looked at my watch. It was almost three o'clock. I'd have to hurry. School would be out momentarily.

The photos in the 2004 edition were all relatively normal: action shots of the cheerleaders, football players, basketball players, the drama club, the band and whatever they called those kids who ran around with giant flags during halftime.

I snapped 2004 closed and opened 2005. *Now we're talking,* I thought, flipping quickly through the pages.

Regis and the group were still together, minus Georgina, but he was no longer smiling; not in any of the photographs. He'd been grinning like a Cheshire cat in the previous years, but it didn't look like the rest of the group had been as affected by Georgina's death as he had. Of course, nobody expected them to grieve forever. They were, after all, children and minutes in the lives of teenagers were forever changing, jumping from one drama to the next. It was perfectly normal. But there was something about Regis that bugged me. He looked... scared.

Another thing I found a little odd about the 2005 photos was that I could no longer tell who was the leader of this pack. Regis had been, but his body language was somehow different... *What the hell happened to the boy?* I thought. There was no telling. The expressions on the five faces staring back at me were blank. I heaved a sigh and closed the book, stared at the gold lettering for a moment, then set it aside and opened 2006, their senior year, and flipped through the pages. Regis had all but disappeared from the publicity pages. His playful demeanor really had changed, but still he'd been voted most rebellious of his class. I didn't see it. Especially when there were kids with nose rings and mohawks who were passed over for the prestigious title. *Hmm... Maybe he had friends on the yearbook committee.*

The smiles were back. Lilith Morris, now Overby, was voted worst driver. Shelly and Junior Cole were both voted most likely to be your boss. I couldn't speak for Junior, but Shelly... well, she certainly was bossy.

I almost laughed when I saw that Buck Halloway had been voted by his peers to be the best candidate for the CIA. Maybe there was something to that self-exile in the crawl space routine.

Only Regis looked lost, like a whipped puppy. I was going to have to speak to him sooner rather than later. I had the undeniable feeling that the boy was hiding something. *Hmm... could he be the weak link I'm looking for?*

The bell rang, and the kids jumped up from their tables and appeared from behind the bookshelves carrying backpacks and satchels. The volume of juvenile humanity in the library seemed to have increased tenfold, and it was even worse out in the hallway. The students staggered toward the library exit like zombies, pushing their way through the fresh group— the detentionees, I assumed—that staggered in and took their places.

"All right. Everyone settle down and get to work. If you don't have any work to do, hold up your hand and I'll find something for you," Mrs. Hennessy ordered.

As quiet descended once more upon the library, I took one last look at all four yearbooks, made notes in my iPad and, try as I might, I couldn't scratch the itch those red threads around their wrists gave me.

Mrs. Hennessy remembered the blood moon of that year, I mused, but was it significant? Doc seems to think it was. Me? Nah, I don't think so. I don't believe in that stupid supernatural crap... But I can't deny the facts: the crime rate does rise when the moon's full. Oh, come on, Kate. You'll be seeing spooks next, and not the CIA kind. I wonder if I should run it by the Chief... dozen messages

Not hardly.

11

B y the time I left the school, it was almost three-thirty. I went back to the PD to find my crew were all out of the building, which was fine; it meant they were busy doing something useful and hopefully making headway.

I went to my office, made myself a cup of coffee, took out my notes and started building my status report. I started, but I had the most difficult time concentrating. At the back of my brain, that blood moon thing kept the spaceship of my mind twisting and turning.

Back when I was a youngster, I'd been a fan of author Dennis Wheatly. He was famous for writing novels of the supernatural, such as *The Satanist, To the Devil a Daughter, The Devil Rides Out* and several more. Those books were pretty intense, and they created images that now came flooding back, those novels and movies like *The Exorcist, Race with the Devil, Rosemary's Baby, The Omen...*

Surely I'm not dealing with anything like that, am I? That stuff's all fiction, right? Just because they were scary doesn't mean there's anything to that crap... Yeah, but what about that woman

—*what was her name—Shirley something... Warden? Yeah, that's it, Shirley Warden. She was a Wiccan, or is it just Wiccan? What's that all about?*

"*The Exorcist* was based on a real event," I muttered out loud and then shook my head at my own silliness. I was letting my imagination run away with me and that was something that never happened. I wasn't like that. Movies were movies. In real life, I had a badge and a gun and was pretty sure my Glock would stop any boogeyman I was likely to run into. Still, the blood moon thing continued to nag at me until I could take it no more. I needed to get back to reality, so I picked up my phone and retrieved my messages.

A half-dozen messages from two lawyers, a beat cop, a low-level politician and, of course, two from internal affairs who aired their grievances and voiced their concern over so much nonsense that I almost thought that dealing with the devil might, after all, be more inviting.

I did, however, accomplish my goal. The nonsensical demands in the messages dragged me back to the present, to reality where there were no spooks or specters lurking in the shadows waiting to eat my soul. I grinned at the thought and settled back down to finish my report.

But I didn't get very far. Curiosity won the day, and I turned to my desktop computer and began to Google. I figured that by the time I finished my research, I'd be either bored out of my mind or laughing hysterically at the tinfoil-hat-wearing weirdos who claimed the moon and stars gave them some kind of supernatural power, or conjured up some kind of entity that made crop circles and increased the sightings of Bigfoot. Whatever! I began to research the phenomenon known as the Blood Moon.

As I expected, there was plenty of mention of Wicca, Satanists and zombies. What I didn't expect was all the crap about doomsday preppers and UFO abductees. At first, I was mesmerized by the diversity of the people extolling such events. Then there were the goth chicks who called themselves witches, potbellied mountain men whose ancestors had participated in some way-out harvesting rituals.

N one of it was much help, not at first. But then, as I delved deeper, I began to run across strange news articles from all over the country, about ritual killings, animal mutilations—sheep, cows and such—strange sightings and plain, old-fashioned weirdness. The rantings and ravings of social media weirdos looking for attention? Maybe, but the truth of it was that, as a cop, I knew that at least some of the happenings described in the articles were factual.

There wasn't anything particularly scary about the blood moon. But there were no clear-cut answers to the effect the astrological event appeared to have on people; not that I'd ever experienced anything... that I knew of. I certainly had experienced some weird crap during my time on the force.

The stories about what people did to celebrate the event ranged from the corny to the downright gross to just plain sinister, even evil.

The desk phone rang, breaking in on my thoughts, startling me so I nearly jumped out of my skin.

"Gazzara!"

"Hey, Cap," Janet said. "I have some information about Regis Taylor."

"So tell me," I replied. "What's he been up to?"

"He's in Riverfront Maximum; has been for the past two years, on a five-year stint for aggravated assault."

"Really?" I said, thoughtfully. "Now that *is* interesting. So that's what Shelly Brenner was hinting at. Okay. We need to talk to him. Make arrangements for us to visit, ASAP."

"Already done," she said. "They're expecting us tomorrow morning. I spoke with the warden myself, and he said it would be best if we were there around ten. That's when the inmates are most pleasant." She said those last words with what I can only describe as a verbal eye roll. But I knew exactly what the warden meant. Heaven forbid the inmates should be disturbed by a visit from the police before they've had their breakfast.

"Well, we wouldn't want to inconvenience Regis too much. Good job, Janet." I looked at the clock; it was almost five o'clock. "Why don't you go on home. I'll pick you up tomorrow morning at seven. We can grab some coffee and a bagel and drive over there. I have the feeling Mr. Taylor is going to be a tough nut to crack."

Janet agreed and hung up. I also decided to call it a day. I got up from my desk and stepped over to the window. The days were getting shorter as fall crept in. It was already getting darker, so I hurried out of the building. For some reason, I felt an urgency to get home before it was completely dark. When I pulled up outside my apartment and exited the car, I did something I hadn't done in quite some time. I found myself looking over my shoulder.

12

I t may sound perverse, but I was thrilled to make a visit to Riverfront Maximum Security Prison. It's like visiting a gallery where your artwork and the artwork of your peers is on display. Eh, you'll never understand; it's a cop thing.

We were greeted by Walter Hicks, the Assistant Warden, a giant of a man, with a barrel chest, big hands and a watch the size of Big Ben on his left wrist.

"Good morning, Detective," he said to me. "Nice to see you again. It's been too long." The man's voice was as deep as his skin was dark.

"Good morning, Warden," I said, smiling as he accompanied us through the first set of steel doors.

We had to leave our weapons but were allowed to keep our badges, my recorder, and Janet's document case, which underwent a thorough search before she was allowed to take it through.

The visitors waiting area was depressing. The walls were painted a faded mint green that turned the skin a sickly color that made everyone look like they were at death's door. The visitors themselves were for the most-part a dejected-looking bunch: some had children in tow and looked as life was barely worth the living. I felt sorry for them. They were all victims of their own *loved ones'* crimes.

"And who's this?" Hicks asked, looking down at Janet as he tapped on the office window.

"Oh, I'm sorry," I said. "Detective Janet Toliver, meet Warden Hicks."

"Nice to meet you, Warden," Janet said, smiling up at the huge man.

"And you, Detective," he said, circling his hand in the air in front of the window.

There was a buzzing sound and a loud click.

"All right. If you ladies will follow me, we'll go see your... suspect, is he?" Hicks said as the steel door slid open.

I ignored the question and said, "Everyone been treating you okay?"

It was an inane question, an attempt to lighten the moment. I didn't know the man well, but I had spoken to him several times in the past. He had a reputation as being something of a hard-liner. He didn't intimidate me, but I certainly wouldn't want to cross him. Not only that, he had some interesting connections that had, although it was never voiced in public, made life difficult for some well-known politicians... and convicts, very uncomfortable. *Politicians and convicts. Hah! They're as interchangeable as water and H_2O... They're the same thing, right?*

"Oh, I guess so," he replied with a lopsided grin. "Even if they weren't, who would I complain to?" He chuckled as he led us through yet another door that clanged as it closed behind us.

Finally, Hicks ushered us into a small interview room and asked us to sit at the table and wait.

"There must be no touching," he said, "no exchanging of materials of any kind. You must remain seated at all times on this side of the table. Is that understood, detectives?"

It was, and we nodded, and he also nodded and said, "Taylor

will be with you shortly. When you're done, tap on the window. Officer Williams will show you out. I wish you good luck, Detectives. He's quite a character, is our Regis." And with that, he turned and left.

Regis Taylor was escorted into the room a few minutes later, his bright orange jumpsuit a stark contrast to the gray color of the walls. His hands were cuffed and chained to a heavy leather belt. We both stood. I was a couple of inches taller than he was, so he had to look up at me. He seemed to be in a good mood, smiled broadly at Janet and then at me, and for a moment, I was afraid things were going to get ugly. It's not uncommon for inmates to try and upset female police officers; it's all part of the game, in fact. The profanities, the crude suggestions, the disgusting gestures: geez, it could be an ordeal. You just didn't let them get to you.

I remembered a story a female detective told me when I was a rookie about her first visit to the State Correction Facility to talk to a stoolie who said he had some information and wanted to cut a deal to lighten his sentence. So this cop—Lara was her name—was rather well endowed, and as soon as the stoolie saw her—he'd already been down for more than five—he... well, let's just say the filthy stuff he suggested is illegal in all fifty states.

It rattled her, not because she was a prude, but because the guy was just across the table from her, like we were from Regis Taylor, and had he chosen to he could have done her some serious damage before the guards could intervene. See, they were not allowed in the room with them, as they weren't with us. And while being just outside the door might be close enough when you are at the dentist's office, that's not necessarily so in jail.

Anyway, I digress. So Regis Taylor wasn't like that, nor was he a bad-looking guy; a little worn, maybe, but days spent in the prison yard using the weights had enhanced his already athletic frame. And, like most inmates, he was bald. His thick eyebrows cast shadows over his eyes, making him look more thoughtful than he probably was. Of course, his arms were covered in blue ink: prison tattoos, but even those were skillfully done. He'd certainly gotten his two packs of cigarettes' worth: the going rate for a high-end prison tat.

"Hey, y'all," he said enthusiastically as the guard unchained his wrists. "You don't know how excited I was when I heard I was to have visitors. I bet y'all are here to talk about Georgie Harrison, right?"

"That's right," I said. "Mr. Taylor, my name is Captain Gazzara and this is Sergeant Toliver..."

"Oh hey, just call me Regis, or Rege, everybody does."

I couldn't help but smile. He wasn't at all what I was expecting. I could see out of the corner of my eye that Janet was surprised, too, and was studying him intently. *Easy now, Janet,* I thought. *Not too obvious. We don't want to send him the wrong message.*

"So talk to me. I'll tell you what I know." He looked at Janet again and smiled.

"Mr. Taylor," I said, turning on my recorder and placing it in the middle of the table. "Before I begin this interview, I should warn you that I'm recording it. Do you have any objection?"

He grinned at me, said he didn't, and I went through the usual declaration of time, date, etc., for the record and then said, "I'd like you to take us through what happened that night in 2004?" I asked, watching his eyes.

"Aw, come on. Call me Regis, please. I ain't been Mr. Taylor for more'n two years."

"Fine," I said, rolling my eyes, "Regis."

He looked hard at me for a second, nodded, smiled, then looked away to the right—*good start. He's trying to remember.*

He sucked in a deep breath, then focused his attention on Janet. "That was September 26th," he began, then he looked hard at me and said, "You were there, weren't you, with that big cop? What was his name now... Starke? Wow, you're still lookin' good, Detective. You don't never date inmates, I suppose? Nah, course you don't."

"Yes, Mr. Taylor, I was there," I replied coldly, ignoring the back-handed compliment, but I'm pretty sure he wasn't joking about the dating question.

"Regis. It's Regis. So what is this? Like a redo?" He chuckled. "Did you pull the short stick and get to do the replay?"

"Not quite," I replied. "Please, *Regis.* Try to focus. What do you remember about that night?"

"What? You want to know if I did it? People have been thinking that for years. But I didn't." He folded his arms and stared at me, a half-smile on his lips.

"Come on, Regis," I said. "You were the last one with her. You... had sex with her, didn't you?"

"You don't need to be talkin' like that about Georgie," he snapped.

"Like what?" I said. "You were using her for sex, weren't you? So what's the matter? She decided she wanted someone else? Someone with a future?" I needled.

He didn't answer. He just sat there, glaring at me. I could see I'd hurt him.

"Look," I said, softening a little, "she was only sixteen-years-old; someone almost decapitated her. Help me find her killer, Regis. Help me put him away."

Right on cue, Janet took the crime scene photos from her document case and lined them up on the table in front of him. Regis stared at them. I watched his reaction as he tilted his head to the right and his eyes filled with tears.

"I never used her. I loved her," he said just above a whisper.

"You have a funny way of showing it," Janet said.

"Shit! I didn't do this to her." He looked up at me, wiped his eyes, took a deep breath and said, "I'm sure you've talked to the other members of our group, right? Or am I the obvious choice so you came here first?" He scooted in his backside on his seat and sat up straighter.

"We've contacted several of your classmates," Janet said. "They all said the same, that you were probably the person who killed her."

He ignored her. His eyes never left mine.

"Do you think that shedding a few tears makes me think otherwise?" I asked, holding his gaze.

"The only thing I'm guilty of is not walking Georgie home that night like I should have."

He looked down at the photographs before he smiled; not the smile of someone who was proud of his handiwork but fondly, as if he was remembering her as she was when she was whole.

"We were a real pair," he said softly, his gaze still on the photographs. "I thought the sun rose and set on her. I didn't have much. I certainly didn't come from money... neither did she, but she had potential. A lot of potential. She could have been anything she wanted. We talked about being together, about leaving Chattanooga, getting a small place together. She'd work at Walmart for the discounts and I'd be a mechanic or something." He paused, obviously living the memory. "They were simple dreams. Teenage dreams. You know how it is. Love conquers all."

"You loved her?" I asked.

"With all my heart." He looked me straight in the eye with an innocent, boyish grin. "Hasn't been anyone since her."

"You expect me to believe that? A guy like you? You're not exactly Father Flannigan, now are you?" I prodded.

"Just 'cause I'm in here don't mean I don't have faith. On the contrary, I've got more faith than the frickin' Pope."

And then he gave me a strange look and said, conspiratorially, "See, I know the truth, and it will eventually set me free."

There was something very sincere in his voice. But I'd been around criminals long enough to know that they are all chameleons; every last one of them.

"Is that why you are in here, Regis?" I asked. "You were charged with felony assault. You attacked an innocent man and almost killed him."

"Ha! That poor innocent man is a sadist pedophile. Two days earlier he'd beaten the shit out of an eleven-year-old boy. He paid some asshole pimp fifty for the hour. I'm only sorry I didn't get that piece of shit too. I'd do it again, no problem."

"So, you played the avenging angel? Is that it?" Janet asked.

"No, Red," he snarled. "I'm a guy who didn't do the right thing one time and look what happened. Georgie died because of it, because of me." He looked again at the photographs. "And when you cops came up with nothing, I wondered what the hell y'all were good for. You want to catch a criminal, you have to think like one. Better yet to be one. There can't be none of that I'm the good guy he's the bad guy shit. That'll get you nowhere, right, *Captain?*"

"Thanks for the sermon, Regis. So you didn't walk Georgina home that night?" I said, my goal being to keep him talking so that he might make a slip and unwittingly provide me with some helpful information.

"No," he said. "I actually left before everyone else did. I never saw the moon like that before. It was huge and with a red tinge... It was almost like another planet had appeared in the sky. Did you see it?"

"I may have. I really don't remember it," I replied.

"How about you?" he said to Janet. "Were you even born yet?" Janet looked at him and nodded, but she said nothing; she just continued her incessant scribbling in her notebook, a bored expression on her face.

"You're really cute," Regis continued. "Too bad you're a cop."

Janet cocked her head and smiled at him benignly and said, "Georgina didn't mind you leaving her like that? You'd just been intimate with her. She wasn't upset?"

"No. Georgie wasn't like that," Regis said. "She was okay with it. And we hadn't *just* been intimate. Yes, we'd had sex. But we did that first. Then we hung out with the others for a little while, but I was getting bored. Plus, my brother had just come back from

Alaska. He'd took a job scaling fish up there for a year. And it was getting cold and I didn't have a jacket."

"So you left, and the next thing you know Georgina's murder is on the news?" I asked.

"That's exactly how it happened. And when I called the rest of the guys, no one answered their phones. Not a single one of them." He leaned back in his chair, staring at the photographs. "My God, she didn't deserve that. And those cowards know what happened, too, but they won't talk."

"Who are you talking about?" Janet asked.

"Who am I talking about? Who the hell d'you think? What the hell are the taxpayers paying you people for?" He took a cigarette from his breast pocket, lit it with a book match, and took a long pull. "The others, the group, of course: Lilith, Junior, Buck and Shelly. They know what happened to Georgina."

"What do you mean they know what happened but won't tell?" I asked.

He blew a huge cloud of smoke across the table, stared long and hard at me, then, shrugged and said, "Look, I don't have any real proof. But my gut tells me they all had a hand in her death. I just know it. That crazy-assed Buck was hiding in his mother's crawl space while Georgie's wake was taking place. Did he tell you that?" His eyes narrowed in disgust at the memory. "Piece of shit," he muttered as I held back the laughter, unable *not* to look at Janet, who was smiling and shaking her head.

"No. We actually haven't talked to him yet," I replied.

"Yeah, I only talked to him for a second the other day," Regis said.

"You spoke to Buck?" Janet asked, astonished. "Why?"

"To remind him of the anniversary of Georgie's death, and to tell him the cops were on their way. I've been doing that every year since she died." He smoked the last of the cigarette, then dropped it to the floor and screwed it out with the sole of his rubber slip-ons.

"Did you call Shelly, too?" Janet asked.

"You bet I did. I called them all. They're not hard to find. Just follow the scent." He chuckled again. "I told 'em all that the cops were on their way. I do it every year. Hot damn. This year I was actually telling the truth." He laughed happily.

"Regis," I said gently, "if you didn't kill Georgina, who d'you think did?"

"I told you: I think they all had a hand in it. They were into some weird shit... Hey, you ask enough questions of the right people, you might get some answers. I told you all I know. She was still alive when I left. Was she when the others left? I kinda doubt it."

"Regis," Janet said. "Is there nothing else you can remember about what happened that night, anything at all?"

He thought for a second, then said, "Only that Junior gave Georgie his coat. I would have given her mine but, as I told you, I wasn't wearing one; I was cold. That's it. That's all there is. She was alive..." He watched as Janet gathered up the photos, tears streaming down his cheeks. "She didn't have to die," he muttered. "God damn them all to hell."

We stood to leave, but Regis remained in his seat.

"Thank you, Regis," Janet said. "We appreciate your time."

"Sure, Officer Toliver. You can come back and visit me anytime. You don't talk much, but that's okay. I've got plenty to say for the both of us, if you care to listen." He winked at her playfully. "Do you have any interest in city planning? See, I have a plan that could change the face of Chattanooga, set her at the top of the heap. Maybe you'd like to visit again, bring me some smokes."

I knocked on the window for Officer Williams to let us out, and we left Regis sitting there staring down at the table where the crime scene photos had been.

I wasn't sure what to think of the interview. One thing I was sure of, though, was that either Regis Taylor was the best con man I'd ever come across, or he was telling the truth.

13

The next day started out well, which should have been a sign that things were going to go off the rails pretty damn quick. I'd had my run—three miles before six o'clock—and the tastiest sausage biscuit from Hardee's, and I was in my office. I'd just had my first sip of coffee when my desk phone rang. It was Chief Johnston.

"Do you have a minute?" he asked.

"Yes, Chief. Of course. What's up?"

"Lennie's replacement will be in today; any minute now, I should think. I wanted you to hear it from me first so you wouldn't be surprised to see someone at his desk," he said. I could tell by the sound of his voice that it was as unpleasant for him as it was for me.

"That's fine, Chief, and thank you. I'll make sure I put him to work right away."

"That would be best. I also think it might be smart if you get in there as soon as possible. I know Robar will have a hard time adjusting to the new guy."

I told him I would, and as soon as I hung up, I jumped up and went to the situation room. He was already there. Someone—I never did ask who—had pointed him to Lennie's desk, and there he sat looking through his welcome packet.

I should have known better. I should have been there to meet him. My bad! Unfortunately, the rest of my team were all at their desks too; something they hardly ever were, and they were watching me, along with the rest of the department, so it seemed.

I squared my shoulders and went to Lennie's desk. Its occupant looked up at me with a somber expression.

"Hi. I'm Captain Kate Gazzara," I said, sticking out my hand for him to shake. "You must be—" I almost said Lennie's replacement. Fortunately, he cut me off before I could finish.

"Jack North, ma'am," he said, rising quickly to his feet. He shook my hand, but he didn't smile. There was no friendly expression. I didn't smile either. There was no point in trying to fake the situation. He knew he was stepping into a dead man's shoes, so to speak, and so was getting the cold shoulder.

"My office, everyone," I said, trying not to sound like a hard-ass. "And bring coffee. You too, Jack."

A couple of minutes later, they all trooped in, North bringing up the rear. It was a cold moment, as you can imagine. But I had to crack the ice, so I did my best to introduce everyone—that resulted in quiet handshakes all round. Only Janet was bright and cheery with him.

"We may as well jump right in." I sighed. "We're working on a cold case, among other things," I told him. "Teenager murdered in 2004." I looked around and saw Ann was about to speak, but she changed her mind, stood and walked around to where Jack was sitting and dropped two files on the table in front of him.

"I'll need phone records, cell tower pings, the works. Soon as you can." And she returned to her seat next to Hawk.

Janet was sitting next to North, fiddling with one of her notebooks. Hawk was seated opposite, his arms folded, rocking back and forth on the hind legs of his chair, an enigmatic expression on his face.

"Things are a little tense right now, Jack," I said. I took another sip of coffee, stood up and went to the board.

"I'll recap what we have so far," I said. "If any of you have anything to say, especially you, Jack, just chime in." I looked at everyone: nothing.

"So, Georgina Harrison," I said, tapping her photograph with a twelve-inch ruler. "On September 26, 2004, she was found in the woods that border Swiss Valley Park. She'd been dead more than ten hours. Her throat had been cut from ear to ear, almost decapitating her." I pointed to one of the three autopsy photographs Janet had added to the board.

"She'd also been stabbed multiple times and—this is the weird thing—these symbols." I tapped a third photo. "Doc Sheddon, the ME, states they are symbolism. The perp... one of them—we think there were more than one—carved them into her skin. I'm not so sure. Any comments, anyone?"

There weren't any so I continued, "Doc also seems to be of the opinion that we're dealing with some sort of cult killing... something to do with the full moon."

North snorted, then said, "Sorry!"

"Skeptical, are we, Jack?" I asked.

He shrugged, then said, "Anything's possible, I suppose. Seems a bit far-fetched, though, don't you think?"

I did, but I didn't say so. Instead, I said, "Stranger thing," and then I continued, "I haven't mentioned this before, but I was partnered with the lead investigator, Harry Starke—"

"Wow," Janet said.

"Janet?" I asked.

"Oh nothing. It was just a surprise, that's all, considering."

"Considering what?" I snapped, aggravated. My past relationship with Harry Starke wasn't something I wanted to get into, then... or ever.

"Well," she said, her face serious. "He has a reputation as being one heck of a good detective. How come you didn't close the case back then?"

I stared at her. It was something I'd often wondered myself, which is probably why it had haunted me all these years.

"I think," I said carefully, "that the problem was the age of the suspects. There were, and still are, five of them. At the time they were all sixteen, minors. Which meant they couldn't be interviewed without their parents being present. So getting answers from any of them was just about impossible. Today, however, they are all thirty-two; big difference."

I looked at the four faces at the table. They were all nodding.

"And here they are," I said, turning again to the board. "Jack, along with the phone records, I want full backgrounds on all five." I tapped each of the five photos in turn, naming them as I did so.

"Okay," I said. "That should do it for now. Hawk, Ann, I want you to go and interview Buck Halloway. Don't take no for an answer. Jack, you have plenty to do. Janet, you give him a hand." That wasn't exactly what I meant, and she knew it. What I really was asking her to do was keep an eye on him.

They gathered their papers, iPhones, iPads, etc., except for Hawk, who'd brought nothing with him, and they left. Me? I took a seat at my desk and picked up the phone; I had messages to retrieve. *Oh joy! There's nothing quite like annoying messages from subordinates—and superiors—to chase the blues away.*

It must have been an hour later when I stepped out of my office and took the elevator to the situation room. Robar and Hawk were not at their desks. Janet was on the phone and Jack had his laptop up and running, with files spread across his desk.

I put a hand on his shoulder and said, "Any luck with the phone records, Jack?"

"With the iPhone, no. Getting there, just waiting for the one now. You know how these providers can be. As to the landlines. I've got all of them."

"I need to know who made the call to Buck Halloway at around one o'clock on the 27th. Do what you can. We'll iron out the details later."

I turned to Janet and said, "What have you got for me, Toliver?"

"It seems Regis Taylor was telling the truth," Janet said, swiveling around on her chair to face me.

"About what?"

"About the guy he beat up, Brady Marvelle. He has one heck of a rap sheet. Listen to this." And she began to list his crimes: "Indecent exposure. Lewd behavior in front of a minor. Possession of child pornography. Solicitation of a minor. Aggravated sexual abuse of a minor." Janet took a deep breath. "The guy had been at it for years. Except for a twelve-month stint for the agro, he never got anything more than a couple months."

I shook my head. It was one of those situations that made me angry, where a civilian—in this case Regis Taylor—did our job better than we did. In my opinion, he deserved a medal. Unfortunately, though, there are rules; laws and vigilante justice went out with the Old West. And sometimes, like now, I thought that was too bad. Regis Taylor would have been made town marshal if he'd lived in that era.

"Okay," I said. "So we've got the one and only honest guy locked up in Riverfront Maximum. He got five years for taking down someone we should have put away for twenty. Where's the justice in that, I wonder?"

"That's not all," Janet continued. "According to his high school transcripts, he had a 4.0 GPA and there were a couple of pretty good colleges knocking at his door, including UTK and Georgia State. He could have gotten out of Chattanooga and started over." Janet shook her head. "Unfortunately, there are also a couple of convictions for possession of marijuana. And, knowing him as we now do, I doubt he gave that stuff up, which probably explains why he lost it all."

"That and having his girlfriend murdered," Jack North piped up.

I looked at him like he'd sprouted a third eye in the middle of his forehead. Then I remembered that he was part of my team.

"What are your thoughts, Jack?" I asked. "You've had time to review the file. Anything?"

He nodded and said, "I think those little-leaguer parents should have been arrested and fined for contaminating the crime scene for starters. How many uniforms did you need to finally get them out of there?"

"It was peewee football, and there were nineteen officers who responded," I muttered.

He was right. It was a damn disgrace. Grown men and women wanting to catch a glimpse of a dead girl that could easily have been any one of their own daughters. I don't know what bothered me the most. Georgina Harrison's dead body or the ghouls who trampled all over the crime scene trying to take photos of her.

"What is that, like every uniform on duty that morning?" He smiled.

"I don't think it's funny," I replied.

"I don't think it is either," he snapped back. "It was simply an observation and a critique of the intruders."

I nodded, about to turn my attention back to Janet when he said something that grabbed my attention.

"What about the student—one of the suspects—who lived within walking distance from the park? I'd be looking at her."

I remembered thinking about her at the time of the crime, but it was a dead end. The girl, Lilith Morris, lived on the other side of the park. I turned and went back to my office to review the file and my notes again. As I walked away, I could hear Janet talking with Jack. I made a pretense of stopping to talk to one of the uniforms and listened.

"...then Regis said that Buck Halloway was hiding in his father's crawl space during Georgina's wake. He was doing that when Hawk and Robar went to his house. At least that was what his wife told them. Hawk said he saw him in the window. What do you think that means?" she asked.

I didn't hear Jack's reply. I was already on my way to the elevator. I did smile though: *Reliable little Janet. She's already taken him under her wing.*

No sooner had I walked into my office and sat down behind my desk when my iPhone rang. I looked at the screen, smiled and answered it.

"Hey you. How about dinner and a couple of drinks tonight?" he said.

It had been almost a week since I'd last heard his voice, and I was more than tickled to hear it.

"You bet, but would you mind if we had delivery and a bottle of wine at my place?" I asked.

"Tough day?"

"You have no idea," I said. "I could use a sympathetic ear and a sounding board. You up for that?"

"You bet," he said without hesitating. "I'm in town, at the recruiting office on Lee Highway. I should be free by six. What do you think?"

"I can't wait, but can we make it around six-thirty? I have a full load here."

"Six-thirty it is. See you then." And he hung up before I had a chance to say more.

And six-thirty it was. When I pulled into my spot outside my apartment, he was already waiting for me. As I came to a stop, his car door opened and he stepped out, a familiar figure and one I was very pleased to see.

Chief Gunnery Sergeant Wilcox Dorman, USMC, six feet four, was in full dress uniform, and it showed his beautiful physique off to perfection. I got out of my car and stepped around front to meet him, unable to hide my smile.

14

"Wow," I said. "Are you ever a sight for sore eyes?"

"If that's true, I hate to think what you've been looking at all day," he said as he approached.

In one hand he was carrying a bag that I assumed was holding our dinner. In the other, he had a small bouquet of flowers. Pretty little things in shades of pink and purple, and I felt myself blush. The last time anyone had bought me flowers had to have been my senior prom. Whatever, I was happy to get them... You know, I often forget that I'm a girl—yes, I am. I'm not that old, not yet, damn it—and sometimes, not often, but sometimes I liked to be treated like one.

Dorman? He's an old-fashioned kind of guy. With his military haircut and what small amount of hair that left him graying at the temples, and his broad shoulders, he reminded me of John Wayne in *The Sands of Iwo Jima*. I hadn't known him long, only since that one case... *Oh hell, I don't want to think about that, not tonight.*

So I'd known him only about six months, and I hadn't seen him more than six... no, seven times since. He was a lovely man, and I couldn't help it; I was smitten. It had been a long time since I'd ended my long-term love affair with Harry Starke, almost five years in fact, and while I had little time for romance, I was certainly happy when a little did come my way.

I couldn't wait to get upstairs, crack open a bottle of wine and devour whatever it was he had in the carry-out paper sack he was holding. What else might the evening hold? I didn't know, but I was hoping.

He set the bag down on the kitchen counter, went to the fridge, grabbed a bottle of red, uncorked it and poured two glasses. And then we sat together on the couch, his arm around me, my head on his shoulder. I told him about my day and that Lennie's replacement had arrived. And then... Geez, I don't know what came over me, if it was the few sips of wine I'd had, or if I was just plain old tuckered out, but quite suddenly I felt downright depressed.

It must have showed, because he squeezed me tightly and said, "It'll be all right, Kate."

I heaved a big sigh, but said nothing, remembering that god-awful case when I first met him. It was his input that not only helped me solve it, but also brought us together. When it was over, I'd asked him if I could buy him a drink, and he'd agreed, and we'd hit it off right there and then... no, not that for God's sake. We just liked each other, damn it.

What I liked most about Dorman—I never called him Wilcox, or Will, no one did, except his mom, and even she called him Gunny sometimes—but I digress again. As I was saying, what I liked about him most, other than the obvious, was that he was always just a phone call away when I needed him. And, this may sound corny, but he'd quickly made it clear how he felt about me. No, I wasn't looking for a ring on my finger, but... well, he was... special, and I liked him, a lot.

He was seven years older than me, getting close to retirement, and had a nice safe desk job with the Marines after having served a half-dozen tours overseas. He hadn't talked much about any of that, and I'd never asked. But he'd invited me into his life, and I'd accepted. And so far, I had no regrets.

"It was tough, Dorman," I said, "seeing Jack North at Lennie's desk. Every time I look at him, it reminds me that it's my fault Lennie was killed. I can't shake it and I'm afraid it's going to affect my job, my life, even my sanity," I said bitterly.

"It wasn't your fault, Kate. Those thoughts are normal, though. Completely normal. I should know," he said. "How many good men have died because of orders I gave them d'you think? See, that's the problem people like us have. We're trained to know how to handle a crisis. But when the crisis becomes too big for us to handle, and there's no one there to help, we blame ourselves for the outcome and not the crisis."

"Lennie was waiting for me," I said. "He was there because I didn't do as I'd been told. The Chief told me to go see a doctor... I'd injured my head. He knows me too well, though. He knew I wouldn't do it, and I didn't, so he ordered Lennie to make sure I did. So he was here, waiting outside my apartment in his car, and that piece of trash shot him. I'll never get over it, never."

I leaned into Dorman and felt his arm tighten around me. It felt wonderful, as if his strength might absorb some of the pain.

"That's right," he said. "She was a piece of trash, and it was she that killed your friend. But you know, I have the feeling that if it had not been him, it probably would have been you." He massaged my neck; his fingers felt like steel rods.

"Oh, you saying that makes me feel so much better," I said sarcastically.

He took my chin in his fingers, tilted my head back and kissed me. I closed my eyes and enjoyed the moment.

"I know how you feel, Kate. Honestly... Unfortunately, I do. Hey, the food must be cold by now; you want to eat?"

We sat down together at the kitchen table, and I opened the paper sack while he poured more wine. The roast beef sandwiches were amazing, and while we ate, Dorman told me about himself.

He never had been a closed book. I already knew quite a lot about him: his family and the little things that people share as they're getting to know one another. Most of it was hard to listen to, but I did, and somehow I was able to understand how he felt. No, I'm not going to go into details, or even try to explain what he told me. All I'll tell you is that suddenly, in that moment, I knew we had even more in common than we realized.

I pushed the wine aside, stood, took him by the hand, and led him into my bedroom. I went to the window to close the drapes, and as I looked out of the window, I saw the crescent moon cutting through the dark scudding clouds, and I shuddered involuntarily. And my thoughts returned to Georgina.

15

The next morning I felt a world of better. Dorman rose first and made coffee. Then, while we showered together, he made love to me, for the third time. *Wow, oh yeah, no wonder I felt better. I haven't had a night like that since... Well, we won't go there.*

We left the apartment together, and I kissed him goodbye. Yeah, I did, right out there in the open for all to see; and screw the neighbors. He followed me out to East Brainerd Road, then up onto I-75, where he turned south toward Atlanta and I went north toward the Chattanooga police department. I was feeling wonderful. I turned the radio up—Willie's Roadhouse station—and was soon singing along with Loretta Lynn to "You Ain't Woman Enough To Take My Man." Kind of appropriate, don't you think?

Jack North was already there when I walked into the situation room. It was still early, almost eight o'clock.

"Good morning, Jack. What are you working on?"

"Hey, Cap. I'm just wrapping up the call records Robar asked for and—"

"Okay," I said, interrupting him. I was anxious to get going.

"Finish dotting your i's and crossing your t's. You're coming with me. We're going to visit a suspect, and I could use a fresh perspective." And, without waiting for an answer, I turned to go to my office.

"What about the background checks?" he called after me.

"You can do those later."

"Great. Give me five minutes," he said. And true to his word, five minutes later he was at my office door and ready to go.

I could tell he was already bored by the routine work Ann Robar had given him. Plus, after my talk with Dorman the night before, I'd decided that since Jack North was the newest member of my team, I was going to apply a little pressure and see what kind of diamond in the rough Chief Johnston had gifted me.

The drive to Lilith Overby's house was a little more than twenty minutes, and quiet. I tried to make small talk, but he didn't seem to be up for it.

"Jack, I don't want to pry but—"

"You don't have to worry about me, Captain. I won't let you down."

He was obviously on the defensive, and believe me, I knew exactly what that felt like, so I nodded and let it go.

"This is some house," Jack said as he parked the umarked police cruiser in the driveway.

"Yes," I said. "Look at the landscaping. It's a perfect symmetry of design and color." I shook my head. "It looks like a show house, perfectly maintained because no one lives in it." I paused, then said, "Look, Jack, before we get in there, if we get in there, I just want you to know that you can chime in at any time. Ask questions but keep it professional. I don't know why I'm telling you this. You've done interviews before."

"I have," he replied, dryly, as we walked up the porch steps.

"All right then. Let's see what Lilith Overby has to say for herself." I rang the doorbell, took a step back, and we waited: nothing. I stepped forward again, and this time I knocked on the door, hard, and then again. It must have been a couple of minutes later, and we were about to leave, when we heard footsteps hurrying to the door and then the sound of locks turning. The door opened.

"*What*, do you want?" she snapped. "My children are still sleeping."

Involuntarily, I looked at my watch. It was not quite nine o'clock and on a Wednesday. *Why are they not at school?* I wondered.

"They're recovering from a bout of the flu," she said, anticipating a question I wasn't going to ask.

"Mrs. Lilith Overby?" I said, holding up my badge.

"Yes?" She looked annoyed.

I quickly introduced myself and Jack, told her why we were there, and then said, "Do you have a few minutes, ma'am? I'd like to ask you a few questions."

"No, I don't. I told you, my children are still sleeping, and I don't want to wake them. They've had a very rough time and need rest. I'm sure you understand." She looked from me to Jack and then back again.

"I'm afraid we must insist, Mrs. Overby," Jack said firmly. "It won't take long. May we come in?"

So far, so good for the new guy, I thought.

"I don't think I like your tone," she said and then looked at me.

"Mrs. Overby, I'm sure—"

"I told you no," she said, interrupting me. "I'm not waking the children." She folded her arms, narrowed her eyes in determination, and shifted her weight from her right foot to her left.

"That's fine," Jack said, "because we aren't here to talk to the kids. We're here to talk to you, Mrs. Overby, about the near decapitation of Georgina Harrison on the evening of September 26th, 2004."

Oh shit! I thought. *Here we go.*

Overby stared at Jack, her mouth hanging open.

"I don't know anything about that," she said, her face pale.

"Have you spoken to Regis Taylor? He's the one you need to talk to, not me. He was with her—"

"Yes, I've spoken to him," I said. "Mrs. Overby, this would go a lot easier if you'd let us in for just a few minutes. All we want to know is if there's anything you can remember about that night that might help us find her killer."

"We promise we won't wake the kids," Jack added.

She looked us both up and down, pinched her lips together, and then said something that really pissed me off.

"Fine," she said, stepping aside. "You can come in, but take off your shoes. My carpets are clean."

I stepped out of my shoes, but I could tell by her long, deep sigh that Jack was trying her patience by taking his time untying his laces and placing his shoes carefully on a square of carpet.

Overby grunted something I didn't catch and, with her foot, she scooted the toe of his right shoe a little closer to the other. And I knew then that we were dealing with a special kind of control-freak.

"Follow me," she whispered, "and don't make a sound."

She stepped past us into a vast, open-plan living room and kitchen. Everything was clean and sparkling. Not a thing seemed to be out of place: there was nothing on the stove, no coffee percolating, no breakfast dishes in the sink, no kids' toys on the floor. It truly was a show house, and she didn't ask us to sit down.

"How old are your children?" I asked.

"Mimi is five, and Lulu is three," she whispered. "I was about to make their midmorning snack and put some black-eyed peas in a pot of water to soak for tonight. We're vegan, you know."

"I would have had no way of knowing," I replied, inwardly smiling at the thought of the delicious roast beef sandwich I'd eaten the night before.

Geez, I thought, *how can anyone live like that? Well, different strokes, I suppose, and good luck to you, so long as you don't expect me to participate.*

"Really? And how's that working for you?" I asked, not that I wanted to know, but I thought the question might break the ice, and it did.

"Well, since you ask," she said enthusiastically. "Since we started our diet, I can tell you that my children behave better, and my husband and I think clearer. All those chemicals they put in food these days: they just destroy your brain. I don't think I've ever felt better in my life."

"That's good to know," I said, "because I'm hoping you can tell us about the night Georgina Harrison was murdered. I'm going to record the interview, if you don't mind," I said, taking my little recorder from my pocket, turning it on, and setting it down in front of her on the island's white onyx top.

She looked at me, her right eyebrow arched. She opened her mouth to speak, then changed her mind, closed it, rolled her eyes and nodded her head.

"Thank you, Mrs. Overby, but please say it out loud, for the record."

"Yes, you can record the conversation, if you must."

I almost rolled my eyes myself. I was slowly losing patience with her. She was one waspy... but maybe I was being a little hard on her. She was, in fact, quite a pretty woman. Tall... well, five-nine-ish, slim, short brown hair, like a pixie, with a heart-shaped face and big brown eyes. No jeans and sweater for her, though. She was wearing a beige blouse, a knee-length pleated skirt, also beige, and a dark brown suede vest over the blouse.

"Just think back and start with whatever you remember," I said.

"I really don't remember much. It was sixteen years ago, you know. You were there, weren't you? Of course you were. I remember you from the interview. Didn't I answer all your questions then? Don't you still have your notes?" she asked, her hand going to her hip sassing me.

"We do, Mrs. Overby. But the case was never solved. Georgina's killer is still out there. We're hoping to do better this time. So please, let me ask you once more to tell me what you remember about that night, and from the beginning," I insisted.

She let out another annoyed sigh but said nothing. I thought that perhaps she was thinking, trying to remember. If she was, she didn't get a chance to tell us. Jack saw to that.

"I don't think we're going to be able to get this done here, Captain," he said. "Do you have someone you can call, Mrs. Overby; someone who can look after the children for you? We'll conduct this interview at the police department." He closed his notebook and waited for her to answer.

Her condescending glare turned to one of anger, which didn't help the situation.

"Oh, very well," she said, focusing on me. "Ask your questions, but quietly, please? And please, keep your dog under control."

Again, I had to smile, but inwardly.

I repeated my question, "What can you tell me about the night of September 26th, 2004?" I wanted to let out a heavy sigh of my own. Hell, I wanted to slap her silly face, but of course I didn't; I kept it professional.

"Oh dear," she said, looking to the left. "It seems such a long time ago. My friends and I... we had a special place in the woods that we used to go to. It wasn't deep in the woods, but it was secluded." She cleared her throat, stared vacantly at the countertop, then continued, "It was a special night. There was a blood moon. Did you know that?"

She looked at me as she said it, as if she thought I was some kind of shut-in and didn't know about such things.

"You must have known," she said, her eyes wide. "It was all over the news for days, and the school offered extra credit to anyone who... They wanted us to go out and observe it, turn in papers, take photos, write poems or do drawings, or whatever we wanted so long as we described the event. They're quite rare, you know, blood moons." She lifted her chin slightly.

"That's what I've heard," I said. "Please continue."

"We all showed up. Georgina and Regis slipped off like they always did. The rest of us had fun talking and joking until the moon made its appearance. You see, they didn't realize how strong the effect of this incredible phenomenon was going to be."

"What do you mean by that?" Jack asked.

Overby ignored him, but instead rolled her eyes and focused her attention toward me.

"Whether people want to admit it or not, many of our moods and actions are governed not by our own free will but by the position of the stars, planets and especially the moon," she said seriously. "If you'd checked the astrology chart for that particular day, you'd have seen the strong predictions for all the signs of the zodiac, but especially for Sagittarius... That's me, by the way. The blood moon was supposed to bring earth-shattering changes for me in the area of love and money."

"And did that happen?" I asked, dryly, and inwardly rolling my own eyes.

She looked directly at me, stared at me without blinking, as if she wanted me to pay special attention to what she was saying.

"It did. Within a week after the event, I met my future husband. And, even though my family already had money, he was financially well-off. Very well-off." She continued to stare at me. "We've been married for twelve years, you know."

"And you're saying that your perceived good fortune comes from the Blood Moon?" Jack asked skeptically. "Are you telling us what happened to Georgina Harrison happened because it was *written in the stars?*"

It was a legitimate question, but he had obviously started off on the wrong foot with Mrs. Overby, and she wasn't going to let him forget it. She ignored him.

"You see, Detective Gazzara, we're all connected to every other living thing in not just the earth but the galaxy, the universe. If we pay attention and treat our planet with respect, nurture and protect it, the galaxy will repay us," she said.

Oh, my God. She's a freakin' fruitcake.

I stared at her, unable to believe or even comprehend what I was hearing.

"Okay," I said, trying to figure out what to say next. "So what do you think happened to Georgina Harrison?"

"I think Regis Taylor did that to her. He doesn't have an alibi, as you should know. And his harassing us every year on the anniversary of her death screams to me that he's guilty and that his conscience is bothering him."

"So, you received a call from him, too?" I asked.

"I did. He's crazy, you know. He always was."

"Why d'you say that?" Jack asked.

Again, she ignored him, wouldn't even look at him.

"We spoke with Shelly Pinkowski," I said, "and we tried to speak to Buck Halloway. Both Shelly and Buck's wife said they received phone calls. When we spoke with Regis, he told us he has indeed been calling his high school friends every year... Have you ever talked to him? You must have. You were friends for four years in high school." I leaned on the counter. Lilith's eyes went to my hands and forearms, looking at them as if I was contagious.

"In the beginning? Sure. I didn't want to believe he did it. But then he seemed to go off the rails, as they say, started going with the wrong crowd. He began doing drugs and drinking, and the next thing you know the police are looking at you like you're a criminal just because you're friends. I couldn't afford that kind of reputation." She huffed. "Only someone trying to run away from the truth goes the way he did—"

"Hey, Mrs. Overby. Let me ask you something," Jack interrupted her, finally getting her attention. "Buck Halloway? Did you know about him hiding in his crawl space?"

Part of me wished Jack would have just shut up. Yet another part of me was as curious as he was about Buck Halloway's weird way of coping with his depression.

"Buck is a very sensitive person," she replied, scowling at him. "You wouldn't understand a man like him."

"You know about the crawl space habit, then?" I asked.

"What Buck does is none of my business; you should talk to him," she hissed.

I sighed and said, "Okay, let's get back to that night. Regis and Georgina had slipped away together to... Well, we won't go into that. Regis said he left the group early because he was cold. Do you remember that?" I prodded.

"You mean to tell me that Regis Taylor, a convicted criminal, says he left the scene early and that's good enough for you? No wonder you haven't solved this case yet," she said.

"So you're telling me that he didn't leave early?"

"I don't remember," she said, looking away to the left.

She's lying. Why?

I let it go, but I could see out of the corner of my eye that Jack had caught it too, and he wasn't happy. He hadn't been since we walked into the house.

"So, let's say he did leave early," I said. "What happened then?"

"Well," she said, still avoiding eye contact, either with me or Jack, "I had done my research and wanted to... oh, how shall I put it? Welcome the Blood Moon. I wanted to invoke its power, its beauty, its majesty to... You see, there was a little ritual I wanted to perform. It just required a little preparation... but no one else wanted to do it." She shrugged and stared at the countertop.

It was all Jack needed. He laughed. She looked up, glared at him, but kept her silence. I had a feeling the interview was just about over.

"Did you see anyone or anything strange after you guys started to leave?" I said.

"I saw Junior Cole give Georgina his coat, and then everyone decided they wanted to leave," she said, staring at Jack.

I thought that little bit of information was interesting since Regis had mentioned it too.

"Did you leave at the same time as the others?" I asked, but she was staring at Jack scribbling in his notebook.

"You know, Captain, I don't appreciate him taking notes while I'm speaking." Lilith scowled.

"It's normal procedure, ma'am," Jack replied without looking up.

"I don't care. I think I've told you all enough. If you haven't caught the killer by now, you never will. This has been a total waste of my time, and I'd like you both to leave my home right now." She folded her thin arms over her flat chest, glared at me, and then walked quickly around from behind the island and almost ran to the front door.

I picked up my recorder, but I didn't turn it off, and followed her. I found her standing at the wide-open front door.

"I have one more question for you, Mrs. Overby," I said. "Did you all leave together that night? Where did Georgina go?"

"I don't remember," she said, annunciating each word slowly. "Now, please go."

I stood there, in my bare feet, staring at her. She looked away and began tapping her foot impatiently.

"If you'll just give us a minute to put on our shoes, Mrs. Overby, and—"

"You can put them on out on the porch!" she said too loudly as she kicked one of Jack's shoes out through the open door.

I looked at her sternly, hoping she wouldn't try to put her hands on either one of us, maybe try to push us out. That wouldn't have ended well.

Fortunately, she didn't get the opportunity, because just then a small voice behind us said, "Mommy?"

A little girl in pink tights and a pink sweatshirt was standing on the stairs, her hands clasped in front of her.

I smiled. I couldn't help it. She was adorable, her big blue eyes looking at Jack and me.

"Oh, that's just great!" Overby snarled. "Now you've woken them up!"

The little girl didn't move. She just stood there, looking at us.

I turned, grabbed my shoes, and quickly stepped outside. Jack? Oh no. He had to bend down and wave at the child. She instantly smiled and came down the stairs toward him, but her mother swooped in and grabbed her up.

"Mommy. Who's that?"

"They are the police, honey. They're not here to make friends."

"What?" Jack said, standing up, shoe in hand.

I stepped back inside, grabbed Jack by the arm and pulled.

"Get your other shoe," I ordered. He tried to shrug me off, but I held fast. "Detective North. Get your shoe. We're leaving."

He did as he was told and gave me a curt nod. I gently pulled the front door closed, and as we put on our shoes, I heard the door locks slam into place: one, two, three. I looked at Jack.

"What?" he said sharply as he pulled his shoes on.

"I thought you knew how to interview people?" I said, stepping into my own flats.

"I didn't do anything that was out of line. If anything, it's she that was out of line. If it'd been me, I'd have hauled her down to the station." He looked at me as he stood upright.

"Get in the car," I said.

We sat there for a moment. Not a word was exchanged. It wasn't that I was really mad at Jack. I wasn't. It was just that he wasn't anything like Lennie. Lennie was... friendly, innocent-looking, non-confrontational. Jack? Just from that one interview, I knew he was a hard-ass. That in itself wasn't a bad thing... No, in some circumstances it could be a good thing, but not inside the house of a homemaker with her children present. Maybe I was nitpicking. I didn't know.

"You didn't do anything wrong, Jack," I said as we sat there. "You just didn't read her all that well. She's a little high-strung, which means you have to treat her accordingly."

"A little?" he said.

"A little," I said, raised my hand, indicating an inch with my thumb and forefinger.

Jack smiled as he looked over his shoulder and backed out of the driveway and headed back to the PD.

"I'm sorry," he said.

"What? For what?"

"I might have been a little aggressive back there. I didn't like her attitude. Most people are willing to help the police when we show up on their doorstep."

"Maybe we need to be a little more aggressive," I said thoughtfully. "Everyone we've interviewed so far, with the exception of Doc Sheddon, the ME, has had an attitude. Wait, I take that back. Regis Taylor didn't. Well, not a belligerent attitude, like that one." I jerked my thumb over my shoulder in the direction of Lilith Overby's house.

Back at the PD, Jack went to his desk and I went to my office to write up my notes and do a little paperwork. The rest of the afternoon went off without a hitch; lovely. And, to top it off, I got another call from Dorman; even more lovely.

"Twice in the same week?" I said. "I should buy a lottery ticket. It's my lucky day."

"And hello to you too," he said. "Dinner tonight?"

"Umm, let me check my appointments," I joked. "Okay. I'm free. Sounds good."

"Great. I'll pick you up at the police department?" Dorman asked.

"The sooner, the better," I replied.

16

<hr>

That night we polished off a bottle of red wine with two heaping plates of pasta and garlic bread. I enjoyed the hell out of it, but I knew that I was going to have to get into the gym sooner rather than later, and I told Dorman as much.

"You're a great cook, Dorman. I don't think I've eaten this well in my whole life. I'm going to get fat," I said, taking another sip of wine.

"You think? Spaghetti's my limit, I'm afraid. That was my mother's recipe. So... your turn next?"

"Oh, Lord. Are you serious? I can't cook, sweetie. I never had the time to learn."

By then we were in my living room, on the couch together. I'd opened a second bottle of wine, and I hadn't felt so good in a long time... No, not because of the wine, but because for the first time in a long while, I felt... oh, I don't know: wanted, maybe. Loved? Oh no, not that. It was way too soon for that. I was as wary as a long-tailed cat in a room full of rocking chairs.

Actually, as I sat there with my head on his shoulder, a glass of wine in hand, I was thinking about the interview with Lilith Overby. *What the hell did happen to...*

"I'm glad to hear things are going well with the new member of your team," Dorman said, breaking into my thoughts. "Jack, you said his name was?"

"Yes. He'll be okay, I think. He's had a rough time, and he's a hard-ass, but he's a good cop," I said. "We were interviewing one of the suspects..." and I told him what had happened.

"It was interesting, to say the least," I said. "She told us she wanted to perform some sort of ritual to harness the power of the moon." I chuckled. "I know that high school kids get into some weird stuff, but they usually grow out of it. It's all about the drama, excitement, being different. Lilith Overby, though... Sheesh, she still believes the moon and stars rule our lives, our destinies. Can you believe that? I didn't think horoscopes were even a thing anymore."

"She wanted to perform a ritual that night?" Dorman asked. His expression had gone from amused to thoughtful.

"That's what she said. Some kind of moonbeam harvesting. Acknowledging the moon and its power or some such garbage. It reminds me of the Wicca craze, you know, when there were dozens of movies showing teenagers dabbling in the black arts." I shook my head.

"It's crazy!" I said. "But let's not talk anymore about my work. There's another bottle of wine in the fridge. We could watch a movie and let all that food digest."

"I think that sounds like a good idea. But..." Dorman looked at me seriously. "When you're dealing with people who really believe —and it sounds like this woman does—well, I'm sure I don't have to tell you how unpredictably dangerous they can be. Please, be careful. The moon brings out a lot of strange behavior in some people."

"That's almost exactly what Doc said," I muttered.

"Who?"

"Doc Sheddon. The Medical Examiner." I smiled. "He remembered that this all happened during the blood moon back in 2004. The funny thing is we're due for another one within the next couple of weeks, maybe less."

I waited for Dorman to say something funny or assuring, but he didn't.

"This girl, Georgina; she died on the same day as the blood moon? That's terrible," he said.

"The fact she died at all is terrible," I replied.

The fact was that this whole blood moon mumbo-jumbo was exasperating enough to make me shake my head and roll my eyes. There obviously wasn't anything supernatural about a phenomenon that had been happening since time began. It's an eclipse, for God's sake. Nothing more. Happens all the time. Yes, that's true, but no matter how hard I tried to tell myself I was investigating nothing more than a cold case, I couldn't help but feel there was something more to it. What that was? I had no clue.

17

I was feeling good when I arrived at work the following morning. But I hadn't been at my desk for more than ten minutes when my phone rang.

"Yes, Janet, what is it?" I asked.

"I think you better come up here, Cap. There's a mad woman here, yelling her head off, says she's Mrs. Lilith Overby and she wants to speak to the captain."

What the hell? I thought, rising to my feet.

"Tell her I'm coming. I'll be right up." I hung up the phone and went to the elevator.

"Where is the Captain? I need to speak to the Captain!" Lilith Overby was standing just outside the elevator doors when they opened and I stepped out into the situation room. She was looking around like she'd lost her keys.

"Good morning, Mrs. Overby," I said as the elevator doors closed behind me. "How can I help you?" As I said it, I happened to look around the room. There were at least two dozen officers present and every single one of them was up and gawking over their cubicles, and all of them were grinning like fools.

She spun around. She was wearing an expensive gray exercise suit over a pink T-shirt with "Find a Cure" printed in tiny letters over the left breast. Her tennis shoes and fanny-pack were also in matching colors.

"I need to speak to your captain," she snapped "I want to file a complaint against your partner over there!" she said angrily, pointing at Jack. "He was completely disrespectful in my house," she continued. "He scared my children half to death. He should not be allowed to carry a gun. That man is not qualified to catch a dog, let alone protect the public! He—"

"Hold on a minute!" I said loudly. "Mrs. Overby. First, I need you to lower your voice. Second, I *am* the captain."

"You? You're the captain? I don't want to see you. You're as bad as he is. I want to see the person in charge."

As she said it, the elevator doors opened again and Chief Johnston stepped out, just in time to hear her next missive.

"Detective Gazzara, I understand that you are beholden to the patriarchy of law enforcement, but I am not. I will not be intimidated in my own home by some fool with a badge abusing his authority and—"

"Mrs. Overby, stop—"

"What's going on here?" Johnston asked, interrupting me.

"I need to speak to someone in charge about that officer over there. I wish to file a complaint!" Lilith hissed.

"Chief, I don't know what Mrs. Overby is talking about." I was angry. There's very little that upsets me more than when someone wrongly accuses one of my team.

"Mrs. Overby? I'm Chief Johnston," he said, turning to her and holding his hand up at me. "Would you accompany me to my office, please."

Lilith scowled at me and everyone else in the bullpen before nodding and following him into the elevator. As the doors closed, I heard him ask her if she'd like a cup of coffee or a bottle of water. It was like a slap in the face. I walked across the floor to Jack's desk.

"Is she serious?" he said as he looked up at me, shaking his head.

"Please, tell me you didn't make another trip to her house, or that you were surveilling her without checking with me first," I said.

He stood up. "I didn't do a damn thing other than go with you to her house," he replied angrily.

Hawk and Robar had crossed paths with the Chief at the elevator.

"What the hell's going on?" Hawk asked.

Before I was able to speak, Jack told him quickly what had happened.

"You're kidding me?" Robar said.

As much as they might have been uncomfortable with Jack being Lennie's replacement, there's a unity among cops that's virtually unbreakable. And when someone accused one of us of wrongdoing, we took it seriously.

Me? I took this one personally. Maybe it was because Jack hadn't gotten the warmest welcome from the rest of the team, or maybe it was because we worked Overby together and I knew she was lying, I didn't know. What I did know was that Jack was on probation and could well lose his career over a single false complaint. Not only that, the last thing I wanted was for the new member of *my* team to feel that he was all alone. I've known that feeling and I promise you, there's nothing worse.

And then Janet's desk phone rang. She picked up, listened for a moment, then offered it to me, mouthing, "It's the Chief."

"Chief," I said.

"My office. Now. And bring North with you."

I didn't answer. I simply handed the phone back to Janet, turned to Jack, and told him to come on.

Two minutes later, we were standing together in Linda's office like a couple of schoolkids waiting to see the principal. And oh, was I ever pissed off.

"You can go on in," Linda said, setting her phone down.

I took a deep breath, squared my shoulders, and walked right on in without knocking, Jack close on my heels.

"Shut the door and sit down, both of you."

Johnston waited until we were seated then said, "This is not how I wanted your reassignment to begin. You've been here less than two days, and already I've received a complaint that you've overstepped your authority and threatened that woman and frightened her children."

"Chief, I was there," I said. "Jack might have been a little aggressive, but that's all. He was totally respectful." I caught Jack looking sideways at me, like I'd just sprouted donkey ears.

"What?" I said to him. "I told you as much on the drive back to the department. Don't give me that look."

"You also said I didn't do a bad job," Jack replied.

"You didn't." I shook my head. "But, as I also said, you could use a little polishing. It takes a while to get used to a new team. Chief, it takes time—"

"Chief," Jack interrupted me. "I didn't scare anyone's kids. They were sleeping when Mrs. Overby reluctantly let us in the house. She made us take our shoes off. Do you have any idea what kind of crazy coot we're dealing with..." He caught the look the chief was giving him and tailed off. He was on the edge of his seat, his hands on his knees, leaning toward the Chief's desk.

"I'm with Jack on this, Chief. As I said, he might have been a little aggressive, but he wasn't disrespectful and he sure as hell didn't frighten the kids. We only saw one of them, and she wanted to make friends with..." I, too, received the look and closed my mouth.

Chief Johnston leaned forward on his desk, folded his hands and looked at both of us. Suddenly I felt cold, angry. Sadly, I'd felt like that before, and in that very office too. But I knew Chief Johnston was a fair man. He wasn't going to let the words of one crazy woman who was obviously exaggerating the situation push him into making a rash decision... was he?

"Jack, you're on a 'three strikes and you're out' probation. I know Captain Gazzara, and if there's one thing she is, it's that she's faithful to her team, backs them all the way, and I respect that. But you already have two strikes against you—"

"Whoa! Wait just a minute, Chief," I jumped in, interrupting him. "Are you saying I'd cover for him when I know he's in the wrong? That's a pretty lousy thing for you to assume, based on that silly bitch's word. What exactly did she say to you anyway?" I snapped.

"She said that she felt threatened by Detective North and in fear for her life and that she wouldn't leave until I recorded the information and filed a report with Internal Affairs," the Chief said calmly.

"So it doesn't mean a damn thing that I was there and can assure you that it wasn't like that at all? Do you think I'd lie to cover for the guy who replaced one of my best detectives? The guy who hasn't been on the job for more than twenty-four hours? That doesn't make sense. And, Chief, you know that if it doesn't make sense it probably isn't true."

"It's okay, Cap," Jack said bitterly. "I appreciate you going to bat for me, but they've been looking to get rid of me for some time. You're friends with Lieutenant Cheryl Blackburn, aren't you, Chief?"

He looked at Chief Johnston, and I felt my gut tighten up like knotted rope. You don't ever put the Chief on the spot like Jack had just done.

"Be very careful, son," Johnston said, his voice so low I could barely hear him. "Don't say anything you'll live to regret."

"What difference does it make?" Jack said. "She's wanted me out for a long time. I don't know why. I never dated her. Was never disrespectful. We just didn't click. And when she made it clear that her intent was to have me removed, not just from her precinct but from the force, I knew it was only a matter of time." He leaned back in his chair and folded his arms. "You can't fight City Hall, or the police bureaucracy, for that matter."

"Those are harsh words, Jack," the Chief said.

"Did you even take a look at my file? Those strikes you were talking about are by a specific group of people. You'll notice that some of them even use the same terminology," Jack said. "And I'll bet you didn't see the two commendations either." He looked at me and continued, "Blackburn thinks it's because she's a woman that we didn't click. I'll tell you it's because she's incompetent."

"Now you hold on!" Johnston said. "She's seen more action than you have, Detective. And she's a damn good cop to boot. You might think the Chattanooga PD is about who you rub elbows with, but I can tell you most of us had to work our way to where we are."

"Most, but not all, right?" Jack said, shaking his head. "Yeah, well, you're not going to find too many willing to work as hard as me. But I can't do my job if I'm called out by every jerk who gets their feelings hurt because I'm asking questions."

I sat there waiting to see what Johnston was going to say to that. I knew there were a lot of cops in high places who didn't deserve to be where they were. Hell, I watched a couple of them sail past me without even looking in the rearview mirror. It happens. It happens in every job. But I didn't want Jack to get fired because of Lilith Overby, especially as I knew personally that he didn't do anything wrong.

"So, am I packing up my desk? It won't take but a minute. I haven't even had time to unpack," Jack said.

"All right, Jack, that's enough," Johnston said. "I believe you. Now, what am I supposed to do with Mrs. Overby's complaint?"

Of course, the obvious answer came readily to mind, and I prayed that Jack wouldn't have the nuts to tell him.

"Do whatever you think is best," Jack said and waited.

"You're on my radar, Jack; you too, Kate. We'll see how it goes. But I have a feeling that woman will be back, and if she does file some kind of formal complaint, I'll be left with no choice but to take action."

Now that really chapped my jaws. Suddenly, I was angrier than I've ever been: *I'm on his frickin' radar? I don't think so.*

"You know what, Chief?" I said after taking a deep breath. "I think I've taken just about enough crap from this department to fill a dumpster. I took four years of Finkle's sexual harassment and you never did a damn thing about it. I had to handle that son of a bitch all by myself. I should have sued his ass, and the department, but I didn't out of respect.

"I'm on your radar?" I continued. "I sometimes wonder where the hell your loyalties lie, Chief... You know what? I'm just about ready to quit this mess and go work for Harry Starke. At least I know where I stand with him, which is more than I can say for you. Now, d'you want my damn badge and gun or are you going to support me as I deserve?

"That stupid woman is a suspect in a murder case. Don't you think it's a little strange for such a person to be acting the way she is? I sure as hell do. And are you telling me that every time a suspect throws a hissy, we're supposed to back off? As to North here. I back him every inch. He goes, I go!"

Jack sat rigid on the edge of his chair, not daring to speak.

Johnston looked at me, a half-smirk on his face. "Are you finished, Captain?"

I nodded, a horrible sinking feeling in the pit of my stomach. *Oh hell, I don't want to quit, much less go work for Harry Starke!*

"Good, because I'm going to say this just once—Jack, give us a moment, please. Wait in Linda's office. I'll call her when I'm ready for you."

Jack jumped to his feet and all but ran from the room.

"Don't you ever talk to me like that again," Johnston said so quietly I could barely hear him.

I didn't answer. I just stared back at him. I sure as hell wasn't going to back down.

"I've always had your back, Captain. If I hadn't, you would have been gone a long time ago. Henry Finkle wanted you gone almost as much as he did Harry Starke. Instead, I promoted you, twice. I agree, you've had it tougher than most, but you've handled it well, until now, that is. I've always admired you for that, but if you want out, I won't stop you. What's it to be?"

I thought for a moment, about what he'd just said. It was true, though he'd never said as much to me before, but then, why would he? He was the chief of police; he answered to no one, much less a lowly captain.

I let my breath escape noisily. He smiled. I was instantly reminded of a great white shark coming in for the kill, and I couldn't make up my mind which was scarier, the shark or the Chief.

"Call Jack back in, Chief," I said, very quietly, "but please, let me handle him from now on."

He nodded and picked up the phone.

"Sit down, Jack," Johnston said when he returned. "How relevant is this Overby woman, Catherine?" he asked, picking up her complaint and tearing it into four.

"She's as much of a suspect as the other four," I said. "She was cleared when she was a teenager. There was no evidence to link her to the crime; still isn't. She was friends with the deceased and that's all. I think we could leave her alone for a while. She's not going anywhere. Maybe have Janet and Robar question her next time."

"So, I'm still on the payroll?" Jack asked.

"For the time being," Johnston said dryly. "But I'll say this to both of you: what was said in here today, especially about Blackburn, goes no further than this office. Understood?"

Johnston sat with his hands still folded on his desk. His eyes in shadow from his gathered brow. He looked like a comic book character.

"Yes, sir," I said without hesitating.

When Jack and I walked back into the situation room, all eyes were on us. There wasn't anything more to say to Jack about the ordeal. It was over and done with as far as I was concerned.

"Look, Jack," I said when we reached his desk, "I think you need to get out of the office for a while, get some fresh air; I know I do. Janet, we need to talk to Buck Halloway again... Sheesh, what am I saying? We never talked to him to begin with. Take Jack with you. Go to the house and tell him that if he doesn't talk with you there, you'll arrest him and bring him in. Tell him we don't have a crawl space here, but we do have a nice warm six-by-eight cell. Got it?" I ordered.

"Sure thing, Cap." Janet looked at Jack. "You ready?"

He nodded and grabbed his jacket from the back of his chair.

"Am I ever," he muttered, and I didn't blame him.

Me? I went to my own office to hide for a while until the smoke settled. I sat down at my desk, safely behind a closed door, and did a quick search of Lilith Overby's social media. I let out a small sigh of relief. It was looking like making complaints was her bag. As far as I could see, she'd filed grievances against almost every business in town.

Unfortunately, though, I knew we weren't done with her and that I needed to talk to her again. That thing she mentioned about Junior Cole giving Georgina his jacket was stuck in my head. It was a nice, simple gesture... and yet... it seemed to carry a lot of weight for both Regis and Lilith. I also needed to talk to Junior Cole.

Junior Cole lived in Monarch, North Carolina. I thought it was time to pay him a visit. You can imagine, then, how surprised I was when he came to me first.

18

I t was about forty-five minutes after Jack and Janet had left
the station to talk to Buck Halloway when the call came in;
there was a shooting at the Halloway residence. Of course,
my heart almost stopped beating. I remember grabbing my jacket
and running out of my office, but I don't even remember getting
into my car, much less how I got to the scene.

When I arrived, the road was blocked off and there were a half-
dozen blue and white cruisers, two ambulances and two fire trucks
parked along both sides of the road, all with their red and blue
lights flashing.

I parked my own cruiser and walked—no, I ran—almost a block
to where I spotted Janet, her hand to her forehead, talking to a
uniformed cop.

"Janet? What happened?" I said, looking around. "Are you all
right? Where's Jack?"

And then I saw him coming out of the house, a uniformed
officer following close behind. He was covered in blood, and my
heart dropped to the pit of my stomach.

"Jack!" Janet shouted. "Are you all right?"

He nodded slowly, his face pale.

"Thank you, Detective North," the officer said.

"You bet," Jack replied quietly. "Let me know if you need anything else, Ollie. I guess I'll be here for a while."

Then he turned to me and said, "I know what you're thinking."

"I don't know if you do," I replied. "What happened? You look terrible. Are you okay?"

"Yeah, I'm okay... Well, sort of." He looked at Janet.

She shook her head, then said to me, "I'll be just a minute, Cap. Let me finish up here, okay?" and she turned again to the uniformed cop.

"So, what happened, Jack? Who's been shot?" I pressed.

"Halloway. He shot himself."

My mouth dropped open. I was stunned.

"*What?*"

Jack shrugged. "He shot himself. He's dead."

"Oh... my God!"

Janet patted the uniformed officer on the arm as he flipped his notebook closed and came over to join us.

"What the hell happened, Janet?" I asked... no, I snapped at her.

She raised her eyebrows, tilted her head, and said, "Really, Captain?"

I was... almost speechless. I licked my lips, stared at her, sucked my top lip, bit it, then said, "Just tell me what happened."

And she did. She told me.

"So, we arrived a little over an hour ago. Mrs. Halloway was in the driveway, and it looked like she was getting ready to go somewhere. So Jack suggested that we wait until she left before approaching the house because, according to Hawk and Robar, she ran interference for her husband." She took a deep breath, then continued, "So that's what we did. We parked down the road apiece and waited until she was gone, then we walked to the house and knocked on the door. We knew he was home because we'd heard Mrs. Halloway call into the house and tell him she'd be back in an hour."

She looked at Jack, then at me. I nodded, "Go on."

"So we knocked at the door, and when he opened it, we identified ourselves and asked if we could come in.

"Well, the first thing he said was..." She looked at her notes and continued, "'This is about Georgina Harrison's murder, isn't it?'

"I told him it was and asked again if we could come in. He said we could, and we did. Whew, did he ever sti—sorry, smell. Anyway, he offered us coffee, which we refused, and I told him we had questions for him. We went into the kitchen, where I told him I was going to record the interview. He said he didn't mind."

Janet looked up at me. "Cap, I think maybe if you listen to the recording, you'll hear what happened."

"I think you'd better give me the short version first," I said.

She nodded. "Well, it's not really so short, but... okay. So, I asked him to tell us about that night. He said he didn't remember much except that they were all excited about the blood moon, and that they went to their usual meeting place, in the woods off the park." She consulted her notes again and then continued.

"I asked him to tell us about it, and he did, as best as he could recall. It was pretty much in line with what the others had said... He remembered talking with Shelly Pinkowski, 'a real heart-to-heart about the world and each other and the future,' he said it was.

"I asked him what the others were doing while he was talking to Shelly. He said Georgina went off with Regis, as usual, and that Lily wanted to perform some kind of ceremony, but the others weren't up for it. Then it got really cold, really quickly, and Regis decided to go home. He, Buck, wanted to stay there with Shelly, talking and stuff until the sun came up... and then he said something really strange. He said..." Again, she looked at her notes. "'I sometimes wonder if I'd stayed, if I'd feel the way I do today. If Georgina would have stayed with us, maybe she'd still be alive today. See, it wasn't until after that I started with the depression.'"

She paused and looked at me and then continued, "Jack asked him what happened next. He said that Regis left first. Lily was pissed because they wouldn't do her ritual and she hung back sulking while he, Buck, walked with Junior Cole and Georgina back toward the park.

"I asked him where Shelly was at that point. He said he didn't remember. Jack told him that seemed kind of strange seeing as they'd had such a meaningful conversation. He kind of laughed at that but said again that he couldn't remember.

"Then I asked him..." She consulted her notes again, and read, "So, you walked with Georgina and Junior. Out of the three of you who left the group first?"

She looked up at me, "He said Georgina did. He said she headed toward the park because it was right off the busy street and she said she felt like she'd be safe walking there."

She read from her notes again, "'She gave Junior back his coat and went on her way.' Buck said. 'I feel like walking. That's what she said.'"

"So why did he shoot himself?" I asked. "How the hell could you let that happen?"

"We didn't... Well, not really," she said.

"So tell me," I said impatiently.

She took a deep breath and nodded. "I asked Halloway why he liked to go down into the crawl space. At first he didn't answer. He just stared at me with a weird expression, like I'd just slapped him. Then he told us it was time for us to leave, and he just... walked away down the hallway and up the stairs. So we did as he asked. We left... that is, we were leaving and were at the door when we heard the gunshot." Janet shook her head. "Jack ran upstairs and found him with a bullet wound to his head."

"He was still alive, just," Jack said. "So I started CPR. That's why all the blood."

I stared at him, thinking, trying to figure out what to do. I needed to get CSI in there and search the place in the hope that they'd find something that would confirm Buck Halloway had killed himself out of the guilt he'd been suffering for the past sixteen years. Unfortunately, I couldn't do that, not without a warrant. It wasn't a crime scene.

Could Buck Halloway have been Georgina's killer? As sick as it sounded, I sure as hell hoped so.

I sent Janet and Jack home. Jack couldn't go anywhere in the state he was in anyway, and both he and Janet were in for a world of paperwork. It was a suicide, which meant a half-dozen internal departments would now have their hands in the pot, including Internal Affairs, searching for the slightest crack in Jack and Janet's story. Business as usual.

19

It was almost four o'clock that afternoon when I arrived back at the police department. I eased quietly past the door to the Chief's office and closed the door to my own office behind me. I made myself some coffee, and flopped down behind my desk, to think, but not perchance to dream.

Truth be told, I was hoping that I could get all my ducks in a row in order to present the Chief with the cleanest and fairest description of what had happened at the Halloway residence. Unfortunately, I didn't get the chance.

I hadn't been seated more than five minutes when my phone rang. *Damn it, Chief. I just got here.*

"My office. Now!" he said when I answered, and then he disconnected before I had a chance to speak.

Oh hell. Here we go again.

"Sit down, Catherine." He glared at me across his desk.

"Chief, I know what you're going to say, but—" I began, taking a seat in front of him.

"Do you? Do you really? Well, I don't think you do. I get a complaint against the newest member of your team this morning, and this afternoon a suspect shoots himself to death, and what do you know? Damned if he isn't being interviewed by the same team member. Talk to me, Catherine."

To put it mildly, Chief Johnston was angry.

"Chief, the man killed himself. That's it. Jack performed CPR until the paramedics got there. He didn't leave his side. And, if the guy killed himself because he was being questioned as a suspect in a murder case, then we should be searching his house right now and patting Jack on the back for cornering our killer."

"Really? Is that what you think we should be doing? Well, the press thinks differently. They think we're out of control. They think the Mayor should appoint an independent council to investigate the way the Chattanooga Police Department questions its suspects."

"You've got to be kidding me?" I said, rolling my eyes.

Johnston glared at me. "Am I?" he said. "You think?"

"Chief, come *on!* You can't be serious. Jack did everything right. Janet was there and witnessed everything. Buck Halloway had mental problems from the word go. You can't possibly blame this on Jack. He's been in town only a few days and on my team even less than that."

"Well, I'm afraid it's not that easy," he said as he stood up.

"You've got to close this Harrison case, and quickly. It was against my better judgment to let you reopen it. I only did so because it was one of your first and had stuck with you. I understand that. But sometimes a fresh set of eyes is what's needed to seal the deal. So you have until the end of the week, seventy-two hours, to put it to bed. If it's not done by Monday morning first thing, it's over. Maybe a couple week's leave will do you good. Kate, I know you've got vacation time you haven't used. Maybe it's time for you to take a break."

"Sheesh," I muttered, more to myself than to the Chief. "What would I do with myself?"

"Get out of here, Kate. Go do what you do best. Find me a killer."

I didn't know what to say, so I just nodded, said nothing, and got my backside out of his office as fast as I could.

Linda was at her desk. The sympathetic shrug she gifted me with did little to raise my spirits.

Seventy-two hours? You've got to be kidding me. Okay then. Let's do it.

I went home, drank a half-gallon of orange juice I picked up on the way, opened a can of chicken noodle soup, threw it into a pan, and turned on the stove.

Yeah, I was in that kind of a mood; the kind that only comes when you've been chewed out by your boss. So, instead of my usual glass of wine, I took a healthy shot of NyQuil, showered, and went to bed.

I don't remember going to sleep, but it must have been as soon as I hit the sheets. I do remember the crazy dreams of creepy crawl spaces, blood moons, and kids hanging out in the woods and doing unspeakable things to each other.

20

I woke early the next morning, jumped out of bed, pulled on my sweats, stuffed my hair into a knit cap, hit the pavement and ran eight miles, four in each direction, on East Brainerd Road.

When I got home, I was literally drenched in sweat.

Twenty minutes later, after a hot shower and two cups of black coffee, I was dressed and ready to face the day: my head was clear and my energy at its peak.

I called in and told the operator I was working a case and would be late into the office and to make sure to let everyone that mattered know. And then I climbed into my unmarked cruiser and went to the Halloway house, to see what there was to see. It was Friday morning, eight o'clock.

Some kind soul had stationed a blue and white outside the house with a uniformed officer therein whose job it was to keep the family from disturbing the scene. I parked on the street behind the cruiser, climbed out of the car, stepped up to the driver's side window and flashed my badge on my hip.

"Captain Gazzara," I said. "Long night?"

"Not too bad. Who is there to complain to?" He chuckled.

"You've got that right," I said dryly. "I'm going to take a look around inside, okay?"

"Be my guest. Ain't nobody going to bother you."

I nodded, thanked him, and walked to the house. I opened the door, ducked under the tape, and stood for a moment listening to the unearthly silence.

Jack had said Buck Halloway had gone upstairs and that it was from that spot the gunshot had sounded. I snapped on a pair of purple latex gloves, looked around, then headed up the stairs. It was so quiet you could almost touch it. I could hear myself breathing, which was even more unnerving.

I didn't have any trouble finding the place where Buck Halloway had pulled the trigger and thus ended his miserable life. To the right, at the top of the stairs, inside the master bedroom, I found the massive stain on the carpet where he'd bled out. There was blood spatter on the walls and even some on the ceiling. Jack's bloody shoe prints were all over the carpet.

I stepped carefully inside the room and then the en suite bathroom to the left. It was nothing special, just a regular bathroom with towels on a rack, makeup on the vanity, hand soap in a dispenser, and a medicine cabinet on the wall. I opened it and wasn't surprised to see several dozen medication bottles, all with long names I couldn't pronounce. Some were to be taken before bed. Some were to take as needed. Some were to be taken daily, some twice a day.

"Geez," I muttered to myself. "Halloway didn't kill himself because of Georgina. He killed himself because of this lot."

I closed the cabinet door and stepped back into the bedroom. I stared down at the bloodstain and wondered what the hell he must have been thinking when he stuck the muzzle of the weapon under his chin and pulled the trigger. *No one will ever know, I guess.*

I stepped awkwardly around the stain to the dresser and began rummaging through the drawers, not sure what I was looking for, but hoping for... something. After searching, I was disappointed: I found nothing, no diaries, no hand-written notes, no indications of an overwhelming sense of guilt. I gave it up and went back downstairs, but I wasn't finished looking around, not yet. I was going to find that crawl space.

It was a pretty safe bet, so I thought, that no one had looked in the crawl space. I doubted if anyone even knew about his strange practices. Even so, I figured it had to be fairly easy to get to, and thus to find. I began my search in the living room and then went from there to the kitchen, looking in all the closets for a trap door, but I found nothing.

"It can't be this difficult," I muttered as I peeked inside the pantry and pushed a box of canned foods aside: again, nothing. The floor was smooth and solid: not a break in the hardwood anywhere. "It's got to be here somewhere."

I looked at my watch. It was already ten after nine. I shook my head, looked around the kitchen once more, then thought, *Maybe it's outside... No, I don't think so. There has to be access in the house somewhere... but where?*

I stood for another minute, made a silly face, then thought, *I guess I'm going to have to call Mrs. Halloway.*

That was something I'd been hoping to avoid. The poor woman was having to cope with the loss of her husband, and the realization that he might be a killer. Me? I had an open mind: maybe he was involved in Georgina's death, maybe he wasn't. She claimed she knew all about what had happened that night, and that Buck had told her everything. *What exactly does that mean, I wonder? Did Buck confess to her?*

"Is she worth questioning?" I muttered to myself. "Sure she is, but not right now."

But now I had just three days to put it to bed, *and I wasn't going to find the solution here in the pantry.*

I gave it up, wandered out into the hallway, taking out my phone to call Mrs. Halloway as I went. I'd already selected her number from the contact list and was about to tap the go button when I noticed a closet door, right there by the front door. Obviously, it was a coat closet, a common feature in most homes these days, and I wondered how I'd managed to miss it. *Walked right on past it, didn't you, girl?*

I opened the closet door and as soon as I did, I knew I'd found what I was looking for. Aside from a couple of winter coats hanging from a metal bar, and a box marked "winter hats and gloves," it was empty. I moved the box to one side with my foot and there it was, a cutout, a square trapdoor, with hinges on the left and a ring pull on the right.

I reached down, grabbed the ring, and pulled. Quietly, almost silently, the trap door opened. The beam from my iPhone flashlight cut through the darkness below. It smelled stale, and I could feel the cold down there, but I didn't smell anything like mold or damp. I knelt down and peered inside. The floor appeared to be made from concrete, and it looked smooth. I sat back on my heels, then took a deep breath and eased myself down into the darkness, swung my flashlight from side to side, and found an electric outlet with a single cord plugged into it that led to a solitary bedside type lamp; there was no bed, of course.

Crouching low, I stepped over to the lamp and turned it on. It was dim, maybe 40 watts, but from its light I could see that the crawl space stretched across the entire foundation of the dwelling. It was about five feet high, maybe a little more, with brick piers—support columns—in rows spaced six feet or so apart. Now I'm almost six feet tall, so you can imagine how uncomfortable I was hunched over, my arms dangling almost to the floor like a damn great monkey.

Buck Halloway had arranged several cushions in a square, beside the lamp; they appeared to be couch cushions. There was also a dustpan and a small hand broom. It was amazingly clean down there, but oh so dark, even with the lamp turned on: there was nothing to contain the light, to reflect it inward.

There were books down there, too, lots of them, but one, in particular, caught my eye. It was a hardcover, red with gold lettering: Eastwood High School 2004. The cover was faded. Its edges scuffed and worn, as if it were some child's favorite book. I picked it up, opened it; the pages were dog-eared. I flipped through them. Every page with a photo of the six friends had its corner folded to bookmark it. I found Georgina's class picture. It would have been taken sometime early in the year, before summer break.

Unlike the books I'd reviewed at the school library, this one was full of signatures and autographs. It seemed based on the number of girls who signed it, that he was quite a popular kid: short notes saying things like "stay sweet" and "U R the Best." Shelly Pinkowski's note read, "I will never forget the night of the blood moon." Needless to say, I nearly choked when I read that. Buck had said that he and Shelly had this deep, intense conversation before they all scattered for the night. I wondered if that's what she was alluding to. I scoured the other students' autographs and found similar entries from Junior Cole and Lilith Overby. A chill ran over me. Could they all have been complicit in Georgina's death?

I closed the book and set it down on one of the cushions. By then, my eyes had become somewhat adjusted to the dim light and I noticed a thin red bracelet on the floor beside the cushions. It was a twin to those the kids were wearing in the photographs. This one, though, was broken. It looked like it had been ripped apart. *Hmmm!*

I continued to look around and then I noticed something else: sticking out from under the cushion closest to the lamp was the corner of a piece of paper. I leaned over and pulled it free. It came out from under the cushion along with several more pieces of paper. They were newspaper and magazine clippings: articles about the blood moon. I was about to toss them down onto the cushions when I happened to notice the date on one of them. I looked again at all of them. Some had dates, some didn't. Those that did... they weren't dated September 2004. They were dated over a period of the last five weeks: they were about the blood moon due in the next few days.

And it was then I knew that it wasn't just the Chief I had to worry about: something dreadful was going to happen if I didn't get this case wrapped up and quickly.

Don't ask me how I knew that. I just did. And as soon as the thought popped into my head, I was overcome by an overwhelming sense of impending doom, and I knew I had to get out of there.

I picked up the book, and, with it and the clippings still in one hand, turned on my iPhone flashlight, turned off the lamp and stooping, headed toward the patch of light that was the trap door. I reached up and set the book and papers on the floor inside the closet and was about to push myself up and out when I had a god-awful feeling that I wasn't alone down there.

I knew I was. There was nowhere to hide. But I tell you, every hair on the back of my neck stood on end. Every instinct was telling me to hurl myself up out through the trapdoor, but the rational side of my brain was telling me there was nothing down there.

Whatever, I gave in to my instincts and scrambled up and out of there like a scalded cat. I flung myself forward out of the crawl space and rolled backward out onto the hall floor, pulling my knees up to my chest as if I was sure something was about to grab them.

I lay on my back on the floor, my legs safely out of reach of anything that might be down there in the crawl space. The open maw that was the trapdoor seemed to stare at me. *Frickin' hell, Kate. Pull your silly self together. You're a grown woman, for heaven's sake. Get your ass up and act like one.*

And I did. Slowly I pushed myself up onto my feet, stepped forward, and peeked down into the darkness: nothing. No demonic, twisted face staring back at me. Just... darkness.

Oh shit, Kate. Whew. That was... just your rabid imagination gone wild, you damn fool. Yeah, well, when you look into the abyss, the abyss looks right back at you, I thought as I shuddered and kicked the trapdoor shut. I walked out of the house, slammed the door behind me and walked quickly back to my cruiser, waving a hand at the officer in the blue and white as I passed, climbed in, slammed the car door, fell back against the backrest, closed my eyes and heaved an audible sigh of relief.

Now you might be wondering what kind of a stupid wimp of a woman I am. Hey, I wondered that myself, but you had to be there. It really did creep me out.

So, with the yearbook, newspaper clippings, and the red thread safely on the passenger seat, I decided that I needed to submerge myself in normalcy, or as near as I could get to it. I headed to the police department and my office.

I made coffee, checked my emails, organized the files on my desk from most important to least, and was about to dig into the Georgina Harrison case file when I saw the flashing red light on my phone. My favorite task, checking messages. They were all routine, all except the last one that, when I checked the time stamp, came in when I was in the Halloway crawl space. It was just silence, a hang up, I supposed... or was it? *There you go again, you silly...*

I deleted the message, but not before another shiver ran down my spine. I got up from my desk and went up to the situation room. I needed some humans to talk to, a little reality.

21

For the first time in a long time, I stayed later at the office than I needed to. It wasn't that the idea of being in my apartment behind closed doors in my warm jammies with a glass of red wine didn't sound great; it did, but I was just a little reluctant to leave the hustle and bustle of the PD and go out into the darkness. It wasn't a conscious decision. I just lingered longer than I needed.

So, I hung around, making work for myself until my desk looked tidier than it had since the day I moved into the office. I think I'd written detailed accounts of everything I'd been working on up to and including the bathroom breaks. Finally, at around six o'clock that evening, I gave it up, sighed, looked around and told myself, "All right, Kate. That's it. You've done enough. Go home."

And so, I put my computer to sleep, slipped into my jacket, grabbed my purse from the floor and walked toward the door... and then suddenly, in the open doorway, Jack North appeared, startling me so that I let out a yelp.

"Jeez, Cap. I'm sorry," Jack said.

"North! Wow, you're going to be the death of me," I said as I let out my breath.

"Yeah, funny. You're not the only one who says that." He looked at me and pursed his lips. "You got a minute. Can I talk to you?"

"Sure, you can," I said, taking a seat at the table, and not just a little thankful that I didn't have to leave yet.

"I've been doing some research. Well, Janet and I have. She went home about thirty minutes ago, but I sometimes have trouble sleeping so I stayed on," he said.

"I know that feeling," I replied. "I didn't see you at your desk earlier. I thought I was the only one here."

"Yeah. Uh, well. Let me explain what I found," he said, taking a seat at the table opposite me.

"You all right, Jack?" I asked.

"Yeah, but I'll be honest. I'm a little freaked out by some of the stuff I found."

"Okay," I said. "Why don't you begin at the beginning."

And he did. He told me that one of his hobbies was... well, he's a UFOlogist; he's into ancient aliens, and a spin-off of that was an avid interest in urban legends, which he tries to keep up to date with.

He mentioned the "usual suspects" like Bigfoot, the Chupacabra, the Roswell UFO crash, the Illuminati, the secret prisons and research facilities. *Boring!*

It was, and it's stuff I'd never paid much attention to, ever. But then he started to talk about the blood moon event, and that did get my attention. He said he would never have even thought to look into it had he not been involved in the Georgina Harrison case.

"Go on," I said. "I'm listening."

"I printed these articles from the internet," he said. "Now, bear with me, Cap. I'm not saying that there is going to be some kind of apocalypse, like the end of days or something. I'm just pointing out something I found interesting."

"Okay," I said and leaned forward to listen.

He began with a short history lesson about the Blood Moon phenomenon. According to his research, this rare nighttime occurrence was something people had been fascinated with since we could walk upright. Without going back to the days of the dinosaurs, suffice it to say that the display was seen by many as a sign of either good or bad, depending upon what happened next. Good crops. Bad weather. Many more babies. Fewer elderly deaths, love or hate, and all sorts of other crazy stuff, and he emphasized crazy, as in psychotic behaviors. Patterns. All of that kind of stuff, so the believers say, could be attributed to the event of a blood moon.

Then science stepped in and explained it all away. The scientists maintained that the blood moon was nothing more than a celestial episode that could accurately be predicted to appear every so many years.

Well, we all know that's true, right? Right, but that didn't stop the true believers.

"You've heard of Freemasonry?" Jack asked.

"Of course, I have," I said skeptically. "You're not going to tell me they have something to do with Georgina's murder, are you?"

"No, of course not, but what d'you know about them?"

"Not much," I replied. Wondering where the hell he was going with it, and if maybe I didn't have some kind of nut on my team after all.

"Right," he said. "No one does. They are a huge secret society. A lot of people give them more power and authority than they deserve. But many of the founders of the United States were Freemasons. They have lodges all over the country. In fact, one of the biggest Masonic populations is in a place I wouldn't even have guessed." He looked at me across the table, scratching his chin.

"Where?" I asked.

"Right here in Chattanooga." He smirked.

"Okay. That's weird. But aren't they just a men's club for

snobs? The Chief is a Freemason, I think... maybe. I'm not seeing the connection."

"There isn't one," he said. "I just thought it was interesting, is all."

He shrugged. I was ready to up and leave, but then he shuffled his papers, taking one out and handing it to me. "Look at this. This article is from 2004, just one week before Georgina died."

The article was titled "The Ugly Side of the Blood Moon Spectacle."

I read it part-way through, then handed it back to him without saying anything.

It gave a brief history of the constellations and the scientific background that made the moon turn red and appear to be the size of Jupiter. And it mentioned the folklore around the farming community, but then it took a left turn into the macabre. I still didn't see a connection. I sat back in my seat and folded my arms.

He shook his head, narrowed his eyes and frowned, then said, "You don't see it?"

"See what?"

He began to read from the article, "In recent years, it has been recorded that the number of suicides increases during this two-day event." He looked at me, eyebrows raised in question.

I looked at him and said, "We know she didn't kill herself, Jack."

"I know that," he hissed, annoyed, shaking his head. "Listen." He raised his hand, his index finger pointing up at the ceiling. "In addition to the increased number of suicides, the murder rate, not just in metropolitan areas but in rural areas, has almost doubled. Every time there was a blood moon, the murder rate goes up. This has been recorded since the mid-1800s."

I sighed, unfolded my arms, and leaned forward.

"Look, Jack," I said patiently, "the murder rate goes up every time there's a full moon. We all know that. I think most people know that. I'm not sure what you are trying to tell me. What are you saying?" I asked. Partially because I wanted to know what Jack's angle was, and partially because I wanted to wrap it up, go home, take a hot shower, drink a couple of glasses of wine and go to bed.

"For one," he said, "I don't know if we are looking in the right place for Georgina's killer. Two, I'm afraid we are going to see more of the same within the next few days. The blood moon will be up again. What are we going to do?"

He looked at me, not expecting an answer. We both knew there was no answer, and I was starting to feel the noose tighten.

"Before we go home," he said, "I have one more thing to show you. But, it's a little delicate," Jack said, looking over his shoulder at the closed door.

"What do you mean?" I asked tiredly.

He took a deep breath, scooted in his seat, and then leaned forward. "When I was a beat cop, I always knew I wanted to be a detective. So, even when I wasn't working a case, I was getting to know the locals, the street people, my neighbors. You know all about that, right? Some of these people walk a very fine line."

"So, you've got some informants?" I said. "So what? We all have them. I still do."

"I know that, too."

"Come on then, cut to the chase," I said. I was getting frustrated. "Tell me you have an informant that saw Georgina being murdered. That would be a great help," I said dryly.

"Not quite that," he replied, "but I do have someone who said he saw some people acting strangely in the woods not far from where Georgina's body was found."

"Is he sure? It was sixteen years ago," I asked skeptically.

"That's the point, Cap. We're not talking 2004. This was last week."

Now that, I wasn't expecting. Nor did I know what to think of it. The woods are still a popular hangout.

"Okay..." I said. "So some kids are doing the same thing as

Georgina's group was doing sixteen years ago: getting high or drunk, having sex, pretending they're witches and trying to raise the dead. Just because people are gathering in the woods after dark doesn't mean they're planning aggravated, ritual murder. Give it up, Jack. I'm going home."

I'd heard enough. I was a captain in the police department and I'd gotten there because I was a damn good detective. I lived by the facts, the hard evidence; that was the procedure. Murders were committed because of greed, love, hate, jealousy, anger, money or revenge. Not because the damn moon turned red.

"But Cap. Don't you think we should at least be keeping an eye out? Maybe assign a couple of uniforms to patrol the area?"

"No! I can't go to the Chief with a couple of old newspaper clippings and a story that kids are still congregating in the woods. He'd laugh at me. Go home, Jack. You've had a rough couple of days. You need to rest, get your head back on straight. I know I do," I added, trying to soften what I'd just said to him.

I could tell he was about to argue with me, but something stopped him, which surprised me because I'd already figured him for a hothead, and hotheads always had difficulty holding back their emotions.

Instead of arguing he said, "Look, Cap, I know it's been hard for everyone since I got here. I heard a lot of good stories about Lennie. I want you to know that I'm not trying to replace him. From what I heard, I don't think I ever could. Guys like him, nice guys with their badges pinned to a big heart, that just isn't me. I walk in the shadows of guys like Lennie. And I'm okay with that. I just want to be seen for doing *my* job, not Lennie's. Does that make sense?"

"It does, Jack, and I thank you for that."

"Thanks. And thanks for your patience, for taking a look at what I found." He shrugged as if he thought I was going to disregard all of his hard work.

I had no intention of doing that.

"Do me a favor," I said. "You said Janet helped you with it. Talk it over with her, and then you guys come to me with a plan. I'll listen."

That seemed to be an acceptable compromise. He nodded, took his stack of printouts and left. I looked at the clock on my computer. It was after nine. I went home to my bottle of wine, a hot shower, and my bed.

22

The Venderden Funeral Home was a quaint, beige brick building that could have been a florist's shop there were so many planters, vases, and window boxes decorating the grounds. The parking lot was full when Janet and I pulled in.

"Are you okay?" I asked after hearing Janet sigh.

"Yeah, I hate funerals, don't you?"

"I do," I said.

"And yes, I'm okay. As long as I stay focused, I'll be fine," Janet added.

"I know you will," I said, patting her on the shoulder. "Let's do this."

I adjusted my badge on my belt, made sure my jacket covered my weapon, and we exited my unmarked cruiser, then together we headed inside.

Buck Halloway must have been a popular guy, judging by the size of the crowd, though how that could have been with him spending all his off time in the crawl space, I couldn't begin to guess. Maybe it wasn't him they were there for, maybe it was his wife.

I felt the need to say something to her, but I could just imagine how she'd receive me. No doubt she was going to blame me, and Jack... and Janet for his death. And so, as I waited in line to pay my final respects to the closed coffin, I looked about the room. Janet had gone to check out names in the registry and I saw her take a prayer card.

There were lots of flowers. They flanked each side of the casket, and there was a large, framed photograph of Buck just to the right, a younger, bright-eyed and happier Buck. *My, how time changes everything,* I thought. I passed on by to where Lena Halloway was sitting on a couch off to the right of the casket, along with an older woman who I figured was either Buck's or Lena's mother. She was tending to two little girls, both wearing simple little navy-blue dresses that matched their mother's.

Even though she'd obviously been crying, Lena Halloway looked very pretty. She saw me, looked me up and down, and I not only saw but felt her eyes focus on my badge. It didn't take long for her to figure out who I was.

"You're with the police?" she asked, rising to her feet.

"Yes, ma'am," I replied, and introduced myself and Janet who'd rejoined me.

"I'm so pleased you came," she said, offering me her hand. I shook it and she continued, her voice trembling, "I hope you're not here because you feel somehow responsible for Buck's death."

What the hell do I say to that? I wondered.

"I'm here on behalf of myself and my team, to offer our sincerest condolences."

"Thank you," Lena said, quietly, her head lowered. "When I spoke with the other officers... I should probably have made him talk to them... I told them that Buck had told me everything about that incident back in 2004. I know he thought the world of Georgina, and I think he did his best to move on, but he was suffering terribly with clinical depression, and those phone calls from Regis Taylor every year always set him back." She took a deep, shuddering breath and continued, "He couldn't get beyond it. He couldn't let it go. So you see, it was only a matter of time before... he..." She looked at the coffin, tears streaming down her cheeks.

"I am so sorry, Mrs. Halloway."

She sniffed, wiped her eyes with a paper towel, then said, "I know it must sound terrible but, in a way, I'm glad it's over." She smiled through the tears. "The one thing I was really afraid of was that he might do something like this when our girls were at home. But he didn't, God bless him. I know he was thinking of them when... when he..." She shook her head, wiped away the tears again and said, "I do hope he's in a better place. He didn't deserve..." and then she burst out crying, turned to her mother, wrapped her arms around her neck, held onto her for a few seconds, and then turned again to me.

"I don't blame you or your officers, Captain, and I hope you don't either. I just pray to God that you find the person who murdered poor Georgina. Her death has caused so much pain for so many for so long. It needs to be over. I'll pray for you, Captain."

"Thank you, Mrs. Halloway," I said. "I appreciate that more than you know."

She nodded and sat down again.

I have to say that Mrs. Halloway was truly a lady, and that after my short but moving conversation with her, I felt somewhat better; not about anything in particular, just an overall feeling of well-being. Of course, she could wake up the next morning cursing me and the department. For now, though, she was okay with us, and I was going to take full advantage of that.

Janet and I moved to the back of the room and began surveying the mourners. Many were obviously family, as we could tell by the greeting they received from Lena and her mother.

The big surprise came when we saw Shelly Pinkowski-Brenner and Lilith Overby walk in, not quite together, but within minutes of each other.

"Janet, why don't you mingle a little, keep your eyes and ears open, and be sure to keep tabs on the two classmates over there."

"You got it, Cap," Janet said, and she slipped away, blending into the crowd.

I watched as the two classmates, separately, offered their condolences to Lena. I found it rather odd that the two who'd been so close in high school had not kept in touch over the years.

Shelly turned from Lena and made her way slowly toward the back of the room. As she did so, Janet approached her, put her hand on her arm, smiled, and spoke to her. I watched for a minute while they talked together.

I smiled to myself. Janet could charm the birds out of the trees.

Me? Knowing Shelly was in good hands, I decided to keep an eye on Lilith. She'd taken a seat two rows back from where Lena was sitting: not close enough to chat, but close enough to listen to any conversation she might have.

But Lilith seemed to be on edge. She kept looking toward the door as if she was expecting someone. And she was.

When an unusually tall, dark and handsome man wearing an expensive blue suit sauntered in, I knew instantly that this was who she was waiting for.

The man was carrying a trench coat over his arm, revealing not only a shiny gold watch but also a loop of red thread around his wrist. *Hmm, interesting.*

I watched in amazement at the transformation as Lilith stood up, and in a not-so-veiled attempt to gain his attention, took off her sweater, revealing a little black dress cut dangerously low in the back. She struck a pose next to the side table... Sheesh, I couldn't help but smile. *She looks like she's waiting for a bus.*

While I was watching Lilith, I was also watching the man. There was something about the way he was looking around. He seemed nervous. His eyes were puffy, almost as if he'd been crying and, he was jingling something in his pocket... his change, maybe? He waited for an opportunity, then instead of going over to Lilith, he went to Lena, bent over at the waist, took her hand, looked at her, then kissed it. Then he stood upright, her hand still in his, said something, shook his head, and let go of her hand. It was quite a performance, and she appeared to know him. They talked together for another minute, then Lena pointed in Shelly's direction.

Gotcha, I thought. *You, my friend, are the missing link: you're Junior Cole, the sixth spoke on the wheel.*

I opened my phone and flipped through photographs until I came to the picture of the group. I looked at it, then at the man. *Oh yeah, you're him all right.*

Between Janet and I, we'd made a half-dozen phone calls to his home in Monarch, North Carolina. He'd never answered. We left messages. He ignored them. Had he not shown up at the funeral, Janet and I would have been taking a trip to Monarch. So, his arrival was an unexpected gift, and not just for me, but more about that in a minute. I watched and waited. What happened next was a snub I never expected.

While Junior Cole was talking to Lena, Lilith was watching him, her eyes bright, licking her lips as if he were a side of beef and she was a tiger that hadn't eaten in a month. Her eyes swept up and down his body as she nervously sucked on her lower lip. But as the man left Lena, after taking her hand again and patting it gently, and then wiping tears from his own eyes, and heading toward Shelly, Lilith stepped in front of him.

He stopped dead in his tracks, looked at her, shook his head, and then hurried on past her as if she was a bag lady begging for change. Lilith, undeterred and without hesitation, gave chase.

"Hello, Junior," Shelly said as he hugged her and kissed her on the cheek. She smirked at Janet but didn't introduce them.

Janet stood by watching and listening as the two one-time class-mates chatted together. They were together no more than a few seconds—Cole, having paid his respects, was obviously eager to get away, and no wonder. No sooner had he wished Shelly all the best and said goodbye, than a breathless, nervous Lilith Overby followed him out into the reception area.

Me? I followed them, while Janet stayed with Shelly.

"Junior!" Lilith called after him. "Junior! Wait!"

But Junior didn't wait; he barged through the front doors and nearly broke into a run as he hurried toward a silver Porsche parked at the far side of the lot.

Lilith, wearing high heels, ran awkwardly after him. It was a wonder to me that she didn't snap her bony ankles.

I watched through the glass doors for a moment and slipped outside to see if I could listen to... Hell, I had no idea what Lilith was up to. Whatever it was, it looked like Junior wanted no part of it.

"Junior! Please! Wait!" she called, waving as she ran: short steps, arms waving like wings.

"Please, Lily! Not here," Junior said when she finally reached him.

I slipped out of sight between the parked cars and inched my way toward the couple until I was able to get within three cars of them.

"... you won't return my calls," Lilith said.

"It's not just you, Lily," he said, his car door open. "You know what time of year it is. Whenever I see a Tennessee area code, I don't answer it because... well, you know; it could be Regis, so I just don't answer the phone at all."

"I can't believe he still does that." Lilith chuckled nervously, somewhat mollified. "He did it to me, too... I'm so glad you're in town, Junior. I was hoping we might get together. Talk about old times."

"Old times? Are you kidding, Lily? One of our closest friends was murdered when we were just kids. Another is in jail, and now Buck's committed suicide." He ran his hand through his hair. "We're cursed, Lily. It was that damned stupid ritual you wanted to foist on us. It's only a matter of time before something bad happens to the rest of us."

"You don't really believe that, do you?" Lilith said, taking a step forward and placing a hand on his arm. "Because I think we've been extremely lucky. Look at you. You have a successful law practice in North Carolina, and from what I hear, there may be political opportunities opening up for you soon. Shelly's also doing well. I'm doing fine. No worries except..." She moved in even closer until her hip was touching Junior. "When are you going to accept it... that we should be together?"

"Lily," he said, took a step back, shaking his head, "we don't belong together. We were never... we never were like that. I don't know where this obsession of yours has come from, but you have to stop it. I'm sorry; I have to go," Junior said, his hands trembling as he fumbled with his keys.

"Oh, just look at you," Lilith said, smiling. "You can't help but tremble when I'm near you, but I promise, you don't have to be scared of me."

"But I am, Lily. I am scared shitless of you, and for you. You need help. You really do. Serious help."

"What are you talking about? You're just being silly. I've never been better. And just wait until the blood moon this weekend." She smiled devilishly.

"Oh, my God! You're not still dabbling in that crap?"

"I'm not dabbling in anything. I'm just saying that the stars are all aligned, and some really exciting things are about to happen. Trust me, you'll see," she said, and moved so close to him her breasts were touching his chest. If she'd gotten any closer to him, she'd have been inside his suit.

"No. No!" he said loudly. "See, there you go again, getting in my head. Lily, please, you've got to stop this silliness. Go on, go back inside. I have to go."

He put his hands on her shoulders, turned her around, and pushed her gently toward the funeral home doors.

"Go on back inside and apologize to Lena," he said. "I did, because we sure as hell didn't do anything to help Buck, did we? What kind of people are we anyway?"

"All right," she replied. "I'll go back inside, but I won't apologize. I've done nothing to apologize for. But don't think for one second that you've gotten rid of me. You won't be going back to North Carolina right away, will you?"

Junior didn't say anything. He just looked away.

"I didn't think so," she said and turned and walked jauntily back into the funeral home, without a backward glance at Junior.

I watched as his body relaxed. His head fell forward until his chin was touching his chest and he was looking down at the ground, his arms hanging loosely at his sides. He shook his head, as if trying to rid himself of some sad, unwanted thought.

I adjusted my badge, stepped out into the open, turned on the record app on my iPhone, and walked toward him.

23

"Excuse me," I said, holding up my ID. "Junior Cole?"

"Yes?" His eyes narrowed. He frowned, his brow furrowed.

"My name is Captain Gazzara. I'd like a word, if you don't mind, maybe ask you a couple of questions?" I smiled. He looked me slowly up and down. *Damn! He's undressing me.*

He must have decided I was attractive enough, because he shrugged and said, "Do I have a choice?"

"Not really," I replied, smiling, looking him slowly up and down. *Two can play your game, fancy pants.*

"I'd like to talk to you about Georgina Harrison."

Junior blinked, looked to his right, then said, "What about her?" *Don't do it, Junior. Don't lie to me.*

"You know what about, Mr. Cole. Georgina Harrison, a close friend of yours, was murdered sixteen years ago on the 26th."

He didn't answer. He just stared at me. I took a deep breath and said, "I was a part of the investigating team. As I recall, you were interviewed by Detective Starke; d'you remember?"

He nodded, slowly, but still said nothing.

"As you know, Mr. Cole, we never found her killer. I've reopened the case. We couldn't interview you properly back then because you were a minor. That's not the case now, is it, sir? I should tell you that I'm recording our conversation." I held up my phone.

He stared at it, then said, "I understand, but is this really necessary?"

"It is, so why don't we begin with you telling me what you remember about that night," I said, placing the phone on the top of his car.

"Are you serious, Detective? I'm here for the funeral of one of my best friends. He killed himself, damn it, and you want me to recall events that happened sixteen years ago? I don't think so, and I really don't have time for this." He reached for his car door handle.

"As you wish, Mr. Cole, but if you don't talk to me here, I'll have a blue and white come pick you up and take you to the police department, and you can talk to me there. Now, what's it to be, and before you answer, you might want to think about how that would look to the members of your firm. The choice is yours, sir."

He sighed, then said, "Oh, very well... but it was a long time ago, Detective. My memory is not that good anymore."

"Really? You're what, thirty-two, and your memory's going already? Just do your best," I replied dryly.

He thought for a moment then said, "It was one of those beautiful nights. The sky was clear, the stars bright, twinkling, and the moon... it was quite a sight, it really was, but not that spectacular, not to me anyway. It was that whole lunar eclipse thing, you see, and we were out there to see it, do school projects and... whatever. It was interesting, yes, but I didn't see what all the hype was about. I mean, if you've seen the moon once, you've seen it a hundred times, right?"

"How long were you all out there?" I asked.

"Well, I'd say about an hour. No, it was more like two before we left."

"What time was that?"

"Ten thirty-ish, I suppose?"

"And?"

"As I remember it, Georgie had forgotten to bring a coat, and she was getting cold and wanted to leave. She was wearing just a white sweater and black pants... shorts," he said, vacantly, obviously remembering something. "I seem to remember that she'd changed her hair. When she got there, she had it pulled back behind her ears, with those clip things, you know? But then she went off with Regis, and when she came back it was loose and tussled. Uh, I think."

"That's quite a lot of detail for someone who said he couldn't remember," I said.

He shrugged, smiled self-consciously, then said, "So, I had a little crush on her when we were kids. So what? It's what kids do, right? But that's all it ever was, a crush. You see, she had a thing for Regis. I never understood the attraction—the man's an idiot—but what do I know about women?"

"He was just a boy back then," I said.

"Yes, but still an idiot. Can't see what she saw in him. Maybe if she'd..." He shook his head and stopped talking.

"Did that make you angry, that she liked Regis instead of you?" I asked.

"Well, a little maybe. I was a little jealous but—"

"Did you ever tell her how you felt?"

"Not exactly. I tried to let her know in little ways. I'd carry her books when Regis wasn't around, open the door for her... That kind of thing. Regis, boy, he really went off the deep end when she died," Junior said, looking off in the distance.

"In what way?"

"He wouldn't talk to us. He just clammed up, dropped out of just about everything. He was angry."

"Mr. Cole, you say you were a little jealous; did you ever lose your temper? Didn't you ever get fed up, making all those gestures only to be rejected?" I asked, watching his eyes.

He was sweating slightly, looking down at the ground, hands in his pants pockets playing with his keys.

"No. I've never lost my temper, ever. Yes, I was a little put out, but it was high school. Everything was a big drama back then. You know how it is." He smiled awkwardly.

"I was watching you talking to Lilith Overby," I said. "You came mighty close to losing it then."

"No, I didn't," he said loudly, outraged. "And what were you doing listening in on a private conversation?"

"What d'you think I was doing, Mr. Cole?" I asked dryly. "You shouted at Lilith, and you just shouted at me. Did you ever yell like that at Georgina?"

"No."

"But you do admit to being jealous? Jealousy can make a person do crazy things. And you were one of the last people to see Georgina alive. You went for a walk with her and Buck Halloway. Tell me about that."

"A walk? Not really," he said. "I left her with Buck." His eyes flicked away to the right. "So I might have gotten upset but..." Then his eyes snapped back to me. He looked incredulous, as if he'd just caught on to what was happening to him. "You're insinuating that I... I didn't kill her. I didn't kill Georgie," he stuttered. "I didn't."

"So you say. Okay, so let's just look at the facts. According to you, the three of you walked from the woods to Swiss Valley Park where you split up: Georgina and Buck went one way, you went the other. But you see, Buck also told us that you walked to the park together and then split up. But he said it was you that went with Georgina, not him.

"Unfortunately, now that Buck's gone, we only have your word for what happened that night." I folded my arms, tilted my head to one side and frowned.

He just stood there, his mouth open, body rigid, staring at me.

"You admit it upset you that Georgina rejected your advances," I continued. "You admit you were jealous. And... I think you lied to me when you said you left her with Buck, which means that you were the last person to see her alive. I think you waited until Buck was out of sight, then dragged her back into the trees and killed her."

"I didn't! I didn't kill her. I—"

"It doesn't look good for you, Mr. Cole."

Yes, I was bluffing. I didn't have enough to book him. I didn't even have probable cause to take him in for questioning. I was merely hoping to rattle his cage, get him to open up and tell me what really happened that night.

"You're crazy," he shouted. "I didn't kill Georgie. If anyone did, it was Regis Taylor. He was sleeping with her. Maybe she got tired of him and wanted to break it off. The man's a violent offender. He's in prison now for aggravated assault. He's the one with the history of violence. Not me."

For a guy who ran his own law firm and was a pillar in the legal community, when it came to defending himself, Junior was no Perry Mason.

"I think you did," I said. "I think you killed Georgina Harrison in a fit of jealous rage. I think you dragged her into the woods, stabbed her multiple times, and then you *cut her throat from... ear... to... ear,*" I said.

"*Nooo,* I did not. Good God, I was in love with her. I'd never have hurt her. I would have given her everything I owned," he said, now sadly. "I'm still in love with her. Or at least I'm in love with what I remember of her. I don't want to talk to you anymore. Either arrest me or let me go."

I nodded, and said, "I'm not going to arrest you, Mr. Cole... Not yet, but don't leave town. I *will* want to talk to you again, and soon." I tapped on the hood of his car three times with my fingertips, picked up my phone, turned off the recording app, and turned and walked away, back toward the entrance to the funeral home, only to run smack dab into a frantic Lilith Overby who gifted me with a look that could've frozen a pot of boiling water.

24

"Haven't you done enough?" she hissed at me as she stormed past me to Junior's car.

I watched for a minute, too far away to hear but close enough to see that there was more trouble in paradise.

Lilith stood in front of Junior, leaning forward from the waist, her hands on her hips, saying something to which he just stared at her. She stomped her feet. He shrugged, his arms bent and his palms up. He shook his head. I could tell he'd said no. And then he looked at his wrist, picked at the red thread bracelet with his other hand, and said something. Lilith stared at the red thread, and whatever it was he'd said, it seemed to make her happy.

She stepped forward, close to him, wrapped her arms around his neck and pulled him down to her. He didn't seem to respond, but he didn't fight it either. His arms hung limply at his sides as she whispered something in his ear, then kissed his cheek and looked up into his eyes. He didn't look happy about that, whether it was the kiss or what she whispered; he was frowning.

Finally, Lilith let go of him, put the palm of her hand against his cheek and said something. Then she took a step back, nodded, and turned and hurried to what I assumed to be her car. But before she got more than a half-dozen steps away from him, he shouted after her.

"I don't ever want to see you again, Lily. Never. Do you understand me?"

"You don't mean that," she said loud enough for me to hear. "You know you don't."

"Yes, I do. Please, don't embarrass yourself anymore." And with that Junior Cole got into his car, closed the door and drove away.

Lilith saw me watching her, stopped dead in her tracks, obviously trembling with rage.

"Bitch," she snarled at me, then marched over to her car, climbed in and sped off, the tires of her Jaguar squealing as she turned hard onto the road and disappeared in the opposite direction of Junior Cole.

I went back inside the funeral home and found Janet on a loveseat with the proprietor. They both stood as I approached.

"Captain Gazzara, Mr. Venderden," she introduced us. "He's the owner," Janet said as I extended my hand.

Venderden was a pleasant-looking middle-aged man and a master of the sympathetic, funerary smile and kind gaze. Hell, even I felt better just looking at him.

"It's nice to meet you, sir," I said.

He inclined his head politely.

"Captain," Janet said, "Mr. Venderden was telling me about an anomaly on the... on Buck's remains. You might find it interesting."

I looked at him. The smile remained static.

"Mr. Venderden," I said, "are you able to tell me about it, officially? I wouldn't want you to violate your contract with the family of the deceased."

"It's not like that," he said. "I intended to call the police when I received his remains, but somehow it got away from me. We've been very busy of late. Normally, I wouldn't even have thought much about it except that... well, I know who Buck Halloway was.

"You see, I was working my way through my first year of mortician school when I heard the news about that teenager's... that schoolgirl's death and, of course, their names, the friends, were in the papers, including our friend in there." He nodded in the direction of the receiving room.

"I've lived in Chattanooga all of my life, and in this business, you get to know just about everyone. My father was the funeral director here when it happened, and even though the girl's funeral was not held here, the people at Hickey's—that's where the teenager was prepared—well, I knew one of the morticians, he passed a couple of years ago, Lawrence Beecker was his name. He told me something very strange. I never forgot it," Venderden said, his practiced, soft Southern drawl offering an extra layer of comfort to his voice.

"What was that, Mr. Venderden?" I asked.

"Well, as you probably know, the autopsy was carried out at the Medical Examiner's office. So, all the morticians at Hickey's had to do was the basic, dare I say, mechanics? There was not to be an open casket." Venderden paused, took a deep breath, and folded his hands in his lap.

"But Lawrence told me that the girl's torso had some sort of symbols carved into it. Apparently, they were reluctant to prepare the poor girl, and it was touch and go for a while whether they would or would not. In the end, old man Hickey put his foot down, told them that the family had been through enough and that they were to get on with it, and they did."

Janet was right; it was interesting. The more so because I had gone out of my way to tell Doc that the scratches on the body were nothing more than the result of the violent attack: the killer's rage, a crime of passion. Maybe Doc was right. What I'd just heard from Venderden seemed to indicate that he was. *Whoa, could I really be dealing with a ritual killer?*

"But now," Venderden continued, "after all these years, you can imagine my surprise that I am burying one of the people involved in that terrible death." He paused, looked at me, the smile still there but now obviously fake. "He also has similar markings carved into his skin."

I was stunned, just as he intended.

"How can that be?" I asked, looking at Janet. "My detective was on the scene when Halloway killed himself. He was fully clothed. Am I right?"

"He was," Janet replied.

Venderden shrugged. "I'm sure he was. The markings are quite old, scars, fully healed, across his thighs. I'm not an expert, but I'd say they were self-inflicted. I did contact his wife, but after hearing her voice on the phone, I decided not to share the information with her. She'd been through enough already. I had made a note on my calendar to contact the police after the service. But you arrived here on your own. Saved me a dime." Venderden smiled.

"Who did the autopsy?" I asked.

"Someone at Erlanger. It wasn't a suspicious death so a medical examiner's postmortem wasn't necessary."

I nodded. "When is the interment, Mr. Venderden?" I asked.

"After the church service tomorrow morning."

"I'd like to take a look at the body, in private, when there's no one here. It's important. Would you mind if my partner and I come back after the visitation? I'd like to take a look at those markings."

"Of course," Venderden said.

And we thanked him, left the funeral home and made a beeline to Doc's office. I needed to hear his opinions about the marks and the blood moon again. No matter how way-out I thought they might be.

25

"What are you two doing here?" Doc said as he opened the front door for me.

"Nice to see you, too, Doc," I replied. "Where's your new receptionist?"

"I had to let her go. She was sexually harassing me," Doc said as we followed him to his office.

Oh Lord, please don't let him say that out in public.

"Have a seat, ladies. Just put those things on the floor."

We grabbed the stacks of files that were piled on all four of the chairs and did as he asked; we cleared two of the chairs and dumped the contents on the floor.

"You could at least have had her clean your office before you booted her out," I said. "What did Mrs. Sheddon have to say about her putting the moves on you?"

"She said she wanted to have a serious talk with her, make her an offer she couldn't refuse," Doc said as he took a seat. "Now, let me guess. You want to talk about Georgina Harrison?"

"I do, Doc." I looked at Janet. "We've just attended Buck Halloway's visitation. Suicide. He was pronounced dead at the hospital. They did the autopsy but... Well, it was pretty straightforward, so I understand. He shot himself in the head. I'll let Janet tell you the rest."

I sat quietly and watched Doc as he listened to Janet while eyeballing me over his half-glasses. He didn't have to say a word. I could see the *"I told you so"* in his gaze.

"That's very interesting," he said to Janet, who'd been reading from her extensive notes. "So, old man Venderden thinks the scars on Halloway's thighs are old and self-inflicted, does he? Well, he would know if they were old. Self-inflicted? I'd need to see the body. I can subpoena it if you like—"

"No!" I interrupted him sharply. "That won't be necessary. We're seeing the body later. I'll get photos. If need be, I can show them to you and get your opinion. What I want to know right now is, are the carvings on Georgina's breasts random acts of violence, are they accidental, or were they made by some sort of lunatic trying to appease his god? More important, do they actually mean anything?"

This wasn't really the time for him to gloat, but I could tell by the look on his face that he was going to. He rotated his chair, picked up a file from the credenza, rotated back again, flipped it open and stared at me. His right eyebrow arched high up his forehead. I looked at him, rolled my eyes, and sighed.

"I had it ready in case you decided you'd like to see my notes." He looked at Janet and winked.

She smiled back at him. Sweetly, as if sugar wouldn't melt in her mouth.

"All right. Quit flirting with my partner and tell me again what you think the *random* scratches are." I scooted my chair closer to his desk.

Doc took out an autopsy photograph of Georgina Harrison's body, a close-up of her upper torso taken before he had begun to cut.

"You see this one here?" He made an imaginary circle around a cut that looked like a small shepherd's crook just over her right breast.

"Doc, that could have been made by a piece of broken glass, part of a beer bottle. She could have fallen on it."

"Normally I'd agree with you, but if you look at this close-up..." He set another photo next to it.

"What am I looking at?" I asked.

"I think I see it," Janet said, leaning forward.

I could see it too, but to me... it could still have been made by broken glass. There were scratches all over the body, but those Doc was pointing out were deeper and obviously cuts.

"Wait!" Janet opened her yellow pad, flipped to a blank page, and said, "This is what I see." And she quickly drew a Shepherd's crook, a half-moon, something that looked like a small "q" and then a squiggly line.

The rest of the wounds were simple stab wounds, not deep, but administered carefully as if the killer wanted to inflict maximum pain before he slit her throat.

"They look like runes to me," Janet said.

I looked at her skeptically. "And you know this because?"

"It's just a hobby... well, it was once. Not anymore, but when I was a kid, a teenager. I think we are looking at symbols for four letters of the alphabet."

"I don't see it," I said.

"Check this out," Janet said, ignoring my skepticism. "This one I think is a T, this one an N, an S, and the last one is an E, I think.

I shook my head. I still couldn't see it.

"To me, they look like nothing more than shallow knife wounds," I said. "Some sadistic bastard wanted to torture her before he killed her. Doc, is that what you see?"

He shrugged, then said, "Make of it what you will... I will say this: I think these four wounds were made by a much smaller knife, a small pocket penknife, perhaps."

I was getting frustrated, which wasn't, isn't, like me. I still couldn't see any intelligent design in the cuts, and I was thinking that what could have been a break in the case was turning out to be a bust. Not only that, but I was also afraid that if they were right, then the implications would be unthinkable. No, I wasn't ready to go there, not yet. At that point, what I *really* wanted to do was go back to the funeral home and check out the cuts on Buck's legs.

"I'll admit it's a bit of a stretch, Cap, but..." Janet said as I stared at the photos.

I didn't answer. I just shook my head, slowly.

"I hope to God you're both wrong," I said quietly.

"Well, I don't know what they mean," Janet said. "D'you have any ideas, Cap?" she asked, snapping me out of my trance.

"I hope they don't mean anything," I said. "But we need to keep digging. We need to get back to the funeral home."

"Are you all right?" Janet asked. "You look pale."

"Yeah, I'm fine," I lied. "Thanks for your help, Doc. I don't know what the hell we're dealing with, but I've got a sick feeling in my stomach that it's more than I was bargaining for."

"Well, let me know if there's anything else I can do to help," he said, as he followed us to the door.

"Kate? Do you think this could be some kind of satanic thing?" Janet asked, as we walked to the car.

"I didn't... It's just that... Oh hell, I don't know what to think."

"I wouldn't beat myself up over it if I were you, Cap," she said cheerfully. "That's why you took it out of the cold case morgue to begin with, to take a fresh look at it. You knew there was something wrong when you and Harry investigated it originally. That's why it's been bugging you all these years."

She was a smart kid. And I probably needed the pep talk, but I didn't acknowledge it. Instead I had to ask the question:

"You studied that silly shit when you were a kid?" I asked as I started the car and pulled out onto Amnicola. "Who the hell has a hobby like that?"

"Evidently, Lilith Overby does."

I gifted her with a look that should have shriveled her right there in her seat, but she simply looked right back at me and gave me a cheeky grin in return.

26

The Venderden Funeral Home was in darkness and appeared to be locked up tight when I pulled into the parking lot just before five-thirty that evening. Only a single tiny light at the end of a long hallway was still on, prompting me to knock loudly on the glass door. Venderden appeared almost immediately and smiled as he approached.

"Hello, detectives," he said as he opened the door. "I'm glad you are here early. Come on in. I'm all alone here. I know you think me strange, but you see, I enjoy the quiet of the sanctuary. Growing up in the funeral business as I did, there's very little I haven't seen, and very little causes me distress, not anymore," he said as we followed him along the hallway. "But I can't say I'll be sorry to see this business with Mr. Halloway settled."

"I understand how you feel," I said.

We followed him to a door almost at the end of the hallway on the left. He unlocked it and held the door open for us. Goose bumps ran up my arms as we stepped inside, reminding me of Doc Sheddon's forensic rooms.

"We keep it cooler in here for obvious reasons," he said as he stepped up to the casket.

I'd expected the body to be fully exposed, but only the lower section of the casket was open.

"I'll need to confirm that it's Buck Halloway, Mr. Venderden," I said.

"Oh, yes, of course," he said, hurrying to open the top section. "I'm sorry, Detective, I should have realized that you must have seen far worse than this. But, if I do say so myself, considering what we had to work with, I think my mortician did an excellent job of cleaning him up. But there was only so much that could be done; it was a devastating wound."

They hadn't bothered to apply makeup. Why would they when they knew that no one would see him? Thus Buck's face was the color of asphalt and, considering the explosive force of the gasses from the bullet, his head was surprisingly intact. Nothing the family should be allowed to see, of course, but for my purposes there was no doubt I was looking at Buck Halloway.

"You understand that we don't actually dress the body; we don't put it *into* the outfit. We split the clothing up the back and wrap it..." He tailed off as I looked at him.

Venderden nodded and gently tugged and unfolded the pants from Buck's cold, gray legs. The scars were indeed old. I photographed them with my phone. And, much as I hated to, I had to admit to myself they looked similar to those on Georgina's body.

"They're the same, aren't they?" Janet said, leaning over the casket for a closer look.

"I'm not sure," I lied, not yet willing to admit it out loud.

"If I had to guess, I'd say they're self-inflicted," she said.

Before I could answer, my cellphone rang, startling me. I looked at Venderden, embarrassed at being so jumpy.

"Sorry to bother you, Captain." It was Jack. "D'you have a minute?"

"Hold on, Jack." I took the phone from my ear and told them I needed a moment, then went out into the hallway.

"Yes. What is it?"

"I found some strange stuff that might just tie in with the case. I've been checking into the symbols carved into Georgina Harrison's chest. They're real, Cap. They're pagan astrological signs."

I put my hand to my head and closed my eyes. "That's not what I wanted to hear," I said, "but go on, tell me." And he did.

I listened while Jack rattled on about ancient aliens, stone circles, and a group of pagans that worshipped the moon: "The Daughter of the Sun," the "Queen of the Night," and other such silly crap. Apparently they regarded themselves as descendants of the gods and found strength, protection, and good fortune by making sacrifices to the Goddess during specific lunar events. The Blood Moon being the grand pooh-bah of all moons.

"I watch the History Channel," I said dryly. "All that silly shit they keep running about ancient aliens that people thought were gods, but I've never heard of the group you're talking about. Are you sure this isn't just some crazy internet conspiracy theory that someone dreamt up? You know. An urban legend like that Slenderman nonsense?"

"It could be," he said, "but you know what happened with Slenderman. There were several sacrificial deaths attributed to the mythical man's followers—mostly young kids—who believed him to be real."

I did, and it was a world I couldn't yet understand... nor believe.

"Okay, I got it," I said, "and I'll think about it. I'm at the funeral home. I'm going to drop Janet off at the PD and then go home. I'll meet you at the office tomorrow morning, and we'll talk it over." I hung up, thanked Venderden for his help, and told him we were leaving.

"Be careful out there, detectives," he said. "As I also deal with death every day, I can assure you that this is not the strangest thing I've ever seen. Hold fast onto your faith. When all is said and done, that's all that there really is... isn't there?" He extended his hand to me and I shook it. Janet did too.

"Thank you, Mr. Venderden. I couldn't agree with you more," and with that, we left him.

I drove us back toward the police department, and we hadn't been on the road long when Janet began to prattle, as she always does. I was in no mood for it, so I told her to shut the hell up. Did it upset her? No. She knows my moods, and when to let me think. Ten minutes later I dropped her off and then went home.

I locked all the doors, turned on the television, grabbed a half bottle of red from the fridge—all that was left from a binge a couple nights earlier. It wasn't much, and it surely wasn't enough to make me forget all that I'd learned throughout the day, but it was enough to help me fall asleep. And I have to tell you, I slept like a log until...

I woke up around three in the morning, startled by something. I lay there for what...? It must have been ten minutes or more, listening, but I heard nothing. Eventually, I crawled out of bed, naked except for my panties, and went to get a glass of water. When I stepped into my small front room, I froze, virtually and literally. It was so cold, and I could hear the wind blowing... *Outside? What the hell?*

I checked the window. It was closed. *Oh no! It can't be.* But it was. The front door to my apartment was wide open. Every nerve in my body was instantly alert, pumped full of adrenaline. I ran to the nightstand, grabbed my Glock, ran back into the living room and stopped dead, my weapon in both hands, extended in front of me. I must have looked one hell of a sight, almost totally naked, my breasts swinging in the breeze. But I had no thought for any of that, not then. I stood stock-still, listening, my ears straining, eyes wide to catch even the smallest movement or shift in the shadows.

Finally, with my heart pounding in my chest, my body coated in a thin film of sweat, thinking it was now or never, I bolted for the door and slammed it shut, frantically slipping the locks in place.

Then, with my back pressed up against the door, I waited for my worst nightmare to materialize. I figured the intruder must now be locked inside with me. I waited, barely breathing, my finger gently resting on the trigger—yeah, I know that was a huge no-no, but you had to be there. Anyway, nothing moved. My apartment was as quiet as Venderden's funeral home after hours.

Quietly and quickly I went to my room, slipped into my robe, then with my weapon still in hand, I flipped on every light in the apartment. I looked under the bed, in the closets, behind the shower curtain and anywhere else I could think of, even under the damn kitchen sink. But I was alone. And the fact that I distinctly remembered locking the door when I came home, prowled around the back of my mind like a nervous rabbit...

And then my cell phone rang, and I yelped like a scalded puppy. I almost leaped out of my freakin' skin. I picked it up, answered it without even looking at the screen.

"Gazzara," I said. Nothing. Nothing but static. "Hello?" Still nothing. Then the phone went dead. I looked at the calls received log: no number. Just one word, "Unavailable."

I looked at the kitchen clock. It was three-twenty-two. I went back to bed, but I didn't sleep, not one wink.

27

I was still awake when my alarm blew up the silence at six o'clock. It was still dark, but I was still very thankful for the arrival of the new day.

I slipped into my sweat suit and a dirty old pair of tennis shoes and went for a run, and I tried to enjoy it, but my heart just wasn't in it, nor was my body; it was bone tired. On any other day, I would have run a solid five miles, sometimes more. On that day, I managed only half that, but it felt good and it did clear my head.

Sadly, about a mile and a half out, I turned around and ran back to my apartment, disappointed in myself. There's nothing more deflating than a half-assed workout. Anyway, it did give me time to think. By the time I returned to my apartment, I'd convinced myself that I must have not only left the front door unlocked, but also unlatched, and the wind had blown it open. The phone call? A wrong number, of course; that's what it was.

I ran up the steps and into my apartment, slammed the front door behind me and locked it—with the deadbolt and the chain—and headed for the shower with some feeling of peace, knowing that this time the door was closed and locked. Even so, I spent less than five minutes in the shower; I'm sure it was the quickest *ever*.

I took my time getting dressed, not for any good reason that I could think of, but more to relax, I guess. I selected a pair of light tan tactical pants and a white roll-neck sweater over a white tee. I put my hair up in a ponytail and applied a little makeup; not much, just a little eye shadow and pale pink lipstick. That done, I slipped into my signature tan leather jacket, clipped my holster and badge onto my belt, checked in the mirror one last time, and headed out the door.

I arrived at the police department twenty minutes later, at ten to nine, to be greeted by Hawk at the ground floor elevator doors. The look on his face was enough to tell me that he had just recounted the number of days until his retirement, and the hours couldn't go by fast enough.

"Oh crap. What now?" I muttered.

"You need to talk to North," he said without any preamble. "He's pretty pissed off."

"Why? What's happened?" I snapped. *Damn! As if I don't already have enough on my plate!*

"That woman who came in yesterday, Lilith Overby," Hawk said. "She came back. She was already here waiting when we arrived at eight this morning, and she was madder'n hell."

"Is she still here? What did she want?" I asked, but I had the feeling I knew what it was about. It had to be about what happened at the funeral home.

"No. She's gone. She threw a fit, called Jack a... some names, and promised to be back."

"So what did she want?" I repeated the question, stepping closer to him, trying to avoid the crush of passing bodies in the corridor.

"Where do I start? Your name came up. Something about you stalking her at Buck Halloway's funeral. But that wasn't the half of it. It's Jack she was really out to get. Nothing like the support of the community to make you feel like you're doing your job, is there?"

"What did he do, Hawk?"

"According to him, he was just doing his job."

"Does the Chief know?" I looked back along the corridor toward his office.

"No. He's in meetings all day over at City Hall. That ought to put him in a good mood," he said sarcastically. "I suggest you get it sorted before he comes back."

"You've got that right," I said. "Go on up and have Jack come to my office."

Hawk nodded, and we took the elevator to the second floor; I turned and went to my office.

Two minutes later there was a knock on my door. It opened, and Jack North stepped inside.

"Cap, that woman is out to get me fired—"

"Calm down, Jack. Sit down."

It was at that point that I realized the morning was already going to hell: I looked around for my travel cup and realized that I'd left it on my kitchen counter.

"Oh shit," I muttered under my breath, then said out loud, "What the hell's going on? What have you done now?"

"Captain, I was just doing my job. You can ask Toliver. She was there. We worked half the night, and some of the stuff we found required we go out and do a little snooping. It was all legit. Look, if people can file claims against us for doing our jobs, what the hell are we supposed to do?"

"Janet was with you?"

"Yeah. See, I told you about the pagans. I'm talking early native Americans and their rituals. Well, I found this place considered to be sacred, and it just happened to be not far from Mrs. Overby's neighborhood. We didn't go to her house or anything, not even her block. In fact, I don't think we were anywhere near her subdivision. And, now that I think about it, I don't know how she could have known unless she was spying on us. Anyway, she claimed I was stalking her."

"But she didn't say anything about Janet being in on this harassment issue?" I asked.

"Nope. Not a peep about her."

"And where is this *special* place?" I asked.

"On the north side of the woods, not far from where Georgina Harrison's body was found." He paused, shook his head and said, "You know, Cap, I'm just trying to do a good job. I know I've messed up in the past, but this case is going to explode in our faces if we don't wrap it up soon. The full blood moon is tomorrow night, and I'm certain there's going to be trouble. All we need is for someone to leak it to the press and it's game over."

I nodded thoughtfully. Jack was right, and I didn't like it that he was being targeted by a woman with obvious mental health issues.

"I'm going to have to have a talk to the Chief," I said. "If I don't, and she gets to him first... well, who knows?"

He nodded and said, "Look, I know my job is research; it's what I do, right? It's why I'm here. I'm a detective and, just like you, I live by what I find. I love facts and figures. They talk to me. I trust them. So if my research tells me there's an old bridge over a dry riverbed next to the cell tower where our victim was last known to communicate, I'm going to verify that. If I can't do what I do because I might hurt someone's feelings, then I'm... useless. There's no point in my even being here. I might as well go work at a frickin' bank."

"I understand what you're saying, Jack. Believe me, I do, but we have to walk a fine line." He opened his mouth to speak, but I held up my hand to stop him. "I know... I know! We're dealing with a nut. Even so... Well, just be careful; stay out of her sight. I'll handle it."

I felt kind of sorry for him. I'd been called on the carpet enough times to know exactly how he felt. I also knew in my heart that he wasn't at fault, and I believed that Lilith Overby was suffering from some kind of trauma because I'd reopened the case: she was going to lash out at anyone who got in her way. Unfortunately, she'd taken an instant dislike to Jack.

"Yeah," he said resignedly. "I know just how it's going to go. It's her word against mine, and we all know which side Internal Affairs will come down on." He pushed himself up out of his seat from the chair and went to the door. "Anything else, Cap?"

"Go somewhere and cool off," I said, as I made a note to talk to Janet. "Put it out of your mind. You're not alone in this so don't go off on your own and make things worse. Understand?"

He didn't reply. He just nodded his head and looked at me like I was offering a band-aid for his slit wrist. He closed the door behind him, leaving me with my thoughts.

I didn't like how things were developing for him. It would have been easy for me to sit there and wish that Lennie was still around. *How much easier that would be,* I thought. But that kind of thinking wouldn't be fair to Jack. Sure, he was a square peg being forced into a round hole, and I couldn't help but feel bad for him.

I decided to get everyone together on Monday morning, talk it through, see where we all were with the case. Maybe together we could figure this thing out before it blossomed into a public relations nightmare. Little did I know it was going to turn into a nightmare no matter what.

28

I didn't emerge from my office until a little after two o'clock. I went up to the situation room, where I found Jack at his desk doing some paperwork. He didn't look up. Hawk, Robar, and Janet were also at their desks. At least they all acknowledged my presence.

Janet looked up at me and asked for a minute of my time. I nodded and was about to pull up a chair when she shook her head and glanced pointedly at Jack.

I got the message, nodded, and said, "Yes, but I have to go back to my office. I'm expecting a call."

"I just wanted to tell you that Jack is a good cop," she said, as she shut my office door and sat down at the table. "I never thought I'd say this, but he makes Lennie look like an amateur."

"Really?" I said sharply. *This had better be good.*

"Really," she said. "I miss Lennie, and I know you do too; we all do, but I think he'd be pretty jazzed to know who had replaced him. That's the kind of guy Lennie was."

"Yeah, he was," I replied but didn't say anything more.

"I just thought you should know," she said self-consciously.

"And I'm glad you did. So... why don't you tell me what happened last night, Janet?"

"That's just it. *Nothing* happened. We went to this place in the woods where Harrison's body was found... well, not *where* she was found. It was some distance away. Anyway, there wasn't much to see. Just a rocky clearing among the trees. A nice place for a picnic, but that's all. Jack said it was some sort of Native American powwow spot, or something like that. He's all taken up with this blood moon thing. I'll be glad when it's over. Just another couple of days, right?"

I nodded and said, "I know that place. It's where Georgina Harrison and her friends used to hang out."

"So that's where she was killed?" she asked.

"No, it was closer to the edge of the woods."

"So she couldn't have been killed at the rocky meeting place, then?"

"No. CSI went over it and found nothing: no blood, nothing. So you guys didn't find anything else? You didn't see Lilith Overby?"

"Not her or anybody else. It was dark and kind of creepy. I was glad I wasn't alone."

"So," I said, changing the subject, "tell me, what did you and Shelly Brenner talk about yesterday?"

"Umm, okay," she said, seemingly surprised. "I asked her why she didn't mention the little shrine when we interviewed her."

"Oh yes, and what did she say?"

"She said it's been there so long she'd forgotten about it. I think she's paranoid. She's still convinced that our questions are just a ploy to get at her husband and damage his political career. I told her we were investigating a murder and that she was a suspect. That... sort of grabbed her attention. I also told her that if that didn't ruin his chances, he was probably already home free and only he, himself, could ruin them. She didn't like that at all."

"Well played, Toliver," I said.

"Thanks, but did you notice the effect Junior Cole had on her and Lilith Overby? I saw her take off after him when he left. You'd think he stole her purse the way she gave chase." Janet shook her head.

I had to laugh because that was the perfect way to describe Lilith's reaction to him.

"I saw him stop and talk to Shelly. What did she say to him?" I asked.

"Not much. They hugged, told each other hello, and she mentioned how sad it was that Buck did what he did, but that it was nice to see him, and then he bolted out the door with Lilith in hot pursuit. I saw you follow Lilith, and I decided to stay inside and mingle, to see what I could see, which was nothing, so I latched onto Venderden. The rest you know... Cap, you never told me what happened when you went outside?"

I gave Janet the condensed version of Lilith's confrontation with Junior Cole and my subsequent conversation with him. What I didn't mention were the strange occurrences at my apartment: the open front door and the phone call.

"I don't get it, Cap," Janet said, her eyes half-closed, frowning in concentration. "It seems to me like everything is tied together, but we don't know who is holding the strings. It's frustrating. Don't you feel we're right on the edge of it? Like it's right there in front of us, just an inch out of reach?"

"Yeah, well... You maybe, but not me, not yet. But I've been thinking... I'd like to talk to Junior again, dig a little deeper, rattle his branches. Maybe something will fall out of the tree. I told him not to leave town, so he shouldn't be too hard to find. Do me a favor, go and tell Jack to see if he can track him down. Then you can go question our Mr. Cole, and take Jack with you."

"Sounds good, Cap." And with that, she got up and left, closing the door behind her.

Ten minutes later she was back.

"Jack's gone," she said, hugging the door frame and drumming her fingers on it. "According to Hawk, he grabbed his iPad and said he was going to run an errand and would be right back."

"Okay, so when he gets back, you do what I said," I replied, not thinking much of what she'd said. It wasn't until I came out of my office at around six that I realized Jack didn't just go run an errand. He was missing.

"That was his ex-wife," Hawk said as he hung up the phone. "I called her and asked if she knows where he is. She said she saw him two days ago and he was fine then, a little grumpy, but not upset or in a bad mood. She hasn't heard from him today."

"Okay, you and Robar go to his apartment," I said. "I'm worried he—" I didn't get the chance to finish. The elevator doors were already closing behind them.

I walked to his desk and looked at his calendar. The only thing he had marked thereon was today's date, circled in red, with the words *full blood moon* written inside the square. Other than that, it was blank.

"Janet, did he mention if he was going anywhere special tonight, the woods perhaps? Was he working on anything in particular?"

"He didn't mention anything, and I don't know what he was working on. He spends a lot of time online... We had covered so much last night, Cap. And after Mrs. Overby came bouncing in here today, I don't think he'd be very much inclined to go anywhere near her neck of the woods again. She never did come back, did she?"

"The woods," I muttered, then shook my head. "You don't suppose..."

Janet waited for me to speak, but I was lost in thought.

"I don't suppose what?" she asked.

"You don't suppose he could have gone to the crime scene, do you?"

"What crime scene? Halloway committed suicide."

"Not that," I said. "The old crime scene, Georgina Harrison's. Hmm. Maybe we should go take a look."

Her face drained of its color. She hesitated for a second, then said, "But it will be dark... Okay, fine. I'll grab a couple of uniforms to go with us."

"You do that. I'll meet you there."

29

The fall and winter seasons were harder on the police since it got darker earlier. By the time I got to Swiss Valley Park, it was dark as midnight. The moonrise was scheduled for approximately seven-thirty. I looked at my watch; it was seven-fifteen. I grabbed my flashlight from the glove box, exited the car, locked it, and began to walk.

A half-dozen teenagers were hanging around the swings, laughing, giggling, smoking weed; I know because I could smell it. I turned on my flashlight, shining it at them. There were six of them: four boys and two girls, all aged about sixteen. *Same age as Georgina,* I thought.

"Police," I said loudly. "What are you kids doing out here?"

"Nothing," they all said together.

"Just waiting to see the blood moon," one boy said.

"Hey, you're a cop, right?" one of the girls said, a pretty dark-haired little thing. "Is it true what they say, that a girl was murdered here?"

I nodded. Teenagers can't get enough of that stuff. "It is."

"No shit?" the girl said, obviously impressed.

"No shit," I replied. "Look, I don't care where you guys go, but you can't stay here, okay? Just go and hang out at one of y'all's houses or garage or a front porch. Just stay close to other people. Okay?"

"Why?" another of the boys asked. *There always has to be a smart-ass.*

"Well, for one thing, you're smoking dope. For another, you're all minors. Finally, so the boogeyman doesn't get ya. Now go on, get out of here."

They started laughing and giggling among themselves.

I shook my head. What did they think was going to happen? That I wouldn't arrest each and every one of them and call their parents to come pick them up? If they did, they were wrong. I would've had two cruisers there in a heartbeat. *Little monsters.*

"I don't believe it," I heard one boy say as he swung on the monkey bars.

"I heard that story," another replied.

"Look, here it is," a girl said, holding up her phone.

"I'm not staying," the other girl said.

"Me neither," another of the boys said.

They climbed off the monkey bars and walked away to the road.

"We're going. Bye," the pretty dark-haired girl said to me. "Have a good night, Officer."

"Yeah, thank you, and you have *a safe* night."

"Good luck catching the boogeyman," the smart-ass kid said, making the others gasp and laugh.

"Good night, kids," I said, smiling to myself, and I began to walk toward the woods. I'd just stepped on a gravelly, dirt path that led around the woods when my phone rang. It was Robar.

"Gazzara," I said

"Hey, Cap," she said. "There's no sign of Jack at his place. Where are y—" My phone went dead. I looked at it. No signal. I swiped it off. Then it rang again. The number ID read "Unavailable." I tapped the green accept button and put the phone carefully to my ear.

"Gazzara," I said. Then, static, loud and harsh. I pulled the phone away from my ear. I could still hear the high-pitched electric whine. Then the screen went black. It just died.

I licked my lips, looked behind me at the playground equipment. All six swings were moving, swinging gently, as if someone had just slipped off the seats. *Well they have, haven't they? All six of them.*

I shrugged, stuffed my phone into my jacket pocket and moved ahead to the tree line, sweeping the beam of my flashlight back and forth.

I could see something through the trees, glowing. It looked like someone was burning something in the distance. *Is there a firepit in there somewhere?* I wondered.

I didn't think so; burning in and around the park wasn't allowed, and not in the subdivisions without a permit. And then I realized what I was looking at. It was the moon creeping over the treetops. It shone through the bare branches, as if covered with black veins.

I stood still, looked straight up; I could see stars twinkling and I wondered how many there actually were. And then I was stricken by a sad thought: *I wonder if Georgina looked up and saw the stars while her throat was being slashed?* My eyes began to water. I wiped them with the back of my hand, sniffed, swallowed hard, and took a deep breath.

With renewed determination, I marched on into the darkness. My flashlight, although it was a police issue high-intensity, LED model, seemed to offer no more light than a candle. The air was at least ten degrees colder inside the forest than the rest of the park. It wrapped around me like a vast, moist blanket. I shivered. My shoulders shook. I squinted into the darkness. I listened. The quiet was disturbed only by the hoot of a lone owl; then something dashed across the trail in front of me, through and under the blanket of fallen leaves on the woodland floor.

Now I know just what you're thinking: what the hell was she doing out there all alone? Why didn't she wait for Janet, or call for backup? The short answer is, I don't know... well, I do. I couldn't call for backup, now could I? My phone was dead, remember. Look, I'm an experienced cop with more than seventeen years on the job, and a captain of detectives for God's sake. And it never occurred to me, not for a single moment, that I needed backup anyway. It wasn't as if I was expecting trouble. I wasn't. I was just looking for Jack. And it was after all a public park, not a creepy haunted house or abandoned insane asylum: just saying.

The path I was following was well-traveled, dry, and smooth. Was I on the right one? I didn't know; there were dozens of them. But I figured that if I was Jack, I'd walk the route that Georgina had.

It felt like I was a million miles from civilization. Yes, I stuck to the jogging paths and walking trails, but that kind of back-to-nature crap wasn't for me. The moonlight filtered through the bare branches casting weird shadows. Yes, it was a little unnerving, especially when I had the eerie feeling that the forest was watching me.

I could smell the earthy scent of decaying vegetation. The air was cold, crisp. Someone, somewhere, had a woodstove burning; I could smell it, a warm, soothing smell.

The moon had risen a little higher among the spidery branches of the trees, and, from what I could see of it, I was a little disappointed. It wasn't blood red at all, not like I thought it would be, how the pundits had said it would be. It was just pinkish, no big deal.

I didn't see the moon the night Georgina was murdered. I hadn't arrived at the crime scene until ten the next morning, and all I could remember were the dozens of people milling around, walking back... and forth...

"No," I whispered. "Only one person was walking back and forth."

I stood still, my eyes closed, and let the memory wash over me. The scene was a mess, and it was huge. We knew that Georgina had been killed in the woods, but we didn't know exactly where. I remember going for a walk that morning, along this very path.

"It was daylight," I whispered to myself. "Everything looked different, not like it does now. And there were people everywhere."

"Police!" I remembered shouting, holding my badge in the air for all to see. "This is a crime scene. You need to leave the park, now!"

I thought then that I was helping. Now I wondered if I didn't shoo away the killer along with the crowd.

Who the hell was that guy pacing? I wondered. I didn't think anything of it at the time. And Harry never mentioned him. I last saw him close to the place in the woods where Georgina, Regis, Shelly, Buck, Junior, and Lilith had said they always gathered, that Native American meeting place where Lilith had tried to persuade them to participate in her ritual.

I didn't think anything of it, of him, then, because Mike Willis and his CSI team had just arrived and I was busy with them. And we had to search the entire forest to make sure we'd cleared everyone out.

Now here I was again, deep inside the forest, almost a quarter-mile from where the body was found. All was quiet. I stopped again and listened just to be sure: nothing. I shook my head, wondering again what the hell I was doing. I almost turned around and went back to my car, but my gut was telling me to keep going, that Jack might be in trouble.

I was almost at the site I thought might have been Jack's destination. I stopped again and listened. I heard nothing. I started forward again, shined my flashlight ahead along the path and then... there it was, a small clearing among the trees, rocky, surrounded by large, irregular boulders, the floor bare, tramped over millennia by the feet of... who knows how many, until it was as hard as concrete. I swung the beam of my flashlight over the boulders and around the clearing.

Jack was lying face down on the ground: one leg straight, the other bent at the knee. His arms were above his head, in the position of surrender.

30

"Jack!" I called to him as I ran to his side. I knelt down beside him and touched his neck. *Oh, thank God!*

His skin was warm, pulse steady. I shined my flashlight on his head. The hair at the back was matted with blood. I grabbed my phone. It was still dead. I looked wildly around. I grabbed for my Glock. I figured if I fired it in the air Janet and the officers would hear it and come running. But before I could pull it, I heard rustling behind me.

In my mind, I raced through a thousand possibilities, none of them good: A masked assailant with a gun. A crazed psycho with a hatchet. Even the shadowy something that had somehow invaded my apartment. My heart raced. I spun around, the beam from my flashlight slicing through the darkness.

"Stop! Stop right there!" he shouted. "Drop that flashlight. Don't touch that gun."

I kept the beam of the flashlight on his face, hoping to blind him. I didn't recognize him, but I could tell behind his wild eyes I saw a hint of recognition. Frantically, I searched my memory. How could he know me? Did he know me? Or was I to be just another of his victims?

"Drop the flashlight. Do it now!" His weapon gleamed in the beam of light.

Slowly, I stood up and raised my hands. I let the flashlight fall to the ground. As far as I could tell, the man must have been close to sixty years old, maybe five-nine or ten, wiry with a thin face and thinning brown hair.

"Now the gun. Take it out slowly. Two fingers... Good! Now drop it and kick it away."

I did.

My mind sped through a thousand different scenarios, my training, close-quarter combat, even knife fighting—and I wasn't even carrying a knife. I knew I could take the guy, given the right opportunity, but that was the problem: opportunity... It was too soon. I knew I had to play along with him until I caught a break. And the best way to do that was to keep him talking.

"You don't remember me, do you?" he asked.

I looked at him. In the moonlight he could have been anybody. All I could see, and not even well, was a middle-aged man in khaki pants, a plain button-down shirt, and a hoodie. The only thing that set him apart, as far as I could see, was a huge gold ring on his right ring finger. You couldn't miss it: that hand was holding the gun.

"No, I don't recognize you," I said. "Should I?"

"I always knew this day would come," he said, his voice trembling with emotion. "But I never expected it to be on the night of the great feast. It's a sign. I know it is."

He smiled. It wasn't the kind of smile that made you feel real good... It was the kind of smile that sent a repulsive shudder through me. He knew something I didn't, and he was reveling in some grotesque memory that I either didn't know or had long forgotten.

"Who are...?" I tilted my head to the right. The words stopped in my mouth as if they had suddenly become big solid brick blocks.

"It is coming back to you, isn't it?" he asked. "We only spoke briefly. You were so young. Trying to sound tough ordering people around like a big shot. You were a little fish in a big pond. It would have been cute if it wasn't so pitiful." He chuckled. "*You* let me go. Of course, it wasn't *you*. It was the great god Moloch that let me go. He is all powerful."

"You were here sixteen years ago?" I asked.

"It *is* coming back to you," he said. "That's good. You were a bitch back then just as you are now, consumed with the need to show people how important you were. You were so busy focusing on my daughter that you didn't even notice me."

I squinted at him. "You aren't Georgina's father. Georgina's father was living in Canada at the time of her death. He's still there."

It was as if I'd flipped a switch somewhere deep inside the guy's head because I watched him go, in a split second, from sadistically amused to violently enraged. *What the hell?* He began to tremble. His hands shook. The moonlight glinted off the muzzle of the gun. I was sure he was going to shoot me. *This'll teach you, Kate. Next time, if there is a next time, wear your damn vest.*

"Not Georgina," he howled. "Georgina Harrison was a slut, a whore. She did nothing but cause pain and torment to everyone around her. I'm talking about *my* daughter, you stupid *bitch.*" Spittle flew from his mouth as he cursed me from between clenched teeth.

My mouth had gone dry. My heart was pumping nineteen to the dozen. I could feel the adrenaline surging through my body. I was wired. *Just give me a chance, you son of a bitch; just one.*

I stood perfectly still, my hands at my sides, fingers curled into knuckled fists. *One straight shot to the throat and you're done. C'mon... Come on. I dare you.*

I listened for any noise that might indicate someone was coming down the path. *Where the hell's Janet and the backup?* But I could hear nothing. Even the owl had stopped hooting. Jack was injured, and things were not looking good, for him or for me. *Keep him talking. Establish rapport. Put him at ease. Wait for your moment.*

"*Your* daughter?" I asked quietly. "I don't understand. Who's your daughter?"

"She was raised in the *Family.* Even though her mother and I were not together, I made sure she was raised to be a *believer.* And I did. She didn't just believe in the Molochian theology, she embraced it and she thrived. Never once did she pollute her body with meat. She offered small sacrifices on each and every sacred day. And she was rewarded; I made sure of that. But certain achievements required a more meaningful sacrifice." And then he giggled to himself.

He's rambling. That's good. Keep him going... Who the hell is Moloch?

I stared at him. The moonbeams were full on his face, giving it an ethereal glow. I was wondering what to say next... when it clicked, and I smiled at him and rolled my eyes, perhaps not the finest choice I'd ever made.

"Lilith's father?" I said and chuckled. "No, you're not Lilith's father. I met him all those years ago when we interviewed her. He died recently. It was noted in the file. Nice guy. I liked him."

"That... that man," he stuttered, waving the gun in the air, with his finger on the trigger. *I guess nobody ever told him...*

"That man... he was the man Lily's mother chose to be with. The bitch couldn't wait, could she?" he raved. "She *wouldn't* wait. She wanted it all *now!*"

Then he seemed to calm down a little, clasped the gun in both hands, closed his eyes and held the slide against his forehead, muzzle pointing upward, as if he was praying, and perhaps he was, but not to my God.

"The pleasures of this world," he said, pointing the gun at me again, "can be so very intoxicating. Had she been willing to wait for me, I would have fulfilled her every dream, her every wish. But no.

She chose him over me. She divorced me and took Lilith away with her." He'd stopped shaking and a smile curled the corner of his lips. He was a proud papa.

"You killed Georgina, didn't you?" I asked very quietly, trying not to spook him. "What did she ever do to you? Why would you kill a helpless teenager? She was your daughter's friend." *Frickin' hell! If I don't do something, and quick, this asshole is going to kill me.*

I glanced around. I couldn't see much. The clouds were scudding over the moon, reducing what little light there was to almost nothing. I wondered if I could make a run for it. *Uh-uh, don't try it. You'll break your frickin' neck!*

Running wasn't an option. I might have made it five feet before he put a bullet in my back. I was trapped. And besides, I couldn't, wouldn't, leave Jack.

"The silly little bitch didn't do anything to me," he snarled. "It's what she did to Lily. She stole the only boy Lily ever loved."

"What? You're telling me that you killed Georgina over a boy? Over Regis Taylor?" I laughed out loud.

"Not Regis Taylor, you stupid woman. Not that piece of excrement!" He took two steps toward me. The look on his face—pure evil—was something to behold. "She took Junior Cole away from my Lily!"

I stood there with my mouth open. *Junior Cole? Georgina had died for him?*

"Junior Cole?" I repeated. "You killed her because of him?"

"Lily confessed her feelings to that boy," he said, his eyes wide. He was barely holding it together. "She opened her heart to him, laid bare her soul, but he rejected her. What was wrong with him? Yes, I had to ask myself that. Why would he not embrace the love, the physical, the emotional connection with Lily? It made me question his heterosexuality. Because even though she's my daughter, there is no denying her obvious sexual allure."

I couldn't believe what I was hearing, but one thing I knew was that he had no intention of letting me live, not after him baring his soul, as he was.

And I shuddered at the way he was talking about Lilith. He was obviously in love with her himself. *Disgusting pig!*

"But that wasn't the sacrifice Moloch needed," he continued. "I couldn't defile my own daughter. That wouldn't bring me the power I needed. No, I needed to offer him the ultimate sacrifice on the most sacred night in seven long years."

I stood there, listening to this loon, unable to believe what I was hearing. *Jack was right! Geez... This crazy is about to confess.*

"Georgina?" I asked quietly. "You sacrificed Georgina, didn't you? You sacrificed her because Lilith couldn't get a frickin' date? You're freakin' insane."

Okay, so that was a mistake. He ran at me like a charging bull, jammed the muzzle of the gun into my ribs, and slapped me across the face, *hard*. So hard, I swear I felt my jaw move. My knees gave out and I almost crumpled on top of Jack. I was on my knees again. I put my shaking hand to my lips; they were split, bleeding.

"I am not insane," he snarled, taking two steps back. "I... am enlightened." He paused, looked up at the moon, then closed his eyes and muttered something that made no sense.

"Junior told Lily that he was in love with Georgina," he said, looking down at me, waving the gun in the air. "He yearned for Georgina, wrote poems about her and watched her from afar, hoping one day she'd notice him and return his love."

He stared at me, his eyes glinting in the moonlight.

"And I knew," he continued, "that the only way I could give my Lily what she desired was to sacrifice Georgina to Moloch. She would no longer be a distraction, and Moloch would be pleased and give the boy to my daughter."

"But he didn't, did he?" I said. "She didn't get Junior. He turned his back on her, just as he did at the funeral home." I figured I'd said too much, again. But this time I'd be ready for him. I put my hands up as if to ward off the blow. If it came, I figured it would be the chance I was waiting for, and I was ready for him... But it never came.

"No," he growled, walking slowly backward, his gun still trained on me. "Because Moloch, in his wisdom, knew the boy wasn't right for Lilith, and so he rewarded her in other ways. And she recognized his wisdom and embraced him. And he continued to reward her. She found the answers to her SAT test on her teacher's desk. She caught her boss in an extra-marital affair. She was in a car accident: the president of a large corporation ran a stop sign and hit her car, then paid her off to keep quiet. She met her husband, and a month later his fiancé died suddenly of the flu."

"Oh, my God," I said. "You really are one sick puppy. You think all of that happened because you murdered that poor girl?"

"I admit nothing," he said, walking toward me. "Who will there be to say I did? Not you!" He raised his hand to strike me again. I readied myself...

"Daddy! What are you doing?" Lilith said, walking out of the shadows.

31

"Lily," he said, surprised, stopping short.

I assessed my chances: not good. I judged Lilith's dad, still holding the gun, to be outside the zone, more than six feet from me.

"I have her, see?" he said. "Here she is."

"Daddy. We don't have much time. We have to complete the ritual when the moon is at its zenith. I have to prepare; you have to prepare."

She practically ignored me and Jack, giving me only a cursory glance.

In one hand she was carrying a small lantern, one of those indestructible tactical things they advertise on TV. In the other, she was holding a stun gun.

"I will. We both will," he replied.

"No. I mean now! We have to do it now!"

I felt something move beside me, and then I felt Jack's hand touch mine. He was awake. My heart leaped. Now we had a chance. I didn't dare look down at him. I didn't dare move, not yet.

"Don't worry, my darling," he said. "We have plenty of time to

get them ready. It's going to be a beautiful night, sweetheart, especially for you." He spoke to her as if he was talking to an
eight-year-old.

"Do you see what I did, Daddy? You didn't expect it to be a
man, did you? I did it. I knew he'd come, and I was waiting for him,
and I hit him with a rock. Didn't I do good?"

"You did, honey. Now pick up that flashlight and turn it off.
We don't need it."

"Lilith, what the hell are you doing?" I said quietly.

She glared down at me, the stun gun within a foot of my neck.
"You didn't have to get involved in any of this," she hissed at me. "It
was him I wanted." And she kicked Jack's leg.

In front of me, Lilith's father, his eyes closed, head tilted back,
began muttering words I couldn't distinguish. With his arms
stretched out in front of him, he made small, deliberate motions
with his hands. He was praying, I could tell. But to what I had no
idea.

"Lilith," I said. "Is this really all about Junior Cole? You're
married and have two beautiful children. Please, stop this. Let me
help you." But as I looked up at Lilith's face, eerie in the pale green
glow of her lantern, I saw only emptiness in her eyes.

She set the lantern down. Her father began to chant some
strange liturgy. I could barely hear the words, and those I could
hear I didn't understand. I rolled my eyes, *Oh... my... God. Are you
kidding me? This can't be for real. This can't be happening.*

But it was real, and it was happening. Lilith Overby and her
father, whose name I didn't even know yet, were performing some
sort of pagan ritual that I had no doubt involved a sacrifice... And
Jack and I were to be the goats. *This silly shit has gone on far too
long. We need to put a stop to it, now!*

I put my hand down and gently squeezed Jack's.

"You can't do this, Lilith," I said.

"Oh, but we can," her father said. "And it's happening everywhere, right now, all over Chattanooga. In the homes. In the fields.

In the forests. We are legion. It's too bad you won't be here to witness the glory."

I rolled my eyes—it was a pity he couldn't see it—and said, "What exactly am I going to miss? Y'all planning on raising the dead or something? When are y'all gonna get neckid and dance? Now that I would want to miss, especially skinny Minnie, here." I guess saying that wasn't too smart to say either. My jaw was aching where Igor, or whatever his name was, had hit me.

I don't know if it was what I'd said or part of their stupid ritual, but he put the gun in its holster and made a great show of pulling a knife from a sheath on his belt.

Well, I thought, *I guess it's now or never. I hope you're ready, Jack.*

I was still on my knees. I nudged Jack with my fist. *Shit.* He made no response.

"Take off your clothes," Lilith ordered, taking a step closer.

"Er... No," I replied.

She looked at her father, her eyes wide. It was as if no one had ever defied her before.

"Do as she says," he snarled. "Take off your clothes. Do it now."

"Screw you, you dirty old man."

"Take off your freaking clothes now!" Lilith yelled, stepping right up to me. The stun gun was almost at my neck when Jack leaped to his feet, swung his fist, connected with her wrist and knocked it from her hand, sending it spinning deep into the shadows.

Jack grabbed Lilith's wrist, twisted it, forced her arm behind and up her back, wrapped his other arm around her neck and pulled her in front of him.

"Let her go!" the man yelled, panicking. Waving the knife in the air.

"Looks like you're going to miss your chance," I said, pointing upward.

The moon was higher in the sky. I wasn't sure exactly when

they were supposed to perform their ritual, but I figured that with the moment fast approaching, he might panic even more and give me an opening.

"Let her go," he replied, his voice much calmer, the glint in his eye deadly.

"Put the knife down and Lilith will not get hurt," Jack said calmly.

He dropped the knife at his feet.

"Daddy! Daddy! He's going to ruin everything! Don't let him!"

He reached for his gun. I looked wildly around, trying to find mine.

"Kill him! Just shoot him!" Lilith yelled, struggling in Jack's grip.

Slowly, he pulled the gun, looked at it, then leveled it at Jack's head. Jack ducked his head behind hers.

"Daddy! Why aren't you doing something! He's going to ruin it all! You are going to ruin it all! You're going to ruin everything!"

"Hush, little one," her father whispered. "Calm down. Leave it to me. Everything will be fine."

"*Shoot him!*" Lilith shouted as she tried to writhe out of Jack's grip.

"Go ahead, Daddy. Shoot me," Jack taunted.

"Daddy! He's got his hands on me! He just squeezed my tits. Shoot him! *Just shoot him!*" Lilith howled.

I watched as her father took aim then pulled the gun back. He took an uncertain step forward then froze. There was madness in his eyes as he struggled to make up his mind what to do.

"The ritual," he muttered more to himself than to us or to Lilith. "The ritual. I must have faith."

And with those last words on his lips, he dropped the gun, picked up the knife, and charged. Without thinking, I dived sideways, grabbed my Glock, rolled, came up on one knee and, just as the blade grazed Jack's cheek, I fired off two rounds.

Lilith's father stopped in mid-stride, stood stock-still, his eyes wide in shock. The knife dropped to the ground. He put his hand to his neck; blood spurted out between his fingers. He looked at me, questioningly, as his life slowly leaked away.

He looked back over his shoulder, as if he was expecting someone to come save him. But the devil he'd made a deal with didn't show up. I had no doubt, though, that the meeting was only seconds away, the time he had left to live.

Lilith began screaming, clawing at Jack like a wild animal. Spittle flew from her lips as she called us every name in the book. *What the hell is a qedesha?* I wondered. I never did bother to find out.

"Lilith Overby, you are under arrest for conspiracy—"

"Hold on, Jack. You can't arrest her for conspiracy to commit murder. There's a ten-year statute of limitations."

"But it was first-degree murder. There's no statute of limitations on that."

"True, but the killer's dead," I said, nodding at the body.

"Lilith Overby," he said, looking at me triumphantly. "You're under arrest for assaulting a police officer," all of that while struggling to remove his cuffs from his belt and wrenching Lilith's arm still further up behind her back.

Finally, he managed to restrain her, her hands anyway, because she proceeded to kick and spit at us until her backside was forced to the ground and the realization of what had happened began to sink in.

I stepped over to her father, who was lying face down in the dirt. I felt his neck but couldn't find a pulse. He was dead. When I noticed a bulge in his back pocket, I put my hand inside while Lilith screamed at me not to touch him. I pulled out his wallet, flipped it open, and, by the light of the moon, looked down at the face of the man who had killed Georgina Harrison. His name was Lawrence Morris.

～

"Where the hell were you, Janet?" I asked when we finally reached the edge of the woods and found her with two uniformed officers waiting for us. "We could have died in there."

"I know, and I'm so sorry. But you weren't here. There must be fifty trails. We didn't know which way you'd gone, not even when we heard the shots. Why didn't you wait for us? That's what you're supposed to do, isn't it, wait for backup? Are you okay? Oh... m'God. Jack, you're hurt. Are you all right?"

"You finished?" I asked, glaring at her. She was obviously devastated. I looked at her silently for a moment, then nodded and said, "You're right, Janet. I should have waited for you; I didn't. Not your fault. Yeah, we're okay, both of us. Lilith whacked him on the head with a rock, is all."

She looked somewhat mollified; I wouldn't have been. She *was* right. I'd broken the cardinal rule and not for the first time. Fortunately, it all worked out, but it could just as easily have ended tragically.

"What happened in there?" Janet asked.

"It's a long story," I said. "I'll tell you all about it tomorrow. Right now, I need to get out of here, take a hot shower, and guzzle a glass of red."

Yeah, that's what I needed, but I wouldn't get either. I needed to go to Morris's home, and there were statements to make, reports to write, and... well, you know the routine. I knew I'd be lucky if they turned me loose before noon the following day.

"*You'll all die,*" Lilith screamed as the paramedics strapped her to the gurney. "All of you. You don't know what you've done. You'll pay with your lives and your children will pay. You've unleashed the beast. Moloch will not sit by idly while you persecute his followers. And you," she screamed through the open back doors of the ambulance. "You will suffer the most. I'll make sure of that. I will avenge my father. You'll pay. You'll beg for death—" And the doors slammed shut, cutting off her wild diatribe.

"Was she talking to me?" Jack asked as a paramedic tended the cut on his head.

"Yeah, you," I said, smiling. "Or me. Nah, I'd say it was you."

"It was you who killed her dad, but I'm willing to share. Geez, what a night," he said, wincing as he tenderly touched the bump on the back of his head.

"Yeah," I said. "The media said it was going to be a humdinger, and they weren't wrong, were they?" I gingerly touched my split lip, and I too winced.

"Do you think he was telling the truth, her dad?" Jack asked.

"About what?"

"About the rituals going on around the city. Do you think that's happening?" Jack looked genuinely angry.

"People all over the world worship false gods, but I don't think many of them are into sacrificing teenagers to some Babylonian god I've never heard of just to get a prom date. So no, I don't."

"We should go search Morris's house, don't you think?" he asked.

"I do, but we also have this mess to clean up. I'll call Mike Willis and have him get started." I looked at my watch. "Look, it's almost midnight. You have a head injury, so you're out of here; you're going to the hospital—"

"I'm fine. It's just a bump," he said, interrupting me

"Nope. It's protocol. It's not your call."

"They'll just tell me to take two aspirin and call them in the morning," he muttered and folded his arms across his chest in defiance.

"Probably," I agreed. "And if they do, you can come and join me at the Morris house, unless you want to go back to the office and get started on the paperwork."

"Well, okay then. That changes everything. You know how I feel about paperwork."

"Janet, you go with him and, if they let him go, bring him on over. Make sure he does what he's told. No more broken rules, okay?"

"Roger that, Cap," she said. "And if he's good, I'll make sure the nurse gives him a lollipop when we leave."

He smirked. It was the closest to a smile I'd seen on his face since he joined my team.

I smiled, shook my head, and looked up at the moon. It was full, it was pink, it was beautiful and I'd be happy to never see another blood moon as long as I lived.

32

J ack was right. They examined his head, gave him a clean bill of health, and told him to take two aspirin and call if anything changed. He and Janet arrived at Morris's house about forty-five minutes after I did.

It was close to twelve-thirty in the morning when I got there. The place was lit up like Grand Central Station; yellow police tape surrounded the entire house, including the garage at the back. I wondered how Harry and I had missed this guy all those years ago. Hell, the house was located less than three short blocks from Swiss Valley Park.

I flashed my badge at the uniform on guard outside and, as I signed the sheet, asked him, "Been here long, Officer?"

He looked at his watch, consulted his sheet, and said, "We got here at twelve-seventeen, twenty-one minutes ago."

I nodded and said, "So how's it going in there?"

"Hah, they're all over it. I've not been in there myself, but it seems like they're having a ball."

I looked at his name badge: T. Jinny. I patted him on the shoulder, thanked him, and walked on in.

What the hell did he mean by that? I wondered as I snapped on a pair of latex gloves and headed for the front door.

The first thing I noticed when I stepped through the front door was the strong smell of incense, and the place was sooo neat and tidy... I wouldn't have been surprised if June and Ward Cleaver lived here. But there was no Mrs. Morris. Lilith's father lived alone and obviously kept the place tidy.

The place was bustling with people: uniforms, junior grade detectives and, of course, the members of Mike's team.

I entered the living room to find Hawk and Robar there too. Apparently, Mike Willis had given them the nod, and they'd taken it upon themselves to join the search team. Of Mike himself there was no sign, but I knew he had to be there somewhere because his CSI truck was parked on the road outside.

Hawk was his usual enigmatic self; Robar looked... I don't know... shaken would probably be a good word.

"What is it?" I asked her. "What have you found?"

She was looking closely at a large, glass-fronted bookcase. She had both doors open and was running her fingers slowly along the spines of the books, Hawk was looking over her shoulder.

"Oh, hi, Cap," she said, shaking her head. "Whew, this is one hell of a collection, 'hell' being the operative word. Have you ever seen anything like this? Look at them. Every book on these shelves is New Age or some such shit. There are books on astrology, astronomy, black magic, satanic rituals, earth worship, spells, witchcraft, seances, I mean, you name it. Look at this one; it's *The Satanic Bible* by Anton LaVey. This one is *Witches and Warlocks*. And look at this one, *Satan Wants You*. Have you ever heard the like?"

I hadn't, but she wasn't done.

"Here are two more by LaVey: *The Satanic Rituals* and *The Satanic Witch*. D'you think Morris really believed all this shit, Cap? You know, when I walked in here, I thought what a lovely, antique bookcase, and then I started looking at the titles. And oh boy, look at them; talk about the devil being in the details."

That was the longest speech I'd heard from her in more than a year.

"Yes, it's a little off the wall, that's for sure... I've never seen one of these before," I said as I pulled *The Satanic Bible* from the shelf and flipped through it, noting the illustrations as I did so.

I slipped it back between the books as Robar said, "And this is not all, Cap. Come on, I'll show you."

I followed her into the hall that led to the bedrooms, while Hawk went to find Mike Willis.

Robar pointed to one of the pictures on the hall wall and said, "Nice country home, right? Take a closer look."

At first, I thought it was a scenic picture of a front porch in some lazy southern country town. But then, on closer inspection as Robar had suggested, I spotted a man hanging by a noose in the corner of the porch where you'd expect to find a porch swing. *That's freakin' bizarre,* I thought. *Who the hell would want something like that hanging in their home? Huh, I guess Lawrence Morris would.*

There were more paintings, all similarly gross, but without being outright gruesome.

A walk through the bathroom revealed nothing of interest except for the medicine cabinet loaded to capacity with a variety of prescription pills that, just by looking at the labels, I could see had the potential to make for one hellish rollercoaster ride after another. No wonder the guy was seeing demons and believing he had special powers.

The bedrooms also revealed nothing interesting. I stood at the open door to the master bedroom and noted how austerely furnished and decorated it was, obviously by the man himself, and I wondered why Lilith hadn't gifted him with a little of her woman's touch. I flipped on the light and stepped inside.

A plain gray bedspread covered the queen-sized bed; matching curtains covered the windows. There was a dresser and two night-stands, one on either side of the bed. I sat down and looked at the digital clock. The red numbers told me it was 12:56 AM. I turned on the bedside lamp and looked around the room. Other than the few pieces of furniture, it was bare: no personal effects. No phone. No photographs. It was a place to lay his head, no more than that.

I pulled open a drawer to one of the nightstands: nothing, it was empty. I stepped over to the dresser and opened the top drawer: underwear, nothing else. I closed it and pulled open the second drawer: shirts, neatly folded. I lifted them and... I was shocked, disgusted by what I found.

There were seventeen candid photographs of Lilith, most of them obviously taken without her knowledge. I shook my head, stunned. *He must have been one sick puppy!*

They weren't pornographic per se, just... sick; well, the photos showed how twisted his mind must have been. There was one of Lilith bending over her daughter, her blouse falling open, the obvious subject of the photo. Another was a closeup of her kneeling down in her yard tending flowers; again, her cleavage was the subject. Another was shot from behind of her bending over in a short skirt. They were all much the same. The man must have been obsessed with his daughter's breasts, because the one I found the most disturbing was of Lilith leaning over a cake with icing that read "Happy Birthday, Daddy," her blouse unbuttoned half-way, wide open revealing her naked breasts as she winked right at the camera.

"Oh, my," I groaned as my stomach folded over on itself.

I slipped the photos into an evidence bag, signed it, added the date and time, and had Robar witness it. Then I went through the rest of the drawers, but I found nothing else of interest.

And then I heard shouting, "Captain! Robar! Come down here."

It was Hawk. He was calling from the basement. We headed back through the kitchen to the open basement door, where we were joined by Janet and Jack.

"What's going on, Cap?" Janet asked.

"More than you probably want to know," I said. "C'mon, Hawk wants us in the basement."

The steps—you couldn't call them stairs—to the basement were steep, barely safe and made from two-by-fours and the like. I followed Jack carefully, Robar and Janet close behind.

At first look it was a basic unfinished basement: a wide-open space with round steel poles set at intervals to support the floor above. There was a washer and dryer set against one wall, a water heater under the steps, and a chest freezer just to the right of the steps against the end wall.

Hawk was standing beside an open double door in a wall that appeared to divide the basement into two sections, or rooms, the one behind the doors being the larger of the two. There was no sign of Mike Willis, so I figured that he was inside the other room.

"Come on," Hawk said, beckoning. "Come and look at this."

We paused at the open door and looked inside. Except for some dim lights and two accent fixtures, the room was pitch black, and I do mean black. The walls, the ceiling, all painted black, even the floor. The two accent lights? Even now I shudder when I think of it. Seated on a plinth, staring at us, its eyes glowing dark red, was a winged, goat-headed statue.

"The fallen angel himself," a voice whispered in my ear, startling me... Not hardly, Mike Willis scared the crap out of me.

"You... you... get your team in here," I said as I carefully stepped forward. "No wonder it stinks in here. We need to make sure none of those bones are human."

The floor around the statue was littered with the remains of small animals: cats, raccoons, opossums.

"The frickin' lunatic," I said to Willis. "He said he and his daughter made small sacrifices to Moloch, this must be what he was talking about."

"That's not Moloch," Janet whispered. "That's Baphomet, the archetypal depiction of Satan himself."

"Oh yeah?" I said, unable to take my eyes off its evil face. "And just how d'you know that, missy smart-ass?" I asked. I should have known better. Janet never opens her mouth unless she knows exactly what she's talking about. And, sure enough, away she went.

"Research, of course. I always found the idea of Satan to be... I dunno... interesting. Baphomet, as you see him there, is a demon supposedly worshipped by the Knights Templars back in the fifteenth century. Modern Satanists adopted him as their depiction of Satan sometime back in the early twentieth—"

"Okay, Janet," I said, interrupting her. "I get it, but if this is Satan, who the hell is Moloch?"

"He is," she said, pointing to a smaller statue off to the right, almost hidden in the darkness. I took out my phone and turned the flashlight on.

Moloch was at the center of a small altar. He was flanked by two huge black candles. A black cross hung upside down on the wall behind him. The altar was also surrounded by the remains of many small animals.

There were two silver chalices, several knives, two heavy silver chains with pentacle pendants, and an incongruous looking pair of tortoiseshell spectacles.

"Holy shit, Cap," Jack whispered. "D'you think all of this is for real?"

"What do you mean?" I wrinkled my nose, took a fresh N95 mask from my pocket, took it out of its sealed wrapper, put it on, adjusted it, then stepped carefully toward Moloch to get a closer look.

He was indeed a strange one: the torso of a heavily muscled man with the head and horns of a bull, a woman's breasts, and with its arms spread wide, welcoming.

Close up and personal it was kind of funny. Seen from the back of the room shrouded in dark shadows, it looked... Scary doesn't get it. It was more frightening, dreadful in the full meaning of the word; the fuel of nightmares. But, as I said, upon closer inspection it was really quite pathetic. The animal remains were... disgusting.

Candle wax had dripped down onto the altar and lay in dirty black puddles. It was a sickening display.

"I mean, d'you think Morris was actually a devil worshiper?" Hawk shook his head. "Because—"

"Are you kidding, Hawk? Look at this... Yes, I do believe he was, and that his daughter, Lilith was too, still is. You weren't there when they loaded her into the ambulance kicking and screaming. She said we'd released the beast and were all going to die."

"Frickin' hell," Hawk said. "If this don't take the cake... I thought I'd seen it all, but this..." He tailed off, lost for words.

"So now you can retire knowing that you *have* seen it all," I replied.

"So, you think it's for real then?" Hawk persisted. "You don't think it's all just bullshit?" Hawk asked. "No one really does this stuff... do they?"

"Lawrence Morris obviously did," I said, "and he must have indoctrinated his daughter at a very early age. Did they believe in what they were doing? Yes, I have no doubt that they did, and that Lilith still does. It's a religion to them. They were true believers. Just as devout to their god as the Pope is to his. The evidence is here for you to see," I said, pointing at the remains. "To him it was all very real." *Boy, am I glad Doc Sheddon isn't here to gloat and say, I told you so.*

"He had to be some sort of mental case, right?" Hawk said. "If you hadn't put him away, he'd have ended up in a rubber room at Moccasin Bend."

"Either that or run for the Senate," Janet said, shaking her head. She was still at the back of the room, just inside the door. "Okay, I've seen enough," she said. "I'm going back upstairs. I have this... this... well, I hope it isn't contagious."

"Me too," Robar said. "I'm gonna dream about it for months, I know I am."

I didn't blame them. I wanted to get out of the basement too.

Another of Mike's CSI techs appeared in the doorway, stood for a moment, staring around in awe.

"Hey, Charlie," Mike said. "Let's get some lights down here and get started."

Charlie turned and left, presumably to get the lights.

"Shit," Hawk said. "You're not going to bring all this crap to the PD, are you Mike? I don't like that idea. It'll bring bad karma."

"And where else d'you think I'm going to take it, Hawk?"

"Hell, take it to Doc's place. He won't give a shit."

"Can't. He doesn't have the equipment I need to process it."

"Shit," I heard Hawk mumble.

"Come on, Hawk," I said, patting his arm. "It isn't like the PD is a beacon for good karma, now is it? Let's get the hell out of here and let Mike get on with it. I have a statement to make, paperwork to do and..." It suddenly hit me that I'd killed a man only a couple of hours earlier.

"Come on," I said. "Let's go find Jack and get the hell out of here."

I found Jack in Morris's office. He'd already gotten into his computer and was hammering away at the keys like a man possessed... Oops, wrong choice of words.

"Cap," he said, looking up at me as I entered the room. "I think we have everything we need here. Morris liked to chat with other people, online, about this Moloch character. There are hundreds of hours of discussions about his beliefs and practices. There's even some on a dating site for people with alternative religious beliefs: Satanism, Wicca, Asatru, Gnosticism, and even Voodoo. I also ran his financial background. The man was loaded, worth almost two million dollars. Where the hell did he get that kind of money, d'you think?"

"Yeah, how?" I said, leaning over his shoulder. "I keep trying to tell people crime doesn't pay, and it seems like every asshole is out to prove me wrong."

"But the big deal is," Jack said, "that he admitted killing Georgina Harrison."

"He posted that online?" I asked, stunned. The idea of that floating around the ether seemed to me to be yet another violation of the poor girl.

"Actually, no. It's all written down in this." He picked up a spiral-bound notebook and handed it to me. "God only knows what's written in the rest of them," Jack said as he turned and pointed to at least two dozen more on a bookcase behind him.

"That one's dated 2004. I guess Morris was reliving his glory days. There's an account of how he sacrificed Georgina; it's toward the back. I put a slip of paper there so you could find it. I started to read it; I just couldn't do it. He was one evil, sadistic son of a bitch, that's for sure. You know she was conscious all the while he was cutting on her?"

I didn't answer, but I could feel his eyes on me as I read the pages of Morris's account of what happened that night. Me? Unlike Jack, I was a little more objective about it. To me it was just another piece of evidence, another nail in a killer's coffin, and his daughter's.

"I'm not so sure Georgina was his first victim—" I started to say, looking at all the notebooks.

"The first one is dated 1990," he said, interrupting me.

"Really?" I said as I did the math. "Lilith would have been two years old. Okay, pack them up and sign for them, Jack. I'll have the others read them... Whew, who knows what we'll find? I bet we're in for some nasty surprises. We'll also need to run his prints and DNA through the national databases to see if there are any matches."

I looked at Jack. He looked tired, like a kid who'd been up all night playing a new video game, but still not quite ready enough to quit.

"Everything he wrote in that book," he said and nodded at the one in my hand, "says that it was all about his daughter. He was obsessed with giving her everything she wanted. It must have been one weird relationship those two had."

"You can say that again," I said. "You haven't seen the photos I found in his bedroom. She was daddy's little girl, that's for sure."

"Eww," Jack said, making me smile for the first time in twenty-four hours.

"Right," I said, looking at my watch. It was almost seven in the morning and already quite light outside. We'd been at the Morris house more than six hours.

"Wrap up here, Jack. Take the spirals with you and go back to the police department, get someone to take your statement, and then go home and get some rest. Tell the others to do the same. I'll see y'all in my office this afternoon at... say three. I'm going to head on over to the Forensic Center—Morris's body should be there by now."

"You got it, Cap. I'll also sign for the computer. I can go through the files while they go through the notebooks."

I nodded, told him good-bye, told the others the same, and I left them with Mike Willis. He'd be there for a couple of days... there and the stone circle in the woods.

Me? I needed to get out of Lawrence Morris's creepy home and go somewhere where things were normal, structured, and routine: Doc Sheddon's little house of horrors. But first I needed a shower and some coffee.

33

It was just after nine o'clock that morning when I arrived at the Forensic Center on Amnicola Highway, only three blocks from the police department. Chief Johnston had called while I was at home, and I had to fill him in on what happened which made me later than I wanted, needed to be. At least the Chief sounded happy, but that's not always a good sign.

"That you, Kate?" Doc asked through the intercom when I pressed the button beside the rear door to his offices.

"Yeah, it's me," I replied resignedly.

"Thought so. I was expecting you."

There was a buzz and a loud click, and I pushed through the heavy metal door; it automatically closed behind me with a clang and a snap.

"Where are you, Doc?" I called.

No answer, but I could see there was a light on in one of the examination rooms. I approached, raised my hand to knock, but before I could, the door opened, and a large Styrofoam cup appeared in a hand wrapped in blue latex. I smiled, so grateful I could have kissed him.

"Oh... m'God. Thank you. I could kiss you."

He looked at me over his glasses and said, "That wouldn't be appropriate, young lady. It's Sunday, and not yet nine. How did you know I'd be here?" he asked, holding the door open for me.

"I heard Janet call you to the scene," I said. "I knew you'd be here. Carol not coming in?"

He nodded absently, "Yes, she's here. Well she was. She's gone to McDonald's for bagels. She should be back shortly." He paused, looked closely at me and then continued, "I heard you had a close one last night, Kate. Glad to see you are all right."

"Yeah, thanks. I'm just a little tired." I nodded.

"What happened there?" He pointed to the corner of my lip.

"Well, you know me, Doc. Sometimes I just say the first thing that comes into my head. And not everyone appreciates my input. Your latest admission, Lawrence Morris, certainly didn't." I touched my lip. It felt like it was sticking out six inches from my face and was still tender to the touch. "Crap, I must look a sight."

"A sight for sore eyes, yes, Kate, as always. Go suit up. Let's get on with it, shall we? Get it done and finished with."

I went back to the locker room and dressed for the occasion: Tyvek coveralls, booties and cap, safety glasses and latex gloves.

By the time I returned, he'd snapped on the bright overhead light, started the cameras and the recorder rolling, and had already begun his examination.

He grabbed a large pair of stainless-steel shears and began to cut off Lawrence Morris's clothes. As his shirt came off, we both gasped at what we saw. Me? I was stunned. Not by the body, we'd both seen more of those than any human being has a right to. To me, he was no longer a person, just a slab of meat. Insensitive? No, not really, because that was all that was left: Lawrence Morris was no more.

What amazed us were the decorations: dozens of symbols, including several that matched the ones Doc had first pointed out on Georgina's body, as well as many others, but none of them had been cut into the skin. Some were obviously tattoos, others... I just didn't know. They were scars, sure, but unlike any I'd ever seen.

"Brand marks," Doc said, answering my unasked question. "Self-inflicted, I shouldn't wonder."

"You think?"

"Yes. By the placement and the angle: he must have been working with a mirror which, in itself, would have been rather difficult because everything is reversed. Most people find that disorienting," he said, looking down his nose at the markings.

"Geez, just look at that one," I said, taking a photo of it with my phone.

On his left breast, over his heart was a tattoo, some six inches in diameter, of a satanic pentacle complete with a goat's head at its center.

"It's quite beautiful, don't you think?" he asked. "If you like that sort of thing."

"No, I don't. It's freakin' sick," I replied.

"He died from a gunshot wound to the neck: entry wound here... and exit wound here. Nice shot, Kate. You completely severed the carotid artery." He looked at me, then said, "Are you all right?"

I knew what he meant. I'd discharged my weapon and killed a suspect, which meant I was going to have to spend time with the department shrink. Strangely, I didn't feel bad about it. Morris was going to kill me or Jack or both of us.

"Yeah. I'm okay. It was him or me," I replied flatly. "And it wasn't a good shot. I was aiming center mass, but he moved."

"Well, I'm glad it's him and not you lying here," Doc said.

"Er... you and me both, Richard."

He looked sharply at me, then smiled and nodded. No one ever called him that. Not even his wife.

He continued on with his autopsy and ninety-five minutes later he was done. Everything about Lawrence Morris was terribly boring and normal. The weights of his organs were exactly what they should have been. His brain had no abnormalities, lesions, or blemishes. He'd eaten vegetables for his last meal. Other than the single gunshot wound—my second shot had creased his shoulder, within two inches of the one that killed him—he appeared perfectly normal and healthy.

While Doc was working the body, I stepped over to the table where Carol had already laid out the few personal effects Morris had had on him: his wallet, necklace, and that huge gold ring I'd noticed on his gun hand. I didn't find anything out of the ordinary in his wallet except for a black credit card.

"Hey, Doc. You ever see one of these?" I asked, holding it up for him to look at. He squinted down his nose through his glasses.

"Of course, that's one of those no-limit credit cards. All Medical Examiners have one," he said. "I have one. Was this man rich, then?"

"That's what Jack said. He scared up his financials while we were searching his house."

"Did he now? Did you happen to find anything else of interest there?" Doc asked. He wasn't very good at pretending he was asking innocent questions.

I rolled my eyes, looked at him sideways and said, "Look at his chest, Doc. What do you think? He was a Satanist, all the way, with his own church in the basement—if you can call it that—with statues of a goat-headed man and some critter called Moloch."

"Fascinating, absolutely fascinating," he mumbled, as he held Morris's brain up to the light and squinted at it through his half-glasses. I wasn't sure if he was talking about Morris's basement or his brain.

I just shook my head and picked up the pendant, a silver circle on a black cord. The circle was filled with what looked to me like onyx, upon which a strange geometric design was engraved along with the letter M, both picked out in white. The M, I thought, must be for Moloch. I put the pendant down and picked up the ring. It was heavy, chunky, and solid gold. It was also huge, the face almost an inch across, and the onyx inset was inlaid in gold with what appeared to be a sextant and a flag and some Latin words that were unfamiliar to me.

"You ever see a ring like this, Doc?" I asked and stepped over to the table.

"No. At first, I thought it was a Freemason ring, but those are slightly different. I'm not sure what the significance of that one might be. Whatever it is, he loved it because it must have been very uncomfortable to wear."

I returned the ring to the table and it was then that I noticed a piece of red knitting wool. Actually it was two pieces knotted together, but it had been only one. Carol must have cut it in order to remove it from his wrist.

"Hey, Doc. What about this?" I held it up for him to see. "It was on his wrist, right?"

He peered over his glasses across the table and said, "Some kind of hippie bracelet, I think?"

"I don't think this has to do with hippies, Doc... Oh hey, Carol. I didn't see you come in."

"Hi, Kate. You want to take a break? I have sausage and egg bagels and coffee in the break room... Ah, I see you noticed the deceased's kalava."

She took the red bracelet from me, looked fondly at it, then replaced it on the table.

"Okay," I said. "I'm listening. What the hell is a klava?"

"Kalava," she said, "the word is kalava. It's nothing really, just a talisman of sorts that's supposed to bring good luck and protect the wearer. Hindu, I think... or maybe Jewish, or both, I'm not really sure. It's a kid thing these days, a sign of friendship, not as much as it used to be... I have to say, I was surprised to see him wearing it. He was kind of old for that sort of thing. Then again," she continued, picking up the pendant, "this guy must have been into some weird stuff. D'you know what this is?" she asked.

"No," I said. "What is it, and how do you know all this?"

"Oh, you notice stuff in this game, and I'm a sponge for weird." Carol held the pendant up by the cord and swung it back and forth in front of my face. "This is the medieval sign for Lucifer, the Bringer of Light, or Satan, as he's better known these days. Nice piece, and expensive, I bet."

She laid the pendant down and said brightly, "So, you want a bagel or not? Doc, I'll put yours in the microwave and set it for you. All you need to do is push start, okay?"

He nodded and mumbled something I didn't hear.

"Sorry, Carol," I said. "Much as I'd like to stay and chat and eat, I can't. I have statements to make and, well... you know how it is. I will take a bagel with me, though, if that's okay."

It was, and I took off my coveralls, and all the rest of the garb, washed my hands and face, grabbed the bagel, said my good-byes, and drove the three blocks to the police department and... You don't want to know.

Of course, I still had a lot of hoops to jump through before I was done with the Georgina Harrison case. But as far as I was concerned that Sunday morning, it was over, case closed. I'd done what I wanted to do. What Lawrence Morris and Lilith Overby believed didn't change the fact that they killed the girl and were going to kill again, had they not been stopped. And that made me wonder why she, Lilith, was so taken up with Jack, and I made up my mind to ask her... whenever I got the opportunity to interview her.

By now, I was convinced that the night Georgina was killed, the group of friends participated in much more of Lilith's little ritual than they'd let on. The secrecy, the matching red wool bracelets, the intricate scars on Buck's legs, the discrepancies in their stories... I doubted we'd ever learn the truth. But maybe, just maybe, in a moment of pride, Lilith would slip up during an interview and we'd find out what really happened that night.

I wasn't holding my breath, though.

The days after Lawrence Morris's death passed quickly. I didn't suffer any aftereffects from shooting him. I knew it was a righteous kill and so was able to put it out of my mind, but I did spend many hours with the department psychiatrist, and even more with IA.

Chief Gunnery Sergeant Wilcox Dorman took some leave and I spent a lot of time with him. He really is a sweetie and just what I needed, in more ways than one.

I also sometimes wonder how those people, Internal Affairs, can live with themselves: they seem to regard everyone they interview as guilty until proven innocent, rather than the other way around. Yes, it was something of a trial for me, but I came through it with flying colors... I even received a commendation. Go figure.

Jack? He's changed. I don't quite know what to make of him. The Chief gave him a pass for the perceived problems of that week, but he's still on probation. Janet seemed to have taken him under her wing, which is kind of strange, seeing as how he's four years older than she is. But if anyone can steer him straight, she can. And she was right: he is one hell of a good IT tech, and yes, I too think Lennie would approve of him. *Lennie... Oh, Lennie. Rest in peace, my good friend.*

Now you might be thinking that's the end of the story, but you would be wrong.

It was on a Wednesday morning, two weeks after I shot Lawrence Morris to death, when I drove to the Hamilton County Jail where Lilith was being held without bail. She'd been charged with being an accessory to the murder of Georgina Harrison.

She had been held at the Moccasin Bend Mental Health Institute for evaluation until her doctors had finally declared her mentally competent and fit and able to answer questions, though whether or not she'd talk to me, I had no idea.

She'd inherited her father's money, and there was a whole lot more of it than Jack had found that day at Morris's home. She was a very wealthy woman and thus able to hire a prestigious legal firm in Atlanta to represent her, two of whom I was about to meet. *Oh, lucky me!*

She was due to appear in court for her preliminary hearing in two days, on Friday. There was no telling how things were going to turn out for her. I was sure her team of attorneys would stop at nothing to get her off, cut her a sweet deal: probation and time served. Maybe it wouldn't even go to trial. After all, what did we really have on her? Only my word and Jack's as to what really happened in the woods that night.

But I wasn't too worried. These days, with the Me Too movement being what it was, I was pretty sure she would be labeled a victim, the victim of her deranged, manipulative overbearing and... obsessed father.

And so as I drove to the county jail, I was daydreaming, thinking about the case, and how it couldn't have gotten any stranger. But it could, and it did. I was absolutely not prepared for the surprise that was waiting for me when I arrived.

The desk sergeant was a caricature of the type: a huge, muscular man, his head shaved, and wearing a tight-fitting uniform shirt with short sleeves, beneath which bulged a pair of exceedingly hairy arms. I handed him my ID. He gave it a cursory glance, then nodded and asked for my weapon. I handed it over.

He looked me up and down—why do men always do that? One of these days... then smiled politely at me.

"You'll need to take a seat, Captain," he said, handing me a visitor badge and pointing to a row of steel chairs set against the wall. "Mrs. Overby has a visitor with her. He should be down shortly."

I smiled back at him, sat down, and opened my phone to check my email. Fortunately, I didn't have to wait long.

It couldn't have been more than ten minutes later when I heard the elevator ping. I looked up and, to my great surprise, saw Junior Cole walking across the lobby toward me.

He looked right at me and actually flinched. It was as if I'd caught him shoplifting. The color drained from his face. I wasn't sure if he was going to smile or run, so I stood and stepped forward.

"Hello, Mr. Cole. How funny, my meeting you here."

Funny? Yeah well, you should have been there. I didn't know what else to say. Whatever, it worked.

He took off his visitor's badge, handed it to Baldy behind the desk, then turned to me, stuck out his hand for me to shake... and there it was, a red braided woolen thread around his right wrist.

"Oh, uh, hello, Captain Gazzara... Yes, I suppose it is."

He smiled self-consciously and looked down at his feet.

"Might I ask what you're doing here? Surely you're not visiting family?" I asked, knowing damn well why he was there. Oh, I know; it was none of my business, and it was rather rude, but you know me.

He shrugged, swallowed hard, wouldn't look at me, shifted from one leg to the other, then cleared his throat.

"No. Not family. Not exactly. I came to see Lily Overby," he said, lifting his chin defiantly.

"Oh. Well, now that's very nice of you. How is she? I am here to see her, too," I said, smirking.

"I know what you are thinking, Detective, but you're wrong. Lily..." He paused, sucked on his bottom lip so hard his top lip went all the way down to his chin. "I don't know how to describe it, but I just had the feeling she needed a friend. I don't know if you are aware, but her husband has left her. He took the children with him and—"

"Yes, I heard that," I said. "It was unfortunate, but also understandable."

"She doesn't have anyone else, you know. And when you talk to her, you'll see... You'll see that she's not who you think she is. She's a gentle, loving person."

Oh, you've got to be kidding me, I thought.

"I think the story about her biological father abusing her is true," he continued. "I also think he manipulated her. And... and I realize now how cruel I myself was to her."

He looked down at the floor again, then continued, "I'm going to make it up to her, Detective. I really am. I'm going to spend the rest of my life trying to make it up to her. That I promise."

I stared at him, unable to believe what I was hearing. No matter what the doctors said, they hadn't seen her like I had. The woman was insane. She tried to get her father to kill Jack.

"The rest of your life?" I asked quietly. "Sounds pretty serious."

"I know it's your job to be skeptical," he said. He was feeling more confident now that he'd gotten it off his chest. "But I feel something for Lily I never thought I'd feel for anyone. It just suddenly hit me. I was totally unprepared for it. She needs me, and I'm going to be there for her, always."

I couldn't find words to answer him. I was stunned, didn't know what to think.

"I'll say goodbye," he said. "I hope you understand."

And then he turned and walked away without a backward look.

Me? I wondered what the hell had just happened. I stepped over to the desk. Baldy looked up at me, his eyebrows raised in question.

"How many times has that man come to visit Lilith Overby?" I asked.

He frowned, then checked his log, and said, "Four times. You want the dates and times?"

"Please."

He wrote them down on a sticky note and handed it to me. I thanked him and headed toward the elevator and the second floor.

The elevators were all on the top floor and I had to wait, and while I did, I had that god-awful feeling that the unbelievable, the incredible had happened.

Did Lawrence Morris's promise to his daughter come true? Was he, himself, the sacrifice that was needed on the night of the blood moon that would push Junior Cole into Lilith's arms?

Was I really supposed to believe all that mumbo-jumbo about stars aligning, planets rising and human sacrifice? I didn't think so... Perhaps Junior Cole's sudden change of heart was due to Lilith Overby now being an extremely wealthy woman.

At that moment I didn't know what to believe. All I knew was that I had Lilith Overby locked up tight, that I was about to take her statement, and that she and her father had tried to kill Jack and me. And that I sure as hell was going to testify against her at her trial, and that she was going to be found guilty of being an accessory to murder...

But was she? I had a nasty feeling that this thing wouldn't even go to trial, that her slick, big-time Atlanta lawyers would get her a sweet plea bargain. All I could hope for was that, plea or not, she'd be locked up and off the streets long enough for me to reach retirement. Whatever! I knew I was going to do everything in my power to put her behind bars for a long time.

This place wasn't so different from the lockup where Regis Taylor was incarcerated. I figured by now he must have heard the news that Georgina's killer had been brought to justice. Maybe it would give him a little peace.

The ping of the elevator bell snapped me out of my reverie. I stepped into the elevator, pushed the button, wondering what the hell was going to happen next.

I stepped out of the elevator to be met by a woman in a very sharp, tailored blue suit, and an even more expensively dressed tall, distinguished gray-haired man I knew quite well. No, it wasn't August Starke. But he was almost as good a lawyer as August, and August is the best. Lilith was spending her money wisely.

Me? I smiled sweetly at them both, shook their hands, introduced myself and said, "Shall we?"

The End

Thank you for reading Georgina, Book 8 in the Lt. Kate Gazzara series. If you enjoyed it - and I sincerely hope you did - you'll probably want to read the next book in the series, Nicolette, Book 9. If so, CLICK HERE.

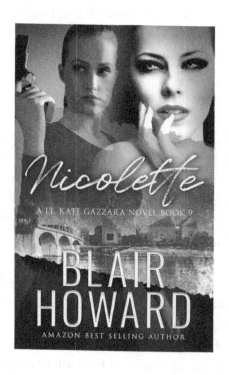

ACKNOWLEDGMENTS

Many people have helped with the writing of this book, and I thank them all, especially my editor Diane Shirke. Great job Diane.

My thanks go also to my friends still in law enforcement and retired, for their help in the past and the present... and for the help I know you'll provide in the future, especially you Ron, Gene, David, CSI Laura Lane.

Thanks also to my Beta readers who managed to find most of those annoying little typos.

Finally, thanks to my ever-patient wife, Jo... and of course to my constant companion, even if she does eat everything that's not tied down, Sally.

NICOLETTE

A LT. KATE GAZZARA NOVEL BOOK 9

ISBN: 9798675312580

"I'll call you later," he said, right before the trailer's aluminum door slammed shut behind Erica.

How many times had she heard that? She stood on the tiny, uneven wooden deck outside the door, holding her high heels in one hand and her bulky purse under her arm, feeling used and dirty. *Crap, this wasn't supposed to happen,* she thought angrily as she looked self-consciously around the neighboring trailers.

Erica Fleck had made herself a promise that she would never sleep with Charlie again. Of course, when he called and invited her over, she'd been in complete control. She wore her best skinny jeans and a tight tank top with her favorite red heels, but only to show him what he was missing. She wasn't interested in getting back together, not even if he begged her.

"Get back together? He won't even drive you to the damn bus stop," she muttered as she descended the steps.

The Tomahawk Trailer Park is really nice when you first pull into it; curb appeal is what they call it. But it's just a facade. Back at the rear of the lot it isn't so pretty. Charlie's silver trailer was nestled between a dilapidated, vinyl-sided mobile home within which the television was on twenty-four-seven and a plywood-covered trailer incongruously surrounded by pretty flowers in flowerpots. It was as if the owner was trying to gussy up a dirty old dress with a little cheap bling. It made the place look suspicious rather than inviting.

"You know you miss me, honey," Charlie had said to her as they sat together on the couch watching some stupid superhero movie.

Erica had no interest in the movie but pretended to be engrossed as if it were the best movie she'd ever seen. She was trying to play hard to get.

How hard could it be when you took a bus to his trailer and were serving yourself up like a piece of steak on a platter? her conscience hissed.

But Charlie knew all the right buttons to push. He was handsome. He was shirtless when he opened the door, and he kissed her hand like an old-time gentleman.

Yeah, he's a real prince. That's why he didn't even offer you a cup of coffee before you left.

As Erica's bare feet hit the grass, the reality of what she'd done hit her. She tried to hold up her head, but she knew without a doubt that anyone who saw her would know exactly what she'd done. People who lived in the nicer trailers up front by the road were already leaving for church. Those that weren't were out tending their tiny yards before it got too hot to mow the ten feet of grass that came with every unit. Others watched her from behind curtains or through the slats of their blinds as she marched the walk of shame.

Of course, no one really cared what Erica was doing, who she'd been doing it with, or where she was going. But in her head, she just knew that all eyes were upon her and that every head was shaking in disgust. That was how she felt, and it was horrible. How could she have been so stupid to fall for Charlie's line of bullshit yet again?

Of course, doing a shot of Jack Daniel's with him as soon as you walked in the door probably wasn't the smartest move you ever made... And following him into his bedroom to watch television when you could have stayed in the living room was also pretty damn dumb. Her conscience sounded just like her mother.

All Erica could think of was getting home and taking a shower. There was no way she was going in to work at the hotel. She'd call in and tell them she had cramps. *Let someone else run the damn desk.*

Finally, Erica reached the entrance to the trailer park on the main street. It was still early. She'd have to sit at the bus stop in the bright sunshine while the morning traffic became heavier by the minute. And she'd have to put on her shoes. There was no way she was going to walk on the sidewalk barefoot, her heels dangling from her fingers for all to see.

Carefully, her arms spread wide to maintain her balance, she tiptoed over to an older model green car and leaned against it to pull on her heels. Not an easy task. Her feet had swollen from the walk. As she slipped the right one on it pinched her toes, making her wince. *How the hell am I going to manage the bus ride and then walk the two blocks from the bus stop to my apartment?*

"Slowly, that's how," she muttered as she shifted from one foot to the other. Just as she was wedging her other foot inside her shoe, she glanced sideways into the car through the window.

"Oh, I'm so sorry," she said to the person slumped over inside. "I was just trying to get my shoes on..."

At first, she thought she'd scared the young woman, and that perhaps she too had had an encounter with a boyfriend at the trailer park and instead of driving home had just parked and went to sleep. But that didn't explain the tape around her wrists.

"Tape? Oh, m'God!" Erica's mind froze. After swallowing hard, she knocked on the glass. There was no response. The woman didn't move.

Erica looked around, her mind in a whirl. There was no one but her on the street. There were no businesses open, no police cars cruising around. She looked again through the window, her heart beating so hard she could hear the blood rushing through her ears.

Oh wow... Oh wow... What should I do? I'll stop a car... No, you could get run over or they'll think you're a hooker... Hell you might as well be you silly b... Damn it, Erica, just call the frickin' police.

She fumbled through her purse. Her hands shaking... *Where the hell is it? Oh no, I didn't... I know I didn't. I didn't leave it in Charlie's trailer. I can't go back... I just can't,* she thought as she continued to rummage wildly around inside her purse. *No. I can't do that. Just the thought of going back there makes me want to throw up. Oh my God, that poor woman... Those bruises, that tape... pretty blouse though... Are you serious, Erica? How can you think something like that with her mouth all taped... Where the frickin' hell IS it? Ah, gotcha, whew. Thank you, Lord!*

Then she had another thought, one that made her look nervously around.

What if the person who did this comes back? Tears filled her eyes.

"Nine-one-one. What is your emergency?" the operator said coldly.

Erica stuttered. The words that were pounding around in her head wouldn't come out of her mouth.

"Nine-one-one. What is your emergency?" the operator repeated the question more forcefully.

Erica thought for a second that she'd just hang up. *Press that little red button and just start walking.* But she didn't. She took a deep breath and started talking.

"I'm at the entrance to the Tomahawk Trailer Park. There is a dead woman in a car," Erica said, her bottom lip trembling.

What are you crying for? she thought. *You don't know the woman. For all you know she deserved to get killed. Maybe she beat her kids or was on drugs.*

Erica's thoughts were churning around inside her head. She didn't want to hang up with the 911 operator. Thankfully, the person on the other end of the line asked for a description of the car and a dozen other questions that kept Erica talking.

"D'you live at the park, ma'am?"

"No. I was visiting a friend," Erica said, feeling guilty because it wasn't true. "Actually, that's not quite true. It was a booty call."

"Well, that happens," the operator replied without judgment. "Does the person you were seeing know about the woman in the car? Is he with you now?"

"No. Hell no," Erica said just loud enough for the operator to hear.

Suddenly, a strange sense of calm settled over her. "No. He probably won't come out of his trailer until he has to go to work tomorrow night. He's like a damn bat."

The sound of sirens rapidly approaching grew louder. Erica let out a deep breath and told the operator the police were just a block away and that she could see the red and blue emergency lights of two police cruisers speeding in her direction.

"Okay, stand by until they arrive, please. The police will take over from here, and they'll want to talk to you," the operator said. "You take care now."

"Thank you," Erica replied. "I will."

Less than a minute later the two blue and white police cruisers screeched to a stop in front of her as she waved them down. The uniformed officers, big and serious, slammed their car doors, hitched up their belts and joined her.

"What seems to be the problem, ma'am?" The tag on his shirt proclaimed him to be "V Short."

No, he's not! The thought jumped unbidden into her head.

"There's a dead woman... in that car, over there."

"Stay here, please, ma'am, while we take a look, okay?"

She nodded. The officers stepped over to the car and shined their flashlights in through the window even though it was broad daylight.

She watched as they walked together around the car, peering in through every window, but not touching the car; one of them talking constantly into what seemed like a walkie-talkie on his left shoulder.

Finally, the officer named Short walked back to where she was standing, her left elbow cradled in her right hand as she nibbled the nail of her left thumb. The other officer returned to his cruiser, opened the trunk, and took out a fat roll of wide yellow crime scene tape and proceeded to cordon off a huge area around the green car.

"So, Miss..." Short said, waiting a beat for Erica to give him her name.

"Fleck, Erica Fleck."

"I need you to make a statement, Miss Fleck, but I think it might be better if we went to my car. It's about to get real busy around here," he said, eyeing the already growing crowd.

Short took Erica's statement, her phone number, her address, and asked if there was someone she could call to come get her and take her home.

"No. I'll wait for the bus," she replied as more and more cops showed up as well as a rollback transporter truck to remove the vehicle.

"No worries," Short said. "I'll have someone drive you home." He waved over another uniformed officer and instructed him to take Erica straight home. As she sat in the back of the police car, her shoes off and her feet feeling better, she knew she'd never go to that trailer park again.

2

My first sip of coffee of the day was interrupted by the telephone.

I'd been enjoying the cool morning breeze wafting in through the open window of my bedroom. The temperature had dropped down to a cozy forty degrees overnight and I'd left the window cracked open a little so that I could feel the cool breeze flow over my face as I lay snug under the covers. I wasn't due at work until nine that morning...

My name, by the way, is Kate... Catherine Gazzara. I'm a captain, a detective, in charge of a small special crimes unit at the Chattanooga Police Department.

It was a little after 7:30 when I got out of bed that morning and went naked to the bathroom, where I pulled my old terrycloth robe from the laundry hamper and slid into it. It was an ugly old thing with coffee stains down the front and a worn hem, but it was warm and comfortable. As a joke I'd gotten a pair of pink fuzzy slippers for my birthday from my team at the office. I'd never admit to wearing them, but I slipped them on and shuffled out to the kitchen to make coffee. As far as my team knew, I slept in tennis shoes so I could run out the door at the drop of a hat. But secretly, I loved those silly slippers.

I'd set the coffee machine the night before so all I had to do was push the button and wait.

Two minutes later, cradling the hot cup in both hands, I sat down at the table, sipped, closed my eyes, breathed in the aromatic fumes and... I was startled as my iPhone began shouting at me, "Don't worry, be happy." I looked at the screen: it was Janet.

My partner, Sergeant Janet Toliver, at twenty-six, is still the youngest female detective in the Chattanooga Police Department and the youngest member of my team.

"Sorry to bother you so early, Cap," she said.

"What's going on?" I asked. It was too early for chit-chatting.

"They're bringing a car to the impound. The ME is on his way," Janet said.

"Okay, so what's that got to do with me? And why is the Medical Examiner coming to the impound?" I yawned. I already knew the answers to both questions. Doc Sheddon doesn't do abandoned cars. There had to be a body involved.

"There's a body in the car," Janet confirmed. "Female. Young. Duct tape around her wrists and mouth."

"Get yourself over there, Janet. Don't let them touch anything until I get there. I'll be there in thirty minutes."

I hung up, took one more gulp of hot coffee, poured the rest into a thirty-two-ounce to-go cup and topped it up. Fifteen minutes later I was in jeans and a T-shirt, behind the wheel of my car and speeding to the police impound. I pulled up next to the only luxury vehicle in the place, a black Lexus SUV with a vanity license plate that read DOA.

Hamilton County's Chief Medical Examiner had beaten me to it, again.

With my to-go cup in my hand, I elbowed my way through the circle of uniforms and technicians gathered around the car. The transporter truck had already set it down, but as far as I could tell no one had touched it... yet.

It was an older model sedan, a mint green Chevy Impala. I made a note of the license plate number and wrote it down on my notepad.

"What? No good morning?" Doc Sheddon said.

"Where are my manners?" I replied as he took my coffee from my hand and helped himself to a big gulp.

"Out on the sidewalk somewhere," he replied. "What is this, hazelnut?" Doc's face wrinkled up like he'd just swallowed unsweetened lemonade.

"I thought I'd try something new," I replied, taking back my cup.

"Ugh. You people. If it isn't broke, don't fix it," Doc grumbled. "Are we going to spend all day here? I'd like to get to the body sometime today."

"Okay, give me a few minutes, Doc." I offered him my coffee cup. "Want another sip?"

"And end up like her?" He pointed inside the car and shook his head.

I smirked and began my inspection. Doc Sheddon and I were used to each other. He grumbled and fussed like a man who had never been given a fair shake his whole life. The truth is, the only thing the man didn't have was hair on his head and twenty-twenty vision, which is why he wore those silly little half-glasses that made him look like a balding Geppetto. But he had enough clout to order the uniformed officers around, and even me on occasion. Plus, he drove a Lexus that must have cost him more than I get paid in a year. No, Doc Sheddon had no reason to be crusty with anyone. But he was. And I could tell by the way he pushed through the officers to find a quiet spot all by himself that he was annoyed he was having to wait before he could process the body.

As much as I liked Doc, he was going to have to learn the virtue of patience.

I made a note of the VIN number under the windshield, checked the bodywork for fresh damage—there was none—and finally checked the tires for mud. There was none of that either. They were, in fact, just an average set of standard Michelins. As I was wearing only jeans and a T-shirt, I took out my pocket flashlight, handed my coffee to one of the uniforms and then lay down on the ground and shined the light underneath to see if there was anything clinging to the bottom. Nothing looked out of place. Even the dirt and wear and tear appeared normal.

"Okay. Let's open her up," I said as I got to my feet, dusted myself off and retrieved my coffee. I walked over to where Doc was standing. He handed me a pair of purple latex gloves and I snapped them on. The man carried them around with him like most people carry spare change.

"Just give me a couple of minutes more, okay?" I asked.

"Take your time, missy. It's not like I have anything else to do," he said, grabbing my coffee and taking another swig. "Ugh. Filthy stuff. Its only redeeming virtue is that it's wet."

I smirked and said, "Hang onto it for me while I take a peek inside the box."

I motioned for one of the uniforms to join me as I stepped back to the car and carefully opened the driver's side door. The smell wasn't as bad as it could have been, but the aroma of death was there mixed with cigarette smoke and something else. Perfume. Cheap perfume that didn't just go up your nose but nestled in behind your eyes and gifted you with a throbbing headache. I leaned inside, careful not to touch anything, and shined my flashlight all over the interior. There was an old rain jacket on the back seat, a pen, a couple of receipts and an empty coke can on the front passenger side floor, and a blunt—a homemade joint made from a cigar—in the ashtray.

"Maybe this was a drug deal gone bad," the officer said.

"I don't know about that," I said, staring at it, thinking that maybe we'd catch an early break with a DNA match. "One blunt does not a drug deal make."

"A hooker then," he said. "Maybe she strayed and her pimp offed her up as an example to the others."

"I doubt that too," I replied. "She's nicely dressed... doesn't look like a hooker. Her nails are natural and well kept. And why would a dealer or a pimp duct tape her up and suffocate her?"

"What makes you think she was suffocated?" the officer asked.

"That bag." I shined the light on the plastic bag on the floor by her bare feet. "I think that's lipstick on the inside. It looks like it from here."

"Here, let me." I stood aside and watched as he leaned inside and carefully, between his latexed thumb and forefinger, delicately picked up the bag, stepped back, held it up to the light and studied it.

"I think you might be right." He looked at me and nodded.

I'd seen this officer around the police department, but aside from a casual glance and maybe an occasional double take at his broad shoulders, I'd never given the man much thought. Who had the time? But now that he was right there in front of me, with a look on his face like he didn't mind a girl getting the answer right, I allowed myself a tiny smile. He was cute, but there was a dead girl in the passenger seat who took precedent.

"Bag it and tag it," I said as I turned my attention back to the body. *Hmmm, nice friendship ring... No wedding band. Someone has to be missing this young lady.*

Her mouth was covered by duct tape... *Painful*, I thought. Her wrists were taped together, but not her ankles. I looked around for the roll of tape, but unless it had rolled under one of the seats it wasn't inside the car. *Maybe it's in the trunk.*

I wondered if this was a standard kidnapping, then why would the kidnapper risk having his victim in the front seat. Wouldn't he be better off throwing her in the trunk? At least the back seat where no one could see her. I looked for the keys. They were not in the ignition.

I looked down and pulled the lever to release the trunk lid and went around back to look inside. It appeared to be almost empty: just the spare tire, an emergency roadside kit and an old, neatly folded blanket. Nothing that indicated anyone had tampered with or even opened the trunk. Still, forensics would scour everything for me.

"All right, boys. The transport has arrived. Let's move her. She's been in there long enough," Doc barked as two EMTs wheeled a gurney close to the passenger side of the car.

I stood back and watched as they methodically moved the young woman from the front seat to the gurney, taking care not to disturb the scene or anything on her person that might be of value to the investigation. My heart jumped. When they had the body on the gurney, I could see the passenger's seat where the girl had been was stained with blood.

"Doc?" I looked at him, hoping he'd tell me she had a laceration on her thigh or that there was a reason for this blood other than the horror I was thinking. He looked over my shoulder at the seat and I heard him make the same sigh that I made. Was she assaulted to this degree that she bled all over the car seat?

"I won't know anything, Kate, until I get her on the examination table," he said quietly. "Don't ask," he said, anticipating my question about the time of death. "I'll get her liver temperature now. Give you a rough idea, but you'll have to wait for the specifics until I've finished my examination." And then he turned and followed the gurney to the ambulance.

I nodded to myself, staring after him as he walked away, and then I turned and looked around at the officers. The place was silent. Everyone had the same expression on their face. I hoped they weren't thinking what I was thinking.

I stepped away, had a quick word with Lieutenant Mike Willis, our forensics supervisor, and asked him to let me know immediately if he found anything unusual. It was a speech by rote I'd made many times before, and one I really didn't have to make at all. Mike is good at his job, the best, in fact, and doesn't need me to tell him how to do it. But he's a doll and grinned at me and said he would, then he told me, in the nicest terms possible, to get the hell out of there and let him get on with it. I did, and as I did Doc waved for me to join him.

"Sometime between eight and ten last night, and don't ask me if I'm sure. Based on the liver temperature, I'd say I'm pretty close. Now, I'll escort this young lady back to my place."

I thanked him, told him that I'd check in with him later, told him goodbye, then turned back in time to see Mike's team begin their work. Within seconds they had vacuums, plastic baggies, lint rollers, florescent lights, tweezers, combs, fingerprint powder and dusting brushes spread out all over the place.

They descended on the car like ants on a picnic. Each member of the forensic team had a specific job to do to ensure every fiber, particle or print was collected and tagged. Something had to come up. But as with every crime that happens in Chattanooga, just when I've got one that stirs my gut and I want to focus all my efforts on, half a dozen other crimes pop up screaming for my attention. Literally.

3

It was just after eleven that morning when I left the police garage. I'd planned to go to my office, make myself some more coffee, maybe answer a couple of emails, make a few phone calls and wait for Doc to let me know when he'd finished his examination of our Jane Doe. On a good day I would have stayed to watch the autopsy, but somehow I just didn't have the stomach for it.

On arrival at the PD, I thought I'd drop in at the situation room and see what was going on. What I didn't expect was to see a hysterical woman sitting at Detective Ann Robar's desk sobbing uncontrollably.

As soon as she saw me, Robar stood and waved me over.

"Captain Kate Gazzara, this is Maureen Lawson," Robar said. "She's here because her daughter is missing."

"Mrs. Lawson." I reached out my hand and cleared my throat. "How old is your daughter?" I asked as my chest tightened. There's nothing worse, in my opinion, than a missing child.

"She's twenty-four," Maureen blubbered.

The tension in my chest eased, and mentally I went back to

figuring out which phone calls I needed to make first and if I wanted to make another cup of coffee or finish what I had left in my to-go cup. I looked at Robar, my eyebrows raised in question.

"According to Mrs. Lawson," Robar said, looking down at her notes, "her daughter had a date last night with a new man. Someone she met online. She never came home."

I looked at Mrs. Lawson. She was a tall woman, well built with eyes a little too close together and a large nose. She wore what I'd call "mom clothes"—comfortable pants with a simple blouse that covered up unwanted middle-aged weight gain. Her nails were expertly manicured... probably the one luxury she allowed herself. I figured her to be about fifty years old. The gray roots were beginning to show at the top of her head, but the rest of her hair was dark brown.

"Mrs. Lawson, Detective Robar will take the rest of your statement but since your daughter is an adult, we have to wait twenty-four hours before we can issue a missing person report. It's like this," I said, sympathetically, "if she went on a date, she probably spent the night with this man and—"

"No! My daughter isn't like that. She won't even try on clothes in a store dressing room because she's so self-conscious. I know something's happened to her. I just know it." The woman began to cry.

I felt bad for her, but there was nothing I could do. She had no idea of the number of people who are reported missing and eventually show up again with a tan because they drove to Florida on a whim, or with a new tattoo because life had just gotten a little too quiet for them. A twenty-four-year-old girl from Chattanooga on a date with a new guy who doesn't come home is either the beginning of the greatest love story ever told or a crime novel. Of course, I said none of this to the distraught Mrs. Lawson.

"Give Detective Robar all the details and anything else you think might help," I told her. "We'll do all we can once she's been missing for twenty-four hours."

I gave her my card, and Robar's from the stack on her desk and that appeased her, at least for the moment, and I said goodbye and left them to it. Before I slipped away to my office, however, I decided to stop by Jack North's desk.

Jack is the newest member of my small team and he and I were slowly getting used to one another. It wasn't easy. Jack was Lennie Miller's replacement. When Lennie died—I should say was murdered—not only did I lose the best computer forensics guy in the entire Chattanooga PD, but I also lost a good friend. And even though everyone said it wasn't my fault that he died, there was a part of me that would always feel that it was.

Geez, how many things in my life would I change if I knew then what I know now? More than a few, you can bet. But, as they say, hindsight is always twenty-twenty. I couldn't have changed what I didn't know.

So now I had to look to the future and not only accept the newest member of my team but do my best to nurture and turn him into a productive member. So far, after only a couple of months or so, I thought Jack seemed to be a good fit. I liked him. But he came to me with a lot of baggage. He's thirty-six, married with no children, maybe five-ten—an inch shorter than me—medium build, maybe a hundred and seventy pounds, clean-shaven, hair cut short... and he's on probation. Yes, I was his last stop before Chief Johnston showed him the door, unless he got his act together and followed the rules. And that makes me the last person he should have been assigned to.

Oh well, so far, so good.

"Good morning, Detective North. I have something for you," I said as I took a seat on the corner of his desk.

"Morning, Cap. Lay it on me," he replied as he leaned back in his chair with his coffee mug in his hand.

"I need you to run this VIN and license plate number. We have a murder victim. She was still in the car when they brought it to impound. The ME has her now, but I need to know if this Jane

Doe is the owner of the car and if not, who is. There was no identification on the body. No purse. You know how it is. It's never easy."

"That's an understatement," he said as he took the scrap of paper from me, glanced at it, nodded and said, "I'll get right on it."

"Thanks," I replied as I slid off his desk. I turned to leave, then thought better of it. *I can do better,* I thought.

"How are you doing, Jack? Anything you need from me?"

He looked up at me, puzzled, and said, "No... I can't think of anything. Why d'you ask?"

"I don't really know. How are you getting along with the others?"

"Fine, I guess. It's a bit overwhelming..." he trailed off, unsure of what he was saying.

"Overwhelming? How so?"

"Well, it didn't take long before I realized Lennie was something special. That can be hard to live up to."

"You don't have to. Just remember that we're a team and do your job. They already accept you, as do I. You know you can talk to me whenever you feel a need. You don't need to ask. I'm there for you, as are Janet, Ann and Hawk, right?"

He nodded, gazed up at me and, for the first time, I noticed the intense blue of his eyes. "You got it, Captain."

I could see he still wasn't quite sure what I was trying to do... or say, and I'm not sure I was either, but he was part of the team and I wanted to be inclusive.

"As soon as you find anything, let me know, okay? Talk to you later." And with that I turned, walked to the elevator and down to the first floor to my office.

"This is his last stop, Kate," Chief Johnston had told me that day when he informed me that Lennie's replacement would be arriving in a couple of days. I remember it wasn't exactly the kind of news I wanted to hear that dark day in September two months ago. "If Jack North doesn't work out with you, he won't work out at all. His IA file is six inches thick and, like you, he doesn't work well with others."

I also remember how that pissed me off more than it should have. Yes, it was true, at least to a degree, that I had a problem with authority... well, some authority. I don't do well with idiots, and the PD has them by the bushel, but that's another story. I told the Chief I'd look after him, and I have. He's a pretty damn good hacker. Not quite in Lennie's class and certainly not in Tim Clarke's—he's Harry's tech genius... And that's another story too. Janet took him under her wing right away. Hawk and Ann not so much, at first anyway. Now? Well, he seems to have made a place for himself.

As I waited for the elevator, I turned to look at him. *Looks like a good cop,* I thought, not for the first time. *Yeah, he'll be all right. Need to keep him on a short leash, at least for now, but he can be a great asset for the team if he stays in line,* I thought as the elevator dinged and the doors opened.

When I sat down at my desk in my office on the first floor only three doors away from the mighty chief himself, I took a swig from my to-go cup. Ugh. The coffee was stone-cold and bitter as hell. *Hazelnut? Doc was right: filthy stuff.*

I stood, tossed the dregs into the trash can, stepped over to my personal, one-cup machine, selected a pod of dark Italian roast—a holdover from days gone by—and made myself twelve ounces of the good stuff. Then I sat down again and thought about the Chevy and the dead girl inside it.

Now I'm not a squeamish person—you can't be if you do what I do—but a shiver ran up my spine as I thought of her demise. *That poor girl... What she must have gone through... What the hell is going to come of this? Nothing good, that's for damn sure.*

After a couple of hours in my office, I began to get the feeling I was actually going to get my work for the day completed. Files had been updated, emails responded to, and just about every voicemail message had been listened to and returned... And that's when Jack came knocking on my door with a huge can of worms.

"I got those numbers you were asking for. The VIN and license plate for Jane Doe," he said, shaking his head. "The VIN belongs to a Nicolette Percy of East Brainerd. But the plate is registered to a Thomas Cowel of downtown Chattanooga. I don't get why either one would be off the beaten track at the Tomahawk Trailer Park."

"Not to mention that the VIN and plate are supposed to match." I sighed. "Is Janet in?"

Janet Toliver is my right-hand, my partner, and an anomaly. She's twenty-six years old and looks sixteen. She's every mother's dream of how she'd like her kid to turn out. A redhead, she's intelligent, street-smart, lovely, and she always looks like she's just skipped off a school bus which is a priceless asset for what she does. My initial visits always seem to go well when she's with me. It's like I brought my kid sister along; not the least bit threatening. The thing is though, it's all very deceiving: the girl has a black belt in Jiujitsu, is an expert marksman with a pistol and long gun and seems to have the ability to see right through the lies.

"She's with Hawk on the Benson case. The fire that burned that restaurant and killed one of the busboys," Jack said, rubbing the back of his neck.

"That's right. So she is. Okay, then. It's you and me, buster, so saddle up. You're coming with me." I grabbed my iPad and keys. "Since Mr. Cowel is in downtown Chattanooga, let's go pay him a visit."

4

The Cowel residence was, in a word, beautiful: a quaint little blue bungalow with flowers in boxes underneath every window, a cobblestone driveway with just the odd weed here and there growing up between the cracks, and a brightly-colored welcome mat that apparently saw a lot of traffic.

Jack thumbed the bell push and knocked on the metal security door that, unfortunately, was a necessity on Conway Street, located as it is just off McCauley. We didn't have to wait long.

"Yes, who are you? What do you want," a tiny voice said from the video doorbell.

"We're with the police," I said, holding my ID up to the camera. "My name is Captain Gazzara. I'd like to have a word with you, sir."

There were two loud clicks and both doors unlatched and swung open slightly.

"Please, come on in." And we did.

The doors opened into a small, completely dark foyer and another room beyond. There could have been a half-dozen men with machine guns aimed right at us and we would never have seen them. The interior reminded me of one of those old vampire movies where the home of the bloodsucker was kept dark inside for fear that a single ray of sunshine might cut through the darkness and sear the monster's flesh.

"Come on through. There's a light switch just to your right."

I flipped the switch and said, "Hello. We're looking for Mr. Thomas Cowel." I held up my badge as did Jack, but we still couldn't see him. "I'm detective Kate Gazzara. This is detective Jack North. We'd like to talk to you for a moment."

"All right. I heard you the first time," he said. "Yes, that's me. Did you close the doors? Are they locked?"

It was a strange question. Most people know if their doors were open or locked.

"Sir?" I asked.

"I'm blind, you see. So, if you wouldn't mind giving the door a jiggle, we'll solve the mystery if it's locked or not."

And I felt like a complete idiot. Shaking my head, I grabbed the metal handle and tried to turn it, but it didn't move; we were locked in with... Instinctively, I laid my hand on my weapon.

"Looks like it's locked," I said.

"Good, thank you. I wasn't expecting visitors," Cowel said, clicking his tongue as he maneuvered his electric wheelchair around to face us.

We were finally able to get a good look at him.

He was wearing a long-sleeved dress shirt and golf shorts and looked to be in his late seventies, bald on top, but with a face that reminded me of an old hound dog, being long in the jowls and droopy around the eyes. It was also quite obvious that his legs were little more than bones covered with a thin layer of skin and that he hadn't been able to walk for some time, probably several years.

"We're sorry to bother you," Jack said, looking at me.

"Well, it's too late for that now, isn't it?" the man snapped. "Come in. Who are you again? You rattled off your names like you were calling an auction. Sit down, sit down," he said impatiently. "What d'you want?"

We stepped inside the living room and repeated our names.

"We're here to talk to you about a young woman that was found dead in her car early this morning."

"Oh, my. How very interesting, but why d'you want to talk to me?" Cowel replied.

"The car is a 1980 Impala. The VIN number is assigned to a woman, but we aren't sure if it's our Jane Doe. Unfortunately, the license plate number is assigned to a 1995 Chrysler LeBaron that belongs to you, Mr. Cowel," I said and watched his reaction. His eyes might not have been able to see, but they certainly registered excitement and shock.

"Are you serious, detective?"

"Absolutely, sir," I replied. "Do you have any idea how a license plate belonging to you might have gotten onto another car?"

"No, I don't. The LeBaron was, of course, my car. But as you can see, I am no longer able to drive; not for several years. However, I only recently got rid of it. I sold it."

I nodded. "We need to know who you sold it to, and when. Do you have those records, Mr. Cowel?" I asked.

"Of course. Yes, I have all that. Wait right here, please. I'll fetch them for you." Cowel backed away, executed a perfect turn and with a noise that sounded like one of those spaceships in a Jetson's cartoon, he disappeared down the hallway. Two minutes later he was back with the paperwork, including a legal and honest bill of sale and a signed, paid-in-full receipt. He sold the car in June, less than six months ago.

"I find this very strange," Cowel said, "because the young man I sold this car to said he'd remove the license plate and leave it in the garage. It should still be there."

"If you don't mind, sir, I'd like to take a look and see if it is... still there," I said.

"By all means. Follow me, please." Again, with a slight movement of his hand, the chair spun on the spot and he whirred away down the hall again with Jack and me following.

We followed him into what I imagined must be a den, or more likely a library filled with books: old books, new books, thin books, fat books, everywhere I looked. The complete works of Mark Twain, at least a couple of dozen books on Great Britain. There were books that looked so old they were falling apart and others about the 2016 World Series Cubs vs. Indians. I think the Cubs won.

"You have a lot of books, Mr. Cowel," I said.

"Yes. I used to be an avid reader. Now I have to listen to books on the computer. It just isn't the same," he said as he rolled on into his kitchen then made a sharp left to the inside garage door.

"There," he said, pointing to the door. "Just slip the bolt. The door should be unlocked. You'll find it on the bench."

Jack opened the door to reveal an empty garage. He stepped across the open space to a long bench set against the far wall. It took but a cursory glance along its length from one end to the other for him to confirm that the plate was missing.

Even from where I was standing behind Cowel, I could see the bench was clean: not a tool, auto part or piece of rag anywhere. The cupboard was bare. Jack turned, looked at me and shook his head.

"It's not there, Mr. Cowel," I said. "I'm afraid he must have taken it with him."

"Oh dear, that's not good is it? Are you sure?"

"Yes, I'm sure... Mr. Cowel, and no, it's not good, because for six months he's been running around with the car still registered to you. You, sir, are still responsible for any problems that might arise during his use of the vehicle: parking tickets, accidents... And I expect you canceled your insurance, correct?"

He sighed, nodded and said, "I just didn't think to follow up. I'm sorry, Detective."

I too sighed, looked at Jack, shook my head.

"How did you find him, this person you sold your car to?" Jack asked.

"I put an advertisement on Craigslist. As you can see on the receipt, the young man paid in cash. He was very polite, and he said he'd remove the plate. I told him to leave it on the bench in the garage. He said he would," Mr. Cowel said.

"Mr. Cowel, I need to hang onto this receipt and bill of sale, if you don't mind," Jack said. "We'll return them, of course, but for now they're evidence, and we'll need to contact the man who bought your car. His name, according to this," he said, looking at the receipt, "is Roger Heddiger. This address though... I don't recognize this street name."

"Yes, by all means. Keep them. I don't think I'll be needing them anymore. The transaction was completed... well, the sale was. The title transfer, obviously not." Cowel shrugged, his eyes looked straight ahead, seeing nothing but sensing everything.

"This reminds me of the old-time radio shows," he said. "You know, the ones where the detectives would find a key clue and then be off to an exciting confrontation. I do hope your experience is just as successful as any Sam Spade encounter."

Mr. Cowel reminded me somewhat of Doc Sheddon. *I bet the two of them would have gotten along well together.*

"Was there anything unusual about this man, anything else about him that you can remember, Mr. Cowel?" I asked. "Anything at all?"

"From his speech patterns I believe he was white. He used the word 'like' a lot, but then so does more than half the population under thirty... On thinking about it, he didn't seem all that bright. I don't mean mentally challenged in any way. But he may have killed off quite a few brain cells using the Jack Daniels and Mary Jane method. If you catch my drift," Cowel mused. "I'm afraid that's about all there is. He was here for less than thirty minutes and left with the car."

"There wasn't anyone with him?" Jack asked.

"Not that I'm aware of. He said he took two different buses to get here."

"Well, we'll leave you to your books then," I said, "audiobooks, that is."

"Here are our business cards if you think of anything else, please don't hesitate to give us a call," Jack said, offering him the two small white cards.

"I told you, Detective, I can't see," Cowel snapped.

"I'm sorry, sir. It's a force of habit," Jack said, flustered.

"Understood," Mr. Cowel replied. "Don't worry. I have your names and number memorized."

"You do?" I asked.

"It's still 9-1-1, isn't it?" Cowel said.

If I hadn't known better, I might have thought there was a twinkle in those blind eyes, and I had to smile. *Crusty old coot, but likable enough.*

"You're a sharp tack, Mr. Cowel," I said.

"I've been called worse," he said, lifting his chin proudly.

And so, as we left Thomas Cowel to his own dark world, we had a lead, which was more than we usually came away with from such an interview. He was a nice old man and quite brave not only to sell his vehicle the way he did but also to be living on his own. I decided I liked him.

"So, are we going to the address on the receipt?" Jack asked, snapping me out of my thoughts as we climbed into the car.

"Yeah, I think that might be a good—" Just then my cell phone rang; it was Robar.

"Hey, Cap. You aren't going to believe this," she said into the phone.

"What is it?" I asked again without any emotion in my voice. I don't like conversations that start that way.

"We've identified that Jane Doe. Her name is Nicolette Percy," Robar said and waited for my reaction.

I sat and waited for her to clarify.

"And?" I asked.

"Come on, Cap. Nicolette Percy is the girl who was reported missing by her mother this morning. You met her, remember?" Robar replied before rattling off the address for Maureen Lawson, Nicolette Percy's mother.

It took me a minute to digest what I'd heard. Nicolette Percy was the daughter of the woman who wanted to put out a missing person's report this morning. And Nicolette Percy was also the owner of the vehicle bearing Mr. Cowel's plates. She was the duct-taped victim.

"We'll be right there," I said as I hung up the phone and looked at Jack.

"That didn't sound like good news," he said.

He was right. It wasn't. It's never a good sign when a case begins to split like cells under a microscope. It would be one thing if the new developments were answers. But in this case, it was a quickly spreading cancer of questions.

It was almost five o'clock that afternoon when we arrived back at the police department. Robar was at her desk speaking on the phone and scribbling notes on her iPad. Jack took a seat next to her desk. Me? I didn't want to interrupt her call so I paced impatiently back and forth.

"That was one of Nicolette Percy's coworkers, a guy by the name of Mr. Don Harrington. He was calling to let us know she didn't show up for work today and that wasn't like her at all."

"Everyone's into Nicolette Percy's business," I said irritably. "Why would a coworker call us? More to the point, what did he have to say? And did you notify her mother?"

"Whew, Cap. Slow down a little. That's a threefer. No, I haven't notified her mother. Not yet," Robar said. She was a mother herself, and I could tell that the idea of notifying the mother was bothering her. She and her husband were raising two boys who were in that wonderful though terrifying—for a parent—stage of life called "the mid-teens."

"I thought it would be best to talk to you first," Ann said. "The coworker, Harrington. He'd already called the girl's mother, which is why he called me. He collaborated the mother's story about Nicolette having a date with a new guy and that she'd met the guy online."

"Of course, she did. Did you get *his* name?" Jack asked.

"No. Harrington said that she, the Percy girl, had the guy's information on her phone," Robar said. "Forensics brought it to me. Oh, yes. You didn't know, did you? Forensics found her purse in the trunk under a blanket. It's on your desk, Jack. Maybe you can work your magic and crack the four-digit code," Robar said, shaking her head.

I knew what she was thinking. Meeting a man or woman online was always a risky business. Yet, people did it all the time. Sometimes, things would work out. The meeting turns into a harmless date and a good time had by all, and then maybe there is a second date, even a third. Yes, it happens. Unfortunately, the only ones that cross my desk are the ones that end like this one seemed to have done, with a mother crying over her missing daughter... or an unidentified body left like a discarded fast-food receipt in a car.

I had a deep-seated feeling, though, that this one was different... That blood on the car seat. It wasn't how much of it there was, rather than how little, and what there was, was smeared all over the seat... I arched my back to conceal the shivers that raced across my shoulders at the recollection. I very much doubted that it was menstrual discharge and if I was right... well, it didn't bear thinking about.

"What else did Willis find, anything?"

"Not much," Robar replied. "He thinks the driver must have been wearing gloves. The only prints he found belonged to the girl. He's sending a sample from the blunt for DNA testing, but you know how that goes."

I nodded and said, "Okay, it's time to wrap things up for today. We'll sit on this until tomorrow. Robar, if you want to talk to the coworker, do so in the morning; take Hawk with you. Jack, get that phone opened for me by tomorrow morning if you can."

I took a deep breath and looked at my watch. I was ready to go home. The case was only a day old and had already become a tangled mess of leads that left me feeling frozen as to which way to go. Then it hit me. There was only one path for me to take and I'd head that way first thing in the morning. I needed to see Doc Sheddon.

5

The Medical Examiner's office is a quiet, lightly trafficked place; not a place most people enjoy visiting, for any reason. Me? I could take it or leave it. I enjoyed Doc's friendly banter and I always learned something new. And aside from his patients—as he calls them, with tongue in cheek—there was something comforting about the routine, the cleanliness, the calm of the place that was a welcoming change from the insanity that plagued the police department.

"What the hell is this?" I heard Doc's voice through the plate glass as I entered the building. I poked the doorbell in the reception area and waited. After a few minutes, an older lady, maybe a decade younger than Doc, appeared on the other side of the glass, and she looked angry; in fact, she glared at me. I held up my badge and smiled.

"Doc's expecting me," I said patiently. "I'm Captain Gazzara." *Damn*, I thought. *He's done it again. This is a different receptionist from the one that was here just a week ago.*

This lady, though, was pissed and wasn't about to take my word for it. She stomped back into the breakroom where I heard her talking, but it came through only as murmurs.

"Well don't just leave the police captain standing there! Let her in, for God's sake," I heard Doc reply, his voice raised in anger.

The woman reappeared, rolled her eyes and without uttering a word to me, pressed the button and unlocked the door. I stepped inside and ran right into Doc.

"Ah, so it is you," he grumbled.

"You were expecting another police captain?" I answered.

"Of course not..." He wrinkled his nose. "Can you smell it?" he asked.

I sniffed the air, wrinkled my nose, then shook my head and said, "Smell what?"

"It seems that some people who've been on the job for less than a week think this place needs air fresheners," he growled, glaring at the offending receptionist. "There's a stick thing in the breakroom that's supposed to smell like vanilla and lavender. It smells like... Oh never mind. It's good to see you, Kate."

I looked at the receptionist who was dragging her purse out of the bottom drawer of her desk, and it didn't look to me as if she was just leaving for the end of her shift.

"Is that so bad?" I asked.

Doc glared at me as if I'd suggested we eat his latest cadaver. I blinked and jerked my head toward the receptionist who slung her bag over her shoulder and stomped out the door.

"Good riddance," he snapped as the door closed behind her, then he calmed down, beamed at me and said, "Tell me, Catherine, do you by any chance know a competent woman who can handle the simple job of answering the phone, making a schedule, and pushing a button to open a door? I'm having a hard time finding one." He looked at his watch. "Mrs. Sheddon will be beside herself when she hears she has to come in again to help out."

I snickered, shook my head and said, "None that I want mad at me."

"What's that supposed to mean?" Doc said as we went to examination room number two. It was not much different from rooms one and three, except that everything was reversed: the two examination tables were to the left instead of the right. Most importantly, however, the coffee pot was on a counter behind the body, at its foot rather than its head. I made my way past the sheet-covered table and helped myself to a Styrofoam cup of burnt coffee.

"It means two things. One, I think I know why you work so well with your patients." I pointed to the body under the sheet. "They do exactly as they're told. And two, you desperately want Mrs. Sheddon to come to work for you."

"Captain Gazzara, I take serious umbrage to those unfounded comments," Doc said as he walked over to the body.

"I'm just stating the facts, Doc," I said as I took a sip of coffee, looking at him over the rim of the cup. "So, what can you tell me about Nicolette Percy?"

"I like things done my way," he said. "I expect my staff to respect the order of things, not set about changing it the minute they're hired... What? We have a name?" Doc looked at me, surprised.

"Her purse was in the trunk of the car. Forensics delivered the news to Detective Robar last night," I said.

"I see. Well then, let's see..." He pulled back the sheet, lowered his chin to his chest, steepled his fingers together a couple of inches below his chin and, over the top of his glasses, contemplated the remains of what once had been an attractive young woman. "Miss Percy died of asphyxiation." Doc adjusted his glasses with his forefinger.

"You were correct about the plastic bag. It's already gone to the lab. Her lipstick was indeed on the inside, but you know they are checking for anything else. I'm sure they'll send the report to you... eventually."

I nodded but said nothing. I let Doc continue. He took a pen from his pocket and used it to point to the horrific bruises that encircled the woman's neck. They reminded me of a sickly purple and yellow snake.

"This is the impression made by the folds of plastic as they squeezed around her skin," he said. "The bag was indeed the cause of death: asphyxiation... She suffocated, poor girl. Her windpipe was only badly bruised but not crushed. Still, her assailant used a lot of force when he tightened it around her throat. She suffered greatly, I think."

I nodded and took another sip of coffee as Doc peeled back her eyelids. The irises had the gray film of death over them. The sclera, the white part of the eye, was specked and blotched with red: petechial hemorrhage. The result of asphyxiation.

"Are those defensive wounds on her arms?" I asked. "I've never seen any like that."

"No, I don't think so. I'm quite sure those marks were made by her assailant when he grabbed her and when he wrapped the duct tape around her wrists," Doc said as he pointed with his pen. "You see here, it looks like a perfect handprint: four fingers and a thumb."

Doc was right. Four dark purple marks were greeted by a single dark purple mark just above them; whoever had made those bruises had left an almost complete handprint: four fingers and a thumb that almost encircled her upper arm. *Hmm, big hands... so her assailant was considerably larger than her. She's petite. Similar in size and stature to Janet.*

I looked down at her face and, instead of seeing the usual expression of sleep or oblivion, there was an expression of what might have been the result of shock or even a reluctant final acceptance of her impending death. I shook my head.

"As for the blood on the car seat..." He paused, then continued. "There was actually less than it first appeared. Bleeding stops when the heart stops beating. What little there is was leakage caused by penetration... Well, need I say more?" Doc shook his head, then took off his glasses and started to clean them on his white coat. "She was, I'm sad to say, assaulted postmortem."

"I knew it. The sick son of a bitch," I said, feeling my stomach fold over on itself. It was rare for anything to upset me the way necrophilia did. There's something about the sheer brutality of it that made me glad Nicolette Percy was dead when she was violated. Oh, I was angry. Enraged that the sadistic piece of garbage had taken such heinous liberties with her corpse.

"I've sent samples to the lab," Doc said. "It'll probably be a while before you get the results, but you can assume I'm right. I doubt there'll be any DNA, though. The perpetrator was savvy enough to wear a condom. There was, however, a stain on her blouse... Well, not exactly a stain, more of a smear; sputum, I think. I think her assailant must have coughed on her at some stage, so we might get lucky. Anyway, I sent her clothing over to the forensics lab. I don't know what they found in the car... more blood, possibly. Trace evidence? Possibly. Mike Willis is nothing if not thorough, and he'll be able to move a little faster in-house than my guys at the lab. You'll know soon enough, I'm sure. Time of death? Between eight and ten pm."

"What kind of person would do something like this, Doc?" I asked. "The textbooks say there are many motives for murder: sex, greed, love, hate, revenge, money or drugs. But what drives a man to do this to a corpse? I don't know about this one, Doc. I may have hit my limit."

"If you're serious, I could use a secretary." Doc smirked as he handed me a copy of Nicolette's file.

"Er... No, but thanks for the offer."

I left Doc's office feeling heavy-hearted. Now I had to go and break the news to Nicolette's mother. I wasn't going to mention the assault. There was no need. Her daughter didn't experience it. But as soon as I got to the police department, I felt like I needed a shower and some mouthwash. If I held the details inside me for too long, they would rot my brain. Thank goodness Janet was back from her insurance fraud case. I picked up the phone and asked her to come to my office.

"Hey, Cap. I've got the details of the Benson case—the busboy who died in the restaurant fire," she said, twisting her mouth to the right. "The restaurant owner's mistress squealed the whole story. Isn't that always the way? I've got everything typed up ready for your signature. It makes for some interesting reading, especially when the mistress decided to talk."

"Come on in and shut the door," I told her. For a second I felt bad. Her expression fell and I knew she thought she was in trouble.

I told her to take a seat and then told her about Nicolette Percy. Janet's expression said it all. She lost the color in her face, her jaw tightened.

"I have to go break the news to the mother. You ready?" I asked.

"Yes. I'm ready," she said.

"Well, give me a minute. I need to see how things are going with Jack."

I picked up the phone and punched in his number. He answered immediately.

"How are you doing, Jack? Have you cracked Nicolette's phone yet?"

"Not yet. I had to quit working on it for a while. The Chief dropped by and told me to tidy up my files."

I knew that feeling. "Soon as you can, Jack."

"You got it, Cap, but it's going to take a while. It's an Android 8. There are ten thousand possible four-digit combinations. A brute force hack... that's where I have to punch in each combination by hand would, including the thirty-second delay every five attempts, take a hundred and eleven hours. Fortunately, there may be a way to shorten that down to maybe less than sixteen hours. I have a buddy who—"

"Okay, I got it," I said, interrupting him. "Just do what you have to but open the damn thing. It's important... Do what you can."

"Leave it to me. I'll get it done as soon as I can." And with that, he disconnected the call.

I also checked in with Ann Robar. She was out of the office, as was Hawk. She'd gone to Nicolette's place of business to interview Don Harrington about Nicolette's date and hadn't yet returned.

"Where's Hawk, do you know?" I asked Janet.

"He was home, sleeping," Janet replied. "He stayed most of the night with me getting the Benson paperwork done. He called in though, and Ann asked him if he wanted to go with her, so he did."

"How come you aren't home, then?" I asked.

"Not tired. Besides, I had a feeling something exciting was going to happen today," Janet said, as if premonitions were an everyday occurrence for her.

"Aren't you glad you stayed?" I mumbled as I made a note of the address Robar had collected when Nicolette's mother had come in to make her missing person report.

"Maybe this isn't it," she said. "Maybe something even more exciting than this is going to happen."

"Bite your tongue," I said as she pulled my office door closed behind her and we headed out to tell Maureen Lawson, Nicolette Percy's mother, that we'd found her daughter.

6

Maureen Lawson lived in a plain home on a plain street in a plain neighborhood. It certainly wasn't the most expensive single-family dwelling on the block, but it was nicer than most. With a white picket fence, a recently black-topped driveway and a large concrete birdbath in the front yard, it was the only yellow house on the block.

We parked on the street and were walking to the front door when it opened and the woman I recognized as Maureen Lawson stepped out onto the porch, her hands clasped tightly together in front of her and tears in her eyes. She stood, shaking her head.

"You found her, didn't you? She's dead, isn't she? I knew it... I knew it." Her voice caught in her throat.

"Mrs. Lawson, it would be better if we went inside," I said. "If you don't mind."

She nodded absently as she backed into the house, leaving the door open.

When Janet and I stepped inside a few seconds later, we found her on the floor, on her side in the fetal position, her hands clamped to her mouth, sobbing loudly. I closed the front door behind us and went to her.

"She was such a good girl," Maureen said. "Why would anyone want to do something like this? Couldn't they see how good she was? Couldn't they see it?"

"I'm so sorry, Mrs. Lawson," I said. "I know this is a terrible shock." I swallowed hard. "Let's get you up into a chair." I turned to Janet and said, "Give me a hand."

The woman was big—five-nineish, and stocky—and it took more than a little effort to get her up on her feet, but between us we managed it. Then we steered her into the living room where she collapsed into an overstuffed easy chair.

"I'm sorry," I said. "I know it's a bad time, but I need—"

"Where did you find her? Did she... Was she..."

"I'm sorry, Mrs. Lawson. I can't answer those questions, not yet. We're still working the c—" I almost said car. "We're still working the crime scene."

"I need to see her," she said. "Please, I need to see her."

I nodded. "Of course. I'll arrange for you to see her as soon as possible. We'll also need you to officially identify her."

"Of course," she said, "but when?"

"I'll have to let you know," I said. "Mrs. Lawson, can you think of anyone Nicolette might have mentioned who might have held a grudge? An old boyfriend or maybe someone at work who might have had an ax to grind?" I handed my iPad to Janet, who tapped the audio app to record our conversation.

"I can't think of a single person." Maureen started to cry.

I shook my head at Janet, who stopped the recording and went to the kitchen. I heard the tap running, and a few seconds later Janet reappeared with a glass of water and handed it to her.

"I'll be all right," Maureen said as she took the glass. She sipped the water then set the glass on a small side table.

"May we sit down?" I asked.

"Of course," she said, rising to her feet. "Please, let's go into the kitchen."

The kitchen was a quaint little room and obviously recently updated. The walls were decorated with windmills; the cabinets, countertops and appliances were all new. *Hmm,* I thought as I sat down at the small island, *I bet this didn't come cheap.*

Mrs. Lawson, tears still on her cheeks, took a deep breath and said, "Can I get you anything? A cup of coffee? A bottle of water? I think I have a couple of cans of Coke in the garage."

"No thank you, ma'am," I said.

Janet shook her head.

"Please, Mrs. Lawson, sit down," I said. "We'd like to ask you a few questions about the night Nicolette went missing. While it is still fresh in your mind. Can we do that, Mrs. Lawson?"

"Please call me Maureen," She sat down on a stool at the end of the island, gave me a weak smile, then focused her attention on a small vase of zinnias at the center of the island.

I told her we'd be recording the conversation for future reference and asked for her permission. She gave it readily.

"Maureen, you told Detective Robar that your daughter arranged to meet someone she met on a dating site. Is that correct?"

She nodded.

"Out loud, please, for the record," I said gently.

"Yes, that's correct."

"Do you know which dating site that was?"

"No, she never said."

"Do you know where she arranged to meet her date?"

"No, she never told me that either."

"Do you know where they were going?"

"No."

Maureen looked vacantly out through the kitchen window. I turned my head and looked too. The white picket fence continued around from the front yard. It was a nice piece of property with a couple of big trees and a small shed in the far corner. It would be a nice place to live, at least it looked that way to me.

"I should tell you that Nicolette wasn't actually my daughter. She was my stepdaughter, but I've always considered her my daughter. I hate the word stepdaughter... or stepson. I think it's disrespectful to the child, and certainly does nothing for their state of mind. I always spoke of her as my daughter." She sniffled as a fresh wave of tears rolled down her face. "Her father and I divorced about three years ago. It was a mutual decision. Things just weren't working out. I take part of the blame. I took back my name, Lawson."

"How long had you been married?" I asked.

"Eight years." Maureen pulled her lips down at the corners. "No one can say we didn't give it a chance."

"Was Nicolette upset?" I asked.

"She was disappointed. I know that. Her father moved out of Chattanooga and back to his home state of Illinois. Nickie doesn't like the cold, so she stayed with me. Her job was here and her friends." Maureen choked back another wave of tears.

Janet got up from her seat, fetched the glass of water from the table in the living room, refilled it and handed it to her.

With a grateful expression, Maureen mouthed the words *thank you*.

"What can you tell me about Nicolette's friends?" I asked.

"Oh, she had lots of them. Everyone liked Nickie. She was beautiful and saw the good in everyone. I don't think there was a single person who could honestly say a bad word about her." Maureen sniffed.

"I know what you're thinking," she continued. "That's what every mother says about their child. But remember, I'm not her mother. I'm only her stepmother. But I saw the beauty in her, the compassion. When she laughed, you wanted to laugh, too. Responsible too. That's what she was, responsible. I knew her hopes and dreams. She was one of the good guys, Captain Gazzara. She really was."

"You say she was responsible," Janet said, "but she arranged to meet someone she met on the internet. Why would she do that?"

"Nickie had an adventurous side. I won't say wild because she wasn't wild. But she was not afraid to try different things, new things. One of her girlfriends had joined an online dating service and met a really nice young man. So Nickie decided to give it a try too." Maureen smiled weakly.

"Did she date a lot?" I asked. I already knew what she looked like and a girl like her, well I couldn't imagine her having trouble finding dates.

"She had a couple of steady boyfriends over the years. But for one reason or another, none of them were The One." Maureen cleared her throat, then continued, "I think she liked to go out with people and find out about them. She was naturally curious, and I think she was willing to give anyone the benefit of the doubt, even if her gut might have told her differently."

"Do you have the names of the boyfriends?"

She thought for a minute, then shook her head and said, "I really can't remember. It was when I was still married to her father."

"So, what did she tell you about this new person she was meeting, anything at all?" I asked.

"Very little," she said. "She just said that she met him online, that he lived nearby and worked with children. That's all." Maureen squeezed her eyes shut. "My God, she was only twenty-four years old. Didn't he see she was something good? Didn't he see she was a gift?"

"So, you believe that this man she went on a date with had something to do with her death?" I asked firmly.

"It's the only logical answer," Maureen said. "This person is the only one I don't know. He's the missing piece of the puzzle. I'm sorry. I know I'm not a detective, but wouldn't you think the same thing if you were in my shoes?"

"Yes, ma'am. I probably would," I replied with a sigh. "If she met him online, she must have a computer. Can we see it, please?"

"Oh, yes. She has a laptop. But I don't have the password," Maureen said.

That's typical, I thought. *A mother who missed the computer generation by a decade or so. She probably knows just enough to send an email and maybe download a photograph.*

"That's all right," I said. "If you don't mind, I'd like to take it with us. We have people who specialize in this sort of thing," I replied and smiled kindly.

Before I could say another word, Maureen was out of her chair and bustling down the hallway. Within seconds she returned with a laptop and handed it over to me.

"Take it. Do whatever you have to. I don't want it back. To me it's no different from a loaded gun." Maureen wept. "If it weren't for that thing, my sweet Nickie would still be here."

"Thank you, Maureen. This is very helpful." I hesitated, then said, "Do you happen to have a recent photo of her we could borrow?"

She nodded, stepped over to the sideboard and picked up a framed photo, then turned and handed it to me.

"This was taken on her birthday three months ago, but please, when you're finished with it, I'd like to have it back. It's the only decent one I have of her."

It was a headshot. The woman was right, Nicolette was, had been, a beautiful young woman: dark brown hair, bobbed; wide-spaced hazel eyes in a heart-shaped face and lips that had I not known better could have been Botoxed.

"I'll have it copied and get it back to you as soon as possible."

Then I had a thought. "Does she have any brothers or sisters?"

"Yes, a brother, Kenny, but they weren't close. He lives in Chicago. I don't have his address or phone number... I think Nickie had it, and her father has it, I'm sure. I met him a few times. He's a nice enough boy."

I looked at Janet, who'd been busy taking notes until now. She nodded, took the computer from me and folded up her notepad. I silently agreed with her gesture. It was time for us to go.

"Maureen, is there someone you can call who can come and stay with you for a few days?" I asked. "I don't think you should be alone right now."

"I'll be all right, Captain," she replied. "Knowing that you are going to find her killer is the only comfort I need. I'll be all right. Honestly."

"I promise you we'll do our best. And we'll be in touch as soon as we know something. In the meantime, if you think of anything that might help us, even if it seems insignificant or stupid, please, give us a call." I slipped our business cards on the table as Janet and I stood. I picked up my iPad and tapped the off button.

"I'll do that, Captain," she replied. Then she stood and began to cry again as she walked us to the door.

"Again, we're sorry for your loss, Maureen." I reached out my hand. Maureen took it in hers, but before I knew it, she was giving me a gentle hug. I'm not a hugger, but at that moment what could I do? I did what came naturally. I hugged her back.

"That was a rough one," Janet said, wiping her eyes as she slid into the passenger seat.

"Yes, it was," I replied. I'd had to bite the inside of my lip to keep the tears back.

7

B y the time we arrived back at the police department, I was
exhausted. It wasn't yet quite one o'clock in the afternoon,
but to me it felt like I'd already pulled a double shift.

I went to my office to regroup and left Janet to put her notes in
the report. I was planning on a quiet moment with a cup of coffee.
Unfortunately, there was a message on my desk that I needed to
call Chief Johnston as soon as possible. My stomach flipped.

Now, a note on my desk saying I needed to *call* Chief Wesley
Johnston, and as soon as possible, the most straitlaced, by-the-book
police chief in all of Tennessee, and probably in all the other
southern states too, wasn't quite as bad as a note that said I needed
to go immediately to his office. At least that's what I tried to tell
myself. But I knew that neither one boded anything good.

I pushed all thoughts of Maureen Lawson to one side and
immediately set about second-guessing what it was the Chief
wanted. I began to rerun, in my head, my latest busts and interroga-
tions trying to figure out who might have lodged a complaint, I
couldn't think of anyone. Yes, I was that paranoid. And rightly so.
I'd been in so much trouble over the past year it had almost become

routine that Internal Affairs would be looking for something to tag me with.

The only person I could think of that was holding a grudge was Officer Karen Peeks in the evidence room. Several weeks ago, I'd watched as she let another officer take a piece of evidence out of the corral, snap a picture of it, and then return it without properly filling out the paperwork. So, I called her on it. And I then reported her.

Why? It's simple enough. At the time, and I haven't changed my mind, all I could think was that if it was a piece of evidence pertinent to one of my cases and she botched it up because she didn't follow protocol, I'd kill her. Needless to say, I get the stink eye from her every time I see her and now, whenever I need anything from the evidence room, she always has something she needs to finish before she'll get to my needs.

Could that be it? I wondered. Somehow I doubted it, so I took a deep breath and dialed his extension.

"Chief Johnston," he grumbled.

"Hey, Chief. It's Gazzara. You wanted me to call you?" I winced.

"Kate. Yes. Good news. You're getting an award," he said, sounding as surprised as I was to hear it.

"What?"

"Yes. You are being recognized by the Chattanooga Women's Auxiliary of VFW Post #63 for the work you did on the Madia Case," Chief Johnston said.

"What?" I asked again.

"Madia. Come on, Kate. Surely you remember—"

"Yes," I said, interrupting him—something I'd never do under ordinary circumstances, but I was in shock. "Of course I do. It's just that—"

Madia was a Korean War vet, a Marine, homeless and a murder victim. It wasn't a high-profile case, but obviously his compadres were happy with the result.

"Good." Now it was him interrupting me. "They want to show their appreciation by honoring you with their Big Dog Award, whatever the hell that is. The ceremony will be held a week from Friday at the VFW on Douglas Street. Be there at 6:30. Good job, Captain."

"Thank you, sir," I said, still in a state of total shock.

He hung up without saying another word, which is always a good thing.

I sat back in my chair, linked my fingers together behind my head, and smiled up at the ceiling. And then, suddenly, I had the urge to call someone and brag a little. I took out my iPhone and tapped in a number I knew by heart.

"Hey, good-looking," Chief Gunnery Sergeant Wilcox Dorman of the United States Marine Corp said when he answered.

He and I had met during one of my previous cases. A real humdinger that had us both comparing notes on the same person. But it was our experiences with death that we had in common, as morbid as that might sound. The truth is no one understands the life of a cop except for another cop or a soldier. Wilcox was the latter, and he saw death through the same kind of lens as I did. Talking to him was like waking up from a bad dream and realizing it was just that, a dream.

The case? It was the one during which Lennie was murdered. Wilcox—no one ever calls him that except his mother—helped me get through it, the aftermath of Lennie's death, that is. He reminded me that things are never as bad as they seem, and even though I might have a dozen people telling me otherwise, only someone like Wilcox could understand why no one else's words sunk in. He understood. It was as simple as that.

And I'll admit that being six feet tall with salt-and-pepper hair, blue eyes, and still maintaining the physique he'd sculpted during his years in the Marines didn't hurt either. And him being stationed at the Marine Corps recruiting office on Lee Highway, as he was,

was yet another blessing. Oh hell, here I go again rambling on like an old woman, which I certainly am not.

"Hi. Guess what happened to me today?" I asked.

"You got mugged," he stated flatly.

"Very funny," I said and proceeded to tell him what the Chief had just told me about my Big Dog Award and that I'd need an escort and was hoping that he'd be willing to make an appearance with me.

"Big Dog? Wow. That's really something. Of course, I'd be honored to escort you," he replied. "But you do know those guys at the VFW really know how to throw a party. Don't be surprised if you are not three sheets to the wind before they present your award." Wilcox chuckled.

"Fantastic. Sounds like the best award ceremony ever," I replied happily.

"Sounds like you're having a good day," Wilcox said.

"Actually, it's been a bad day." And then I proceeded to tell him about my having to break the news to Maureen Lawson about her daughter. "It's never easy."

"No. I'll bet not. Hey, you want some company tonight?" he asked, his deep voice cutting through the tension in my body like a hot knife through butter.

Geez, do I ever, I thought.

"You were reading my mind," I replied.

"Call me when you're leaving. I'll meet you at your place."

"Sounds good. See you tonight," I said and hung up.

That was all it took. After I finished the call I felt better; even so, it didn't change the fact that Maureen Lawson was now living with the reality that her daughter was never coming home. And I was no closer to identifying a prime suspect. In fact, I barely had anything to go on at all. But I was going to see Dorman tonight, which meant for a few hours, at least, I'd be able to laugh and talk and enjoy those things consenting adults did behind closed doors. I'd take it.

In the meantime, I collected my thoughts and focused back on the Nicolette Percy case. Replaying my recording, I listened to everything Maureen Lawson had said. It broke my heart again to hear the sadness in her voice. And the really tragic part was that the woman was in shock. The full reality of what had happened hadn't even hit her yet. That might happen tonight or maybe tomorrow, but soon enough the full weight of the truth that she was never going to see her daughter again would fall on her like the house crushing the Wicked Witch of the East.

I called Doc and asked him when he could release the body to the funeral home and told him that sooner would be better. He said it would be at least a couple of days, but he'd do what he could.

I called Mrs. Lawson and told her to pick out a funeral home and that I'd let them know when they could pick up her daughter.

She called back an hour later and gave me a name.

8

The next few days went by quickly with little to show for them. It was mid-afternoon of the fifth day of the investigation when there was a knock on my office door. It opened and Robar and Hawk peeked in.

"Do you have a minute, Cap?" Robar asked. "We just got back from Freedom Communal Insurance Company. That's where Nicolette Percy worked."

"Sure." Of course, I did. Actually, I was thrilled to be able to postpone the humdrum work of the day. If the opportunity for a spontaneous root canal had presented itself, I would have been first in line.

"We interviewed several of her coworkers, including Don Harrington, the guy who called us the other day," Robar said, pulling out her notepad as she took a seat across from me.

Sergeant Arthur Hawkins, or Hawk as we all called him, took a seat at the round conference table off to the side. He was inching his way closer and closer to retirement, and I couldn't help but wonder what he was going to do with himself when the time came for him to turn in his papers. Somehow, he didn't strike me as the kind of guy who would easily turn over his badge and gun in exchange for a rod and reel.

I knew one thing: he was going to miss Ann Robar. They worked well together and came across like an old married couple. He was a big, teddy bear of a guy. She wasn't quite as tall as me. She was... eh, homely is an unfair description but accurate, I suppose. Anyway, she wore her hair short and had enough attitude to go around the whole team. But the thing that made them click was the way they bantered with one another. Well, Robar argued with just about everyone.

"Tell me all about it," I said, shoving my iPad to the side of my desk.

Robar looked over at Hawk.

Hawk nodded, then said, "Nicolette Percy worked at FCIC for almost two years. According to her boss, Pamela Horowitz, she was a good employee with a pleasant attitude and a better than average work ethic. The thing Horowitz said she noticed most about her was her punctuality. She was never late and never called in sick. She was absolutely reliable and did her job without any issues." Hawk said. "I looked at her employee file. Her annual reviews were all positive. There was only one incident, though, that caught my eye." He paused, as if he was thinking it through.

"And?" I asked.

"When she first started work at FCIC," Hawk continued, "she crossed paths with a young man by the name of George Cruz who filed a complaint against her with the HR department."

"Cruz filed a complaint against her?" I asked.

"Yeah, he had only been with FCIC for two months when Nicolette started working there. According to Horowitz, it seems Cruz thought there should have been some kind of office romance between them, but Nicolette wasn't interested. According to the paperwork and the statements taken by HR, Nicolette actually told him she didn't like him." He consulted his notebook; something he rarely ever did, then continued, "'Look, I don't like you and I won't go out with you, ever, so please stop bothering me or I'll report you for sexual harassment.' I copied her exact words from the report. This was after he'd pursued her relentlessly for more than a month, so she said. I guess he beat her to it," Hawk said, closing his notebook.

"Oh, brother." I sighed. This was even more of a red flag than the internet dating angle.

"So how did he get HR to take a complaint against Nicolette?" I asked.

"He's one clever little son of a bitch," Robar said. "What he did was kind of sly, to say the least. He said that Nicolette's cruel and insensitive rejection caused him to suffer anxiety, and he wanted her to maintain a professional relationship toward him and refrain from any excessive communications."

I gasped. "And FCIC went along with that?"

"We're in a Politically Correct world, are we not?" Robar smiled grimly.

"That we are," I said, slowly shaking my head.

"So," Hawk continued, "she got written up for that. Now for the kicker: less than two weeks later Cruz was fired on the spot for showing up to work high," Hawk said. "He cleaned out his desk and was escorted out of the building without incident. I'd say we have ourselves a suspect and we need to follow up, find out where he was the night Nicolette was murdered, see if he has an alibi."

"Right. I assume no one's seen or heard from him since he was let go, then?" I asked.

They both shook their heads.

"Okay, Hawk, you and Ann follow up. Time of death was between eight and ten, a two-hour window. What's next?"

"As I said," Robar replied, "we talked to several of her coworkers, but it was Don Harrington who seemed to know the most about her."

"He's the guy who called in, right?" I asked.

"Yes. We actually talked to him first. He told us that Nicolette was his good friend and that he still hadn't heard from her and that he was very worried. When we told him that she was dead, well, he broke down."

"Did he seem genuine?" I asked skeptically.

"He did," Robar replied.

"I agree," Hawk said. "He was genuinely stunned, started to cry. It took him a couple minutes to compose himself."

"Did he and Nicolette date?" I asked.

"No. Harrington is homosexual, and married," Hawk replied.

"Okay," I said, thinking hard. "Even so, we can't rule him out. Not yet. What did he have to say?"

I've dealt with many cases during my years in homicide, and one thing I learned very early was that things are rarely ever what they seem. Just because someone claims to be gay doesn't mean they are incapable of committing murder. I know from first-hand experience that they are: Natalie Cassidy being a case in point.

"He told us that he and Nickie—that's what he called her—that he and Nicolette became friends soon after she started work at FCIC, in their office. His mother was an insurance saleswoman and that's how he got his job. He was happy when Nicolette started because, according to him, she was a bubbly, fun, pretty woman who he could talk to. They had adjoining cubicles.

"According to Harrington," Hawk continued, "Nicolette wanted to find her Mr. Right, get married and start a family. He said she was getting kind of desperate to get herself a man."

"Yes, that's what he said," Robar confirmed. "He actually used the word desperate. He said she'd gone on several dates in the time he'd known her but nothing significant ever developed. He also said that most of the men she'd dated were beneath her, intellectually. Apparently she was one smart kid."

"Not smart enough, obviously," Hawk said caustically. "Anyway, Harrington also said that he and Nicolette would often go out after work for a couple drinks, or to get something to eat." He paused, opened his notebook again, and continued. "He also said that she was finicky about the men who approached her. According to him there were always guys sniffing around, checking her out. But she didn't want a boozy construction worker or some stiff suit. She was picky. And according to Harrington, she was a really good judge of character. At least at work, she was."

"What did he mean by that?" I asked.

"If a new person got hired and Nicolette didn't like him or her for whatever reason," Robar said, "she would rate them, give 'em so many weeks until they either quit or were fired. He said it was freaky how spot-on she often was, scary in fact."

"So, what did Harrington say about the day Nicolette didn't show up for work?" I asked.

"He said that she was supposed to start work at eight. When she still hadn't arrived by ten o'clock, and hadn't called in, he was freaking out, literally. He called her five times in the two hours, but his calls went straight to voicemail. Finally, he called her mother and then both of them were panicking."

"Okay," I said, nodding thoughtfully. "She found her date on an online dating site. Do we know which one?"

"No, Harrington said he didn't know."

"Right," I said. "Her mother said she didn't know either... So... Okay, here's what's puzzling me: why does someone who is supposedly such a good judge of character resort to online dating? To me, it doesn't make any sense. There are plenty of nice guys here in Chattanooga. You're telling me she couldn't use her spider senses to find one guy decent enough to date?"

"I asked Harrington that same question," Hawk said. "The answer's easy enough. One of the women in another office met a guy online, and apparently it's really working out well. There's talk of marriage. You know how it goes."

Sadly, I did. What these people don't want to acknowledge is that for every success story about internet love, there are at least a hundred epic failures. But that never seems to stop anyone. I motioned for Robar to continue.

"So, according to Harrington," Robar continued, "Nicolette wanted to cut through all the bull. She didn't like trolling for dates in the time-honored way. She told him that the clock was ticking and she needed to quit messing around, and that if it worked for someone else, it could work for her. So, she joined the same online dating service that her coworker had joined. She met a guy and they talked online and over the phone. She liked what she heard so she arranged to meet him for drinks after work."

"Please tell me Harrington got the man's name," I said.

"Nope," Hawk said. "He said she told him, but he couldn't remember. All he could remember was that she said he was some sort of teacher with special needs kids. She said she thought that was different and sweet and that he was someone she could admire."

"How about the other woman, the one on the dating site? Do we know who she is?"

"Sorry, Cap. No. He didn't know that either."

"So," Robar continued, "again according to Harrington, Nicolette and her date were supposed to meet at Flannigan's after work. Well, he texted her to see how the date was going. She texted back and said her date didn't show up."

"That's when the interview turned into a real mess," Hawk said. "Harrington broke down, burst into tears saying he would have gone to meet her himself, but he had a bad leak under his kitchen sink and the landlord was on his way over to fix it."

Robar nodded and said, "Harrington was distraught, kept saying if he'd only known, if he'd thought she was in any trouble, he would have dropped everything and run right on over to meet her. We had to give him a few minutes to compose himself.

"When he finally stopped crying," Robar continued, "I asked him if he heard anything from her after she left Flannigan's. I was surprised when he said that he did. Twenty minutes later, she texted him again saying that her date had called and told her he had car trouble and was at another bar on the other end of town waiting for them to fix his flat tire."

"Did she say the name of the place?" I hoped.

"No," Robar said. "He said that she'd always wanted to meet someone like this guy, you know, steady job, modest but steady income... From what she told Harrington, she'd learned from their phone conversations that he was unmarried and lived alone in a small house he bought with an inheritance from his deceased parents. She thought he sounded like a great guy, and that he had great potential to take her away from all the drama."

"Drama? What drama?" I asked.

"Harrington said she was having problems at home," Robar said, reading from her notes. "Apparently her stepmother was over-protective and maybe a little overbearing. But Nicolette was the only girl in the family—she also has a brother, Ken, by the way. Her father had moved back to Chicago. She and her stepmother were all they had."

Remembering Maureen Lawson's reaction to the news of Nicolette's death, it wasn't a big stretch to see how she could be protective of her stepdaughter. Everything that Robar said fit with Maureen's account of things. A young, attractive woman wanting a family, to be a housewife and mother in her own home with her own husband was what most women wanted. And the idea of leaving Chattanooga or even just moving to the other side of town could be an adventure of epic proportions to some. It made Nicolette's death and her mother's grief all the more tragic. I hated this case.

"He also said that whenever Nicolette tried to talk to her stepmother about moving out, she—her stepmom—would remind her how dangerous it was," Hawk said. "Ain't that a kick in the nuts?"

I shook my head and smiled at him. "Yes, I suppose it is," I replied. "Okay, if there are texts, we'll have those once Jack cracks the phone. If she has an online dating profile, we should be able to find out who this guy is. Jack has Nicolette's computer. That's where we'll find some answers.

"We do this one by the book," I continued. "Ann, have Jack run a background check on Don Harrington, just to be sure. Also, check up on the coworker who got fired."

"George Cruz," Robar replied.

"Yes, him. If he's carrying a grudge, we'll want to talk to him about it. You did good work, guys. We have a lot to work with. Let's keep our fingers crossed that something will break." I thought for a minute, then continued, "We also need to find and talk to the coworker, the one on the dating site. She'll be able to tell us which one it was, and then we should be able to find out who the date was. Okay, go to it. Oh, and if Janet's still here, tell her I need to see her, please."

After Hawk and Robar left my office, I leaned back in my chair, put my hands behind my head, linked my fingers together, closed my eyes and rocked, thinking that we were making progress.

We now had several leads, and I was confident that something was going to come out of at least one of them. That was the shot in the arm I needed. Nothing was going to make me feel better about this case except bringing Maureen some kind of closure. Of course, the victim's families always say they never really get closure. But it was something. It was the best I could do.

"You wanted to see me," Janet said, poking her head around the door jamb.

"Yes, come on in and sit down. I should have had you join us, but I didn't know it was going to take so long."

She took a seat in front of my desk, and I spent the next twenty minutes bringing her up to speed.

"So," I said finally, "I want you to go to FCIC and find out who this woman is, then go talk to her. When you get the information, work your magic and get the warrant for... Jack to get into the website's back door."

"Today?

"Yes, today. The first forty-eight hours, remember?"

"But they were up three days..." she caught the look I was giving her. "You got it, Cap," she said hurriedly, "but it's already after five-thirty. Won't they be closed?"

"No. It's an insurance company. They have staff there around the clock."

"Okay then," she said, rising to her feet. "If there's nothing else..."

I smiled at her and shook my head. And she left.

I looked at my watch. She was right. It was after five-thirty, so I packed up for the day, called Dorman and asked him to give me an hour and then come on over to my apartment, and then I slipped out of the building. It wasn't like the situation was going to change much by tomorrow or even the next day.

9

I arrived home at just after six that evening. Dorman arrived some thirty minutes or so later; I'd barely had time to shower and freshen up. Still, he didn't seem bothered that my hair was still wet and that I was dressed in shorts and a tee.

Fortunately, for me at least, he'd taken the time to drop by a Chinese restaurant for take-out: chicken curry and steamed rice. Simple but, along with a nice bottle of white wine, it hit the spot.

I really don't know why he puts up with me. We spent most of the evening talking shop, my shop. His day is pretty routine. I guess it must be what came after... is why he puts up with me. Anyway, he left at a little before eight the following morning, having made coffee, toast, and scrambled eggs while I was in the shower.

They don't come much better than that, now do they, Kate? I thought as I parked in my allotted space at the rear of the PD.

That thought was still floating around in my head when I entered my office, dumped my purse on my desk, flopped into my chair, and sipped what was left of the coffee in my to-go cup. I looked up at the wall clock above the whiteboard opposite my desk.

It was five after nine, late for me, and I wondered if anyone had noticed.

Inevitably, my gaze dropped from the clock to the whiteboard. It had been updated. Someone, probably Janet, had plastered the thing with autopsy and crime scene photos, including a copy of the latest headshot of Nickie Percy.

I leaned on my elbows on my desk and stared up at the happy smiling face... and then my thoughts drifted to the face as it was on Doc's autopsy table. *I'll get him, sweetheart. I promise.*

It was an easy promise to make, but I had a feeling that it wouldn't be an easy one to keep. *They never are.*

"Hey, Cap?" Janet said as she poked her head in my open doorway. "You up for a road trip?"

"Where to?" I asked without telling her good morning. Even though I had the equivalent of three cups of coffee, I was in no mood for a lot of chit-chatting, and Janet liked to chatter, a lot.

"I thought we'd pay Roger Heddiger a visit." She raised her eyebrows and looked at me as if she was asking if I'd extend her curfew from ten-thirty to eleven. I had to smile, inwardly, to myself, of course.

"Who's he?" I asked, squinting, knowing I'd heard the name but couldn't place where.

"He's the guy who bought Tom Cowel's LeBaron. He kept the license plate and somehow it ended up on Nicolette Percy's car... I can't see him putting it on it. Why would he? He would have known that we'd trace it back to him... unless he's totally dumb, which wouldn't surprise me seeing as how he kept it in the first place, the plate. Anyway, Jack gave me the receipt and it has his address on it, so I thought we should... go... and..." She caught the look and, to my relief, tailed off the diatribe and looked expectantly at me.

"How about the coworker, the one that's internet dating?" I asked. "Did you find her?"

She shook her head and made a face. "Nothing yet. She's in

another department. No one in Nicolette's office knows who it is. We need her name. Maybe Jack will find it in Nicolette's phone. If not... well, I'll keep trying."

"Anything from Willis on that smear on Nicolette's blouse?"

"No, I called him when I came in and asked him if he could put a rush on it."

I nodded. "Okay. Have Hawk or Robar come in yet?" I asked.

"Hawk was here, but he said something about going out to get some information on George Cruz. Ann called in to let him know that she has to take her kids to a friend's house. They're spending the weekend. She should be here soon," Janet replied.

"All right. Heddiger it is. You drive," I said, knowing that Janet had purchased a new—to her—used Ford F-150 pick-up truck and was more than proud to drive it around.

As she drove, she talked constantly, about how since she'd gotten the truck, she'd been able to pick up a new dresser and a bookcase that people had put out at the roadside with their garbage.

"It just goes to show how one man's trash is another man's treasure," she said proudly.

Now I'm not above dumpster diving myself. Hell, I've dived into enough dumpsters for evidence, but furniture? I couldn't help but remember that episode of The Big Bang Theory and the easy chair. I shuddered to think what creepy crawlies Janet might have introduced to her apartment.

"Are you sure you haven't brought home some... unwanted guests?" I asked.

"I don't... think so... No, I'm sure. Look, I'd rather be diving for furniture than into the mess we usually have to dive into," she said, visibly shuddering.

"You've got that right," I said, glancing sideways at her as she drove with one hand on the wheel and the other resting on the ledge of the open window.

It was a warm day. The sun was up and the sky was a lovely cobalt blue with just a couple of white puffs of cloud drifting high above.

The highway smelled of diesel fuel, noisy with the sounds of the other vehicles as they raced past us, drowning out most of my thoughts.

"Where are we going?" I asked.

She looked sideways at me, grinning widely, and said, "The Tomahawk Trailer Park. Where else?"

"What? You're kidding me!"

"Nope. There's only one Crystal Lane in all of Hamilton County and that's where it's at," Janet replied. "I don't think it's too much of a stretch seeing as that's where Nicolette was found, right?"

I nodded absently, then started shaking my head. *It can't be that simple... Can it?* I thought. It never was.

I continued shaking my head as I stared, unseeing, out through the windshield. *He lives in the same damn trailer park? I don't see it. He'd have to be... insane, or crazy as an outhouse rat to put the old man's plate on a car with a dead body in it...*

Then again, I did recall that Cowel had said he didn't think that Heddiger was all that bright. *But could he really be that stupid?* I wondered, then shrugged, catching Janet's eye. *Stranger things have happened.*

I had Janet pull over on the opposite side of the road from the entrance into the trailer park. The yellow and black tapes were all gone, and there was nothing left of what only a couple of days ago had been a crime scene. To me, it looked like any other trailer park in the greater Chattanooga area: nice up front, but farther back the quality and the curb appeal deteriorates, and the trailers become little more than shacks with wheels.

I told Janet to drive on in. Crystal Lane was four streets into the trailer park. We turned right off the main drag and found Roger Heddiger's trailer two lots in. It was an older model, but it looked clean. White lace curtains hung in the windows. The steps to the screen door were even and neat. The deck in front of the door was small and painted white, recently by the look of it.

Low and behold, sitting next to the trailer on a small patch of gravel was a Chrysler LeBaron. Its plate was missing and there was a homemade paper tag in the back window that proclaimed "Tag Applied For." *Bullshit. All it takes is a trip to the DMV. What does he think, that we're all stupid? I could write him a ticket just for that... except I don't do tickets. I don't have any.*

"This looks like the place," I said. "Why don't you take the lead on this one."

"You got it, Cap."

Janet got out of the car, stood for a minute, staring up at the front door as she waited for me to join her and, together, we mounted the steps and she knocked on the door.

The door was opened almost immediately by a young man wearing a pink, worn-out terrycloth robe. Janet flashed her badge, made the introduction, and said, "Are you Roger Heddiger?"

He nodded, his mouth hanging open.

"May we come in and talk to you?" she asked.

"Um...uh, can you give me a second?" he stuttered.

"Mr. Heddiger," she said brightly, "we don't care what you're smoking or inhaling or anything else you might be doing. We need to ask you about that car out there. It's yours, right?" Janet blinked as she jerked her head to the right.

He looked like a deer caught in the headlights and was trying to form a thought and wasn't sure if he should say something or run to the bathroom.

"Uh, yeah," he said. "I bought it from this blind guy."

"Mr. Cowel. Yes. He said you did and that you paid him and removed the license plate," Janet said. "Mr. Heddiger, may we come in now?"

Roger swallowed hard, then shrugged and nodded as he stepped aside for us to enter his home.

Like the outside, the inside of the trailer was clean enough, but far from tidy. There was a faint smell of marijuana in the air. The kitchen looked messy: food on the table, dishes in the sink, even clothes on the floor, but nothing really out of the ordinary.

"I was going to take it off, the license plate," he said, "but I was so excited to get the car I forgot." He sat down on the couch, his knees held tightly together, his hands folded on top of them. "I didn't even think about it. I'm sorry."

I sat down on a kitchen chair opposite him and looked down on him; Janet remained standing, walking slowly around the room, taking note as she went. I opened my iPad, turned on the recording app and nodded at Janet. She informed him that we were recording the interview. He shrugged and said okay, his mouth all the time hanging open.

Cowel was right. Roger Heddiger wasn't very bright, and I do believe that he thought saying he was sorry would be enough for us to pat him on the head and tell him, "It's okay, son. But let's be more careful next time. Bye."

"Mr. Heddiger, that license plate was attached to a car belonging to a woman who was brutally raped and murdered," Janet said as she sat down next to me.

That got his attention. He lifted his head and looked from Janet to me.

"Uh?"

"Did you know Nicolette Percy?" she continued.

He shook his head, making his lips flop back and forth. "No. I don't know anyone by that name."

Aside from his slack mouth, he wasn't a bad-looking young man. His hair was long, wavy, almost as if it had been profession-ally coifed. He was thin but muscular. I could see the definition of his pecs in the open "V" of his robe. I figured he must work out. Either that or he was in construction or something similar.

Oh, yes, I thought. *He could easily have strong-armed Nicolette and strangled the life out of her... but for the plastic bag. That would indicate premeditation, and I don't think he has the wherewithal for that.*

"D'you mind if I get a drink of water?" I asked and stood up.

"Go ahead," he said.

I went into the kitchen, turned on the tap, turned it off again and returned just in time to hear him say, "Look, the license plate went missing off my car about a week ago. I kept meaning to take it back to Mr. Cowel. But he wasn't driving anywhere. He's a cripple and he's blind to boot. It wasn't like he could go anywhere and..." He shrugged, looked away to his left, his eyes lowered, guiltily.

I wandered slowly around the room looking for any signs that Nicolette had been there. Nothing!

"And? So why didn't you take it back to him?" Janet asked.

"I work nights at the UPS distribution center. When I get home, I usually have a couple beers, smoke a joint," he said bashfully. "Then I fall asleep. By the time I get up again, there's other stuff to do and then I gotta go to work again. That's why when I saw it was gone, I supposed Mr. Cowel came and got it himself."

"So you just didn't bother to change the registration then?" Janet asked. "You figured he couldn't drive so no one would know and you'd save a dollar or two, isn't that true, Mr. Heddiger?"

"Well no... Yes... No. Look, I was going to get it done, but as I said, I work nights and by the time I wake up... well, it's usually too late to get to the DMV."

Janet nodded, seemingly unconcerned and said, "You say you thought that Mr. Cowel had come and taken the plate. And yet you just told me that you knew he was handicapped, blind. So just how did you figure he might have done that?" Janet clicked her tongue and looked at Roger like she was really expecting a good answer.

"I...I don't know. Maybe a friend brung him to come get it?" Roger asked questioningly. "Look, it was an accident. And I really did mean to take it back to him. But I didn't murder or... rape some girl." He sat there shaking his head and looking from Janet to me and back again.

"You said the plate went missing a week ago? How d'you know it was a week? It could have been two days ago, five; how d'you know?" Janet asked as she continually scribbled on her yellow legal notepad.

It always struck me as odd that she didn't use her pocket notebook, or the iPad I'd gotten for her more than a year ago, but instead, like a straight-A student in high school, she insisted on writing meticulous notes on a big pad of paper. Her scribbles filled the lines quickly.

"I know because it was a Saturday and I was coming in to work at UPS and we have to pass through security. I'm friends with the security guard. I mean, we all are because we see them every night. Well, Keith, that's the security guard. Keith commented on my new car when I first got it. Anyway, he come out of the guard shack and stopped me as I was pulling in and told me my plate was gone.

"I didn't think much of it, right? I thought Mr. Cowel had come to get it himself. So, I figured it just saved me a trip from having to go back to his house. But then Keith said that I better get the car properly registered or the cops would pull me over. And I didn't want that," Roger said.

"That wasn't it, was it?" I said quietly. "It's not that big of a deal, driving without tags. What were you afraid of?"

Roger swallowed hard, his Adam's apple bounced up and down. "Yeah! Right! No, but sometimes I smoke a little before coming home. Keith sometimes does it with me. The last thing I needed was getting busted with pot in the car."

"Yes. I could see how that would be a concern," Janet said.

She continued to scribble for several more minutes without saying anything. Roger watched her anxiously. The look on his face was very worried, and I got the feeling he was telling the truth. He fidgeted in his seat, tugging at his robe and pulling it tightly closed around his legs.

"Look, I'm telling the truth," he said, finally breaking the uneasy silence. "I don't know what happened to the plate. All I know is that Keith told me it was missing so I took an afternoon off and registered the car in my name. Had to pay damn sales tax too;

that was a bummer; cleared me out. I did that just yesterday." He looked us both in the face without flinching.

"Mr. Heddiger? Do you mind if I use your bathroom?" I asked politely.

"Sure. Uh, it's just to the right past the kitchen." He pointed then tugged at the top of his robe, pulling it closed a little more.

I went inside the bathroom, pulled the accordion-style door closed and looked around. It was a little gross. Bits of stubble stuck in dried shaving cream were caked in several spots on and around the small sink. There was a large patch of black mold in the corner of the shower. The medicine cabinet had a box of condoms in it along with toothpaste, cold medicine, shaving cream, some plastic razors and a set of tweezers. The space below the sink was stocked with toilet paper.

I flushed the toilet, which sounded like a clap of thunder, pulled the door open, stepped out into the hallway and looked to the right to see in the bedroom. There was a bed, unmade, and there were clothes hanging haphazardly in a closet that had the same kind of accordion-style door as the bathroom. The carpet had some serious stains on it but nothing that resembled dried blood. I slowly walked past the kitchen, adjusting my badge and my weapon. Nowhere did I see anything out of the ordinary.

"Mr. Heddiger, we appreciate you taking the time to talk to us," Janet said, taking my cue. "If you think of anything that might help us, I do hope you'll give us a call." Janet handed him a business card.

"And go to the DMV and reregister the car," I said. "That piece of paper in the back window will get you a ticket."

"I will, Detective. I promise." Roger took the card from Janet, nodding his head enthusiastically, his lips flopping around like those of a donkey enthusiastically asking for a carrot.

I was sure he'd be racking his brain trying to come up with something that might help. But I was afraid he'd probably just give himself a headache.

"Dumb as a box of rocks," I muttered as we stepped out of the trailer and into the fresh air. It was then that I noticed the curtains in the trailer next door move.

"I think we have an audience," I whispered to Janet.

"Yeah, I noticed through the tiny window in Roger's living room that someone was very interested in what was going on," Janet replied.

"That's a good eye you've got, detective. Let's go say hello," I said.

10

The trailer next to Heddiger's was not in great shape. The drooping gutters were held in place by duct tape. Two wooden crates, obviously being used as outdoor seating, were positioned in the dying grass to the left of the steps. Cinder blocks and random bricks held up one end of the trailer, while the other was supported by wheels that had sunk deep into the mud. The same kind of architectural ingenuity was holding up the rotting front deck.

I went up the steps first and knocked loudly on the door. I could hear someone shuffling around inside, but no one came to the door. I knocked again, but still there was no answer. I looked at Janet who was staring up at me. She shrugged.

"I guess they don't want to talk," I said quietly.

"Yeah, but I get the feeling they want to watch, don't you?" Janet replied as we walked back toward her truck.

"Excuse me?" a female voice said from the other side of Heddiger's trailer.

Janet and I looked up to see an elderly woman in a long shapeless dress and bare feet standing on her little patch of grass.

"Yes, ma'am?" I said as I walked over to her.

"Are you the police?" she asked.

I prepared myself to be inundated with complaints about anything and everything, including noisy neighbors who cut their grass too early on Saturday mornings to strange lights in the sky that she just knew are not airplanes or weather balloons.

"Yes, ma'am." I introduced myself and Janet. "What can we do for you?"

"Are you here about the girl?" she asked carefully.

I looked at Janet but didn't dare get my hopes up.

"Which girl?" I asked.

"The one who they found in the car up on the road. That car had been here, right there." She pointed to Roger's neighbor's trailer, the one we'd just visited but no one had come to the door.

"It was that strange pale green color," she said. "I know it was the same car because I saw it again the next morning, up on the road."

"When was it that you first saw the car parked next door, Miss...?"

"Mrs. Nielsen. It was last Saturday night, just after nine-thirty. I know because I let Missy out to do her business each night at the same time right before we go to bed. She's my little girl."

"Your little... Oh, I see. Missy's your dog."

She gave me a sharp look and then nodded.

"What exactly did you see, Mrs. Nielsen?" I asked, taking out my notebook and starting to write, as did Janet. I put mine away again. *No sense in going over the same ground twice.*

"It was dark out, but I saw the car. It was parked right there. It was backed all the way in." She pointed at the gravel spot at the end of the trailer.

"I'm eighty-two years old, you know, and I've lived here for over twenty years, and I can tell you it was a decent place to live until that Harvel Brady began squatting next door." Mrs. Nielsen glared at the trailer as if it was offending her personally.

"Did you see the girl? Was there anyone in the car?" I asked. I wasn't about to get my hopes up. After all, the old girl could have been suffering from dementia.

"No, I didn't see her, and I didn't get close enough to see the driver. I just assumed it was him. I saw him going round to the back of the car. He was squatted down when I passed by, and I couldn't tell if he was trying to hide from me or was looking at something on the car. He's a strange man, you know."

I looked at Janet. She was busy writing.

"And you didn't see anything else?" I asked.

"No, ma'am, but I did see the car parked up on the road when I was leaving for church early the next day. I attend St. Anthony of Padua Church and they have rosary every morning."

"Do you drive?" I asked. She looked about as capable of driving as did Thomas Cowel.

"Heaven's no. I take the bus, or on nice days I sometimes walk. It's only three blocks from here. You obviously don't go to church around these parts." She looked me up and down as if she could tell I didn't go to church at all.

"No, ma'am," I replied, feeling embarrassed.

"Well, a police officer ought to find a nice church to attend. You all need it most," she said gently. Her tone changed again as she continued, "So, I do hope you teach that man a lesson. He doesn't even own that trailer. He stays there when the owner is out of town."

"Do you know the owner's name?" Janet asked.

"McGee is his last name. I don't know his first name. Young fella but overweight. Drives a truck for a living. That Harvel Brady, though, I don't believe he has a job. Not a legal one, anyway," she said, scowling.

I nodded thoughtfully, then said, "Well, I thank you for your help, Mrs. Nielsen... Can you tell us what Harvel Brady looks like?"

"He's an ugly SOB. Big in the shoulders but that's only to

support his meathead. Fat face, florid I think is the word, and he's losing his hair. Combs it over, but it's all just wispy straggles." That was the best description she could give. She didn't like Harvel Brady; that was clear.

We thanked her for her help and promised we'd look into it. Mrs. Nielsen nodded, and we left her standing there, staring at Harvel Brady's temporary home.

"I hope the old duck doesn't turn up dead," Janet muttered. "If this guy had anything to do with killing Nicolette, there's nothing to stop him from offing an old lady who reported him to the police."

"Oh, he had something to do with it all right. She saw him messing with the car, and we know that's a significant fact, don't we?"

"So what are you thinking?" Janet asked, closing her notepad.

"I'm thinking Heddiger's car was conveniently parked next door and Brady took his plate, and she saw him putting it on Nicolette's car. I'm also thinking that we need to move pretty damn quick. I'm going to have another go at that trailer."

I went back to McGee's trailer, mounted the rickety steps, knocked hard on the door and shouted, "Police. Open up." Nothing. Not a sound from inside. I knocked again, even louder. Still nothing. I tried to look inside. The curtains were closed. I couldn't see anything.

I dismounted the steps, drew my weapon and, with Janet on my heels, I circled the trailer until we reached the gravel parking space. I stood for a minute, staring at it. In my mind's eye I could see the car parked there, Nicolette inside.

I rounded the end of the trailer. The rear door was perhaps fifteen feet from where the car had been parked. I climbed the steps to the rear door, hammered on it, called for whoever was inside to open up, but the result was the same. Nothing. I tried the door handle. It didn't move. It was locked. I came back down the steps, holstered my Glock, walked back around to the front and stared up at the door.

"I know what you're thinking, Cap," Janet said. "Don't do it. We don't have probable cause."

She was right. The word of one eighty-two-year-old woman wasn't enough to justify me breaking in. I needed a warrant.

I nodded, frustrated, and said, "When we get back to the PD, I want you to run this Harvel Brady's name. See if he has a sheet. Get his last known address, where he works, if he works, and any other information; I want to know which end up he likes his boiled eggs. If Nielsen potentially saw him taking the license plate off Nicolette's car and swapping it with Roger Heddiger's, that's pretty significant. Plus, she said she saw the car on the street. Unlike the other witness, Erica, who leaned on the car and saw the body inside, Mrs. Nielsen was walking to church. I think this has turned out to be a profitable road trip. We also need to find the guy who owns the trailer, McGee. That should be easy enough."

"I'll get right on it," Janet said as she opened her truck door and climbed in behind the wheel.

"And," I said, closing the passenger side door and reaching for the seatbelt, "when you find out who this McGee character is, go to Judge Strange and see if he'll sign a no-knock search warrant. Mrs. Nielsen's eyewitness account should be enough probable cause, but you never know. Tell him we're looking for evidence that Nicolette Percy was inside that trailer."

11

I   t was maybe a fifteen-minute drive back to the office, so I took those few minutes to catch my breath and try to filter through the new information.

The Harvel Brady thing was a promising lead, but I had to follow through and check out the neighbor, Mrs. Nielsen. The old duck was wearing glasses when we talked to her. She could have misidentified him, though I didn't think she did. Even so, I'd have to track the guy down and make sure. If I jumped all over him only to find out that Mrs. Nielsen had a history of mental illness or was constantly reporting other tenants to the park manager for minor indiscretions, real or imagined, it wouldn't go down well with my superiors, and that was something I wanted to avoid.

Janet parked her truck out back and we went our separate ways: me to my office, Janet to her desk in the situation room. I didn't even get to sit down before she called.

"Hey, what's up?" I said.

"Cap. I think you need to come up here."

"What's going on?" I asked, frowning.

"There's a guy here by the name of Don Harrington. He was

looking for Hawk or Robar. It's about Nicolette Percy. They're out, but I told him you'd talk to him," she said.

"I'll be right there," I said and hung up the phone.

After what Robar and Hawk had told me about him, yes, I was interested in meeting this Harrington character. I grabbed my iPad and went up to the situation room where a big, hulking guy with long brown hair tied back in a ponytail was sitting beside Janet's desk. He was wearing an expensive-looking pair of black slacks, a white button-down shirt and a red silk tie. Long hair or not, he presented well and could easily have been taken for a maître d' at an expensive restaurant.

"Mr. Harrington?" I asked as I approached.

He looked up at me with a worried expression, stood up and offered me his hand.

"Yes?" His voice was soft, feminine. He had a diamond stud in his right ear.

"I'm Captain Gazzara. I understand you are here regarding Nicolette Percy?" I said, shaking his hand. His grip was firm, his palm dry.

"Yes, ma'am, I am," he replied. "I've just come from her funeral and..." His eyes flooded with tears. "I'm sorry. I'm still in shock, I guess."

"Janet, please take Mr. Harrington down to my office. Can I get you a bottle of water or perhaps a cup of coffee?" I said.

"A bottle of water would be nice. Thank you," he said with a sniff and quickly composed himself.

This is going to be interesting, I thought. I also thought that if the guy was here to cry and didn't have anything more to offer, I was going to slap the cuffs on him for wasting my time.

"Okay. I'll be right with you," I said and went to the break room to get him a bottle of water.

When I returned to my office, I found that Janet had seated the man in front of my desk and was herself seated at the conference table, her yellow pad open in front of her.

"Here you go, Mr. Harrington," I said as I handed him the bottle. "Now, tell me. What's this all about?"

"I don't know if you are aware," he began as he unscrewed the top of the bottle, "but this morning was Nicolette's funeral."

"I did know it was today, yes, but we didn't feel a police presence was necessary." I watched his expression as he took a sip of water.

"Well, I don't know if it was necessary or not, but it might have been nice to have someone in authority witness what the mourners, myself included, witnessed at this supposedly somber event," he said and took another quick sip.

I opened my iPad and tapped the record app.

"For the record, Mr. Harrington, I'm going to record our conversation, but I need your permission to do so."

"Yes, of course."

"Please tell us what happened," I said.

"I guess I'll just have to start from the beginning." He sighed and then took a deep breath. "Several of my coworkers and I had planned to go to Nickie's funeral together—there was a viewing first, in the funeral parlor. We wanted to go and pay our respects, then have lunch afterward... at the Boathouse. I know that sounds a little cold now that I hear myself saying it, but we just figured that since we were all together, we'd get something to eat after the ceremony then go back to work."

"That's not entirely unheard of, Mr. Harrington," I said without smiling. *Where the hell is he going with this?*

"Well, even if it weren't, we all lost our appetites as soon as we arrived. It was just terrible." He started to cry.

Janet fetched a box of tissues from the credenza—a left-over from a cold I'd had a couple of months back—placed it on the edge of my desk in front of him, pulled one out and handed it to him and then returned to her notes.

"Thank you, sweetheart," he said, sniffling. "Now, I know what y'all are thinking... that I'm some catty person who just has to make a comment about what the corpse is wearing, but that isn't it at all. Honest Abe, it's not."

"Er... no, sir. That's not what I'm thinking at all," I said quickly, and it wasn't.

"I'm sorry," Janet said, "did you say, what the corpse was *wearing?*"

I was glad it was Janet who said that. Harrington was looking more and more like a loon with every word that came out of his mouth. I studied his expression and body language. But so far, there was nothing to see other than the man was a little embarrassed. Understandably so.

"I did," he said, twisting the tissue in his fingers. "But before you think I'm really a horrible person, please let me explain."

"Please," I said. *And for Pete's sake get on with it.*

He looked down at the tissue, cleared his throat, then continued, "Nickie and I were very close. I considered her one of my best and dearest friends. Never once did she ever make me feel like I was less than a man just because my lifestyle is different. Of course, we worked together so we did gossip about some of the other employees. I'll admit that, but we also talked about our goals and dreams and likes and dislikes. That's why I know that Nickie would never have wanted to be buried in the horrifying ensemble her mother dressed her up in."

I looked at Janet whose eyebrows shot up to the middle of her forehead. "Excuse me. Her ensemble?" I asked.

"Yes. Please... just listen to me for a minute. Nicolette had wonderful taste in clothes even though she rarely ever bought herself anything new. I blame Maureen for that," he said angrily.

"You knew her stepmother?" I asked.

"Yes... well, I only met her twice. Both times she came to the office to demand money from Nickie, usually on paydays. I don't think the poor girl was ever able to keep even half of her paycheck. Between the crazy "rent"—he made air quotes with his fingers— "that Maureen charged her and the times she, Maureen, came up short budgeting her own money, I do believe Nickie was left with maybe just one hundred dollars every two weeks, at most."

Harrington's eyes had dried, and he was by then openly angry. "So," he continued, "to see her being sent off to her eternal rest in a T-shirt and jeans, well, that just made my stomach flip. She'd bought a lovely dress at a thrift store not a month ago. It was beautiful, a rich brown color that flattered her figure, but was modest, like she was. I knew for a fact it was hanging in her closet. That's what she should have been buried in."

Harrington dabbed at his eyes and began sobbing again.

"So, her mother buried her in a T-shirt and a pair of jeans. Why is that so bad?" I did think it was kind of strange but hardly an arrestable offense.

"You know what?" he said huffily. "I could count on one hand how many times Nickie wore jeans, much less a T-shirt. Even on casual days at work she always wore a skirt or nice shorts that never reached higher than her knees. She was just that kind of girl, you know. She had such a nice figure... she could wear a potato sack and still look like a million dollars. That's why Maureen put her in jeans. She was so jealous of Nickie she might as well have had a neon sign over her head."

"According to Maureen, they were very close," I said.

"Oh yes. That's typical of her. That's what she wanted everyone to think," Harrington sneered. "But I knew what Nickie told me. Her stepmother was horrible to her. But I never thought she'd be this horrible. So, after my coworkers and I saw what she'd been dressed in, we all looked around for her stepmother. Well," he said, conspiratorially, "you can imagine how shocked we all were to find that Maureen had not arrived yet. When she finally did arrive, what I saw almost made me... Well, I thought I was going to faint."

I was intrigued. I couldn't help it. Harrington was spinning one hell of a yarn. I looked across at Janet. She rolled her eyes, but I could tell she too was intrigued because she was leaning forward—

as was I—her arms crossed on the table. And, rare for her, she'd stopped taking notes.

Harrington cleared his throat again, took another sip of water, put the bottle down on the edge of my desk, put his right hand to his chest and took a deep breath.

"When she did finally show up, she wasn't alone. She had a dog with her, a new dog, a black toy poodle named—now hold on to your hat, Captain..." He paused for several long seconds staring at me, then said, dramatically, "Nic-o-lette. There. Now then. What d'you think of that?"

I tried to keep my face straight, as void of expression as possible. But the shock of what I'd just heard was just a little too much for me to swallow. I know I let my mouth fall open in amazement.

"*What?*" Janet piped up, saving me from an embarrassing moment. "She called her dog Nicolette?"

"Yes. Would you even believe it? And then when she brought it up to the casket, well," he said. "Right there, in front of all the mourners. And let me tell you for the record that there was literally a parade of people coming in and out to say good-bye to Nickie." Harrington teared up again but continued. "You know when her mailman took time out from his route to come say good-bye that she was a good person, that she made the world a better place."

"What did Maureen do with the dog?" I asked, trying to move the story along.

"Well, the first thing she did was she introduced everyone to the dog saying that the house was so quiet and lonely she'd needed a friend. We all just sort of stood there, frozen. What do you say to someone like that? So, she went up to the casket where Nickie was laying and sat the dog right on top of her." Harrington gasped and fanned his face with his hand as he cried. "It was the most disrespectful and ignorant thing I've ever seen."

I had to sit there for a minute and really think about what I'd just heard. *Could this be the same woman I talked to the other day?*

Is she a total phony? Have I been had? As much as I hated the idea, I was beginning to think that maybe I had.

"It was like she was taunting Nickie," he said, grabbing another tissue from the box. "She didn't seem to be at all concerned about what we thought of her behavior. She just stood at the casket, holding that poor dog on her stepdaughter's dead body and whispering to it. I heard her tell the dog that Nicolette was her sister.

"Everyone heard her, and they just froze. Juanita from accounting looked at Maureen and gasped so loud that Maureen looked up at her with this shocked look on her face like she didn't know what Juanita's problem was."

"'Take the dog off of her.' Juanita told her. 'Show a little respect. It's her funeral.' Well, Maureen didn't like that at all. 'She's my stepdaughter!' She actually snapped at Juanita."

He paused, looked at me, then turned and looked at Janet. I didn't know what to say to him, so I said nothing. And, for the first time since I'd met her, Janet was speechless.

"But it was obvious," he continued. "Well, it was obvious to me that no one thought she was behaving normal. Finally, I guess Maureen thought she'd wasted enough time—she'd been there no more than about fifteen minutes—because she just... she just left. She didn't even wait to see her buried."

I opened my mouth to speak, but Harrington wasn't done yet.

"I happen to know the funeral director—he's a nice man, a Mr. Coleman—anyway, I asked him if Maureen had acted strange when she made the arrangements. He said that all she said was to keep it under five thousand dollars and do whatever was necessary to make it look decent. So, that's what he did. There were no flowers from Maureen or prayer cards or anything. Maureen had the viewing for only two hours to save money. The whole thing was crazy."

"It does sound that way," I said.

"I'm sorry to have unloaded on y'all this way," he said. "But I just thought someone should know about it. It was no way to treat a beautiful person like Nickie, or anyone for that matter. I just didn't think it was right." He sniffled. "I don't know. Maybe y'all deal with this sort of thing all the time. But I found it horrible. Scary, really."

"Did Maureen talk to anyone there?" Janet asked.

He nodded and said, "Yes, me. Before she left, I asked her if Nickie's father was coming. I knew she and her dad had a strained relationship, but when they spoke on the phone, the few times I was present, she always told him, 'I love you, Dad.' And I never heard them arguing. I think they loved each other, you know what I mean?"

"What did she say?" Janet asked. "Was he coming to the funeral?"

"You know what? Maureen looked at me as if I'd just pooped in her hand. Pardon my crude terminology, but that's the only way to describe her expression. She said no... and that was it." He shrugged and wiped his eyes. He'd obviously run out of things to say.

"Is there anything else you want to add?" I asked.

"Isn't that enough?" he replied bitterly. "That was it. She left."

"Well, that's quite a story, Mr. Harrington," I said. "I'm not sure what to make of it, you've been very helpful. Thank you for coming in." I nodded at Janet.

She stood up and said, "I'll show you out, Mr. Harrington. If you think of anything else," she said, handing him her card, "please don't hesitate to call."

"Oh, my Lord," he said. "I don't think I could handle anything else. But thank you for listening. I do hope you find whoever did this to Nickie." His eyes filled with tears again. "She was a good person. A real friend."

When Janet returned to my office, we both just sat there for a minute. Me? I was still trying to get the picture of the dog on Nicolette's chest out of my head... It seemed so out of character. Janet had seen the same grieving Maureen Lawson that I had, and we'd both felt terrible for her. Maybe she was suffering from Post-Traumatic Stress Disorder. But even that didn't quite fit.

"I don't know what to think about that, Cap," she said, finally. "What do you think?"

"Beats me," I said thoughtfully. "Maybe Maureen Lawson is not all she would have us believe... For now, though, I think we need to pursue the leads we've got. We need to find Harvel Brady. We need to find that damn dating website. We need to find out if Nicolette communicated with him on the website. We need to talk to McGee. We also need for Jack to crack her phone," I said, feeling like I'd just gotten mugged.

12

"Nicolette's disgruntled former coworker, George Cruz, is a bust," Robar said the following morning as she tossed the file and her notes onto the conference table. "He was killed in a head-on collision a year ago. His blood-alcohol level was one point three. I doubt he felt anything."

"Okay. So we know he didn't do it," I replied. "Let's move on."

It was eight o'clock and we were in my office for our morning briefing. We had a lot of ground to cover.

"Jack, what have you got? Have you gotten into the phone yet?" I asked.

"Yes, this morning, actually. Fortunately, it's an older model, an Android 8 with only a four-digit passcode. As I told you yesterday, it could've taken a week to brute force the thing. Fortunately, though, a buddy of mine, a hacker, gave me a USB Rubber Ducky. It took just less than eleven hours. Six hundred and sixty-three minutes, to be precise, not bad considering."

"What the hell is a Rubber Ducky?" Hawk growled.

I must admit, I was wondering that myself. I had visions of bathtime when I was a kid dancing around in my head.

"It's... well... it's a fairly simple piece of software. No, actually it's a flash drive... Okay, so a USB Rubber Ducky is a kind of generic keyboard programmed with a preset set of keystrokes... in this case it's programmed to input the full series of four-digit combinations from 0000 all the way through to 9999, ten thousand in all, with a thirty-second pause after every five attempts. Even so, it can take up to sixteen hours to complete the task. In this case, though, a little less than eleven hours. Not bad, huh?"

"Right," I said. "Can you look in her contacts?"

He looked a little downcast at my lack of enthusiasm, but said, "Sure. Anyone in particular?"

"See if she'd been talking to a Harvel Brady."

"Harvel... Brady?" he said and flipped through her contacts. "Nope, I don't see that name, but there are texts from some guy I assume is her internet Romeo."

"It is. Is there anything useful in the texts?"

"Not much. Just playful banter back and forth. She had the guy's name listed as Pete McGee," Jack replied.

"McGee? That's the name of Harvel Brady's roommate or landlord or whatever he is at the trailer park. Have we gotten that warrant yet, Hawk?" I asked.

"Judge Strange told me he'd sign it today. I'm heading over there as soon as we're done here. You want me and Robar to go tear the place apart?" He tapped Robar on the arm.

"Good idea... No... Wait. I want to be there when we crack that sucker. Give me a call when you're heading that way and we'll meet you there. Okay, Hawk, Ann, off you go." And they got up and left.

"Jack," I continued as the door closed behind them. "Is there any way to confirm the phone number Nicolette used to contact McGee? If you can, pull his phone records for the past six months. Let's see what he's been up to." I folded my arms.

"No problem. I can do that." He nodded.

"Good. Do it fast because I'm going to need you to crack Nicolette's computer before Hawk and Robar get back."

"More work for Rubber Ducky. I'll call my buddy. We're going to need a backdoor hack for Windows 10."

"Good," I said, then took a deep breath and looked at Janet. "Ready to take another trip to Tomahawk Trailer Park?"

"I was hoping you'd say that," she replied, grabbing her yellow pad and tucking it under her arm.

"You look like you're running late for homeroom," Jack teased, shaking his head.

"Yeah, I was thinking the same thing," I said, smiling at her. "If you don't finish all your paperwork by five o'clock, it's detention for you, young lady."

"Ha, ha. Like I've never heard that before. You guys need to come up with some new material," Janet said, trying not to smile.

"Let's go," I said, grabbing my iPad.

We decided to take my car in case anyone recognized Janet's truck and gave the target the heads-up that we were on site.

It seemed like only minutes later we pulled up in front of the crappy-looking trailer next to Roger Heddiger's. Janet immediately reached for the door handle. I put a hand on her arm and told her to take a minute. It was still quite early, and I needed to mentally gather my thoughts.

"Okay," I said, a few seconds later, "let's do it."

We exited the vehicle and made for the rickety steps. I could already see that the curtains were open and that there was movement inside.

I climbed the steps, hammered on the door with the side of my fist and shouted, "Police! Open the door!"

I heard heavy footsteps approach the door and a muffled shout, "Who did ya say it is?"

"Police! Open up!"

I heard the lock turn and the door slowly opened to reveal a...

Even today I have a problem trying to describe the guy. I know it's not politically correct to use the word, but there's no other word for it. The guy was fat, huge, and he was wearing what once must have been a brightly colored Hawaiian shirt, but those days were long gone; most of the color had been washed out of it. Add a pair of dirty, khaki cargo shorts that came all the way down to his mid-calf along with black boots and white socks and you begin to get the picture.

"Mr. McGee?" I asked.

"Yuh," he replied. His whole face, head and neck were red, and he was sweating. His eyes, although wide, had a confused look about them.

I told him who we were and that we were investigating the rape and murder of a young woman found outside the trailer park. He opened the aluminum screen door and let us in.

I turned on the recording app on my iPad and said, "Have a seat, Mr. McGee. I just have a couple questions to ask you, but before I do, I need to inform you that I'll be recording this interview. Do you have any objections?"

He flopped down on the couch, looked at the iPad, and then shrugged and nodded.

"Out loud for the record, please, sir."

"Yes, I don't mind. Go ahead, but I didn't do nothin'."

I had him confirm his name, then recorded name and rank for Janet and me, then the date and time, and... well, you know the routine.

"What do you know about a young woman by the name of Nicolette Percy?" I asked, as Janet slowly took in the entire perimeter of the room, her hand on her weapon just in case our large friend decided to try anything.

The trailer was old. With a little care it might have been a cute, retro-style home, but long years of neglect had taken their toll. The window frames were buckled. The linoleum floor covering had seen better days, being worn and scuffed. The kitchen cabinets had, at some time in the distant past, been painted light pink, but were now dark and dirty. There were stains on the floor and what looked like water damage. The walls were a grungy, dark brown paneling dulled by years of dust and smoke. The air conditioner in the corner had made red streaks down the wall where the water had dripped from the condenser. Cobwebs laced the corners of the ceiling, dead flies peppered the windowsills, and there were gouges and scuffs along the baseboard. The kitchen faucet dripped continuously.

"Nothing," he said, leaning back on his couch with a grunt as he spread his arms wide along the top of the couch, his belly a thing of wonder and amazement. The couch was old, upholstered in a red and black plaid pattern, that long ago had sacrificed its springs to the weight of Pete McGee.

He put his left foot on the coffee table, a thing of dubious beauty tastefully decorated with newspaper pages, a couple of porno mags, dozens of beer bottle rings and cigarette burns. The whole place stunk of stale beer and cigarette smoke. I doubted that it had been aired out in years.

"You never met her on an online dating service?" I asked, but before he could answer, my phone rang. I checked the screen. It was Hawk. I took the call.

"Yes, Hawk?"

"I've got the warrant. We're on our way."

"Good, come on. Bring some uniforms with you. We're already inside." And I hung up.

"You were about to say?" I said.

"What was that about?" he asked.

"The phone call? You'll see," I replied. "Now, are you going to answer my question?"

"I'm not on no online dating service. It's kind of hard for me to meet anyone on account of my job," he said.

I wanted to suggest the size of his stomach might have more to do with it than his job, but I kept it to myself.

"What kind of work do you do?" I asked.

"I'm a truck driver; on the road two weeks at a time. I service Chattanooga, Lexington, Louisville, Indianapolis, Chicago, Wisconsin and Birmingham, Alabama. I just travel back and forth, almost in a straight line." He pointed a plump finger in the air and made a line up and down.

"You didn't have a date scheduled for last Saturday evening? You made arrangements to meet her at a bar, but you had car trouble and asked her to meet you at another bar not far from here?" I paused for a second, stared hard at him, then continued. "Because, Mr. McGee, that's exactly what's in her texts. They pinged off a cell tower not half a mile from here. So did your responses."

"Hell, that wasn't me. I wasn't even here. I was on the road. I had a shipment of carpets from Dalton going to Chicago. I picked up a load of appliances there and headed on up to Eau Claire, Wisconsin, and then I had to have my truck serviced in Peru, Indiana. See, I had an issue at the weigh station on the Indy state line. They're always hassling me in Indiana. That kept me there for two extra days. Cost me over a thousand bucks 'cause the delivery ended up being late." He swallowed hard. "It's all in my logbook. You can check that with my boss."

"I'm sorry, but those logs are filled out by you. Who's to say you didn't fudge the timeline?" I smirked.

"You're a bit out of date, lady. The logs are electronic these days. You can check where my truck was any minute of any damn day. I wasn't here, I tell ya. It wasn't me. I was in Indy most of the time. I just got back last night."

Geez, I knew that about the logs. What the hell's the matter with me today?

"I'll take your word for it, for now, but we will check the logs. Now, tell me about your roommate, Harvel Brady?"

At the mention of Harvel, the man's face went gray. It was like an eclipse. I watched him swallow hard and take a deep breath. He licked his lips and blinked nervously.

"He's not my roommate. He just stays here sometimes. But he doesn't have a key. So, I don't think he was around," he replied, shifting in his seat.

"What's your relationship with Mr. Brady?" I asked.

"Oh, you know. We just hang out together sometimes. Drink. Play video games. Sometimes he crashes here, he does. But only when I'm around. I think he has a girlfriend over on East 38th Street. At least he did at one time. She might know where he is. I think her name is Christine... or Kathy. Something like that."

"Can I take a look at your cell phone, Mr. McGee?" I asked.

"I... don't have it. I lost it," he stuttered.

"Where did you lose it?" I asked.

"If I knew that it wouldn't be lost, would it?" There was no humor in his smart-ass answer, but there was a thin layer of sweat forming on his forehead. It was becoming shinier by the second.

He caught my look and hurriedly said, "Maybe at the weigh station? I dunno. I stopped for a couple of hot dogs at one of the truck stops. Maybe I left it there?" He slumped his shoulders.

"That doesn't sound too good, now does it, Mr. McGee?"

"I'm telling you, Detective, that I don't know where my phone is and I don't know any Nicolette Percy. I never arranged a date with her or anyone else. I was on a run up north, like I told ya. Check the logs, you'll see."

"You could have paid someone to make that run for you. And your friend, Harvel Brady, can't corroborate your story because you say he wasn't here, even though I've got a witness, a neighbor, who puts him here."

I still hadn't checked Mrs. Nielsen's background, but I figured there was no harm in tossing the claim out there.

From the look on Pete's face, I must have hit a nerve. Either that or he'd eaten something that didn't agree with him. Like something organic.

"I wasn't here, I tell ya. I was on a run... My iPass! My frickin' iPass," he shouted excitedly. "My iPass can confirm I was on the road. They even have video. You'll see... You'll see me in the cab. And I haven't heard from Harvel in weeks. So, I don't know who you were talking to, but they're all mixed up."

"Fine," I said. "I have to tell you that two more of my detectives are on the way here with a search warrant, and when they get here, they're going to scour the entire place from top to bottom for any trace of Nicolette Percy." I leaned forward. "You see, a rape leaves behind all kinds of almost invisible traces. If I find so much as a hair from her head in here, I'll have you in cuffs before you can say, yikes."

"No problem," he said. "I got nothin' to hide. Search all you like. You won't find nothin'."

But I could tell he was trying to hide something. He kept avoiding my eyes, looking away to the left, chewing on his bottom lip and picking at his cuticles.

I heard two cars pull up outside.

"That's good," I said, "because it sounds like they're here."

I stood up, picked up my iPad and turned off the app. "I'm going to leave you to them. For your sake, I hope you've been telling me the truth. If they find anything... well, God help you. In the meantime, here's my card. If you can think of anything that might help us, give us a call."

I placed a business card on the coffee table. "And if I were you, I wouldn't accept any long routes from your employer for the next couple of weeks."

I opened the door and stepped out. Hawk, Robar and two uniforms were approaching the bottom of the steps.

"He knows," I told Hawk. "He seems cooperative, but you never know. Let me know if you find anything." And we left them to it.

"What do you think?" I asked Janet when we were on our way back to the PD.

"I'm not sure what to think. His body language came across as someone who really didn't know what we were talking about. But you can't get around the fact that his name's on Nicolette's cell phone. Those texts had to have originated from his phone, but if he killed her, wouldn't he have tossed it, in the river or at least in a ditch somewhere?"

"You'd think so, wouldn't you?" I said. "But if he really did lose it..."

"Then somebody else made the calls," Janet finished for me.

"Don't forget, the roommate," I said. "Mrs. Nielsen saw Harvel Brady with Nicolette's car." I shook my head thinking of how scared Nicolette had to have been.

"Do you think McGee's covering for Brady?" Janet asked.

"Maybe," I said, squinting in the bright sunlight. "He certainly has something on his mind. Whatever it is, we'll know soon enough. A guy like him, I doubt we'll have to turn up the heat too much before he spills his guts."

"What if he didn't lose it?" Janet asked. "What if Brady stole it from him?"

"I was thinking that myself—"

Just then my cell phone rang. "Gazzara."

"Hey, Cap. It's Jack. I got that address and phone number you wanted. The address linked to Pete McGee's cell phone is 56 Crystal Lane in the beautiful city of Chattanooga. The number is 555-201-0884." He sounded pleased.

"Good work. How're you doing with the computer?"

"Still waiting for the hack," Jack said. "It shouldn't be too much longer... I hope."

"Well, soon as you can," I said.

"Roger that," he replied and hung up.

Whew, I thought. Even though there were a lot of lines in the water, I couldn't help but feel like I was drifting. I couldn't decide which way I wanted to go first. Funny, though, how sometimes if you just sit still, a push in the right direction comes from out of nowhere and gets you moving again.

13

My phone was ringing when I walked into my office, almost an hour later—we stopped off at Smokey Bones for lunch. I didn't even have a chance to make a cup of coffee and I was dragging. I quickly sat in my chair, picked up the receiver and pressed the button with the blinking red light.

"Gazzara."

"Captain Gazzara?" It was a voice I didn't recognize.

"Yes, this is Captain Gazzara, Homicide. What can I do for you, Mr...?"

"I was given your name by Don Harrington. My name is Charles Percy. I am Nicolette Percy's father."

I sat up straight. He had my full attention.

"Mr. Percy, thank you for your call. First, I'd like to say I'm very sorry for your loss. When I spoke with Mr. Harrington, he told me about the kind of person your daughter was. You had a lot to be proud of," I said. I heard him sniffle.

"Thank you, Captain. Can you tell me what happened to her? Her stepmother... Maureen hasn't exactly been forthcoming."

I took a deep breath and told him everything I could without revealing anything that might prejudice my investigation. I did not tell him about the postmortem assault. Those kinds of details are best kept from the family. It's something no parent should have to live with. Even so, I could hear him choking back his emotions.

"I knew it would come to this," he said. "I just knew it."

"What do you mean, Mr. Percy?"

"Maureen is a sick person. She's sick," he said. "She didn't use to be. I was a widower, you see. She and I met at a church bingo. Can you believe that?"

I didn't want to say it, but that was a rather hard pill to swallow especially after meeting Maureen. But then again, the more I learned about the case, the more I doubted my own gut instincts. Nothing was turning out the way I'd expected. Why should Mr. Percy's story be any different?

"She was a beautiful woman. Or so I thought, until the day I told her 'no.'" He sounded bitter. "My kids liked her. Nicolette was her maid of honor. We had a lot of fun together as a family. We went out for breakfast most days and attended a lot of family get-togethers. That was my side of the family, of course. Maureen didn't really have a family. Just a brother. We'd only met him once and that was one time too many. He was scary and strange. That's why I thought she was so involved with the kids. Even though Nicolette was her stepdaughter, she treated my daughter like she was her own."

"What changed, do you think, Mr. Percy?"

"We'd been married about four years. Things were good. They weren't great like they had been in the beginning. The real world had crept into our lives and we both had routines, obligations, family commitments that needed to be tended to, like Nickie's college.

"I'd mentioned to Maureen that I was saving for the kids to go to college; I had been for years. As it turned out my son, Kenny, didn't have any interest in going to college. He's an apprentice with a well-respected plumbing outfit here in town. Chicago is a good place for blue-collar workers. But Nickie didn't want to go. She wanted to go to art school. I'm not sure what for. One day she wanted to go into fashion. The next it was sculpting. After that she wanted to be a writer. I thought she could have done all of it if she really wanted to. But that's what Dads are for, isn't it? To tell their daughters they are the most beautiful, the most wonderful... I'm sorry."

"It's all right, Mr. Percy. Take your time," I said as I scribbled my notes.

"But when Maureen found out I had money for the kids in a separate account, she went behind my back and started dipping into it. I'm not a rich man, Captain Gazzara. But I made sure I had money set aside for a rainy day, that I was prepared for those unexpected things that pop up in life. Maureen took all that away."

"If her name wasn't on the accounts, how did she get her hands on the money?" I asked.

"Simple. She told the bank that I'd lost my debit card. They sent a replacement within two days. She made sure she met the mailman, and within a month she'd withdrawn more than seventy-five thousand dollars. That was just about everything, all of Nickie's college money. The only reason I found out about it was because I had been going to the same bank for years and was friendly with the tellers. One day I walked in and one teller, who was especially nice, asked me if everything was okay. Of course, I didn't know what she was talking about, so I said 'yes, why d'you ask?' You'd have done the same, I'm sure."

"I would," I admitted.

"Well, the teller, she tells me some story about how her church can sometimes help people with bills or food if they need it. That it was all done quietly to protect the recipients from feeling they were getting a handout. I nodded and said that was great and that she should be proud to be a part of something like that, and then I asked her why she was telling me about it? To be honest, I thought she was going to ask me for a donation... and I would have been happy to give her one, but then she asked me if I'd like for her to add my name to her list of needy families. Well, I tell you, Captain, I almost choked." He paused, and I heard him take a deep breath.

"Apparently, Maureen had told everyone at the bank that I was gambling away our money. She needed to take money from Nickie's college fund to make ends meet. I was absolutely mortified. Mortified," he said.

"What did you do?" I asked.

"Well, I confronted her, of course. I asked her where the money had gone. She had no answer for me. She begged me not to tell Nickie. She said that the relationship between stepmother and stepdaughter was already a hard one and she didn't want me to ruin their friendship. But what was I supposed to tell Nickie? I told Maureen she was going to have to tell Nickie herself, and I left her to it."

"What do you do for a living, Mr. Percy?" I asked.

"Back then I owned a small hardware store. Nothing fancy. But it was mine." His voice dropped. "I had to sell it to pay off Maureen's debts. Then I filed for bankruptcy and then filed for divorce. I'm in real estate now. I'm an agent."

"How did Nicolette handle it when Maureen told her what she'd done?" I couldn't imagine how Nickie could have remained with her stepmother after hearing what she'd done.

"She told her the same story she told the woman at the bank. Maureen had been manipulating her since the day we were married. There was nothing I could say or do to convince Nicolette that it wasn't true, that Maureen had stolen the money. When I decided to divorce her, Nickie insisted that she'd stay with her.

"'She has nothing now, Dad,' Nickie said. 'I can't just leave her all by herself, can I? She'll never be able to cope.'"

I heard him sigh, and then he continued, "But that was my daughter. She thought she was helping. But I knew that as soon as I moved back to Chicago that Maureen would turn on her, and she did. She took just about every cent Nickie earned, and... she told me she often slapped her," Mr. Percy said.

"Why didn't she ask for your help?" I asked.

"Captain Gazzara, I know you must have dealt with many women in abusive relationships? You tell them to leave, to not stay with a guy who treats them bad, right? It should be simple. But it isn't, is it?" he asked.

"No, sir. It isn't, not at all."

"Every time I spoke to her, I told her she should come to Chicago and start over. And every time she told me she had her life there in Chattanooga, with her friends... The last time I spoke to her she said something I'll never forget. She said she'd always wanted to go to the top of the Sears Tower. Of course, they don't call it the Sears Tower anymore. I thought that perhaps she'd reached some sort of turning point, that she was going to ask to come visit and maybe stay. I had room for her."

"What happened?" I asked, my fingers numb from writing everything he said as fast as he said it.

"The next time I spoke to her, she said that Maureen had borrowed some money from her so she didn't have enough to come visit. I offered to pay, but my Nickie... well, she wanted to do things on her own. She said, 'no, Dad. I'll have the money in about two more months if I'm frugal. Then I'll come.' That was the last time I spoke to her." His voice was strained. He sounded as if he was crying.

I took a deep breath and asked the question that had been on my lips for the past twenty minutes, "Mr. Percy, do you think Maureen might have had something to do with your daughter's death?"

There was a moment of silence, and then he said, "If she didn't, I'd place all my money on her brother, Harvel Brady."

What? WHAT? As soon as I heard that name, I froze.

"What did you say?" The words tumbled out of my mouth. I was sure I'd just hallucinated and that I didn't really hear what I thought I did. That I was confused, that I'd been daydreaming about the situation with Harvel Brady and it just seeped into my mind as Mr. Percy was speaking.

"Maureen's brother," he said. "His name's Harvel Brady."

Nope. I'd heard him right and my stomach flipped.

Percy continued, "I bet if you run his name, you'll have a file on him. He's a real nasty piece of work, a junkie and a thief, and God only knows what else."

Percy was talking, but I was only half listening. My case was quickly turning into a nightmare, as confusing and tangled as a string of Christmas lights.

"Harvel Brady is... Maureen's brother?" I asked, finally pulling my thoughts together, but still not quite able to grasp what I just heard.

"Yes, that's right. You... you sound like you know him."

"No... That is, I know of him, but I've never met him. Look, Mr. Percy. There's something I need to do. Is there anything else you want to tell me before we hang up?"

Fortunately there wasn't, because by the time I'd gotten off the phone with him, I felt like I'd been sitting there all day and that I needed to stretch my legs. Anyway, I put the phone down and just sat there staring at my notes. After several minutes in a semi-comatose state, I shook myself, picked up the phone again, called Janet and had her gather the rest of the team and come to my office. We needed to find Harvel Brady... like yesterday.

I needed coffee! I got up from my desk, shoved a CPD mug under the coffee machine, put in a pod and set the brew to eight ounces—I needed it strong—and pushed the button.

14

Over the next several minutes, they all came trooping in, one by one. They took their usual seats—Janet sat down in the guest chair in front of my desk and propped her briefcase against her chair leg; Jack, Hawk and Robar spread themselves out around the conference table. I picked up my notes from my conversation with Charles Percy, stared at them for a long minute, looked up at my team, glanced at each one of them in turn, then said, "There's been a... development." And then I spent the next fifteen minutes going over what Nicolette's father had told me, all the while mentally kicking myself for not recording the conversation.

When I was done, I emphasized that we needed to find Harvel Brady as quickly as possible, and everyone was to drop everything and concentrate on that until we found him. Everyone that is except Jack, who was still working on Nicolette's computer. Then I handed my notes to Janet and asked her to see if someone in the pool could transcribe them and make copies for everyone.

"How did it go at McGee's trailer?" I asked. "Did you find anything?

"We didn't," Hawk said. "The place is a mess, as you know. I think we need to have Mike Willis's people go through it. They're way better at that kind of search than we are."

"Yes, I agree," I said. "I'll give him a call. Leave the warrant with me. It's still good."

I leaned back in my chair, linked my fingers behind my head—a habit I'd picked up back in the day from Harry Starke—and said, "Okay troops, if there's nothing else..."

"There is," Robar said. "As you know, before we did the McGee thing, we stopped by to see Maureen Lawson. I think you'll be interested in the outcome of that visit, short as it was."

"Oh yes," I said, perking up. "Do tell."

"At first she didn't want to talk to us," Robar said. "When she came to the door, she wouldn't even let us in. It wasn't until I threatened to cuff her and bring her in that she finally took the chain off and let us in. She had that little dog in her arms. The one you briefed us about."

"Yes. That would be Nicolette," I said sarcastically.

"Right," Robar continued. "So, I asked her if we could see Nicolette's room. She hesitated, then said it was a bit of a mess, that she hadn't had time to tidy it from the last time she slept in it. I told her it didn't matter and that we wanted to see it anyway. Well, she huffed and puffed and finally agreed to let us see it.

"I have to tell you, Cap. It was a mess. If one of my kids... well. There were clothes all over the place. It was like Nicolette had had a temper-tantrum and thrown her things around. The bed wasn't made. The covers had all been dragged off and were in a heap on the floor. All of the drawers were open—"

"Hell, Kate," Hawk growled, interrupting her, "it looked like someone ransacked the place."

"Did you ask Maureen about it?" I asked.

"Of course, I did," Hawk said. "When I came out of the room— we didn't find anything, by the way—I asked if that's the way she, Nicolette, kept it, and why hadn't she tidied it up."

"What did she say?" I asked.

"She told me it was always that way, that Nicolette was a slob and that—and I quote"—he looked at his notes—"'contrary to popular opinion, Nicolette was not an easy person to live with.' She told us that her life was very much like her room. There were certain aspects she kept neat and orderly like her appearance to others and her persona at work. But the truth was that she had a lot of secrets and played a lot of parts that Maureen didn't feel needed to be shared with the world. She also said she'd been meaning to tidy it up but hadn't had time." Hawk made a face like he'd smelled something bad.

"I tell ya, Kate, the woman really pissed me off." He paused, shook his head like an old dog, then continued.

"I told her. I said, Ms. Lawson, if you know something about Nicolette that you haven't told us, now might be a good time to tell us. And damn me if she didn't use what I'd just said as an excuse to start in questioning us about the case.

"'Why?' she said. 'Have you got any leads? Who d'you think might have killed her? Have you found any clues? Do you think you'll be able to wrap it up quickly?' That's what she said, didn't she, Ann?" Hawk looked at Robar who nodded in agreement.

"'We are not at liberty to say at the moment,' I told her," Hawk said.

"Then I asked her if there was anything she'd like to share with us?" Robar said. "And she became all over-dramatic. She let out a huge, false sigh and shook her head as she looked at the floor, still stroking the dog's head. And then she came out with it. 'I didn't want to say anything,' she said. 'It feels like I am betraying my step-daughter, but I found her journal.' Then she said she didn't even know Nicolette kept one, and before I could say anything else, she walked off down the hall and came back with this."

Robar held up a cheap, Dollar Store journal that had smiley faces on it and the words Dream Big. She stood, walked around the table, handed it to me, then returned to her seat.

"It looks new to me, Cap," she said. "Like she'd only recently started keeping it."

"Has Maureen read it?" I asked.

"Yup," Hawk interrupted. "Ann was holding the book. and Maureen pointed at it and told us she had no idea that her daughter had led that kind of double life."

"Give me a minute, okay?" I said as I opened the journal and began to read the neat, clear handwriting about a visit to one of Chattanooga's sketchier neighborhoods: *Met some guys. Had some beers. Can't wait to go back.* The entries were pretty boring. No descriptions of anything or anyone. There were no names. Just references to some shady places that could have been any of a half-dozen places around that particular neighborhood. Hell, they were so vague I was sure I'd been to most of them myself.

"What do you think?" I asked without looking up, still reading.

"I don't think it's hers, Nicolette's," Hawk said.

I looked up. Robar was nodding her head in agreement.

"You think Maureen staged it?" I asked.

"I do," Hawk said.

"Anyone get a sample of Nicolette's handwriting? I'm sure if we contacted the people she used to work with, we'd be able to get one," I said.

"I've already put a call in," Robar said.

"Good," I said and looked at Janet, who'd been sitting quietly with her notepad on her knee, scribbling away. "What about you, Miss Toliver? Anything to add?"

"I checked out Pete McGee's alibi," she said. "He's in the clear. He was in Indianapolis when Nicolette was killed. There are eyewitnesses who can put him there."

"Okay. That's good to know. We can cross him off the list and focus on Harvel Brady, but I want McGee's phone. He said he lost it. If he did, we need to know who found it, because it's for damn sure that someone did, and that someone is probably the killer. And I'm thinking Harvel Brady." I paused, thinking hard, then continued, "I also find it really strange that Maureen didn't think to mention her brother." I looked at Hawk. "Did she say anything to you guys about a brother or family?" I asked.

"Nope. Not a word," Hawk said.

"Okay." I turned my attention to Jack. "I'm waiting on you to save the day. How much longer are you going to be with Nicolette's computer?"

"I'm meeting Sarah in... at four-thirty. She's bringing me a USB stick with the hack on it. Once I have that it shouldn't take but a few minutes."

"Sarah?" we all asked in unison.

"And just who is this... Sarah, pray tell?" Ann asked. "Are you keeping secrets from us, Jackie-boy?"

"No," he said, standing up. "She's the buddy I told you about."

"Woo-hoo," Janet said, laughing.

"Woo-hoo, yourself," he said as he walked out of the room. "I'm happily married, remember?"

"I also ran Harvel Brady's name through the database," Janet said as she leaned down, picked up her briefcase, opened it, pulled out a file big enough to prop open a door, and dumped it with a thud on my desktop.

"No." I gasped.

"Oh yes. Mr. Brady is what some people might call a career criminal." Janet smirked as she flipped the pages.

"Career criminals don't get caught very often," Hawk said as he moseyed over, looked over her shoulder and started reading Brady's list of charges. "This guy's a loser. Look at this. Possession. Possession. Possession with intent to sell. Whoa, here we go. Attempted rape."

"That's not all," Janet said, leaning back in her chair. "Since he turned twelve, he's been in and out of the system. At first it was for vandalism and drugs. But when he was sixteen, he was convicted of raping a fifteen-year-old girl and stayed in juvey hall until he was eighteen, and then he slipped out with a squeaky-clean record."

"Are we sure it was rape?" Hawk asked. "The only reason I ask is because she was fifteen. He was sixteen. The parents don't like him. They catch him with their daughter. To save face the next thing you know it wasn't consensual, it was rape. How many times have we seen it?"

"Too many to mention," I muttered.

"I thought that too," Janet said, "but he beat her up bad and choked her unconscious. I don't think she signed on for that." Janet handed the arrest papers to Hawk.

"What was he last incarcerated for, and when?" I asked.

"Six months ago, for possession and public indecency. He thought he'd enjoy a little afternoon delight in his car outside an ice cream shop."

Janet frowned. "Gross. He was given thirty days in the county jail because what he did wasn't dangerous, just plain disgusting. And get this. On all of these arrest warrants, he's listed the Tomahawk Trailer park as his home."

"He doesn't ever list Maureen Lawson's address?" I asked.

"There's no mention of her at all. It's like they are hiding their relationship," Janet said.

"Would you want to admit you were related to a guy like that?" Robar asked. "She's weird and acting suspicious. But I know I wouldn't want the world to know I had a junkie perv ex-con for a brother. Plus, her daughter was murdered. You don't know how people will talk."

"True. Okay," I said, "here's where we are: we need to find Harvel and we need to find the phone. Janet, Robar, you go visit Maureen again and ask what she knows about him. Hawk, you do some digging and see what you can find out about Charles Percy, Nicolette's father. I'm not giving him a complete pass just because he's the girl's father. Also, see if you get any hits on Maureen Lawson. Now get out of here, all of you. I need to think."

15

I needed to think and to stretch my legs. I grabbed my purse, phone, and plastic to-go cup and left the building to walk across the road to McDonald's directly opposite the police department.

I hadn't had the steaming cup in my hands even a minute when someone tapped me on the shoulder, startling me so I almost dropped it.

"Captain Gazzara, can I talk to you?"

I turned around and got the shock of my life.

"Pete McGee," I said. "Of course you can talk to me. What are you doing here?"

"I was in the parking lot at the police department. I was gonna come in, but I saw you come out so I followed you across the road. I nearly got run over. There's some crazy-ass people out there... Anyway, I need to talk to you," he said, his face even redder than it had been when I first talked to him; beads of sweat dotting his forehead. He was wearing a Chicago Bulls sleeveless tank top and the same oversize shorts. His gnarly feet were exposed in a cheap pair of flip-flops.

"All right. How about we have a seat?"

I pointed to an empty table in the far corner of the restaurant. As soon as we sat down, his right knee began bouncing nervously, especially when I asked if I could record the conversation.

"I guess it's all right. It's probably good to have someone record me saying I'm not suicidal." He chuckled.

I looked at him sternly.

"I just wanted you to know so if anything happens to me, you'll know I didn't do it, I didn't whack myself."

"If you have something to say to me, Mr. McGee, just go ahead and say it," I said as I pushed the iPad a little closer to him.

He looked at it as if it were a cobra readying itself to strike. I just sipped my coffee and waited.

"Yeah. Okay. Well... Look, I didn't know what to say when you showed up at my trailer this morning." He took a deep breath. "You caught me off guard, see? If I'd known you was comin', I would have been ready."

"Like you are now?" I asked.

"I know what you're thinking," he said. "You're thinking that I've had time to concoct a story. Well, that's not it at all. The truth is, I am scared shitless of Harvel Brady. See, I met him at a bar a couple of years ago. I kinda liked him then. He liked to party; I liked to party. He had a way with some of the ladies, not all of them. But some were more than happy to come home with us. It was a fun time. But then he started getting into the heavier drugs. Heroine. Meth." He rubbed his knees.

"Okay?" I said to let him know I was listening.

"Well, he came over last night an' he told me he and a friend was with this girl the other night, while I was on the road. He said that things got out of hand and that if anyone asks, I haven't seen him." Pete swallowed hard. "I didn't want to know what it was all about. I didn't. But he told me anyway. He said that this girl had double-crossed this friend of his and they was supposed to scare her."

I listened as McGee told me how Harvel Brady had supposedly duped the girl into meeting him and his friend and told her what was going to happen to her if she didn't hold up her end of the bargain, whatever that was supposed to mean.

"Harvel didn't say what the girl had done," he said. "He just kept saying that he was only supposed to scare her. Only scare her."

"Go on. Then what?" I said as I glanced at the iPad to make sure it was recording. It was, which was good because I knew I needed a record of the conversation and was in no position to take notes for fear of him realizing what he was doing and quitting. I no longer heard any of the traffic on the busy road outside, nor the chatter of the people at the surrounding tables. I was in the zone; all I could hear was McGee's voice.

"So, I said to him, big deal, Harvel. So you scared her. What's the issue?" McGee looked at me, swallowed hard, then continued. "You see, he was on one of his meth kicks. He was at the house pacing and talking and scratching himself and sweating like it was ten degrees hotter than hell in the trailer... It was warm, but not that warm. Anyway, he went on to tell me how the girl had been leading him on for years. Then he changed his story. He said he just wanted to scare her into giving them some money, but when she said she didn't have any, he got mad. That's when he said they did more than scare her. He didn't tell me what, and I didn't ask. I didn't want to know."

I looked at him. His right knee was still bouncing nervously. He was breathing hard like someone who'd just carried a heavy load of groceries up a steep flight of stairs. I got it. He *was* scared.

"Pete," I said, gently. "I want you to help me understand why you didn't tell me all of this when I was at your home this morning?" I watched him as he stared out through the window at the rush hour traffic on Amnicola.

"I was scared," he replied pitifully, still staring out of the window.

"A big guy like you? Scared? Of what?" I asked, already knowing the answer, but I wanted to get it on record.

"You don't know Harvel," he said. "He's one crazy son of a bitch, not the kind of guy you ignore... ever. If he says for you to hold a secret, then by God you'd better hold it. And if he says he needs to sleep on your couch, you don't tell him no. I've seen him get angry at people. It doesn't take much to set him off, especially when he's high. He becomes a maniac. Really, he does." Pete shook his head, then leaned his elbows on the table and put his head in his hands.

I was afraid he was either about to throw up or pass out. Thankfully, he did neither.

I gave him a minute to compose himself, then said, "Go on, Pete. It's best you get it off your chest. Who was this friend?"

"I don't know. He didn't say an' I didn't ask, an' I didn't want to know what they did to that girl," he said, finally. "And he didn't tell me, but he said that now I knew about it I was an accomplice."

He looked up at me, then continued, "Harvel said he was coming into some kind of inheritance and that he'd give me a cut if I'd keep my mouth shut. I don't know if that's true or not. He was completely lit. I just kept my mouth shut. Finally he just keeled over on the couch and went to sleep. So I snuck out and came over to see you. He's there now. You gotta help me, Captain. You gotta protect me."

"It doesn't make you an accomplice, Mr. McGee. It makes you a bad judge of character. But that isn't a crime," I said. Inside, I felt bad for him. "However, your name is on the victim's cell phone and you say you 'lost' it. That doesn't look good. Now all of a sudden you're ready to throw your roommate under the bus and blame him for what happened to Nicolette Percy. You can see why I might be a little skeptical."

He looked crestfallen.

"How can I reach you?" I asked.

"Well, uh, I'm gonna have to get me another phone, I guess, but you could call my work. Leave me a message there. I'll be calling in to check my work schedule. They'll take a message for me." He blinked his eyes like he'd just woken up. "Does this square things with you?"

"What do you mean, Mr. McGee?" I let the iPad keep recording.

"Well, after what I told you, does it get me off the hook for anything Harvel did? You know, because I told on him?"

He looked at me like a kid waiting for Santa to tell him he'd been a good boy.

"That isn't up to me, Mr. McGee. That will be up to the prosecuting attorney." I watched his face droop. "But I'll be sure to tell him how you cooperated and that you put yourself at risk by telling me what you know."

He nodded. His lips curled up a little in the corners, and he said, "Thanks, Captain."

"Mr. McGee," I said, looking at my watch—it was almost six-thirty, "you say you left him asleep on your couch. D'you think he's still there?" I literally crossed my fingers under the table as I asked the question.

"He should be. If he's not, he'll be at the Clover Bar. It's just a couple of blocks from the Tomahawk Trailer Park on Rossville Boulevard. He likes to go there. But..." He looked out into traffic.

"But what?"

"It's a rough place. You'll need to be careful... And he's going to know I told you." He sighed.

"He's going to know eventually anyway," I said. "And I think I can handle a rough bar."

"If he isn't there, he might be at his sister's house," he said. "I don't know where she lives, though. But I know he has a sister somewhere in Chattanooga."

"Okay, well, you've been very helpful, Mr. McGee. Thank you. I'll send a message if I need to talk to you again. Oh, and don't go home for a while, not for at least an hour. You got that?"

He nodded, but he didn't look happy, not one bit.

I stood up, put my iPad under my arm and my coffee in my other hand, stone-cold that it was—it felt like I'd been drinking nothing but cold coffee since I started the case—and I left Pete McGee sitting at the table with his head in his hands. I hustled back across Amnicola to the police department. Thankfully, when I got back to the office Hawk was still there. As much as I liked to think of myself as a badass, there were some situations that called for testosterone. This was one of them.

16

I
t was almost seven o'clock that evening when I walked back across Amnicola and into the PD. Janet and Ann had gone home, but fortunately Hawk was still there. Jack was at his desk sifting through Nicolette's computer. I asked if he'd had any luck. He said he had and that there were half a dozen naked pictures of her that she'd texted to McGee's phone the day she disappeared.

"I don't know that they are actually her. They're just body shots, very suggestive, but no head. Very little in the backgrounds. Funny thing is, it's not like her; it seems out of character, to me anyway. In all of her other emails and postings on social media, there's not so much as a single cuss word, let alone this kind of thing, but I'm still making my preliminary search. I'll get in deeper as I go, but it'll take time."

"Good job," I said. "And you're right. They're not just suggestive, they're gross. Anyway, we'll talk about it when we get back," I said. "Hawk, you're with me."

Jack looked up and said, "You guys are going for drinks... without me?"

"Yeah, you can't come with us," Hawk teased. "They don't have booster seats where we're going, Jackie boy. You're out of luck."

Jack clicked his tongue and pointed at Hawk while shaking his head, unable to hide the smirk on his lips. It wasn't that Jack was short, he wasn't. It was just Hawk's way of telling him he'd been accepted and was now one of the team, and that since they were the two men in my team, there had to be some traditional ball busting between them. I was glad to see it. After all everyone had been through over the loss of our friend Lennie, it was a relief that Jack had finally been able to fit in.

"How do you want to play this, Captain?" Hawk asked as he drove in the direction of the Tomahawk Trailer Park.

"We're going to find him, grab him, and take him in. No more, no less."

Well, that was my plan, but you know what they say about plans and mice and men, right?

I knocked on McGee's door, hoping he'd done as I asked and stayed away. He had, and so apparently had Harvel Brady. No one came to the door, and I couldn't hear anyone moving around inside.

I knocked again. "Police. Open the door." Nothing.

I looked at Hawk. He shrugged. I reached for the door handle and turned it. It was unlocked. I opened the door and yelled, "Police. Don't move. We're coming in." No answer.

I stepped inside, weapon in hand. Hawk followed and we proceeded to clear the trailer room by room. The place was empty. Brady wasn't there.

"Now what," Hawk said, holstering his weapon.

"We'll try the Clover Bar," I replied. "It's on Rossville Boulevard; not far."

"I know the place," Hawk said as we got back in the car. "It's a real dump. How they keep their licenses is beyond me. You know what this dude looks like?"

"Only from his mug shot. Here, take a look." I handed him a five by six photograph.

"Shit! He's an ugly-looking son of a bitch," he said.

I grinned sideways at him and said, "That he is, but a mullet never does any man justice."

In the photograph, Harvel Brady did indeed sport a mullet. His skin was tan, and his jaws and cheeks blended almost seamlessly into his neck and shoulders. He had the kind of muscles that came with temporary construction jobs, or brief stints in prison. He wasn't on a strict fitness regimen so he had some flab, but he was strong enough to hurt someone if he felt the need. Obviously, he'd felt the need when he murdered all one-hundred-and-ten pounds of Nicolette Percy—Yes, by then I'd convinced myself that he was Nicolette's killer. If I had to compare him to an animal, he looked like a bull... with a mullet.

The Clover Bar was a simple corner place: old, built of cinderblock and stucco, with a metal roof, a solid front door and bars on the windows. It was a multifunction business, a combination of liquor store, bar, and a check-cashing establishment.

I entered first with Hawk close behind and found myself under the bright florescent lights of the liquor store. I paused just inside, looked around and was amazed at the variety of the stock. A person could buy anything from a case of beer to Wild Turkey, Jack Daniel's and Absolut vodka. There were even a couple bottles of Boone's Farm wine. Hell, you could even buy lottery tickets. And a sign behind the register proclaimed that the staff would cash checks up to two-hundred dollars, no credit check. *Oh yes,* I thought. *I bet you will, and at what cost?*

There were three people at the register, which was being manned by a wrinkled old woman with gray skin and patches of white hair on her head. A cigarette dangled from her lips. Her voice as she rang up her customers sounded like a metal rake being dragged across gravel. She must have been in her eighties. She looked like a tough old bird and I had an idea that you didn't want to mess with her, and I'd have bet good money that she had a sawn-off twelve-gauge behind the counter. I had no doubt that if she couldn't handle the situation, big Bruno sitting on a bar stool by the door would handle things quite adequately.

Hawk, who looks more like a cop than anyone I've ever seen, walked to the front of the line and said to the old lady, "Where can we get a cold drink, darlin'?"

"Straight back," she grunted, pointing the way with a gnarled finger that reminded me of the Ghost of Christmas Future.

"Much obliged," he replied.

I looked at the convex circular mirrors high up in the corners of the room and saw the old woman, Bruno at the door, a guy in the far corner at the coolers trying to pick out a beer brand, and a clerk who was sweeping by the entrance to what looked like the stockroom.

We strolled through the shop and walked into a long narrow bar that looked more like someone's basement. There were boxes of inventory piled into pyramids behind the bar and along the far wall. There was an old, worn-out pool table that was more gray than green. A dartboard hung on the wall in the furthest corner of the room, no doubt to make sure that the drunks were less likely to hit any of their fellow patrons, I assumed.

The place smelled of stale beer and cigarettes. It felt as if fresh air hadn't permeated the place since the Carter Administration.

We entered together, Hawk slightly in front of me. And wouldn't you know, every head turned to give us a once over; there had to be more than forty of them. The majority looked as if they just walked in off a construction site, and they probably had. The rest of the bunch looked like men and women of leisure, independently wealthy receiving a monthly stipend from the American people.

We stood together browsing the faces. It took only a couple seconds to spot Harvel Brady. He was parked on a stool at the far end of the bar. As soon as he looked up from his drink, he spotted us. He stared at us for just a second too long, then he made a mistake; he upped and bolted for the back door. By then, Hawk was already halfway across the room.

Brady hit the emergency crash bar on the door, bursting it wide open, allowing a dim shaft of light from the security light in the parking lot to cut through the swirling cigarette smoke while at the same time a tired, outdated fire alarm started clanging. The bell was loud, causing the old woman at the front counter to utter a string of curses that would have made a sailor blush. I have to tell you, I was laughing as I ran, following Hawk, my weapon drawn and my badge on display. I darted outside and followed Hawk as he made a left turn into the alley behind the bar. Boy could he move! For a guy who was just a couple years from retirement, he moved like a rookie just out of the Academy.

The alley behind the bar was like so many others—just wide enough for a dumpster truck—with the hot smell of decay from the food tossed into the single dumpster, and the pungent aroma of urine; a gift from the drunken patrons at the bar who, over the years, decided it was easier to relieve themselves out back at closing time than it was to stand in line at the single urinal in what was optimistically called the restroom.

The back alley was hot, hotter than the street, and I could feel the stink clinging to my skin and clothes like an invading virus. *Damn*, I remember thinking. *If I get this stink out of my hair with two washes, I'll be lucky.*

There was no telling how many drinks Brady had had before we arrived, but I could tell he was at least three sheets in the wind, for which I was more than a little thankful: he was younger than Hawk. Had the man been sober, or worse, on one of his drugs of choice, there was no telling how many officers it might have required to take him down.

I ran after the two men and saw Brady grabbing at anything and everything in his path: garbage bags, black plastic crates, stacks of broken-down cardboard boxes, tossing them over his shoulder trying to slow Hawk down. All it did was make him mad.

"Police! Stop!" Hawk shouted, but either Brady didn't hear or he ignored him and staggered onward, the thud-thud-thud of Hawk's size thirteens getting closer and closer.

I still had my weapon drawn, but as we neared the end of the alley I holstered it and put on a spurt. I was afraid that if he made it to the road, he'd either get run over or we'd lose him. Neither one was an option. If the man was a killer, and I was pretty sure that he was, I needed to bring him in before he could kill again.

I needn't have worried, though, because sometimes Lady Luck intervenes and things work out. And there she was, waiting for him. Just as Brady was about to make the turn, he stepped onto something nasty. I thought it was a puddle of water or urine, but it wasn't; it was some kind of oil spill, and his feet went one way and he went the other. He slid to the right then, his arms flailing like out of control windmill sails, his legs became entangled and he went down hard. Hawk was on him like a flea on an old coonhound.

Hawk cuffed his wrists behind his back and then rolled him over.

I stood, feet apart, hands on my knees and said, "Harvel Brady. You're under arrest for the rape and murder of Nicolette Percy. You have the right to remain silent..." and so on and so on.

Hawk stood, grabbed him by his arm and hauled him to his feet.

"Do you understand your rights as they've been explained to you?" I asked as Hawk spun him around to face me.

He didn't answer.

"The detective asked if you understood your rights," Hawk said, "Do you or don't you?"

"Yeah, yeah," he snarled. "Leggo, Grampaw. You're hurtin' my arm."

Just then, a blue and white police cruiser appeared at the entrance to the alley, and then they were all over us: two more cruisers, two fire trucks and an ambulance, and more than a dozen firemen and EMTs milling around and looking disappointed there was no blaze to put out.

"What have you got, Detective?" the uniformed cop asked Hawk as he approached. As soon as he told him the charges, the officer took over, grabbed Brady by the arm and steered him to his cruiser, crammed him in the back and slammed the door.

I glanced into the cruiser through the back window. Brady glowered back at me. He didn't look at all happy. His lips moved as he muttered to himself, squinting at me with eyes black and filled with hate. Maybe it was the darkness, but he even looked evil. I smiled at him, gave him a pinky wave and a wink. If he thought for one minute that I was scared of him, he had no idea who or what he was dealing with. I'd tackled and arrested guys three times his size and with even worse rap sheets. Still, I will admit, knowing what he'd done to Nicolette, he was one scary son of a bitch.

"Why do they do that?" Hawk asked me as the cruiser pulled away. "Why do they always have to run?"

"Well," I said, laughing. "They take one look at you and think, I can outrun that silly old asshole. Little do they know that you are like a damn Pit bull and that the laws of physics don't apply to you."

"Gee, thanks, Cap," Hawk growled. "I love you too."

"Well done, Detective," I replied.

By the time we got back to the police department, it was almost ten o'clock and I was... tired. So we locked Brady in a holding cell and I told Hawk to go home. After all, Brady wasn't going anywhere and eight hours behind bars might loosen him up a little. It had been a good day.

17

I rose early the following morning and decided to go for my usual run. I say usual, but I hadn't done it for more than a week, nor had I worked out, and I knew I was going to be stiff. I also knew that it would do me a lot of good and that a hot shower when I returned would set me up for the day, and it did. By eight-thirty I was at work, in my office and raring to go.

I picked up the phone and called Jack. He didn't answer. I called the front desk and asked if he'd checked in. He had, so I figured I'd go looking for him. I eventually found him in the forensics lab diligently working on Nicolette's computer.

"Tell me you've got something for me," I said as I walked in.

Jack looked confused. His dark hair was a mess, and he rubbed his eyes as he looked up and saw it was me.

"I've got something but I'm not sure what it is," he said. "Nicolette was registered at a site called LookingforLove.com. She had quite a few hits. Based on her profile description and what I've read in her file, she was honest and upfront about herself. So, there were quite a few takers." Jack stopped and took a gulp from a can of Coke.

"No nude photos?" I asked.

"No, none."

"She was a pretty girl," I said.

"Yeah. She was. And a lot of guys thought she was too. Come and look at this."

I walked around to the other side of the desk and looked over his shoulder.

"See, here's a guy who is a senior teller at one of the community banks downtown. I have a buddy who works in a similar job. Those guys make sixty-kay a year. He's no deadbeat. And this guy's a dentist. And here's a web designer."

"I don't know what you're getting at," I said.

"Nicolette was corresponding with all these guys," Jack said. "This site offers features like you can give them a wink or you can send a smile before you really start to communicate. I guess they consider it flirting."

"Good grief." I had to roll my eyes.

"My sentiments exactly. So here she is flirting with these guys and one of them rises to the top of the heap."

"Let me guess. Pete McGee," I said.

"Nope. Daryl Leeds. He's a little older than her. A widower. A nice-looking guy, right?" Jack clicked on the thumbnail photo of a handsome-looking man in his late thirties and enlarged it. I nodded. He looked up at me quizzically.

"He is."

"They exchanged over thirty emails together." Jack took another swig of Coke. "But then, from out of nowhere, Pete McGee swoops in and starts blowing up her message board."

"Do you think this Daryl Leeds is involved?" I asked.

"Not at all. I ran a background on him. He's a straight arrow, good credit, no sheet other than a speeding ticket back in seventeen. As I said, he's a widower. His wife died of lung cancer. Heavy smoker right till the end."

"So what does he have to do with Nicolette?" I asked.

"Nicolette had already arranged a date with Daryl. They were supposed to get together the following week, but then McGee stepped into the picture and began messaging her. We're talking a heavy dose of sugary sweetness. I'm surprised she didn't become diabetic—he was so sweet and sugary... I can make copies, if you like."

"Maybe later. Tell me what happened between her and Daryl."

"Right!" Jack said. "So after several messages from McGee, Nicolette decided that she wasn't going to meet with Daryl after all. She sent him a message telling him she was sorry but that she'd promised to meet someone else and that she didn't think it was fair to not let him know. It's like a freakin' soap opera."

"So what did Daryl do?" I asked, hoping for a response that might help me understand where Jack was going with it.

"He said he understood and was totally cool with it, and he thanked her for being so honest. He wished her the best and that was that," Jack said.

"Okay, Jack. I'm not getting your discovery. Spell it out for me like you're talking to a third grader."

"What I'm getting at is this; had Nicolette kept her date with Daryl, she might still be alive today. But McGee was a real Casanova. Hell, Cap, I would have picked Pete over Daryl, too, if I'd been her." Jack shook his head.

"Why do you say that?"

"The guy's a romantic. He said all the right things and had that sweet job of helping kids and oh, wait until you see his picture." Jack pulled up an image of a good-looking man who didn't look anything like Harvel Brady even on his best day, nor was it the real Pete McGee.

"Who the hell is that?" I asked.

"Mister Stock Photo," Jack said and folded his arms across his chest. "The entire profile is bull, fiction. And I'm pretty sure all the romantic things he said were quotes from bad movies and cheesy song lyrics."

Now I understood what Jack was saying. Someone had entrapped the girl, Brady. There was a real guy who was interested in Nicolette. He was decent and average, and nothing any woman would ever be afraid of. And she pushed him aside for some flowery words and cheap lines. How lonely Nicolette must have been to just fall for it. It made me sad.

"But I haven't gotten to the real heart of the matter," Jack said.

"There's more?" I asked.

"Maybe it's just a coincidence, but you tell me what you think. Nicolette already had a date with Daryl. Then Pete showed up. He pursued her like he knew that she could be on the hook with another guy and that he had to move fast. From what I found out on Nicolette's search history, she liked a little poetry, she liked old movies and wanted to buy a dog. An English bulldog. It was in her search history that she was researching this. And BOOM, she's pursued by a guy who claims to have an interest in all of those things and more." Jack shook his head. "I think Pete, if it was Pete, was being fed information by someone."

"It wasn't McGee. It was Harvel Brady. Do you think it could have been Don Harrington feeding him the information, electronically?" I asked. "He and Nicolette were close."

"Maybe. Or maybe it was someone even closer to her," Jack said.

I swallowed hard. "Her mother?"

"Makes sense," Jack said.

"What about the nude photos? Can you tell if they are Nicolette or in Nicolette's house? Anything like that?" I asked.

"No. But so far they were the only ones ever sent, and on the day she went missing." Jack shrugged.

I nodded and told him to keep working and let me know what else he found and headed back to my office. On the way I ran into Hawk.

"Hey you," I said. "I was just about to call you. You ready to go talk to Mr. Brady?"

"I wouldn't rush down there, Captain. The guy isn't talking," Hawk said.

"You talked to him already?"

He nodded.

"Did he lawyer up?" I asked.

"Nope. Just sat there picking at his nails, yawning and looking at me like he had an ace up his sleeve," Hawk replied.

"Do you think he does?"

"If he does, I don't know what it could be. They let him make his phone call, but he didn't call an attorney. I'm not sure who he was talking to. Maybe his dealer. Who knows?" Hawk yawned. "But he wouldn't say a damn thing to me."

"We'll see about that," I replied. "Have 'em pull him from holding and set him up in an interview room."

"I already did. He ain't happy."

I nodded. "Let's go," I said. "I just have to stop at my office first."

I had no idea what we were about to be in for, but I had an idea it wasn't going to be pleasant.

18

Janet was at her desk surrounded as usual by stacks of yellow notepads and dozens of case files. She looked up as I walked past. "Cap?" she called after me.

"Not now, Janet," I said, and went to my office. I quickly dumped everything on my desk, grabbed my iPad and headed to the interrogation room where a sobered up and agitated Harvel Brady was sitting.

"Good morning, Mr. Brady," I said. "Did you sleep well?"

He looked terrible, as if he'd aged ten years overnight. *A dimly lit bar can do wonders for the skin*, I thought as I sat down at the table opposite him. *Florescent lighting not so much.*

The door opened again, and Hawk walked in and sat down next to me.

I turned on the camera and the voice recorder, and we began.

I read the time, day, date and those present into the record, and then Hawk said, "All right, Mr. Brady. Now that you've had a good night's sleep and a chance to think about things, we're going to try this again. But first, can I get you anything? A cup of coffee? A soda?"

"Sure. Coffee. Why not..." He paused, then continued, "I don't believe it." He chuckled. "You're letting her be the bad cop?" He looked me up and down, leering at me.

As if that's a tactic I've never experienced. He had no idea how many killers sat in that chair doing the exact same thing and still ended up behind bars. It would take a lot more than a pair of bleary eyes to scare me.

"Cap, you want a coffee?" Hawk asked pleasantly, rising to his feet.

"Thanks," I replied. *When didn't I want coffee?*

"Black with sugar," Brady called as Hawk left the room.

"Detective Hawkins has left the room at eleven oh nine," I said for the record.

Brady's hands were cuffed and he stank like a polecat. I could smell the stench of cigarettes and sweat as his body desperately tried to expel the poisons, the sickly, sweet smell of a career junkie.

"Mr. Brady, why don't you tell me about the night of the eighth when Nicolette Percy went missing," I said, leaning back in my chair.

"I don't know what you are talking about," he mumbled and began to pick at his thumbnail. It looked as if he'd torn the cuticle to the quick.

"Where were you that night, between eight and ten? Did you have a date? Maybe you hung out with some friends? What?"

"Yeah, that's what I did. I had a date, then I hung out with some friends." He leaned across the table closer to me.

"Okay, Mr. Brady. You don't have to talk to me, but we would like to get a DNA sample. Just a quick swab of the inside of your cheek," I said as I took the sterile kit from my pocket.

Harvel looked like I had just produced a set of rusty pruning shears and told him that we were going to skip the formalities and castrate him on the spot.

"Nope. I'm not consenting," he said.

"You're not?" I asked. "There's a surprise. Well, suit yourself. I'm sure we'll be able to get a sample from Pete McGee's place."

"G-go ahead an' try," Harvel stuttered, sneering at me. "I never spent more than ten minutes in his place, ever. You won't find anything."

It was hard not to notice the man's knee bouncing nervously up and down just like his friend Pete's was when he told me what he knew about Harvel and Nicolette.

"I'll be back," I said, rising to my feet.

I left him there alone and went next door to the surveillance room where Hawk was sipping his coffee. He tilted his head, nodded at the desk and said, "Your coffee."

I picked it up and took a sip. It tasted like... well, you don't want to know, but it was wet and it was hot, and it hit the spot, sort of. I turned to look at Brady through the one-way glass. He was fidgeting nervously, his right knee still bouncing rapidly.

"I told you," Hawk said before taking a loud slurp. "You ain't gonna get anything out of him, much less a DNA sample."

"Oh, I don't know... Hell, Hawk, there's more than one way to get a sample," I replied. "Take his coffee to him. We'll let him sit and stew for a while, literally," I said as I walked over to the thermostat that controlled the temperature in the interrogation room. It was set at a comfortable seventy degrees. I bumped it up to eighty and watched as Hawk took Brady his coffee.

"I don't want no damn coffee. Take it away."

"Suit yourself," Hawk replied and left, taking the coffee with him. The door closed with a solid thud and Brady sat there alone, twisting his fingers together. He knew we were watching him. He gave us the finger, then put his head down on the table and closed his eyes.

We watched patiently as the temperature in the interrogation room continued to rise, and within minutes we could see the beads of sweat begin to form on his forehead. He fidgeted. He took deep breaths. Finally, he sat up and wiped his brow. I smiled when I saw the damp spot on the steel tabletop.

Then he stood up, walked around the room, then lay down on the concrete floor and stretched out, trying to cool off like a dog that had been basking in the sun a little too long. With his hands still cuffed, he cradled his head as he lay on his stomach. Then he rolled over and put his hands behind his head.

"What do you think?" Hawk asked.

"Let him cook in there a little while longer. I'm going to go check my email. Let me know when you think we should stick a fork in him." And that was a mistake.

"Will do," Hawk said, taking another sip of coffee.

I left the observation room and headed toward my office when Janet stopped me.

"I'm sorry, Janet," I said. "What did you need?" Truth be told, I was feeling a little guilty about blowing her off earlier, but I'd had to see where we were with Brady before I could even think about anything else.

Janet flipped open one of her yellow pads as we walked together to my office.

"I received a very strange phone call last night just as I was about to go home," she said.

"You did? What was it about?" I asked.

"Maureen Lawson."

19

I ushered Janet into my office and closed the door.

"Sit down. What about her?" I asked.

"She took a course at the Lewis Marquette Junior College," Janet said as she took a seat in front of my desk.

"Really?" I can't say I was impressed.

I took my seat behind my desk and turned my computer on. It groaned and clicked as it warmed up and, within the usual couple of minutes, flashed to life telling me I had thirty-two unread emails. That being so, I was happy to adjust my focus and listen to what Janet had to say about Maureen Lawson and her community college project.

"You know Nicolette's murder was given almost no coverage by the media, the television stations," Janet said.

"Of course, it wasn't," I said. "Just a passing comment before it was shoved aside to make room for the latest imaginary offense committed by some spoiled-rotten celebrity or half-baked politician."

"Right," Janet said. "Well, last night I got a call from one of the teachers at Marquette, a Ms. Paula Wells. She did see it, and it rang a bell... Apparently, Maureen Lawson was in her screenwriting class," Janet said as she looked at her notes. "According to Ms. Wells, Maureen wrote a screenplay about her daughter's death."

I took a deep breath, narrowed my eyes, and said, "So? Some people grieve differently. I don't know if this is any different from Eric Clapton writing a song about his child who died, or Pope Leo XIII who wrote the prayer to Saint Michael after he had a vision of the angel fighting demons. So what's the point?"

"Where did you hear that?" Janet asked.

"You didn't pay attention in Sunday school, did you?" I teased, grinning at her.

"Well, those two things make sense, because they happened *after* the events took place. Ms. Wells said that Maureen was in her class a year ago," Janet said, grinning back at me.

"Really, now that is interesting. What else did she tell you?"

"Not much. She was about to give a lecture. I told her I'd call her back."

I shook my head and said, "No, here's what you do: you and Robar go talk to her and get back to me as soon as you can. Maybe Maureen wrote the ending to our story and we can wrap this thing up."

"You got it, Cap. I'll be in touch," she said, rising to her feet and heading for the door.

I shook my head as she closed the door behind her.

Just when I thought things couldn't get any stranger, I thought, *I get a news flash like that.*

I made myself a cup of coffee and then headed back to the interrogation rooms to see what was going on with Harvel Brady. I stepped into the observation room just in time to see him haul himself gasping up onto his feet using the steel table as leverage. He staggered to the door and began pounding on it and screaming.

Oh shit! I thought. *I'll not be getting any awards for this.*

20

I was right. Less than twenty minutes later I was standing in front of the Chief like a schoolgirl in front of the principal.

"What the hell did you do to Harvel Brady, Gazzara?" Johnston all but shouted at me.

"Nothing. He was fine when I left him," I replied. "Hawk took him a cup of coffee, which he refused... He was fine, perfectly coherent. Chief, he was only in there for twenty minutes. The temperature barely hit eighty degrees. I don't even think it's possible to pass out from that."

"Not you, maybe. Not someone who hasn't made a habit out of huffing paint or injecting meth."

"He huffs paint, too?" I asked innocently.

"I don't know what the hell he does, but we are all well aware of his drug use. That crazy tactic you just pulled on him could have killed him. And now he's in the hospital and Internal Affairs is already sniffing around. What the hell were you thinking?"

"I had to get a DNA sample. He refused. I knew if I turned up the heat, he'd sweat and I'd get one, and I did." I smirked, but Johnston only flared his nostrils and stared at me like a bull about to charge. "When it comes back a match for Nicolette Percy's assailant," I continued, "there won't be anything for Internal Affairs to bark about, Chief."

He shook his head, looked at me and said, "Kate, I think you might need to take a step back for a while. You've been running nonstop for more than three months. I've been watching you—"

I put my hand up to stop him.

"Oh no," he said. "You're going to hear me out. Now sit down and shut up."

I sat.

"You're always here early," he continued. "You always leave late. I don't think I've ever seen you eat anything, but there's always a cup of coffee in your hand. Yes, you're a good detective, and nobody in this department works harder than you do, but therein lies the problem."

"It's the nature of the job, Chief. You know that," I said quietly.

"Well, it's not going to end well for you if you keep it up, Kate. And you can take that any way you want to," he said. "When cops start thinking that the streets will explode into chaos if they aren't around, it's a sign that they need a vacation."

"No, Chief. No. Not yet. Look, I'm close to locking this one up, really close. Let me finish it out, and I promise I'll use half my vacation time. I've got more than two months owing, I think. I'll take the time off. I will. Please, don't take me off the case. Not now." My heart was racing.

"You have two months' vacation owing? There you are. That's just what I'm talking about. Two months. That means you haven't taken any time off in almost three years..." He paused, then said, "I have your word that you'll take a month?"

"I promise," I said, nodding my head enthusiastically.

"Harvel Brady will be released back into police custody as soon as the hospital discharges him," he said. "In the meantime, I'll do my best to keep Internal Affairs at bay until he's back behind bars, but I want you to stay away from him, and the hospital."

"You mean, I can't go visit and take him a get-well-soon bouquet?" I asked.

"I'm in no mood for jokes, Kate. Do you ever think of what you are doing and how it affects the department? How it affects your team? Because I know for a fact you don't care one iota about the perps," Chief said.

"Am I supposed to?" I asked angrily. "Chief, Harvel Brady raped and murdered Nicolette Percy... No, he did worse than that. He raped and suffocated her to death, and then he sexually abused her dead body. You're right that I don't care. What is there to care about except nailing his ass to an execution table?"

"I think you need to remember who you are talking to, Captain."

"I'm sorry, sir." I wasn't, but I had to say it.

The sad part about it was that I liked the Chief. He was a good guy, and most of the time he had my back. But there was also a phenomenon among the top brass that once they reached the northern end of the totem pole, it was really easy for them to forget the rules they'd bent or broken to get there. I could count on one hand how many of my superiors in the CPD didn't bend the rules when they were climbing the ladder.

He nodded. "Apology accepted. Now, you stay away from that hospital and go home. I'll notify you when Harvel Brady is back in police custody and not a minute sooner. Understood?"

"Yes, sir," I replied, "but Janet and Robar were going to talk to a witness about—"

"I said go home, Kate. I mean it." Johnston glared at me then looked down at the stack of papers on his desk. "That'll be all."

"Yes, sir," I said as I rose to my feet.

I was sure I left skid marks on the floor as I peeled out of his office and went to my own.

I was gathering my stuff together with the intention of leaving when my phone rang. It was Hawk.

"How'd it go in there, Kate?"

"Not as bad as it might have. You?"

"Likewise. He's not so bad."

I nodded to myself and said, "So what's up?"

"The whole thing was an act, Kate. He was fine when I brought him some water. He wouldn't touch it, so no prints or DNA."

"Don't worry about DNA. I got some from the sweat he left on the table... You really think it was an act?" I asked.

"I know it was. You know how I know?" Hawk asked.

"Enlighten me."

"One of the beat cops brought in a hooker. He was taking her to booking. Harvel almost broke his damn neck trying to catch a glimpse of her ass. No, that boy was fine. He knows the system, and I think he played us just to get into the hospital so he could get his fix. He'd been here fourteen hours. He already had the shakes."

"Has anyone been assigned to watch his room?" I asked. "It would be just like the brass to call the EMTs to pick him up and then forget to send an officer to escort him."

"Oh, yeah. That would be me. I'm here. I'll stay with our friend until it's time to bring him back to his cage. I'll be the first face he sees when he wakes up tomorrow morning."

"Oh, don't I wish I could be a fly on the wall to see his expression."

I wished Hawk luck and told him to give me a call if he needed anything. Chief Johnston obviously didn't give Hawk as big an ass-chewing as he did me. I wasn't surprised. I was the Captain. It would always fall back on me and rightfully so. That's why I got paid the big bucks. *Yeah, right!*

I grabbed my bag, shut off my computer. At that point it was showing I had sixty-one unread emails. *Oh hell... Well, they'll just have to wait!*

The message light on my phone was blinking, too. But orders were orders, and I wasn't about to upset the Chief by staying after he told me to leave. But, as with all well-laid plans... It was just as I was leaving through the back entrance that I bumped into Janet and Robar; they were walking in as I was walking out.

"Should we go to your office?" Robar asked

"No. I've been sent home for the rest of the day. The last thing I want is for the Chief to catch me still working," I muttered.

"How about McDonald's then?" Janet asked. "I'm hungry."

"Fine. What did you guys get from Paula Wells at the college?" I asked as we dodged the traffic on Amnicola.

"I think you should wait until we're sitting down to hear it, Cap," Robar said.

I could hardly wait.

21

I t was a good time to be at McDonald's. It was early afternoon and the crowds had all gone back to work. Janet ordered a cheeseburger with fries and a cherry Coke. Robar ordered a large fries, and I did a fish sandwich and fries along with a large coffee. The Chief was right: I really did need to cut back. We grabbed our orders and found a table in the corner, far from the maddening crowds, and Janet took her yellow pad from her brief-case, looked at Robar and then me.

"Are you ready?" she asked.

"Yes." I sighed.

"It was like going back to high school," Janet said, shaking her head, and then went on to fill in the details.

Apparently, Marquette Junior College was a friendly little place set on a couple of acres of land not far from the University of Tennessee, Chattanooga. It offered all the crappy classes—math, English and so on—the kids needed to get through before they could focus on their true passions at a more reputable, and insanely more expensive, institute of higher learning. But there were also a lot of night classes for people who wanted to try their hand at sculpting or painting or furniture reupholstering or, as in the case of Maureen Lawson, screenwriting.

Paula Wells had been a screenwriting professor at UC Berkley for over ten years. According to her biography, her biggest accomplishment in the screenwriting world was a television show about an all-female private investigator team in Los Angeles that was scooped up by one of the big networks. After a pilot and two episodes had been filmed, they canceled the show. She fell back to teaching what she loved and was never canceled again.

"We called ahead to make sure Paula Wells would be there," Janet said, checking her notes, "and she was, and she was waiting for us when we arrived. She was pacing nervously back and forth. A tall, slender woman without much in the way of a figure. She looked distraught, right, Ann?"

"She did," Robar replied. "She told us she was pleased we'd come to talk to her. I recorded the conversation. I think it might be good if you heard what she had to say. That okay, Cap?"

I nodded. I had all the time in the world. Fortunately, it wasn't a long interview. Ann tapped the playback button on her mini-recorder and set it down in the middle of the table.

I heard Janet and Robar introduce themselves and then ask for permission to record.

"Yes, please do." The voice sounded tinny on the small recorder. "I'm so glad you came. I'm sure this is all much ado about nothing and that there is a totally reasonable explanation. But I couldn't help thinking..." she tailed off.

"We appreciate any information, Miss Wells," Robar said. "You just never know. Even the smallest piece of information, even though you might think it's insignificant, could be extremely helpful. So, if you wouldn't mind, please tell us what you know."

"Please, call me Paula. I'm glad you feel that way. As I said, Detective Toliver, Maureen Lawson attended one of my classes about a year ago. My classes aren't all that big, so it's very easy for me to remember my students and very often I get to know them quite well. Some even become good friends. That's not what happened with Maureen Lawson, however. Oh, I remember her vividly. But we never became friends."

"Why not?" Robar asked. "Didn't you like her?"

"Well, it's like this, you see?" Paula said, "As a way of getting to know the members of my class, I have them introduce themselves and tell us a little about their life: I ask how they would describe themselves as they would if they were a character in a story. I ask them to highlight what they think is memorable about them. I get some funny answers, as you can imagine.

"When describing a person, beginning writers often describe just hair and eye color," Paula said. "But adding say a limp or a habit, a nervous tic, chewing their lip or even an expression to the character makes them more memorable. Anyway, I had a class of eight people that semester. Out of all of them I only really remember Maureen, and that was because of what she said that first evening in class.

"She said her daughter had been murdered and they never caught her killer."

I grabbed the recorder and hit the pause button.

"What?" For a minute my mind didn't register what I'd just heard. Did I really drop the ball? Did Maureen have another daughter who was dead? Who was she talking about because at that time Nicolette was very much alive?

"That's what Wells said she said," Robar said, wiping her lips on a paper napkin. "Apparently, everyone sort of froze and waited for Maureen to explain but, and I am quoting Wells, here, 'Maureen just sat there basking in the glow of attention and sympathy.'"

"Okay. Give me a minute..." I muttered as my initial interview with Maureen flashed into my head.

I remembered how bad I felt for her, having lost her daughter to a murderer. For some odd reason I kept thinking that there had to be some reason for her to be acting so... out of sorts. Then I thought about Harvel Brady. He was a drug addict and a violent man. And then my thoughts switched back to Maureen again. Had Brady abused her daughter when she was a child and the story she told in class that night was her way of unloading? I didn't know, and I couldn't wrap my head around it. Maureen was a grieving mother... but a night school class on screenwriting?

"Okay," I said. "What else?"

"That's not even the best part, Kate," Robar said, looking down at her own notes. "The class project was to write and perfect one screenplay that could be submitted to a production company for consideration. You'll never believe what Maureen's plot was about."

"Are you sure you want to make that bet?" I said over the rim of my coffee cup. "What happened next? There's more to it than that, surely?"

"There is indeed," Janet said as she opened her briefcase, took out a sheaf of paper clipped together at one corner.

"She gave us this," Janet said as she handed it to me. "It's a copy of Maureen's screenplay."

I took it from her and glanced at the title page, and I shuddered when I read the title.

"*Why Would Anyone Kill Her?* That's the name of her screenplay?" I took a sip of coffee and then flipped through the pages to the end.

"I already checked, Captain," Robar said. "She left it as a cold case. But get this, the daughter... the victim was strangled to death by an unknown assailant who she'd met online," Robar said, nibbling on a fry. "The best bit, though—she paints the cops as a bunch of morons who do everything wrong and are crooked to boot."

"Of course, they are," I muttered, more to myself than to them.

"Wells also said that during class Maureen would talk about her daughter without ever naming her," Robar said. "At first, she, Paula, thought it was just a coping mechanism Maureen was using to shield herself from what had happened. But it wasn't that at all, was it, Janet?"

"No," Janet said, taking up the story. "Paula said Maureen would talk about her daughter, saying that she didn't have good judgment where men were concerned and that she had questionable friends. It's not exactly the way you'd think a mother would talk about her deceased daughter."

I flipped through the manuscript seeing the words but not really reading them. The few sentences I read came across as stiff and childish. If she was hoping to land a television deal, I had a feeling it wasn't going to cut it.

"Then, she started talking to the other students," Janet continued. "One kid was writing a police procedural and Maureen told the class he'd gotten his facts wrong, that Medical Examiners only check a body for drugs if the family gives the okay, which is not true. She also said that Maureen was mean, and critical of the other students' work, and made snide remarks."

By the end of the interview, Paula Wells had painted a strange portrait of Maureen Lawson. A scene from an old movie popped into my head: the image of Dorian Grey growing uglier and uglier by the day.

"Did Wells mention anything about a brother?" I asked.

They shook their heads.

That struck me as strange. The only person ever to mention that Harvel Brady was Maureen Lawson's brother was her estranged ex-husband, who claimed the two were eerily close.

"All right," I said. "We've more than enough to chew on. I'm under orders. I've got to go home. I'm going to take a hot bath, drink a bottle of wine and try to think this thing through. In the meantime, you guys write up your reports. Hawk is at the hospital with Brady, and Jack is still dissecting Nicolette's computer." I took a deep breath. "We'll get together in my office tomorrow morning; nine o'clock sharp." And I left them to it.

When I left the girls, I had every intention of doing as I was told and go home, but a part of me wanted desperately to go visit Brady in the hospital. But to do that I'd have to break my promise to the Chief and risk getting Hawk into trouble. But I wanted to find out what his reaction would be if we brought his sister into the equation. So, instead of going to the hospital, I called Hawk.

"You are supposed to be at home," Hawk said, clicking his tongue.

"Yes, well, I'm not," I said. "Not yet, anyway. Look, I want you to ask Harvel about his sister Maureen Lawson. Tell him that we already know everything."

"Do we?" Hawk asked.

"No, we don't have a clue," I replied. "But maybe he has an ax to grind now that she's left him to take the fall."

"You think they're in it together?"

"No... Yes... No, Hawk, I don't know what to think. So see if you can screw something, anything, out of him."

"Okay, Cap. I'll give it my best shot. I'll call you when I get done."

"Sounds good. I'll be at home, sipping on a glass of red."

"That sounds like a stellar plan, Captain. I'll be in touch."

I smirked as I hung up, put the car in drive and headed home. Hawk was a good detective. If anyone could get Brady to talk, he could. I had a feeling that Brady might be planning to escape. And I didn't give a damn. That jerk had caused me enough grief. But as it turned out, after a left and a right and another left and driving a few miles out of my way, I somehow found myself in Maureen Lawson's neighborhood. That being so, I thought I might as well pay her a visit. Since it was on the way home.

Sorry, Chief.

22

There were several cars in the driveway when I arrived at Maureen's house, which was something of a surprise. Not only that, but it also looked like every light in the house was on and I could hear music coming from inside.

So much for the grieving period, I thought as I parked on the street in front of the house. I didn't get out of the car, not right away. Instead I sat for a few minutes watching the house. As far as I could tell, there was nothing untoward going on. Nothing really suspicious except that... Maureen's stepdaughter had been murdered just a few days ago. Hosting a party that soon didn't seem like normal behavior to me.

Technically, I was off duty... and I was thirsty. *I could use a cold drink.*

So, I got out of the car, left my iPad behind and walked to the front door. I didn't knock, not right away. Instead I stood there for a moment, listening. There seemed to be a lot of chatter and the music was much louder, the kind of music they play in the background in trendy bars where a half-way decent wine costs twenty dollars, by the glass. I shook my head and rang the doorbell. I heard a male voice call for Maureen.

"Someone's at the door," the mysterious voice called. "Is it the party favors, d'you think?"

"Shh. We don't want to have to share with the whole neighborhood," I heard Maureen reply, and then she started giggling. When she opened the door and saw me standing there, though, she gave me a look like she'd just stepped in a pile of excrement.

Me? I smiled sweetly at her of course, and said, "Maureen. I do hope I'm not interrupting anything," I lied. I was absolutely hoping I'd interrupted something and, from the look on her face, I had.

She was wearing a spaghetti-strapped top with a pair of cropped pants that were just a little more than snug around her hips and strappy sandals.

She squinted at me, her eyes narrowed until they became little more than slits, and she clamped her lips together. For a moment she was speechless. I continued to smile at her.

"Captain Gazzara," she said, looked over her shoulder toward her guests then back at me. "Why are you here?"

She was holding a small dog under one arm while she smoothed the hair on the nape of her neck with the other.

"I was passing and... well, I just wanted to talk to you for a minute." Another lie. The fact is, I didn't know what had brought me to her door. Some might call it intuition. Then again, the fact that her brother Harvel had decided to lie his way out of holding and into the hospital and ruin my day might have had something to do with it.

"Really? About what?" she asked as if there were nothing between her ears but air.

"About your daughter's death, of course," I replied. "May I come in?"

"Well, I'm in the middle of—"

"Of a party. I can see that," I said, stepping over the threshold and pushing past her into the foyer. There was a faint smell of marijuana in the air but nothing I'd ever bust anyone for. The music continued to play but the chatter had almost ceased, though I did hear a couple of whispers and shushes as everyone turned to look in our direction.

"No!" she snapped at me. "It's not a party. Well, it is a party, but it's really a celebration of my daughter's life. Just a few of my closest friends. We've come together to reminisce about Nicolette's life," Maureen said, and a calmness settled over her face. She must have been pretty proud of herself for thinking that one up so quickly.

"That sounds like a perfectly normal thing to do," I replied as I studied the group of revelers. It wasn't the classiest looking group I'd ever seen. Although everyone was around the same age as Maureen, they all looked kind of cheap, thrown together in a hurry. *I wonder if she picked them up at a local bar.*

"Well, umm, it's what Nicolette would have wanted. She told me that if ever she died, she wanted me to have a party, like the Irish do, and try not to cry. In fact, she even suggested that I take a trip somewhere. But then," she said coyly, looking up at me through her over-long fake eyelashes, "that's the kind of girl she was. She never wanted anyone to be sad." Maureen sniffled, but her eyes were dry; she was putting me on.

"And will you be taking a trip, Maureen?" I asked, frowning at her.

"Uh, I was considering it, you know, to honor her last wishes," Maureen said. "I thought I might possibly go on a cruise to somewhere nice."

I nodded, trying not to look surprised by what I was hearing. It was the strangest and most bizarre tale I'd heard in a long time.

"Sure," I said. "That's what most normal people do when tragedy strikes." Yes, I was being sarcastic, and she caught it.

"I don't quite understand that remark, Captain Gazzara, but if it means what I think it does, I don't like what you are insinuating."

"I'm not insinuating anything," I replied, smiling innocently. "I just wanted to stop by and make sure you were doing all right and give you an update on the case. Would you be able to step away from your guests for a minute?"

"If... it's just for a minute," Maureen said and then she stepped outside onto the front stoop.

Now I'm no dummy. I was about to get the bum's rush and I knew it, but I followed her out onto the porch anyway.

It was quite dark outside, but I could see a head of dark clouds rolling our way.

"Looks like we might be in for a storm," I said pleasantly.

"Will you please get on with it?" she said. "Will you please tell me what this is all about? What have you found out about my daughter's case?" Maureen asked, suddenly morphing into a concerned mother, kneading her fingers and clutching at her throat.

"We arrested Harvel Brady today for Nicolette's murder," I said, carefully watching Maureen's eyes as she froze. Her mouth dropped open and she began to make a tiny mewing sound.

"And there's more, I'm afraid," I said gently, still watching her eyes. "I'm sorry I didn't tell you before, Maureen, but your daughter was sexually assaulted post mortem... that means after her death. We were able to match Harvel's DNA," I lied.

"What?" She gasped. "*What?*" she shrieked.

The door opened and a man stuck his head out and asked if everything was all right.

"Yes, of course it is," she snapped as she pushed him back inside and closed the door.

"I thought you'd already been through too much and I didn't want to add to your burden... and your grief," I said gently. Though inwardly I was smiling like a loon.

"Fortunately," I continued, "Nicolette didn't suffer that additional humiliation. She had already passed," I continued, thinking what a stroke of luck it was that I'd decided to withhold that bit of information. Maureen's response was... expected.

"She was raped *after* she was dead?" she asked quietly. Her entire attitude had changed. The funny thing was she'd looked more disgusted when she first opened the door and saw me standing there than she did on hearing the news that her daughter had been heinously violated after death.

"I understand that Harvel Brady is your brother, Maureen. So my question is, why didn't you tell us about him when you first came to the station or when we first visited you here in your home?"

I'd barely gotten the words out of my mouth when there was a rumble of thunder off in the distance. A portent of things to come? Maybe, and didn't think I could have planned a more intimidating setting. I was grateful for it.

"Well, it's simple enough," she huffed. "I haven't seen Harvel in years," she said quickly, a little too quickly. "We don't get along. We never have... Detective, my brother is a drug addict. He also has a very bad temper. If he knew that I was even talking to you, well, I think I'd be seeing Nicolette a lot sooner."

That, I thought, *is an interesting choice of words.*

I didn't interrupt. I wanted to hear what else she had to say. So I tilted my head slightly to one side and raised my eyebrows wide, a silent question.

"My brother also mixes with a very rough crowd. Very rough. As I said, I don't have anything to do with him. He's into all sorts of drugs. I really do believe he might be capable of murder."

I couldn't believe what I was hearing. She was throwing her brother under the bus.

"Do you think he killed your daughter?" I asked.

"Are you serious, Detective. You just told me his DNA was found inside her. That would make it pretty open and shut, don't you think?"

I did think, but at that moment I didn't know if it was his DNA on her blouse or not, and I sure as hell didn't know what to think about the way she was acting... and talking.

"Maureen, I'm sorry, but that's not good enough. You knew

where your daughter had been found. She was in her car outside the Tomahawk Trailer Park, where your brother stays, and you didn't think to tell us that you even had a brother, much less that he lives in the trailer park. As you say, he has a police record and is known to be violent. So, I hope you can understand how I might find that a strange omission," I said, feeling the cooler air rush across the back of my neck as the dark, rain-filled clouds quickly approached.

"I'm going to tell you something, Captain Gazzara. Until you walk a mile in my shoes, don't you dare judge me," Maureen hissed. "Most of the time, I was afraid for my life. And Nicolette was not the little angel everybody thinks she was. She had a... a reckless side. She was not much different from Harvel in many respects. But if I was to confront him and ask if he'd done anything to my daughter, you'd be looking for my body, too. And from the way you're handling Nicolette's case, the chances that anyone would ever find it seems less than likely."

What the hell is she talking about? I didn't understand a word of it.

"That's something you won't have to worry about, Maureen," I said, struggling to stay cool. "Harvel's in police custody right now. Actually, he's in the hospital. He suffered some kind of episode at the police department," I said, hoping to get some kind of reaction from Maureen.

She stared at me but said nothing. Her attitude seemed to have hardened, her lips were drawn tightly together and her face, now in shadow, looked like something out of a horror movie.

"A member of my team is posted outside his room," I said. "He's to be released in the morning and will be heading straight back to jail under escort. You've nothing to worry about... Maureen, didn't you think that your brother could be Nicolette's killer?"

"It crossed my mind. You said you had his DNA. Isn't that enough?"

"It's enough to prove he was with her, but it's not proof that he killed her."

That was sad but true. Then again, I knew that any reasonable jury would convict the man for murder because the chances of Harvel having killed Nicolette, and raping her after she died, were better than a bet that the sun would rise in the morning. But I didn't think Maureen knew that and, call me crazy if you like, her behavior was damn suspicious.

"Like I said, Captain," she said, "I haven't spoken to my brother in ages. I don't want to be mixed up with the likes of him. You've got your man. Anything he says, any word that comes out of his mouth, will be a lie. He hallucinates from the drugs he takes and then thinks he sees and knows things, but it's all a figment of his imagination. His brain is fried, not that he was ever that smart, not even when he was a child." She folded her arms and closed her mouth, tight.

I got the message: the conversation was over.

"Just one more question, Maureen," I started to say, but she cut me off.

"I'm sorry, Captain Gazzara, but I'm going inside before it starts to rain. My guests are waiting, and I think I've been more than accommodating. I've answered your questions. Goodbye, Captain." And, without another word Maureen Lawson whirled around with her dog still under her arm and went back into the house, slamming the door closed behind her.

Me? I stood for a moment, listening, trying to hear what was going on inside. All was quiet for a few moments. The music continued. But then, as if nothing had happened, the conversation picked up again... just as the rain started to fall.

I jogged back to my car. I'd barely closed the car door when it really started coming down. It became a gully washer, but I didn't mind. Driving in the rain didn't bother me at all. Yes, I was forced to slow down some, but the sound of the raindrops hammering on the roof of my car was soothing, in a way.

I let my thoughts roam free inside my head. There was no doubt that Maureen was acting strangely. But that, in and of itself, didn't mean a whole lot. Maybe she didn't care that her daughter was dead. Maybe she was glad. Who knows? If so, it wasn't a crime. Horrible and cruel, yes. But not a crime.

When I finally made it to my apartment, I was thrilled to close the door and lock it. Before I took off my shoes, I grabbed the bottle of wine from the fridge, pulled the cork and took a swig. Not at all ladylike, I know. But who was there to care? Hell, I felt entitled. I kicked off my shoes, stripped off my clothes and slung them on the bed, went back to the kitchen, grabbed a glass from the cupboard, filled it almost to the brim, then flopped down on the couch in my underwear. I put on the television, found some stupid sci-fi show that I had no idea what was going on and let the world melt around me.

It was like I turned my brain off, and it felt good. I needed to recharge the little gray cells and then take the time to look at the new information I'd gathered with fresh eyes and a clean brain, which meant I'd wait until the next morning. I'd go for a run, have a nice big cup of steaming black coffee and then pick Maureen Lawson apart. For now, though, I had to let the batteries recharge. I sipped at my wine almost continuously, enjoying every milliliter until the glass was empty, then I lay my head back against the couch, closed my eyes and, just as the wine was beginning to do its job and I was feeling warm and fuzzy all over, the buzzer to my downstairs door snapped me wide awake.

"Hello?" I said into the little box on the wall next to my kitchen door.

"Hey, it's me. Can I come in out of the rain?" It was Dorman.

"Sure." I smiled and didn't bother to get dressed. Instead, I buzzed him in, poured another glass of wine for me and one for him and waited. And boy was he worth waiting for.

23

Dorman left at eight the following morning, and I was late; no time for a run, but who cares? The workout I did get more than made up for it.

So, I went to work that morning feeling refreshed and ready to tear into my case and get it wrapped up nice and tight. Of course, I should have known that something would go wrong. Doesn't it always?

The rain had continued through the night and was still bucketing down as I drove to the PD that day. So when I walked in through the rear doors to find Jack waiting for me with some surprising information, I wasn't sure whether to be pleased or apprehensive. As it turned out, it was the latter.

I opened my office door and he followed me inside, with a coffee mug in his hand, and sat down on the chair in front of my desk.

"I've dug as deep as I can go in Nicolette's computer," he said as I busied myself behind my desk.

Actually, I was trying to get my act together: purse, laptop, iPad, phone, desktop...

"And?" I asked.

He took his notebook from his breast pocket, leaned back, crossed his right ankle over his knee and took a deep breath. "Before I tell you this, I did double and triple check my information to make sure I'd gotten it straight because it wasn't making any sense."

I blinked at him, indicating he needed to get to the point and be quick about it.

"I thought it was kind of weird that as soon as Nicolette had gotten an invitation from a man on the website our friend Pete McGee showed up," Jack said. "Not only was the guy pushy, but it all seemed just a little too convenient. So, I called in a couple of favors from a techie I know who owes me for a surveillance gig I did for him on his girlfriend. Or should I say ex-girlfriend—"

"Is this one of the minor indiscretions that got you assigned to me?" I asked.

"No. But if I were you, I'd forget I told you... just in case." He looked at me warily.

I rolled my eyes. "Continue."

"So, my friend jumped in and was able to show me a few neat tricks."

Jack went on to describe how they were able to trace the unique IP number of the computer that was communicating with Nicolette's.

Could this be the confirmation I needed to prove Harvel Brady set Nicolette up with the intent to kill her?

"And let me guess. It led to Tomahawk Trailer Park." I smirked.

"Yes and no," Jack replied, making me frown.

"What the hell does that mean?"

"Captain, the correspondence from McGee to Nicolette came from the same address as Nicolette's computer," Jack said.

"I don't understand what you are saying. She sent them to herself?" I asked, totally confused.

"No. Not at all. Whoever this "Pete" was—we know it wasn't

the real Pete McGee because he was on the road—he was in Nicolette's house on another computer," Jack said and leaned back in his chair and looked at me expectantly.

I must have looked completely dumbfounded because he unfolded his arms, leaned forward and continued to explain.

"Did you ever see the old movie *When A Stranger Calls*? It's about a babysitter who keeps getting these creepy calls to check the children she's babysitting. So, she freaks out and calls the cops and they say they'll trace the caller."

"Because that happens all the time," I replied.

"Right. Well, the twist in the movie was that the calls were coming from inside the house all along, and the killer was right there the whole time, in the house."

"Now, I talked to Maureen just last night and she said she hadn't seen her brother in a long time," I replied. "And that she was scared of the man. So I don't get it... Could it be that she was lying?"

"Well now, Captain," Jack said. "You know how people always tell the truth when they talk to the police. Nah, she couldn't be lying."

I shook my head and smirked. I knew Jack was pulling my chain. The people we talk to rarely, if ever, tell the truth, even when they've nothing to hide.

"So, what did you mean when you said yes and no about it leading to Brady at the trailer park? Sounds like no to me, that it didn't lead to him at all."

He shrugged and said, "Well yes, I suppose... if he wasn't at Maureen Lawson's house, but we don't know for sure that he wasn't, do we? You only have her word for it that she hasn't seen him. And we still have the phone record. That puts him in the vicinity of the trailer park at the time of Nicolette's death."

"No, it puts Pete McGee's phone in the vicinity of the trailer park. And that means absolutely nothing unless we can get a confession from Brady. And that's not going to happen." I shook my head.

"I'm betting Brady stole it," Jack said.

"Maybe he did, but that's not enough to charge him with killing her. Even if the substance Doc found on her blouse gives us a DNA match, that doesn't mean he killed her, or even raped her after death. Hell, he used a condom. He could have found her body and seen an opportunity and took it... But see, this business with the computer messages coming from inside Nicolette's house... If it wasn't Brady, then that means there's only one other person it could have been, her mother."

But does it? I thought. *What about the people in her house last night? Any one of them could.... Oh hell, that's all I need.*

"We need to look at Maureen's computer," Jack said.

I grinned at him, then said, "Oh, this is going to be fun. Let's go."

And I really did believe it was going to be fun, visiting Maureen Lawson for the second time in eighteen hours.

It didn't take long for us to drive to Maureen's house. The cars from the previous evening were all gone and the place looked undisturbed and tranquil in the morning light; that is until we stepped up onto the front porch where we found a half-dozen stamped out cigarette butts and several plastic cups lying around and in the flower pots.

I rang the doorbell and took a step back. Jack went back down the steps and watched the windows.

There was no answer. I rang the doorbell again and knocked on the door. After waiting a few minutes, I pressed my ear against the hardwood door. There was someone inside shuffling around, but no one came to the door.

"I think we are being ignored," I whispered quietly to Jack.

"Can we get a search warrant?" he asked.

"Oh, I think there might be a way for us to do that," I said as I felt that uneasy feeling growing in the pit of my stomach.

24

Every cop knows a judge who will walk the fence, at least to some extent, and be a little lenient when it comes to issuing search warrants. Some of them, though, are so by the book they could be accused of plagiarism every time they cited a reason for not issuing the warrant; the reasoning was so word-for-word exact. Others would carefully consider the facts and judge each case on its merit. And then there were judges like Mickey O'Donnell.

I'd known Judge O'Donnell since he first made a pass at me at a Christmas party when I was still a beat cop. It never hurt to have a judge as a friend, so when he made a pass at me again a couple of weeks later at the New Year's Eve party, I reminded him that he'd done it before and that it was a no-no.

When I was promoted to detective and there was a retirement party at a local watering hole for the outgoing detective, Judge O'Donnell was there, and once again he propositioned me... Only this time he offered cash.

I know. Sexual harassment. Blah, blah, blah. The truth was the old boy's harmless and it never bothered me all that much. And he was so drunk I got a buzz off his breath. And it was never malicious, not the way it was with Henry Finkle... but that's another story, and one I've told many times before. And besides, it never hurt to have a trick up your sleeve for when you needed something a little... shall we say, off the wall? So, whenever I needed a quickie warrant and didn't want to wait for the wheels of justice to slowly creak to a decision, I headed over to Judge O'Donnell's chambers. And so that's where we went.

Judge O'Donnell had a good heart. Sure, he was a horny old man. The only difference between him and the rest of the judges, lawyers, bailiffs, stenographers, janitors and anyone else in the courthouse was that he took no for an answer and never laid a hand on anyone. His secretary had been with him since the earth cooled and she'd never complained, not even once.

"Knock, knock," I said, poking my head around the door jamb—the door was open.

"If it isn't my favorite detective," Judge O'Donnell said, smiling broadly. "Do come in, my dear. Sit down, sit down. What can I do for you?"

"Hi, Judge. Do you have a minute?" I asked.

"For you, I have all morning."

I looked at my watch. It was ten after ten. *Surely he can't be drinking already... can he?*

I stepped inside. Jack followed. As soon as the Judge saw him, his attitude did a one-eighty and he frowned.

"Who are you?" he barked.

"This is Detective Jack North," I said as Jack stood politely just inside the door. "He's new to my team. We're currently working on a murder case and need—"

"Wait outside!" Judge O'Donnell shouted.

"What?" Jack snapped back.

"You heard me! Wait outside!" the judge hollered again.

I looked at Jack and shrugged. He went outside and shut the door behind him. Judge O'Donnell's face changed from a scowl to the most angelic smile. I could tell that in his younger days when he had all his hair and his real teeth, he must have been a real charmer.

"Now that we are alone..." he said practically purring.

"I need a favor, Judge," I said, shaking my head.

"Oh, you do? Detective Gazzara, you've always been my favorite, you know that," he said as he scooted in behind his huge oak desk and folded his hands in front of him.

"Really? I had no idea," I joked.

"What is it you want?" He narrowed his eyes at me and looked me up and down.

So, I took a deep breath and told him about Nicolette's case.

"I saw that on television. Terrible case. I'm glad you're on it, Detective. So, you need a warrant?" He pulled a pen from a bouquet of pens and pencils in front of him.

I handed him the paperwork Jack had drawn up quickly, probably too quickly, I was sure, and I hoped it was free from typos.

"Thanks, Judge." I smiled.

"Now you owe me, Detective," he said as he signed the warrant and handed it back to me. "And I'll be collecting sooner rather than later."

"Judge, I've never once uttered a word about your little advances. Doesn't that prove my dedication to you?" I said, playing the game. "Come on. Any other female cop would have run to Internal Affairs and you know it. But not me."

"Why is that, Kate?" he asked.

"I'm a sucker for a handsome face, Judge," I lied. The old man in the black robe smiled like a boy who just stumbled across a stack of porno magazines in an alley.

"You're my kind of woman, Kate. Come on. Let's make a plan to meet and throw caution to the wind. I know the staff at the Moxy Hotel. Very discreet. Very accommodating." He winked. "They let me use their private elevator, you know."

"That's a tempting offer, Judge. But I've got to serve this search warrant. I need this lady's computer before she scrubs it," I said, and this time I was telling the truth.

"That's the problem with you young women today. A man offers to provide you with a pampered life in exchange for a little roll in the hay and you put your careers first. What a sick and twisted world we live in." He sighed.

"I couldn't agree more," I said, playing along. "But I'll make you a promise, Judge." His eyes lit up. "I'll meet you under the mistletoe at this year's Christmas party. And I'll make sure we are next to each other at the stroke of midnight on New Year's Eve."

"You tease," he purred.

"You bring out the worst in me, Judge. Thanks for this," I said as I stood and waved the warrant.

"Until next time, my dear," he said.

And I left, feeling his eyes all over my backside. I knew he'd have forgotten my promise by the time happy hour rolled around, so, in my book there was no harm and no foul. You can think whatever you like.

I stepped out into the hallway and closed the door behind me. Jack was leaning against the wall opposite, his arms folded across his chest, looking at me suspiciously.

"What happened in there?" he asked as he walked across the hallway toward me, his hands now stuffed deep in his pockets and his eyes full of suspicion.

"I got the search warrant. Let's get some uniforms, just for show," I said.

"Cap, what did you have to do to get that?" Jack asked.

"Are you frickin' serious?" I asked. "Nothing! I get along with that old man, that's all."

Jack looked like I'd just slapped him across the face with a cold fish. I couldn't help but chuckle. I don't know if Jack thought I'd really done something to appease the old pervert in black robes or if he knew deep down that I didn't, but still I wondered.

"Look, Judge O'Donnell likes the ladies. Sometimes you do

better with sugar than with vinegar. Besides, he's harmless. If I actually took him up on one of his offers, I think the old goat would have a heart attack on the spot," I said as we hurried to the car.

Jack radioed in for a blue and white and two uniforms to meet us at Maureen's house. I could tell that he wasn't too sure about my methods, but so what? I'm a big girl, and for a guy who'd gotten himself into as much trouble as he had, so much trouble it had gotten him assigned to my team as a last resort to save his career... Well, at that moment he was behaving like a rookie... And then I got it: *Geez, he's freakin' jealous.* And at that thought, I chuckled out loud.

"What?" he asked as I put the car in drive and stepped on the gas.

"Not a thing, Jack. Not a thing."

25

Ten minutes later I pulled my unmarked cruiser into Maureen Lawson's driveway and parked behind her Lexus. This time, though, she was waiting for us. Well, maybe not. Maybe she just saw us arrive. Whatever, she opened the door before we even stepped up onto the porch, and she had a scowl on her face.

"Not again," she snapped. "What d'you want this time?"

She was no longer wearing the strappy blouse and tight-fitting slacks. Instead, she was wearing yoga pants and a baggy T-shirt. Her feet were bare, and her makeup was a mess: there were still little clumps caked around her eyes which were surprisingly bright; thanks probably to eye drops or perhaps the effects of too much hooch.

"I have a search warrant," I said, waving it in front of her nose as I pushed past her into the house.

The place was clean and tidy, but there was a definite smell of marijuana in the air. I walked through the living room into the kitchen, looking around as I went. I spotted what was left of two joints in an ashtray on the coffee table, and a half-dozen empty beer bottles in the trash can.

"Captain Gazzara, this is harassment," she said, standing in the kitchen doorway with her hands on her hips. "I'm going to call your Chief and tell him what you are doing."

"You're going to call Chief Johnston and tell him I'm doing my job?" I replied, waving the warrant at her. "Good. It's about time someone had something positive to say about the police. I have a warrant to seize any and all of your computers, tablets, cell phones and any other electronic devices you own."

"You can't take those things. I need them for work." She nearly screamed. Maureen's face went from red to white and she pushed her hands straight down by her sides and clenched them into fists. For a minute, I was sure she was going to throw herself down on the ground again and start kicking and screaming.

"I'm afraid we can. Don't worry. We'll return them as soon as we're finished with them," I replied. "If you wouldn't mind, please tell the officers where they are so they won't have to tear your nice home apart."

Just then there was a ruckus upstairs and suddenly a man appeared at the top of the stairs. He was wearing nothing but blue jeans—still unbuttoned at the waist—and then he came running down the stairs. He had long dreadlocks, but his skin was as pale as a corpse.

We all drew our weapons and stepped back

"Police! Freeze," Jack shouted.

The man staggered to a halt at the bottom of the stairs, his eyes wide, his hands up as far as they would go.

"The stuff's not mine! It's hers!" he yelled.

"Oh, shut up, Sean!" Maureen shouted.

"Wow. He's a keeper," I said.

Maureen shot me a look that would have killed a lesser person.

"Come on into the kitchen, junior," I said. "Take a seat for me." I waved my Glock at him and, with his hands still in the air, his feet bare and his pants just barely defying gravity, he did exactly as he was told. I figured he was less than half her age.

"This is too much," Maureen snapped, but she did tell the uniformed officers where they could find her laptop, iPad and cell phone.

Jack stayed in the kitchen with the lovebirds while I toured the house.

I found some evidence of drug use, but not enough to make a bust. I figured most of the narcotics were already swimming around inside Maureen and Dreadlock-man's systems. The master bathroom smelled like the alley behind the Clover Bar where we'd apprehended Harvel Brady.

I went to Nicolette's room. One of the uniformed officers was already there making sure we had everything we needed. He left me, and I stood there for a moment looking around. It had been tidied since Robar's visit. It was a nice room and typical for a young woman. There was a stack of pictures on the dresser which, I assumed, noting the creases at the corners, had once been tucked between the frame and glass of the dresser mirror. Most were of a smiling Nicolette. Some were of her with girlfriends. None had males in them.

I turned to head back downstairs, but then I had a thought and stopped. The bed was unmade. I knew the uniforms had already searched the room, but I somehow knew it wasn't them that had disturbed the bed.

I stepped over to the closet and opened the doors; Nicolette's clothes were gone. I peeked inside her dresser drawers. Her clothes were still there, all neatly folded and properly organized. I looked again at the unmade bed. Something was out of whack and I thought I knew what it was; it had been slept in... and recently.

I went back downstairs and into the kitchen.

"Maureen, was Nicolette a neat person?" I asked.

"What?" she snapped as the frustration of Jack's presence

keeping her from whispering instructions to Dreadlock-man bubbled to the surface.

"Your daughter. Was she neat? Organized?" I asked again.

"Yes. She had a place for everything and everything in its place," Maureen said, snarkily.

"Have you made any changes to her room since her death?" I asked.

"I gave away some of her clothes. I took down her pictures. But that's all. I just can't bring myself to do anything else." Maureen sniffled.

I wanted to slap her.

"Who slept in her bed?" I asked.

"What?" Maureen looked confused.

"Someone slept in her bed. Who was it?"

"Oh, that would be me. I slept in there," Dreadlock-man said.

"Shut up, Sean!" Maureen swatted at the man with her hand, but he dodged it.

"Hey," Jack said sharply. "Knock it off, or I'll cuff you."

"You wouldn't dare!" she hissed.

"Ms. Lawson," Jack said, softly, "if you don't calm down right now, I *will* cuff you and put you in the back of that blue and white cruiser, for your own safety and mine."

She got the message. The idea of the neighbors seeing her perp-walked to the car was too much for her. She bit her lip, glared at us, but said nothing.

"So, you slept in her daughter's room?" I asked Sean, but I was looking at Maureen.

"I didn't know he was in there!" Maureen's voice was loud. "He's a left-over from our get-together last night."

"I didn't think you'd mind since we'd slept in it before," Sean said. "Look, I don't want any trouble. I just want to go home."

Jack asked where home was, took down his full name and then began to question him as Maureen sat helplessly by listening to him blather on. He didn't have much to tell us; nothing we didn't already know... except for one small detail: he and Maureen did more than just sleep in her daughter's room and not just once. My stomach flipped as the images of the two of them writhing together in her bed floated unwanted into my head. There was no way I could hide my look of disgust.

It was then that one of the officers wearing blue latex gloves appeared with the laptop and iPad in plastic bags and not just one but two cell phones.

I looked at the officer and said, "That it? You're sure there are no more devices?"

"Yes, ma'am. If there are any more, they're well hidden."

"Okay," I said. "Jack, have him sign the evidence log and give her a receipt. Then you can leave, officer..." I looked at his tag. "Malone."

He and Jack completed the paperwork, and Jack handed them off to me.

"Thank you, Malone."

"Thank you, ma'am." And with that, the two of them left.

I looked at Maureen. She glared back at me.

"You bitch," she said. "I'll have your job for this. How am I supposed to work without my laptop?"

I didn't answer. Instead, I said, "Two cell phones? Why do you have two?"

"Is it against the law to have two cell phones?" she asked with a huff. "One is for business. The other is personal. I really don't believe what's happening here. While the man who killed my daughter is still out there, you are here harassing me."

Sean sat there quietly as if he thought if he didn't move, no one would notice him.

"That's not quite true," I said. "The man we think killed your daughter is in custody. I told you that last night, remember?"

Maureen stared at me, her eyes wide. Her lips moved slightly, but she said nothing.

"You do remember me dropping in, don't you, Maureen? I'd say your little party must have been a smashing success... Wasn't it, Maureen?"

She didn't answer.

"How about you, Sean? I know you had a good time... Might want to get yourself tested though. God only knows who else she's been with."

He didn't answer either. He just sat there, mute, head down staring at his feet.

Maureen bit her lip then said, "You've got what you came for. I think it's time for you to leave."

"Maureen, we'll get these back to you as soon as we can," I said, rising to my feet. "Thank you for your help. We really appreciate it."

I barely got the words out before she jumped to her feet and stomped past me out of the kitchen and up the stairs.

I smiled and looked at Jack, "She's right. It's time we weren't here. Grab the swag and let's get out of this hellhole." And we did.

We slowly walked the few yards back to my car and then I stood for a minute by the driver's side door and said, "How long do you think it will take?"

"That depends on how tough her security is," Jack said. "I don't see her being any kind of tech-savvy genius. The phones won't be a problem. They're both Androids so I can use Ducky again. That's if she even has a passcode. If she does, we're talking hours. Do you want me to do the phones or computer first?"

"Whatever is easiest, quickest. You call the shots on this stuff. It's all Greek to me," I replied. "By the way, are they both turned on?"

"One is, why?"

"I think you'll find the one that's turned off belongs to Pete McGee."

He made one of those faces, his mouth turned down at the corners, stared at the bags containing the phones and nodded, "I think maybe you're right. I wouldn't bet against it."

I nodded and said, "Let's get out of here."

"What about me?" Sean asked.

He was standing at the curb, properly dressed, if you could call it that.

"You're free to go, Sean. We'll call you if we need you again," Jack said through the car window as I backed out of the drive.

Sean was a big boy. He'd find his way home.

26

Jack grinned happily as he exited the car at the PD carrying the goodies we'd retrieved from Maureen Lawson. It was nice to see him in his element and enjoying himself. He hurried away to the forensics labs like a kid with a new toy.

Me? I took the elevator to the situation room where I found Janet and Robar at their desks. Hawk, so Robar said, was on his way back with Harvel Brady. I took a seat on the edge of her desk.

I could hardly wait. I wanted to know if the guy cracked between here and the hospital. If anyone could get him to talk, it would be Hawk. He wore his years of experience well, did Hawk. He could be a hard-ass, and if a perp wanted to play games during an interview, he knew how to handle them. But it was when Hawk spoke to the perps like real people that he got them to talk. And he was alone, one-on-one with Brady for the entire ride back to the PD.

Brady though? I didn't know. I had a feeling he would be the exception.

Hawk did have one thing going for him, though. He knew what

Brady had done to Nicolette after death. There might be a chance he'd talk if Hawk offered him some sort of deal.

The prisoner code has been glamorized by Hollywood, but most of what you hear is true. The pecking order inside is very real and important to the inmates. They even have a moral code. Child abusers and necrophiliacs are in for a world of hurt. Hawk would lay it out for him, tell him the truth, offer him a deal that might just save him from being castrated with a dull knife. Oh yes, I was hopeful, but again, this was Harvel Brady.

Hawk appeared some thirty minutes later after having secured the prisoner in a holding cell.

When I saw him exit the elevator, I could tell immediately by the look on his face that I was going to be disappointed.

"The guy had nothing to say to me," Hawk said as he rolled up a chair and sat down.

"Nothing at all? Not even when you mentioned his sister?" I clenched my jaw.

"Well... no! He just clammed up."

And then Hawk proceeded to tell me what had happened while Brady was in the hospital, and what a pain in the ass he'd been.

"He didn't know that I was stationed right outside his door," he said. "I heard him harassing the nurses and saying disgusting things to them, things you wouldn't want your mother to hear. Sheesh! Even though he was cuffed to the bed, he's still one slimy son of a bitch. Not someone those nurses should be exposed to. So, after I heard him tell the fourth nurse what he'd like to do to her and after she left as if the devil himself was after her, I decided to step in, and he didn't like it." Hawk smirked.

"What did you say to him?"

"Well, since he was cuffed to the bedrail, I grabbed his wrist and the rail and squeezed till his eyes popped. But since I couldn't beat the shit out of him, I explained that it wasn't smart to hassle the ladies who brought him his meds. The dumbass had never even thought of that. The guy's head's in bad shape; he talks like Rocky Balboa. The drugs must have turned his brain into mush a long time ago. It's like he has his basic instincts, but don't ask him to solve a crossword puzzle or give you directions."

Hawk might be a tough guy when he needs to be, but he's also smart and criminals don't expect that from him.

"So," Hawk continued, "I pulled up a chair and put on whatever sports was playing on television." He took a deep breath. "And what a surprise that was. Harvel knows his baseball, and we had quite a pleasant chat about that. He's a Cubs fan, you know."

"That's too bad," I said, smiling. "As if he doesn't have enough strikes against him." I'm a Braves fan.

"Right. Anyway, I played nice. I asked him how he was feeling. He said that we'd used brutality, unnecessary force when we arrested him, and he was going to sue us and have our jobs. I told him he wouldn't be the first to try it and go for it."

"Oh, that never gets old," I replied. And it doesn't. If I had a dime for every time a perp said that to me or one of my team members, I'd have been able to retire at thirty-five.

"Yeah, he told me he's got it all figured out. He's going to file a complaint against us for what we did to him. All the charges will be dropped and we'll be out of work while he'll be sitting on a mountain of money." Hawk looked up at me, his eyes dark, brooding.

I didn't reply. I had nothing to say. Actually, I did, I had a whole rant to say about it, but there wasn't time for me to vent to Hawk and call Harvel Brady all the names that were spinning around in my head.

It was a typical response from someone who was up to his eyeballs in heat and as dumb as Harvel. I let out a deep breath and motioned for Hawk to continue.

"So, I skipped all the formalities and asked him right out if there was anything he wanted to tell me about the night he spent with Nicolette. He didn't answer."

Hawk rubbed his hands together, then continued, "I didn't

think the usual method of smooth-talking him, offering him some sort of deal was going to work. So, I tried something else and I probably should apologize for what I did next."

"What did you do, Hawk?" The hair on the back of my neck instantly stood up. If he'd roughed up the suspect in the hospital, I was in a heap of trouble and was going to have to jump through a lot of hoops, and that was never fun. Even Judge O'Donnell wouldn't look the other way if someone from my team threatened or roughed up a perp *while in the hospital*. Even if the son of a bitch deserved it.

"Don't worry, Captain. I didn't lay a hand on him, but I sure as hell wanted too. I practiced restraint." Hawk smirked. "What I did ask him, conversationally, as if I was personally interested, was what it was like to take Nicolette after death. I got really graphic. I didn't hold back. You should have seen the look of shock on his face. He was embarrassed... No, not embarrassed. Humiliated. You remember those days when we were young and after a dozen beers and after last call, you thought you'd met the love of your life? Then when the sun comes up and you roll over only to discover the carriage turned back into a pumpkin?"

I had to laugh at his analogy.

"That, Hawk, never happened to me, but I get your drift," I replied.

"Yeah well, lucky you. It happened to me more than once. Anyway, I don't think Harvel knew what he was doing when he did what he did. Not that that lets him off the hook. I'm just saying, I think it was the drugs that made him do it. That in itself should have him begging to be locked up. If he mistakes a corpse for a willing participant in his lovemaking, something's seriously wrong with him. I tell you, Kate, by the look on his face he had a very different memory of what happened that night."

"Did he admit to anything?" I felt like I needed a shower to wash off the grime that came with Hawk's story.

"I told him that if he didn't have anything to do with Nicolette's death that he needed to tell me, and if he decided to keep quiet, he needed to remember that once a jury heard what he'd done to her body after she was already dead, they'd scream for the death penalty. And there was a damn good chance he'd get it. But the guy didn't even flinch." Hawk shook his head, unbelieving.

"Do you think he had understood what you were telling him?" I asked. "Because if as you say his brain is fried, he'd be found unfit to stand trial, for any of it."

"Oh yeah. He knew what he'd done. He just wasn't going to admit it," Hawk replied. "I don't think it's worth interrogating him again today. I'd let him stew overnight and then see if we can offer him some kind of bargaining chip."

I nodded, thoughtfully, digesting what Hawk had told me. We could let him stew, but I didn't think it would do any good: it sounded like the man was a moron. But I agreed to do it anyway.

It was at that point that Jack came knocking on my office door.

"The computer's been wiped," he said.

"What?" I stared at him, not wanting to believe what I was hearing.

"Wiped clean. Clean as a damn whistle. She knew we were coming and she scrubbed it."

What the hell? Jack was excited, but he didn't seem too upset. In fact, he had a devious smile on his face.

"I need to call in an expert, someone I know and—"

"Are they on the department payroll?" I asked firmly.

"No ma'am... but..." He looked at me then Hawk.

"This boy fits right in," Hawk muttered.

"Anyone I know?" I asked.

He slowly shook his head.

I just knew it was going to bite me in the ass, but what choice did I have?

"Okay. Do it, and do it fast," I ordered.

All we could do now was wait.

27

It was like the calm before the storm while we waited for Jack to tell us if he'd been able to get anything from Maureen's computer. In fact, it wasn't until the next day before we heard from him, but I'm getting ahead of myself.

Later that same afternoon, after he'd been put into holding for the night, Harvel Brady kept his word and filed a formal complaint about the treatment he'd received during his arrest and interrogation. Within an hour Internal Affairs came sniffing around.

Chief Johnston was so mad at me that he ignored all my calls and emails. Actually, he often did that, but this time I got the feeling that he was more angry than usual.

If only he knew how the case was shifting, I thought as I sat at my desk. *He might understand that not only did we need to turn up the heat on Brady, literally, but also that I have a hunch that this thing has roots that go deeper than just a simple homicide.*

"Captain?" Janet knocked on my door, interrupting my thoughts.

"Hey, come on in," I said. "I feel like I haven't seen you in a month. What's going on?"

"I'm not sure where to start," she said as she closed the door behind her and took a seat. Her usual stack of yellow pads was in her hands.

"This doesn't sound good," I said.

"I wouldn't say it isn't good, Cap. I think I discovered a motive." She wrinkled her face and shook her head slowly.

"Okay." I waited. "But?"

"I got a call from Kenny Percy. That's Nicolette's brother," Janet said. "He said he had something to tell me that his father didn't know. It seems that just before the divorce papers were served, things were difficult in the Percy house."

I watched Janet keep looking down at her notes. She was fidgeting as if hesitant to jump right in, and that wasn't like her. She rambled on about the arguments between Charles Percy and Maureen, the needling and the issues with money that Kenny had heard them fighting about.

Then Janet took a deep breath and said, "But it was what happened one day when Kenny came home early," Janet swallowed hard and shook her head.

"Spit it out, Detective," I said.

"Kenny said he walked into the house and immediately knew that something was wrong. Maureen's car was in the driveway, as usual. Nothing looked out of place inside the house. But then he noticed the smell. He said it was like the cheap incense you get in those bodegas by the bus stops."

I knew what she was talking about. It was what I smelled at Maureen's house the night before, mixed with the marijuana, a hint of cherry or strawberry mixed with the smoke. It induced a headache more than it did anything else. Head shops and meth dens smell like it too.

Janet went on to tell me that Kenny thought the smell was coming from the garage. His first thought was that something had caught on fire and was smoldering. But then he heard voices.

"He said he had never been so scared in his life. All he could think was that some homeless hobos had come into the house and were going to rob them or worse. So, he grabbed a knife from the kitchen and tiptoed up to the garage door. When he pressed his ear against the door, he realized that the people on the other side of the door were doing more than just talking." Janet took a deep breath.

"Did he know who was out there?" I asked.

"He said he heard Maureen and another man," Janet said.

"Well, I don't find it too hard to believe that she was having an affair. That doesn't really surprise me at all." I leaned back in my chair thinking how I needed another coffee.

"No," Janet said. "I guess Kenny didn't think so, either. But he didn't like the fact that she brought some stranger into his dad's house. Even if it was just the garage, so he opened the door."

And then Janet read from her notes—she has her own brand of shorthand—repeating exactly what Kenny had told her.

We kept all of the usual things people keep in their garages: bicycles, a lawn mower, lawn chairs and a wheelbarrow. Dad likes to do small projects so he also had a workbench. It was nothing special, just a long wooden table with a light hanging over the top. He had a toolbox at one end and a cardboard box with random pieces of sandpaper, PVC pipe, a jar of nuts and bolts and stuff like that at the other end. He used an old worn-out barstool as a seat sometimes.

I had the knife in my hand. I didn't know what I was going to do with it. I was sweating and scared, but I was angry more than anything else. And I'd had enough of Maureen stomping around the house muttering at me all the time. When my dad was home, she focused her attitude on him. It's one thing to fight because you don't love each other anymore, but she disrespected him, completely.

Anyway, I opened the door and the smell was much stronger. From where the door was there were three steps that led down to the garage floor where the workbench was.

I saw the needle first. Then the spoon with the brown stuff around the edges. I knew what that was. I'd seen it in the movies.

But I never imagined I'd see it in my own house. I don't know what was worse. Seeing that or what I saw next.

"*What did you see? I asked him,*" Janet said.

I saw Maureen. She was with the guy who we all knew was her brother, Harvel Brady, and they were... naked.

Janet looked at me as she set her notes down.

"Are you sure you heard him right?" I asked. "Are you sure you heard *that* name?" My mouth had gone completely dry.

"Oh yeah, that's definitely what he said, Harvel Brady. How could I make a mistake? But to be sure, I did a little digging with the information that came back on his saliva kit, his DNA. We already have his rap sheet, so I ran a full background check.

"So, he's got a record, we all knew that. But what we didn't know is this: when he was nineteen years old, he legally changed his name from Harvey Lawson to Harvel Brady. I also confirmed that he and Maureen had the same birth parents, so if you are anything like me and trying to think that there was any way that they might not be siblings, you can just forget it. They are. They are full brother and sister. And I don't mean to make light of it, Kate, but I think I'm about to puke."

Me? I actually shivered.

"Did Kenny say anything else?"

"Oh, he didn't stop there," Janet said. "He said that he gasped when he saw them and nearly fell down the steps. They spotted him. Harvel grabbed him in a headlock, and Maureen told him that if he ever told anyone what he'd seen, his dad or anyone else, they'd kill his father and sister, Nicolette."

I just sat and stared at her. I was stunned, didn't know what to say.

Fortunately, I didn't have to. Janet being Janet, she chattered on telling me details I can't even now remember until finally she gave me Kenny Percy's number, telling me that if I needed to, I could call him any time.

"Wow," I said when she finally ran out of steam. "You did good, Janet. Very good. I think I will call Kenny and talk with him."

Janet nodded, stood, walked to the door and opened it.

"Hey, Janet," I called after her. "Do me a favor. Check on Jack for me. See where he is with Maureen's computer and her phones."

"Sure thing, Cap," and she pulled the door closed.

I dialed Kenny's number and he answered right away. I didn't waste any time. I introduced myself and told him I was recording the conversation. I had to validate this story before it could be of any legal use.

Something deep inside me was hoping that maybe Kenny was full of it, just an angry kid, bitter and upset that his parents split up. But as Kenny repeated what had happened that day when he came home from work early, almost verbatim to what Janet had read from her notes, I became sure he was telling the truth. There was no hesitation in his voice. No stuttering. No backtracking.

"I'm sorry you had to deal with this, Mr. Percy," I said, even though I knew it hardly made a difference now.

"It's okay, Detective. I'm just glad that you guys are catching up to her. I don't know if Maureen did this to Nicolette, or if it was her brother, but if they did, I want them to pay for it."

"Mr. Percy," I said. "Why is it, d'you think, that Maureen insisted that Nicolette stay with her instead of letting your father take her back to Chicago with him?" I asked.

"Oh, that's an easy one. The guys."

"The guys? What guys?"

"Any guys. Nicolette was pretty and she had friends. Maureen didn't, and she wanted to be Nicolette's age again. She wanted to party and have guys chasing her like they did Nicolette. Look, she was so jealous of Nicolette it drove her crazy. She could never look at her and tell her how beautiful she was. Instead, she'd look at her and point out her faults, what few she had, like the mole on the side of her nose, that her toes were bent or some other stupid issue... and she'd blow it up out of proportion to make herself feel better.

Always as a joke, though. Narcissistic bullshit is what it was," Kenny snarled. "All the money in the world can't erase the ugliness inside that woman."

I thanked Kenny for his time, hung up the phone and groaned again, thinking what a wicked pair they were: Maureen, an incestuous woman who stole her ex-husband's money. Harvel, her incestuous brother who murdered Nicolette and defiled her corpse, and who wouldn't talk to anyone but Internal Affairs.

"There is more to this than just Harvel," I muttered to myself. "I just know it. Come on, Jack. Hurry up and tell me some good news. I sure as hell could use some."

But, as it turned out, it wouldn't be that day.

My phone rang. I looked at the screen. It was Dorman.

"This is a nice surprise," I said.

"What time do you want me to pick you up?" he asked, his voice sounding velvety.

It was refreshing to talk to a guy without ever having to use the words, murder, time of death, weapon, method, or evidence.

"Pick me up? Tonight you mean?"

"Yes. Isn't tonight your award thing from the VFW?" he asked.

"Holy crap!" I slapped my forehead. "I totally forgot. It completely slipped my mind. Oh, gosh." I looked at the clock and it was already four-thirty.

"How about you pick me up in an hour?" I asked as I grabbed my purse and shut off my computer.

"I'll see you then," he said and hung up.

I picked up my desk phone, called Janet and had her tell the team where I was going and that I was leaving. I heard her tell them, and I heard them wish me luck or maybe they said they didn't give a damn. I don't know. Two minutes later I was in my car and racing home trying to figure out what the hell to wear.

28

Dorman was right. The folks at the VFW do know how to have a good time. They had the place simply decorated with red-white-and-blue streamers across the ceiling. The tables were covered with white tablecloths with votive candles at the center. There was a huge, fully stocked bar to the left and a small dance floor with a DJ to the right. And as soon as we walked in, the Grand Marshal, Mr. Brian Pekin, approached us with a drink in his hand and a smile on his face.

"Captain Gazzara, it's so nice to see you. Welcome," he said, shaking my hand and complimenting me on my dress.

I had to smile. It was one of those stunning little black numbers I keep handy for emergencies such as this one. That and a pair of four-inch heels that pushed me up to a full six-foot-three so I was looking down on him. Still, it was really nice to hear it from him considering I felt like a stuffed sausage. I hadn't been out running as regularly as usual and damn if it didn't suddenly feel like I should have been on one of those reality shows that feature people tipping the scale at five-hundred-pounds. Dorman had told me not to be silly, that I looked beautiful, but he would, wouldn't he?

Pekin didn't have to, but I was grateful for the boost in self-confidence.

I introduced Wilcox and, of course, there was the instant flash friendship that often occurs when brothers-in-arm meet, even for the first time. Before I knew it, I had a martini in one hand while the other was being pumped by every person in the place.

Ms. Marie Madia, Jose Madia's daughter, was there. I remembered her from the case. She looked good and was smiling, although the mere mention of her father brought tears to her eyes.

"You have no idea what you've done for my family," Marie said. "The rest of them could not be here. They had prior obligations and well, I think now that it's over they are tired. But I did want you to hear it from at least one of us how grateful we are to you."

"It might sound cliché," I said, "but I was just doing my job." I smiled as Marie's eyes filled with tears.

"That is what you think, Captain Gazzara." She smiled. "My family and I would say that you were the answer to our prayers."

Okay, I'm not one for the mushy stuff. Anyone will tell you that. Hell, if I kept it a secret that I love my fuzzy slippers, I'm certainly never going to admit to having any kind of softer side. But I was touched. And when Marie gave me a big hug—something else I'm not a fan of—I couldn't help tearing up just a little myself. As soon as she left to join the other veterans, her father's friends and compadres, I quickly downed my martini and asked Dorman to get me another.

After about a half-hour of drinking and socializing, the guys finally got it together enough to present me with "The Big Dog Award" that was given only after careful consideration by the members of the Ladies Auxiliary. It was a heavy brass cast of the Marine bulldog mascot with a cigar, helmet, and three stars on the shoulder of the coat he was wearing. It was cute. I was touched.

I didn't like these kinds of ceremonies and always thought awards or any kind of recognition should be done in private without an audience or pictures. But this group was different and allowed me to say just a simple thank you without demanding a speech before they welcomed everyone to get a refill at the bar and let the music begin. After a few oldies but goodies a slow song came on, and before I knew it, I was in Dorman's arms feeling like a teenager at the high school dance.

"You do look lovely tonight, Kate," he whispered.

"Thanks. You don't look too shabby yourself," I replied.

Just then a woman let out a squeal behind me. I turned and saw Marie Madia waving and shouting. When I looked to the door, I saw her brother and a couple of cousins who had been at her house when I was talking with the family about the case. They all hugged me and fetched me drinks, and we all wiped away a few tears.

"That's a nice family," Dorman said.

"Yeah. This kind of shit always happens to nice families," I grumbled.

It made me think of Nicolette. That was the problem with being a homicide detective. One among many, I should say. The case I was working on, no matter what it was or where I was, always managed to haunt my every waking moment. Whether it was while I was doing my laundry or grocery shopping or even when I was supposed to be having a good time, the thoughts were like cock-roaches, always looking for a crack where they could slip quietly in and ruin everything.

"Want another martini?" he asked.

I shook my head. "No, I think I've had enough... Dorman, I have something interesting I want to run by you. The Madia family... when Jose was murdered, they all pulled together. They helped me and the team in every way possible. I know for a fact they had at least a couple of dozen prayer services said for us and for Jose while I was working the case. There wasn't a single part of their day, for any of them, that wasn't somehow tied to trying to help us find his killer."

"Is that so strange?" Dorman asked.

"No. Just the opposite, it's the norm. What's strange is when a family doesn't do that," I said as I snuggled in a little closer.

"Okay, you want to talk about it?"

"No, I was just thinking out loud." The truth was, I was thinking it was about time we took a closer look at Maureen Lawson.

Without putting up too much resistance I had one more martini, and by the time Dorman and I arrived back at my house, I was dying to get out of my dress for more reasons than one.

When I woke up the next morning, I had only a slight headache from the previous night's revels, and for that I was thankful. Dorman, still on Marine Corps time, had been up since five and brought coffee. I sat up in bed, grabbed it gratefully and took a sip. It was heavenly.

"I'm going to go for a run to clear my head," I said. "Want to come with me?"

"That sounds like a great idea, but I don't have a gym bag with me," he said and winked at me.

I looked at him. He was sitting on the edge of the bed wearing only boxers. I shivered, and not from the cold.

"Well, if you like you can bring a pair of shorts and running shoes and leave them here. That might work out okay. Then we could run together when the opportunity presents itself," I said, knowing my cheeks were burning, and hating it.

"I concur. Until then, I'll leave you to your workout." He took the last sip of his coffee, stood, leaned over and kissed me.

"I need to go and change for work," he said.

Ten minutes later he was out of the door. I got up and went to the living room to finish my coffee. I could still feel his kiss on my lips, and I smiled, and then I was back to thinking about the Nicolette Percy case.

It was just after six when I left my apartment and headed east on East Brainerd, running fast. Ten minutes into the run, my phone rang.

29

It was twenty minutes after six that morning when Jack called, and I was a little more than a mile out from my apartment and running quickly toward the turn. I stopped, zipped open my race belt and took the call.

"Yes, Jack. What the hell are you calling me for at this time in the morning?"

"Sorry to bother you, Cap," Jack said, but I could tell by his voice that he wasn't at all sorry. He was bouncing with excitement.

"Tell me something good."

"We cracked Maureen's computer. Sarah and... we were able to reconstruct the wiped files. You won't believe what we found."

"Have you called the rest of the team?" I said as I turned around and began walking back toward my apartment.

"Not yet. I thought I'd call you first."

"Wake them up. Get everyone there, in my office. I'll be there in... give me an hour."

I hung up without saying good-bye, ran back to my apartment, stripped, and jumped into a scalding hot shower. Oh, how good it felt, for a few minutes anyway. I stood under the showerhead and let it wash away the remnants of too many martinis and a night with Wilcox Dorman, wonderful though it was.

The reality of finally closing in on Maureen Lawson had me moving swiftly through my apartment as I turned on the coffeepot. I dressed quickly in jeans and a white blouse, tied my hair back in a ponytail, applied a little makeup and grabbed a yogurt to put something solid in my stomach. I didn't like yogurt, but it was on sale and was better than nothing. For years I'd survived on just coffee to get me through to lunchtime. But I had the feeling it was going to be a busy day and I might not get a lunch or dinner.

I filled my to-go coffee cup, took a last quick look in the mirror, liked what I saw, slipped by Glock into its holster, clipped my badge to my belt, donned a tan leather jacket, grabbed my keys, my bag and headed out the door.

It was a few minutes after seven. The sun had not yet peeked over the horizon.

I pulled into my spot at the rear of the police department just as Janet and Robar were getting out of their cars.

"Good morning, Captain," Janet said cheerfully as if she was always at work by seven in the morning and this wasn't a crazy inconvenience. On thinking about it, though, she probably was always at work by seven.

"Morning, Cap," Robar said, taking a bite of a huge golden croissant.

"That looks good. Did you bring enough for the class?" I asked her.

"Are you kidding? I had to hide this one from the savages at my house. It's like Doomsday Prepping, hoarding, trying to save myself something to eat. Two boys and a husband in the house is worse than a plague of locusts," Robar said as she proceeded to greedily eat her croissant.

We walked in together. It was a typical early morning at the Chattanooga Police Department. There were a couple of hookers waiting to be processed, a penny-ante thief who couldn't run fast enough to dodge the uniforms, a couple of junkies and half-dozen rough-looking dudes in the drunk tank. We passed them by and went straight to my office where I found Hawk already seated at the table with a mug of coffee and reading a newspaper, and Jack pacing about like a caged lion.

"Hey! Hey, good morning!" he, Jack, waved. "I'm sorry I had to drag everyone in this early, but I found some big stuff. I mean, I wasn't sure how savvy Maureen was but as it turned out, and as I originally guessed, she must have read a couple articles online about how to scrub your laptop and thought she'd done the job. So anyway, Sarah and me, we were able to reconstruct most of the files... She went home, by the way, Sarah did. She was here almost all night."

Hawk took a sip of coffee and then looked at me. "He's been like this since he emerged from the forensics lab about an hour ago. I wouldn't let him have any coffee; he's wired as it is."

"How long have you been here?" I asked Hawk.

"What are you talking about, Cap? Since when are we allowed to leave?" he grunted.

I smiled. "Yes, it sure feels like that sometimes," I said as I sat down behind my desk.

He gifted me with a half a grin, the most I'd ever gotten from him, and he folded his newspaper and laid it down. Jack already had Maureen's laptop open on the table. The flat-screen monitor on the wall was already turned on and was showing a Windows 10 desktop display, Maureen's, I assumed.

Jack waited until everyone was seated and then he began, "Okay, so, Maureen thought she was being pretty sneaky. She deleted everything and then went a step further following the Wikihow.com advice on how to wipe your computer," Jack said before grabbing his huge, two-liter bottle of Coke and taking a gulp. "But what she doesn't know is that we might be just some down-home country boys here in the Digital Forensics lab, but Sarah is not, and she has better toys than hers: Yeah Boy!"

He shouted the yeah boy and pumped his fist like he'd just scored the winning goal between Alabama and Tennessee. Janet burst out laughing. Robar, who was busy chewing the last bite of her croissant, started to choke, grabbed Hawk's coffee and took a huge gulp before he could grab it back. Me? I was more than a little intrigued by this mysterious Sarah person.

"Jack," I said quietly. "This Sarah person... she's a friend?"

"Ye-es?"

"I hope you're not playing away," I said.

"Playing away? Having an affair you mean? No. *No!* I wouldn't do anything like that. I love my wife!"

"Okay, okay. Settle down, Jack," I said. "I was just asking. Now please tell us what you found."

Jack cleared his throat and launched into a tirade of technical geek-speak that would have put the entire team so deep into a coma that we'd never get out of it.

"Whoa," I interrupted him. "Just the facts, okay? It's only seven o'clock and all of that is way above my head."

"All right, I'll skip to the meat and potatoes," Jack said. "So, not everything that was recovered is in pristine condition. But what we do have is golden. Take a look." And he began typing so fast his fingers were a blur.

The images on the monitor changed to show something that even I knew was a string of chatroom messages from Nicolette on her LookingforLove.com message board. We could read everything everyone had written to her and what she'd written back.

"That's Nicolette's account," I said. "I thought you were working on Maureen's computer." I was ready to jump over my desk and slap Jack silly if he'd spent all his time working on the wrong laptop.

"Yes. It is Nicolette's account..." he said, smiling broadly and pausing for effect. "But it's Maureen's computer. And all of the communications from Pete McGee to Nicolette came from this computer." Jack clicked his tongue and looked at me.

"I don't get it," Hawk said.

Robar cleared her throat. "You're saying that Maureen Lawson or someone was communicating with her as Pete McGee from Lawson's computer?" Robar asked with her shoulders pulled up to her ears. "Is that what you're saying?"

"That is exactly what I'm saying," Jack said. "She, or Harvel Brady, made up a profile, put up that Mr. Stock Photo image, gave the guy a history, education—using a lot of cutting and pasting from internet sample documents—and presented her own daughter with a phony Romeo," Jack said.

We all just sort of sat there.

"Well, that presents us with a major log jam!" I said thought-fully. "We have her brother Brady's DNA on Nicolette's body, which tells me he killed her... And we have his DNA on the blunt found in her car. But, as far as a jury will be concerned, there's now an ocean of reasonable doubt we've got to cross; I don't even see a murder conviction."

"Well, I found a couple more things," Jack said. "Well, one that's really weird and makes no sense. And then there's also some email correspondence from Maureen to an insurance company. It's just bits and pieces, but the name of the company was Anchor Insurance. I think she took out a policy. Can't say on who or for what amount."

"That's good, Jack," I said.

"Janet." I looked at her, but she was already scribbling in her yellow pad.

"I'll get right on that," she said and smiled.

"What was the other thing that was weird?" Robar asked.

"Yeah, that. I can't figure it out, but two days before Nicolette died, Maureen was also corresponding back and forth with Harvel. Something about him taking out the garbage for her and in return she'd let him work in the garage." Jack shrugged.

"Can you pull up that correspondence?" I asked.

"Sure." Once again Jack's fingers flew across the keyboard,

and the next thing I knew, I was looking at an email chain that made some rather disturbing references to garbage and the garage. Jack was the only one who hadn't been briefed on the phone call I received from Kenny Percy. I had wanted him to finish getting what he could from the computer before I brought him up to speed. I let Janet fill him in and he reacted appropriately.

"Okay," Jack said. "So Maureen is asking her brother to take out the trash. 'Time is running out,' she says. And then she says, 'if I bag the trash, you'll have to take it out like you promised. If you won't, I will have to find someone else to take it out.'"

I stared at the screen and continued reading the emails aloud.

"'Look, if you'll do what I ask, there will be more money for you when it's done. But you are going to have to take it out.'"

"And look at the dates," Robar said. "The day before Nicolette's death."

"She's not talking about garbage," I muttered. "She's talking about her stepdaughter."

"Right," Robar said. "She said that she would bag it, which means that she was planning to kill her."

"And Brady replies, 'I'll do it, but I want to play in your garage,'" Hawk said. "Maureen's replies don't seem like she's too into that, but what's a quick tryst between brother and sister after a murder's been committed?"

"Holy shit!" Jack said. "Then this is some kind of code for sex for murder, because all I could think of when I was reading it was who the hell cares so much about working in someone's garage? I thought it must have been one hell of a man-cave for Harvel to beg like he did. Damn! Is that sick, or what?"

"Do you know where the communications from Maureen's computer were sent to?" I asked. "The real Pete McGee doesn't have a computer and neither does Brady."

"One step ahead of you, Cap," Jack said. "He was using the Chattanooga Public Library. Just your basic Gmail account. I've got a time stamp. Their computer tech can corroborate the address. Maybe they'll have surveillance footage that puts him there."

"Great. Robar, you and—" I started.

"Library opens at nine-thirty," she interrupted me. "Hawk, you ever been to the library before? It's a big place with lots of books. Some people actually like to read."

"Very funny. Come on, I'll buy you breakfast before we go," Hawk muttered as he stood up.

Jack was about to say something, but before he could Hawk clapped him on the shoulder, hard. "Good work, newbie. Proud of you, son."

"Thanks! You know I haven't eaten in a couple days. Except for some Chinese food and a bag of Doritos. I'd like some breakfast," Jack said.

"You buyin'?" Robar asked.

"Well, I guess I could. I think I've got enough—"

"Shut up, newbie and come on," Robar said. "Hey Janet. You had breakfast yet?"

"Not yet. The insurance companies don't open until at least nine-thirty." She smiled, then stood from her seat and headed toward the door. "Cap, are you coming too?"

I thought about the yogurt and winced. "Yeah, I'm coming, too."

30

There are a handful of restaurants in Chattanooga that we like to use. I would have been happy with any of them, but since Robar was the only one with a car big enough to haul all five of us, we left it to her to choose where we'd eat. She liked IHOP. So that's where we went.

It was a rare thing for all of us to go out to eat together, and I couldn't help but wonder why we didn't do it more often.

As usual, I was the quiet member of my team, the least noisy anyway, I suppose. There was a lot of banter, especially between Hawk and Robar. There wasn't a smartass remark that Hawk wouldn't make, and Robar compared everyone to one or the other of her kids whom she threatened to kill on a daily basis. Jack and Janet listened to the seasoned officers as they talked about previous busts and bad guys. Me? I was away with the birds, my mind on other things, including Dorman.

"Have you ever had a case like this before?" Jack asked. "Like... with incest?"

"You were reading my mind," Janet said. "I took the phone call from Kenny Percy when he verified Maureen and Harvel were indeed brother and sister. I put the phone down and just sat there, all stupid and dumbstruck for about ten minutes... Well not really ten minutes, but long enough."

"It's the drugs," Hawk said. "They do funny things to your brain."

Robar and I nodded. We knew it was true.

"Junkies will do anything when they are high," Hawk said. "Reality? Out the window. Morality? The same; anything goes: fathers and their daughters, mothers and their sons, brothers, sisters... It's pretty common, especially in the more remote areas of the country, but it's not often we run across a dynamic duo like Maureen and Harvel Brady."

"But it isn't always the tweakers you've got to worry about," I said. "Isn't that right, Ann? Sometimes the scariest thing can be as innocent-looking as a cat."

I watched Hawk's face as his jaw dropped. Robar nearly spit out her coffee as she nodded, gulped and then started to laugh.

"What's scary about a cat?" Jack asked.

"I get the feeling Hawk is going to be mad when we get back to the station." Janet chuckled as we all watched Hawk shake his head and look down in his lap.

The food came just as Robar was trying to describe Hawk hanging half in and half out of a window on a fire escape after a cat had scared him. It wasn't that he was afraid of cats. And he wasn't afraid of heights, but when the angry cat took a swipe at him, knocking him off balance, he'd had enough. He opened the nearest window and tried to climb in, scaring the living daylights out of some old woman.

"He was waving his badge trying to tell the old girl that his pants were caught," Robar gasped. "I was afraid she was going to take advantage of him."

Of course, Hawk had a story of his own to tell, and so it went, back and forth until Jack and Janet had finished their food and were on their second cups of coffee. By the time we finished breakfast, the sun was up. It had been a nice respite. I was proud of my team, and I was sure that we were going to wrap this case up nice and tight and quickly too. *Then maybe the Chief will forget that he's mad at me.*

I paid the tab. It was the right thing to do.

"Jack, you did a good job on Maureen's computer," I said as we walked into the PD. "So why don't you go to the library with Hawk and Robar and help there. Then go home and get some sleep. I'll call you if we need you."

"Thanks, Cap. Yeah. I can do that. They wouldn't know what to look for anyway. I'll make sure we get what we need."

"I'll contact the insurance agency and see what I can find out," Janet said as soon as we stepped inside.

Hawk, Jack and Robar had left to go to the library. Everyone had an assignment so I went to my office. I now had almost a hundred unanswered emails and messages. I spent the next hour digging into them. Fortunately, almost all of them were routine and quickly dealt with. It seemed like no time at all before Janet tapped on my door and peeked inside.

"Did you find anything?" I asked, waving her to the seat in front of my desk. I could already tell by the excited look on her face that she had.

"Not one. Not two. Not even three, but four different companies issued policies on Nicolette Percy's life totaling four hundred thousand dollars," she said triumphantly. "And the beneficiaries?" she continued. "Maureen Lawson. And as crazy as it may seem, so far only one of them has paid out. The other three are wanting more information, and at one company I talked to, they said they found her behavior, and I quote, 'rather strange.' When I asked the adjuster what she meant, she said the way Maureen keeps calling and emailing, asking when they're going to release the cash. He said it threw up a red flag, and they'd opened an investigation." Janet looked at me, smiling, then said, "So what d'you think about that?"

"Wow." Was all I could say, trying to figure out the implications. Then I nodded, smiled and said, "Four hundred thousand, huh? I wonder if dear old brother knows about that? How about you and I go talk to him."

And we did. Janet and I went to the county jail where Harvel Brady, aka Harvey Lawson, was currently residing. As it turned out, there was a lot he didn't know about his dear sister.

31

Harvel Brady didn't have a real home of his own, and for some odd reason his sister didn't allow him to use her address for house arrest. Until a trial date was set, he was being held on remand in the Hamilton County Jail in downtown Chattanooga, a short ten-minute drive from the PD.

The holding area is pretty much like a regular jail except not as spacious, and it was two sometimes three guys to a cell. The inmates came and went depending on the docket. The corrections officers—the guards—were on a strict schedule and every movement, every document, every minute of the day was cataloged and videotaped so that none of the inmates slipped through the cracks, had any excuse to file complaints or were hurt while they were in custody: Jeffery Epstein's shadow loomed large, even in our small city. I say inmates, but none of the people in holding were actually inmates. They were in a kind of limbo until their trial was set.

So, Janet and I flashed our badges and filled out the appropriate paperwork, handed over our weapons to the officers behind a window of three-inch-thick plexiglass and then we were escorted to an interview room where we sat and waited at a steel table with a plexiglass divider at the center. A uniformed officer stayed with us until another officer brought Brady to us; he didn't look good.

He was sweaty and fidgety and obviously suffering from withdrawal. He took one look at Janet and me and rolled his eyes.

"I told you. I ain't talking," he said. "And you ain't supposed to be here talking to me. I filed a complaint with your Internal Affairs department. They said they were going to look into you. You'll be out of a job real soon."

If he really didn't want to talk to us, he would have turned right around and told the guard to take him back to his cell and that would have been the end of things. But, like most of the people being held on remand, I think he was probably glad to get out of his crowded, noisy cell, if only for a few minutes. He sat down and looked at us, his eyes flicking back and forth from one of us to the other.

I looked at the guard and nodded. He took the hint and left the room, locking the door behind him.

"That's all right, Mr. Brady," I said sweetly. "I understand how you feel. So why don't you let me do the talking and we'll see how you feel when I'm finished?"

By then, Janet had her yellow pad out and was already diligently taking notes.

He stared at me for a moment, folded his arms across his chest. I stared back at him. He was a mess. He hadn't shaved. His hair stood out at wild angles and his eyes were bloodshot. The effects of his long addiction were beginning to show.

"Harvel, I'm not here to get you to confess to anything. I know you killed Nicolette: either you or your sister Maureen. We got your DNA. Your sweat was all over the table in the interview room. It matched the saliva we found on her blouse, and on the blunt you left in her car," I lied—we wouldn't get the DNA results for at least another couple of days, but he didn't know that.

"I didn't kill her. Look, I ain't stupid. I screwed her, yes. And you got a DNA match. So what? That just means we had sex, consensual sex, not that I killed her."

"Oh, she consented all right; she was dead, you sick f—" I managed to catch myself before I swore at him, something I rarely ever do. Then I continued, "Abuse of a corpse is a felony in Tennessee, Harvel." I paused for a second, then continued, "So you had sex with her. Where? At Maureen's house? In McGee's trailer? Her car? Where?"

"I told ya. I ain't talking to you!"

"And you stole McGee's phone, didn't you?"

He didn't answer, but the look in his eyes told me I was right.

"Who did the texting? You or Maureen?"

Again, he didn't answer.

I nodded, then said, "So, Harvel, tell us about the garbage."

"Garbage? What garbage?"

"Maureen asked you to take out the trash, and in return she said you could play in her garage. What was that about?"

His face drained of its color; his mouth opened and closed several times, then finally, "I told ya I ain't gonna talk to you. I wanna see a lawyer."

I nodded, then said, "I can't say I blame you. But you're broke so they'll assign you a public defender. How d'you think that will go, Harvel? I don't think that things will work out well for you... But hey, maybe you can ask your sister to pay for a good attorney now that Nicolette's life insurance policies have paid off." It was a long shot, but I saw Harvel blink.

"You didn't know?" I asked innocently. "Maureen took out four policies on her stepdaughter for a total of four-hundred-thousand dollars. She already has the money, directly deposited into her bank account." It was a half-lie. Only one had paid out so far. "That's a lot of money," I continued. "And since you only *took out the trash* after she *bagged it,* you probably don't deserve half of the payout.

But you'd think she'd at least make sure you had a decent lawyer. Now she's living the good life; all that money, and you're stuck in here. Isn't that always the way, though?"

"I don't... believe you. How do you know?" he asked.

"You know, Harvel, it's a funny thing. The moment you mention that you're investigating a homicide to an insurance adjuster, they'll tell you just about everything you want to know. Insurance companies are like that; they hate paying out money. You know that, right? Still, it's too late now. They already did... pay out." I winked at him. "So, is there anything you want to tell me? I'm going to see your sister when we're done here. Maybe you'd like me to give her a message. Something about the garage, perhaps?"

Harvel's face went white, but still he said nothing. He swallowed hard, kept his arms folded across his chest and chewed his lip.

"You do know that incest is a felony in Tennessee, too, don't you, Harvel? So even if you aren't charged with Nicolette's murder, they're going to lock you up for a good long time. Boy, the other inmates are going to love you... and by that I don't mean they'll *love* you. What d'*you* think they'll do?" I shrugged. "Don't answer that question. We both already know the answer. Look, Harvel, I can put in a word for you with the DA, but you're going to have to work with me. I'm in no hurry. Why don't you take twenty-four hours?"

I took a business card from my pocket and put it on the table in front of him, then Janet and I stood up and walked to the door. I banged my hand against it and the metallic echo filled the room. I could hear the sound of the lock turning, then the door opened and the guard appeared.

"You don't have anything on Maureen!" he called out to us before the door slammed shut behind us. "And you won't. You hear me!"

The echo of the metal door shutting shook the hallway.

"Well, did we accomplish anything?" Janet asked as we walked slowly back to my car.

"I don't know. But I think now that he knows about the money, and he's stuck in here while Maureen's still a free woman, it might just work to our advantage," I said.

The truth was, though, that I really didn't know if what I said had sunk in. For all I knew Harvel could have made up his mind to take the fall and go to jail for his sister's sins for the rest of his miserable life. Maybe this was how things worked in the Lawson family. All I knew was that I'd planted the seed and maybe, just maybe, it would take root and he'd flip on his sister. Considering all the other things he did with her, ratting on her should have been easy... and so much less gross.

"So what do you think happened that night?" Janet asked.

I shrugged, made a face, then said, "I don't think he killed her. I think Maureen did."

"What makes you think that?"

"Motive," I said. "He didn't have one, not that we know of. But she did: four hundred thousand of them. I think she planned the whole thing.

"Look, we know Brady was there that night, at McGee's trailer, with Nicolette's car. That old girl, Nielsen, she saw the car parked there at around nine-thirty, so she said. It was dark and he must have been driving. So Maureen must have killed Nicolette at home, before she was due to leave on her date but, as we know, there was no date... Well, Nicolette thought there was."

"What about the text messages that Don Harrington received from Nicolette that night? Telling him that she'd been stood up?" Janet asked.

"According to Harrington, he initiated the sequence. He texted Nicolette to see if the date was going well. Since Nicolette was either already dead or taped up, Maureen must have replied using Nicolette's phone. But then she realized texting that Nicolette had been stood up was a mistake. Maureen needed to keep the date going... to throw suspicion onto Nicolette's "date" as the murderer. So Maureen texted Harrington again using Nicolette's phone,

saying that she was meeting her date somewhere else. She needed
to make it appear that the murder was committed by her online
"date," just like in her screenplay. Then Maureen put the phone in
the trunk along with Nicolette's purse. That would be when the
text messages stopped."

Janet nodded, and I continued.

"Anyway, I think Maureen killed Nicolette just as she planned
and then Brady took the body, to dump it, only he didn't; he had
other plans. Instead he put her in the passenger seat of her car and
drove it to McGee's... took advantage of the darkness, hauled her
body into the trailer through the back door and... spent the night
with her."

"Oh, come on, Cap," Janet said. "She would have been stiff as a
board by morning."

"That would depend on what time she died and the temperature inside the trailer. Doc said between eight and ten. The
Nielsen woman said she saw the car at nine-thirty, which means
she hadn't been dead for more than an hour. McGee said it was
warm inside the trailer, so that would have slowed rigor down. Hell,
Janet, he could have spent three or four hours with her then
returned her to her car when he was done... when he'd finished
with her. It wouldn't have been hard for him. She weighed what? A
hundred and ten? He's a big guy. No problem!"

"That's quite a stretch, Cap."

"For a normal person, yes, but Harvel's far from normal, and he
was probably strung out on drugs." I shrugged.

"But why would he swap the license plate?" I shook my head
and closed my eyes, then opened them again and said, "I have no
earthly idea... except that in his burned-out befuddled brain, maybe
he thought he could somehow blame Heddiger for the girl's death.
Unless he talks..."

Jack had called in while we were talking with Harvel and left a
message that the library did indeed have a surveillance camera at
the front door and another in the computer room.

It was what I wanted to hear, but I found myself wishing things would move a little faster.

32

Lee Hensley Day Spa was an appointment-only oasis where the finer ladies of Chattanooga go when they feel that the pressures of their world are just becoming too much to bear. It's located off Shallowford Road, three blocks east of Highway 153. From what I'd heard, the packages they offered included a steam bath, cryogenic therapy, massage, acupuncture, skin rejuvenation treatments that included a seaweed wrap and a mud bath, and a whole bunch of other things, none of which I could afford.

"Can I help you?" a woman said as she rose from behind her desk in the reception area.

She looked to be in her late forties and was wearing tight black slacks and a black blouse that matched her jet-black hair that hung to the middle of her back. I could tell by her attitude that all ninety pounds of her was ready and willing to try and stop us from disturbing the peace and tranquility of the spa. It was, after all, sacred ground and not just anyone was going to be allowed to traipse right through it without an appointment.

I smiled at her and held up my badge, as did Janet and Robar at the same time, making sure she'd spot our holstered weapons.

"I'm Captain Gazarra. Chattanooga PD. You have a client here, a Ms. Maureen Lawson."

"I can't divulge that information, Captain," the woman said defiantly. "I believe you need a search warrant."

"You watch too much television, lady," I snapped. "That being so, tell me what happens when someone obstructs a police investigation and allows a murderer to escape? Hmm? Do you know what usually happens to that person?" I asked.

The woman in black blinked nervously. She knew darn well what happened to those characters, and I could tell she wasn't going to risk getting shanked in a holding cell by a prostitute or a drug dealer.

"Uh, oh. Yes, Captain. I'm sorry," she said as she perused the names in her ledger, her long, manicured nails scrolling over each name. Even upside down I could see Maureen's name. She'd been in the spa since ten o'clock that morning. It was now almost two. She was enjoying her newfound wealth.

"What's your name?" I asked the receptionist.

"Elisandra," she replied.

"Okay, Elisandra. Here's how this is going to go. We'll try to do this as quietly as possible and not disturb the rest of your clients, but I want to see Maureen Lawson... Now!"

She visibly let out a deep sigh, nodded, looked at her watch and then the clock on the wall.

"Maureen should be finishing up her manicure and pedicure. If you go down this hallway to the very end, there's a door to the right and several windows just before you reach it. You'll see her," Elisandra said nervously.

"Thank you," I said. Out of the corner of my eye, I saw Robar grab one of their pamphlets and stuff it in her pocket.

"Really?" I asked as we walked down the hall.

"I've got a twenty-two-year anniversary coming up," she replied. "It's the least I deserve."

Elisandra was right. It wasn't hard to spot Maureen. She was wearing a white robe and was sitting high up in a perch alongside two other customers, a glass of champagne next to her and a young woman at her feet slathering them with lotion. Apparently the pedicure had not yet begun.

Her hair, though, had been done and her skin glowed from the exotic treatments. I didn't knock. I just opened the door and walked right on in, followed by Janet and Robar. The air was toxic from the smell of nail polish remover.

I stood for a moment, not saying a word. Maureen had been chatting with the woman next to her and had just picked up her champagne glass, about to take a sip when she saw me. And she gasped.

Everyone in the room froze. The new age music continued.

"Maureen Lawson, I'd like you to come with me, please," I said, with Robar and Janet just behind, flanking me, one on either side. I waved for her to come down off the seat. I didn't expect what happened next.

"I'm not going anywhere," she hissed and sipped her champagne. Then she turned her head back to the woman she'd been talking to and tried to continue the conversation, but the woman wasn't listening. She was staring at us.

"Maureen. It's time to go," I said, taking a step toward her. "Let's let these people finish their visit in peace."

"I'm not going anywhere with you," she said. "I haven't done anything, and you can't make me." And she clamped her teeth together so tightly I thought she'd crack them.

"Maureen, we found your emails," I said gently. "You thought you'd scrubbed your computer. You didn't do it properly. You talked to your brother about taking out the trash. That was Nicolette, wasn't it? You were talking about your stepdaughter, weren't you? She was the trash you wanted taking out. Come on, Maureen. It's time to go."

"I'm not going anywhere!" she screamed at the top of her voice, making everyone in the room including me jump.

"I didn't do anything! You can't prove it! You don't have anything on me!"

"Maureen, calm down!" I said sharply.

"I will not calm down!" she screamed. "*I will not calm down!* That little bitch ruined everything! Everything! She was young and pretty and soft! She didn't do one thing for me! Not one! I gave her a place to live and she repaid me by abusing me! Me! I'm the victim! Not her."

She was hysterical. Her face had changed from glowing and pampered to a twisted, red mask filled with hate. She kicked out at the girl who had been massaging her feet, knocking her flying. She swatted at the woman she'd been conversing with only seconds ago. And she threw the champagne glass at me. Fortunately she missed by more than a yard and it shattered against the wall on the other side of the room.

"Maureen, you aren't helping yourself!" Robar shouted, taking a step forward. "Come down from there. Talk to us. We'll listen. Tell us your side of the story! All we want to know is the truth about what happened to Nicolette."

But, it wasn't working. Maureen was having a full-blown temper tantrum.

"I will not come down! I will not, I will not, I will not," she screamed and began to stamp her feet. With her eyes squeezed shut and her hands clenched into fists, she pounded away on the arms of her chair. Her ranting scared the woman next to her so much she jumped out of her chair and joined the employees who'd scattered to the opposite sides of the room.

"Maureen!" I shouted. "We don't want you to hurt yourself! Now come down off that chair and let's talk. If there's another side of the story, we want to hear it, believe me."

"Another side to the story?" she screeched. "There was only one side to the story. I'll tell you! Nicolette was a selfish, manipulative little brat! She was a slut, a whore and some guy she never met before killed her! You have it all on her computer! All of it!"

"Maureen," I said gently, trying to calm her down. "Those communications came from you. We know they did. And so did the naked photos. They weren't of Nicolette. You did that. You put them on her laptop to make her look bad. To make her look like she was something she wasn't. And you didn't scrub your computer, Maureen. You set your daughter up. The day she was supposed to meet Pete McGee you put a plastic bag over her head and you killed her," I said coldly.

Unlike Robar, who with two teenagers was a master at negotiations, I was blunt. The truth was often ugly and hard to take. But facing it was often the first step to getting justice. Unfortunately, Maureen didn't want to face it.

"But it all went badly wrong, didn't it, Maureen?" I said. "Harvel was supposed to dispose of the body. He was supposed to dump her or bury her or whatever. But he was high on drugs, so he violated her corpse, raped her dead body, and then he left her in her car outside the trailer park where he stayed with the real Pete McGee. Just some poor truck driver who didn't even know you or Nicolette. What the hell Harvel thought he was going to achieve by switching her license plate I have no idea, but that's exactly what he did. Now get down off that chair or I'll come up there and drag you down!"

Maureen started to cry hysterically. The sounds that came out of her mouth weren't even words. She shook her head and clamped her hands tightly over the arms. She pounded her bare feet and shook her head.

"Fine. Have it your way. Maureen Lawson. You are under arrest for the murder of your stepdaughter, Nicolette Percy. You have the right to remain silent. Anything you say or do may be held against you in a court of law. You have..." Everyone knows the words. I walked up to the chair, took hold of her hand and yanked her to her feet.

It was like pulling a feisty, screaming toddler out of a department store. I continued to read her her rights as Robar slapped the cuffs on her.

"Where are my clothes! I want my clothes! They won't even let me get dressed!" she screamed as we led her out of the salon.

Janet did collect her clothes and her personal belongings, including her car which was parked outside the salon. And, since she was under arrest for murder, we now had probable cause to search those belongings. And, lo and behold, we found a roll of duct tape in the trunk of her car. It was bagged and tagged and sent immediately to Mike Willis for processing.

I'd already called ahead to make sure Hawk and Jack had picked up Brady from the county jail and had him settled in interview room one. They had, and they were waiting for us.

If Maureen thought that the worst was over, she was in for a rude awakening.

33

B y the time we walked her into the PD, Maureen had calmed down. She was still dressed in the salon robe, and I was pretty sure that they'd tack another seventy-five dollars onto her bill for that.

Her hands were cuffed in front of her and she stared straight ahead, her lips pinched tightly together, her chin raised and her eyes barely deviating from what was directly in front of her. That is, until we led her past the open door of interview room one... and she saw her brother.

The gasp was audible. As soon as she saw him, I watched her body begin to shake. Not out of terror, but rage. I walked her into the adjoining interview room, sat her down and closed the door. Janet said she had something she needed to check and she left, so did Jack. Robar and Hawk went together to the observation room.

"Maureen," I said, after taking a seat and cautioning her again for the record, "you do know that you are in a lot of trouble. Are you willing to talk to me, help me to understand what happened?"

She glared at me. "I assume Harvel has already told you."

"Actually, Harvel hasn't said a word," I said. "The only thing he's told me is that he didn't know about the insurance money and he admitted that he'd violated the body, and I tend to believe him."

Maureen took a deep breath. Her color had returned to normal, but I could see the crazy light lingering in her eyes. Her mind must have been working overtime, trying to spot a life preserver or a plank of wood or anything that might save her from the vast ocean of trouble she was in, but there was nothing. I spent the next forty-five minutes talking to her, questioning her and trying to get under her skin, but I got nowhere, and I was becoming frustrated and angry. I decided to take a break, let her stew for a while.

Before I could, however, there was a knock on the door and Janet stuck her head inside. "Cap, can you come out here for a minute?"

Now I never liked these kinds of interruptions. They were always urgent and rarely brought good news. So, with no little trepidation, I stepped outside, leaving a uniformed officer to keep her company.

"I'm not getting very far with her," I said.

"Well, maybe this will help," Janet said. "After I learned what I did from the insurance companies, I decided to do a little more digging into Maureen's background. She's more than two-hundred-thousand dollars in debt. There's a lien on the house. She was going to lose everything." She handed me a stack of papers printed from twelve different credit card providers. "And that's not all—"

"Captain?" Jack said, interrupting her as he came toward us along the corridor.

"Oh shit! What is it now?" I grumbled.

"I found some more emails."

I sighed, shook my head, and said, "Are you serious?"

"Yeah, but not that kind. If they had been you would have heard me puking all the way here," he said, smiling broadly while Janet chuckled.

"No," he continued. "There are emails from Maureen to Nicolette demanding money for rent and utilities. It's pretty clear she was charging Nicolette a lot to live there and wouldn't tolerate a late payment. But I don't think she ever used the money to pay bills. I talked to the electric company. They were about to cut her off. She was four months behind but brought herself current only last week, after she received the hundred grand."

"That's good work," I said. "But I don't think it's going to make a difference. I think she's gone, gone, gone." I tapped my temple.

Janet spoke up again. "I was going to say, when I was so rudely interrupted by the boy genius here..." She glanced at him. He grinned happily back at her. "I was going to say that I don't know what it will take for Harvel to turn on her since he's made it clear that he's not going to, but I also found that he was also in debt... to the tune of more than twenty-thousand dollars. How does a guy with no job, a rap sheet a mile long and not even a place to live get that much credit?"

Jack made a sound. "That's not unusual. I know several people who're in that boat."

"Okay," I said wearily, "So we have more than enough information to prove that Maureen had a problem with money. That's a pretty solid motive. A confession from her would be better than one from Brady, because he's a con and a jury will naturally assume that he's lying," I clicked my tongue.

And then, just when I thought things couldn't get any worse, the screaming started.

34

At first, I thought it was one of the female uniformed cops having a row with one of her peers—those guys can get kind of rowdy when they're getting off a shift—but then I realized it was coming from Harvel's interrogation room.

The observation room door opened.

"What the hell is that?" Hawk demanded. "Brady! I'll..." And before I could stop him, he barged into interview room one.

"Shut the hell up, Brady," he yelled at him. "You're disturbing the peace. I don't care what kind of inner demons you've got! Tell them to pipe the hell down!"

"I want to make a confession!" Harvel sobbed. "I did it! I killed Nicolette! Maureen had nothing to do with it! Nothing at all!"

"Oh, isn't that just sweet how he wants to take the rap for his sister-girlfriend," Jack whispered in Janet's ear.

She shook her head and dug him in the ribs with her elbow. I didn't smile. The whole scene was just too bizarre. He was right, though.

"I'll tell you everything." Brady was by then sobbing almost uncontrollably. "Maureen had nothing to do with it. You can let her go."

Brady was cuffed with his hands behind his back. Tears and snot were running down his face. He was shaking violently, looked like an oozing, melting mess. He really was suffering from withdrawal.

"That's very nice of you, Harvel. Would you like to tell Detective Hawkins your story?" I asked quietly.

"Yes. Yes, yes! I'll tell him everything. Just let Maureen go. She didn't do nothin', I swear."

Of course, there was no way I was going to let Maureen go. She had the motive, the method and the roll of duct tape. She wasn't going anywhere even if I wanted to let her go. Which I didn't. But I just nodded and let Hawk take over. He shut the door behind him and everything went quiet. *Sheesh,* I thought. *What a frickin' relief. I gotta get me another job. This kinda crap is about to get to me. Maybe the Chief's right. Maybe I need a break...*

And then, when I walked into the other room where Maureen was being held, I almost screamed myself. She was sitting there all prim and proper, her robe pulled tightly around her, her hands folded together on the table and the biggest shit-eating grin on her face I'd ever seen in my life. She'd obviously heard every word Brady had said, or should I say shouted?

"I'd like to talk to my lawyer, please," she said calmly. No one would have guessed this same woman had, only thirty minutes earlier, thrown the hissy fit of the century.

I nodded and said, "My pleasure." And I closed the door and shivered, involuntarily.

I turned to Jack and said, "It's over. She murdered Nicolette. No doubt about it. And Brady aided and abetted her by getting rid of the body... and he abused the body; no doubt about that either. So book her, Jacko! Book them both. Charge her with Murder One and insurance fraud. Charge them both with conspiracy to commit murder. Charge him as an accessory to murder, with abusing a dead body, with... Just throw the frickin' book at both of them. Let a jury sort out the mess."

35

T hat day, day ten of the Nicolette Percy investigation, was one of the longest days of my life. By the time Maureen and Brady had been charged, photographed and finger-printed and all the paperwork had been completed, filed and distributed to the appropriate departments, including the copy I personally handed to Chief Johnston—which got me a minimal grunt and nod in return—I felt like I'd run a marathon in high-heeled shoes, no bra and an itchy sweater. I was exhausted and annoyed all at the same time. It was almost seven when I left the building and went home.

I locked the door, shut off my phone and stripped off my clothes.

I'd closed my case and the bad guys were in jail awaiting their preliminary hearings, but I wasn't happy. Even on bad days—and this one should have been a good day—a glass of wine and maybe some television was usually enough for me to be able to forget about the job long enough to settle my nerves, get my bearings back. But this time it wasn't like that.

I pulled the blinds in the front room and in the bedroom. A

quick shower was all I wanted. No food, no wine, nothing. My bed looked inviting so I lay down, and as soon as I did, I realized it was a trap. I couldn't rest. I couldn't close my eyes. The Percy case had been a bad one, and I couldn't get it out of my mind. It bothered me.

So I got up again and went into the living room and sat down on the couch. And, for a long while I just sat there, listening to the silence. There were no computer keyboards clacking. No phones ringing. No uniformed officers gossiping. No file cabinets being slammed shut.

It felt like... It felt like I hadn't experienced so much quiet... ever. If only my mind could have wound down, but it didn't. Inside I felt like an old-fashioned watch that had been wound too tight, and there was nothing to do but patiently let the gears go through their slow motions before I'd feel like normal again. But that, so it seemed, wasn't going to happen any time soon.

"Why, Kate?" I asked myself, out loud, my voice sounding over-loud in the quiet. "Why are you so wrapped up in this case? You've certainly seen more gruesome murders."

It was true. I'd seen machete attacks and satanic rituals, dismembering and stinking rotted corpses and good old-fashioned shootings. But there was something about the Nicolette Percy case that told me it was going to be one for the books, a case to remember.

She was a nice girl, Nicolette. One who was looking forward to meeting a nice man, one she could spend her life with. Her step-mother played a cruel and deadly trick on her all for an insurance payout. And I couldn't forget Harvel Brady. Something must have happened to those two when they were children for them to have turned out the way they did. I don't believe Hawk was right when he said it was all about the drugs. I'm sure they didn't help, but I just couldn't believe that was all there was to it. Something bad must have happened to them to turn them into the monsters they'd become.

Something was needling me. My gut shifted and I could feel an idea nibbling at the edge of my mind, but I was afraid to take a look and see what it was. Deep inside I knew I wanted to look for an answer to my questions about why the Lawsons were the way they were. It wasn't the most common last name. Marriage certificates, birth records and doctor records are all available... If you know where to look, and I certainly did.

"You're going to have to do this on your own," I muttered. "Chief Johnston isn't going to allow you to blow your nose let alone investigate the extended family of a murderer and her sidekick."

Maybe there was something wrong with me. I've seen first-hand the way people can be cruel to each other, to their blood children, let alone stepkids. And not one of those cases ever made me want to search out the root of the problem. This one did.

"This one was different."

I had ten weeks of vacation time I hadn't used. Add in the fourteen sick days I was due, and I had nearly three months.

"What are you going to tell the team? Or Chief Johnston?" I muttered.

Nothing. Not a damn thing. I was going to do my homework, find out about this family and then head off to wherever their roots were planted. As far as anyone else was concerned this was a vacation, one that I needed in the worst way.

I was going to take the road less traveled and maybe learn something that would help me be a better cop. Because if I just kept to my same routine, if I kept on working case after case, catching the bad guys, locking them up, only to turn around and do the same thing over and over again... "It's like I'm a machine. A frickin' machine!"

I took a deep breath.

"Ah, you're just burned out, Kate. It's that simple. For once, you want to find a way out for yourself, and not because the Chief is breathing down your neck or because the Mayor and the press are beating up the department again."

A calmness I can't ever remember feeling before had settled over me. My mind that had been racing in a dozen different directions for so long was beginning to catch up with my already exhausted body. I needed a glass of wine.

I got up and went to the fridge. The only thing in there was half a bottle of white; it would have to do.

I poured myself a glass and then went back to the couch. I figured I'd call the Chief and tell him I was putting in for my vacation time, all of it. I was sure he'd approve it. Hell, he'd already made me promise I'd take a month. So, having me out of the office might be a vacation for him, too.

The wine was sweet and cold on my tongue, and before I knew it, the glass was empty and my head felt like it was surrounded by soft, fluffy pillows. I went into the darkened bedroom and lay down. The sheets were cool. The clock read nine pm. It was wonderful. There was still a whole night to sleep and no need to get up early tomorrow.

Now some people might think I'd gone a little crazy. Certainly my world had tilted, a little, but I felt a whole lot better for having decided that I wanted to find out about the Lawson family. I felt like I had purpose. *We all need a purpose, don't we?* I thought as I slipped easily into sleep. It was three in the morning when I awoke.

"Oh boy," I said as I stretched and yawned.

The idea of taking my vacation time to search out the mystery of Nicolette Percy's family was still fresh on my mind, so much so that I thought I'd cut out some of the process and call Chief Johnston's office and leave him a voicemail, telling him I wanted to take my time off and ask him to approve it.

Unfortunately, when I picked up my phone, I saw I had nearly a dozen voicemail messages and ten texts—I'd turned my phone off, remember?

36

"What the hell is all this?" I tapped in my code and connected to voicemail. The first message was from Hawk.

"Hey, Kate. I hate to bother you, but there's a reporter here who says that he had a call from Harvel Brady's attorney complaining and detailing allegations of brutality when he was placed under arrest. I'm just giving you a heads-up, okay? I'll toss the guy out, but be on the lookout."

The next message was from a reporter. How the hell did he get my number? He, too, was asking about Harvel's trip to the hospital.

There were three more messages from reporters all looking for comments. Then Janet called saying she too was being questioned about my interrogation methods and that they wanted to know if I'd ever done anything that made her question my authority.

"I said of course not and told them you were one of the best cops out there. Don't worry, Cap. This will blow over, soon," she finished cheerfully.

"Famous last words," I muttered. There was a call from the Mayor's office. I deleted that one without even listening to it. The

Mayor's Office never called a cop to tell them what a good job he or she was doing and that their work was appreciated. Oh no. A call from the Mayor's is never good news.

Another message from Hawk. "Kate. You might want to turn on the news. Looks like Internal Affairs is talking to the press. What else is new? Who do they think is going to come to their house when someone breaks in and is pistol-whipping them?"

"Screw 'em," I muttered. "Frickin' talking heads. I hate them."

But it was the last message that got my attention.

"Kate, it's Chief Johnston."

Oh, that's just great! Whenever he calls me at home, it's usually Wesley. But not this time. I've just wrapped up a difficult murder case and he has an issue with it, so it's Chief Johnston. I continued to listen nervously, chewing my lip.

"Kate, we've got a problem. Harvel Brady's lawyer has contacted every news agency in the city, claiming that you put him in a hot box for an undetermined amount of time and that he suffered a breakdown and had to be taken to the hospital. We have a PR mess that makes the Exxon oil spill look like a kids' bedtime story."

"I don't believe this," I whispered to myself.

"Internal Affairs is all over it," he continued, "and I'm afraid they're out for blood. The Mayor, Kate... The Mayor is threatening to come down here and personally kick some ass if I don't address this issue."

"I have a side too, you know!" I yelled to the dead voice on the line.

"I need you here, in my office, first thing tomorrow morning. I'm sorry, Kate. I know you are a good cop and you've solved a lot of difficult cases, but this is the game we have to play. I'll plead your case to the sharks as best I can. You need to tell me what you are willing to do. You've got a reputation, Kate. I think it's just about caught up with you." End of message.

The worst-case scenario would be that I'm fired, I thought. *But if that was the case, Wesley would have said so. No, he was looking for a way to drag me out of the mess I've made, that Brady made for me.*

I was sure of it. But there was no denying I was in deep, and it was going to require not only some severe groveling, but I was also going to have to make a grand gesture in order to take the wind out of IA's sails. Morally, if for no other reason than to protect my team from having the stink of their Captain on them, I had to do it. Fortunately, I already had something in mind. I called Hawk. Late as it was, he was awake.

"Are you sure that's what you want to do, Kate?" he asked when I'd finished telling him what I was thinking. "We've worked together for a couple of years now, and I think there might be another way, a better way... I can tell 'em it was me, that I left him alone."

"Not a chance, my friend. It was my idea; I'll take the blame. This is what will work, Hawk. You know it as well as I do... And you have less than a year left to retirement. I couldn't live with myself if you lost your pension because of me."

"I've been through this kind of crap before, Kate; many times. It's nothing. It's part of the job, you know that. We always have each other's back. I have yours. The press hates cops. Internal Affairs hates cops. People wonder why police protect one another. We have no choice. This department is a freakin' jungle," Hawk said angrily.

"Yeah, you're right about that. I remember my old dad. He always said it doesn't pay to be a nice guy." I chuckled, but it wasn't funny.

"Your dad was right," Hawk said. We chatted for a few minutes more. We'd all but forgotten about the Percy case. Now it was all about Harvel Brady, the corpse raper. According to the press, he was now some sort of victim.

I told Hawk not to worry, thanked him and hung up.

I sat for a moment, considering my options. There was only one. I called the Chief at home.

"Yes, who is it?" he growled sleepily.

"Wesley. It's Kate."

"What the hell, Kate? It's four o'clock in the morning. Whatever it is you want, it can wait. I left you a message. I told you to come in first thing... Look, I understand what you're going through, but I don't want you to worry. I think we can turn this thing around and—"

"Chief," I said, interrupting him, "I want to put a request in for my vacation. I've got more than two months owing. I'll come in like you said, and we can make it look any way you want. But I need to take some time off and if it will appease IA... If you can keep my team out of trouble, I'll even agree to a visit to a shrink. ONE visit. But I want this time off. I need it." I waited for his response.

"If that's what you want, Kate. I'll approve it. But you'll be in tomorrow, right?" he asked.

"Yeah, I'll be there. First thing."

The next morning I did as I promised. I spent thirty minutes with the Chief talking things over. I explained fully what had happened with Brady and how he was after the pot of compensatory gold, and all the time Johnston sat there, leaning back in his chair, his fingers steepled in front of him. I had the distinct feeling I was talking to Obi-Wan Kenobi. Then I had to listen, on speaker, with the Chief listening, to a lecture over the phone from the Mayor. That done, I promised the Chief I'd meet with the department shrink for two sessions. That done, he signed off on my vacation, and I went to my office and flopped down behind my desk. I was officially dead to the rest of the department for the next two months and I didn't know whether to be happy or to cry.

I hadn't been there more than a few minutes when there was a gentle knock on the door and Janet came in. Her eyes were wide with worry.

"You okay?" I asked.

"Yeah. What about you?"

"Yes, I'm fine," I replied.

We talked for a few minutes, then I said, "Janet, would you mind doing me a favor? Would you get me Maureen Lawson's and Harvel Brady's... No, Harvey Lawson was his birth name. I need their dates of birth... and where they were born."

"Sure, Cap. Anything else I can do?" Janet asked.

"Yes." I chuckled. "For Pete's sake don't tell anyone."

She smirked, blinked, nodded and slipped out of the room.

I picked up the phone and dialed Dorman's number.

"What's cookin', hot stuff?" he asked.

"Hey. I'm taking a vacation."

"Where to?"

"I don't know yet. You want to come?"

The End

Thank you. If you enjoyed Nicolette, you might like to read the next book in the series, Catherine. The story begins where Nicolette left off and leads Kate on a wild and dangerous investigation into the heart of Appalachia. It's a nail biter you won't want to miss. Click here to download your copy now.

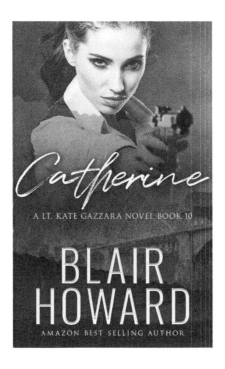

ACKNOWLEDGMENTS

As always, I owe a great deal of thanks to my editor, Diane, for her insight and expertise. Thank you, Diane.

Thanks also to my beta readers whose last-minute inspection picked up those small but, to the reader, annoying typos. I love you guys. Thank you.

Once again, I have to thank all of my friends in law enforcement for their help and expertise: Ron, Gene, David for firearms, on the range and off. Gene for his expertise in close combat, Laura for CSI, and finally Dr. King, Hamilton County's ex-chief medical examiner, without whom there would be no Doc Sheddon.

To my wife, Jo, who suffers a lonely life while I'm writing these books: thank you for your love and patience.

Finally, a great big thank you goes to my oh so loyal fans. Without you there would be no Kate, no Harry, Tim, Doc... well, you get the idea.

FREE BOOK

Now for a little something extra. You've just read Book 9 in the Lt. Kate Gazzara series so you're up to date, at least for now. My question is, then: would like to try something new, for free? How about you join my mailing list and I send you Harry Starke GONE... for free? If you're a fan of Stuart Woods, Baldacci, Connelly, Coben and Hoag, you should get to know Harry Starke. He's a detective, dedicated, dark, dangerous, driven, and has a wicked sense of humor. He's addictive: you can't read just one. Click here to Download your free copy of GONE

Made in United States
North Haven, CT
10 August 2024

55906671R00359